WINDFLOWER WEDDING

Windflower Wedding

ELIZABETH ELGIN

11/02

1068 5243

COMPASS PRESS

★ OXFORD ★ MELBOURNE ★

First published in 1997 by
HarperCollins*Publishers*.

Compass Press Large Print Book Series; an imprint of
ISIS Publishing Ltd, Great Britain, and Bolinda Press, Australia
Published in Large Print 2002 by ISIS Publishing Ltd,
7 Centremead, Osney Mead, Oxford OX2 0ES,
and Bolinda Publishing Pty Ltd,
17 Mohr Street, Tullamarine, Victoria 3043
by arrangement with HarperCollins*Publishers*.

British Library Cataloguing in Publication Data
Elgin, Elizabeth
  Windflower wedding. –
  Large print ed.
  1. Sutton family (Fictitious characters) – Fiction
  2. World War, 1939-1945 – Great Britain – Fiction
  3. Domestic fiction
  4. Large type books
  I. Title
  823.9'14 [F]

Australian Cataloguing in Publication Data
Elgin, Elizabeth
  Windflower wedding/ Elizabeth Elgin.
  1740307720
  1. Large type books.
  2. Domestic fiction.
  3. Sutton family (Fictitious characters) – Fiction.
  I. Title
  823.914

ISBN 0–7531–6783–2 (hb) ISBN 0–7531–6784–0 (pb)
(ISIS Publishing Ltd)
ISBN 1–74030–772–0 (hb)
(Bolinda Publishing Pty Ltd)

Printed and bound by Antony Rowe, Chippenham

For my own 'Clan'

Sally, Tim, Maria
Joanne, David, Angela
Rachel, Rhiannon
Jayne and Rebecca

The Pendenys Place Suttons

The Rowangarth Suttons

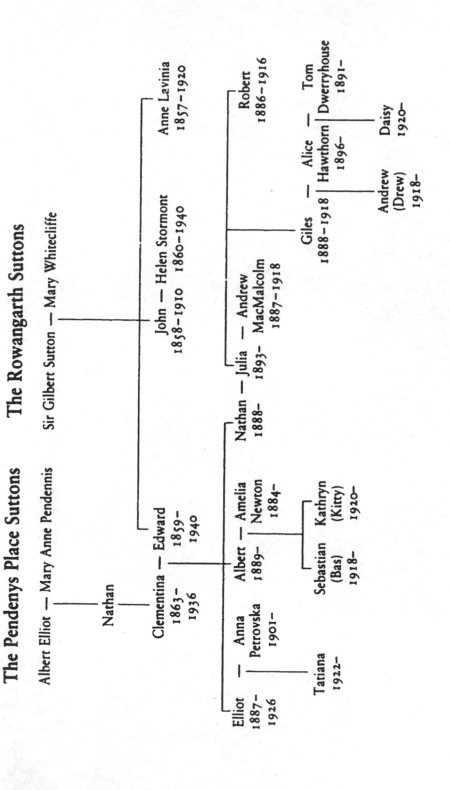

Albert Elliot — Mary Anne Pendennis

Sir Gilbert Sutton — Mary Whitecliffe

Nathan

Clementina — Edward
1863–   1859–
1936   1940

John — Helen Stormont
1858–1910 1860–1940

Anne Lavinia
1857–1920

Elliot — Anna
1887–   Petrovska
1926   1901–

Albert — Amelia
1889–   Newton
        1884–

Nathan — Julia — Andrew
1888–   1893–   MacMalcolm
                 1887–1918

Robert
1886–1916

Giles — Alice — Tom
1888–1918 Hawthorn Dwerryhouse
          1896–   1891–

Tatiana
1922–

Sebastian   Kathryn
(Bas)   (Kitty)
1918–   1920–

Andrew
(Drew)
1918–

Daisy
1920–

CHAPTER
ONE

1942

Home. Keth Purvis smiled with pure pleasure. Where he was being driven he had no idea, and cared still less, because this morning he had disembarked at Greenock. Not quite home. Holdenby in the North Riding of Yorkshire was home, but Scotland was near enough! Now he was only a telephone call away from Daisy; now, the Atlantic no longer separated them.

"So do you want the good news first, or the bad?" his superior in Washington had asked.

"Whichever, sir."

They had turned him down, he'd thought; turned down his request to return to England, but the bad news was that that request was approved — with conditions. The good news was that when he returned to England, when a passage could be arranged for him, he would be promoted to the rank of captain.

He wasn't, he recalled, offered any details. It was a take-it-or-leave-it deal, with no questions asked and no answers given.

He had taken it; had grasped it eagerly, for what condition could be so demanding that Daisy was not worth it?

That had been on his birthday in July. Now it was September and the heather on the hills fading, the bracken turning to gold. Days of waiting became weeks, then months. His elation turned to dejection. They had forgotten him, he was sure of it, until one day he was on his way on a troopship filled with American soldiers and airmen and, though he only once glimpsed them, a score of nurses, carefully chaperoned.

They had not sailed in convoy. The *Queen Mary* was too fleet to be so confined. She sailed alone, keeping a zigzag course the whole way across the Atlantic to outwit submarine commanders who would give eyeteeth and more to sink her or her sister ship the *Queen Elizabeth*. The Mary and the Lizzie — and the Mary had borne him safely home. To Daisy.

"Where are we?" he asked of the woman driver.

"Sir — I don't rightly know . . ."

"Somewhere in Scotland, surely?"

"Yes, sir. Somewhere in Scotland." She stared ahead, her cheeks pinking.

"So if you don't know where we are," he teased, "how will you know when we get there?"

She could well be lost, he thought mischievously. It was two years since signposts had been removed — even the one at Holdenby crossroads — so that the enemy, when he parachuted in, should not know where he had landed. Then, Britain daily had expected invasion and though it was almost certain that invasion would never happen now, still the signposts and names of railway stations had not been put back.

"Sir. I know *approximately* where I am." She glanced at him sideways and saw the smile on his face. "And I know *exactly* where we are going, but you know I can't tell you!"

"Of course, Sergeant." He didn't care where they were going. He had always thought — when They had told him his request to return to England had been approved, but with conditions attached — that he would be sent to some out-of-the-way, hush-hush place. Another Bletchley, only in the wilds. Doing exactly the same thing he had done at Bletchley. And where more wild than this, with the road they travelled little wider than a cart track and getting narrower by the mile?

A beautiful wilderness, for all that. To their left, the head of a loch, circled with hills, and to their right, mile upon mile of pine trees and tangled undergrowth and the sun, big and orange, beginning to sink behind those purple hills.

He looked at his watch. Ten o'clock. Daylight lasted longer the further north they travelled. In London — and in Liverpool too — blackout conditions would already be in force, he supposed.

"What time is blackout?"

"Depending on where you are — and give or take a minute or two — round about ten o'clock."

"Should you have told me that, sergeant?" he said with mock severity.

"Oh yes, sir. I got it from the newspaper this morning."

She was biting on her bottom lip to suppress a smile. She was really rather nice. Married, of course. Her wedding ring was the first thing he noticed about her capable left hand. There were many married women in the armed forces, he supposed, and soon, given luck and seven days' marriage leave, Daisy would be another of them.

"I don't suppose," he hazarded, shifting his position the better to see her face, "that if we were to pass a phone box you could stop? I'd like to ring my fiancée. We haven't spoken to each other for —"

"*Sir!*" She cut him short, her face all at once very serious. "There are no phone boxes around here. All removed. Security, see. But even if there were and you ordered me to stop — we-e-ll, I'd be bound to report it as soon as we arrived because it would be more than my stripes were worth if I didn't!"

"And you'll report this conversation?"

"No, sir." She was smiling again. "Not this time. Only you've got to realize the way it is."

"Yes. I realize." Phones, where they were going, would be listened-in to or scrambled, and every letter he wrote censored. He expected it and he didn't care. "I suppose we *are* allowed to have phone calls?"

"With permission, yes, sir. You'll be able to phone out, sometimes, but there are no calls allowed in. I've been there a year now, and I still don't know

4

the phone number. And when you do phone, you'll have to get used to the fact that someone will almost certainly be listening."

"Hmm." He folded his arms and stared ahead. More hush-hush than Bletchley Park, this new destination. At Bletchley he had at least been trusted with the phone.

Then he shifted in his seat, straightened his shoulders and allowed himself a small, secret smile. He was home and soon Daisy would know it in spite of all the petty restrictions.

And that was all that mattered!

Wren Daisy Dwerryhouse, summoned to the phone in the hall at Wrens' Quarters, Hellas House, said, "Dwerryhouse," and waited, breath indrawn. It was always like this now, when anyone at all phoned.

Keth? whispered a voice inside her, even though she knew it would be Mam or Drew or Tatty.

"Hi, Daiz!" Only Drew called her Daiz. "Just thought I'd ring, see how you are and if there are any messages for Rowangarth."

"Drew! You're going home!"

"Only seventy-two hours. We're getting de-gaussed again so most of us have got a spot of leave."

"Is Kitty going with you?"

"She is. She managed to wangle it. Well — you know Kitty!"

Daisy knew her, and liked her; liked her a lot in spite of the fact that Kitty's coming to England had

5

resulted in near heartbreak for Lyndis, with whom Daisy shared a cabin.

"Well, enjoy yourselves. I'm just fine, tell Mam and Dada. And give my love to Aunt Julia. I should be home on long leave myself before so very much longer. That'll put a smile on Mam's face. Oh — and give my love to Kitty too, won't you?"

She smiled into the receiver as she replaced it; just as if she were smiling at Drew, her brother — her *half*-brother. Dear Drew who was so in love, just as she was, and planning a wedding as soon as They, the faceless ones, allowed it because in wartime, *They* could do anything they wanted and without so much as a by-your-leave.

She opened the door of Cabin 4A, closed it carefully, then paused to think about what she would say.

"That was Drew on the phone." Leading-Wren Lyndis Carmichael said it for her. "And he's in dock and taking Kitty out and not you and me." Not any more, since Kitty.

"Yes, but they're going home. He's got seventy-two hours' leave. He just phoned to see if there were any messages."

"I see. And you don't have to look so guilty. I brought it on myself, didn't I? Fell hook, line and sinker for him and then he ditches me for Kitty Sutton, one of your hallowed Clan!"

"No, Lyn! Drew liked you a lot — then Kitty happened along and that was it! It was nothing to do with the Clan."

"You're right. It wasn't. And I should've got used to it by now, but being dropped still hurts, Daisy, because I still love him — more than ever, if that's possible. Even though he's going to marry Kitty, it doesn't stop me wanting him."

"Lyn, love — what can I say? Both you and Drew are special to me, and Kitty too, so I've got to sit on the fence as far as you and he are concerned. Don't ask me to take sides."

"I won't. Only you can't turn love off. You can try, but the loving is always there."

"I know. It would be the same for me if Keth found someone else. And don't think I'm all smug, Lyn, because I've got a ring on my finger. I worry, sometimes, that we'll be so long apart he'll forget what I look like. I mean — why did he have to be sent back to Washington? Three years away, then one day, out of the blue, he's on the phone — back home. And just when we think we'll be getting married They send him away again. Who do They think They are, then? Almighty God?"

"Of course they do! Has it taken you all this time for the penny to drop? We are only names and numbers to that lot! But I'll tell you something, Dwerryhouse D. I'm going to have the time of my life cocking a snook at Authority the minute I get back to civvy street again. Just imagine seeing an officer and saying, 'Hullo, mate,' to him instead of saluting! Or maybe even winking!"

" 'When I get back to civvy street again.' How many millions of times must that have been said, Lyn?"

"Lord knows, and He won't tell! Anyway, now that we've done our stint for King and Country for the day . . ."

"And eaten a mediocre, kept-warm lunch."

"*Very* mediocre. So what say we take a walk in the park? There won't be many more lovely afternoons left. We're well into September, now."

"Mm. Had you realized that we're three weeks into year *four* of the war?"

"I had. But if it hadn't been for the war, I wouldn't have met Drew, had you thought?"

"Drew is *taboo*!"

"Okay. And worrying about Keth in Washington?"

"That too."

"So what shall we talk about? Shortage of lipsticks and face cream?"

"Or the blackout?"

"And the pubs always running out of beer and never a bottle of gin to be seen!"

"And my wedding dress, hanging at Rowangarth!"

"Now we're back to Keth again!"

They began to laugh, because it was best you laughed about things you were powerless to change, then pulled on hats and gloves and made for the park, just across the road.

Navy-blue woolly gloves and thick black stockings on a beautiful Indian summer day in September, Lyn thought. *Yuk!*

8

"By the way," she said, when they had fallen into step and were making towards the Palm House, "I know it's taboo, but what did you say they were doing to Drew?"

"Not Drew — his ship! And surely you know what de-gaussing is?"

"I don't — except the entire ship's company gets a seventy-two-hour leave pass when it happens."

"De-gaussing is passing an electric current through the copper wire that's fixed round the ship. It neutralizes it, sort of, so that mines won't go off when they sail over one."

"Clever stuff — especially if you happen to be on a minesweeper like Drew is. Does it really work?"

"It has done, this far." Daisy crossed her fingers. "I suppose they're having a top-up, or something. So what shall we talk about?" Daisy said very firmly.

"Heaven knows!" What was there to talk about that didn't lead back eventually to Keth or Drew? Lyn brooded. Or more to the point, how Drew Sutton was crazily in love with Kitty, his cousin from Kentucky and had proposed to her and spent the night with her within the space of twenty-four hours? "I suppose we could talk about what we would do with a hundred clothing coupons; if we were allowed clothing coupons, that is."

"I'd rather talk about pay parade tomorrow," Daisy said. After all, pay parade every two weeks was just about the only thing you *could* be sure about!

Unspeaking, they walked past the shattered Palm House and on towards the ornamental lake. Life got tedious, sometimes, for those serving in His Majesty's Forces, and often — much, much too often — very lonely.

Alice Dwerryhouse was well pleased. She had been to a salvage sale and come away with enough flower-printed cotton to make two dresses — one for Daisy and one for herself. And after thinking long and hard she bought five yards of pale blue fine woollen material, smoke-stained and in parts water-marked too. She had worried about the pale blue wool, washing it carefully, thinking she had been a fool to waste good money on something that could shrink into nothing as well as wasting precious soap flakes.

She need not have worried. It had blown dry on the line and come up fluffy and soft — and stain-free and pre-shrunk, into the bargain. Now Daisy could have a nice going-away costume and the beauty of salvage sales was that material sold there came not only cheaply but without the need to hand over clothing coupons for it! You paid your money and you took pot luck, she supposed. And it wasn't very nice, if you let yourself dwell on it overmuch, that such windfalls were the result of some fabric warehouse being bombed and the bolts of wool and cotton knocked down for salvage.

She pulled the iron carefully over the pale blue length, trying hard not to gloat that now Daisy would not only have a proper white wedding dress but a going-away outfit too. Indeed, she sighed, coming down to earth with a jolt, all her daughter lacked now was a bridegroom and Keth Purvis was miles away in Washington.

It was all Hitler's fault, though. Evil Hitler who was the cause of it all, and why the air force lads didn't bomb him to smithereens she didn't know. Or maybe, she thought, smiling wickedly, how would it be if the good Lord worked a crafty one so that Hitler and half a dozen mothers of sons and daughters away in the forces could be locked in a room for ten minutes. Ten minutes, that's all it would take!

"Alice! You were miles away. Penny for them!" Julia Sutton closed the kitchen door behind her — Julia never knocked — then sat down beside the fire.

"A penny? No, they're worth much more than that!" They were too, considering what she had just done to Hitler. "But there's good news written all over your face — so tell me."

"Good news indeed! Were you going to put the kettle on?"

"You do it. Just want to finish pressing this material. It's come up real well, though I can't say I didn't have second thoughts after I bought it. But what's happened?"

"Drew and Kitty, that's what." Julia set the kettle to boil. "Kitty phoned. Can I put up with the pair of them for three days, she said. Drew's been given leave!"

"Leave? A bit sudden, isn't it? He's not —"

"Not going overseas? No, I don't think so. Something that had to be done to the ship, she said. Very vague. You know what Kitty's like. She didn't even get round to saying what time before the pips went, but I take it they'll be arriving on the six-thirty into Holdenby — if not before, of course, if they hitch a lift from York."

"And you're still pleased — about them getting married, I mean?"

"Delighted. Kitty is so adorable — she always was, come to think of it. Quite the naughtiest of the Clan, but such a way with her. You like her, don't you, Alice?"

"You know I do. I always did. We're very lucky, you and me both." Carefully she draped the precious material to air, then folded the ironing blanket carefully. "And I've got news for you too. Daisy's leave has been approved. She'll be home a week from now. And I'm not supposed to tell you, so you'll have to be very surprised when you see him in uniform. Tom's been made a sergeant. There'll be no living with him now!" Alice smiled fondly. Tom — a marksman in the Great War; now a sergeant in the Home Guard. Funny how being married to him got better with each year. Different, but better. Two more years would see their silver wedding anniversary. Mind, she sighed, if the war

12

hadn't happened she could well have been a grandmother now.

"Why the sigh?"

"Oh, just thinking about Keth and Daisy being apart. I ought to be glad he's where he is and not in the thick of the fighting, but I would, just once, like to see the six of them together again, just like they used to be when they were growing up."

"My Clan? Drew, Daisy, Keth, Bas, Kitty and Tatty. And five of them are in England now. Only Keth to will and wish home, then I shall take their photo again, just as I did in the Christmas of 'thirty-six. 'Thirty-seven, remember, was the last summer they were all together. And I'm sure they'll be together again one day."

"When the war is over, happen?"

"No, Alice. Long before then. I know it!"

"Then fingers crossed that you'll be right."

"I *am*." Julia stirred her tea thoughtfully. "Did you see it in the paper, by the way, that the milk ration is being cut?"

"I did. It's down to five pints a week now, between the two of us!"

"We-e-ll, I suppose Home Farm will slip us the odd pint, now and again. It isn't as though milk has to be brought here by sea. I don't feel so bad about getting extra milk — not like sugar, or tea or petrol. Wouldn't touch those. Wouldn't risk a seaman's life."

"I should think not, and us with a sailor son!" Alice drained her cup, then upended it into her saucer, gazing at the tea leaves clinging to the sides. "Wish Jinny Dobb were here to read our cups. Jin wasn't often wrong, was she?"

"No. Dear Jin. It'll be a year on the fifth of October since they were all killed — and a year on the tenth since Mother died."

"I know." Alice reached out for Julia's hand. "I loved her too, don't forget — I loved all of them. But they wouldn't want us to fret. None of them would."

"Mm. And we've still got each other, you and me. Sisters to the end?"

"Sisters," Alice said, gravely and gratefully, "to the end . . ."

"Have you ever stopped to think, Gracie Fielding, that if this dratted old war goes on much longer you'll be a time-served gardener?" Jack Catchpole, sitting on his upended apple box, blew on his tea. "That is, of course, provided you don't go getting any ideas about getting wed and wasting all the knowledge I've passed on to you!"

"Married, Mr Catchpole?" Gracie blushed hotly. "Now whatever gave you an idea like that?"

"Gave me? When it's sticking out a mile and that young Sebastian never away? Don't know how he manages to get so much leave!"

"Well, he won't be able to get away so often in future. It was quite easy, once, but now the aerodrome — er — *airfield*, is ready, Bas says the bombers will start arriving soon and things will be different." A whole new ball game, he said it would be.

"Ar. I did hear as how the Americans down south are already going bombing, and serve those Nazis right, an' all! But young Bas won't be flying bombers, will he?"

"No. He wanted to, but his hands — well, his left hand in particular, put paid to that." She added a silent thank goodness.

"Never mind. His hands didn't stop him getting to be a vet'nary with letters after his name, so they can't be all that bad. And it was a miracle he wasn't taken in that fire like Mrs Clementina was."

"I never notice his hands, truth known," Gracie smiled.

"Of course you don't. Just a few old scars. Mind, I shall want to know good and early when you and him set a date. I shall take it amiss if you don't let me do the flowers and buttonholes for you. And think on! We want no winter weddings when there's only chrysanths to make bouquets of. See that you plan it for the summer when there's flowers about."

"Mr Catchpole!" Gracie jumped to her feet. "I've told you time and time again that I don't think it's at all wise to get overfond of anyone in wartime. You could get hurt. Look what happened to Tatty."

"Aye, poor little wench. But wisdom has a habit of popping out of the window, Gracie lass, when love walks in at the door, and don't you forget it."

"I won't. I'm not likely to. I've told you that often enough!"

"Aye, but it seems no one has told young Bas. He's a grand lad, you can't but admit it."

"Yes, and he can get pipe tobacco in their canteen and he brings you some every time he comes. You *encourage* him!" Gracie said hotly. "But you've no need to worry about losing me. I want to do my apprenticeship. I want to be a lady gardener when the war is over. I don't want ever to go back into an office so you'd better accept that you're stuck with me, 'cos I'm *not* going to marry Bas Sutton."

"Now is that a fact?" Jack Catchpole slurped noisily on his tea. "Well, you could've fooled me, Gracie Fielding," he chuckled throatily. Oh, my word, yes!

CHAPTER
TWO

The army car, camouflaged in khaki and green and black, turned sharp left and the driver stopped at a guard post where a hefty red and white gate barred their way.

"Hi," the driver said laconically, offering her identity pass, even though she obviously knew and was known by the soldiers who stood guard. "One passenger, male." She turned to Keth. "Your ID sir, please."

Keth fished in his pocket, offering his pass. The corporal of the guard switched on his flashlight, studying it in great detail. He handed it back, then shone the light full in Keth's face. "Carry on, driver!" he rasped, satisfied with the likeness.

Saluting smartly he motioned an armed guard to open the gate, winked at the driver, who winked back, then waved them forward.

"Very officious," Keth remarked mildly, blinking rapidly as black spots caused by the torch glare danced in front of his eyes.

"Just a couple more miles — and another checkpoint," the sergeant smiled. "Have your ID ready."

The black spots were fading and Keth looked around him. The sun had sunk behind the hills, and in the half-light a crescent moon hung silver white at the end of a long avenue of tall pines.

The driver braked hard as a large bird ran across their path. "Damn it!" she muttered. "I should have got it, but I always brake. Instinct, I suppose."

"What was it?"

"A cock pheasant. Wish I wasn't so squeamish. He'd have done nicely for the pot!"

She accelerated, drove at speed down the long, straight drive then slowed as they approached a second checkpoint.

This time only a pole barred their way; Keth offered his identification without being asked for it, closing his eyes against another beam of torchlight, which did not come.

"'Night, Mick." The driver wound up her window then said, "There you are. Home sweet home, sir."

Keth let out a whistle. Silhouetted against the sky it could have been Pendenys; Pendenys Place, Holdenby, but with more towers. Pendenys was in the North Riding of Yorkshire, though, and the great bulk ahead was in the wilds of Scotland. Somewhere in Scotland, and hidden and guarded and secret.

"What's it called?" It was worth a try.

"Home sweet home, sir, like I said."

They slowed to a crawl as the car wheels crunched into the gravel of the circular sweep in front of the forbidding entrance.

18

Good security, Keth thought. Gravel made a lot of noise, even to walk on. It reminded him of the curving sweep of the drive at Denniston House, where Mrs Anna and Tatty lived, and he wished he were crunching up it now.

One of the massive double doors swung open, revealing a dimness beyond. The door closed again and torchlight picked them out.

The ATS driver got out, stretched, then rotated her shoulders.

"Captain Purvis, sir — this way, please."

Keth made to pick up the largest of his cases but it was at once grasped by a lance corporal and carried up the steps, together with his canvas bag, a second case and his respirator and steel helmet.

One, two, three . . . Mentally Keth counted the steps. Eight in all. He always counted steps as he climbed them; always had done. It irritated him, but still he did it.

The half-door grated open again, then slammed shut behind them. To his left an armed sentry sloped arms and stamped loudly as Keth passed.

This must, he reasoned, be the great hall. There had been a great hall at Pendenys with a floor patterned in highly polished tiles, massive arches and a grandiose staircase. The great hall in this secret Scottish castle was higher, its floor slabbed and worn and cracked in places. The staircase was oak, turned black with age, and a canvas strip covered its treads, though whether to protect the stairs or to deaden sound Keth couldn't be sure.

To his right a massive iron fireplace crackled and spat wood sparks and it gave him strange comfort. He smiled his thanks to his driver who said, "Good night, sir. Good luck," then walked away down a long, echoing passage.

"The CO is expecting you if you'll come this way," said a regimental sergeant major, picking up Keth's cap. "I'd take this, if I were you, sir."

Keth thanked him, and settled it on his head, realizing he would be expected to salute.

They began to climb the stairs. Twelve steps up — dammit, he was counting again — the staircase branched to left and right. They turned left and the RSM knocked twice on the third door on the right.

"Enter!"

"Captain Purvis, *sah*!" He did a smart about-turn, opened the door and closed it behind him with a bang.

Keth came to attention and saluted, all the while wondering about Pendenys and if army boots stamped all over Mrs Clementina's floors and up her stairs and if everyone banged her doors like the muscular sergeant major.

"Sir!" Keth stared ahead, arms rigid at his sides.

"At ease, Purvis. Take a pew." The brigadier nodded towards a leather chair opposite.

Keth sat, then removed his cap, placing it carefully on the floor at his side.

"Good journey over? No bother?"

"The best ever. The *Queen Mary* doesn't waste time."

"Hm. Always fancied a trip on one of the queens. Comfortable, was it?"

"Yes, sir, but very — er — basic."

The liner had been stripped of all her luxury. A cabin intended for two now slept eight in iron bunks. He remembered his first luxurious crossing of the Atlantic in 'thirty-seven, then wiped all thoughts from his mind.

"Drink?" asked the senior officer. "We do manage to get the odd bottle of whisky from time to time." He rose to pour two measures.

"A very small one for me; I haven't eaten since morning."

"Water with it?"

"Please, sir."

"Welcome." The brigadier raised his glass. "Good to have you with us."

"Thank you, sir. Glad to be here." How glad they would never know.

The brigadier had poured very small measures. He tilted his glass and drained it. Keth thought him a decent fellow but then perhaps he was a very senior boffin in khaki. Perhaps everyone here were mathematicians or scientists disguised as soldiers, just as he was.

"How was Washington?" He poured another small measure of whisky, nodding his head in the direction of Keth's untouched glass.

"Not for me, sir. I'm fine, thank you. And Washington has hardly changed."

"Hm. You were there before — at the Embassy?"

"Yes, sir. In the cipher room. A civilian."

"And you volunteered to return — correct me if I'm wrong?"

"I asked to be drafted home. I was told there would be conditions and I accepted them — though I don't know yet what they are."

"All in good time. Tomorrow's another day. Right now you'll be wanting a kip, I shouldn't wonder. Sorry you missed dinner but your batman will go on the forage for you." He glanced at his watch, a signal for Keth to get to his feet.

"No hurry. Finish your drink." The brigadier pressed a button beneath the lip of his desk and almost at once the lance corporal who had carried in Keth's kit appeared to stamp his feet and stand to attention.

"Take Captain Purvis to his quarters, please."

"Er — good night, sir." Keth emptied his glass. "Thank you."

"'Night, Purvis."

The interview was over and he had learned nothing save that tomorrow was another day when doubtless the conditions would be explained to him, and where he would be working, and with whom.

"Will you be going down to the mess, sir, while I unpack your kit?"

He was being asked to clear off out of it and not make a nuisance of himself.

Obstinately he said, "No, Lance Corporal, I don't feel like socializing tonight. But I would like a couple of sandwiches and a very large mug of tea.

Milk, no sugar. And then I would like a bath and maybe, afterwards, make a phone call."

"Oh, deary me, sir." The batman shook his head mournfully. "The sandwiches and the bath — no trouble. The phone call, oh, no."

"But why ever not?" Keth indicated the bedside telephone with a nod of his head.

"That, sir, is only internal, between you and the switchboard. Won't get you to the GPO, not that instrument."

"Then how do I go about it?"

"Sir, you don't. There's a ban on outside calls. Only in the direst emergency would you be allowed one. But I'll see Cook about your sandwiches. I might manage beef . . ."

"Beef will be fine."

"Righty-o, sir. I'll get them now, then I'll come back and unpack for you while you have your bath. I believe you've come from the States?"

"I have."

"Then you won't know about baths, here. Six inches of water, no more, per person. There's a black line painted around all our baths, and over that line we dare not go!"

"Of course not." Keth bit on a smile, then rummaged in his canvas bag for his toilet things. He had brought several tablets of soap with him and rose-geranium bath salts for Daisy — a bottle of perfume too, to use on their honeymoon because as sure as God made little apples, they were getting married on his next long leave. "But are you sure there is no way I can phone my fiancée?"

"Not that I know of, Captain. Letters is the only way and they'll have to be seen by the Censor. Even ours." He shook his head dolefully. "But that's what comes of working in a place like this. You take the downs with the ups, and since I was pulled off the beach at Dunkirk with one in the shoulder, I count my blessings, in a manner of speaking. Rather be here, for all its faults, than holed up in Tobruk or in a prisoner-of-war camp."

"Faults? You mean there's nothing much to do here?"

"Oh, there's the recreation room and the NAAFI van comes twice a week. They bring ciggies and we're allowed a couple of bottles of beer. But mostly it's — well, you know what I mean, sir? I'll see to your sandwiches. And if you'll give me your soap bag I'll reserve you a bath on the way down. It's customary, around this time of night, to put your soap and towel in a bath, otherwise you'll be unlucky."

"Thanks, Lance Corporal," Keth smiled. "And what am I to call you?" He seemed a decent sort, in spite of his sorrowful expression.

"Call me? Why, Lance Corporal, that's what, sir! If you'll pardon me, it doesn't do to get too familiar here — what with the fluid nature of the place, if you get my meaning." He left the room, leaving Keth to wonder about the fluid nature of the place and why phone calls were strictly not allowed. Frowning, he picked up the telephone.

"Switchboard," a female voice answered at once.

"Can you tell me, please, how I can make a call to Liverpool?" Dammit, it was worth a try!

"See the adjutant, sir. He'll refer your request to the brigadier," came the ready reply.

"Thank you." Carefully, thoughtfully, he replaced the receiver. But hadn't the brigadier said that tomorrow was another day, and with a couple of sandwiches inside him and a mug of tea, things would seem better. One thing was certain; no one here gave straight answers to straight questions and he hadn't yet discovered the name of the place, nor where, in Scotland, it was located.

The lance corporal returned, looking even sadder, placing a plate and mug beside Keth, shaking his head gloomily.

"Sorry, sir. No beef. You'll have to make do with cheese."

"Cheese is fine."

"Then I'll be back, sir, in ten minutes. Oh, and the adjutant's compliments, and will you see him in his office at nine sharp in the morning?"

Keth bit into the sandwich, realizing how hungry he was and how surprisingly good the cheese tasted.

He kicked off his shoes then lay back on his bed. Even though the telephone mocked him, he knew there would be some way to speak to Daisy, tell her he loved her and that soon they would be married.

Darling, he sent his thoughts high and wide, *I love you, love you, love you — and I'm home!*

Drew and Kitty walked hand in hand beneath the linden trees.

"I'm so happy," she sighed. "Everything is so perfect that sometimes I worry."

"Worry, when we'll soon be married and you'll be mistress of Rowangarth and we'll live happily ever after?"

"I'd rather be *your* mistress, but I suppose I am, really."

"No. You're my lover," Drew smiled. "Are you truly happy about us, Kitty?"

"Truly, truly happy. I don't want to come down off my lovely pink cloud."

"You'll have to, to marry me — and that's another thing. When?"

"Look, let's sit down." She linked his arm, then entwined his fingers in hers, sitting on the stone seat at the side of the walk. "All this — you, me, meeting and loving, Rowangarth on a September afternoon — even the war can't spoil it. It's our own special world and no one has ever loved as we love, nor ever will. I love you and I'm in love with you. I'm so devastatingly happy that I want this gorgeous madness to go on for ever — can you understand, Drew?"

"Of course. It's the same for me too. But I want us to be married."

"We *are* married. We met on a scruffy dockside in a bombed city and all at once every light in

Liverpool blazed brightly and I felt dizzy, and oh, Drew, I'll never be able to tell you how wonderful it was, that first loving. That was when we were married, don't you see? That very night we slept together. We've even got same names — Drew and Kitty Sutton."

"I want you to be *Lady* Sutton. I want Uncle Nathan to marry us. I want you to have my — *our* — children."

"And we will be married, of course we will, and we'll have kids — four, at least. But, darling, I want this unbelievable happiness to last a little longer. Let me get used to being in love?"

"And if I'm sent foreign — what then?"

"Then we'll get married on your embarkation leave, though wouldn't it be just marvellous if Mom and Pop could be there? Oh, she's delighted about us. She always knew my English half would get the upper hand and I'd marry an Englishman. I think she even secretly hoped it would be you, darling. So let me wallow deep in my pink cloud — just for a little longer? Let me stay starry-eyed — *please*?"

"Kitty Sutton, you always speak in superlatives! You always did. To you, everything must be larger than life — even being in love."

"And you, my darling, are dour and sensible and you're still reeling from the shock of being bowled over by my glittering personality. So why don't you come and join me on my pink cloud? I stayed awake ages last night, thinking you might knock."

"Yes, and I lay there for ages, wanting to come to you."

"So what happened?"

"Don't know. Suppose I dropped off, eventually . . ."

"No, you wanted to sleep with me, but when you think about it, darling, it wouldn't have been right — not here, at Rowangarth."

"Me creeping along the passage, you mean, like we were using Rowangarth for a dirty weekend?"

"Mm. We'd get caught, anyway . . ."

"Yes. Those boards creak something awful in the upstairs passage."

They began to laugh, then agreed that not for anything would they sleep together at Rowangarth until they were married. Any place else — every place else — but not Rowangarth.

"When we get back to Liverpool," Kitty whispered, "will you have to go back on board right away?"

"No. I'll just report to the quartermaster, then push off to the Adelphi, I suppose. Shall you come with me, darling?"

"We could spend the night at my digs. Ma won't mind."

"The Adelphi would be better and I could sign the register Andrew and Kathryn Sutton without so much as a blush."

"And I'll twist my ring round on my finger so it looks like a wedding ring and then everybody'll be happy! And we've got to be together every minute we can, because you never know the day I'll get sent to London. I've been expecting it for a while now."

"I'll hate it if you go."

"Yes, but had you thought — I could lodge with Sparrow and it would be just great sharing the spare room with Tatty. Do you suppose Aunt Julia would let me?"

"Sure of it. And I know Sparrow would like it too. But don't let's talk about you being sent away, Kitty — not till it happens?"

"Okay. And when — *if* — it does, we'll think about Daisy and Keth who are miles apart. At least you and I will be able to ring each other. We'll have to do what your gran did; count our blessings and oh, Drew, wouldn't she have been pleased about you and me? Didn't she always just love a wedding?"

"Mm. If I'm at sea, darling, will you phone Mother when it's the first anniversary of her death next month?"

"I will — word of a Sutton. And my bottom's getting cold on this seat; let's skip afternoon tea and go for a walk? Let's go to the top of the pike so I can say hullo to Pendenys. And, darling, when we're married and the war is over, will Uncle Nathan and Aunt Julia go to live there? Well, it's his now, or will be when the military gives it back."

"Mother will only go there under protest. She doesn't like Pendenys. Well, who would when they've lived all their lives at Rowangarth? But we'll worry about that when the war is over and the Army gives it back."

"I'm surprised the soldiers are still there. I'd have thought Grandmother Clementina would've haunted them out of it ages ago."

"Kitty Sutton, I'm surprised at you! You're getting as bad as the locals. It isn't haunted. It's just that the army lot are so secretive about what goes on there and it makes it sort of mysterious."

"What d'you think they're *really* doing there? Spying? Cloak-and-dagger?"

"Can't make up my mind. There's all sorts going on that most people don't know a thing about. I'm sure Keth's a part of something like that. He's so vague when you ask him what he's doing."

"Yes, well whatever it is he's doing it in Washington, which is rotten luck for Daisy."

She held out her hand and they began to run; across the lawn and the wild garden and over the stile, into the wood. And when they had passed Keeper's Cottage and were hidden in the deeps of Brattocks Wood, they kissed long and hard.

"I love you, darling," he whispered. "Have I ever told you?"

"Not in Brattocks, you haven't. So kiss me again and then we'll climb to the top of the pike and you can tell me there that you love me. And I shall stand and shout it out to the whole Riding. Kathryn Norma Clementina Sutton loves Andrew Robert Giles Sutton and they're going to be married in All

30

Souls, and you're invited to the wedding, all of you!"

"I do love you," Drew laughed. "Don't ever change, will you? Don't ever stop being dotty?"

And she said she wouldn't, then asked him to kiss her again.

Keth blinked open his eyes, looked questioningly around him, then realized he was in a castle in Scotland and that he was *home*!

"'Mornin', sir." His batman had opened the blackout curtains and placed a large mug of tea at his bedside.

"'Morning, Lance Corporal." Keth stretched, then swung his feet to the floor, making for the window. All around were wooded hills and in the distance, the glint of early-morning sun on water. The loch they had passed on their way here, perhaps?

"What did you say this place was called?"

"I didn't, sir, but you'll doubtless be told. It's Castle McLeish."

"And it's — *where*?"

"Somewhere in Scotland, Captain, though if you was to press me, I'd tell you it was in deepest Argyll and more than that I'm not prepared to say."

"And who lived here, before the Army took it?"

"A gentleman who made his money from whisky. He passed the business on to his two sons, then came here to spend the rest of his days in peace and solitude — or so he thought. But now he lives in a croft about five miles away and both his sons are in the Navy. It's a funny old world, isn't it?"

"A funny old world, Lance Corporal."

And a wonderful world with Daisy only hours away. Argyll. On the west coast of Scotland and directly north of Liverpool by about two-hundred-odd miles! So near, and if only he could find a telephone she would whisper that she didn't believe he was home again and it was true, wasn't it? He really *was* home? And when was he getting leave and when would they be married?

"When you're shaved and dressed, sir, I'll explain the geography of the castle."

"Oh — er — yes. Think you'd better."

"It's a rambling, up-and-down sort of place. You could get lost in it and not be found for days. You'll want the mess, then the adjutant's office. One in the east wing," he said, mournfully, "the other in the north tower. Them stone floors play havoc with your feet."

"I'll survive," Keth grinned.

"Yes, sir. Let's hope so. Some do." And some didn't. His melancholy was on him again. He'd seen them come and he'd seen them go and all of them fine, upstanding young men. Yes, and women, too, which wasn't right, to his way of thinking. "They'll be serving breakfast now, if you'd like me to show you the way . . . ?"

When Keth returned to collect his cap in readiness for his visit to the adjutant, he found his bed made, his room cleaned and the windows open to the September morning.

And it was a beautiful morning, he thought, breathing deeply on the brisk, tangy air. His whole world was set fair and if he was not to be given a posting to England, then this beautiful part of Scotland would suit him very nicely — once he had sorted a few things out, like where and with whom he would be working — and phoned Daisy or, at the very least, written her a letter. Somewhere in Scotland, he would head that letter, and when she opened it her cry of disbelief would be heard on the other side of the Mersey.

He straightened his tie, brushed away a speck, then tucking his cap under his left arm, made for the north tower and the adjutant who would answer all his questions and explain the intricacies of phoning your girl and why there was such an air of secrecy over the place. He found the north tower with no trouble at all and knocked firmly on the door marked "Adjutant".

"You'll be wondering why you are here," Keth was asked when pleasantries had been exchanged and hands shaken.

"Not really. I put in a request for a posting home and I suppose I'll be doing what I did before. What I really want to know is how I can phone my fiancée, and I'd like an address to give her when I write. She doesn't know I'm back, you see, and —"

"And you're impatient to get in touch? Well, I'm sorry, but there'll be no phone calls and no letters

— at least, not with this address on them. You can write," he hastened, prompted by the agonized expression on Keth's face, "but you will have to write your letters exactly as if you were still in Washington. No hints that you're in UK; nothing to give the game away.

"This office will have them censored and appropriately franked, and your young lady will receive them in due course and be none the wiser as to your whereabouts — and that's the best we can do, I'm afraid."

"But I don't understand. I used to work at Bletchley Park and I'm not telling you anything you don't know, because it'll all be on my service sheet. And I imagined — wrongly, it seems — that I would take up where I'd left off. Before Washington, I mean . . ."

"Yes, it's all here." The adjutant opened a drawer, taking out a bulky folder. "You have a knowledge of, er, Enigma?"

"As much as the next man. Nobody knows, really, what's going on in that direction — not all of it," Keth said guardedly.

"But you are familiar with Enigma?"

"I've done my fair share of code-breaking." Watch your tongue, Purvis!

"Wehrmacht and Luftwaffe codes — yes. But how about the U-boat codes? How familiar are you with them?"

"Now look here," Keth flung, all at once on his guard. "I signed the Official Secrets Act not so long

34

ago, so if you want to know what went on, I suggest you quiz someone else."

"Your attitude does you credit, Captain, but I know what goes on at Bletchley; I know there's a fair amount of success with the German army and air force codes, but I know they can't break the naval code and it's become a raging priority. Orders from the Cabinet Office, in fact."

"We did break the U-boats' code — sometimes," Keth offered uneasily. "It took a lot of doing, though, for some reason. Only managed it a couple of times a week and very often what we gained was yesterday's knowledge."

"Exactly. And we'd rather like to be more up-to-date on it. Either that," he shrugged, "or we're going to lose the entire merchant fleet in the Atlantic, and Hitler will have done what he wanted to all along: bring us to our knees by starvation. Our shipping losses are phenomenal and we can't go on losing ships the way we are. We think there is a variation between the machines used by the Army and Air Force on the one hand and the Navy — which includes U-boats — on the other, and that is why you are here, Captain.

"From now on your sole preoccupation will be the breaking of the U-boats' code and that is all I can tell you at the moment. During the next few days the MO will take a look at you, assess your fitness. It'll be likely you'll need a day or two toughening up. Your file indicates that you've done a small-arms course and the usual rifle drill and are fairly familiar with other forms of self-defence."

"Like what?" Keth scowled.

"Like using a hand grenade and a basic knowledge of booby traps and explosives."

"Self-defence? Sounds more like commando stuff to me. But yes, I did go on one or two courses, though what use they were was always a bit of a mystery."

"You'll find out — in time. Meanwhile, I've fixed you an appointment with the medical officer. Be there at ten. It's likely he'll prescribe a spot of PT and a few cross-country runs. Oh, and see the dental officer, will you? Best that you should." He folded the file with a finality that indicated that the interview was over, then rose to his feet. "And don't look so perplexed. It'll all be crystal clear by the end of the week."

Indeed, thought the adjutant, it would have to be.

"End of the week? Okay — I'll accept that but —" Keth raised his eyes to those of the adjutant and held his gaze steadily, "but just tell me one thing. Is this another of those peculiar billets — like Pendenys Place in Yorkshire, I mean?"

"And what do you know about Pendenys?" He lowered himself into his chair, his gaze as steady as Keth's.

"Not a lot and most of it rumour, I suppose. The locals think something is going on there — and it's securely guarded, like here, and like this place it's secluded."

"You've been to Pendenys, then?" The adjutant reached for the file again.

"Many a time — but before the powers that be took it off Edward Sutton. I live near there. I'm engaged to the daughter of the head keeper on the next estate."

"To Daisy — er — Dwerryhouse, who's in the WRNS?"

"Yes." Keth looked down meaningfully at the open file. "Tell me something I don't know."

"Very well — if I must! When you came back to England from Washington — the first time, I mean — you met her down south. You were stationed briefly at Bramble Hill, not far away. And you stayed the night with her at a Winchester hotel. You'll not want me to tell you that you signed in as Mr and Mrs Purvis. You were under surveillance even then!"

"That's enough!" Keth was on his feet again, his face an ugly red. "I know all about the Official Secrets Act and the Defence of the Realm Act too, but leave Daisy out of it — okay? What she and I do is damn-all to do with you, or anybody else for that matter! Did it give you a kick, reading through my file? Because you'll know we stayed the night at a Liverpool hotel too, not long before they sent me back to Washington without the chance to say goodbye to her — like it was some stupid cloak-and-dagger thing!"

All at once that hotel room with its cornflower and poppy bedspread and curtains and the electric fire that guzzled shillings seemed to have been dirtied.

"No, we don't seem to have any record of that one," said the adjutant mildly, "but by then you'd have been pretty well cleared security-wise. Your fiancée is in the clear too."

"I should damn well think so! And all this because of Enigma! Have you got my mother's blood group in your records too?"

"Steady on, Purvis. Nobody sees these records but the high-ups — and me. And you got it right. This place — and Pendenys, if you must know — are very secure establishments, so your details are safe here."

"I couldn't give a damn one way or the other!" Keth was calmer now, though his heart still thudded much too loudly. "But leave Daisy out of it — right?"

"And you calm down, Purvis or —"

"Or you'll put it on my file: given to sudden rages!"

"Not on this occasion. But if I were you, I'd take a turn in the garden — do a spot of deep breathing, sort of — or your blood pressure isn't going to look too good when the MO takes it. And Purvis —" he hastened as Keth opened the door, "don't take this to heart. It's nothing personal. We like to know everything about our operatives — we have to — so you'd better get used to the idea that what you do during the next few days here will probably be closely watched and recorded."

"Remind me to let you know, then, every time I flush the toilet!" Keth hissed. Then closing the door again, leaning on it in what he hoped was a perfectly controlled and relaxed pose, he said softly, "Just what goes on here?"

And the adjutant, equally controlled, replied that he would be told very soon.

"Thank you — *sir!*"

Keth opened the door again, then closed it behind him very quietly. Then he shut his eyes tightly, took a deep breath and said, "Arrogant bastard!" He even permitted himself the smallest smile, thinking that his words might have been heard — and noted on his file!

And why was he worrying? he thought, as he walked through the immaculately kept grounds. He was back — for the second time. He had asked for a draft home, had accepted there would be conditions attached to it, so why get het up over the adjutant? They had to be careful till they had cleared him — a second time. He must accept it. It was the price to be paid for getting back home. To Daisy. He was to carry on his work with Enigma. He was a mathematician — a boffin, a back-room boy — doing his bit for the war under the disguise of a captain in the Royal Corps of Signals. And as soon as his security check was okayed, he would know exactly what went on, what was required of him and how soon he would be allowed that phone call to Daisy.

Calm again, he looked at his watch. Best cut along sharpish. Best not keep the MO waiting.

CHAPTER
THREE

"Pity we missed Drew and Kitty," Tatty sighed.

"No, it isn't," said Daisy firmly. "Well, from your point of view, I mean."

Daisy, home from the Wrens on seven days' leave; Tatiana Sutton, home for two nights from her translator's job in London.

"Why isn't it?"

"Because you're hurting still over Tim, and seeing them together would have been awful for you. I miss Keth till it hurts, but at least I'll see him one day. You don't even have that to hold on to."

"No. Just memories. I often wonder what would have happened if I'd got pregnant. Sometimes, I wish I had; it would have been some part of Tim. I know there'd have been the usual upset — Tatiana Sutton getting herself into trouble, and all that cant — but I wouldn't have cared. Grandfather left me comfortably off — I could have kept the little thing."

"Well, you didn't have Tim's baby, love, but if you had I'd not have pointed a finger. It could've happened to me and people who live in glass houses don't throw stones."

40

"You're a good friend. It's nice to be able to talk to someone about Tim and I appreciate you going up the pike whenever you can to let him know he isn't forgotten. I got up early this morning and went there. I felt very near him."

"Good." Daisy reached for Tatiana's hand and they walked on, glad to be together for just a little while. "How's London, by the way — and Sparrow?"

"London's okay; better, now that we don't get so many air raids. The Blitz was awful. I feel like a Londoner now. There's so much kindness about — everyone being nice to each other; smiling, and all that. It's because we've been through all that bombing together, I suppose."

"I know what you mean. I felt very close to the Liverpool people, knowing I'd seen their blitz out with them. You and me have really grown up, haven't we, Tatty?"

"Me especially. I defied Mother and Grandmother over Tim and then I walked out and went to London. I only wish Tim and I could have been married — even though it would have been only for a little while.

"And another thing — Uncle Igor is quite nice to me these days. I go and see him every week now. At first I did it because I felt sorry for him — all alone in that house in Cheyne Walk — and I suppose I went because I wanted to find out about my father."

"What about him?" Daisy said sharply. Not that it was any business of hers, but she was as sure as anyone could be there was something not quite right about Tatiana's father, even though he'd been dead for ages. For one thing, both Mam and Dada changed the subject if, innocently, she had mentioned him and for another, Aunt Julia's mouth went positively vinegary when anyone said Elliot Sutton's name. "Did you find out, whatever it was you wanted to know?"

"Oh, yes, I did. Uncle Igor couldn't stand him. He said he warned my mother not to marry him, but she was determined to have him — and all the while Grandmother Petrovska and Grandmother Clementina encouraging it. It seems that Grandmother Clementina was so rich she could buy anything she wanted and she wanted a title in the family."

"Hm. By things I've heard — in passing, sort of — I believe she had money but no — er — well, she was a little bit bossy."

"Grandmother Clementina had, as they say around these parts, plenty of brass, but no breeding. I'd believe it, too. What little I remember of her was that she was a bit — well — *loud*. Anyway, my mother had a title. In Russia in the Czar's days, the daughter of a count was entitled to call herself a countess and Grandmother Clementina seized on it like it was the answer to all her dreams. A real countess at Pendenys Place! Uncle Igor thought it was pathetic."

"And what else did he tell you?" Daisy was intrigued.

"I'll tell you — one day. Right now, I'm enjoying being home — when I can keep out of the Petrovska's way, that is. I wish she'd take herself back to London and look after Uncle Igor at Cheyne Walk, but I think she's still scared of the bombing. I notice Uncle Igor isn't falling over himself to persuade her back. I think he's quite contented on his own. He lives in the basement kitchen now. The rest of the house is closed up except for what was once the servants' sitting room, next to the kitchen. That's where he sleeps."

"I wonder why Mrs Clementina ever bought a house in London," Daisy frowned. "She hardly ever used it."

"A whim. That's all it was. Did you know," Tatiana giggled, "that when the Petrovska and Mother and Uncle Igor first went to live there — when they had to get out of Russia because the Communists took over — Grandmother Clementina complained bitterly that Eastern European refugees had taken over the property next door, and the value of her own house would go down."

"I bet she soon changed her mind about her next-door neighbours when she found they had titles! Is Cheyne Walk as nice as Aunt Julia's little house in Montpelier Mews?"

"No. The Cheyne Walk house is much, much bigger and not half so cute. I love being at Montpelier with Sparrow. She's a darling. We might even have Kitty living with us if she gets sent down to London to work."

"You won't get yourself upset though — Kitty going on and on about Drew, and you — well . . ."

"Loveless, and wanting Tim? No. That part of my life — and it wasn't much more than three months, remember — is most times locked up inside me. I only let it out when I feel very brave, but one day I'll be able to think of him without hating the world, I suppose. Sparrow says I will."

"Mm." When Tatiana talked about Tim, Daisy felt guilty because Keth was safe in Washington and it made her want to hug her friend and tell her she understood, but there was still a coldness around Tatiana that warned everyone away.

"Well, that's life, as they say." Tatiana's attempt at a smile failed dismally. "And here we are at the crossroads so do we go to Denniston or your place?"

"Whichever you want." Daisy would rather not go to Denniston House because Countess Petrovska always looked at her in a very peculiar way. As if, almost, the daughter of a gamekeeper had no right to be best friends with the daughter of a countess. And that was very stupid of her, Daisy thought hotly, when that gamekeeper's daughter was rich enough to buy the entire Rowangarth estate and Denniston House too, had she wanted to.

But she tried not to think about the money because it must not be allowed to come between her and Keth. Hardly anyone knew about it; only her parents, Aunt Julia and Drew and Keth — not even Keth's mother knew. Money left to her by an eccentric old bachelor when once they lived in the New Forest. Money that never seemed quite real because she had only got it legally on her coming-of-age last June, and now there was nothing to spend it on because the shops were empty and Wrens were not given clothing coupons, so she couldn't go raving mad and buy a fur coat — just for devilment, of course!

"Hey!" Tatiana was snapping her fingers in front of her nose and Daisy blinked and smiled guiltily. "You were miles away in a trance!"

"No. In Washington," Daisy said without so much as a blush. "So where are we going then?"

"Your place," said Tatiana promptly. She liked Daisy's parents and she loved the cosy kitchen and always being made to feel wanted. "And you never showed me what Keth gave you for your twenty-first. A case full of make-up, you lucky dog! Are you sure you won't use it till your honeymoon?"

"Absolutely sure. I keep it in the pantry where it's cool so none of the pots of cream will go off. It would be awful if they did."

"They'll be all right, but shall we just have a gloat over them and maybe a sniff? It'll be positively sinful to see so much make-up all at once. It's ages since I got even a pot of cold cream. I suppose that now Keth's been sent back to America he'll be sending you silk stockings and all sorts of things."

"I wouldn't mind a few pairs of stockings, for going out in, I suppose, but such a lot of parcels get torpedoed these days, crossing the Atlantic. Mind, the last one Kitty's mother sent from Kentucky got through, and would you believe it, she had sent glacé cherries? Tilda was speechless — well, she hasn't been able to make cherry scones for ages, there being no cherries in the shops. I shouldn't wonder if she didn't bake some for Drew, when he was on leave."

"They were lovely days, weren't they?" Tatiana sighed. "When we were all young, I mean, and Bas and Kitty came over on one of the liners and the Clan was together. Will we be together again, do you think?"

"Yes, we *will*. There are five of us here already. Whoever would have thought Bas and Kitty would make it to England with a war on, an' all? And Aunt Julia says she feels it inside her that Keth will get home too. She's getting as bad as Jinny Dobb, but oh, if only he could come back . . ."

They had climbed the far fence of Brattocks Wood and were standing beneath the elm trees where the rooks nested. Daisy looked up at the big black birds that circled overhead.

"Have you ever told it to the rooks, Tatty?"

"Told what to the rooks?"

"Oh — *things*. Special things like secrets and wishes and fears — anything, I suppose. They always keep secrets and sometimes I think it helps to tell them your worries."

"Isn't that a bit pagan?"

"No. Country people often do it. Some people tell things to the bees, but Mam and I tell it to the rooks."

"Your mother does it?"

"Yes. Always. And it wouldn't surprise me if Aunt Julia doesn't have the odd word with them from time to time, even though she's the wife of a vicar!"

"But how do you do it?" Tatiana wasn't at all sure that Grandmother Petrovska would approve of such things, her being devoutly Russian Orthodox still, and always crossing herself and praying to her icon.

"Well, you lean your back against the tree — any tree where rooks nest, then you put your arms behind you, palms touching the tree and you close your eyes and you do it."

"But what if someone saw you, or heard you?"

"Oh, they'd have you branded a witch and it would be the ducking stool for you!" Daisy gave a shout of laughter. "You don't actually *say* things out loud. You think them and your thoughts go up to the rooks."

"And it works?"

"I'm not sure — but it's worth a try, isn't it?"

"And could I talk to Tim?"

"No. You'd need a medium for that, and only Jinny Dobb was any good at it."

"And Jin's dead."

"Yes."

"The same night as Tim died. When his bomber crashed."

Daisy nodded her head. She didn't want Tatty to talk about that night.

"It'll soon be a year since he died, Daisy."

"I know, love. But Reuben died that night too, and your Grandfather Sutton and Mrs Shaw and Jinny."

"And all Tim's crew!" Tatiana's mouth set traplike. "Bastard Germans!" she hissed.

"Don't, Tatty . . ."

"Don't hate that pilot who shot Tim down? So what do you think I'm made of — grit and granite?"

"No, I don't. You know I don't." Daisy grasped her friend's hands, squeezing them tightly. "I hate them too for what they did to Reuben that night. He was the nearest I ever got to a grandfather and I loved him every bit as much as you loved your Grandfather Sutton!"

"But it was special between Tim and me. Grandfather Sutton and Reuben and Mrs Shaw and Jin were old. Tim had hardly lived!"

"Tatty — *please*. I'm sorry we came here, started this. I shouldn't have told you about the rooks."

"Yes you should and I'm glad you did! Oh, I'm not going to tell them how much I love Tim — not yet, anyway — because I'm too bitter inside me. But show me how you do it, because I'm going to tell those rooks how much I hate German fighter pilots who shoot up an aerodrome just because it's a wizard prang and how especially I hate the one who got Tim's plane."

"If you think it will help, but I don't think the rooks much like bitterness and hatred. Leave it, Tatty? Leave the fighter pilot who killed Tim to God, why don't you?"

"Yes. I'm being awful, aren't I? And I suppose I should remember that Tim's plane dropped bombs on the Germans — and maybe killed old people like Grandfather Sutton and Reuben, and little children, too . . ."

"Yes — well that's what wars do to people like us, Tatty. Mam says the old ones make wars and the young ones have to fight them. And let it come, love, if it'll help." She gathered her friend to her as tears filled Tatiana's eyes and ran down her cheeks. "Let's give the rooks a miss today, and tomorrow we'll go up the pike. You'll be nearer to Tim up there."

"Yes. That was where he died." She dabbed her eyes, then blew her nose furiously. "Thanks for being so nice about it, Daisy. It's awful trying to be normal when you know you'll never be normal again."

"I know, love. You'll feel a lot better once we've heard the curlew call at the top of the pike."

"I will, won't I? And do I look awful? Will your mother know I've been crying?"

"No, Tatty. You don't go all red and blotchy when you cry like I do. And if you did, she would understand. Don't forget Mam knows what it's like. For a whole year she thought Dada was dead."

"Yes, and for almost a whole year I've *known* Tim is dead and that I'll never see him again. But I'm glad for the time we had together, Daisy. No matter what, no one can take that away from me."

"No, love. And no one who cares for you as much as I do would ever want to. So let's go and see Mam and have a look at my make-up?"

"Okay." Tatiana looked up sharply as a bomber flew low overhead. "See it, Daisy? That's a Halifax, a new one. They've got them at Holdenby Moor to replace the old Whitleys."

"Do you still do your aircraft recognition, Tatty?"

"I do. If it flies, I can tell you what it is — ours or theirs. Come to think of it, why didn't I join the ATS as an aircraft spotter? I'd have done very well at it."

"Well, you're stuck with being a translator now. We're both of us stuck with what we've got for the duration. And who's to tell, Tatty, maybe you were intended to go to London? Maybe it was in your stars that you should."

"And meet someone else, you mean? Oh, no!"

"I didn't mean that. But you've made friends with your Uncle Igor, haven't you, and somewhere in London something might just happen to at least help you to come to terms with losing Tim."

"Help me accept what I can't change, you mean?"

"Something like that — yes. I hope you will, Tatty. I can't bear to see you like this. And maybe there's some truth in what Mam always says — that

50

nothing lasts; not the good times nor the bad. Maybe soon it's going to be your turn for something good to happen."

"Maybe. And I really am learning to count my blessings, Daisy. Did you know I'm helping the WVS now; a sort of escort. I've done it twice. It was Sparrow's niece Joannie started me off. She asked me to do it as a favour the first time, and I'm thinking of doing it regularly: taking airmen out. I don't mean dating them, but they're mostly aircrew, in need of an escort, really. And don't look so bemused. The first time I did it I was shattered; didn't think it was for me. But then I felt so sorry for them, you see."

"Wounded airmen, you mean? You go to the hospital and talk to them and walk with them?"

"No. They could walk fine, those I met. But they have been in hospital and now they're going out some, you see. Facing the world again, I mean."

"Facing the — Tatty, you don't mean they've been burned?"

"I mean just that. They're all young men, Daisy, and some of them look awful. It's mostly their hands and faces. Their hair and their ears are just fine; protected by their helmets. But their poor faces — oh, the first time I saw them I felt sick inside."

"Were they so bad, then?"

"Yes. Their features all gone. But that wasn't why I felt awful, Daisy. We were going to the theatre, you see — me and three other girls and four airmen. It was their first time out of hospital blues and into their uniforms again. And it was the first time they'd been out since — since it happened."

"It must have taken a lot of doing — for them, I mean."

"It must. Like I said, I felt sick, but I didn't let it show. I smiled when I was introduced to my airman. I looked right into his eyes and smiled and do you know what, his eyes looked relieved. His face didn't, because he can't smile yet. But his eyes smiled.

"He was a navigator called Sam. He held his arm out so gallantly, and I took it because that man could have been Tim. My wonderful Tim could have looked that way, and just for a second I was glad that he hadn't suffered like that."

"I know what you mean, Tatty. All of them intelligent and good-looking — then for that to happen is awful."

"Yes. I know Tim dreaded it. Do you know he once said to me that he'd rather die than fry?"

"Tatty! Don't say such things!"

"Tim said it, not me. Most aircrews say it. It made me cry so much he promised never to say such a thing again. And he got his wish in an awful kind of way. At least it was clean for him, and quick."

"Tatty — *don't*. Tim wouldn't want you to be like this."

"No, but he'd have wanted me to go out with those wounded airmen because they are worse than wounded, Daisy. They said there's some wonderful work going on — skin-grafting and things like that.

They can even build up noses again. Sam said he was glad about that because his original nose was awful. Said he hoped he got a better one second time round."

"I don't know how he could joke about it."

"Nor me, because it isn't just their poor faces that are wounded, it's their pride too. Sam got a bit serious and told me that when he was in hospital, the girlfriend of the airman in the next bed came to visit and she started to scream and make a fuss when she saw him. He said the Ward Sister just got hold of her and all but threw her out. The girl never came back. She wrote later, and broke it off.

"So they are really marvellous and that's why I shall go out with them and dance with them and help them to come to terms with what's happened. They'll learn to accept it, I hope, and that special hospital helps a lot. But it's still awful for them. Tim would have hated it."

"Oh, lovey!" Daisy reached for her friend, hugging her, blinking away tears that filled her eyes. "Tatty Sutton, you're a truly lovely person and I know why Tim loved you so much. He'd be proud of what you are doing."

"You think so?"

"I *know* so, and I'm proud of you too! So let's go to Keeper's and take a peek at my make-up — and why I'm saving it I just don't know!"

"I do," Tatiana whispered. "And thanks, Daisy."

"Why, for heaven's sake?"

"For being my friend — and for understanding. And tomorrow, before I leave, we'll go to see the rooks — okay?"

"The good old rooks," Daisy smiled. "You bet we will!"

Keth had not done so much writing since his student days. He put down his pen, rubbing the back of his hand, frowning.

He would be gone for ten days, they told him — certainly no longer than two weeks. So write your letters to the people you usually send them to, they said; address them and date them as if you were still in Washington, and write them as if you were still in Washington too.

"But my mother and fiancée will carry on writing to that address — I won't get any letters!" he had protested.

"They'll be redirected to you. You'll get them — eventually."

"But why? And where am I going for ten days?" Surely not another stupid course trying to make a soldier out of him when all he was good at was mathematics and code-breaking.

And then an awful thought filled his head and he quickly dismissed it because they couldn't be sending him to make another parachute jump? He shuddered to remember the last, the only, jump he had made; tried to shut out the look of disbelief on his instructor's face. And far worse than that had been the awful bruising he got on landing and how lucky he was, he'd been told, not to have been badly injured, and to go back to signalling because surely he was better at signalling than parachuting out of a plane!

"Where you're going you'll know when you've been kitted out," he was told. "And you can leave your stuff here because here's where you'll be coming back to."

"I see," he'd said, but he hadn't understood a word of it because they still weren't giving straight answers to straight questions. All he knew was that the muscular sergeant major he encountered on his first night at Castle McLeish was a drill instructor who supervised assault courses and who took great delight in putting officers with soft hands through it time and time again. He could also be very insulting — respectfully insulting, that was!

So Keth had written two letters to his mother and four to Daisy and he would have to write at least two more because usually he wrote to Daisy every day.

Two of the letters he had supposedly written from Kentucky where he was having a weekend with Bas and Kitty's parents, told how delighted they were that Kitty and Drew were engaged and how sad Mrs Amelia was not to be having the time of her life organizing engagement showers and fussing over her daughter's trousseau. He felt all kinds of a heel as he wrote them.

Trouble was, he had seen no evidence yet of anything in the least familiar to him. As far as he was concerned, Castle McLeish was little better than a drill camp and Keth Purvis was being toughened up for something that this far had nothing to do with Enigma nor *bombes* nor code-breaking. Something, somewhere, didn't fit and the more he thought about it, the more apprehensive he became.

If only somebody would say — in answer to his oft-asked question — "Yes, Purvis, *this* is what you are here to do," then go on to explain exactly what it was they wanted of him and why he was going away for ten to fourteen days. It was a simple enough request to make but it had not been answered. Nor had anyone looked him straight in the eye and *that*, he decided, was what made him even more apprehensive.

Well, he'd had enough! He laid down his pen, picked up his cap, in case it became official, and made his way to the mess where he knew he would find the adjutant. And he would have answers to his questions; eyeball-to-eyeball answers, or his name wasn't Keth Purvis!

He had waited his time in the mess; waited until the adjutant was alone, then walked across the room to face him.

"A word, if you please — sir!"

The adjutant recognized the narrowed eyes and jutting jaw and asked him if it wouldn't wait until tomorrow.

No, Keth said, it wouldn't. Either he got a straight answer *now* to a couple of questions he wanted to ask or he would put in a request to see the Commanding Officer!

That was why he sat here now, in the outer office. Wait, he had been told. The Commanding Officer would see him in just a minute. The minute had stretched out to fifteen; the customary waiting time for all subordinates intent upon wasting the CO's time. A heel-cooling period.

Yet Keth did not want to cool down. He wanted to know why he had come from Washington only to do physical jerks and be ignored when he asked the sane and sensible question: what the hell was he doing here?

The phone on the ATS sergeant's desk rang. Keth wondered why every army girl here was a sergeant. This one was a good-looker; hair like Lyn Carmichael's. She smiled and told him to go in. He jumped to his feet, hoping his stare hadn't been too obvious, then knocked on the door she indicated.

"Enter!"

Keth closed the door behind him, came to attention and saluted.

"At ease, Purvis." He was not invited to sit, so he stood feet apart, relaxing his shoulders, hands behind back. "Now the way we do things here, Purvis, is not to make a b. nuisance of ourselves. We speak only when spoken to and we don't ask questions — right?"

"Sir . . ." Keth acknowledged cautiously, because he *had* been speaking out of turn and he *had* made a nuisance of himself, he supposed.

"Has the nature of what goes on in this establishment been lost on you, then? Did you never wonder why you had been asked to leave letters behind you?"

"Yes. And I wondered — with respect, sir — what kind of a course I was going on, for about a fortnight. I thought I would be doing the work I did at Bletchley Park, but I can see no indication of it here."

"Enigma, you mean? Well, you're right. We only *know* about Enigma here. We know about a lot of things."

"Yes, sir." Keth's mouth had gone dry. He was beginning to wish he had left well alone.

"If you'd kept your mouth shut for just another day, I could have given you the whole story, but since it seems you *can't*," the senior officer paused to let his words sink in, "since you want to know why you were brought back from Washington, I'll tell you.

"We had your card marked, Captain — just in case we wanted something done by someone who had a working knowledge of the Enigma machine. And then we found we did and we want you for a courier's job. And please let me finish," he snapped as Keth opened his mouth to speak. "There are any of a dozen other men could do the job and a damned sight more efficiently than you; men who don't ask questions nor throw their weight about as you have been doing! But none of those men has your knowledge of Enigma, you see."

"Courier?" Keth breathed, running his tongue round his top lip. "Deliver something?" Was *that* what all the fuss was about, for Pete's sake?

"No. We — *They* — want something picking up. From occupied France."

"*Ha!*" Keth's body sagged. Then he straightened his shoulders, stared ahead and asked of the regimental photograph on the wall, "And if I don't want to be parachuted into occupied France, sir?"

"Then you can start packing your bags now and I'll guarantee you a seat on the very next plane back to Washington! You asked to return to UK. You knew there would be conditions attached. You were specifically told so! What's the matter with you, man — got a yellow streak?"

"No, sir. Only when it comes to parachuting!"

"Hm. Understandable, I suppose, when your one and only jump was an utter fiasco, according to your records. That's why you won't be parachuting in."

"Then that's fine, sir." He didn't like being called yellow.

"I'm glad, because you'll be leaving here tonight. SOE will kit you out and brief you. It will be in no way dangerous. All you have to do is pick up something and bring it back. It's the operators in the field who'll be taking the risks."

"Yes, sir." Of course it wasn't dangerous. He hopped over to France every week of the year! "Am I to start packing my kit?"

"No. Leave it all in your room. Anything personal or private you will place in an envelope, seal it down, and initial the flap. One of your drawers has a lock and key. Lock anything away that you want to and give the key to the adjutant when you leave. Afterwards, you'll be coming back here so you can pick up your bags before you move on — back to Bletchley. Any questions?"

"Just how will I be — er — going in, sir?"

"All depends. On weather conditions. It'll either be by Lysander — that's an aircraft," he said, as if explaining to an idiot that a Lysander was an extremely efficient, small, light aircraft that could land on a postcard, almost, "or by sea — the submarine boys will put you ashore. Like I said, it'll all depend."

"Yes, sir. Thank you, sir."

"Right, then. Dismissed."

Keth remembered to salute, to do an efficient about-turn, then left the room, also remembering to smile and nod his thanks to the red-haired sergeant on the desk, as if what he had just been told hadn't knocked him for six!

Then he opened the door of his room, sat heavily on the bed and gasped, *"Flaming Norah!"*

CHAPTER
FOUR

Telegraphist Drew Sutton, having handed over the middle watch to his opposite number, stripped off to his underpants and swung himself into his hammock. Hammocks were very adaptable. On a boat as small as HMS *Penrose*, you slung them wherever there was a space, be it in the mess or beside the engine-room bulkhead. Hammocks moulded themselves to your body and gently swung you to sleep with every rising and falling of the *Penrose's* bows. Double beds, on the other hand; large, sinful double beds with soft shaded lights either side, took a lot of beating.

He smiled into the darkness. Kitty Sutton. From Kentucky. His kissing cousin and the woman he would marry just as soon as he could get her down the aisle. At this moment, Kitty was wallowing in being in love. She was in love with love and didn't want to spoil it, he suspected, by getting married. Yet they were morally married, he supposed. If sharing a bed on every possible occasion constituted a marriage, then they were well and truly wed. And he could understand Kitty's reasoning. To her, he supposed, sleeping together in delightful sin was more thrilling, more risqué, than the church-blessed union after which you not only could sleep together as much as you wanted, but were expected to do so. The intonations of a priest, the pronouncing of them man and wife was all very well, but his adorable Kitty, he was almost sure, preferred the former and the element of risk it carried with it.

Take Thursday night. He smiled fondly. She had stood demurely beside him as he signed the hotel register Andrew and Kathryn Sutton, Rowangarth, Holdenby, York. She had fluttered her eyelashes coyly, and the new lady receptionist — who didn't know Drew at all — asked her, if Modom wouldn't mind, of course, to produce her identity card.

Drew pulled in his breath and hoped she wouldn't blush furiously. And Kitty had not blushed at all! Having, on her arrival in the United Kingdom, acquired a British ration book and a British identity card which stated she was Kathryn Norma Clementina Sutton of Rowangarth, Holdenby, York — her official English address — she placed it on the desk with the sweetest of smiles and said she wouldn't mind at all!

Then the red-faced receptionist had stammered her apologies, explaining that one couldn't be too sure these days, and she hoped Mrs Sutton would forgive her.

At which Kitty smiled even more sweetly, pocketed her identity card, and all at once very serious, said, "It's *Lady* Sutton, if you don't mind."

Then she swept to the lift, jammed her finger on the button, leaving the squirming receptionist looking for the smallest crack in the floorboards in which to hide.

"Kitty Sutton, you really do take the plate of biscuits!" Drew had collapsed, laughing, on the large, bouncy bed beside her, imploring her never to change; always to be his outrageous, adorable Kitty. She had laughed with him and promised him she never would, then proceeded to undress with indecent haste.

"Kitty." He whispered her name softly. It would be strange, in church, marrying Kathryn Norma Clementina when it was really Kitty he was in love with. His life now could be divided into two phases; before Kitty and since Kitty — and he wondered how he had even remotely existed before the night, barely three months ago, when she came back into his life like a hurricane. He was still breathless from the impact.

The same ATS sergeant drove Keth away from Castle McLeish in the same car in which he had arrived, only this time he sat in the back seat. He sat there because he needed to think and uppermost in his mind was SOE, which any fool knew was Special Operatives Executive and differed from MI5 and MI6 in that it was concerned solely with getting agents into occupied Europe, listening for their W/T call signs and getting them out again when they had completed their operation or when it became imperative to remove them quickly for their own good. The Army, the Royal Air Force and the Royal Navy, Keth knew, all co-operated in the delivery and collection of those agents. You didn't work with Enigma and not know it.

Now, it seemed, either the Submarine Service or the Royal Air Force was taking him to France — ostensibly as an unimportant messenger, charged only with making a collection. There would be little risk to himself, he'd been told, and he grasped that assurance to him like a warm, comforting blanket.

On hearing his immediate destination he had, after the initial shock subsided, written two more letters to Daisy, then addressed nine envelopes, two to his mother and seven to Daisy. In the last letter, dated ten days ahead, he told her that the course he had been sent on was almost finished and soon he would have a more permanent address to give her.

Then he posted the unsealed envelopes in a box not unlike those used by the general public which was marked, *Missives for Censoring* but which really meant *Stick your love letters in here, chum, to be read by the po-faced adjutant.*

He had disliked the adjutant at Castle McLeish on sight, labelling him pompous, upper class and insensitive; wondering when it would be *his* turn to be deposited into occupied Europe; hoping it would be very soon! Yet Daisy was worth it. Just to think of her mellowed his mood.

He said, "I don't suppose you are allowed to tell me where you are taking me this time, Sergeant?"

"No, sir. Just another place Somewhere in Scotland — about an hour away."

He could hear the smile in her voice so he said, "And did they give you those stripes for being button-lipped?"

"Yes, sir, they did — and I don't want to lose them."

"Well," he expanded, "I can't say I'm sorry to be leaving Castle McLeish — for a while, at least. Especially I won't miss the adjutant. Is he always so snotty?"

"No, sir. Far from it." Keth sensed the sudden edge to her voice.

"Oh?"

"Yes, Captain. He's one of us — *really* one of us. He's done more drops into you-know-where than I dare tell you. About six weeks ago his wife was killed in an air raid. They haven't sent him back since. He has children, you see."

Keth did not speak for the remainder of the journey.

The only train into and out of Holdenby Halt on a Sunday bore Tatiana away to York and thence to King's Cross. Daisy stood and waved until the little two-carriage train disappeared round the curve in the track, then she cycled back to Keeper's Cottage, thinking that during the next seven days five of Aunt Julia's Clan would have been to Rowangarth, though not all at the same time, of course. Drew and Kitty had been and gone, then she, Daisy, arrived on leave and the day after, Tatiana had come home on one of her rare weekend visits.

And then Bas phoned, begging a bed for the night. Kitty's brother Bas was real sweet, Kitty said, on Rowangarth's land girl, Gracie. Gracie, on the other hand, was giving Bas a run for his money, though Jack Catchpole reckoned it was only a matter of time before he caught her.

Daisy looked forward to seeing Bas again. She had last seen Sebastian Sutton in the late summer of 'thirty-seven when she stood at the waving place where the railway line ran alongside Brattocks Wood for about thirty yards. Exactly five years ago. She and Bas had grown up since then. She smiled, wishing the Clan could be together again, just once for old times' sake. But the Clan was incomplete because Keth had been sent back to Washington and only the Lord knew when he would be home again.

She missed Keth desperately. A part of her would have given anything to have him back; the other part — the sensible part — wanted him to stay safely in America and no matter how long the war lasted, she always reasoned, she would at least know he would come home safely and that one day they *would* be married.

She told herself she was lucky; that Tatty would have given ten years of her life to know that one day, no matter how far away, she would see Tim Thomson again. Tatiana Sutton, the spoiled and cosseted child, had grown into a woman who once loved passionately, then dug in her stubborn English heels and defied her Russian mother and grandmother, taking herself off to London out of their meddling reach. Tatty lived at Aunt Julia's little white house now, with Sparrow to care for her, to understand and love her without reservations as only Tim had done.

Probably, if Kitty was sent to London to join up with ENSA, she would live at the little white mews house, too. It would be good for Tatty — provided Kitty didn't talk too much about how happy she was, and about getting married to Drew. But Kitty Sutton never did anything by halves. It wasn't in her nature. Bubbling, volatile Kitty, whom everyone noticed the minute she stepped into a room; sparkling, notice-me Kitty, whom Drew loved desperately. She would be good for him, Daisy thought as she pedalled down Keeper's Cottage lane. Drew had always been serious. He'd changed some since joining the Navy, but then you had to adapt. If you didn't, life in the armed forces could be hell.

"Hi, there!" Gracie, carrying cabbage leaves, making for Keeper's Cottage and the six hens she looked after at the bottom of the garden, beside the dog houses. "Just going to see to the hens — are you coming?"

Daisy said she was; she liked Gracie.

"Did you know Bas will be over at the weekend?"

"Yes. He told me. Twice. Once in a letter, then again on the phone."

"My word — letters *and* phone calls," Daisy teased. "Where's it all going to end?"

"Heaven only knows. Sometimes I think I should finish it all; times like now, I mean, when I can think straight. But when we're together it's an altogether different ball game, as Bas would say."

"It's called being in love, Gracie."

"Well, I'm not in love! You know I won't fall in love till the war is over!"

"Then you should try it. You might even get to like it."

"Even though we might be parted, like you and Keth? And I haven't got all day to stand here talking. Mr Catchpole will be giving me what for for wasting time. Here!" Carefully she put four brown eggs into Daisy's hands. "Take these to Tilda, will you? And don't drop them!" And with that she was off, up the garden path, making for the wild garden, striding out defiantly.

Never going to fall in love? Daisy thought, shaking her head. But Gracie *had* fallen for Bas the minute they had met, did she but know it. Pity, she thought, about that Lancashire common sense of hers getting in the way.

"See you!" she called, but Gracie strode on.

Another isolated, heavily guarded house, Keth thought; about thirty miles west of Castle McLeish if the position of the sinking sun was to be relied upon and the speed at which they had travelled. In this house there was more of an urgency in the air and, for once, the first question he asked had been answered with surprising frankness.

"How long will you be away, Purvis? Just as long as it takes, I suppose. There's a submarine flotilla not far from here and that's how you'll be going in. You might think things are ponderous slow when you get there, but you'll only have one contact — two, at the most. You'll just sit tight. Things get passed down the line, sort of. Better that way. And don't think that being a courier is paddling ashore, swopping passwords, then paddling back to the submarine. It's never that straightforward."

"No." They were sitting on the terrace, drinking an after-dinner coffee and brandy in the most civilized way; so ordinary and normal, Keth thought, that he couldn't believe that soon he would assume another identity and be sent to —

"Where exactly am I going — or shouldn't I ask?"

"Not out here. We'll go inside. It's getting cold, anyway." The man, dressed in civilian clothes and whose name Keth did not yet know, picked up his glass then murmured, "My office, I think it had better be."

When they were seated either side of a log fire and their glasses topped up, Keth said, "France, I gather."

"Yes — occupied France."

"Good. I speak the language passably well." Better than passably. Tatty's governess, herself French, had seen to that such a long time ago, it seemed. When Keth Purvis had lived at Rowangarth bothy, it was; before the war when Rowangarth garden apprentices lived there and were looked after by his mother — and she glad of the job. "I don't suppose I'd fool the locals, but I could get away with it with a German."

"Then let's hope you don't meet any. Oh — and you'll have to see the photographer first thing in the morning. Your papers are ready, except for that. Better see the barber too. Your haircut looks a bit English, I'm afraid. Apart from that, there's a resemblance to Gaston Martin about you."

"That's whose ID I'll be taking? A pretty ordinary name, isn't it?" The surname Martin was as common in France as Smith was in England.

"Nevertheless, Gaston Martin does exist. He was invalided out of the French artillery just after Dunkirk. Deaf, in one ear — remember that. But you'll be given details."

"And where is he now?"

"He's here, in the UK. He got taken off the beaches with our lot and our lot invalided him out. He's working in North Wales, so you're not likely to cross each other's paths — not where you'll be going, anyway."

"That's a relief." Keth was glad of the brandy because ever since he'd been told about France, his stomach had felt distinctly queasy. He wondered if he would sleep tonight or lie awake turning it over in his mind, telling himself he was a damn fool.

Yet a bargain was a bargain. They had told him when he asked to be sent back to England there

70

would be conditions attached and he accepted without a second thought; anything to get back to Daisy. But not in his craziest dreams had *anything* embraced cloak-and-dagger stuff, because that's what this escapade boiled down to; downright bloody stupid, to put not too fine a point on it. Times like now, he could accept it — just. But how would he feel when they dumped him on some dark beach? Not very brave, he knew.

"When it's over and done with — well, what I'm trying to say is — when I'm back, what's going to happen? To me, I mean."

"You'll pick up where you left off — at Bletchley Park. I take it you don't want to go back to Washington?"

"I don't! I'm only in this predicament now because I wanted to get home."

"Getting cold feet?"

"Got! I'm not the stuff heroes are made out of, I'm afraid; but conditions They said, and conditions I accepted."

"Good. Only a fool isn't — well, slightly afraid. And in SOE we don't ask for heroes. We'd rather our operatives stayed alive. I hate sending women in, you know," he said gruffly, picking up the brandy bottle, asking, with a raising of his eyebrows, if Keth wanted another. And Keth, who drank little, nodded and pushed his glass across the table.

"Good man. Help you to sleep. And don't worry, we aren't trying to recruit you."

"Then why now?" Keth tilted his glass.

"Might as well tell you now as tomorrow or the next day. We knew of your request — to come back to UK, that is — and you wouldn't have had a hope in hell if we hadn't needed a specialist, so to speak. You're familiar with Enigma." It was a statement.

"Yes. It's still something of a hit-and-miss thing — breaking their codes; well, breaking the naval codes."

"*Exactly*. That's the whole crux of the matter. Luftwaffe and Wehrmacht codes are little problem, or so I understand."

"That's right."

"But the naval codes — well, we can gather in their signals with no trouble at all. What is so annoying is that they chatter all over the Atlantic airwaves — especially the U-boats — and there's damn-all we can do about it. Can't break 'em."

"We can, sir, but most often it's too late."

"Far too late for our convoys, yes. We're losing one merchant ship in every four that crosses the Atlantic and it's got to stop. It's immoral!"

"So I'm to be part of an operation that's going to get hold of an Enigma machine the German Navy uses?"

"Yes. But don't get butterflies, Purvis."

"I've already got them and they're wearing clogs!"

"Then don't worry — at least not too much — because we think we've managed to get hold of one. Don't ask me how or where. One thing we don't do is expect our radio operators over there to transmit long-winded messages. But the information this far is that one is ready for collecting. That's why we need someone like you to check it over and bring it back. I take it you'd know what you were looking for?"

"No. But I'm familiar with the ones their Army and Air Force use, so I reckon I'd spot anything different."

"Then that's all we ask. Churchill would give a lot to break the U-boats' codes. We can't go on losing ships the way we are, nor the men who crew them."

Keth agreed, then asked, "So you don't know the exact location of the machine?"

"Only approximately. Like I said, our wireless ops in the field don't waste time on claptrap. They set up their sets, hook up their aerials and make their transmissions as fast as they can. The Krauts have got special detector units and they like getting hold of one of our men — or women. That's why our lot don't go round like Robin Hood and his Merry Men. They're mostly loners. The fewer operators they know, the better. You'll rely on your contact and trust him, or her. Your contact will tell you only as much as you need to know, so don't ask questions, or names, because you won't be told. I understand," the older man chuckled, "that you asked a lot of questions at Castle McLeish."

"I suppose I did, but I'm learning." Keth tilted his glass again. "Can I ask when I'll be going?"

"In about forty-eight hours."

It was, Keth supposed, like going to have a tooth filled, only worse. He drained his glass then got to his feet. "If you don't mind, sir, I think I'm ready for bed now."

"Yes. Off with you. By the way, you don't usually hit the bottle, do you?"

"Hardly ever. But on this occasion, it has helped calm the butterflies. Good night, sir."

"'Night, Purvis." The elderly man watched him walk carefully to the door, relieved to find himself thinking that the young officer, inexperienced though he was, would fit the bill nicely. Strangely dark, he brooded. Black hair, black eyes. Gypsy blood, perhaps?

"Purvis!" he called.

"Sir?" Keth's face reappeared round the door.

"Any didicoy blood in you?"

"No," Keth grinned. "My mother was a Pendennis. Cornish. They're a dark people."

"Ah, yes."

Didn't take offence easily, either. And no matter what they'd said about him at Castle McLeish, *he* liked him. Purvis should do all right — as well as the next man, that was . . .

Grace Fielding was picking the last of the late-fruiting raspberries when a tall shadow fell down the rows. Without turning she said, "Hullo, Bas Sutton."

"Hi, Gracie. Marry me?"

She put down her basket and turned impatiently.

"No, I won't — thank you. And you always say that!"

"Can you blame me when you always say no?" He tilted her chin, then kissed her mouth.

"And you can stop that in working hours!" He always did it and in public, too! "Mr Catchpole's going to catch you one day and you'll be in trouble!"

"No I won't. I've just seen him — given him some tobacco. I shouldn't wonder if he isn't sitting on his apple box right now, puffing away without a care in the world."

"You're devious, Bas Sutton, and shameless." She clasped her arms round his neck, offering her mouth because even if Mr Catchpole were not sitting on his box, smoking contentedly, the raspberry canes hid them. And she did like it when he kissed her, and she wanted nothing more than to say yes, she would marry him; would have said it, except for just one thing. Her sort and Bas Sutton's sort didn't mix. Not that she was ashamed of her ordinariness. She was what she was because of it and she loved her parents and her grandfather. She even loved Rochdale, though not quite as much as Rowangarth.

Rowangarth. Bas was sprung from the Rowangarth Suttons — the Garth Suttons, Mr Catchpole called them. His grandfather Edward Sutton had been born at Rowangarth, even though he married into Pendenys. And the Pendenys Suttons had the brass, she had learned, and one day Bas would inherit that great house — or was it a castle? — simply because his Uncle Nathan, who owned it now, had no children and in the natural order of things, the buck would stop at Sebastian Sutton — or so Bas once said.

But even if Bas refused Pendenys, he'd be rich in his own right because one day he would inherit one of the most prosperous and prestigious studs in Kentucky, while Gracie Fielding lived in a red-brick council house and would inherit nothing except her mother's engagement ring. And the silver-plated teapot that had come to her from a maiden aunt.

"What are you thinking about? You were staring at that weather cock as if you expected it to take off."

"I — oh, I was thinking it's time for Mr Catchpole's tea so you'd better kiss me just once more, then you can stay here and finish picking this row till I call you. And don't squash them. They're for the house, for dessert tonight, and Tilda Tewk doesn't like squashy fruit!"

"Yes, ma'am." He kissed her gently, then whispered, "I love you, Gracie."

He always told her he loved her because one day she would let slip her guard and say she loved him too. One day. And when it happened, he would throw his cap in the air, climb to the top of Holdenby Pike and shout it out to the whole Riding!

"I'm sure you do, Bas Sutton," she said primly. "But in the meantime get on with picking those rasps!"

76

"You're not interested in the candies I've brought you, or the silk stockings or the lipstick, then?"

"Pick!" she ordered, then laughing she left him to find Jack Catchpole, who was puffing contentedly on a well-filled pipe.

"I've come to make the tea," she said. "Bas is carrying on with the picking."

"Ar. He's a right grand lad, tha' knows."

"I'm sure he is, but that's between me and Bas, isn't it, and nobody else!"

She stopped, horrified at her cheek, her daring, but Mr Catchpole continued with his contented puffing and his wheezy chuckling and didn't take offence at all. Because he knew what the outcome of it all would be, despite the lass's protestations. He'd said as much to Lily.

"Mark my words, missus, young Bas isn't going to take no for an answer. Things alus happens in threes and there'll be three weddings round these parts, mark my words if there isn't."

And in the meantime, may heaven bless and protect GIs who brought tins of tobacco every time they came courting his land girl!

"Make sure it runs to three mugs, Gracie lass," he called over his shoulder. "And make sure I get the strongest!"

Life on a mid-September afternoon could be very pleasant, be danged if it couldn't — even if there was a war on!

CHAPTER
FIVE

Her watch over, Leading Wren Lyndis Carmichael scanned the letterboard beside the door at Hellas House. Everyone did it. It was automatic on entering quarters.

She reached for the one addressed to Daisy, recognizing Keth's writing and the Censor's red stamp. She would put it in Daisy's top drawer with the one that came yesterday — a kind of welcome back after her leave.

It was only then she saw the letter bearing her own name, and a bright orange 20-cents Kenyan stamp. It had taken almost three weeks to arrive. Sea mail, of course. Very few letters came by air now.

She closed the door of Cabin 4A behind her, placing the letters on the chest of drawers. The midday meal was being served; she would read her own letter when she had eaten because it was from her father and the first since he had written telling her of her mother's death — the woman she had thought was her mother, that was.

She glanced round the small, empty cabin. She missed Daisy. It was almost a year since a woebegone Wren in an ill-fitting uniform and flush-faced from a raging temperature came to Cabin 4A.

A lot had happened in that time. They became close friends, and shared runs ashore with Drew Sutton when his minesweeper docked in Liverpool. Lyn tried not to think about Drew Sutton now, because she had fallen crazily in love with him and ached for him to love her.

And so he would have, she thought despairingly, had not Kitty Sutton arrived from America. It had been a love-at-first-sight job for them both — or so Daisy had said on one of the rare occasions on which she now mentioned her brother.

It had been that, all right. Love, and everything else! Drew and Kitty spent that same night together and in the morning they were engaged. That was what hurt, Lyn acknowledged. Them sleeping together, because she had practically offered herself on a plate, only to be gently turned down by Drew Sutton. As if he were waiting for Kitty to come along, she thought, and amusing himself with Lyn Carmichael meantime, damn fool she had been for letting him.

She lifted her chin and bit on her lip. She no longer cried just to think of Drew, and Drew kissing Kitty and making love to Kitty. Not outwardly, that was. Her tears were gone because she had no more left to cry; only those inside her that hurt like hell; tears that didn't leave her eyelids swollen and her nose red, but which writhed through her to stick in a hard knot in her throat and refuse to be shed.

She let go a deep sigh, then made her reluctant way to the mess. After early watch, kept-warm dinners were served and kept-warm dinners offered hard peas and gravy dried leathery. And it was the same with the custard, spooned over a sugarless pudding. Leathery, like the gravy she thought miserably, and at this moment she wanted to be miserable because a letter had come from her father and she didn't want to open it.

Nor would she, she thought defiantly, taking a kept-warm plate from the serving hatch. She would not open the letter until Daisy came back from leave; pretend it had arrived only that morning. And then, because Daisy knew all about what had gone on in Kenya, and *before* Kenya, reading what her father had written wouldn't seem so bad.

She speared a chunk of meat on the end of her fork, looking at it distastefully.

"Roll on my leave," she said out loud to no one in particular. Roll on October when she would collect her travel warrant and her leave pass, and a seven-day ration card, and go to stay with Auntie Blod in Llangollen. At least in Llangollen there would be no chance of accidentally meeting Drew Sutton — with Kitty.

She began to mull over the idea of volunteering for overseas service and knew at once she would never do it; knew that she lived daily in the hope of seeing Drew, even with Kitty, because she loved him that much.

She would always love him.

Tatiana Sutton left the Underground at Knightsbridge and turned left into Brompton Road, thinking with pleasure of the rabbit, already skinned, and the pheasant, already plucked and wrapped in newspapers, in her leather bag. Daisy's father had given them and Daisy's mother prepared them, sending with them her very best love to Sparrow. And not only meat enough for four meals, but two large brown eggs given by Gracie, fresh from the nest only that morning and not weeks old like the rationed shop eggs Sparrow had to break into a cup and sniff suspiciously before using.

Sparrow would be pleased too with the bunch of Michaelmas daisies and chrysanthemums sent with Julia's love, and the grave instructions to take care of herself now that the nights were drawing in, and to keep warm.

Dear Sparrow. So full of love and caring and cosseting. She had made life bearable again, and when the war was over and she had to return to Denniston House, she would miss Sparrow a lot.

She smiled as she crossed the road into Montpelier Mews, once upon a time the stables belonging to the big houses in the square. The little white house with its red tiled floors and shining brass doorknobs and handles was home to her now, and Sparrow her best-loved person — apart from

Tim, that was. It shamed her, sometimes, that if asked to place her right hand on the Bible and state who was most precious to her, she would in all conscience have to answer that it was Sparrow, hurt though her mother would be to hear it.

"I'm home," she called, banging the outer and inner doors behind her. "Have you missed me?"

"I'll miss the peace and quiet now that you're back. Are those flowers for me?"

"You know they are. Aunt Julia picked them herself. She sends love and says you are to look after yourself."

"And is the dear lady well?"

"She is."

"And happy?"

"Very happy, Sparrow, and chasing around the parish doing her vicar's wife bit and looking after Bas, who's on leave for a couple of days."

"Your Aunt Julia should have had children of her own," Sparrow sighed, "but she left it over late. I suppose, now you're back, I'd better make a pot of tea."

Truth known, she had been waiting this hour past to make one and would have, were it not wasteful of the tea ration to use a precious spoonful for one person only, when that same spoonful could provide tea for two.

"Yes, please. You put the kettle on whilst I unpack my gifts, *food* gifts! I tell you, Sparrow, you and I will be eating like lords this week!"

"Hm. Well, I hope the food was honestly got, and not black market."

"It was — honestly got, I mean. Daisy's father said he was sorry he couldn't supply the butter to roast the pheasant in. And did any letters come whilst I was away and did Uncle Igor phone?"

"No letters and no phone call — leastways, not from your uncle. But our Joannie rang to ask if you'd be busy on Tuesday night and I told her you wouldn't be."

"But I'm doing escort duty with Sam from the convalescent home. We're going up West to see *The Dancing Years*."

"She knows that. What she rang for was to see if you could manage an extra one. She thought the music might cheer him up. He's at the same convalescent home as Sam, and waiting his turn to go for treatment."

"And is he —?" There was no need to finish the sentence; no need to say the word.

"Yes. Like all the others and in need of a kind word and a smile. Those smiles mean a lot, Joannie said. I'll ring her back when we've had our cuppa and tell her you don't mind taking one extra."

"No trouble at all, Sparrow."

"You're sure, now, 'cos what I didn't tell you is that he's not only got burns — this lad got blinded as well."

"Hell!" She shuddered, covering her face with her hands.

"You don't have to take him if it's going to upset you."

"But of course I will. I want to. It was just that it doesn't seem fair, does it?"

"Life never is, girl."

"You don't have to tell me. And I'll manage all right. Sam will give me a hand, tell Joannie."

"You're a good soul, Tatiana Sutton. You'll get your reward in heaven."

"I'd rather have it here on earth. I'd swap all that heaven nonsense just to have ten minutes with Tim; say a proper goodbye."

"What do you mean — 'heaven nonsense'? Blasphemous, that is!"

"Well, I don't believe in heaven and sometimes I don't believe in God either — only in Jesus," she added hastily.

"Well! I'm surprised at you! And what would your mother think to hear you say that?"

"Nothing, because I wouldn't say it in front of her."

"And you'd best not say it in front of me again either! Do I make myself plain?"

"Yes, Sparrow, you do. And I won't say it again if you'll promise not to go on about it and try to convert me."

"Convert you? Now would I do that, and you so bitter inside that you can't see the wood for the trees? Come here and let's you and me have a cuddle because Sparrow understands. She really does."

"I know you do, and I'm sorry if I upset you," Tatiana whispered, hugging her close. "And I ought

84

to be ashamed, shouldn't I? At least I'm not injured, nor blind."

"No, girl, you aren't." Sparrow shuddered even to think of that beautiful face burned and blistered and those big, brown eyes never to see again. "And that's something to be thankful to God for, 'cos it's all in His hands, and by the time you're as old as I am you'll have come to realize it, I hope."

"And how old are you, Sparrow?" She didn't want to talk about God.

"As old as my tongue and a bit older than my teeth! So are you going to pour that tea before it's stewed to ruination, and give me the news from Yorkshire?" She had never been to Holdenby; probably never would, but that didn't prevent her feeling a part of Rowangarth.

And Tatiana said she was, then whispered again that she was sorry, because not for anything would she upset Sparrow, who must be *at least* seventy-five.

Keth shook the hand of a colonel from Army Intelligence, who did not offer his name but asked him, pleasantly enough, to sit down and make himself comfortable.

"So! The MO and the dental officer have given you the all clear; have you made a will?"

"Yes." Talk of such things made him uneasy. Wills were for old people, he had always thought. "When I was first commissioned, I took care of that."

"And your next of kin is your mother?"

"Yes." Mention of next of kin gave him the same feeling.

"Just a precaution. Nothing sinister, but in view of the fact you'll be under some slight risk . . ."

"Slight!" Keth jerked.

"You're having second thoughts? Because now's the time to say so . . ."

"No second thoughts. I was told there would be conditions and I accepted them. But don't think I shall enjoy going, because I won't! So does that make me a coward?"

"No. I wouldn't give much chance for the safety of any of our operatives who had no fear. Nor would I believe them if they said as much. And a man who admits fear, but still goes ahead with the job is far from being a coward."

"I'm a mathematician, sir. There's not one iota of derring-do in my entire body."

"Then be glad of it. It's the careful ones who make it home every time. But you aren't a trained operator, as such. We've given you only enough knowledge to help you survive. The less you know, the better. We'll put you ashore, you'll be met and taken to a safe house. You'll wait there until you hear that what you have gone to collect will be delivered to you.

"Then you'll hang on to it — study it all you can within the bounds of safety — and keep your head down until we can have you picked up. It will depend on weather conditions, and suchlike. Either the submarine that will take you out will bring you back, or we'll send a Lysander in."

"And I'm definitely going in by submarine. No jumps?"

"No parachuting. According to your records, you wouldn't survive another jump!"

"You could be right, sir." Keth managed a smile; one of relief rather than pleasure. "It's an experience I'd rather not dwell on. The sea route sounds a lot safer."

"It *is* safe. There's a submarine flotilla not five miles from here — the fifteenth. They've done a fair bit of toing and froing for us in the past. We've been in touch with their navigating officer about tides and things. We want a flowing tide; one that will wash away any evidence like footsteps — allow the dinghy to get as far inshore as possible. Provided the Met boys give us the okay weatherwise, you'll be on your way within hours and back within a couple of weeks. Then you'll completely forget your little errand to France."

Little errand? Typical, that was, when just to think of it made his teeth water, Keth brooded.

"I'll be happy to — forget it, I mean."

"You'll be in all sorts of trouble if you don't! Anyway, good luck, Purvis. Get yourself over to Room 22. Your papers are ready — and all you need to know about Gaston Martin. Read them over and over. Think yourself into his identity. He was born in a little place near Lyons, which is in unoccupied France. You won't be going anywhere near there, so you're unlikely to run into anyone who might have known him. His family probably have been told that he's missing, believed killed in action.

"If anything happens, though, make for the unoccupied sector. You'll be safe enough there. This far, the Krauts have respected their boundaries and left them alone."

"Vichy France, you mean, sir? And what constitutes *anything*?"

"Anything going wrong. You can get to the Pyrenees from unoccupied territory, and over into Spain. Or you'll be told by Room 22 where you can get help. In one of the Marseilles brothels, for instance, the madam can be relied upon."

"*Brothel?*"

"Yes. Places where men can come and go without being noticed overmuch. Don't look so holier-than-thou, man. There *is* a war on, don't forget, but you can ask all the questions you want of the Room 22 people. They'll be rigging you out with clothes and all you need. Ask a lot of questions. What may seem trivial might just stand you in good stead *if* anything were to go a bit wrong — which it shouldn't."

"No, sir. A straightforward pick-up."

"Absolutely." The colonel rose to his feet, holding out his hand, wishing Keth good luck, assuring him that if he kept his ears open and his eyes down, the entire operation should go like clockwork.

Keth pushed back his chair, put on his cap, then saluted and left the room, hoping with all his

88

thudding heart that the colonel knew what he was talking about.

Clockwork. He would say it over and over again. It would be his good-luck word. The submarine boys would get him there and someone would get him out. With the package. And he would want to know more about that package and about what he would do when he stood up to the ankles in sea water and the submarine lads were getting the hell out of it!

He thought about the last war and men who were given no choice but to crawl over the tops of trenches into No Man's Land through barbed wire and uncharted minefields, to face the machine gunners. His thoughts went back to a churchyard in Hampshire; to the grave of the man who had gone over the top many times. And in that moment he felt a strange, fatalistic calm and very near to Dickon Purvis, his father, who, if there really was a hereafter, would be looking down tonight on his son. And understanding.

"Well, that's everybody been and gone — well, almost everybody," Gracie sighed. "Drew and Kitty, and Tatty. And Daisy goes tomorrow."

"You've forgotten young Keth. He hasn't been. And what about Bas, then?" Catchpole demanded.

"The idiot!" Bas had decided not to take the one Sunday train to York, saying he would rather stay a few hours longer, then hitch a lift back to his billet at the Army Air Corps base at Burtonwood. "He was absent without leave, you know. Someone was covering for him, but I hope he made it back all right. Stupid!" Gracie fretted, pushing her hoe angrily into a very small weed. "One of these days he'll run into the Snowdrops and his feet won't touch the ground!"

"*Snowdrops?*"

"Their military police. They call them that because they wear white gaiters and white helmets."

"Hm. Snowdrops is nice little flowers. Pretty and dainty — and welcome. You alus know winter is almost over when the snowdrops flower."

"Well, those military police are neither pretty nor dainty. Big bruisers, Bas says they are, and some of them real nasty with it. And he didn't phone me last night, either!"

"Last night," said Catchpole severely, "he was busy thumbing a lift back to camp — or avoiding those Snowdrop lads. On the other hand, he might have got hisself caught . . ."

"Oh, Mr Catchpole, you don't think he has?"

"He could have, but I hope not." He would miss his tins of tobacco.

"And so do I! Going AWOL is a serious thing."

"It is. In the last war they shot 'em for it, but they're a bit more civilized now. Reckon these days he'd only get three months in prison!"

"You're joking, Mr Catchpole!" It didn't bear thinking about; three months without seeing Bas!

90

"Happen I am, lass. There'll be a phone call for you tonight, don't fret. He's as taken with you as you are with him. He'll get through."

"He can please himself!" Gracie jammed her hoe deep into the ground so it stood upright between the rows of early chrysanthemums, shivering and swaying. "I'm going to make tea," she called over her shoulder. "Not that you deserve any!"

Head high, she made for the potting shed, heels crunching the gravel. Then she filled the little iron kettle at the standtap and set it to boil on the hob, taking deep, calming breaths, chiding herself because she'd let Mr Catchpole get under her skin, because there was more than an element of truth in what he'd said. She *was* taken with Bas Sutton. She looked forward to his visits, to dancing with him and kissing him. And the way he smiled made delicious little shivers run all the way from her toes to her nose.

Yet shivers apart, she always managed to count to ten; always refused to say she loved him and always said no, very prettily, each time he asked her to marry him. She was losing count of the times he'd said, "Marry me?"; losing count of the number of times she had closed her eyes, taken a deep breath and thought, really hard, about Daisy and Keth being so far apart and them not knowing when they would meet again. And Drew, fretting because Kitty could be sent to London to work for ENSA. And as for poor Tatty and Tim . . .

She tipped the twist of tea and sugar into the pot, determined not to get upset next time Mr Catchpole teased her about Bas or blush furiously or say things she didn't mean because she was almost sure she could fall in love with him, though not for anything would she admit it to a soul!

She glared at the kettle, willing it to boil and all the time thinking about Bas and the Snowdrops and hoping they hadn't stopped him and asked him for his leave pass. Because Bas getting caught just didn't bear thinking about!

CHAPTER
SIX

Daisy removed the *On Leave* disc from the hook beneath her name, replacing it with one bearing the words *In Quarters, Cabin 4A*. Then she glanced at the criss-crossed letter board. None there for her, but in all probability Lyn had taken them.

Returning from leave was less traumatic now, she acknowledged, as the cramped familiarity of Cabin 4A reached out to her. This, for most of the year, was home; this small space with room only for a two-tier bunk, a chest of drawers and two wooden chairs she had shared for a year with Lyn who would soon be returning from watch. And shared it amicably, too. They were firm friends, their only cross words caused by Drew who was now engaged to Kitty. His feet-first fall into love with Kitty was sudden and thorough. Exquisite disbelief rocked him on his heels to find that after five years apart, his tomboy Kentucky cousin had grown into a head-turning beauty. The engagement pleasantly shocked everyone who knew him — with the exception of Lyn Carmichael, who was still devastated by it.

Daisy removed her hat, then pulled her fingers through her hair, smiling to see two letters on her pillow just as she expected and a sheet of notepaper on which was written large and red, "WELCOME BACK. YOU'VE HAD IT, CHUM!" Had her leave, that was, until the New Year. Lyn, on the other hand, would start hers next week, which was a crafty move when you considered she would miss her week of night duties.

Daisy smiled, pushed the note into her drawer, determined to leave it on Lyn's pillow in two weeks' time, and carefully opened the two envelopes. Then she kicked off her shoes and lay back on her bunk to read them at least twice. The first time to savour their contents; to close her eyes and recall kisses and whispered love words; the second time to read between the lines for small phrases, names deliberately misused; any irregularity, no matter how small, that would hint at something the Censor had not seized upon.

Yet there was nothing, save that he loved her, missed her, wanted her. Nothing about the work he did in Washington nor if there was even the slightest chance he might be sent back to England with the same indecent haste They had sent him away. But They could do anything They wanted and usually did. Without explanation; without giving Keth even a forty-eight-hour leave pass to let them say goodbye. By the time this war was over, *They* would have a great deal to answer for!

A glance at her watch told her it was time for evening standeasy or, had she been a civilian, a bedtime drink and a snack. She had not eaten since midday and all at once realized she was hungry. She wondered as she spread viciously red jam on her bread what news Lyn would have and thought that in all probability there would be none. These days some of the sparkle had left Lyn's eyes and a lot of her *joie de vivre*, which was a pity because she and Drew seemed so good together. Until Kitty, that was . . .

She balanced her plate on her mug and walked carefully back to Cabin 4A. Eating in cabins was forbidden but rules were there to be broken. Life would be very dull without the occasional tilt at Authority and at the moment the common room was cold and cheerless without the fire which could not be lit until October because of the shortage of coal.

It made her think of the leaping log fire in the black-leaded grate at Keeper's Cottage and Mam sitting by it alone because Dada would be out with the Home Guard until ten o'clock at least.

A pang of homesickness hit her and she quickly ate her bread and jam, licked her sticky fingers, then fished in the pocket of her belt for three sixpences.

She would book a call home. Trunk calls almost always took ages to come through, but tonight she might be lucky and get through before lights out.

"Could I have Holdenby 195, please?" she asked the operator, who answered almost at once. "Holdenby, York?"

"Have one shilling and sixpence ready, please."

Daisy smiled. Operators never asked you to have your money ready if they didn't have a line to Trunks. She pushed three sixpenny pieces into the slot, with a ping, ping, ping.

"Press button A. You're through now."

All at once life was not good, exactly, but at least bearable. A phone call home with no bother and Lyn back off watch in less than an hour. If only there were some way to ring Keth or even send a message on the teleprinter at Epsom House, then life would be really good. If only Washington — and Keth — were not so far away!

"Mam! It's me! I'm back safe and sound. Thanks for a lovely leave . . ."

Keth spread the papers on the table in his room, gazing at them with disbelief.

"Read them," he was told in Room 22. "Read them over and over. Think yourself into Gaston Martin. Bring them all back here, though, before you go to sleep. They'll be safer with us."

Sleep? Would he ever sleep again? He hadn't felt too bad about what was to come until he was faced with another man's identity. That was when it really hit him.

An identification card with Keth Purvis's photograph on it; a card skilfully forged to look as if it had been in his pocket — in Gaston Martin's pocket — since his discharge from the French Army in the winter of 1940.

Gaston Martin, his work permit said, was a labourer. Keth looked at his hands and shrugged, then looked again at the equally worn discharge certificate, taking in still more of the details of Gaston Martin's life. He must, he had been told, commit it to his memory; must imagine himself into another man's ego — into his psyche, his soul. He must, from now on, even try to think in this other man's language.

Born to Belle Martin in her mother's apartment at Nancy at three in the afternoon; two months after his father's death in the trenches. Left in the care of his grandmother when his mother returned to her former occupation of seamstress. A sewing-maid, like Daisy's mother?

Daisy. He was back home, yet she did not know; just the distance of a phone call away, yet he must not ring her. And of course he could not, because Keth Purvis no longer existed; not until he returned from France, that was. *If* he returned, he thought distastefully.

Gaston Martin. Born on 3 September 1917. He would remember the date easily because another war, this war, started on 3 September.

He didn't know his address because as yet no one knew just where he would be put ashore. When they did, an address would be written in in the same faked faded ink, he supposed. They were thorough, he'd grant them that.

Put ashore. Words to start the tingling behind his nose. Somewhere, probably, between La Rochelle and Biarritz, Room 22 said vaguely; somewhere very near, Keth hoped, to the package he was to pick up.

That part of the coast would be safer, wouldn't it, than the highly fortified northern ports of Calais and Dunkirk? The journey would take longer, though. How many days' sailing time by submarine and did submarines travel submerged during daylight hours? How many miles an hour could they do? *Knots* per hour, wasn't it?

He wondered how it would feel to be submerged. Submariners couldn't suffer from claustrophobia on the sea bed, could they? So much water around and above them. How much pressure, his mathematical mind demanded, could the hull of a submarine take?

But that was nothing to do with him and he forced his thoughts back to the business of getting to France. A crossing to the north would have taken less time; but the South of France was nearer to unoccupied country — to Vichy France; nearer, too, to neutral Spain — if you could call Franco neutral in his thinking.

Yet why had Room 22 laid such stress on the nearness of Vichy France, and Spain? Was his trip — hell, *trip*? — to France more dangerous than they wanted him to believe?

He was afraid. He admitted it. Not necessarily of being killed quickly and cleanly. That took seconds and most times you didn't know it was going to happen, his father once said. But he was really afraid of being taken and interrogated and then killed and worse even would be the knowledge that he would know, just before it happened, that he would never see Daisy again, nor Mum, and that they would probably never know how he had died. That really hurt.

He reached in the pocket of his jacket for his flask, poured a too-large measure of whisky, then tossed it down. It stung his throat and made him gasp for breath, but he felt better for it.

Once, when he worked in the boring safeness of Bletchley Park, Daisy had demanded to know why he was so secretive about what he did, and was he really a spy?

Keth Purvis a spy! His laugh had been genuine, yet now he *was* a spy. An enemy agent the Germans would call him if they got hold of him. He was to assume another man's identity, carry false papers, wear specially provided civilian clothes obtained in France. What else could he be called but spy?

He wanted Daisy *now*, yet who was Daisy? Gaston Martin did not know of her existence. Gaston Martin had been discharged from the Army because his hearing was impaired. His papers said so. He must remember that, always. Not to hear properly might be an advantage if people started demanding answers to questions.

The whisky inside his empty stomach was beginning to relax him and he found he could think of Daisy without feeling sick at the thought of losing her. He *wasn't* going to lose her! *They* were sending him to France as a courier because he knew about Enigma. That was all. He wasn't an agent. Agents were highly trained and he was an amateur. Even that stupid lot at Whitehall didn't send amateurs into danger — not real danger. He was to be taken to France by submarine, met, then hidden until it was time for him to bring back the package. They would take good care of him. Not that Keth Purvis was of any importance. What was important was the machine he would bring back. Any boffin with a knowledge of Enigma could have done it, couldn't they? They had chosen him because he owed them one for his passage back to England, so he had to do it, if only to save lives at sea. Keth Purvis wasn't at sea, was he? Didn't cross the Atlantic again and again in a slow-moving convoy, nor go on the Murmansk run — that suicide trip to the north of Russia with tanks and guns for Stalin.

When it was over and done with he would return to Bletchley Park. They had told him that. And when that happened, he would never again complain of the mind-blowing frustration of it. He would even be glad that in some small way, perhaps, what he had done would help decode German U-boat signals more easily. Breaking their code only one day in five wasn't on. When they could break it as easily as the Wehrmacht and Luftwaffe codes, then the Atlantic would be a whole lot safer for Allied seamen.

He looked at the flask, then screwed the top back firmly. Gaston Martin had no need of more.

He picked up the closely typed papers he had been given. Gaston Martin, born to Belle and the late Jules a year before the end of the last war.

His mother was dead too. In hospital, following complications after an operation for appendicitis and no, he had not been with her when she died. It was too sudden, too unexpected. Only *Grand-mère* was with her. *Grand-mère* died a year later. Both she and *Maman* were buried at — Hell! *Where?*

Frantically he searched through the papers. So much to learn, but learn it he would, because he was going to France and coming back safely. All in one piece.

D-watch, relieved by A-watch, arrived back at Hellas House at twenty minutes past midnight or, in naval time, 00.20 hours.

"Hi," smiled Lyn, carefully pushing open the door, depositing tea and jam and bread on the chest of drawers. "I thought you'd be awake still. Brought you up a drink. Good leave, then?"

"Great. And thanks for leaving the letters — and the welcome-back greeting."

"Keth all right?" Lyn took off her jacket, eased off her shoes.

"He's fine. He still loves me, which isn't a lot of use, him over there and me here. Any news? Scandal?"

"News — yes. You know the buzz about the hats? Well, it's official. New caps in clothing stores soon and we're to swap the old ones for the new type.

Not before time, either. Just like school hats, these things. The new ones will be a sort of cross between a matelot's cap and a beret, I heard. Cheeky. Worn low on the forehead, an inch above the eyebrows. At least I'll be able to wear my hair in a pleat and not have to screw it into a roll." Lyn Carmichael refused, unlike most other Wrens, to have her hair cut short. "Oh, and we needn't carry our respirators everywhere now. Seems Hitler isn't going to gas us! We're only to take them when we go on leave. They're going to let us carry shoulder bags. I've actually seen one, though we have to buy them ourselves. Fifteen bob, I think they'll be. Quite smart. It's all been happening whilst you were away."

"Things are looking up," Daisy smiled. "No more news?"

"We-e-ll, yes." Lyn took a steadying gulp of tea. "I had a letter from Kenya. From my father. It took me ages to open it because for some stupid reason I hadn't expected to hear from him again — well, not until the war was over. It seems, though, that he and Auntie Blod have written to each other regularly since my mother died."

"The lady you *thought* was your mother," Daisy corrected.

"*Thought*. I never really liked her; that was why she had me sent to school in England, I suppose."

"But you like your Auntie Blod, don't you?"

"If you mean am I glad she's my real mother and not my aunt, yes, I am. My father should have

102

married her, though, knowing he'd got her pregnant."

"I think he might have done, Carmichael, if your Auntie Blod had told him."

"Then she should have and they could have married and I'd have had a proper mother and father!"

"You're still annoyed about it, aren't you — annoyed with your father, I mean?"

"Yes, I am. The randy old goat!"

"Lyn! That isn't kind! It must have been awful for your Auntie Blod, giving you up to her sister and thinking she would never see you again. And I think she still loves your father, else why did she never marry and why are they writing to each other all of a sudden?"

"Why indeed, and me not being told about it! But I suppose it'll all come out in the wash. Auntie Blod will tell me about it when I go on leave. And if she still loves him, well, what the heck!"

Blodwen Meredith, her *real* mother, if she wanted to be picky, must truly have loved her father, just as Lyn loved — would *always* love — Drew Sutton. It was like Auntie Blod once said: you couldn't turn love off to order.

"It's their life," Daisy said softly.

"Yes, it is. Want some bread and jam?"

"Just tea, thanks. And, Lyn — about your father. You once said you liked him better than your mother; that he was quite decent to you, when *she* wasn't there."

"I should think so, too! After all, I was his natural daughter. My mother must have hated it really, having me around. The one I *thought* was my mother," she amended, sighing.

"Well, it's all coming right for them now, and you should be glad about it if they want to get together after all those years."

"I suppose I should. I'll try to be, if only for Auntie Blod's sake. I love her a lot. Always did."

"Probably because some part of you knew she was your real mother."

"Probably. Sure you don't want this bread and jam, Dwerryhouse?"

"Sure. Eat it yourself, then get into bed. I've put a hot-water bottle in for you. Chop chop! Some of us want to get to sleep! And by the way — I missed you. I'm sort of glad to be back in the old routine."

She pushed the empty mug beneath her bunk, then wriggled down into her blankets. Come to think of it, Liverpool wasn't a bad old place to see out the war in, for all its faults — provided the Luftwaffe didn't come back and blitz it again!

But anywhere would do really. Without Keth, one port was much the same as another. And Lyn was smashing to be with — when she wasn't all quiet, thinking about Drew marrying someone else, that was. Poor Lyn . . .

"Where are they, then?" Tatiana Sutton smiled a greeting at Sparrow's Joannie, who was quite high up, really, in the Women's Voluntary Service.

"You're sure you don't mind — taking on another one?"

"Not at all. They aren't a bit of trouble. It's the one or two civilians who look at them as if they've got no right to be out in public that bother me!"

"The air gunner is blind. Did Aunt Emily tell you?"

"She did." Tatiana drew in her breath sharply. Tim had been an air gunner. "But he'll like the music, even though he won't be able to . . ." Her voice trailed off, because it was awful enough having your face burned beyond recognition; to lose your sight as well must make you want to rage against the injustice of it.

"The music will be an extra bonus," Joannie said. "Just going out on the town will be really something. It's his first time out since — since it happened. You'll have to play it by ear. You realize that, don't you?"

"I do. What's his name?"

"Bill Benson. How's Aunt Emily, by the way?"

"She's fine. Sent her love. Joannie — just how old *is* she? I've asked, but she won't tell."

"So have I and got one of her looks for it. But it's my guess she's nearer eighty than seventy."

"She's a love. She bullies me, you know."

"I do know, but it's really affection. She's got to have someone to love. Here are the tickets." She handed over a re-used envelope, stuck down with an economy label. "They're good seats. You're to meet the chaps outside the theatre."

"The Adelphi, isn't it? I'm looking forward to it. How are they to get back afterwards?"

"There'll be transport provided. There are quite a few lads out on the town tonight so wait with yours, can you, till a driver comes to pick them up?"

She said of course she would and that she knew which line to use on the Underground and where to get off. She was getting to be quite a Londoner.

"One last thing, Tatiana. If there's an alert, I think it would be best if you got them to the nearest Underground — then stay with them, till the all clear."

"I'll look after them." There were fewer air raids on London since Hitler had invaded Russia. Very few people left a cinema when "Air-Raid Warning" was flashed on the screen now. Usually it was only air-raid wardens, ambulance drivers and fire fighters who left to report to their nearest centre; just as Uncle Igor did. It was the same in the theatres. Someone — usually a pretty girl — stood at the side of the stage holding up a notice to the same effect.

But Londoners were getting blasé about the Luftwaffe. They had paid their money and were staying to see a show! It was as simple as that. And London was a big place, they usually reasoned; the bombs would probably drop miles away!

"I'll take them if they want to go," Tatiana smiled. "But best be off. Don't want to keep the RAF waiting!"

She wouldn't, she was to think afterwards, have been so eager had she known what would be there outside the Adelphi Theatre to greet her.

"This is Bill," Sam said. "Sergeant Bill Benson." Which would have been all right, Tatiana thought when she had got the better of the cold, cruel pain that sliced through her, had he not turned, his hand searching for hers, and spoken to her with Tim's soft way of speaking; had he not had a shock of fair hair like Tim's, nor the wing of an air-gunner above his left tunic pocket.

Tim come back to her, his beautiful face burned beyond recognition; Tim, wearing dark glasses over sightless eyes. Not smiling, because to smile she knew to be difficult. But the hand she grasped was Tim Thomson's hand and the voice that said, "Tatiana. Nice to meet you," was Tim's voice. Even his height belonged to a sergeant air-gunner she had not seen for a few days short of a year.

She clasped the hand in hers, said, "Nice to meet you, too, Bill," then covered that hand with her free one and closed her eyes and whispered silently inside her, "God! How could you do this to me? How could you?"

"We're in good time." Sam speaking. "What say we find the bar and sink a crafty half?"

"A crafty half it is!" said a voice not a bit like Tatiana Sutton's. Then she pulled Bill Benson's arm into the crook of her own. "That okay with you, Bill?"

107

And he said it was and asked her to tell him — quietly, if she wouldn't mind — when there was a step up or down; otherwise he could manage just fine.

And Tatiana thought it was just as well one of them could manage just fine, because *she* couldn't. She was light-headed and hot and cold, both at the same time. And it hurt, almost, to breathe.

"Give me your stick," she heard herself saying, "and you, Sam, walk on the other side. Relax, Bill. We've got you."

Yet all the time she was shaking inside her. And her mouth had gone dry and it was hard, even, to think; think about getting Bill Benson up and down steps and stairs, that was, and fixing him up with a beer; finding a corner of the noisy, heaving bar where he could manage to drink it without being pushed or elbowed.

"What are you drinking, Bill?" Sam had asked when they had found a place to stand.

"Heavy, please." There was no smile on his tight, rough lips, but there was a smile in his voice.

"That's bitter, in Sassenach," she heard herself explaining to Sam. "And I'll have a glass of light, please, if that's okay?"

"You know your Scottish ales," Bill said with Tim's voice.

And she took a deep breath and said, "But of course, hen."

She hadn't meant to be flippant, had not meant to use one of Tim's words because Tim had often called her hen. And you shouldn't be flippant, should you, when nothing about and around you was real; when all you could be sure of was the voice that wept inside you?

God! Why did you do this? Why did you take Tim away from me then send Bill Benson into my life?

Because Bill was Tim and Tim was Bill. Only sightless eyes and a cruelly burned face disguised them.

She found herself wondering if Bill liked to dance, only to hear a ragged voice whispering in her ear: It doesn't matter if Bill Benson dances or not. He isn't Tim. Tim is dead! He will never come back; you know he won't.

She was grateful that Sam returned at that moment, carrying three glasses on a tin tray.

"Y'know, Tatiana — there's one good thing about being a wounded hero! You get served first!"

She took a glass, then said, "Bill," and he turned in the direction of her voice. "Your drink . . ."

He held out his hand and she arranged his fingers round the glass, then said, "Cheers!" even though his hands had not been burned and could have almost been the hands that once touched and gentled her body.

Did you hear me, God? Why . . .?

Keth tapped on the door and pushed it open.

"Hullo, sir. Come for your homework?" asked the pleasant-faced ATS corporal.

"Please. But tell me, Corporal, why are all the army girls around here sergeants but you?"

He felt pleased that his voice sounded so normal.

"Because I'm not old enough. You have to be twenty-one in this setup. Only three months to wait!"

She looked very young; certainly not twenty and three-quarters. He wondered how much she knew; how far she was trusted, until she turned the dial on the safe to the left and right, then handed him a folder marked "237".

"This is yours, Captain. Will you sign for it, please?" There was a docket stapled to the front of it and she wrote the date, the day and the time on it then offered it for his signature. "And will you sign the office copy, too?"

"You look very young to be working in a setup like this." Keth initialled the second copy. "Do you find it a strain?"

"No, sir. My own choice entirely. I wanted, initially, to be sent out into the field, but —"

"Work for SOE, you mean? An agent?"

"I work for SOE now," she smiled. "But yes, one day I'd like to go to France."

"But *why*?" She was too young, too pretty, too vulnerable-looking.

"For the same reasons as yourself, I suppose."

"Hey! Don't get any ideas about me! I'm here because I made a bargain. I owe them one — and I suppose I'm going because I know more about — well —" he faltered, "I'm going because I know

110

more than most about what this particular trip entails. I'm certainly not going because I like danger, or anything like that. I want to get it over and done with, then settle into my boring routine again. And get married," he added, almost as an afterthought. Which was stupid, really, because he had become Gaston Martin only because he so desperately wanted to marry Daisy. "And should we be talking like this, Corporal?" he asked more severely than he intended to. "What I mean is — well — will our conversation be reported to Himself in authority?"

"No, sir," she said softly. "Not by me it won't."

"Thank you." He smiled, relieved. "But tell me why someone like you should want to go on active service with SOE? Working here you must surely know what it entails?"

"Yes, I do. But I love France, you see. All the special things in my life happened there. We went there a lot before the war, on holiday and every year to the same *pension*. I learned to swim in France when I was four. France was a happy place for me and my brother.

"Then my parents sent me to school there, to finish me off, as they called it. I went when I was sixteen. When I came home for my seventeenth birthday they wouldn't let me go back; they thought we'd soon be at war, you see, and home was the safest place to be. I've been trying to get back ever since."

"A young man?"

"Partly," she said, without even the hint of a blush. "There was someone I was fond of, but his letters stopped. I suppose I'd be happy just to know what has happened to him — if he is still alive. But really, I just want to go back to France. Can you understand?"

"Yes, I can," he said softly, knowing they shouldn't be talking so intimately and that probably the place had hidden microphones. "But do you think —?" His eyes swept the walls and ceiling.

"They might be listening in?"

"Nothing would surprise me here."

"No. This room is all right."

"But not Room 22?"

"I didn't say that. And, sir — can you go there now? They said I was to tell you."

"I'm on my way. 'Bye, Corporal."

"Goodbye, sir."

He closed the door softly, walking slowly across the bare, echoing hall, turning left towards the staircase. He should have asked her name, he supposed; would have, had he even remotely imagined she would give it to him.

But how could she want to stick her neck out — walk headlong into danger; or be parachuted into it, or flown into it, or go there by submarine?

Because she loved France, she said and because there had once been someone special there. It was, he supposed, why Keth Purvis was about to do something equally stupid. Because he loved Daisy.

Love, he supposed, was the most powerful motivator of all — unless it was hate.

He knocked twice on the door of Room 22 and a voice called to him to enter.

Reaching for the ornate iron door handle, he wondered how much more he would know by the time he left.

CHAPTER
SEVEN

Keth lolled in the armchair, feet straddled, legs stiffly outstretched, and glowered at the pile of clothes on his bed and the cheap suitcase at the foot of it.

He was annoyed. Damned annoyed. With himself, but most of all with the slab-faced stranger who had made him a laughing stock. Because not only, it seemed, was he an idiot when it came to parachuting; now he had gone one better.

Half an hour ago he had acted — or was it *reacted*? — like an absolute fool and all because Slab Face had caught him unawares.

He jumped to his feet and strode to the window, kicking out childishly at the case as he passed it. One lock on it was broken. He would have to tie it round with string, he supposed.

He stared moodily across the grounds to the dense pinewood beyond. The clothes on the bed were all second-hand and he wondered if they had been washed. Did they have jumble sales in France and did SOE send a bod over regularly to buy up old clothes?

But he was being childish, not entirely because of what had happened in Room 22, but because, if he were completely honest, this stupid, what-the-hell-am-I-doing-here mood of bewilderment was because he was afraid. He had always been afraid, only now was the first time he'd admitted it.

In Room 22 he'd been greeted with a nod by the civilian with whom he'd drunk brandy last night. The stranger who sat behind the desk — the one with the face like a concrete slab — had not even nodded, indicating with a frugal movement of his hand that Keth should sit in the chair facing.

"We will conduct this interview in French, Captain. Name?"

That had been the start of it.

"Gaston Martin."

"Age?"

"Twenty-five." Easy. Just two months younger than himself. "Born the third of September." That was easy, too. The day war started.

"Mother?"

"Belle."

"Father?"

"Jules Martin. Killed 1917."

The questioning was rapid; his answers without fault. He let himself relax because his French was better in every way than that of his interrogator whose French was too perfect, too correct. Parisian French. Learned at university, no doubt. But Keth Purvis spoke the language with mam'selle's Normandy accent; used her clichés and her colloquialisms and she had told him his pronunciation was almost perfect.

That was when his complacency was shattered.

"Mon capitaine!"

Keth had turned his head sharply in the direction of the voice, his guard completely down, to gaze across the room, eyes questioning. That was when it happened.

The blow to his face caught him unawares. He turned, startled, knocking over his chair as he lunged across the desk.

"What the hell!" He grabbed at the coat lapels with angry hands, heaving the man to his feet. "What was that in aid of?"

Slab Face did not reply. Still shaking with anger, Keth hissed "Tell me!" at his brandy-drinking companion, who shrugged without even moving his position.

"I'll tell you!" With a practised move, the interrogator freed himself from Keth's grasp, then delivered a chopping blow to his shoulder that sent him reeling across the room to fall, legs in air, near the door.

"Get up, Captain," the voice drawled and because apart from being reluctant to continue the conversation from floor level, Keth needed to look his tormentor in the eyes; calmly, and without wavering, and listen to the offered explanation. Slowly he rose, dusting his sleeve, pulling straight his jacket. Then he took three steps to stand in front of the desk, jaws clamped tight.

"All right! I'm listening!"

"Sit down, please." A command, not an invitation. "So, Captain Purvis . . ."

"*Why?*" Keth demanded, all at once realizing his cheek throbbed painfully and wondering how soon it would show bruising.

"Drink?"

"Thank you, sir, no."

Without moving a muscle of his face the man turned to the table behind him and poured from a decanter. Then he sat down, sighed, and said, "Why did I hit you? So shall we take it that you, an Englishman in German-occupied France and posing as a native, is asked for his papers by a passing patrol — which often happens, I might add — and something prompted the corporal in charge of that patrol to take you in for — er — questioning. Just a routine arrest to let his superiors know he was doing his job efficiently.

"Let us say that I was the young, zealous officer who asked questions of you — perhaps, like the corporal who brought you in, a little overzealous because I had no wish to be sent to the Russian Front. And I would have to admit that you seemed genuine. Your answers were correct, though not too readily offered; your whole attitude, I might have thought, was entirely that of Gaston Martin."

Keth waited unspeaking.

"Then I, who might have been a Gestapo officer, slapped your face, unexpectedly and seemingly without reason. And not only did you let your guard down, but you reacted exactly as your interrogator hoped you would. It's the oldest trick in the book and you signed your own death warrant when you fell for it!"

"Yes, but dammit, how was I to know? Wouldn't you, I mean?"

"You mean, dammit wouldn't I have been annoyed, too, and the answer is yes, I would! But a Frenchman — Gaston Martin — would have called him all kinds of a pig, *in French*, maybe even spat in his face. Yet you, *mon brave*, reacted in English! One sudden slap, and your cover is blown!"

"Okay. So I know now. It won't happen again."

"It had better not. In this line of business, second chances aren't very thick on the ground." The man with the face like a concrete slab emptied his glass, then left the room without a sideways glance at either of those remaining.

There was silence as the door closed softly and they listened to the unhurried tread of receding footsteps.

"There's a name for people like him!" Keth muttered to his companion of the previous evening.

"There is." The unknown, unnamed man who wore civilian clothes and poured generous brandies allowed himself a small smile. "But one day you might have reason to be grateful to the miserable bastard for saving your life. So how about a quick one before lunch? I'd like you to eat with me in my office. There are a few things to go over before you leave."

Keth almost demanded to know when, exactly, but his new-found, painfully acquired caution warned him to wait.

"Thanks, sir. I'd like that."

He had tried to smile but could not, because his heart was hammering still, though whether from anger, or the sudden realization that even an unimportant operative could not close his eyes to what could happen, he did not know. In this setup, he was forced to admit, there were no milk runs and even the most straightforward in-and-out job was no piece of cake.

Now, in his room, he turned from the window and stared again at the neatly folded clothes; clothes, he supposed, that those in charge of such things would expect a French labourer to wear: well-worn trousers, a jacket and shirt, collar attached. Brown shoes which looked as if they would fit — he hadn't tried them on yet — and a raincoat.

He snapped open the one good lock on the case to find underwear — none of it new but clean, at least — a pair of working trousers, overalls and a cap. He'd have bet on a beret, though he was now prepared to admit that the people here knew what they were about.

To complete Gaston Martin's worldly goods were two towels and a spongebag — even that looked used — and inside the bag a razor, shaving soap, a toothbrush — *new!* — and a cake of dentifrice in a silver-coloured tin.

Before he left he would be given a cheap, French-made watch and franc notes and coins. Not too many, of course, because labourers weren't expected to carry a lot of money. Gaston Martin probably lived from job to job within the boundaries of his work permit and what was left over from the purchase of his strictly rationed food, he would doubtless spend on wine. Red wine, Keth decided.

He made a note to ask more about his ration card. His food-ration documents bothered him almost as much as his claustrophopic mode of transport to an isolated inlet north of Biarritz.

He found himself wishing he had been allowed to bring a photograph of Daisy because in his present state of perplexity he found he could not bring her face into his mind's eye, nor hear her voice nor her laugh at will. Something to do with shock, he supposed, or apprehension, or a mix of both. All he could remember was the way her hair slipped through his fingers and the feel of her lips on his. Her face, though, and her voice were gone from his rememberings. What a mess. What a damn-awful mess!

He reached for his cap and slammed shut the door of his room behind him. He needed to walk. He would walk around and around the grounds until some perplexed sentry asked him what he was about. And when he was tired of walking, he would write to his mother and again to Daisy; tell her how much he loved her and wanted her. Hell, how he wanted her!

Briefly he returned the salute of the sentry on the garden door, then stuffing his hands into his trouser pockets in a most unsoldierly way, began to walk along the crunching, gravelled paths in the direction of the distant hills, wondering just how near to them he would get before being stopped.

What was Daisy doing now? His diary was at Castle McLeish so he had lost track of her watches. The wireless was freely available here, so he was fairly sure there had been no air raids on either Liverpool or London.

He kicked out at a stone on the short-cut grass beside the path, trying yet again to bring Daisy's face, her smile, into focus. But she remained elusive, so he straightened his shoulders, set his arms at an easy swing, and began to walk the boundaries of the grounds.

So he was nervous and apprehensive, but who in his right mind wouldn't be? He was a mathematician, a back-room boy. He was a breaker of codes and not one iota brave. Not for him flying a bomber over Germany in the blackout; not for him prowling the seas in a submarine nor dropping out of a plane at the end of a parachute. He was lucky that he knew his limitations and being brave — *foolhardy* — was not one of them.

So he was going to occupied France and knew now where he would be put ashore and that he would be picked up and hidden away until he was needed. He was not being asked to take undue risks. Even the Enigma machine would be brought to him by some foolish brave man — or woman. Then he would be brought out again with the precious package and if he couldn't do something as uncomplicated as that for Daisy; do it, even, for the merchant seamen who risked their lives every time they left port, then it was a poor lookout.

Wherever you are, my darling, he whispered with his heart, it's going to be all right for us. I'm all kinds of a fool, but we *will* be married on my next leave and nothing on the face of the earth will stop us because I love you, love you!

It was then that it all came right and he was able to recall her smile, hear the softness of her voice as she whispered that she loved him too; that she would always love him and yes, they would be married. Very soon.

It was at times like this, he insisted as he walked briskly back to the forbidding stone house that was forbidding no longer, that he *had* to believe. But believe in who, or what? In God, perhaps; in miracles? On this early October afternoon he *needed* to believe in miracles and yes, in God too. It was all down, he supposed, to loving Daisy so much and if *conditions* meant taking a calculated risk, then she was worth it.

He was going to France and coming safely back! Oh, too damn right he was!

"So how did things go, last night?" Sparrow demanded as they cleared the table after supper. She was downright curious if only because Tatiana had volunteered nothing on her return from the theatre — except that the music had been lovely.

"Just fine," Tatiana shrugged.

"And you didn't get yourself upset?"

"Of course not. Why should I?"

"No reason at all — except that you *are* upset! Is it the new one — the blind one? Did you find it all too much?"

"No, Sparrow. Oh, *no*."

"Then tell me." She filled the bowl with water then added a fist of washing soda. "Because the first time you took an airman out you were full of it, and wanted to go on helping Joannie's lot."

"And I still want to." Tatiana watched, fascinated, as the older woman lathered a block of primrose soap into a sud. "I really do. It was just that — well, it all seemed so spooky. Not spooky-frightening but spooky-strange, sort of. And rather nice."

Sparrow continued her lathering without comment, agitating the water into bubbles.

"You see, Sparrow, I'm trying to tell myself that something wonderful hasn't happened — and it has. I told you about Tim?"

"Y-yes."

"Well last night it wasn't Tim, exactly. He was called Bill Benson. And he was Scottish and just about Tim's height. And he had fair hair, too, and —"

"And he was an air-gunner, like your Tim was?"

"Yes." She picked up a plate, drying it ponderously. "It threw me, at first."

For just a little while it had been too much to accept. It got so out of hand that in the dimness of the theatre, when Bill leaned close to whisper to her, he sounded so much like Tim she had wanted to get away; push past everyone, run out and never go back.

"So now you're going to pretend it's your young man come back to you with his face burned?"

"No, Sparrow! Don't say that! It's cruel!"

"It's fact, girl, and you're being morbid! Your young man *hasn't* come back. The one you took to the theatre last night *wasn't* Tim. And I'm not being cruel about their poor faces. Far from it. I think they should all have a medal, Lord love them! But don't get entangled, Tatiana. Your mother put you in my care and I won't have you getting yourself upset all over again. And maybe this Bill has a young lady — maybe even a wife. Did you think to ask?"

"I didn't, Sparrow, because it isn't important," she said softly, though she knew as soon as she spoke that it *was* important because she was so certain in her dreamings that the young man who sat beside her had some part of Tim in him, that she had wanted to reach for his hand, entwine her fingers in his, just as she and Tim always did in the intimate, shoulder-to-shoulder darkness of Creesby picture house. Would have, only a voice, very much like Sparrow's, had called a warning, and she was forced to tell herself it was not Tim who sat beside her and that even to think such a thing was being unfaithful to his memory.

124

But for just a moment, until she regained control of her feelings, Tim had not died in a crashed bomber on Holdenby Pike. Tim survived, dreadfully burned and blinded, too, her foolish heart insisted, and had come back with a different name. And even his name was uncanny. Tim Thomson. Bill Benson. Even the cadence was there.

"Well, if it isn't important, you'll maybe stop trying to rub the pattern orf that plate and shift yourself so we'll be done in time to listen to Tommy Handley! And maybe it'd be better if our Joannie sent you someone different next time."

"No!" She said it much, much too quickly. "I mean — well, I promised Bill and Sam I'd see them both again next week. We got on well together the three of us, and Sam is such a help with Bill. I couldn't go back on my word, Sparrow. Not the word of a Sutton."

"Well, if you say so. Only don't go filling your head with day dreams or you'll get hurt again — especially if he's married. And there was a letter for you from Liverpool. I left it on the hall table. Did you see it?"

Sparrow knew Daisy's handwriting; had known Daisy since she was a little thing in her mother's arms, and living in Hampshire.

"Sorry — I didn't look, actually. I'll read it later. And don't worry about me, Sparrow — though I'm glad, really, that you do. It was just that meeting Bill Benson last night was a bit of shock, that's all. I'm fine now. It's all under control. I know what I'm doing."

But did she know what she was doing, she thought that night as she lay snug and cosseted in bed and thought about Tim Thomson and Bill Benson. Because she didn't know what she was doing if she were scrupulously honest, and to say she did was like spitting into the wind, which was a very unladylike thing to do — apart from being messy!

She turned over with an exaggerated sigh, then plumped up her pillows. Frightening though that meeting had been, she knew there could never, ever, be another man in her life after Tim. And that was a pity, really, because never to be able to fall in love again was a terrible thing to have to accept; like becoming a nun and not being able to go back on your word.

But those three wonderful months she and Tim spent together were worth a lifetime of being alone. Indeed she was, she thought, very lucky to have met Tim at all. If she hadn't gone to the dance at Holdenby Moor aerodrome she would never have known the joy of loving completely and being completely loved in return.

She smiled softly and sadly and said good night to Tim as she always did, then made her mind a blank, because she must not think about Bill Benson. Perhaps Sparrow was right and Joannie should ask some other volunteer to take him out on the town.

Trouble was, she had promised, and anyway, next week she would most probably wonder why she had ever thought Bill Benson was in the least like Tim. There could never be another Tim Thomson. Not ever. It was as simple — and awful — as that.

Drew and Kitty leaned against the landing-stage railings, thighs touching, hands clasped, gazing across the river to the Cheshire side. Sharp against the skyline the jagged outlines of bombed buildings were gentled by a setting sun that scattered the river with a sparkle of rubies.

"Kind of beautiful, isn't it?" She smiled up at him. "If it wasn't so sad, I mean. Wish I could paint. It's so dramatic."

"Then I'm glad you can't because knowing you, your canvases would either be terrible, or very good indeed."

"And in this case," she pointed to the wartime skyline, "scary. Y'know, honey, it's like we're standing back, looking at something we've no power to do anything about; all of us puppets, having our strings pulled."

"We're nothing of the kind! You and I are living, breathing people. We have minds of our own and we're going to be married," Drew said firmly. "And one day, all this will be behind us. Last time, Mother said, when they thought their war would never end, it was suddenly all over."

"Sure, and they had to pick up the pieces and wonder if it had all been worth it, just as our generation will wonder." She turned her back on the stark outlines that were already being dimmed and softened around the edges by the blocking out of a scarlet sun behind a tall, distant building. "And I know we have minds of our own, darling, but sometimes there's no choice but to do things we don't want to."

"Like?" He pulled sharply on his breath.

"Like me coming over here to work with ENSA and being willing to go anywhere, kind of . . ."

"So you *are* leaving Liverpool! Why didn't you tell me?"

"Because I didn't want to spoil tonight, I guess. Because in a few hours you've got to be back on board and next time you dock I'll be gone. To London."

The river ferry came broadside on to the landing stage and they looked down, not speaking, to watch the gangway fall with a clatter and people hurrying across it.

"Let's not go dancing." It was Drew who broke the uneasy silence.

"No. Let's go back to the digs." To Ma MacTaggart's cheap theatrical lodgings; to Ma, who never thought to remark that the bed in the room Drew took for the night was never slept in.

"Mm. You can tell me about it, then." It wouldn't seem so awful when they lay close, and warm from loving, Kitty telling him she was to be based in London as they feared she might be; would not seem so bad when they were so relaxed they could imagine London to be only a sixpenny tram ride away. "And London will be good for your career — all the theatres."

And the bombing, his mind supplied, because it would start again, nothing was more certain. When Hitler was done with Russia the full force of the Luftwaffe would be hurled at Britain once more. Not that Hitler was getting all his own way there now. The German armies had been halted and held, and in some places thrown back. And Moscow was no longer threatened, though Leningrad's siege had yet to be broken.

"What are you thinking about?" Kitty whispered. "You sure were scowling."

"I was thinking about the war in general and Russia in particular and how it might not always be very safe when you get to London."

"I'll be just fine, darling." There was a churning of water between the landing stage and the ferry as it made its way back towards the Cheshire side. "For one thing, I'll be with Sparrow and Tatty, and for another I'll be out of London on tour a lot of the time.

"On tour," she giggled. "Sounds like I'll be doing the provincial theatres before the show opens in the West End, when really we'll be playing gun sites and aerodromes and village halls; any place there are men and women in need of cheering up. You've no idea, Drew, what a wonderful audience they are. They stamp and whistle like crazy. It makes me feel real good, like I'm a star and they've all paid pounds and pounds just to see me."

"You always did like an audience, Kitty Sutton. You knew even when you were little how to play to the gallery. Do you know what a precocious brat you were?" Smiling, he tweaked her nose.

"Guess I must've been pretty awful," she laughed.

"You still are. You come into a room like a force-eight gale, demanding to be noticed — just like you slammed into my life that night on the dockside. Suddenly I knew what it was like to be hit amidships by a torpedo."

"And I love you too." She reached on tiptoe to kiss his lips lingeringly which was something nice girls shouldn't do in public, then they began to walk towards Bold Street and the little street off it, where Ma MacTaggart lived. Now, Drew thought, he had another picture of Kitty to store in his memory and take out and live again when they were apart.

Kitty, silhouetted against a red evening sky and the stark, bombed buildings on the far bank of the river; Kitty so beautiful that it made him wonder why it was him she loved and not someone as good to look at as herself; Kitty's English half that loved the Mersey and to stand at the Pierhead watching the river ferries that churned across it. Kitty, warm and flamboyant, whose lips silently begged him to make love to her each time they kissed.

He had been so ordinary before the night he saw her behaving so badly in the too-small, too-cheap red costume. That night he fell in love with his Kentucky cousin; deeply, desperately, in love. What Gracie would call, he supposed, a hook, line and sinker job. Kathryn Norma Clementina Sutton, his *raison d'être*.

He quickened his step, the sooner to get to Ma's and the bed he would share with her. They would love, then she would fall asleep in his arms, her ridiculous baby-soft curls tickling his nose. And in the morning when she opened her eyes and smiled and said, throatily, "Hullo, you," they would make love again because it would be the last time for only God knew how long.

He took her arm and she demanded to know what the hurry was and he told her she knew damn well.

"And, Kitty, hear this! Next time I get long leave we're getting married and no messing — even if it's a special licence job!"

She said that was fine by her, because maybe being deliciously unconventional and doing what nicely-brought-up girls shouldn't do every time they found themselves within spitting distance of a double bed was wearing a bit thin now.

"You're right, Drew. Reckon we've come as far as we can and I guess you should make an honest woman of me. Come to think of it, it might be nice to be Lady Sutton."

She stopped walking and gazed up at him with eyes so blue and serious and appealing that he took her in his arms, right there in the middle of Bold Street, and kissed her hard and long.

And didn't give a damn who saw them!

CHAPTER
EIGHT

Keth stood unmoving in front of the mirror and, unmoving, Gaston Martin stared back. Those who kitted him out had done a good job, he grudgingly admitted. The clothes fitted; even the shoes and the socks, of which one pair was neatly darned, could have been worn by himself — times past, that was, when Keth Purvis wore darned socks and cheap, well-worn shoes.

Yet he must forget his other self. He was Gaston Martin now. In the pocket of his belt was five hundred francs in notes; in his trouser pockets a knife, a handful of small coins and a packet of Gauloises, even though he did not smoke. Inside one of the three very ordinary buttons on his jacket was a compass, though why a compass was necessary if he was to be taken to a safe house, hidden away, then returned to his point of departure, he had no idea.

In a brown paper carrier bag which he was told to get rid of at once if there was even the slightest risk of being picked up, were carefully packed valves and a small, heavy packet. Valves for wireless operators to replace broken ones — valves were notorious for their fragility, it seemed — and spares for the firing mechanisms of two automatic revolvers. Just to be carrying such things gave reality to his journey; a shivering awareness that began when he was checked and checked again for incriminating evidence by a man who could once have been a police detective.

No English brand names on any of his clothing; no London Tube tickets or bus tickets in his pockets or evidence that his underwear and handkerchiefs had been laundered in England. Laundrymarks were a big giveaway, the man said as he left, satisfied.

Keth dug a hand into his trouser pocket, bringing out the coins, placing them on the window-ledge to familiarize himself with their values. The coins made sense to his mathematical mind; tens were easier to calculate than twelves; you just stuck in a decimal point. Twelve pence to the shilling was all wrong, really.

He turned as the door opened to admit his inquisitor of yesterday; the man Keth had dubbed Slab Face and against whom he still felt resentment, even though his cheek had not bruised.

"You've had your final check?"

"Yes, sir."

"Feeling all right?"

"No, but I'm working on it." Why did the man irritate him so?

"You'll be leaving in the morning about ten; arrive at the naval base about eleven. When you sail will be up to the submarine people. Their ops room will work out your expected time of arrival and tell us so we can alert our people at the other end."

"Seems all very straightforward, sir."

"We like to think we know what we are doing, Captain. Good luck." He held out a hand and Keth was surprised its grasp was firm and warm. It comforted him until the man turned, hand on the doorknob and said, "You'll be given your D-pill in the morning, by the way."

"My . . .?"

"Dammit, man — do I have to spell it out?"

"But I hadn't thought —" Keth stopped, all at once feeling real fear.

"What hadn't you thought?"

"That I was all that important. No one told me about anything like — well, *that* . . ."

"Then you should have been told. And we do not consider any of our operatives unimportant, Captain. You are being sent to France because you have special knowledge of the machine you are to bring back with you and not because of your prowess as an SOE operative — nor your ability to survive under questioning."

"No, sir." He was doing it again: putting him down.

"You have more knowledge than you think. Under duress not only would you tell them why you were in France, but before they'd finished with you you'd have told them about Bletchley and how much we know already about their Enigma

134

machine. They think their signalling system is safe because they change the code every day, but with persuasion you would tell them that we are breaking their army and air force codes whenever we want to, and that soon we hope to be breaking their U-boat signals, too."

He paused, breathing deeply and loudly as if allowing time for his words to be given fullest consideration.

"So that is why, before you leave, Captain, you will go through your final briefing, be given your codename — Gaston Martin's codename — and advised where best to hide your pill. And that when you swallow it you will be dead in fifty seconds.

"I have had grave doubts about sending you, but it is too late now to do anything about it. But of one thing I *am* sure. You, as an individual, are of little value; what you know *is*. Never forget that. Good day to you. Good luck."

Keth stood transfixed, wanting — *needing* — to yell, "*Bastard!*" at the top of his voice, wanting to tell him to find some other fool to do his dirty work. But he did not because now there was no going back and anyway, all at once he seemed incapable of speech or movement. All he could be sure of was his love for Daisy and his need to hold her close.

Damn Slab Face! Petulantly he swept the coins from the window-ledge and into his pocket. And in the morning when he left this place, he would not think of Keth Purvis nor his mother, nor Rowangarth. And especially he would not let himself think of Daisy because Gaston Martin was going to France and only when he returned could Keth Purvis be himself again.

"I love you, Daisy," he said out loud. "I'll love you till the day I die."

Then he thought of the D-pill and wanted to weep as he had not wept since the day his father died, but instead he sucked in his breath and said very slowly and deliberately, "Wherever you are, my darling — take care . . ."

Grace Fielding gave the apple a final polish then laid it carefully on the rack. She knew all about the storage of apples and pears now; had no need to ask instructions. Yet the trouble with grading and wiping and storing fruit for the winter, Gracie frowned, was the time it gave her to brood; think that for three days had there been neither a letter nor phone call from Bas — which was unusual.

The crunch of footsteps on the path sent her hurrying to the door and down the wooden steps of the apple loft to find not Bas, nor Tilda, who had said she would call in for apples, but a tall army sergeant who smiled and said, "Afternoon, miss. Can you tell me where I can find Mr Jack Catchpole?"

"He's over yonder in the far corner, seeing to the winter chrysanths."

She pointed to where late-flowering chrysanthemums, grown to bloom at Christmas, were being transferred into pots, ready to be carried into the shelter of a greenhouse at the first sniff of frost on the air. But Catchpole, who missed nothing, was already advancing, garden fork in hand, in the direction of the trespasser.

"Afternoon, sir." The soldier held out a hand which was reluctantly taken. "Sergeant Sydney Willis. Would you be the orchid expert I've been hearing about?"

Catchpole's expression softened. He liked being addressed as sir and having his undoubted knowledge in the cultivation and propagation of orchids deferred to.

"Happen I'm the gentleman you'm looking for." He laid aside his fork and reached for his pipe to clamp it, empty, between his teeth. "But you wasn't expected, sergeant," he admonished in order to establish that visits to his garden were strictly by appointment.

"No. I'm sorry, but I took the chance, in passing, of finding you. I was told of your experience with orchids, you see, and —"

"By who?"

"By sergeant Tom Dwerryhouse. I was talking to him in the pub. Famous for your orchids, he said, and being a gardener myself I took the liberty of calling. Leeds Corporation Parks and Gardens," he added hastily, eager to establish a rapport. "Keen to learn more about orchids, they being a favourite of mine."

Catchpole, mollified, returned his pipe to his pocket, dolefully remarking that he'd clean run out of tobacco, but if the sergeant would care to stay for a sup of tea, his apprentice would soon be making one. At which, Sergeant Willis offered a fill from his own pouch, then settled himself eagerly on the proffered apple box.

"You have a fine garden, Mr Catchpole. I envy you." He gazed with a practised eye at near perfection.

"'S now't like it should be. No specialist growing now on account of there being no coke for heating the glasshouses. Time was when I had two under-gardeners and at least three 'prentices." His eyes took on a yearning look. "But nowt's the same with two dratted wars to contend with, though my land girl is a grand lass and willing to learn. Had me doubts when Miss Julia landed me with her," he murmured through a haze of tobacco smoke, "but her's got the makings of a gardener in her if she don't go getting herself wed like most females do."

It was then that Tilda, in search of her apples, appeared by way of the small back gate, eyebrows raised questioningly at the stranger who had inveigled his way into the garden.

"Now then, Tilda! Gracie's got your apples. Her's in the shed, mashing a pot of tea."

"Who's he, then?" Tilda demanded in a whisper to which Gracie whispered back that he was a gardener, or had been in civvy street, and was here to see the orchid house — she thought. And when she had delivered two mugs of tea she gave Tilda the bag of apples, remarking that as far as she knew the sergeant's name was Sydney Willis and he came from Leeds.

"But you'll stay for a cup, Tilda? The kettle's almost boiled again. Think I can squeeze a drop more out of this pot. I should have brought those apples to the house, but I was running late this morning," she offered when they had settled themselves in the shelter of the now empty tomato house from which there was an uninterrupted view of the two men. "And you know what a stickler for time-keeping Mr C is."

Which wasn't true, really. She was late this morning, there was no denying it, but only because she had hung around, waiting as long as she dare for the red Post Office van — which hadn't come, of course.

To which Tilda replied that it was no trouble at all to collect them, it being a nice afternoon and she having time on her hands on account of there being little with which to cook; demanding to know more about the soldier who seemed to be getting on like a house on fire with the crusty head gardener.

"Don't know any more'n I've told you," Gracie blew hard on the hot, pale liquid in her mug, "'cept that he said he worked for Leeds Corporation."

Tilda nodded, keeping to herself the knowledge she had gained in a passing glance; that the soldier belonged to the Green Howards, a Yorkshire regiment; that he was middle-aged, like herself, and like herself was showing signs of greying in places though he was tall and straight and wore a Clark

139

Gable moustache with great aplomb. She nodded again, sipped her tea, and wondered if he was married.

She was still asking herself the same question as she skirted the wild garden on her way back to Rowangarth, and it came as a pleasant shock to hear her name being called in strong, masculine tones.

"Miss Tewk! Wait!"

She turned to see the soldier, bearing a carrier bag of apples.

"You forget them, miss," he smiled. "I volunteered to deliver them."

"Oh! That's very — er — kind of you." She felt the flush of colour to her cheeks because she'd been so interested in Catchpole's visitor she had clean forgotten the apples. "But you shouldn't have gone out of your way, sergeant."

"Sydney," he corrected, smiling, "And I didn't go out of my way, exactly. I offered to bring them because I wanted to ask you —"

"Yes?" Tilda whispered, snatching on her breath.

"To ask if I might call on my next spot of time off."

"*Oooooh!*" She felt distinctly peculiar.

"I'd like a closer look at that grand avenue of lindens over yonder, you see. Mr Catchpole told me his grandfather planted them more than fifty years ago."

"Now that I couldn't say." Tilda, distinctly disappointed, found her tongue. "You'd have to ask Mrs Sutton's permission for that, her being in

140

charge whilst Sir Andrew's away at sea. I could mention it to her, though I'm sure it'll be all right if Mr Catchpole says it will — him being head gardener."

"He did give me permission, Miss Tewk. I just thought it might be nice to have the pleasure of your company, you being familiar, so to speak, with the trees on the estate. He did mention that Rowangarth has some very fine English elms."

"We have. On the far edge of Brattocks Wood."

A walk in the woods with a soldier — next Wednesday, weather permitting, at half-past two, she thought tremblingly as later she fretted over unaccustomed lumps in her bechamel sauce.

She wondered yet again if Sergeant Willis was married and knew, deep within her love-starved heart, that he was, which was just Tilda Tewk's bad luck, she supposed, sighing deeply. She, who had always wanted a gentleman friend of her own, had never been lucky in love, there being so many young men taken in the last war and plain girls like herself shoved to the back of the queue. She had given her young heart to the Prince of Wales, him so boyishly handsome and with such a wistful smile. Her love for him was pure and from a great distance and she had only removed his picture from the kitchen mantel when Mrs Simpson got her claws into him.

At one time, Tilda pondered, as she squashed another lump against the side of the pan with her spoon, she had longed for a husband and children, then downgraded her hopes to perhaps just one passionate love affair. And since passion had never chanced her way, she had long since decided to settle for a dalliance, however brief. Now it seemed as if her prayers had been answered in the handsome form of Sergeant Sydney Willis and she would walk in Brattocks with him on her next afternoon off and show him the elms and the old, propped-up oak that folk said was almost as old as Rowangarth itself — if looking at trees was what interested him, that was. And if asked, she would continue their friendship until he admitted he had a wife and children when, as had happened with the Prince of Wales, she would be forced to give him up.

But until that happened, she decided with stiff-lipped determination, she would make the most of what the Fates allowed and be thankful for small mercies. And a dalliance.

"I hoped you'd come." Alice dried her hands and took off her pinafore.

"You knew I would." Julia pulled out a chair and leaned her elbows on the kitchen table. "It's just a year now since . . ." She glanced at the clock on the kitchen mantel.

"Since we were celebrating your wedding anniversary and Mother-in-law's birthday. And then the bombers were shot down and —"

No need for words as they clasped hands across the table top; no cause to say that Reuben, whom Alice looked upon as a father, and Mrs Shaw and

142

Jinny Dobb had died that night. Nathan's father, too.

"How's Nathan taking it?"

"Not too badly. He asked prayers for them all at early Communion and for the two aircrews who died. He's over Creesby way tonight. A young wife six months pregnant in need of comfort, he said. She got a telegram this morning. Husband killed in the Middle East. Should have gone myself. I know what the poor woman is going through," she said flatly.

"Of course, love," Alice said gently. "I went through it as well, 'cept that Tom came back. I took flowers to the graves this morning — had a little weep. And I won't forget Lady Helen, either."

"It was a swine of a week, wasn't it? Four deaths and two of our bombers, then Mother died too, just days after. It was as if the old ones had had enough. Two wars in anyone's lifetime is cruel."

"I'll be there if you want me, Julia, like always — if Nathan won't think I'm interfering, that is."

"He won't. You and me have always remembered things together. Mother's first anniversary isn't the time to stop. And I've booked a call to Montpelier Mews; told the exchange that if no one answers at Rowangarth I'd be here — that's okay, isn't it? Don't want to block your line or anything."

"You won't be. Daisy got through half an hour ago to let me know she hadn't forgotten — sent her love to you, too. And I'm glad you're ringing London. Folk are inclined to forget Tatty and her airman. She'll be a long time getting over that night. By the by, Daisy met Drew and Kitty; briefly, she said. They were both fine, though Drew will be back at sea now."

"And Kitty away to London. Well, at least she'll be good for Tatty, and Sparrow will have two of them to fuss over." Julia pushed back her chair as the phone in the passage outside began to ring. "That'll be my call."

"Then remember me to them all — and say special love from me to Tatty, won't you?"

Alice filled the kettle and set it to boil, wondering how many times she and Julia had shared a comforting cup.

Too many to count, she thought sadly. Far, far too many.

CHAPTER
NINE

"There now, lovely girl!" Lyn Carmichael was kissed and hugged. "Home for a week this time, is it?"

"A week and a day, Auntie Blod. Am I welcome?"

"As a pound of black-market butter! Of course you're welcome, *cariad*. There's foolish to ask!"

"No butter, I'm afraid, but I've got a card for a week's rations with me. Oh, it's good to be home!" Lyn hung up her raincoat. "I've brought some dirty shirts and collars, if you don't mind . . ."

"I'll do all your stuff on washday. Get yourself upstairs and out of that uniform. And where on earth did you get that hat?"

"It's a cap, not a hat — our new, official-issue Wren-type headgear. Like it?"

"No, I can't say I do. The old hats were more ladylike to my way of thinking."

"And *very* fuddy-duddy. We all think the new ones are cute, sort of."

"Saucy! But I'll bring you up a jug of water for a wash. Want it out of the tap, or the butt?"

"The butt, please." Lyn liked to wash her face in rainwater.

"I'm out of toilet soap, *cariad*. Mine's down to a sliver."

"I've brought my own and there's a soap coupon with the ration card. Oooh, Auntie Blod — let's pretend the war is a million miles away? Let's shut it out for eight nights and seven days, shall we? Let's you and me just talk and talk?"

"We'll do that, *merchi*. Talk about everything under the sun."

And about Kenya, too, she thought grimly, because ever since she had known the truth about, well — *things*, Lyn had clammed up when Kenya was mentioned, just as she went all poker-faced when Drew Sutton's name came into the conversation.

Talk, because there were things to be brought into the open whether the stubborn little miss liked it or not. And before so very much longer, too!

Keth sat in the back of the camouflaged army staff car feeling distinctly uncomfortable. Beside him was a fresh-faced lieutenant and driving them, a staff sergeant who looked as if he'd be a good sort to have beside you in a backs-to-the-wall situation, Keth decided.

The man at his side he wasn't so sure about. A youngster, really, who would doubtless report back to the stone house that Gaston Martin had been safely delivered to the 15th Submarine Flotilla.

Keth studied the passing scenery. It was especially beautiful to one who was to leave it. Bracken and

146

heather were taking on their autumnal colours; the hills shaded from grey to purple to black, with slants of sunlight slicing between them to glint on the little loch to his right.

He was no longer afraid. He had asked for a posting home and was given it, with conditions attached. This was where the pay-off started, and after his first wave of terrified disbelief, Daisy was still worth it.

The car slowed and pulled over to let a farm tractor pass. It was driven by a land girl and she smiled and raised her hand. Not unlike Gracie, he thought, wondering at the normality of the encounter; trying to imagine what the girl would think could she have known that inside that car was a man who was on his way to occupied France. But everything about this morning was precious and normal save Gaston Martin.

Last night, instead of sleeping, he had carefully calculated Daisy's watches and was almost sure that until Friday she would be working a week of nights. Which meant, of course, that on Friday morning, instead of sleeping, she would be on the train, heading home on one of her unofficial weekends.

They all did it, it would seem, after a week of night duties. Authority turned a blind eye to an entire watch disappearing without trace and without a leave pass, too. Perhaps they accepted that it was only a matter of time until one of the miscreants was stopped by a naval patrol, and that would be that. In the rattle, Daisy said, for going absent without leave and AWOL usually merited at least one week's stoppage of privileges and extra duties in quarters. But until someone was caught, then what the heck, she had laughed. Live dangerously! And for the coming weeks, Keth Purvis would be living dangerously, though if he were caught it would be something altogether different.

Yet why should he be caught? He had worked out the odds against it and they were in his favour. He had also accepted there were millions of men and women doing military service with all its attendant dangers: young girls on gun sites, or manhandling barrage balloons, and men and women of the fire service and rescue teams, who put out fires or dug with bare hands to free women and children from shattered houses even though bombs were still falling.

It was all a question of which way the dice fell and your name and number. It had been the same in his father's war. "If your name and number was on a bullet, lad," he'd once said, "it would find you sooner or later. No use worrying meantime."

Keth smiled inside him as a clump of late-flowering foxgloves slipped past the window to remind him of Brattocks Wood. They comforted him, too; made him think that Someone up there was wishing him luck — Godspeed, he supposed.

Yet did God exist? Most times, his father had said, you didn't believe — especially when you'd had near on four years in the trenches and blamed God for letting it happen. Yet there came a time to believe, Dickon Purvis had conceded gravely, and that was when you were in a foxhole in the middle of No-Man's-Land with shells screaming over your head. God was a good sort then to have beside you.

So now that Gaston Martin was on his way Keth felt calm and glad, almost, that from here on every passing day was one day nearer to lifting the phone and whispering, "Hullo, you. Guess who loves you?" And now he had accepted that he was just as brave and every bit as afraid as millions of other men and women, he would do his best — *better* than his best — to get back safely with the Enigma machine our merchant seamen were so desperately in need of.

"Nearly there, sir." The driver put an end to Keth's broodings.

"Where is *there*, Sergeant?"

"Am I allowed to say?" The question to the young lieutenant.

"Don't see why not. We're about two miles from Loch Ardneavie. Once there was a thriving yacht club there — sailing boats and dinghies — but it's all changed now. No more pretty little yachts nor weekend sailors messing about in boats since the Admiralty collared the entire loch. It's bursting with submarines, now. HMS *Omega*. The 15th Flotilla, and to which Staff and I are to deliver you."

"You seem well informed," Keth observed drily.

"I'm not telling you anything Gerry doesn't already know — sir." He emphasized Keth's rank after the mild reprimand. "Anyway, that's just about it. What happens when you get to *Omega* — well, your guess is as good as mine. And I'm well informed because I've been here before. The last time was with a woman — a WAAF officer."

"And a real good-looker, wasn't she, sir?" the staff sergeant offered.

"They send women!" Keth was shocked.

"Why not, if they volunteer? But look over there." He pointed in the direction of a shimmer of water below them. "We're missing the town. Coming in the top way. That's the head of the loch you can see. Saw some smashing Wrens at *Omega* last time we came."

"Surely they don't have Wrens on submarines?" Keth was becoming uneasy.

"No! They have them on the mother ship, though," the lieutenant laughed. "And they crew the dinghies and launches. Lovely little bottoms . . ."

"My fiancée is a Wren," Keth said stiffly, ending the conversation abruptly as they dropped speed to drive through a small village, then on to the loch where the car drew up at the head of a long jetty.

The sergeant opened the rear door and Keth got out to stare across the vast stretch of water, his shabby suitcase and the carrier bag at his feet.

All at once it was very real and he knew there was no going back. And all at once he knew he didn't want to call it off. He wanted to go; get it over with. Luck didn't enter into it. Now he felt no fear; merely a vague apprehension and a niggling irritation that getting to this point of departure had been such a long-drawn-out affair with everything checked and checked again. Just as if he were a village idiot from wildest Yorkshire and had to be watched every inch of the way.

The lieutenant tapped on the door of a low, square building at the top of the wooden jetty. It had a small sliding hatch in it which was immediately opened.

"Good morning, sir." The face of a Wren appeared. "Can I help you?"

"You can indeed! Will you let someone know we would like to get on board." He nodded towards the great ungainly ship at the centre of a cluster of submarines. "Transport for three if you'd be so kind, Jenny Wren."

"Don't let him fool you," the sergeant said softly to Keth. "He likes to put on a Jack-the-lad act but he's a damn fine operator. Been to France three times already. Not as stupid as he makes out."

"Can do, duckie?" smiled the lieutenant.

"Can I have your names?" asked the Wren.

"No names, sweetie; no pack drill. Just let your lot know we're here. They're expecting us."

"Very well. I'll get a signal over to the bridge. You can walk down the jetty if you like — the gates are open. Watch out for the iron ladder when you climb down into the launch, sir — the rungs are very slippery."

The hatch was slammed shut and a bolt pushed into place. One smashing Wren was having no truck with the charming lieutenant.

"Send a signal to *Omega*, will you?" she called to a signalman. "Shore Station to quarterdeck. Please send boat. Two pongos, one civvy."

The sergeant picked up Keth's luggage, then fell into step as they walked briskly down the jetty. From behind them came the flashing click of an Aldis lamp; ahead of them lay the 15th Submarine Flotilla to whom he would be handed like a parcel, Keth thought wryly, for onward transmission to France.

The air that swept the sea loch from the mouth of the River Clyde was salty and fresh, and it made him wish that Daisy could be here and not three floors underground where most times the air was stale and dusty.

Unspeaking, he followed the progress of a launch as it rounded the stern of the mother ship. It was crewed by women, dressed in sailor's trousers and thick, navy sweaters. All were undeniably attractive. They handled the launch that bucked through the waves as if they had been born to it and when one of them jumped ashore, rope in hand, Keth noticed she did indeed have a lovely little bottom. All at once he was glad that Daisy worked three floors down in Liverpool and out of the gaze of lecherous lieutenants. And he was even more glad that just as soon as he got back from France they would be married. *When* he got back — not *if*!

Mealtimes, Blodwen Meredith considered, presented the best opportunities for what she called essential

152

chats because if what she said didn't suit Lyndis, it was hardly likely the girl would flounce off in a huff, leaving a half-eaten meal on the table. And today was the day for such a chat.

"Well, that's the last of the tomatoes till next year I shouldn't wonder." She placed a bowl of salad on the table. "Remember once you could buy them all the year round."

"So why didn't you tell me you've been writing regularly to my father since —" Lyn left the sentence hanging in the air, concentrating on cutting a piece of cheese.

"Well, you know now," came the defensive reply, Blodwen wondering how it was that her daughter seemed able to read thoughts. "I told you last time you were home we'd been in touch."

"But not regularly. Are you having an affair with him — again, I mean?"

"Affair! How can we have an affair with me here and him there? And as for *again* — well, since it never finished as far as I was concerned, you can call me an old fool."

"No, *cariad*, I'd never call you that. Do you remember once telling me that you can't stop loving someone to order? Well, you were right." Lyn gazed at her plate. "I won't ever stop loving Drew, so who am I to say you shouldn't still love my father — though what you see in him is a mystery!"

"But you're not me, are you? And you might as well know we're going to be married."

"*Married!* Then why didn't he tell me when he wrote?"

"Because he doesn't know. He won't have got my letter yet. But I reckon the time has come, now that our Fan is gone, God rest her, for him to make an honest woman of me."

"You'd propose to him?" Lyn speared a forkful of lettuce with great concentration.

"I would. I have. I wrote a while back, suggesting it. When I get his reply I'll know if he still wants me."

"B-but what good would it do either of you?" Lyn spluttered. "You just said it yourself; you're here and he's in Kenya."

"Not a lot at the moment, I'll grant you that, our Lyn. But this war isn't going to last for ever and I've always had a fancy for your father; never wanted anyone else."

"So you'd marry a man who was engaged to one woman and carrying on with another? Because that's what he was doing!"

"Yes, but it takes two to make love, *merchi*, and I didn't say no to Jack even though he and my sister had named the day. And I couldn't tell him about you being on the way because I didn't know till they were married, and him gone to Kenya. So I'm not losing him again. As far as I'm concerned, I'd have him tomorrow if he's willing. Can you understand?"

"Yes, I can. I know that if Kitty Sutton ever ditched Drew I'd be there waiting, pride on my sleeve — damn fool me!"

154

"Well, that's the way it goes. There's no pride in loving. And I'm sorry about your Drew." She pushed back her chair. "Oh, come you here and have a bit of a cuddle. Your Auntie Blod understands how it is and she'd give anything to see her girl happy."

"I know you would," Lyn sniffed. "And I'm glad you're my mother. I truly am."

Keth looked again at Gaston Martin's cheap watch, then lay back on the narrow bunk, hands behind head. This cramped sleeping space was where he had spent the better part of four nights and three days since sailing from Loch Ardneavie. It stood to reason. A submarine was a tight ship to run and there was no room in all the clutter of wheels and tubes and wires and instruments for a wandering civilian.

Soon they would be there, off the French coast. Enemy-occupied France. HM Submarine *Selene* had brought him safely this far and in a few hours he would be put ashore.

He would be glad to see the last of this bunk; had endured near-claustrophobic conditions only because he knew they could not last and because each night the submarine would surface to recharge the batteries and listen-out for any signals bearing *Selene*'s call sign.

That was when the welcome rush of cold air filled the boat, replacing air gone stale; was when submariners walked the upper casing, filling their lungs with damp salt air.

Some remained within the confines of the conning tower to smoke the cigarettes forbidden them when submerged. Everyone kept a careful lookout for intruders; for swift enemy E-boats and reconnaissance aircraft. At such times, when it seemed they were the only beings on a never-ending sea, Keth would close his eyes and let the quiet of the night wash over him, his mind a blank.

Few spoke when *Selene* rode on the surface. Sound carried far at sea. Some believed you could smell a man sucking a peppermint almost a mile away or see the glow of a cigarette end.

Keth blinked into the darkness, trying to define where the horizon merged with the land mass. A scudding night cloud covered the moon and someone said softly, "That's more like it." Moonlight was not always a friend.

"How far away now?" Keth asked of the First Officer.

"Far enough, but until we take you in we'll stay in water deep enough to dive in."

Number One. That really was his name. Not Tom nor Dick nor Harry. Not even Sublieutenant Smith, or Jones. Everyone with whom Keth came into contact was nameless and he, in return, was called Captain. Best that way, he supposed. What Gaston Martin didn't know he couldn't tell.

"Do you want to eat, sir?"

Keth shook his head. Lately, he hadn't even thought about food. These few remaining hours his thoughts were of the pill hidden in the cuff of his shirt; that obscene, fifty-seconds death pill. He thought, too, about *Omega*, the safe and solid mother ship, far away now in Loch Ardneavie and to which, before so very much longer, *Selene* would return. Without him.

Dot-dash-dot. Dit-da-dit. The letter R flashed from the shore and to which, when he landed he would reply with four short flashes: H — his own sign. For *Hibou*, owl, Gaston Martin's codename. Someone, code-named Hirondelle would meet him. *Hirondelle*, a swallow. He wondered who thought up codenames.

"I think you should eat, Captain."

"Maybe you're right." Best he should. Only God knew when his next meal would be — and where. Keth felt his way carefully down the conning-tower ladder, then made for the galley.

"Fancy something hot, sir, or a sarnie?"

The sea cook spoke with a Liverpool accent and it made Keth think of Daisy.

"Whatever is going, thanks." It would all taste the same.

"Mustard on your beef?" The cook was buttering large slices of bread.

"Please." The man was trying to be kind, Keth thought; sorry for the poor stupid sod they would soon put ashore. Rather him than me, mate!

Keth carried the plate to his bunk. He would never forget this bunk nor the fuggy, blankety smell of it. It had been his womb and soon now they would cut the umbilical cord.

"They're looking after you, then?" *Selene's* skipper, wearing canvas pumps, creased trousers and a navy-blue sweater, appeared. "You're okay?"

"Fine." He was not fine.

"We'll go further inshore about midnight when the tide turns. A leading seaman will be in charge of the dinghy. You'll take your orders from him. He's all right — done it before."

"Good," Keth shrugged.

"Sparks has just had a signal from your lot. Everything's okay at this end. No problems."

Keth thought about Castle McLeish and the stone house. Of course there would be no problems. How could there be? Slab Face did not tolerate problems.

"You've got your stuff handy, Captain?"

"Ready and waiting." One suitcase; one brown paper carrier bag.

"And you'll go through your pockets beforehand? No duty-free cigarettes . . .?"

"I don't smoke."

"Nor submarine lollies?" The lemon-flavoured sweets a submariner sucked when cigarettes were forbidden.

"Nothing at all like that, but I'll check."

"I'll leave you then. You'll want to get your head down for a couple of hours."

"Might be an idea. Thanks a lot." Sleep? Oh, no! Think of Daisy, then? No, no, *no!*

Think instead of dit-da-dit, and *hibou* and *hirondelle*; think of Gaston Martin and the leading seaman who had done it before.

He chewed on his sandwiches. They were tasteless and hard to swallow.

All at once, Keth wanted it to be midnight.

"I thought you'd be alone." Julia offered a spoonful of tea in a twist of paper. "Tom home-guarding again? Put the kettle on, there's a love."

"You on your own too? Is Nathan out then?"

"About the Lord's business. I suppose you've got to accept that when you marry a parish priest."

"Tell me," Alice arranged cups on a tray, "I've often wondered: what's going to happen when the war is over — to you and Nathan, I mean? When he took holy orders he couldn't have known he'd inherit Pendenys."

"No. Nor half of his mother's money either. But *when* it's all over and the Army give back Pendenys, I'll worry about it. I couldn't live there, not for anything!"

"Drew's going to want Rowangarth," Alice persisted.

"I know. He and Kitty living there will make me feel better about leaving it. I suppose Nathan and I could live in the bothy — when the land girls go home," she said absently.

"Had you thought —" Alice filled the small earthenware pot, "there'll be a second-generation

Clan for you. Drew's children, I mean, and Daisy's."

"And Bas and his brood." Julia's eyes took on a yearning look. "Coming over every summer and Christmas . . ."

"Bas isn't married yet. Give the lad a chance!"

"He will be," Julia smiled smugly. "And talking about courting — Tilda's got a follower!"

"What? *Our* Tilda?"

"Oh my word, yes! Name of Sydney. She met him in Catchpole's garden. He's with the Green Howards, guarding Pendenys — and he's single, would you believe! His father was killed in the last war and he looked after his mother till she died two years ago."

"Then here's to Tilda and Sydney." Alice raised her teacup. "She was always a romantic; always had her nose in a love-book, as Mrs Shaw called them. I'm glad for her — even if nothing comes of it. Tilda was very kind to me when I came home from France — till Miss Clitherow put her foot down, that was."

"But wasn't everyone kind?"

"Not exactly. I'd been a servant at Rowangarth, like themselves. You couldn't blame them for being a bit wary — Miss Clitherow, especially. She put me very firmly in my place. I was no longer Alice Hawthorn; I was the future mistress of Rowangarth. But how *is* Miss C? Haven't seen her lately."

"Her rheumatism is bad — and it'll get worse when winter comes. When she came back from

160

Scotland I thought she'd be just fine in one of the almshouses, but now I think she'll be better staying at Rowangarth — after all, she's got every right. She's lived there longer than I have. But what news of Daisy?"

"She's fine. Had a letter this morning. Drew rang her. You'll know Kitty has gone to London?"

"Mm. Another for Sparrow to fuss over."

"Daisy was a bit puzzled. Said Keth's letters are arriving all higgledy-piggledy; completely out of date order. But maybe some of them were posted in Kentucky, she thought."

"Probably. Amelia is always glad to see Keth. And I still think he'll get home sooner than anyone expects."

"Doing a Jinny Dobb, are you?" Alice laughed. "By the way, Daisy has written her first cheque! Made her go all over queer, she said."

"What did she buy?"

"Nothing, it seems. She thought about all that money in the bank and nothing in the shops to buy, so she drew out five pounds; just about as much as the Wrens pay her in a month! She's taking Lyn out when she gets back from leave, she says."

"I liked Lyndis," Julia murmured, "what bit I saw of her, I mean."

"But you like Kitty better?"

"Kitty is adorable! I shall hand Rowangarth over to her with never a qualm." She jumped to her feet as the dogs outside set up a barking. "There's Tom back, and just look at the time! Eleven o'clock."

"Watch the blackout, love," Alice called as Tom stomped into the kitchen in his army-issue boots. "And see Julia home, will you?"

"No! I'll be fine, thanks all the same. There's an almost full moon tonight."

"Aye. It's grounded the bombers. Bright as daylight, out there. But I'll walk you as far as the wild garden, Julia." Tom didn't hold with a woman walking alone in Brattocks Wood; not even when moonlight made a mockery of the blackout.

"Mind the leaves." Tom offered his arm. "They're falling thick and fast, now. It's slippy underfoot, tonight."

"I wonder if that man in the moon knows there's a war on." Julia looked upwards.

"Not if he's got any sense he won't," Tom laughed, offering a hand as she climbed the stile. "Good night, lass."

"'Night, Tom." She reached on tiptoe to kiss his cheek then ran swiftly across the lawn, turning to wave as she reached the side door because she knew he would stand there until he saw her safely in. Briefly she closed her eyes.

"Thank you, God," she whispered, "for Tom and Alice."

CHAPTER
TEN

"Ten past ten," Daisy said as they stood outside Hellas House. "Shall I go in now, or shall we hang on till half-past?"

"Not in any hurry, are you? I'd like a chat."

"We've been chatting all evening, Drew!"

"Yes, but not about —"

"Not about Lyndis? She's on leave — but you know that."

"I know she's on leave, Daiz. You wouldn't be out with me otherwise."

"No. Not like the old days." Not when once he always took them both out, Daisy brooded, and Lyn had fallen badly for him. "Seems awful that you and I can't meet as much as we'd like to, but I've got to think about Lyn's feelings."

"I know. And I liked her a lot. If Kitty hadn't happened along, I should think the three of us would still be going out together every time we dock."

"You're missing Kitty, aren't you? Poor love — I do know how it is. But London isn't Washington. You'll see her soon."

"On my next long leave, I suppose. Hope she can get time off. I'll go to London if she can't, though I'd rather go home to Rowangarth. I miss it, Daiz."

"Well, you can't have it all ways! And surely ENSA will give Kitty leave? After all, you've got a wedding to arrange. But it's Lyn you want to talk about, isn't it? And you'd best be sharp; I'll have to be in, soon."

"How is she, Daiz? I'm not so big-headed as to think she'll have gone into purdah over me when she could have any bloke she wanted."

"Except Drew Sutton." Daisy set her mouth button-round.

"I'm sorry about that. The Rowangarth Suttons seem good at it — falling heavily and suddenly, I mean."

"And what would have happened if Kitty hadn't come along? Be honest, Drew."

"It would have been Lyn, I'm almost sure. There was something holding me back, though."

"Some*one* called Kitty. And Lyn didn't just like you, Drew. She was mad about you. I think she still is, though she's getting good at pretending she isn't."

"I wouldn't have hurt her, Daiz. Not for anything."

"You mean you wouldn't have *deliberately* hurt her? I know that, but you did, Drew, and there's nothing anyone can do about it."

"You can be quite bossy when you set your mind to it!"

"Sister's privilege. And I'm as sad about it as Lyn is because I like Lyn *and* Kitty — and you, too, you great soft ha'p'orth. I'm piggy-in-the-middle, I suppose. But c'mon, bruv; give me a hug and a kiss."

"I've enjoyed tonight." He circled her in his arms, laying his cheek on hers. "Take care of yourself. See you."

"You too, Drew Sutton. When are you sailing?"

"Morning tide. And remember to say hi to Keth for me, next time you write."

"I'll do that. Careful how you go, sailor. Be lucky."

She stood at the gate of Hellas House until he rounded the corner. He didn't turn and wave. Sailors never did. They never said goodbye either.

Her eyes filled with tears; not for Drew nor Lyn nor Kitty but for herself, because she loved Keth so much and wanted him so desperately.

Take care of Keth, won't you — and Drew? she pleaded silently. And God — *when* is this war going to end?

"I really must get this lot cut." Tatiana wound strands of hair round her finger, pinning them flat to her head. "Yours suits you short, Kitty."

"Mm. Easy to look after, too. When you're out on the road there never seems to be a hairdresser around."

"That's because a lot of them have been called up," Tatiana laughed. "Shampooing hair isn't regarded as war work exactly!"

"Guess you're right." Sighing deeply, Kitty lay back on her bed, hands behind head. "We're going to Norfolk tomorrow, doing a show for the Air Force, there. Then after that we'll be in Scotland. Some godforsaken place called Scapa."

"Scapa Flow. We've got a lot of ships, there."

"But not a minesweeper called HMS *Penrose*. Oh heck, Tatty! I'm sorry! I shouldn't have said that. I've been trying like mad not to mention Drew. You know I wouldn't hurt you for all the world, don't you?"

"I know. And, Kitty — I want you to talk about Drew. I don't know how you can *not* talk about him. I used to talk to Daisy and Gracie all the time about Tim. They'd alibi me so I could meet him, you see."

"Y'mean you never took Tim home? Why ever not?"

"Because Mother was like that. I suppose it's the Russian in her; overprotective. And as for the Petrovska! Well, only a Romanov would have been good enough for me — if they'd never left St Petersburg, that is, and if *that rabble* hadn't murdered the Czar-God-rest-him." She crossed herself devoutly, fluttering her eyelids, mimicking her grandmother. "But I wanted Tim the minute I saw him."

"Guess it was like that for Drew and me too. We'd grown up together — well, twice a year together, kind of — and then, after five years we meet at a crummy dockyard concert and *Wham*! Both of us! Suppose I realized it first. Drew was mad at me for showing too much. But what the heck — I was wearing a borrowed costume!

"Guess there was a lot of me oozing out," she giggled, "but the other sailors just loved it! Drew was real mad at me, though, and said I was common, so I said I was sorry and all at once it came right."

"And was it marvellous, like for me and Tim?"

"We-e-ll, Drew was a bit sniffy, but it was only because he didn't like those sailors ogling me. In the end we went back to my digs. That was when we decided we'd fallen in love."

"And you stayed together all night?"

"All night!"

"Wish Tim and me could have."

"Poor Tatty. You never — not once?"

"Yes, but not all night. I told him I loved him, but in Russian at first. Then we got to talking about me being too young to marry him and him thinking he mightn't live long enough to wait for me — tail-gunners take a lot of flack, you know. Anyway, we decided it was going to happen between us and Tim said that when it did I wasn't to worry. I wouldn't have cared if I'd got pregnant though I suppose now it's best I didn't. When Tim was — was killed, my period was five days late, but it didn't seem to register. I was too numb."

"You'd have been just fine, Tatty. The Clan would've stood by you."

"I know that. But imagine Mother trying to hide the shame of it in Holdenby — and as for

Grandmother Petrovska! She'd have had me whipped! But Aunt Julia and Uncle Nathan would have been all right about it — I know they would. And I could have kept the baby. Grandfather Sutton left me Denniston House and some money, too."

"We were all very sad about Grandfather. When Aunt Julia wrote to tell us we just couldn't believe it. Not so suddenly and cruelly, I mean. And we couldn't get across for the funeral either. Pa was real cut up about it."

"Tim died the same night; probably about the same time, though it wasn't Tim's bomber that crashed on the village. It came down on the pike. I wish I knew how to ill-wish, Kitty. Those German pilots who shot up the aerodrome that night would be dead now if I could do it. D'you think I'm peculiar?"

"Of course I don't!"

"The Petrovska thinks I am. She doesn't like my Englishness. Uncle Igor is the better for knowing, though. We've got quite close lately. He told me things . . ."

"What things?" Kitty's eyes sparked.

"Oh, nothing like *that*!" If only I could tell you, Kitty. If only I could tell *anyone*! "He told me things about living in St Petersburg before the revolution and the way life used to be for the rich. Sometimes I'm glad the Bolsheviks kicked them out!"

"I reckon they call them Commies now," Kitty offered.

"I know. But *she* still calls them Bolsheviks; the rabble, the great unwashed! I'm glad my mother married an Englishman, even though she wasn't happy with him."

"She wasn't?" Kitty breathed. "Ooooh! Do tell."

"No! I mean — there's nothing to tell. Not actually." Hell, she'd nearly let it slip! "What I meant was that she must have been unhappy, starting four babies and only me living. And it must have been awful, having Grandmother Clementina for a mother-in-law." Her cheeks burned. She must watch her tongue, in future! "But I don't want to talk about *them*. Let's talk about us and how glad I am you're here, Kitty. It's a shame you won't be able to meet my airmen just yet."

"Your wounded pilots, you mean — the ones you take out?"

"My burned aircrew, poor brave loves. Sam is getting over it a bit. He's going to have hospital treatment soon; see if they can make him a new nose, he says — a better one."

"And the other one, Tatty?"

"The other one — Bill — is the reason I can bear to talk about Tim; the reason why seeing you so happy with Drew doesn't make me want to end it all."

"*End it all!* Gee, Tatty, don't ever think of that!"

"I wanted to, once. When I knew Tim really wasn't coming back and after I realized I wasn't going to have his baby. If there'd been a pill I could have swallowed — something not painful — I'd have taken it.

"But now there's Bill. I'm not in love with him — it's nothing like that. But when I'm with him I can pretend he's Tim. Bill's got no features, really, and he was blinded. But his hair is like Tim's hair and his accent, too. And he's an air-gunner like Tim was."

"You mean that when you're with him," Kitty breathed, "you act out a fantasy? Bill is Tim, really — is that what you're trying to say? But, Tatty, that isn't fair! Not to you nor to Bill! What if he falls in love with you? Or what if you fall in love with him?"

"So you *do* think I'm peculiar? I knew you did!"

"No I don't, Tatty! I truly don't! But what if your Bill is married, eh?"

"He isn't. He told me so. He hasn't got parents, even. He's got no one in the entire world! And now he's blind! Well, at least he can't see his poor face!"

Tears filled her eyes, then ran unchecked down her cheeks and Kitty was at her side in an instant, holding her tightly, rocking her, hushing her.

"Don't cry. Please don't cry, Tatty. Heck, if only I could do something — anything! I can't bear to see you like this! Please, honey, don't upset yourself."

"I'm not upset. And I was fine till I told you. My own fault, I suppose, for even allowing myself to think Bill could be Tim. I tell myself that Tim is dead, but the minute I see Bill, hear his voice, take his arm — because he can't see, so I have to — then it's Tim I'm with. But sometimes I want him so

170

much, Kitty, I feel real pain! He isn't a prisoner of war, or even missing. He's dead! It's so cruel and uncaring and — and *final*!"

"Tatty, what am I to say to you? There's nothing I can do to help. I'd do it if I could. But if you want to go on with your fantasies, then I hope I'm there for you when the bubble bursts and you have to accept it isn't Tim."

Now Kitty was weeping but for whom she did not know. For Tatty, was it, and Tatty's tearing grief? Or was it for herself, because she was too happy and couldn't even begin to imagine how it would be if one day a telegram came to Rowangarth and Aunt Julia had to tell her? *Oh, please not Drew*.

They held each other tightly, then Tatiana pulled away, sniffing loudly.

"You look a mess, Kitty Sutton. Your mascara's run all down your cheeks. Serves you right for having mascara when we can't get it in here!"

"You look pretty rough yourself, Tatty. Guess we'd better wash our faces and powder our noses or Sparrow's going to notice and you know what she can be like!" Kitty forced a smile.

"But you won't tell Sparrow I was crying over Tim and don't ever tell her about Bill, or her Joannie won't let me do escort duties any more."

"I won't tell. And I think you're very brave, honest I do."

"So I'm no longer that brat Tatiana? And don't deny it, I *was* a whinge. But that spoiled-rotten kid has grown up now and knows what she's doing.

Well, mostly she does. It's just that at times like these she sometimes goes to pieces still."

"You can borrow my cold cream if you'd like," Kitty whispered, offering a pot. "Go on! It's okay. I brought loads of make-up over with me."

So Tatiana said thanks, she'd like that, and since her cousin was in such a generous mood, how about the loan of her dusky-rose lipstick next time she went out?

And Kitty laughed, relieved, and said, "Sure, honey. Anything you want! Be my guest!"

The Commanding Officer of HM Submarine *Selene* stood on the bridge within the conning tower, his first officer at his side. The stars were gone now, and drifts of low cloud streaked the horizon.

"Everything close up, Number One?"

"Yes, sir. Dinghy inflated. Crew at the ready." He lifted his binoculars, sweeping them from left to right and back again. "Seems quiet, over there . . ."

"Yes." The CO did not like operations such as this. It was his first drop and he resented hazarding his boat, engines stopped, silhouetted against the skyline. *Syrtis* usually put agents ashore — knew how it was done. Apart from the seaman loaned from spare crew for the trip, no one on *Selene* had a clue about such things and he wondered why the SOE bod couldn't have parachuted in!

Below, clinging to the running rail on the upper casing, one of *Selene*'s seamen held fast to the

172

dinghy; beneath him a sailor climbed the ladder to the bridge, the SOE man at his heels.

"Any questions, Leading Seaman?"

"Thank you, sir, no. Think we'll make for that far headland — get to the lee side of it."

The headland cast a long, wide shadow and the sailor had done it all before, knew that there they could blend into shadows and the sea, on the lee of the jut of rocks, ran calmer.

"Recognition signal R-Roger. Dit-dah-dit."

"Got it. Reply with H-Harry."

"All set, then?" The submarine commander turned to Keth. "Climb over. I'll pass your case to you. And the leading seaman is in command of the dinghy. Take your orders from him and don't try to pull rank."

"I will — and I won't. Thanks a lot, skipper." Keth offered a hand which was shaken firmly. "Best press on . . ."

His throat was dry as he arranged himself in the bows of the dinghy, his case wedged between his knees, arms clutching the bag of precious spares. He felt nothing; neither hope nor fear. He only knew his mouth made little clicking sounds as he pulled his tongue round his lips and his heart beat too quickly. He could feel its insistent thuds in his throat, his ears and behind his nose.

The leading seaman waited, paddle poised, on the port side of the fat, bouncing craft; a second seaman took his place beside him. From the conning tower came the hoarse whisper, "Good luck!"

Keth raised his hand in acknowledgement. The dinghy bucked as, at the push of a paddle, it left the submarine's side.

Carefully, strokes matching, the paddles cut into the water with hardly a sound, a splash. Keth fixed his gaze on the submarine. He had felt acute discomfort so closely confined on board; now, as the vastness of sea and skyline opened up, he wanted nothing more than to be back in its claustrophobic safeness.

The paddles picked up speed, racing for the shadow on the far side of the headland. Keth sucked in a deep breath, then let it go in little huffs. The seamen knew what they were about.

They reached the shelter of the headland just as the cloud drifted away from the moon and the sea was again lit with silver. The two men breathed evenly, paddles lifting, slicing. The blur that had been France was sharper, darker, now. Keth wanted to cough and swallowed hard on it.

The paddling ceased and they floated in on the breakers to a scraping stop. The younger seaman jumped out, heaving the dinghy onto firm, wet sand, holding tightly to the mooring rope. The elder man reached for the battered case, leaning over to pass it out. Paper bag in hand, Keth swivelled round, then stepped ashore.

"Thanks," he whispered.

"We'll wait," came the brief reply.

They stood unmoving, eyes ranging the dark of the landmass.

"That's it!" The leading seaman pointed to a briefly flashing light.

Keth reached for his torch. His hand was shaking. He pressed four times on the switch.

"Right, sir. They're over there. Stay here, close to the rocks. The beach could be mined. They'll know the way through if it is. They'll fetch you. Good luck, Captain."

Hands grasped his, then he was alone. The seamen dipped their paddles deep, straining against the incoming tide. Soon, they would be back on board *Selene*; back to the stifling, protecting closeness. Soon, the commanding officer would give the order to start engines and they would make for deeper, safer water — and home.

Keth stood very still, holding his breath then letting it go in a little hiss. Soon someone would take him to a safe house, and soon a signal would go out that Hibou had arrived and the whole thing would be set in motion. It might only take days, or a week, two weeks, but for Keth Purvis, the messenger, the risk was small compared to that of the men of the secret, hidden army of partisans.

Close ahead of him a light flashed briefly and he heard slow, measured footfalls on the sand. Then, to his left, from the shadow of a rock, a voice whispered, "Hibou?"

"*Oui*. Hirondelle?"

"You've brought them?" The man picked up the carrier bag.

"Spares."

"Good. Follow behind me."

Keth walked unspeaking, case in hand, frowning because he had expected a Frenchman and not someone with the unmistakable accent of an English public school. He matched his steps to those of his companion, walking where he had walked, glancing left and right, wondering what next.

"That's better." Hirondelle stopped, listening, in the shelter of bushes that grew thickly on the edges of a wood. "We'll wait," he said, squatting on the springy turf. "For your contact," he added, almost as an afterthought.

Keth nodded, taking his cue from the other man, speaking as little as possible, pushing his case beneath a low bush though he had no idea why.

They did not wait long. Keth saw the figure, walking quickly and without sound at the side of the path. Despite the darkness, he knew it was a woman.

He watched as she stopped, listening. Hirondelle reached for a twig, then snapped it. The woman began to walk again, eyes ranging the bushes.

"Hirondelle?" She stopped and Keth could see she wore short dark socks, and a dark skirt and jumper.

"Natasha?"

He rose to his feet. Keth did the same, wondering in a surge of panic why they had sent someone so young; sent a girl of no more than fourteen to do the work of a man.

Keth held out his hand; hesitantly the girl took it.

"I'll leave you, then," Hirondelle said in French, picking up the carrier bag. "You know what to do?"

"Yes," she whispered as the man crossed the path then slipped silently into the deeps of the wood.

"One minute," she said softly, "then we go."

"Right." This was stupid. A slip of a girl sent to collect him! What were they about?

"Sorry," she said as if she could read his mind. "The patrol went past ten minutes ago. They'll not be back for an hour. Moonlit nights are not good . . ."

"No." Keth wondered if Natasha was her real name or her codename. "Is it far?"

"Half a mile inland. We'll be all right," she urged.

"Yes." All at once, Keth recalled a fourteen-year-old Daisy, and felt a sudden longing to protect the girl called Natasha. "We'll be fine."

"Come," she ordered, still speaking in French. "We go to the village."

She beckoned with her hand and Keth felt shame for his lack of trust, accepting the risk she was taking.

"Okay. I'm with you," he smiled, and hearing that smile on his voice she turned, returning it tremulously.

They walked quickly across a clearing where recently trees had been felled, making for the denser cover of the woodland. Natasha did not speak but turned often to check he was following or to indicate that he walk on the grassy edge of the narrow path.

"That is the village ahead," she said softly. "We can't walk through the streets; someone might see us and there is a curfew in force."

"And they would tell?"

"They would *all* tell," she shrugged, "or we must presume so. But some — just *some* — might inform. That is why we trust no one. We'll go across the fields, away from the houses. Dogs might bark, you see . . ."

They did not cross the fields directly, walking instead in the cover of hedge shadows. Keth marked her fragility as a sudden slant of moonlight held her for a second; a child who should be at home with her mother.

"This is it." She opened a gate and set dogs barking. "Sssh!" She clicked her tongue to silence them. "They know me," she said briefly, beckoning him to follow her into the shelter of a shed. "We'll wait a moment. You are to stay here with Madame Piccard — Tante Clara. She is a widow, and old. I live with her now."

"I see. Tell me," Keth whispered, "how old you are."

"I am sixteen — and a little bit — and I am an unimportant part of — of *this*, you understand?"

Keth nodded.

"I carry messages, Hibou. Because I look so young, the soldiers do not suspect me."

"But how will your aunt explain me away?"

178

"Don't worry. She has already made it known she is expecting a man to dig her garden. And do I speak too quickly for you, Hibou? Do you understand what I say?"

"Yes — but it would help if you could speak just a little more slowly."

"I will try to remember. And we will speak English, you and I — when it is safe, that is."

"Do your parents know what you are doing tonight?"

"My parents," she whispered, "are Jewish. That is why I live here with Tante Clara. She is not my aunt and she is not Jewish. When the Germans invaded France, I was sent here from Paris, where we lived, to my mother's old friend. But for a year now there has been no word from Paris and we think my parents have been — *taken*."

"They're in prison? And don't you worry too that you might be arrested?"

"Not prison. I think they are dead. And I don't worry too much. I am dark, but I was not born Jewish. I am an adopted child and my nose is small and tilted. It would pass the test."

"*Test?* What is that?"

"You do not know? People suspected of being Jewish have their noses measured. The Germans have a special instrument for doing it. It's true! And may God bless the woman who gave me my nose!"

"So Jews really are treated badly by the Nazis?"

"Not badly, Hibou; like dirt. I feel I shall never see my parents again. It is why I do all I can to help."

"But you are too young to get involved, Natasha."

"If my nose had been a different shape, I would not be too young to be gassed, and my body burned. Ssssh!" she hissed as heavy footsteps trod the path; footsteps which paused briefly, then went on.

They stood still, breath indrawn, then heard the low muttering of an old voice, speaking to the dogs.

"It is all right. It is Madame," Natasha whispered. "She wears boots . . ."

The footsteps returned and stopped again. "Are you there, child?" The women peered into the darkness.

"Yes. And he's here." Natasha stepped out of the shadows.

"Come inside." The woman clumped down the path. "You are late, Monsieur. I expected you days ago."

"I am sorry, Madame Piccard. I had to wait for my papers."

"But you've got them? They're in order?" she demanded sharply.

"All in order." Keth reached in his inside pocket but she held up her hand.

"No matter. I know who you are, M'sieur Martin."

"Perhaps if you could speak more slowly, Tante . . ." Natasha hesitated.

"Of course. He is hard of hearing. I forgot." She shaped her mouth round her words as if she really believed Gaston Martin's deafness, then walked to the hearth, lifting a pan from the hob, stirring it slowly. "There is soup, M'sieur, and bread. You will eat?"

"If you can spare it, please." All at once the tension of the past days left him. Here, in this low-ceilinged, lamp-lit kitchen, Keth felt almost safe.

"What we have, we share. You are welcome."

"I have ration cards and, Madame, am I to be told where I am?"

"You haven't told him?" she asked of Natasha.

"No."

"And *They* did not tell you?"

"No, Madame. Just that I would be met and brought to a safe house."

"Then you are in Clissy. It is as well you know, since you came here by train!"

"Of course!" He smiled across the table and Natasha smiled in return with the mischief of Kitty's smile, he thought in amazement. Kitty, in the summer of 'thirty-seven, with long, black, bobbing curls; hair as black as his own.

He glanced down at his bowl as Madame Piccard and Natasha murmured a grace, then blessed themselves before picking up their spoons. And because he was now Gaston Martin, Keth imitated their actions.

Gaston Martin, he insisted silently. He must tell himself again and again that Keth Purvis was a long way away in Washington. And while he was here in

Clissy, he must not allow himself to think of Daisy, because Gaston Martin would not think of her.

He did not even know she existed.

CHAPTER
ELEVEN

"So, Anna, they still hold out at Tsaritsyn." Olga Petrovska turned off the wireless. "The Bolsheviks are putting up something of a fight — at last!"

"*Something!* Mama, the Luftwaffe bombed the city almost to the ground. They left little standing, yet the Russians are fighting for every ruin, every cellar; even for heaps of rubble! And when they have no guns, they fight with pickaxes and petrol bombs — women, too!"

"Ah, yes." The Countess picked up her embroidery frame. "I read in *Picture Post* that Nazi soldiers are becoming afraid of the Russians. They are calling them men possessed — devils. Hitler has lost a quarter of a million men. Those Bolsheviks in Tsaritsyn have one ambition, it seems; to kill at least one Nazi each day, every day." She jabbed her needle viciously.

"That is gruesome and horrible! Not all those soldiers are Nazis. Many are decent boys like Drew and Bas! And you must *not* call it Tsaritsyn. It is Stalingrad. It has been Stalingrad for nearly twenty years."

"Indeed? So those soldiers who try to take Tsaritsyn are changing their tune now. They were all fervent Nazis when the war was going well for them and no country stood up to them!"

"And you, Mama, had not one good word to say for the Communists, yet now you side with them!"

"I do, Anna, because they are defending Mother Russia. And if they rid it of those arrogant Huns, I will accept they have earned their right to my country."

"Even though you will never see our home again — nor Peterhof?"

"Even though. And I would be proud, Aleksandrina Anastasia Petrovska, to be fighting alongside those women in Petersburg and Tsaritsyn."

She said it softly, almost as though it were a whispered prayer and it gave Anna the courage to say, "Then you will approve of what I am going to do this morning."

"Try me."

"I — I'm going to Creesby, with all the other women whose surname begins with R or S, to register at the Ministry of Labour. All women of my age have to do war work now."

"I see. You will work on munitions or some other demeaning thing! You, a countess born, who has no need to work!"

"I have every need, Mama. And my Russian title counts for nothing here. I am *Mrs* Sutton. I was glad enough to come to England to safety so now I can't refuse England."

"It is preposterous! First Tatiana and now you! Those people seem to think they can do as they wish!"

"They can, Mama. They do! There's a war on, remember."

"Ha! A Petrovska in a factory! Have you seen those munitions workers? They go yellow!"

"I've seen them. Their work is dangerous. They must wear special soft shoes and cover up wedding rings with tape — nothing to make a spark, you see. I hope they don't send me to that kind of war work."

"They had better not! They will hear from me if they do!"

"They would take no notice, Mama. This is everybody's war and we must all help to fight it. Drew is fighting, and Daisy and Bas — and Tatiana is in London, braving the bombing."

"You owe this country *nothing*! Your loyalty must first be to Russia, where you were born!"

"So what would you have me do, then? Will I stow away on a ship going to Archangel? And will I tell them — if I get there safely, that is — that I am the Countess Aleksandrina Anastasia Sutton, daughter of the late Count Peter Petrovsky of the bourgeoisie and have come to make Molotov cocktails to throw at the Germans! Oh, Mama . . ."

"Do not be flippant! I can see now where your daughter gets her impudence from!"

"I'm sorry — truly I am!" Anna hastened, because her mother's bottom lip had started to quiver, which heralded either a prolonged burst of weeping or a fit of rage, guaranteed to bring on a migraine. She dropped to her knees beside her mother's chair, taking her hands. "I'm sorry for your Russia and all the poor people there, but now we live in England, and I must work. I've no say in the matter. But they can't send me away from my home because I am a married woman — and married women are not directed into the armed forces."

"What about married women with children — you have a child, Anna Petrovska!"

"My child is nearly grown up. Only women with a child under fourteen years are allowed to stay at home now. Women of my age are being sent to fill jobs to free younger, single women for the armed forces. Almost any useful job will do, as long as I work."

"So what is there for you to do in Holdenby, will you tell me, please?"

"We-e-e-ll, I could help Winnie on the telephone exchange, or I could work at Home Farm or I could — could . . . Oh dear, there isn't a lot I could do locally, is there? But I'm sure there will be work in Creesby. The Labour Exchange will tell me where to go, and I'm sure they will bear in mind that our bus service isn't very frequent and that I don't get enough petrol coupons to drive there every day. But I mustn't complain; not when the young ones risk their lives every day."

And night, too, she thought for no reason at all — except that she was thinking for the first time with real compassion of a young air-gunner who had been given no choice. And of Tatiana, far away in London, who loved him still.

Keth lay down the axe, pausing to wipe his forehead, closing his eyes, breathing deeply on the salt air that blew in cooling gusts.

It was difficult to believe after all the frustrations and delays that he was actually here at Clissy-sur-Mer, less than half a mile from the coast, doing something as safe and ordinary as chopping logs. Then he smiled because it was a long time since he'd chopped logs at Rowangarth bothy.

The breeze was welcome. In all the turmoil of getting here, not once had he given thought to the fact that so much further south it would be warmer. And had times been normal, he supposed that this part of France would have been a holiday resort.

"Hullo." He looked up, smiling, as Natasha walked towards him carrying a fat, earthenware mug of coffee.

"Good morning, Hibou — or now I think I should call you Gaston. You are honoured. There is very little coffee in the shops, so don't expect it every day. The Boche takes most of it, just as they think they have the right to all the wine the château produces."

"But they don't get it, of course?"

"No. M'sieur at the big house sees to it that we locals have our fair share. Tante Clara left me to sleep in this morning because I was up late last night."

"And you have missed school?"

"Ha! I left school a year ago. Book-learning isn't important at this time."

"It was when I was sixteen," Keth scolded.

"Really? Well, as far as I am concerned, school is a waste of time; learning to stay alive is not!" She went to sit on the chopping block, arranging her skirts prettily.

"Where is Madame?"

"Gone to the village to buy your food and to let it be known, I suppose, that her hired help has arrived."

"Is that wise, Natasha — and should we be talking like this in the open?"

"It would be unwise *not* to let them know you have come. Why shouldn't they know Tante Clara's gardener is here? Now, if they walk by and see a stranger, no one will think anything about it.

"And talking out here is safe enough. The dogs would bark if anyone came." She dropped her voice to a whisper. "This place is a good walk from Clissy. It is why *They* decided it should be a safe house." She touched her nose with a warning forefinger.

"Who are *They*?"

"If I knew I wouldn't tell you; but I don't know. There are many people around here who — *help*, but it wouldn't do for me to know them."

188

"The Nazis wouldn't suspect a child?"

"They would. And when they looked at my papers they would see I wasn't as childish as I look! But this far they've left me alone."

"Aren't you afraid, Natasha?" All at once Keth remembered the pill in the cuff of his shirt.

"Of course I'm afraid. It would be stupid not to be. But I don't intend to go the way of my mother and father."

She said it with such matter-of-factness that he wondered how anyone so young could have known so much heartbreak.

"But you know who *I* am, Natasha, and that Madame Piccard hides people like me, for instance. What about Hirondelle?"

"Hirondelle? Before last night I hadn't seen him and I doubt I will see him again. You brought something for Hirondelle, I suppose?"

"I was told someone would be waiting for the bag." Now Keth was wary.

"There you are then. Next time that man comes out of hiding he will have a different codename. No one knows more than two people at the most. Until you came, Tante Clara was the only other contact I knew. Here in France people like us don't play games. It is all very serious, though I'm not important. Anyone could be a messenger," she said scathingly. "I know very little and I like it that way. The less I know, the less I can tell *them*."

"But how would you explain being here, at Clissy, if you were stopped and asked for your papers?"

"My papers are false, like yours. It wouldn't do to have a Jewish name on them. My parents took care of it all long before I was sent here. They knew, you see, what would happen to them eventually. And when France was invaded, they sent me to Tante Clara at once. We heard, later, there had been a search in Paris and that every foreign-born Jew was taken away. After that, I had no more letters from them. They probably went to Belsen. I think it is one of those places; killing places."

"Natasha! How can you talk like this?"

She rose, shrugging, throwing logs into the wheelbarrow.

"My papers say I lived at Dunkirk, not Paris, and if anyone asked they would be told my parents were killed there at the time of the evacuation of your army, Gaston. Many civilians were killed there."

"Yes." He had been in America at the time.

"It's strange, but I have had three names in my life. The name I was born with, the name I was given when I was adopted and the name on the papers I use now. The first I do not know. I wasn't told until the war started that I was an adopted child. When I asked about my parents all they would tell me was that my father was unknown and my mother's name was Natasha.

"It's why I used it when I met you; it is the only name you will know me by. It is unlikely you will get into conversation with anyone from Clissy — you won't be here long enough — but if you do, you must refer to me as Madame Piccard's niece."

190

"Very well. But how can you be so blasé about it all? How can you bear to talk about your parents without —"

"Without breaking down; without weeping?" She lifted her shoulders in an unchildlike gesture. "Because although I tell myself they are dead, I refuse to weep for them until I know for certain they are.

"When I was three months old, I was adopted. I had black hair and brown eyes — Jewish colouring even if my nose was not kosher. I was reared in the Jewish faith, though now, of course, it is wisest I worship with Tante Clara. She belongs to the Roman Church, and believes in miracles. It is why she thinks I should pray to St Jude. He's the patron saint of lost causes, you see."

She said it without bitterness, wheeling the barrow to the woodshed beside the gate, back stiff, head high and he ran after her.

"I'll help you stack them, Natasha!"

She turned and smiled — to let him see she was not crying, he supposed — and for the second time since their meeting he felt a wash of tenderness for her. Had he had a sister, he thought, she would probably have looked like Natasha. The same dark hair and eyes as his. Funny, that, when you thought about it.

"Pass them to me. I'll pile them up. I'm good at it. When I was sixteen, I always chopped the logs at home. But tell me," he felt safer talking to her within the confines of the shed, "you said 'every foreign-born Jew'. Where were your parents born?"

"My adoptive parents? In Russia. In Moscow. They got out before the Czar was shot and came to Paris to live. I think my natural mother was Russian, too, her name being Natasha, I mean. She went to the nuns to have me but that's all I know, except that I was born in Paris."

"I know someone who had to leave Russia," Keth offered. "Were your parents rich, then?"

"No, though I suppose you might have called them middle class. My Jewish mother was a milliner — had her own shop she told me — and my father was a musician. Most of what they had was taken. What they could carry away helped them bribe their way out of Russia. They never had children so they adopted me," she said softly, sadly. "I can tell you no more. I would like to know about you, Gaston Martin, but I won't ask, though I think you were born in the country, the way you can use an axe," she smiled as Keth began splitting logs again.

"The country," he nodded.

"And your French? Where did you learn that?"

"In school, and then by speaking it to a governess. Not my governess," he added hastily. "I have no father, and my mother isn't well off. If I see this war through, though, I'll make sure she never wants."

He turned sharply as the dogs began their barking and Natasha ran to the gate, smiling. "It's Tante Clara!"

192

"So! You have got yourself out of bed," Madame Piccard admonished. "Here — take my shopping into the house and be careful of the eggs!" Then turning to Keth she said, "You, too, M'sieur. The kitchen, if you please."

She clattered down the path, then closed the door behind them, taking off her hat.

"They know you are here — or they will before so very much longer."

"*They?*"

"The people who are expecting you. I mentioned in the *boulangerie* that my gardener had arrived. That was all I needed to do. Now it will go down the line and you will be contacted."

"How, Madame?" Excitement beat in Keth's throat.

"How do I know? You must learn not to ask questions. You will not be given what you came for until your way out has been planned. It takes time. Be patient — and meantime do what you came to do — tidy my garden and dig over the vegetable plot! I hope you can use a spade, too?"

"I can. But how will I recognize my contact?"

"I don't know yet. Perhaps tomorrow, when I go to buy more bread, someone there will tell me. You must learn to wait for things to happen."

"Patience," Keth smiled, because he liked Clara Piccard in spite of her brusque way of speaking; appreciated, too, the risk she ran taking him in. "I'll chop the wood first, then get on with the digging.

And, Madame," he said as he opened the door, "thank you."

"Ha!" The elderly woman made a dismissive gesture with her hand. "Your thanks are not needed — and anyway, I do it because I hate Germans. They killed the man I married in the last war. Just a few weeks a wife — I didn't even have the joy of a child. What little I do is for my Henri. He would want me to."

Keth closed the door gently. Tomorrow, they might know more. Things were moving and of course, he conceded, plans took time. Messages to be passed, London to be contacted. Here, in occupied France, a wireless operator must always be on the move; must never transmit twice from the same place. He, who knew more than most about the interception of signals, knew that detector vans were always vigilant, hoping to home in on an operator.

He wondered if the valves he had carried were now in use, and, more soberly, if some secret armourer had been able to repair the firing mechanism of two pistols.

Keth looked down at his right hand and the blister already forming there. A long time since he chopped logs, he smiled wryly, wrapping his handkerchief around his hand.

He took up the axe again, thinking that the first day was almost over — day one to be crossed off his mental calendar, his first day as Gaston Martin. To forget that identity, even for one unguarded moment, could cost him his life. And the lives of others.

He raised the axe then swung it with such force that the log splintered into two at the first stroke and flew in opposite directions.

It made him think of the morning the letter came telling him he was not to be given a free place at university. That day he had chopped wood; slammed the anger out of himself.

Yet that was in another life, another country. Now, Gaston Martin chopped wood in a French cottage garden. And waited.

"Mrs A. A. Sutton?" called the clerk at the Ministry of Labour office in Creesby.

"Aleksandrina Anastasia," Anna smiled as she walked to the desk. "Quite a mouthful, isn't it?"

"But lovely names. Unusual." The clerk returned the smile.

"Russian." Anna sat opposite at the desk, pulling off her gloves.

"It's Mrs Sutton of Denniston House, near Holdenby? You'll forgive me for interviewing you immediately you registered, but I have a job I think might suit you; one which wouldn't entail too much travelling. Do you know a Dr Pryce?"

"Ewart? But of course! He's our family doctor."

"He's desperate for help."

"B-but I'm not — well, medically minded. I wouldn't be very good with sick people, I'm afraid."

"It's a clerk and general factotum he needs. He told me he's given up all hope of ever getting a partner, the way things are, and he does have the district nurse to help ease things. It's more someone to organize appointments he needs, send out the accounts, and most important, he said, be there when the phone rings. The work would be confidential, but I don't have to tell you that, do I?"

"N-no. But do you think I'll suit? I'm afraid I don't know a lot about anything."

"Whatever work you take — and the Government expects you to take work — might be a little strange, at first. Your details say you have no children."

"Not small children. Just Tatiana, and she's in London."

"Then won't you at least think about working for Dr Pryce? I'm sure you would fit in well."

"All right! If he's willing to give me a try — I'll do my best."

"Then better than that you can't do." The clerk was already filling in a green card. "If Dr Pryce decides to take you on, will you ask him to complete this card, and return it to us?"

"And if I don't suit?"

"Then he'll fill in the appropriate section and return it just the same. We'll fit you in somewhere else then."

"Thank you." Anna rose to leave. "What would my hours be?"

"Full time, almost. Eight until four in the afternoon or nine until five. Half an hour for lunch.

Sundays off and every alternate Saturday. Your wages you would agree between you. Good luck, Mrs Sutton."

Later, at Creesby terminus, Anna sat on the bus, waiting for it to start. Already she had decided not to get off at the crossroads but to go on into the village and call on Ewart Pryce. It would have made more sense, she supposed, to ring for an appointment, but the more she thought about it, the more she liked the idea.

It would be her first job. Imagine! Well turned forty, and never been out to work. It made her feel useless; a lily of the field. But Tatiana seemed to be doing well in London; why then shouldn't Anna Sutton have a job, too?

Ewart was a friend as well as her doctor; she knew he would be a reasonable and kind employer. And she had no choice, did she? It was either the surgery on the Creesby road, or work as a bus conductress or perhaps in munitions. She might even be sent to work in the chip shop! Only one thing was certain: under the Emergency Powers Act she was now required to work, so why not for someone she knew and liked? And being away from Denniston would be a relief from her mother's demands, though just to allow so unfilial a thought made her blush.

She had pleased — obeyed — her parents; she had married and tried to please and always obey her husband. Now she was a widow and tried to please a society which demanded a strict code of conduct from a woman alone.

But the Government said she must work and it might be rather nice, being at the surgery with most of the patients people she knew. And imagine leaving Denniston in the morning and not returning until late afternoon! She could cycle there, too; no waiting for buses!

The more she thought about her new-found key to freedom, the more giddy she became. She was still high on a cloud when she pressed the bell of Ewart Pryce's front door.

"Anna!" It was opened almost at once. "Business or pleasure?"

"Were you asleep? Did I waken you?"

"I was just catching forty winks, but I'll put the kettle on. Have you time for a cup of tea?"

"This isn't a social call, but I'd love a cup of tea. And I'm not ill either, so you can wipe the concerned expression off your face."

"So tell me," he said as they settled themselves at the kitchen table.

"I believe you want a clerk to work in the surgery and take phone messages."

"Y-yes . . .?"

"We-e-ll, the Labour Exchange sent me and I'm willing to try, if you are." She rummaged in her handbag, cheeks burning, for the card.

"You mean — but Anna!" He threw back his head and laughed. "This is marvellous!"

She knew, even as she offered him the green card, that the job was hers. Now all that remained was to tell her mother.

Clara Piccard swished the curtain over the staircase door, then pulled her chair closer to the fire.

"The nights are getting colder," she remarked. "Not the days, just yet, but the nights . . ."

"Natasha is asleep?" Keth stirred lazily, shifting his stockinged feet on the hearth.

"She had little sleep last night, and after all she is still only a child."

"A very brave child. She told me about her parents. Do you think she will ever see them again?"

"I don't know. It is in God's hands. I'm glad her mother sent her to me. I was alone and lonely. The child has made a difference to my life."

"But isn't it strange," Keth pressed, "that you should know her family — Jewish, and Russian, and you of a different faith and nationality?"

"Not strange, exactly. When the last war ended I was nursing in Paris. A refugee was brought in, ill with pneumonia and he was in my ward. He and his wife were lonely and bewildered; I was lonely, and bitter. We became friends. They took a small apartment near mine, then from somewhere they adopted Natasha. I loved the little thing. She called me Tante Clara.

"Two years before this war started I retired and spent my savings on this little place. There were rumours, even then, of war and about terrible things happening to Jewish people in Germany. We decided that if those things should ever happen in France, then I was to take the child."

"And now you both help people like me?"

"We do what we can. I dream, M'sieur, of the day we wait at Clissy station and those two lovely people get off the train. I fear they never will, but still we pray. Are you hungry?"

"Not particularly, thanks."

"The fire is red; I thought to make toast. We never have butter on our toast now, but I have some apricot preserve left from the days when there was sugar to be had. And I need an excuse to go into Clissy in the morning."

"Visit the *boulangerie*?"

"Exactly."

Clara Piccard did not cut bread for toast. The urgent knocking on the back door caused her to lay down the knife.

"Ssssh!" she said sharply, listening.

There followed three sharp taps on the window, then three more.

"It's all right." She turned down the paraffin lamp. "Stay where you are. Who is there?" She opened the door.

"It's Bernadette." A woman with a shawl over her head pushed her way into the room.

"Who is he?" the visitor demanded.

"You know who he is, woman! I told you a man was coming to work in my garden!"

"I have something to tell you, Clara."

200

"Then tell it. Gaston is deaf. He was a soldier and the big guns did things to his eardrums. You've been listening to the wireless, Bernadette?"

"Yes. The news from the BBC. It seems there is all hell let loose for the Boche in North Africa. A barrage of shells such as this war has never known. I thought you should know."

"And that is all?"

"Isn't it enough? Now Hitler is getting it on all sides! I'll listen to the next broadcast."

"Then be careful, Bernadette Roche!"

"What did she say?" Keth asked when they were alone again.

"You didn't hear?"

"I did, but she spoke too quickly for me. Something has happened?"

"In North Africa. I have no wireless because I have no electricity. Sometimes I think it is as well. But Bernadette has one — in spite of the fact they are forbidden. She hides it and only brings it out for broadcasts from London."

"What if she were caught?"

"Then someone else would listen. It is essential we do. London sends coded messages for — *people*, as well. But tonight they tell that there is a great offensive in North Africa and, for once, the Allies seem to have the upper hand!"

"That's wonderful news!" Keth gasped. "Do you still have need to visit the bread shop tomorrow?"

"I do!"

"Then all at once I am hungry for toast and apricot jam!"

"So! You are home — at last!" Olga Petrovska wore her hurt face. "You have been out all day and not a living soul do I speak to! Where have you been, all this time?"

"I've been to Creesby, Mama!"

"That was this morning!"

"Registering for war work takes time. And I called on Julia." She had, but only briefly.

"Then you will have heard the six o'clock news?"

"No! What's happened? I left Rowangarth just before six, and walked home."

"There is a battle in the north of Africa. They didn't say where, but Hitler's tanks are being pushed back! And serve him right, too, for starting the war!"

"Have there been heavy losses?"

"That they didn't tell us, but I hope many Germans were killed."

"Mama! Please don't! Our soldiers — *their* soldiers; most of them are young men like Drew and Bas and Keth! Don't hope for anyone to be killed. Bad thoughts can rebound on the sender!"

"So you want me to be sorry Germans are being killed when killing is the only way to end a war!"

"Mama — *please* . . ." Anna closed her eyes wearily. "I'm hungry. Have you made anything to eat?"

"I have not!"

202

"Then it will have to be a cheese sandwich and leftover soup. And I'm sorry, Mama, but you're going to have to learn to look after yourself. I've got a job, you see."

"So it has come to this! Peter Petrovsky's daughter in a factory!"

"No. There was work for me in Holdenby after all. Ewart Pryce needs help at the surgery. I start on Monday." She said it almost defiantly.

"So you not only called at Rowangarth, but at the doctor's house as well? Never a thought for your mother! And had you realized, Anna, the doctor is a single man!"

"And I am a widow — and there's a war on, had *you* thought?"

"Is a single man," the Countess insisted. "What will they say in the village — you and he in that house alone!"

"I — I don't . . ." Anna shook her head. What was she to say in answer to such an outdated, rather nasty insinuation? "I'll put the soup on," she said wearily, quietly closing the door behind her, leaning against it, eyes closed.

Then she set her jaw and marched to the kitchen, holding tightly to her breath because if she did not she would explode! How could her mother cling so tenaciously to the past? Would she never realize that in a country at war everyone was equal; that every man, woman and child was a number on an identity card and without that card no one could buy the food allowed each week in the same exact amounts?

War was a great leveller, yet Olga Petrovska lived on the banks of the River Neva still, and spent every summer at Peterhof. And in her faraway dreamings the Czar-God-bless-him still ruled and all was well with her world.

Anna reached for the cheese-grater. The cheese ration seemed to go further if you grated it. Absently she spread margarine thinly on four slices of bread, then set two trays, prettily, the way her mother liked it to be.

Well, whatever her mother said, now, she was going to work! For three pounds a week! Out there was someone who rated her capabilities highly enough to pay her a wage. It was a pleasing prospect, she thought as she carried her mother's tray to the sitting room.

"Alice — Mrs Dwerryhouse — has been given war work, Julia told me," Anna smiled, in control again.

"But she already war-works! She sells saving stamps for the war effort and helps run the Mothers' Union! And she has given her daughter to fight in the Navy! What more do They want of her?"

"Alice is to work for Morris and Page, that nice shop in Harrogate. Daisy once worked there, in the counting house."

"And what is Mrs Dwerryhouse to count?"

"Alice is to work there Mondays and Thursdays — doing alterations. She was a dressmaker, remember? The rest of the week they will phone her if anything urgent comes in. Julia thinks she will

204

only be busy when the sales are on. People can't buy a lot of clothes now. Alice is quite pleased about it, I believe. Part-time will suit her nicely and the Labour Exchange has agreed to it."

"How old is Mrs Dwerryhouse?"

"A little older than me and a little younger than Julia, I believe. She registered a week ago with the C to Fs."

"She gets part-time work yet you, Anna Petrovska, land yourself with a full-time position."

"You are right, Mama!" Anna said as if she had only just thought of it. "But we must take what we are given and not complain." She hoped her feelings did not betray her because all at once she was looking forward to starting work at the surgery. "I must try to remember what Daisy once said when she joined the Wrens; that if anything I can do will shorten the war by even an hour, then I must do it, whether I want to or not."

She looked down at the tray on her knees to hide the pleasure in her eyes. She hoped she didn't sound as smug as she felt.

"After all, Mama," she said softly, "we must never forget there's a war on!"

CHAPTER
TWELVE

A war that brought Gaston Martin into her life, into her garden, could not be all bad, thought Madame Piccard.

Her woodshed was full in readiness for the cold weather; her paths had been weeded and wayward shrubs and bushes cut back. Each day when Bernadette came to share the good news the BBC was sending to France, she commended Gaston's hard work, wishing sniffily that her Denys was as good with a spade. But Bernadette's husband sometimes disappeared for days on end and she had more sense than to ask where he had been.

"The Boche is finished in Egypt," she announced on her last visit. "I thought you would like to know."

"You'll get us all into trouble, listening to that wireless," Tante Clara grumbled, though she suspected it was not only news broadcasts Bernadette and her man listened in to. "What else did it say?"

"That Italians and Germans are surrendering in their thousands and that Spitfires and food have got through to Malta, at last. But I must go, make a meal for Denys."

"He's back, then? Beats me where that husband of yours gets to. Has he got a mistress?"

"Tante Clara," Natasha scolded when their neighbour had left, nose in air, "that wasn't kind. Perhaps Denys can't tell anyone where he goes. For all we know, he may be —"

"Child! How many times must I tell you that we don't *know* anything! Don't I always say you must never let your right hand know what your left hand is doing? And that applies to neighbours, too, who tune in to broadcasts from London!

"I'm going into Clissy now for bread. I won't be long. See that the kettle is on the boil by the time I get back and you might as well grind the last of the coffee beans." And only God Himself knew when she would be able to buy more!

"I'll go to the *boulangerie!*" Natasha, bored, sprang to her feet. "I'll go on my bike and save your legs."

"*I* will go for the bread! If you are bored, child, you can always give Gaston a hand — and mind what you say to him!"

"Say! He doesn't talk about anything but digging and the garden and when the wind will be in the right direction to burn all the rubbish!"

"Then you should have told him bonfires are not allowed unless I get permission from Monsieur le Commandant!"

"And you will not do that, Aunt!"

"Not until Gaston has gone," she answered flatly, throwing on her shawl, taking the basket that hung

207

from a hook in the ceiling and leaving by the front door, which she rarely did.

Natasha riddled the ashes from the stove so the fire glowed red. Then she filled the kettle from the little iron pump that stood beside the sinkstone and set it to boil.

She knew why Tante Clara was going to the *boulangerie*; the bread shop was the centre of village gossip. Even people who baked their own bread called there. And the Boche, stupid that they were, hadn't realized it was a clearing house — or so she *thought*, Natasha frowned. It made sense, didn't it? Gaston had come for a better reason than to dig an elderly lady's garden. The young, dark-haired man was waiting, though for what and for how long she had better sense than to ask. Tante Clara was right, though. You kept your thoughts to yourself and you certainly didn't juggle them from your right hand to your left.

"I have never seen this garden looking so tidy," she smiled, and Keth, in need of a rest, went to sit beside her on the wooden bench. "You don't look like a labourer, Gaston, but you know how to use a spade."

"I've had plenty of practice." His father had not been able to dig the garden. A man invalided out of the Army with a crippled foot could not.

"Do you have your own garden?" Curiosity was getting the better of tact.

"No. I used to dig my mother's garden."

208

"Used to?" She wanted to know if he were married.

"Before the war — before . . ." he shrugged.

"Oh — I know! I know! We can't talk about anything interesting!" She jumped to her feet. "I think I'll take the dogs for a walk. Tell my aunt I won't be long."

He watched her go, liking her, pitying her, wanting to talk to her about Daisy; knowing he could not. Even though she had met him five nights ago and brought him safely here, he still thought her too young, too vulnerable, to be mixed up in business such as his. He was still leaning on the gate when Madame returned, eyebrows raised.

"I was watching Natasha." Clearly an explanation was necessary. "You've just missed her. She took the dogs. Will she be all right?"

"We must hope so. She knows not to speak to soldiers. Some girls do — in exchange for bonbons. But it does not end at bonbons. I have told her."

"She'll grow up into a beautiful woman, Madame."

"She will — and keep your eyes off her!"

"Don't worry," Keth smiled, allowing himself a rare glimpse of so-blue eyes and pale yellow hair. "I prefer blondes myself."

"I see. Then I wish you well, Monsieur. Now come into the house." She clattered down the path. She reminded him of Jinny Dobb, Keth thought, and wondered if Madame, too, told fortunes.

"I have had a bargain today," she said when Keth had closed the door. "A half-price loaf, just because it had risen too much and was a funny shape. See — the top is hanging off."

Deftly she lifted the crust; from beneath it she pulled a piece of folded paper, reading it, throwing it on the fire, standing to watch it burn.

"What did it say?"

"Wait," she shrugged. "It said to wait. But it would seem things are moving."

"When?"

"How do I know?" she shrugged. "I'm told little. I'm like Natasha — a messenger," she said sharply.

"Yet you take in people like me . . ."

"Yes, and I'm a fool, too! Would you like some coffee?"

"No, thanks. Water will do." He filled a mug at the pump and drank deeply. "Will it take long?"

"I can't say. I would think — though it is only my own guess — that arrangements will have to be made and arrangements take time."

Like coding up a message, getting it to an operator, Keth thought. And the operator needing to find the right place from which to send it, and the right time. Then waiting, listening for an answer and getting word, somehow, to the *boulangerie*.

"Take time," Keth nodded, smiling. "I'll be getting back to the digging."

Wait, he thought, driving the spade deep, for the machine to be brought to a point of departure. Yet who would bring it, and when? But first a way out must be organized and Madame was right. It all took time. Even the weather could hold things up.

"Hullo!" He smiled to see Natasha standing beside him.

"'Allo, yourself," she grinned.

A tight lump of emotion rose in his throat and he felt affection for her. All at once it was important that her parents should still be alive. "Leave the dogs with me. I'll give them a drink and shut them up."

He dipped a bowl in the water butt and the animals drank thirstily. Two elderly greyhounds; quiet, unemotional. He wondered how Madame managed to feed them.

A man climbed a fence into the lane then walked past the gate. He nodded, and Keth said, "M'sieur," wondering who he was, swivelling his eyes sideways as he walked on. Denys, perhaps?

He cleaned his spade with a sod of grass then rinsed his hands in the water butt, shaking them dry.

"A man came past the back gate," he said, unlacing his boots at the back door.

"So? People do walk past our gate. There is no law against it — until curfew. Fair, was he — with a moustache?"

"Yes. Was it Bernadette's husband?"

"No, but he's no one to worry about. Did he speak?"

"We nodded, in passing . . ."

"That's all right then. I got some fish today down at the quay. Supper will be ready soon."

She turned, unconcerned, to stir a pan and Keth felt less tense, taking his cue from the elderly woman who dismissed passing strangers with a shrug.

He had been in Clissy for five days, now, his presence accepted as though he had every right to be digging Madame Piccard's back garden. Why then should he panic because a man walked past? Madame had let it be known he was here, hadn't she, and the Germans billeted in the cluster of huts beside the quay had not come looking for him? Why, when they must surely know of his presence at the cottage on the edge of the village?

He took a deep breath, telling himself he was a fool, that one strange face should not throw him into a panic. Everything was going fine; it was! And hadn't the people at the stone house told him it could be several days before they could get him out again — as long as two weeks?

Trouble was, Keth admitted, things had gone too easily this far and instinct warned it should not be so. He had expected to be hidden away, yet was unconcernedly asked to work in the garden. Already Bernadette had seen him, and now the man with the moustache.

All at once he wanted his hands on the Enigma machine and to be away, through the trees and across the scree to where a dinghy would wait. At this moment of unease, he needed the claustrophobic

212

safety of a submarine called *Selene* and to be a boffin again at Bletchley; sleep in the monotonous safety of a bare room he had once shared with a pilot called Robbie. Keth Purvis wasn't cut out to be a hero. All he asked was to fight the war the best way he knew — with figures and ciphers and clicking, rotating *bombes*. But more than anything, he wanted Daisy.

Lyndis, back from leave, closed the door of Cabin 4A, leaning against it, eyes closed. She was still upset.

"Damn, damn, *damn*!" she whispered as the door opened and Daisy stood there, back from her watch.

"Well, hi! Had a good leave, Lyn?"

"Great." She rose to her feet, taking off her jacket and cap, hanging them up.

"How long have you been back?"

"About ten minutes."

"Then why didn't you wait for the transport at the Pierhead?"

"Because I left Auntie Blod's early this morning. I got here about noon because I'd intended doing a squad drill. I'm behind with them."

Unlike at training depot, they were no longer formed into a squad and marched everywhere. Now they were watchkeepers, they fitted in their two-a-month drills as their duties allowed.

"Oh." No longer interested, Daisy kicked off her shoes, then lay back on her bunk to read the letter from Keeper's Cottage.

"Well, what do you know? I told you Mam had to register for war work, didn't I? Well, she's only ended up at Morris and Page, where I used to work. And Tatty's mother is going to work for Doc Pryce. Can you imagine Mrs Anna working? And you're not listening to a word I say! Something wrong?"

"No — oh, dammit, *yes*." Lyn turned abruptly to stare out of the window. "I didn't go to squad drill. I ran into Drew!"

"Oh Lor'. And what happened?"

"What do you mean, *happened*? I slapped his face!"

"Lyn! You *didn't*!"

"Of course I didn't!" She wouldn't have been able to, had she even remotely felt like doing it. The sudden encounter had unnerved her, thrown her into a panic because until that moment she was sure she could cope with it as she had done the day she wished him every happiness on the phone. But bumping into him, literally, and speaking to him face to face was altogether different. On the steps of the Liver Building it had been, he coming out, she going in.

"Drew!" Dear, sweet heaven, why couldn't she think of anything better to say? And why was he so good to look at still?

"Lyn! Leading Wren, no less! Congratulations on your hook." Which was a pretty stupid thing to say, come to think of it, when all he wanted was to say how sorry he was.

214

"And congratulations on your engagement — but I said that, didn't I — ages ago?"

"You did. And thanks, Lyn — for everything . . ." His cheeks burned. Lyn was still good to look at, still had the most kissable mouth. Once they were close, could have been lovers — until Kitty . . .

"Think nothing of it. I enjoyed the good times, don't forget. But I thought you'd have been at sea still." Why were they standing so close? She stepped backward because she wanted to touch him and she must not.

"Only a short trip over to Douglas and back. Been delivering signals to Flag Officer. And you, Lyn?"

"Just back from leave. Was going to do a squad drill on the roof."

"Then I mustn't keep you . . ."

"No bother. I'm late now. They'll have started."

"So why don't we nip over to Charlie's for a wad and a mug of tea? I don't have to be back yet." The tension was easing. Lyn seemed all right.

"N-no. Best not, Drew." They had eaten cheese sandwiches, drunk strong, sweet tea served from the back of Charlie's rusty van on their first date. Their first *real* date, that was. Without Daisy. And that night, outside Hellas House, their first proper kiss. "Best press on. I'll tell Daisy I ran into you. She's on afternoon watch today."

"I'll ring her, later."

"Okay." Lyn held out her hand. "So long, sailor. Take care. Be lucky."

"You too, Lyn. I'm glad we met."

"Yes." He was still holding her hand so she pulled it away, then turned, running blindly, not caring where she was going.

She ended up at the Pierhead stop of the Overhead Railway; at the place, dammit, where first they met — in another life, it seemed.

She bit hard on her lip. Fate could be cruel. Bloody cruel.

"South end — all the way, please," she asked of the ticket clerk, slamming down a florin, not waiting for the change.

Bloody, *bloody* cruel!

"Then what *did* you do?" Daisy — pulling her back to Cabin 4A.

"Do? We said, 'Hi! Fancy bumping into you! How have you been?' of course, like civilized human beings. No bother! Drew was delivering something to Flag Officer. He said he'd maybe ring you later."

"And that was all, Lyn? You're sure?"

"Of course I'm sure," Lyn flung. "Think I'm still nuts about him, then? What do you suppose happened — that I burst into tears or something? I'm over him, Dwerryhouse! Meeting him again was easier than I thought!"

"That's fine, then," Daisy whispered. "Shall we go down to supper?"

It was all she could think of to say.

Natasha sat on the floor at Clara Piccard's feet, gazing into the fire; Keth rocked gently in the

216

wooden armchair. The fire had been built up against the cold of an early November night, the shutters made fast against lights they must not show.

Keth closed his eyes, tired, now, at the end of each day, and tried to clear his mind of all thoughts.

Tante Clara knitted. The piece of work that fell from her four needles was long and black. A stocking. She always made her own. At first the movements of her fingers intrigued Keth, for he had discovered she could knit with her eyes closed, or when holding a conversation. She never seemed to look down at her work.

"Ssssh!" Natasha jumped to her feet. "The dogs! Someone's out there!" She made for the door.

"Stay here!" Tante Clara rapped. "Wait!"

There was a beating on the door. "Shall I go upstairs?" Now Keth was on his feet.

"No! Answer the door!"

"*Me?*" The dogs still barked frantically.

"*You!* Who else?"

Natasha reached to turn down the lamp; Keth ran his tongue round lips suddenly gone dry, then pulled back the door bolts.

He was at once pushed aside. A gendarme entered the room, followed by two soldiers of the Wehrmacht.

"Papers," rapped the Frenchman. "This is a routine check!"

Natasha turned up the lamp again, then went to stand behind her aunt's chair.

"Get them, child." Madame Piccard nodded towards the dresser. Natasha offered the papers to the gendarme.

"No." He indicated the more senior of the two men with him. "This is not a civil matter. I am here only to act as interpreter."

Wide-eyed, Natasha did as she was ordered.

"Clara Piccard." The young lieutenant looked at the identity card, the ration card. "How long have you lived here, Madame?" he asked in German.

"He asks . . ." The gendarme's command of the German language was not good. "How long have you lived here?"

"You know how long! Five years!" She held up five fingers.

"I see." The gendarme took the folder which held Natasha's papers. "And what are you doing here, Mam'selle? Did you obtain a permit to travel?"

"She did. More than a year ago. She came to me when her parents were killed at Dunkirk. I am her godmother, though she calls me aunt!" Clara Piccard's needles clicked steadily. She looked the gendarme straight in the eyes. "Tell him. You know she did!"

"*Oui.*" He returned the papers to their holder, nodding. "And you, M'sieur?"

"Look at him when you speak," the old woman rapped. "And speak slowly. He's hard of hearing!"

Keth, glad of the sharp reminder, cupped an ear with his hand and whispered, "*Comment?*" Then

218

getting a hold on his bewilderment, he offered his discharge papers.

The gendarme read them then turned, nodding assent, to the officer.

"A soldier. Discharged." He placed a forefinger to his own ear, then offered the papers.

The officer inspected them, understanding little of their contents, though they looked official enough. "Why is he here?"

"I know of him," the gendarme said. "He is a gardener."

"And does he have a work permit?"

"Of course!" Clara Piccard snapped. "He would not be here otherwise. Show him your permit, Monsieur Martin."

Keth offered it. He felt like an idiot and hoped, wildly, that he looked like one.

"It is in order," the gendarme nodded, then fixing them with a long, hard stare he said, "I am to warn you all to be on your guard. People come and go from the unoccupied zone. They are up to no good! You must, by order of the Wehrmacht," he said in his best official manner, "report anything out of the ordinary to me!"

"We will do that," the woman shrugged, "though I have reached an age at which I do not look for trouble. I mind my own business as well you know!" Her eyes sparked a warning to the gendarme.

"I know it, Madame." He turned, nodding to the Germans to signify his satisfaction. The lieutenant clicked his heels, saluted, then turned to leave. The soldier hurried to open the door for him, then they were gone as suddenly as they had come.

All at once galvanized into action, Keth hurried to the door, pushing home the bolts, leaning against it, eyes closed.

"I'm sorry, Madame. I don't know what came over me. A shock . . ."

"Yes. They sometimes search, and each time they do it takes people by surprise," Clara Piccard nodded.

"Not you, though!" Keth was still shaking. "They didn't upset you!"

"They did. They always do, but I have learned not to let it show. I see Germans most days. I am used to them. In your case, M'sieur, it was a first encounter. No blame attaches to you."

"It does! I was scared!"

"You are not a coward or you would not be here in France."

"But I should have said something."

"No! Sometimes to say too little is better than saying too much. Next time you will know how it is done. And I think," she smiled, "that after that, we deserve a cup of coffee."

They deserved a cognac, too, had there been any to buy.

Keth returned to his seat, deliberately relaxing his hands on the chair arms, though it did nothing to stop the thudding of his heart.

He had thought things were going too easily, too smoothly, and now he knew why. The sudden check had been a part of the way it was in an enemy-occupied country. Men — and women — could be arrested at the whim of the local commandant with no questions asked. What alarmed him more than anything was the certain fact that the German garrison knew of his presence here — if only as a jobbing gardener. He was a stranger in Clissy-sur-Mer and must expect to be suspect. Had not the gendarme been there, he would probably have been taken to German headquarters. And once there, he dare not begin to imagine what might have happened.

Clara Piccard poured boiling water on the coffee grounds, stirring them, setting the pot on the stove top to infuse.

"Do you think there was a reason for the visit?" Natasha whispered.

"Not particularly. They like to make a fuss from time to time to remind us who is boss! I'll find out tomorrow, when I go to the bread shop, who else had visits."

The dogs were quiet again; the silence in the stone-flagged kitchen was uncanny and complete. Natasha took mugs from the dresser; Clara Piccard filled them with a steady hand. It seemed, Keth thought, that everything was normal again, yet the visit had unnerved him. Now, the caution instilled into him at Castle McLeish and the stone house made sense, even though his part in the mission was only that of a courier.

He raised his mug in silent salute and Madame raised hers and said, "To France — and all hell to the Boche!"

Later, when Keth lay in bed, he heard a tap on his door and Natasha's voice asking if he were awake. He groped for the matches at his bedside, lighting the candle, hissing, "Natasha! What are you doing here?"

"It's all right. We will leave the door open to make it proper. I want to talk to you." Her wide brown eyes were accentuated by the candlelight and she sat at the foot of the bed, pulling her feet beneath her. "Tonight I too was afraid."

"You, Natasha? But you met me, brought me here. Weren't you afraid, then?"

"Of course I was! But tonight I was more afraid, I think. I have been here more than a year, yet tonight was the first time the Boche have been. Oh, they have searched other houses in the village, but it was as if they've realised for the first time that you and I are here."

"And why does that make you more afraid?"

"I can't really say. I've seen German soldiers before, passed them in Clissy and looked down at the ground as I did so. But this is the first time they have asked for my papers — been interested in me personally. They were too close, Gaston, and I didn't like it. Living so far from the village I thought we were safe but now, perhaps, something — how do you say it? — has been placing the cat into the pigeons!"

"The cat amongst the pigeons," Keth forced a smile.

"So! And I think they all at once get the wind up."

"They're getting suspicious?"

"Like I said — I don't know why. And perhaps it's just that I am feeling a little more sad because today would have been — *is* — my mother's birthday. On days like this I hope and pray more than ever I shall see them both again."

"It isn't a lot to ask," Keth smiled. "Just to have your parents with you."

"No. But in my country, which is defeated and occupied, things we took for granted seem gone for ever. I thought we would all live happily in Paris; that I would have a sweetheart and one day marry and have children of my own — keep them, and not have to give them away as my mother had to. I sometimes think sadly of the way things have turned out for me, and then I remember people who are sent to camps just because they are Jewish, or gypsies, maybe. And I think all of them would be glad to be me."

"Yes," Keth said softly. "Being alive is all that matters." And staying alive, his mind urged. "We are lucky, you and I."

He said it to comfort her because her eyes were still wide with apprehension and shone almost black in the candlelight. And she was only a child, really; a bewildered child who wanted, needed, to live and hope.

"I've been thinking about tonight," he said, "and I'm pretty certain it was a nuisance raid, just to remind people who is boss around here."

"Maybe you are right. And, Gaston — I am thinking too. If they'd suspected anything, *really* suspected, then they would have searched the house and outbuildings."

"Of course! I never thought of that. You are right, Natasha, so why don't you go back to bed? I'm sure Madame isn't worrying."

"She is not! She is asleep and snoring!"

"There you are then. Off you go!"

"Good night, Gaston." She touched his cheek with hesitant fingertips.

"Good night, Natasha. Try not to worry."

He left the candle burning to light her way down, then blew it out as he heard the click of her door sneck.

Try not to worry! Keth plumped his pillow, then lay listening to the ruttling snores from the room below him.

Madame Piccard seemed unworried, but hadn't she said that at her age she didn't look for trouble? Madame was old, had lived her three score years and ten most likely. Keth Purvis was young and greedy for life!

He closed his eyes and thought of Daisy; of her hair, her smile, the way she laughed; thought of her body, soft and giving, naked against his own.

224

No two people loved as he and Daisy loved, nor ever had, nor ever would. He loved her so much he would die for her.

But he wasn't going to die. He was staying alive and getting back home. To Daisy.

He tensed his body, then let it relax with a jerk. He closed his eyes and listened, ears straining, to the night sounds around him.

No hunting owl cried as it did in Brattocks Wood; there was no harsh *kaaark* of a nightjar. All he heard was the creaking of old timbers in the roof above him and below him, Madame's snores, softer now, like a blocked tin whistle.

Eventually he slept.

CHAPTER
THIRTEEN

Amelia Sutton returned from the post box, a small smile on her lips, selecting the letter she knew to be from her son.

"One from Bas?" Albert Sutton looked up from his desk.

"It is! And there's something inside it, Bertie. A photo, I think." Despite her excitement, she slit the envelope carefully "I was right! *Two!* Oh, darling, just look!" She turned it over to read "*Gracie, Rowangarth*" in her son's hand.

The girl who had smiled into his camera was beautiful — happy-beautiful — her eyes reflecting her laughter. She wore a pale blue, short-sleeved shirt and dungarees. Her skin was the colour of an apricot, her teeth even and white. "It's Bas's girl."

"Hm! And wheeling a barrow of manure with a fork stuck in it!" Albert grunted. "Just the damn-fool snap Bas would take!"

"Since when have you ever baulked at good, honest manure, Bertie Sutton? Our children have cleaned stables since they were big enough to lift a shovel! Perhaps that's why Bas took it — to let us know he'd found a girl who didn't mind a bit of muck, as they call it in Yorkshire!"

"You think he's serious about the girl, then?"

"If we're to believe what Kitty writes, he is," Amelia sighed. "I'd like it to be. I want grandchildren before I'm too old to enjoy them. Don't you want grandchildren, too?"

"Haven't given it a lot of thought; always believed that grandchildren happened whether you wanted them or not, though it might be a new experience, I suppose, sleeping with a grandmother." He smiled, kissing the tip of her nose, asking to see the other photograph. "Taken at Rowangarth, this one."

Bas in army uniform; Gracie in a blue dress, her hair newly curled, their little fingers linked.

"A couple, Bertie, if ever I saw one. Taken beside the linden walk, at the stone seat."

"It looks as if both our children have a liking for English spouses. I'd have thought they might have married good American stock."

"Like I did?" Amelia teased. "Well, if our children end up half as happy together as we are, I won't complain. Julia is fond of Grace, you know; says she's fitted in well at Rowangarth and it seems she's giving Bas a run for his money, which can't be bad. That young man is so laid-back he needs something to shake him up!"

"At least they don't seem to be rushing into marriage as if they've got a shotgun behind them." Albert shook his head gloomily. "Seems Kitty is determined for she and Drew to marry as soon as they can get down the aisle!"

"Kitty is different. She always was. I'll be sad to miss her wedding — but that's war for you! Remind me to pop a couple of films in the next food parcel I send. I shall want lots and lots of snaps of that wedding so I can imagine I was there."

"Come here, wife." Albert Sutton pushed back his chair and gathered Amelia to him, all at once thinking of his mother and how glad he had been to get away from Pendenys and marry the first woman with money enough of her own to support him. Now he loved that woman as she had always loved him.

"You're a very lovely lady, Mrs Sutton. You know how much I love you, don't you?"

"I know it, Bertie. And d'you know what? I can't wait to go to bed with a grandfather!"

Keth leaned on his spade, surveying the weed-free path, the newly turned soil. He rested not because he was tired but because what remained of the digging would take little more than a day to complete and he had no way of knowing, yet, how long he would stay at Clissy.

The morning had started chill; until the autumn sun came out to shine warmly. The scent of newly dug earth soothed him and it was difficult to believe that only last night two German soldiers had walked down this path.

The experience left a bitter taste on his tongue that now the normality of the morning was beginning to dispel. A routine visit, that was all. A zealous lieutenant, eager to be seen to be doing his bit for the Fatherland. It was nothing to worry about. Madame would say just that when she returned from the village.

What he supposed was correct. When Natasha and Clara Piccard appeared at the back gate, there was nothing in the older woman's face to betray emotion of any kind. She merely slid her eyes in the direction of the house, as she walked past him.

Keth rinsed his hands in the water butt, then kicked off his boots at the door.

"Come in, M'sieur. Shut the door." The terseness in her voice warned him something had happened.

"Last night?" he prompted.

"It wasn't only us. Several houses at our end of the village had a visit. Just the Boche throwing his weight about. But I left my purse at the bread shop."

"And you want me to go back and get it?"

"No! I left it on purpose. There were soldiers waiting to be served, and I knew she had something to tell me."

"But with Germans there how —"

"How did she tell me? She said, 'A very good morning to you, Madame Piccard. The weather still holds good, for November.' Leaving my purse gave her an excuse to return it."

"But is it unusual to say good morning, or remark on the weather?"

"No, but the way in which she said it — I knew . . ."

"And then what?"

"When we had gone, the girl would say, 'Oh, Madame has left her purse on the counter!' Then she would smile and shake her head and say I was always leaving something behind; that last time, it was my gloves! 'Someone will take it back to her!' she would say for the benefit of the soldiers, and slip it in the pocket of her overall."

"And will there be a message inside it for you when you get it back?"

"I doubt it. Messages are rarely written. Word of mouth is safer."

"So we wait?" Always *wait*!

"You are learning, Gaston Martin! Waiting and watching is what it's mostly about. These things can't be hurried."

"No." Of course they couldn't. Like the nameless men at the stone house; everything checked and checked again. There was more at stake than an Enigma machine. "I'll get on with the digging."

He smiled at Natasha, who was chopping vegetables for soup, and at Madame, who did not return his smile because already, Keth knew, her thoughts were racing ahead.

Wait, he thought, returning to his digging. Wait — and watch — then wait some more. At least the blister on his hand had healed!

★ ★ ★

"Hi, Bill!" Tatiana called, waving her hand to the WVS lady who was guiding the airman through the foyer door. "Over here!"

"Here's your date, Sergeant! What time shall I do a pick-up?"

"The picture finishes at ten so how about quarter-past?" Tatiana took Bill's hand, then tucked his arm in her own.

"That'll be fine! There'll be a couple more to collect from the Windmill — if I can manage to drag them out," she laughed. "See you, then. Enjoy yourselves!"

"Wouldn't you rather have gone to the Windmill?" Tatiana teased as they walked carefully up the balcony stairs.

"I did give it a thought, but it's more a visual thing, if you get my meaning."

"I'm sorry, Bill." Damn! She should have thought!

"Don't be. Normally, I'd have been there like a shot. They say the costumes are really something!"

"Not only the costumes!" Tatiana laughed. "And, Bill — if I sometimes don't think . . ."

"Forget I can't see, you mean?"

"Yes. We-e-ll — I *am* trying."

"I know you are. You smell gorgeous, by the way!"

"My cousin's perfume. She brought it over with her from Kentucky. They can still get things like that, would you believe? I'm wearing her best lipstick, too! But about the flick, Bill — it's really a cartoon, but set to music. I thought you'd like the music. *Fantasia*, it's called."

"I'll like anything where I can sit beside a pretty popsy and sniff her scent and hold her hand. You *will* hold my hand?"

"If that is sir's pleasure," she said primly, though there was laughter in her voice.

"It is. And Tatiana," he stopped as they reached the half-landing, feeling for the wall with his stick, then stopping to let those following pass them, "you'll have to take what I say with a pinch of salt. I like fine to tease the lassies. Thanks for putting up with it. It can't be a lot of fun, shepherding the likes of me around."

"What do you mean by that?" She flung around to face him, even though he could not see the anger in her eyes.

"I know what I look like. I've seen aircrew, all burned, but I thought it couldn't happen to me! I can feel my face, Tatiana, with my fingers! Thank God I can't see it!"

"Then thank Him, while you're about it, that you're alive!" she hissed. "I wouldn't be here if I didn't want to be — don't think for a minute I would! And if it's pity you're after, Bill Benson, don't look to me for it!"

"So that's it," he said softly. "It isn't likely a lovely girl like you would be short of dates — and you *are* lovely because Sam told me. So why isn't there a steady in your life, Tatiana?"

"I'd rather you called me Tatty," she said, taking his arm again, urging him on. "Steps ahead . . ."

"*Why?* Tatiana's a lovely name."

"Because I've always been Tatty — ever since I can remember!"

"And *he* calls you Tatiana — is that it?"

"I don't know what you're talking about! And get a move on, Bill. We're blocking the stairs and everyone is looking at us!"

It was not until the newsreel and the trailer for next week's big film were over that Bill reached for her hand, holding it tightly, leaning close.

"I'm sorry, Tatty — for hitting a raw nerve, I mean. I won't ask again."

"That's okay."

"Truce, then?"

"Truce." She wound her fingers in his, then turned to smile. "I'm smiling at you, by the way!"

"Then if I'm forgiven will you light a ciggie for me — I'm no' very good at it yet?"

"Only if you're careful with it!" she scolded, fishing in his pocket for cigarettes and lighter. "And sssssh! It's starting."

She reached for his hand again, hurting inside because Bill had guessed about Tim and she didn't want to share her memories. All she had wanted was to pretend, just sometimes, that she was with Tim again; listening to Tim's voice, holding an arm that could be his; feeling the rough serge of his tunic sleeve.

"I know it's starting, hen. Think I'm blind or something?"

Smiling, she shook her head, realizing that only seconds ago she had been angry with him for spoiling her dreamings. Yet she could not be angry with one who spoke with Tim's accent, was Tim's height, had corn-yellow hair, too. And just to make it even more real, the man at her side in the half-dark wore three stripes on his sleeves and the brevet of an air-gunner.

She squeezed the hand in hers, smiling gently, then relaxed her shoulder against Tim's. Just for two hours. It wasn't a lot to ask . . .

Keth sat at the fireside, listening to the spitting of logs, fondling the head of the greyhound at his side. He stroked it because it was restless, unused to sleeping beside the warmth of a fire. But Madame's purse had not yet been returned which indicated, she explained, that a visit was to be expected after curfew. Dogs which barked, therefore, must be kept under supervision. It stood to sense.

Madame's chair rocked softly, rhythmically; Natasha knitted. All at once, because the silence and the waiting made him nervous, Keth wished he could listen to a wireless. But neither the antics of Tommy Handley's crazy crowd, nor dance music played softly, intimately, would have stilled his listening apprehension.

Think of Glenn Miller records and the bare room at Bletchley. Think of Robbie blowing smoke rings,

234

saying "Smoooooth, eh, Purvis?" and that at the end of the corridor outside was a wall telephone. Eight paces from the door to the phone; he always counted. Eight paces away from Lark Lane 1322 and Daisy whispering that she loved him.

His hands gripped the chair arms. Useless to try not to think about Daisy, especially tonight when perhaps things might begin to happen.

Things, but not ordinary things like his mother sleeping in Rowangarth bothy under the waning moon that hung above the trees in Brattocks; the same moon he would see if he looked from his window tonight. And Daisy, working lates, because now he had her watches straight in his mind again he knew that was what she would be doing. Sitting at a teleprinter and an hour still to work before the night watch arrived to take over.

He brought the flat of his hand down hard on the chair arm and Madame glanced in his direction, then glanced back again to the fire.

"I told you this game is almost all waiting and watching," she murmured. "Tonight there will be a message — or tomorrow."

The dog at Keth's side growled softly, lifting its head. On the window came three short taps, then three more. Without speaking, Natasha lay down her knitting, reaching to turn down the light; Clara Piccard rose to her slippered feet, then drew back the door bolts.

The man on the step whispered, "The weather still holds good, for November," before the door was opened sufficiently to let him inside. He had fair hair and a moustache. The man in the lane.

"You left this at the shop." He laid a brown leather purse on the table.

"Thank you, M'sieur. You'll have coffee?"

"Please. And you are . . .?" He nodded in Keth's direction.

"Hibou." Keth's lips were all at once stiff.

"It won't be yet." The man sat on the bench in the ingle, holding his hands to the fire. "Not for three nights — when the moon has gone."

Madame clucked at a kettle that refused to boil.

"Hibou and I will meet. I will have the thing with me. I don't know where yet."

"The submarine?" Keth asked.

"No. This time a plane."

"But where will a plane land around here?" Madame demanded. "Always it has been by submarine!"

"A plane," the man said flatly. "Where, they'll tell us later. And thank you, Madame, but I won't wait for the coffee. Another time, perhaps."

"Very well." Clara Piccard quickly opened and closed the door. The dogs whined to be let out.

"Quiet!" she snapped, listening to soft, receding footsteps. "And where, in God's name, can a plane land around here?" she demanded of a kettle just beginning to puff steam. "What are they thinking about?"

"If it's a small one, it could touch down on the meadow behind the big house," Natasha frowned.

236

"On the field where la châtelaine schools her horses."

"But that is two kilometres away and across open land most of the way!"

"It will be safe enough when there is no moon. And there is some cover. I know the place. I have taken the dogs there."

"But you won't be going, child! I had doubts about allowing it last time!

"Then how will Gaston find his way — and in the dark, too?"

"Why must they send a plane? Noisy things! And are we going to have that coffee or not, child?"

"I think your aunt is right," Keth offered gravely. "You are very young, Natasha, to be —"

"*Natasha!* Call me Hannah! It's my real name! Hannah Kominski — or maybe you'd prefer the one on the papers I carry now — Elise Josef. And I am not a child!" She turned pleading eyes to the older woman. "Wars make children grow up sooner! Why won't you let me help again?"

"Because my dearest friends entrusted you to me," Clara Piccard said softly.

"I won't wait for a drink." Thwarted, Natasha jumped to her feet. "I'm going to bed."

"And will you take your anger with you, Hannah Kominski?" Madame held out her arms, gathering her close. "I know how it is for you. I hate the Boche, too. But there are things we can do, and things we must leave to God, though old as I am I still haven't learned the difference.

"But in this I am right. I don't want you to go out any more after curfew. Last time, you were lucky. It was only a short distance from the beach and the way was familiar. And we are only supposing the plane will land behind the château. Let's leave it? In the morning, everything will seem different — it usually does."

"I'm sorry for being cheeky. Forgive me, Aunt Clara. My parents would be ashamed if they'd heard me," Natasha whispered.

"Of course I forgive you. You're all I've got in the world, and dear to me. Go to bed and say your prayers — your way, and mine. God bless you," she whispered, closing her eyes wearily. "You know, M'sieur, two wars in any woman's lifetime are two too many."

"My mother says that, too." Keth took the old hand in his. "But she says that our lot always muddle through — lose every battle, but the last one."

"Muddle through? Is that what you'll call it when it comes to throwing Hitler out of France?"

She thought with terrible fear of the lives that would be wasted before peace came. Would it be like last time: brave young lions led by asses?

"You're tired, Madame. Go to bed. I'll check the doors and see to the fire. Are the dogs to stay indoors?"

"Yes. Leave them be. I wonder if they know there's a war on," she said softly, absently.

"I doubt it," Keth smiled, opening the staircase door.

"Lucky dogs. Good night, Gaston Martin."

238

★ ★ ★

Matilda Tewk, spinster of the parish of All Souls Holdenby, was in such a tizzy that she switched on the kitchen lights without checking that the blackout curtains had been drawn.

"Oh my word, Tilda!" she whispered to the wide-eyed, flush-faced woman in the mirror. "Whoever would have thought it?"

Tonight, in the intimate cosiness of the picture house, Sergeant Willis had held her hand and when she was obliged to pull it away to fish for her handkerchief — there were some very weepy bits in *Mrs Miniver* — he had offered his own, clean and neatly folded. Sydney's handkerchief was in her handbag now, and she would wash and iron it and return it to him next Wednesday afternoon when he called.

But not ten minutes ago the most wonderful thing happened in a starburst of delight. On the back doorstep, no less, Sydney had asked if he might kiss her goodnight.

Her first real kiss. She almost choked on the words in her eagerness to say he could. A tender kiss, for all her lips were very cold. She had known exactly how to do it. Hadn't she read of more first kisses than most and hadn't she waited longer than most for hers?

Their second kiss was beyond believing. He had drawn her into his arms, whispering, "Good night, sweetheart. See you next Wednesday."

She wanted to faint at the wonder of it but managed to whisper, "Good night, Sydney dear.

Take care," before closing the back door behind her and pushing home the bolts with fingers that shook.

And now, wouldn't you know it, there was no one, *no one at all*, with whom to share her triumph. Once, when she was young, she would have given a quarter's wages to be able to announce to Cook and Mary and Bess and Alice that she was walking out.

But Cook was gone, and Mary and Bess and Alice all married — Alice long ago. And married twice, like Miss Julia, when some hadn't had the chance of a dalliance, even.

But tonight she bore those ladies no grudge, for hadn't Tilda Tewk's turn come at last and wasn't Sergeant Sydney Willis worth all the yearning years? And tonight, hadn't he tilted her chin, looking at her exactly as Rhett Butler looked at Scarlett O'Hara when he kissed her? Mind, it had been blackout-dark on the back doorstep, but she knew in her heart his eyes were full of love.

She took off her hat, then set the kettle to boil, wishing the bottle of cooking brandy hadn't been empty these last eighteen months. It would have been good to drink a toast to her future happiness with that flush-faced woman in the mirror, but she was willing, in view of the circumstances, to make do with tea.

Good night, sweetheart. Were such beautiful words ever spoken? Now Tilda and Sydney were to join Mark Antony and Cleopatra, Romeo and Juliet, Jane Eyre and Mr Rochester and Jeanette

240

MacDonald and Nelson Eddy in the gallery of famous lovers.

She closed her eyes and prayed fervently that Sydney's regiment would stay at Pendenys Place for the duration, guarding whatever it was they guarded, and not be sent overseas to North Africa.

Not North Africa, she amended. Rommel's army was all but finished there. Such a victory! There was talk, even, of Mr Churchill ordering church bells to be rung, and what a lovely sound that would be!

With no trouble at all she turned her thoughts back to Sergeant Willis. Victory bells would sound like wedding bells for Tilda Tewk. Tilda Willis. Mrs Sydney Willis. Just to think of it sent shivers through her.

"Tilda!" Nathan Sutton crashed into her dreams, toppled her from her pink cloud. "That teapot is a sight for sore eyes! I don't suppose you could squeeze a cup for me, too? I've been out on a call and —"

"Why bless you, Reverend, of course I could!"

Tilda was herself again; cook to the gentry at Rowangarth and if Sydney's regiment marched away tomorrow, she would still have the Reverend and Miss Julia to look after and young Drew and Kitty, when they were wed. And memories of a dalliance and doorstep kisses.

Because when there was a war on you lived each day as it came and were grateful, if you had any sense, for any small mercy that chanced along. Those kisses had been worth waiting nigh on thirty

241

years for, yet wouldn't it be marvellous if one day Sydney whispered, "Marry me, Tilda?"

"Is anything wrong?" The Reverend butting in again.

"No, Mr Nathan — just thinking about the film. Parts of *Mrs Miniver* were very sad. Just a bit of a lass and newly wed she was — and then she got killed."

And Tilda Tewk would never go to heaven, telling lies to her parish priest!

"There you are, Reverend." Smiling, she offered the cup.

CHAPTER
FOURTEEN

Keth laid aside his spade. That was it! All finished. In the normal course of events, the hired help would move on to another garden or farm. But Gaston Martin must stay here at Clissy because there was a night and a day more to wait.

"So you have finished, Gaston! The garden looks well." Natasha, smiling, back from walking the greyhounds.

"Where have you been?"

"In the direction of the château," she shrugged, filling a water bowl.

"Then don't tell your aunt. You know how she feels about it."

"The field is sheltered by the château. It would be a good place," she whispered. "A small plane could land there easily."

"Natasha! Don't be a fool! Madame wouldn't —"

Keth cut short his warning as Clara Piccard walked up the path.

"See! Gaston has finished all your digging, Tante," Natasha beamed, unconcerned.

"Hm. Do you know, M'sieur, that when I first came here I planted just three small plants." She pointed to a bed of arum lilies. "And look at them now! They have spread into quite a carpet."

"I'll thin them out if you'd like." Keth was eager to fill in his last day here. "Shall I dig up a few clumps and put them in plant pots?"

"That is a good idea! Fill me a large pot and I'll take it to Madame at the bread shop! She has no garden — only a yard. A pot of lilies will look well at her back door!"

"She's happy now," Natasha said when Madame had left by the front door to walk purposefully to the village, the plant in her arms. "She wanted another excuse to go to the shop and there's a limit to the amount of bread anyone can buy!"

"Is something going to happen, then?" Keth dug the garden fork deep, easing out another clump of lilies.

"That's just the trouble. Tante Clara hasn't heard anything."

"And she's getting restless?"

"She always does at times like this and I haven't made it any better for her, saying I wanted to go again."

"Times like this?" Keth jerked. "It's happened before, then?"

"Ssssh!" She walked away from the gate, towards the house. "I think, Gaston, that a few clumps would look well at our own back door. Shall we put some in?"

"Tell me, Natasha! How many times?"

244

"How do I know?" She spread her hands eloquently. "She is involved — that's all I can tell you."

"And you are involved?"

"We help where we can. She and I carry messages. I don't know a lot," she shrugged. "Until you came, Gaston, I had met no one; not Hirondelle nor the man who came to the house two nights ago.

"It's best we don't know, you see. I have wanted to talk about you and your family — what your life will be when this war is over — but I can't. Even to know a little is dangerous the way things are in France. So you say nothing to anyone because you might be talking to a sympathizer."

"You mean some people might actually like having them here?"

"*Mais oui!* Some accept them. They tell themselves they are making the best of a bad job. Others — women, mostly, who either want a man at any price or need the food they can scrounge from the soldiers — fraternize openly. They'll be sorry when Hitler has to leave France; *very* sorry!"

"Who says?"

"No one *says*. Everyone knows it, though. Those who collaborate and the women who sleep with Germans are skating — how do you say it? — on thin ice."

"So where shall we plant them?" Keth smiled, reminded once again that Natasha was not all child. "A clump either side of the path, do you think?"

"Tante Clara will like that. Shall I help you, Gaston? The waiting is not good for me either."

"Of course you can help." And perhaps, he suggested, it might be a good idea to fill more pots with lilies — in case Madame needed to take another trip to the village?

"Of course! I'll bring pots. Perhaps Bernadette would like a plant, too."

They had potted two lily plants and planted more either side of the back door when the clump of Clara Piccard's boots could be heard in the lane. Her usual measured steps, Keth thought, as he brushed soil from the path. But once inside her own garden, she hurried down the path, noticing neither plant pots nor the lilies they had just finished watering in, calling, "A word, M'sieur!"

They sensed the urgency in her voice, following her into the kitchen, closing the door.

"It's tonight!"

"But what has happened?" Natasha whispered. "I thought —"

"Then don't think, child! Orders from London, just come! Tonight — from the château!"

"Something is wrong?" Keth prompted. "Sit down, Madame. You are shaking." *Tonight!* Not tomorrow! "Tell me."

He was shaking, too, because he was being pitchforked in, without having the chance to adjust himself to leaving — and all the dangers that leaving brought with it.

246

"Do you remember when you came, M'sieur — the man who was there, too?"

"Hirondelle?" The Englishman. "He was there for the spares I brought, then disappeared. Will he be at the château?"

"No! He was with someone else — they didn't tell me who. They were bringing it to Clissy — the thing you came for. Hirondelle didn't get here, but the other man did!"

"The package?" Strange, Keth thought, but the shaking had stopped. Now, he felt cold and calm.

"They ran into a patrol. The man carrying the package made a run for it and managed to make Clissy. Last night, it was. The patrol took Hirondelle with them — for breaking the curfew I suppose they'd say, but it won't be long before they get suspicious. He isn't one of us. Even the Boche isn't so stupid as not to recognize it. We can rely on twenty-four hours. Hirondelle will try not to tell anything for that long. After that, God help him, he might be pleading to talk."

"So it's like Natasha said," Keth said softly. "A plane *can* land at the château — and is going to?"

"Yes, but earlier than we expected. They've excelled themselves this time! They can shift themselves when they need to. It's easy enough to get a plane in the air — I imagine they have them always at the ready — but what about us? It isn't so easy here to make changes in plans, and especially now!"

"What do you mean, Tante Clara — *now?*"

"Think, child! Someone breaks the curfew; someone gets suspicious. Before so very much longer all the garrison will be out looking for the other man. They'll be on the alert, and all down the coast, too! Thank God there is no moon or their guns would be on to that plane before it had crossed the coast, let alone landed!"

"I'll make coffee." Natasha's eyes were wide, her face drained of colour. "Then we will think."

"There is no thinking to be done! Gaston will be met at the château — near the line of poplars, they said, at the back of the stables. That man will see to the lights — he's done it before, it would seem, and he will have the machine with him. I don't know his field name yet, but we will be told."

"And who will take me there, Madame?"

"That, too, we will know later. It takes time. We aren't able, here, to lift a phone and talk without being listened to! And we can't go where we like, when we like, because we never know who might see us — nor if they can be trusted."

"So we wait," Keth said flatly. "Again."

"Someone will come." Clara Piccard took mugs from the dresser. "We will know soon what is to become of you. All I know is that a plane will be here, and I was told that the pilot will allow no more than two minutes! Two minutes to get you and your belongings on board, M'sieur, and away!"

"Am I to take my things with me? Had I better start packing?"

"I think you better had! Everything! I don't want so much as a fingerprint left behind. And, M'sieur! Leave out your darkest clothes for tonight. Nothing light-coloured, remember!"

Keth ran upstairs, pulling his case from beneath the bed, staring at it. Only then did it register that he had slept in this attic, bumped his head on the low-sloping ceiling, for the last time. Tonight, if his luck held good, he would be in England.

But *if* was a powerful word. If someone could be found to get him to the château; if the unknown man got there safely with the machine; if the plane came on time and if the pilot managed to pick out the landing lights.

Lights were dangerous, a giveaway. Would they be seen from the château? Could everyone who lived there be trusted?

A small pulse began to beat behind his nose. He swallowed hard, then began the systematic packing of Gaston Martin's belongings. It was eleven o'clock. Soon now he would be on his way. Or dead!

Daisy! Think instead that she would be on her week of night watches and on Friday would be going home for the weekend. And imagine, *just imagine*, that by then he would be able to lift a telephone and whisper, "Hullo, darling, I love you so much."

He willed himself to be calm again, trying not to think about Hirondelle who would be made to tell what he knew. Did Hirondelle have a D-pill? Would he find the courage to swallow it?

Keth took his other shirt, searching for the tiny gap in the stitching at the cuff, slowly manoeuvring the pill out. He must put the thing that looked like a saccharin tablet somewhere more easily accessible. Soon, he would think of a place. He tore a corner from the newspaper at his bedside, twisting the pill inside it, pushing it into his trouser pocket.

He felt sick and afraid. He wanted to get out of this place now; yet he wanted not to go until tomorrow night. He looked up to see Natasha watching him from the doorway.

"Come down for your coffee, Gaston. Tante Clara has taken a pot of lilies to Bernadette."

"So Bernadette knows things, too?"

"I don't know." Her reply was flat and decisive. "There is no sugar left."

"That's all right. I can drink it without." He took a gulp, burning his bottom lip, swearing under his breath.

"Is your stomach making noises, Gaston? Mine is."

"Dreadful noises." He set down the mug, taking her hands in his. "In case we don't get another chance, Natasha, thank you for all you've done for me — for the risks you and Madame have taken. I won't ever forget you, I promise."

"And I shall remember you always, Gaston. Every time I see the lilies at the door, I will remember."

"Will Bernadette tell Madame anything? Are she and Denys in it too?"

250

"I told you I don't know. Denys is not at home at the moment."

"He seems to be away a lot. Beats me why the Germans haven't made him work."

"He has a medical certificate to say he has a bad heart."

"Like I am supposed to be hard of hearing?"

"Yes. Things can be arranged. Tonight, Gaston, I shall stand outside and listen for the plane. When you fly over, will you remember to think of me?"

"Standing beside our lily clumps, wishing me well?" He kissed her cheek affectionately. "I'll do that, Natasha. I'll think of you both."

He felt calmer. Just to think of those he would leave behind him as he flew to safety made him realize how lucky he was. He lifted his mug in a salute and Natasha, smiling, did the same.

"Is she very beautiful, Gaston — the girl in your life?"

"Very, very beautiful. As beautiful as you will be when you are twenty-one. Only she is as fair as you are dark."

"You are dark as I am. Have you Jewish blood in you, Gaston?"

"No — Cornish. Pendennis blood."

"And will you tell your girl about me?"

"When the war is over, be sure I will. And be proud to!"

The camouflaged bus drove to the Pierhead to pick up the night watch from Flag Officer, Port of

Liverpool's offices, and Lyn climbed on to flop wearily beside Daisy.

"My eyes feel like they're full of grit," she said, "and my mouth tastes awful. Just a cup of tea when we get back to the Wrennery, then it's me for my bunk!"

"Rough night? Didn't you get any sleep, then? I managed to get my head down for an hour," Daisy yawned, "then I got a shake at half-past two. All the printers suddenly going mad. Marjie said she hadn't a clue what was going on." Daisy never knew what was in the signals she passed — the important, worth-reading ones, that was — because they were in code. "Probably a convoy coming in, wanting destroyer escorts and fighter protection."

"Mm. Did you know it's official now about El Alamein? Special church services on Sunday and all the bells ringing."

"It'll be a wonderful sound, even if it's only the once," Daisy sighed. "Mam will insist I go to church in my uniform and Dada will be there with the Home Guard, too. It seems for ever since All Souls' bells rang. Remember we once dreaded hearing church bells?"

"Too right — when we were waiting to be invaded! I'll be in chapel with Auntie Blod, I suppose, though they haven't got a bell. Wonder what they'll do to celebrate? Suppose the Minister and congregation will do a conga round the chapel and the Elders will bang tin trays, or something. Okay! Only kidding, though it's great winning

252

something at last — and Hitler's lot bogged down in Russia, too. Maybe things are going our way for a change."

"Hope so. I sent a couple of signals last night to Washington on the direct line and I wondered how far from Keth they would end up. I wish I knew what was going on."

"Going on?" Lyn was instantly alert. "You don't think something's up, do you?"

"Common sense says no; instinct says yes. It's his letters, Lyn. They aren't arriving in date order, you see."

"And is that all? You're lucky even to get them when you reckon on all the fuss and bother it takes getting them here! Don't start imagining things, for heaven's sake!"

"I'm not — I mean, I don't — usually."

"Look — you're tired. We all are. You'll feel better after a sleep. And don't forget we'll be up and away on Friday morning on another crafty weekend."

"Mm. I wonder how long it'll be before we get caught — going AWOL every four weeks."

"*Caught!*" Aghast, Lyn wriggled down in her seat, pulled her cap over her eyes, and folded her arms. "Just *shurrup*, Dwerryhouse, and never say such a thing again!" At the wheel of the transport, the driver whistled loudly and cheerfully. At so ungodly an hour on a drab winter morning, Leading Wren Lyndis Carmichael did not appreciate his chirpiness. "You and Tommy both!" she hissed.

★ ★ ★

The soup bubbled on the hob; the kitchen table had been long since laid for *déjeuner* when Clara Piccard returned to the house. She slammed the door, the expression on her face warning Keth and Natasha into silence.

"*Merde!*" she spat. "The idiots!"

"What is it?" Natasha whispered. "Has something gone wrong?"

"Not *wrong*, exactly, but the soldiers are out, searching for the other man. Please God they don't find him!"

"Amen to that." The churning in Keth's stomach was back. "What will happen if —"

"If he doesn't make the rendezvous, M'sieur, with the package you have come for? I don't know. It takes time for an operator to get a message to London; it might go out too late to stop the plane taking off. The other man *might* get to the château, of course, but someone will have to be there, whether or not, to stop the pilot landing or at least tell him if there is to be no pick-up."

"But the man who is to organize the landing lights — surely he could warn the plane off?"

"Of course he could!" Madame snapped. "But for all we know, the package might make the château. You will still have to be there, Gaston, in case it does."

"But there is a chance it might not?"

"M'sieur, I don't know what to think! If all goes to plan, you and whatever it is you came for will get away safely. If it does not, then I'm of the opinion you should not go back with the plane. The pilot will alert London and they will make other arrangements for you."

"Did Bernadette tell you this?" Keth asked. She and her husband listened to BBC broadcasts from London. What other equipment was in their house?

"You think I'd tell you even if she had?"

"No." Just as at Castle McLeish and the stone house, straight answers seemed never to be given to even ordinary questions. "I just wondered if Denys was in a position to help." Keth said the first thing that came into his mind.

"Help? That man is never there when he is wanted!"

"So we wait?" Keth smiled wryly.

"Again," Madame nodded. "Maybe after dark, someone will come to take you to the château, since you have no way of knowing the way there alone."

"And if no one comes?"

"Then I will take you." Natasha spoke the words quietly yet still Madame spun round, startled, as if someone had thrown a grenade through her kitchen window.

"You will *not* go, child!"

"So I'm a child! It's always *child* when you are being unreasonable, aunt. I want to go!"

"And I say you shall not! *I* will take Gaston."

"With me to help you, Tante Clara. Short of locking me in my room, there is nothing you can do to stop me!"

"Be quiet, and let me think! *Dieu!* If only the patrols weren't out!"

"But they are, and Gaston must go to the château. And someone must be there to bring him back here if things go wrong. With you or without you, aunt, I shall be at the château tonight! You know it makes sense."

"I know nothing any more. One man is taken in for questioning, and suddenly the place is alive with soldiers. They'll probably take him to Bordeaux. They say there's a Gestapo place there. And to think that not so long ago the worst that could happen in these parts was a poor grape harvest!"

"This is all wrong," Keth frowned. "No one seems to know what's going on. I agree it's best not to let your left hand know what the right one is doing, but how can you be expected to get anything done when all you are told is to wait!"

"It must seem like that to you," Madame sighed, "but we do what we can. Even when things do go right, it is still not easy. But we do our best because we don't like being defeated and humiliated. And perhaps things will improve; maybe we *will* get better organized and become strong. Until then, though, we can only take each day as it comes and try — how do you say it — to muddle through."

She spoke not with anger or reproach, but with a strange bewilderment that was tinged with sadness, and Keth felt ashamed that he had even allowed himself to think such things, let alone give voice to his thoughts.

"I am sorry, very sorry, Madame. I didn't mean to criticize. You are all very brave. You took me into your home knowing the risk and have made me welcome. I'm sorry for what I said."

"No matter. I got my garden dug, didn't I? And find me a reel of blue thread, child. I want to go back to Bernadette's."

"What is she making?"

"She is making nothing. The thread is an excuse."

"You will go nowhere, Tante Clara, until you have eaten something." Natasha took a ladle, filling three bowls. "The soup is good. Just a little?" she coaxed.

"I suppose it will wait." Clara Piccard rinsed her hands at the sinkstone, drying them on her pinafore. "And maybe if I give it another half-hour, there'll be something to tell." She lifted her spoon. "I said, didn't I, M'sieur, that most of it is waiting and watching?"

"You did," Keth smiled, trying to act as if there wasn't a writhe of knots in his stomach and at the same time realizing it was almost certain that Bernadette — or her husband — was a wireless operator, and that Tante Clara knew more than she was prepared to admit, even to Natasha.

"When I've had this," Madame said, crumbling bread on her plate with nervous fingers, "you must stay here, child, and you too, Gaston. If the soldiers come, tell them where I am and what I have gone for — *blue* thread, remember. And have your papers ready, don't forget."

"You think they'll come here, too?"

"They came the other night for no reason at all. They'll be here again, be sure of it — unless they've already found the other man."

"And what I came for," Keth said soberly.

"That, too, Gaston Martin." The old woman got wearily to her feet. "I'll be back as soon as I can. And don't look so worried, M'sieur. It may never happen!"

But it *would* happen. It must, and all at once he was worried, though not for himself. His sudden apprehension came because he knew he was the cause of the trouble in and around Clissy-sur-Mer; himself, and an Enigma machine.

"No, Madame." He opened the back door for her, watching her go, trying to smile.

But how did you smile, he demanded silently, bitterly, when you were hating someone with all the feeling you had inside you; hating the nameless, slab-faced man who wanted that machine at any price?

CHAPTER
FIFTEEN

When Madame Piccard returned, still clutching the reel of blue thread, some of the tension had left her face.

"Good news?" Natasha breathed.

"*Better* news. Denys is home — at least he was for the time it took him to wash and eat. He's gone again, to the château, to see to the lights tonight for the pilot."

"So it's on, then?" The pulse behind Keth's nose began to beat again.

"It would seem so. The other man, the one with Hirondelle, made it to the château. They're hiding him and the package until it's dark, and safer for him to slip away."

"Leaving the package behind?"

"But of course. With Denys."

"The people at the château are sympathetic?" Keth urged.

"How do I know? It's common gossip round here that they have given hospitality to Herr Kommandant, but in times such as these it is sometimes politic to sup with the devil."

"But they must know people are hiding up there?"

"If they do, they won't be shouting it from the rooftops and anyway, there are so many stables and barns and coach houses at the back of the place they'd be hard put to it to know exactly what goes on. I'd bet good money on the châtelaine, for all that. She'll know that the jumps and fences in the back paddock will be getting moved after dark. La châtelaine's twin brother was killed in the last war, and old grudges die hard."

"So everything is in hand?" Keth's relief was obvious. "It's all straightforward?"

"Nothing is ever straightforward, M'sieur, never forget it! We'll have to get you to the château and this far there is only Denys to do it."

"Denys and me!" Natasha said softly. "I've done it before, and isn't it best that Gaston stays out of sight until the plane comes?"

"I know you can do it, child, but I'd rather you didn't. It isn't far. I can go with Gaston."

"If you do, I shall come with you! You can't stop me!"

"You'd defy me?"

"I would."

"Bernadette could go." Madame frowned. "She has other things to do, though . . ."

"Of course she has." Making sure that no searching soldiers found the transmitter Natasha was certain Bernadette used. "That is why you should let me do it."

"What am I to do with her, Gaston? She is too old to spank and too young to get caught up in this business."

"I don't know, Madame." Keth's eyes were sad. "I only know that I'm the cause of all this."

"No, Gaston! I don't ask why you are here. I only know you came at risk to yourself to collect something and take it back to England."

"And if I make it, that *something* will help save a lot of lives. But I'm no hero, Madame. The people who found that thing and hid it and got it to Clissy are the brave ones. I wouldn't want any of them — Natasha especially — to take risks for me."

"We do it because we want to. And it is not you who causes trouble. It is the Boche! They are not welcome here! So what we do, M'sieur, is for France and to help redeem the pride we lost when they goose-stepped through Paris.

"And you may go to the château, child. God alone knows who you are, but you were reared by two good people to love the country that gave them sanctuary. I think they would be proud of you tonight, and may God forgive me if I have broken their trust."

"I'll be all right," Natasha said with a small smile. "You mustn't worry. When Gaston is safely away, Denys will see me home — or hide me until the curfew ends. And after tonight, Tante Clara, will you do one thing for me?"

"If I can, you know I will."

"Then will you remember I am in my seventeenth year, and stop calling me 'child'? From tonight on, will you?"

"After tonight, Hannah Elise Natasha, I will never call you child again, I promise!"

Natasha stood waiting. She wore black trousers and a long grey cardigan. Her hair was covered by a scarf; on her feet she wore black gym shoes.

"You are both ready?" Clara Piccard asked, almost in a whisper.

"Ready, Madame." On an impulse, Keth gathered the sad-eyed woman into his arms, hugging her as he had hugged his mother when they said goodbye, laying his cheek on hers. "I'm grateful for all you've done for me."

Unspeaking she pushed him to arms' length, looking into his eyes; then with her thumb she traced the sign of the cross on his forehead.

"God go with you, Gaston Martin, and bless you for what you are doing for us. And you, you wilful young miss — kiss your old aunt and tell her you'll take care." Again the cross of benediction.

"You know I will."

"You'll be back soon after?"

"If Denys thinks it is safe, we'll be back about an hour after you hear the plane. Listen for it, aunt, and wish Gaston a safe flight home."

"I'll come as far as the gate with you — bring the dogs into the kitchen so they don't bark when you come back."

262

"Yes. They'll be company for you."

Keth picked up his case, then opened the door, closing it swiftly behind them. Unspeaking, they stood for a while until their eyes adjusted to the blackness, then Madame opened the doghouse door and the greyhounds sprang out, whining at Natasha's feet, trying to follow her through the gate.

Natasha leaned over to kiss her aunt, then turned abruptly and walked away. Clara Piccard watched them go. Just a few footfalls, then the darkness had swallowed up their shapes.

She inhaled deeply, holding her breath, letting it go in little huffs. Then she gazed up into a sky where no moon shone, nor any stars.

"Mother of God," she whispered, "take care of the child."

"So what do you do," Nathan Sutton asked of his wife, "when you have a full peal of bells and are four ringers short?"

"You find four people willing and able and tell them to pull like mad," Julia laughed.

"But they'll make a terrible noise!"

"Good! That's what we want! They used to ring bells to scare away devils, remember, and the more noise the better. So on Sunday let's make a noise in Holdenby; a glorious, jangling cacophony, and to hell with the purists!"

"Can you ring, Julia?"

"You know I can't, but bags I a rope on Sunday!"

"So who else can we ask?"

"Just tell Will Stubbs you're looking for ringers, with or without experience, and I'll guarantee a queue wanting to join in. It's an occasion, Nathan! We haven't heard our bells for two years and we've got something to celebrate!"

"Do you suppose we'll be allowed a chime of bells for every battle won?"

"I doubt it. I suppose the next time is when Hitler throws in the towel! But it's going to be such a day! Something to be glad about at last. Daisy will be home for the weekend and Tom says she's got to wear her uniform to church. And maybe Bas will be here, too . . ."

"I think you can bank on Bas," Nathan said drily. "But the service on Sunday isn't just about a victory. A lot of men died in that battle."

"Yes, and I'm sorry if I got carried away. A lot of women will have opened a lot of telegrams these past few weeks; we should remember them, too."

"We will, Julia," he said softly, knowing that in another war — in another life, it seemed — the woman he loved so much had opened a telegram. Regretting . . .

The blackness was less absolute now, and on his left Keth made out the darker bulk of a house.

"Bernadette's," Natasha said.

Keth looked at the outline of a high, sloping roof and knew that beneath it hung a wireless aerial. Strange that he had only distantly glimpsed that roof through the trees; that apart from crossing the lane to gaze in the direction from which the man with the moustache had come, he had never left Clara Piccard's garden.

Now he had been thrown out into a world where soldiers searched. He could be shot without warning for breaking the curfew, though he knew that someone like himself would be more use alive than dead. It made him think of the twist of newspaper in his trouser pocket and a small, obscene pill.

"We are at the road," Natasha whispered. "If you hear any sound, get down!"

She walked on the grass verges of the narrow road. Keth counted her footsteps. Dammit! Why did he always count?

"There it is." She turned right. Stars showed in the sky again and Keth was able to make out the outline of a gate.

"Over here. Keep to the side of the hedge."

"Is it very far?" Keth whispered.

"No."

Ahead of them, a night bird called and she stopped again to listen.

Keth pulled in his breath, held it until his ears sang, then he let it go through rounded lips.

"All right." She began to walk again towards what seemed like a break in the hedge ahead of them, not making diagonally for it but keeping to the hedge bottom.

"Don't open it. It creaks."

They had come to a small iron gate which swung on its hinges inside a curve of fence. A kissing gate. There was one at Rowangarth at the end of the linden walk. Natasha climbed it, then whispered for him to pass over his case.

"We are on château land now. There's a wood ahead. We'll do better once we're in it."

"How much longer?"

"Fifteen — twenty minutes . . ."

Keth followed closely behind. The wood was free of undergrowth and to walk from tree to tree on a well-kept path helped him to relax.

Natasha placed each step carefully, stopping as a plane flew high over the treetops. One of theirs? Keth all at once thought of Holdenby Moor; of the crossroads and the elm trees at the far edge of Brattocks Wood. Daisy would be going there soon.

He changed his case to the other hand, wayward thoughts in check. Daisy was a million miles away in another world. For just a few more hours, here and now was all that mattered!

"Look!" Natasha whispered. Ahead and to their right was another dark bulk and Keth knew it was the château. "We must keep away from the house. This way." She walked on through the trees, then turned sharply left, taking his hand, placing it on solid brick. "We're almost there. Keep to the wall for a hundred metres."

Almost at once, Keth smelled hay and horses. The stables were surely close by.

"Make for the trees, now . . ."

His eyes had become adjusted to the darkness and he could make out a long row of tall trees. No mistaking the poplars. They were there!

No lights shone from the château nor from any of the outbuildings to the rear of it. Keth touched the trunk of each tree as they passed it, refusing to count.

"There now — we wait." They had come to the last tree in the row and faced a high, thick hedge. "Someone will be here soon, Gaston."

Keth put down his case, squatting on his haunches to lean against a poplar. Natasha sat beside him, reaching for his hand, squeezing it briefly. Then she searched the ground with her fingertips for a twig.

"What time is it?"

"Don't know." Natasha carried a torch in her pocket, but dared not use it. When the patrols were out, even the briefest flash of light could spell danger. "It will come soon. Listen for it."

Wait and watch, and listen for the plane, though not only they would hear it. It was bad luck that tonight the garrison should be on the alert. Normally, the sound of a light aircraft might not have attracted so much attention.

It would have to be a light aircraft, Keth reasoned; one which could land and take off again in a few hundred yards. How big was the field behind the château? Was it level and smooth? How would the pilot know where to land? Lights, wouldn't there be, placed there by Denys, who, when he was at home, lived in the house nearest that of Clara Piccard?

What was Madame doing now? Standing outside her kitchen door, perhaps, near the clumps of arum lilies he and Natasha had planted only this afternoon? Would she be wearing her black frock, black stockings and boots, with a shawl thrown over her head and shoulders? Would she, too, be waiting and watching and listening?

The evening air had turned suddenly chill, there were no stars to be seen. Covered by cloud, perhaps, and low cloud they could well do without. Clouds blotted out landing lights.

"There!" Natasha grasped his arm.

"I saw it!" He stared ahead and a pinpoint of light winked again.

Natasha got to her feet aiming her torch steadily, switching it on and off, twice.

"Denys?" Keth rose clumsily, feeling for his case with the toe of his shoe.

"Let's hope so."

They stood, breathing noisily. The light flashed again, much, much nearer. Natasha snapped the twig she held and they heard the low, slow call of an owl.

Owl. Hibou. His recognition name.

"Hannah?" a voice asked softly.

"Denys?" She held out her hand and the man grasped it. "Is everything all right?" In her relief, she forgot to hide the shaking in her voice.

"This far, yes, thanks be. Come with me. It isn't time yet . . ."

He turned abruptly, setting off in the direction from which he had come, then stopped to let them catch up with him. They reached a high, wide archway and he said, "This way."

Taking an iron key from his pocket he unlocked a door, motioning them inside ahead of him.

"There now, we're safe. Hibou, is it?" Without waiting for an answer he struck a match, lighting a small piece of candle.

Keth gazed around the small, brick storeroom where empty, dusty bottles were stacked in rows and, along one wall, large wooden vats. The two windows were shuttered and Denys drove home the door bolts before speaking rapidly to Natasha.

Keth frowned, trying to understand what was being said. Only when the other man paused did Natasha ask, "Did you get that, Gaston?"

"Sorry. He was too quick for me." Denys spoke in a dialect difficult to follow.

"It's okay. I'll tell you later. He is deaf," she said to Denys, who shrugged, gesticulated, then began the dialogue once more. Then, red-faced, he finished, stuck his hands in his pockets, and began to pace the floor.

"Tell me," Keth demanded.

"Some of it you already know — that Hirondelle was caught. He is held at the barracks in Clissy and Denys thinks the Gestapo will come for him."

"That's bad."

"Yes, but perhaps they won't arrive yet. Maybe the soldiers at the garrison have given us time, wanting the Gestapo here. But for Hirondelle, it isn't good."

"And it isn't good for you either, nor for Madame nor the people at the bread shop — if he's made to talk, that is."

"He will tell them eventually." Sadly, Natasha shook her head. "But he doesn't know of anyone in Clissy. His group is further south. He only came once before for the spares you brought. Apart from the other man who was with him —"

"And who got away?"

"*Oui.* Apart from him, our Clissy people are safe enough. Remember I said we are told as little as possible? Now you know why."

"I can see the sense in it, now. But why is Denys so nervous? Has anything else happened?" Denys had slipped silently out again.

"Denys is always nervous. He always expects the worst and if it doesn't happen, he reckons he's done well. But soon the plane is due and he'll place the lights."

"That's all very well, but did the other man bring what I came for?"

"He did, and left more than an hour ago. Denys hid it. It is safe, and the other man well clear of Clissy by now."

"And is it undamaged?"

"That I don't know. Why do your people want it, Gaston?"

270

"They need it very badly. Once they know what it looks like, how it works, then it will do a lot of good."

"Save lives? Help win the war?"

"Both." He lapsed into silence, thinking of the man who would soon face interrogation. Was Hirondelle's life to be in payment for the Enigma machine? And when that machine finally arrived in the secret back rooms of the technicians and boffins, would it prove to be worth the price?

"Here! Take this!" Suddenly Denys stood there with the machine in his hand; the naval-type Enigma so needed to help in the fight against U-boats. It looked like a wooden box, its corners dovetailed, the carrying handle of brass. It would open out, Keth knew, to make a complete unit of keyboard and mechanism. He had never seen one like it before. Was it a new type? Would it tell them what they wanted — needed desperately — to know?

"Thank you, M'sieur." Keth ran his fingertips over its surface. The polish had been dulled and was watermarked with white smudges. Had it been immersed in sea water or damaged by an explosion and, more important, how had some person found it and sensed its value and importance? "Am I allowed to look at it?"

"Best not." Denys picked up Keth's suitcase, then blew out the candle. "It's time. The lights must be in position so the pilot sees them on his first approach. He's only allowed two minutes!"

Keth nodded and stepped outside, grateful that Denys had spoken slowly and clearly. He blinked rapidly, then looked at the sky, glad to see the stars again.

They passed beneath the high wide archway once more, then walked in single file along the line of poplars, making for a field. On a moonlit night, Keth realized, the outline of the big house and the jutting line of tall trees would make an excellent marker for a pilot. Perhaps this was not the first time the field behind the château had been used.

They walked through an iron gate which swung open without a sound, then turned left, making for the corner of the field.

"There is no wind so he'll be able to approach from the west, from corner to corner, across the field. Give him a better run, when he takes off again." There was relief in Denys's voice.

"We have three torches," Natasha whispered.

"Is that *all*?" Keth had expected more.

"It's enough. One to show touchdown, two at the far end to show where he must stop. Like a capital L . . ."

"And that's usual?"

"It is. The plane is called a Lizzie — there will be room enough for it," Denys nodded.

Lizzie, Keth smiled; a pilot's pet-name for the Lysander aircraft. A small, ramshackle-looking thing weighing only five tons, Keth's mathematical mind supplied; fixed under-carriage, its up-tilted wings giving it the appearance of a drunken moth.

272

A Lysander could land on a postage stamp, boasted every pilot who flew it. With seating for two and storage space in the short fuselage behind, it was ideal for quick pick-ups and drops. A Lizzie, Keth thought almost fondly, would suit him very well indeed.

"*Sssssssh!*" They listened, breath indrawn. The aircraft was above them, and with minutes to spare!

"Quickly! Over there!" Denys placed his hands on Natasha's shoulders, turning her to face ahead. "You and Hibou will place the far lights three metres apart. When you see mine go on, turn yours on, too. Not until — you understand?"

Natasha ran diagonally across the field. Keth picked up the box and suitcase, following closely behind. By the time he caught up with her she had already placed one torch and was hacking a hole for the second. It was possible, now, to hear the plane clearly as it circuited the château, searching for three small lights.

From the far opposite corner, a light appeared. Natasha gasped, switching one torch, then the other. Then she stood back, running her tongue round her lips, eyes to the sky.

The Lysander came at them from behind the château. It had cleared the poplars and was dropping low, its engine revs slowing. Then it bounced down and came rushing towards them.

Natasha flinched and turned away, sucking in her breath. The engine stammered and coughed. The

Lysander ran on a few more yards then spluttered to a stop.

The canopy was pushed back; the pilot called, "Get your stuff on board, then I'll swing her round!" No greetings, no pleasantries. Even as he indicated the rear seat with a nod of his head, the tail-end of the aircraft was already turning.

"Gaston! Good luck, God bless!" Natasha called.

Keth turned from stowing his case behind his seat, reaching down for the wooden box she held.

"Be sharp," the pilot yelled.

"Natasha!" The plane was moving. "Thank you!" So much he wanted to say! He shoved the Enigma machine beneath the seat. "Take care!" Two minutes. So little time!

"*Halt*!" Above the revving of the engine, Keth heard the command, heard the sound of firing behind them and the short, surprised scream. He looked down to see Natasha spread-eagled on the ground, heard more shots.

"Don't go!" he yelled. "She's been hit! She needs help!" Natasha lying there, like a small wounded bird.

The engine revs increased to a roar, the plane hurtled forward. Keth called, "Didn't you flaming hear me?"

The plane lifted, then climbed sharply, flinging Keth back against his seat. His stomach lurched. They were leaving Natasha behind! Even now, the soldiers would have got her!

"That young kid has been shot!" Keth raged. "They might have killed her!"

"Then let's hope they have!" The pilot's words came clearly over the intercom. "For her own sake, let's hope so!"

"*Bastard!*" Keth shook with anger and shock.

The Lysander hit an air pocket and dropped with a lurch. The pilot put the nose up, making for cloud cover, flying into its protecting blackness.

Keth wanted to flail his fists, hit out. It was beyond belief that Natasha had been left there, defenceless. He sat stupefied in the drifting blackness, letting the noise of the engine fill his head, his thoughts.

For a long time they flew low, into and out of clouds; then all at once banked sharply and climbed into a clear, star-bright sky. Only then did the pilot speak.

"Now hear this! When I touch this thing down — if ever I do — I'll have your guts for garters! Even if you're the pesky bloody head of SOE, I will! Now — *keep it shut!*"

Keth closed his eyes, trying to block out the madness. His brain was functioning again and registering sounds and sights and smells. And memories.

Natasha was dead, he knew it. He wanted her to be dead because not even a young girl would be spared Gestapo methods. And they would find her false papers, which would lead them to Madame and the bread shop; and to Denys — if he'd got away from the château.

The Enigma machine lay awkwardly against the backs of his knees; lay like the dead weight of his conscience. Hirondelle arrested, Natasha shot, and soon the soldiers would knock on Clara Piccard's door. They would take her up the path of the newly dug garden, past the lily clumps and the doghouse and she would never return.

And what of Bernadette and Denys and the people at the bread shop? How many lives for one small machine? He felt white-hot hatred for the ranting lunatic who had started the war; for the soldier who shot Natasha.

But mostly he hated himself.

They touched down at an aerodrome Somewhere in England. Their landing was smooth and without incident. The pilot taxied onto a track beside the runway, making for a blue light ahead. They had landed without permission being asked or given; the Lysander came to a sudden stop and men with rifles came out of the darkness to surround them. A sergeant and a boy-faced officer stepped forward to order them out. The officer carried a pistol and demanded to know who they were.

"Special flight," the pilot rapped, dropping to the ground, motioning Keth to do the same.

"I'm taking you both in!" The officer was very officious.

"That's all right," the pilot shrugged. "Leave a guard on the Lizzie, will you? I'm clean out of fuel. We've got a leak . . ."

Keth remembered the whining, snapping bullets and realized they'd been lucky to make it back to England.

He walked a step behind the pilot, not wanting to talk to him or look at him. He carried the wooden-boxed machine but had deliberately left his suitcase — Gaston Martin's suitcase — behind.

He wanted to forget Gaston Martin. Keth Purvis was safe, alive. He was back home with the Enigma machine *They* wanted. He should be glad, relieved, thankful. He ought to think of Daisy and that he'd fulfilled the conditions of his posting back to England, but he could not. Even Daisy seemed unreal and remote.

He stared into the blackness, listening to the tramping of boots ahead of him and behind him. To hell with the lot of them, he thought, suddenly defiant. Whoever had got him into this mess could get him out of it. He didn't care even if they were taken for spies.

He shut down the turmoil of thoughts in his head. He needed the lavatory and a mug of tea. He wondered how long it would be before he was allowed either.

He tried again to think of Daisy, but could not. Only Natasha filled his mind and the remembrance of that one startled cry. He hoped she was dead. He wished Keth Purvis could be dead, too. He stopped suddenly, clutching his stomach.

"Look out!" he managed to yell, before he vomited all over Gaston Martin's cheap shoes.

CHAPTER
SIXTEEN

Keth stood at the window, staring at the black, leafless trees, at grass rimed with frost, and at mist-covered hills. Here at the stone house, all the things he left behind him — things he'd locked away at Castle McLeish — had been gathered together and placed in drawers. It was as if he had never been away and the nightmare that was Clissy-sur-Mer happened to someone else.

Two nights ago, when they made an emergency landing because the Lysander had leaked fuel all the way back, they were first taken to the guardroom and then, after many phone calls, to the commanding officer's quarters.

Keth's suitcase was brought from the plane and he was able to clean his teeth, and bathe with Gaston Martin's soap. Then he was given a bed and he blanked out all thoughts and slept, even though he knew there was a guard outside his door.

Yesterday morning, after breakfast, he collected the Enigma machine from its safe overnight storage and was escorted from the officer's quarters to stares of curiosity.

Outside that door he was almost relieved to see a familiar camouflaged car and the ATS driver from the stone house. She locked the machine in the car boot, held open the back door and shut it with a bang. Only when she was behind the wheel again did she say, "Hullo, sir. Had a good trip?" Asked it, Keth thought, as lightly as if he'd been to Brighton on a dirty weekend.

"Thank you, yes." He'd got their precious machine but she would never know just what it cost to get it here! "Where are we going?"

"We're going back." She let out the clutch, uncommunicative as ever.

"And they are trusting me to you? No minder, I mean? No armed escort?" He still wanted to hit out and the ATS sergeant was the only whipping-post.

"I can handle almost anything, sir, and the less fuss, the better."

They were stopped at the guardroom gate. The driver showed her pass, the red and white pole that barred their exit was lifted.

"Where are we?" Keth demanded when they had been driving for several minutes.

"You don't know," her eyes met his in the mirror, "that you should have landed a lot further north?"

"I only know we touched down with an empty fuel tank." *We*. He had not, Keth frowned, seen the pilot since they left the guardroom. He had no wish to either. "So where are we now?"

"You landed at a fighter station called Wood Vale. It's near Liverpool."

"But my girl's stationed at Liverpool!"

"That's life, Captain." She smiled at his look of utter disbelief. "We're in Cumberland now, though it's a bit awkward, there not being any signposts or anything."

"And heading north-west, I suppose?" Back to the stone house.

"That's it. I've got a flask of coffee with me. We'll stop in about an hour, if that's all right with you?"

Keth said it was, then lapsed into brooding again. No use asking her to stop at the next phone box. He'd tried that before. But now he was back he could wait as long as it took to be given permission to phone Daisy. He was home and alive and more than that, at the moment, he daren't even begin to hope for.

He wondered if, perversely, they would send him back to Washington. The slab-faced man at the stone house had a peculiar sense of humour. No! Wrong! Slab Face had *no* sense of humour.

Keth took off his cap and laid it on the seat beside him. Then he unbuttoned his jacket and the top buttons of his shirt. He wanted to kick off his shoes, but thought better of it.

Instead, he closed his eyes. Despite sleeping soundly for most of last night, he was still tired. He did not remember drifting into sleep. Only the stopping of the car and a voice saying, "Mind if I have a drink, sir? I could do with a break for ten minutes."

"Where are we?" Keth straightened his back and blinked his eyelids rapidly. His mouth tasted foul.

"Somewhere in Scotland. We've just left Dumfries. I'm making for Gourock and the car ferry over. It'll cut out a lot of driving, that way." She passed him the cap of the vacuum flask, half-filled with milky coffee. "No sugar, sorry."

"That's okay." He managed a smile. "How long did I sleep?"

"About an hour and a half and no, sir, you didn't snore!"

"Good." He wanted to go back to the dreamless oblivion he had just awakened from; wanted to think of Daisy so he might, with luck, dream about her. But his thoughts centered on Natasha; always Natasha, who refused to leave his mind.

"I'm going to pop over that gate. Is that okay, sir?"

"Fine by me." Normally he would have teased her, asking why on earth she wanted to climb a gate. Instead he said, "I might drive away with the car, hadn't you thought?"

"With respect, sir, don't be silly." She held up the car keys. "The gents is to the left, by the way. Mind the nettles!" she called.

She was a decent sort, really; could handle a car well. She had dropped him off at the doors of the stone house Somewhere in Argyll, a little after three in the afternoon, then disappeared without giving him the chance to thank her. He hadn't seen her since. Come to think of it, he had only seen his batman, who suggested he might like to take his meals in his room until further notice, and the civilian who poured generous brandies.

The batman had passed on a request from high up, that the Captain should wear his uniform again and pack his civilian clothes into the case, which would be collected later.

That much he had done gladly; had stripped off then stood naked to pack them. Only when he had shut the case and pushed it beneath the bed and turned on the bath taps, did he begin to feel more apart from what had happened.

Deliberately he let the taps run, ignoring the black line painted inside the bath at a height of six inches. Then he opened his own soap bag, recognizing it like an old friend, took out his soap and flannel and stepped gladly into the hot, cleansing water to wash away Clissy-sur-Mer and Gaston Martin and the Lysander pilot's disgust.

He soaped and lathered his hair, then slipped beneath the water to rinse it. He rubbed and scrubbed all memories of the past two weeks away. He was Keth Purvis again. He had done what was asked of him the best way he knew how, and soon he would be free of this place.

Yet how could he ever be free of Natasha's eyes, her pert nose and a voice that breathlessly insisted she was in her seventeenth year? How did you get someone like her out of your mind, out of your conscience? he asked of the waiting world outside the window. Would he ever?

He looked at his watch. He was due to see the slab-faced man in five minutes. Yesterday, when he arrived, a meeting was not possible because the chief was away, they told him.

But earlier that morning, Keth heard his voice in the hall below. Would he be pleased with the Enigma, even though it wasn't in working order? Would it tell them what they needed to know?

Keth brushed down his jacket, noticing that its brass buttons had recently been polished; the badge on his cap too. Should he take his cap with him? Would the interview be official or covered in secrecy like almost everything else here?

A gust of wind hit the window, rattling it. It had not been so bleak at Clissy.

He picked up his cap. Best not to keep the man they called the chief waiting. Slowly he walked down two flights of worn, twisting stairs.

A light above the chief's office door glowed green. Keth stood very still, breathing deeply, counting to twenty. Then he knocked on the door, surprised it sounded so confident. Aggressive, almost. The light turned to red. A voice called, "Enter!" and Keth did so unhurriedly, pretending an aplomb he did not feel.

"Sit down then, man! At ease!"

Keth selected one of the chairs facing the precisely tidy desk, took off his cap and placed it on the floor at his side.

"So, Captain." The chief leaned forward, elbows on the desktop, making a tent with his fingertips.

Keth made no answer because no answer was expected. He disliked the man as much as before; remembered that humiliating slap. He reached into his pocket, laying the pill on the desk. The other man picked it up, turning to throw it on the fire.

"You made your pick-up, then — after a display of dramatics."

"Dramatics? That's what the pilot called it?" Keth looked his inquisitor in the face. "I'd have said it was more like normal reaction to seeing a girl gunned down."

"You had two minutes, you knew that! What was more important then — a pilot, a plane and what you were carrying, or the girl?"

"The machine, sir — have you seen it?" Keth chose not to answer the question, suddenly determined to stand his corner.

"Of course! Haven't you?"

"No. It was given to me just before take-off and there wasn't time afterwards. I only know it seemed water-damaged."

"How come there were soldiers about? It's pretty lax there usually. Why the breach in security?"

"There was no breach. You don't know, then?" There was sarcasm in his voice.

"Not everything. There's been nothing from that area for forty-eight hours."

"There wouldn't be. The pick-up was put forward twenty-four hours."

"I know that! Did you discover why?"

"I did. The two men who were bringing the Enigma to Clissy were stopped by an army patrol. It was after curfew — they shouldn't have been out. The man carrying the machine got away. The other was taken in for questioning. And it was just bad luck that a patrol was in the area of the château and heard the plane. Those people of yours take a lot of risks."

"Yes. I know what it's like in the field. I'm not a boffin!"

"The machine, sir?" Keth clenched his jaw and stared ahead again.

"I want to know what went wrong at Clissy first."

So Keth told him; about Madame and Natasha and about Denys and Bernadette — and what went on at the bread shop. "I think Bernadette had a transmitter in her house, though no one told me so. I do know they listened to news broadcasts from London, though. Bernadette would tell Madame and Madame — if she could — passed it to the lady at the bread shop."

"It's a good setup at Clissy," the chief acknowledged. "An efficient group. Madame Piccard runs it well."

"*Madame?* But she said she knew little, that she was only a messenger!"

"She would . . ."

"Then what's going to happen there now? I don't know if Natasha is still alive, but either way, they'd see her papers. The couple who adopted her were

286

Jewish, and were taken. Natasha went to Madame with false papers. There'll be trouble if they decide to check up on them."

"There'll be trouble. Period. They'll trace the girl back to Madame. Did you know, Captain, that on the day you left the Germans marched into unoccupied France? It was probably why the soldiers in Clissy were on the alert for a change."

"Well, that's explained away Natasha," Keth said with heavy sarcasm, "and Hirondelle. But you got your machine, and —"

"Hirondelle?" The chief's head jerked up and he sucked air through his teeth. "You knew him?"

"No. He operated in another area, but I met him once, the night I went in. He was there for the spares I took. Tall — very fair. English. One of the men bringing the Enigma."

"Which is now in the lab. The technician got quite excited. Seems it *is* different. An extra wheel and drum, he said. He'll be taking it apart, cleaning it, then within a month it'll go into mass production. By the end of the year all the people who matter will have one."

"And it'll help?"

"I never hazard guesses. It'll be up to the Bletchley Park people to see how useful it is. It's got possibilities."

"Only possibilities? You mean that two people could already be dead and a group in France split up — maybe even arrested — and all for a *possibility*?" Keth was staring him in the face again. "Doesn't anything please you, then?"

"Some things do. And forgive me if I can't work myself into a sweat over your machine, Captain. All right, I'm sure it will help. I saw another just like it yesterday."

"You mean you already had one? You hazard the entire crew of a submarine, an aircraft and its pilot, and God alone knows how many more people, *and you had one*? What were you after — a pair for your mantelpiece?" Keth jumped to his feet, his eyes blazing anger.

"Sit down, Captain." The words were little above a whisper. "Sit down at once."

"Why should I? All right, do me for insubordination if that's what you want! I couldn't care less! Send me back to Washington if it pleases you! It's what you intend doing anyway, isn't it?"

"You are going back to Bletchley, Captain. And you'll most likely be working on the naval-type Enigma — on a prototype of the machine you brought back from France, or maybe like the one that came into our possession *two days ago*. Perhaps they are alike — I don't know yet. All I know is that the second of my pair, as you see fit to call it, was taken off a U-boat in the channel. One of our ships caught the submarine on the surface, recharging its batteries and our sailors boarded it.

"The Germans were too quick for them — opened the seacocks quick as you like. The submarine crew jumped into the sea and our lot

288

picked them up, though I'd have left them to swim! Anyway, two of our sailors searched that U-boat. They knew what they were looking for! They brought out a naval-type Enigma, then went back for the manuals and code books. Pity, that, because the U-boat sank before they could get off it. Churchill should give those two sailors a medal!"

"And what good are posthumous medals? Don't you think both those sailors would rather be alive?"

"I know they would. But they did what they had to do and without a second thought. That's what war does to people; makes heroes of them. Don't deny them their medals."

"I'm not. I wouldn't. Only I'm not brave like they were. I'm a boffin and I'm fighting my own war the best way I know how! I'll be glad to work on that machine at Bletchley, and doubtless every time I see one like it I'll remember those sailors and Natasha and Hirondelle! Do you think I'd forget them, write them off as heroic statistics?"

"I hope you never will." Almost wearily the man rose to his feet, his eyes distant. Then the mask was back and his face became a slab again.

"Goodbye, Captain. As soon as our Intelligence bods have finished with you — and they'll want to know all you can tell them about Clissy — you'll be going back to Bletchley." He opened the door, standing beside it. "Likely you and I won't meet again, though doubtless you'll always remember me as the bastard at the stone house. If ever we do meet, though, and each of us has the time to spare,

I would like to talk to you about Hirondelle, and how he seemed that night you and he met. He was my nephew, you see."

The door was quietly closed on Keth's amazement, on his sudden shame for being such a big-mouthed fool.

"I'm sorry," he said thickly as the light above the door changed to green.

But it was too late now for regrets and anyway, the matter was closed. Clissy-sur-Mer had never happened.

That night, kit packed, Keth lay on his bed, listening to the nine o'clock news. Such jubilation, such joy for a victory in North Africa. This afternoon, read the announcer, churches had been filled with congregations giving thanks for something to be glad about, at last. And afterwards, church bells rang out all over the country; bells people thought they would next hear to warn of an invasion.

But invasion would not come now. The war was turning in favour of the Allies. At last the light at the end of the tunnel. Not the end, nor even the beginning of the end, Winston Churchill said in a triumphant speech. But it was, he promised, the end of the beginning!

The bells in Coventry Cathedral's only remaining tower went out as part of the news, and to the people in occupied Europe the BBC broadcast a recording of the chimes of Westminster Abbey.

How many would hear them on their secret wireless sets, Keth wondered. In Clissy-sur-Mer, would Bernadette listen, then hurry to tell Madame she had heard the bells that rang for a great victory?

"No," Keth whispered into the empty room. Neither Bernadette nor Madame nor Denys would hear them. They would be locked in a cell waiting interrogation; Hirondelle too. And pretty, dark-haired Natasha would never hear church bells again. A great knot of tears he could not release rose in Keth's throat.

He turned off the set. Tomorrow morning he was leaving for Bletchley Park and there, doubtless, he would be working with a naval-type Enigma for the first time. And that machine would save the lives of many merchant seamen crossing the Atlantic. Soon, instead of breaking the U-boats' code only one day in four, sometimes accidentally and often too late, they would be able to decode every signal gathered in by silent listeners; exactly as now they broke every coded message the Luftwaffe and Wehrmacht transmitted.

And every time he saw or touched one of those machines, he would remember Clissy-sur-Mer and clumps of arum lilies that he and a child called Natasha had planted outside Madame's kitchen door, and that when they parted she had said, "Goodbye, Gaston. Good luck. God bless . . ."

Tomorrow he would be a part of the monotony and frustration and safeness of Bletchley Park. Tomorrow Daisy would be on early watch and tomorrow evening he would speak to her, tell her he was home again, and that he loved her. He had fretted and ached and yearned just to hear her whispered, "Hullo," yet now that they were only hours away from it, he wanted to stretch out the waiting, savour it. Tomorrow, that was; a tomorrow which might never have come.

Tonight, though, he would think of Natasha and send her his love and gratitude; send it to a child who wanted to grow up, yet now would always be sixteen.

Good night, Natasha, Elise, Hannah — whoever you are. I won't ever forget you; it isn't possible. Goodbye, and God bless you too.

Tilda placed logs on the kitchen fire and plumped the cushions on the rocking chairs either side of it. She was in a dither. Sydney was calling to sit with her and listen to the wireless!

In the old days, when Mrs Shaw ruled the kitchen like a martinet queen, followers would not have been allowed, but two wars had changed all that.

Of course Sergeant Willis could call, Julia said when asked, her delight that Tilda seemed to have found a gentleman friend at last showing plainly on her face.

"I'm only sorry you can't entertain him properly, rationing being what it is."

"Oh, he don't expect food, Miss Julia. They get well fed up at Pendenys, 'cept that he says he misses the way his mother used to cook. Him and me are alone in the world; I suppose that's why we get on so well."

"Are things getting serious?" Julia asked with her usual frankness, and Tilda was bound to say she wasn't at all sure, though her red cheeks must surely indicate it was what she had been hoping for since reading her first happily-ever-after love story.

"What I'm trying to say, Tilda, is that I hope you'd never let your loyalty to Rowangarth stand in the way if Sydney asked you to marry him!"

"Oh, miss!" She had known Julia Sutton for more than thirty years, yet never would she learn to cope with her directness. "I don't know if I could bear to leave Rowangarth. It's my home, you see."

"Then when this war is over, your Sydney is going to need a job and where better, Tilda, than Rowangarth? He gets on well with Jack Catchpole, doesn't he? Think about it!"

"But he hasn't asked me!" Tilda wailed.

"Then give him a little shove!"

"*How?*" Tilda knew how it was done in romantic novels — the dear Lord knew she had read enough — and that handsome heroes produced small, velvet-lined boxes inside which a ring sparkled, and went down on bended knee and said those lovely words.

But Tilda Tewk was plain and ordinary, though good-hearted, and most folk she knew took it for granted she liked the shelf Fate had left her sitting upon.

"How?" Julia smiled. "Just take your chance when it comes, that's how! I'm on your side, Tilda. I'd like to think that Rowangarth wouldn't be losing a treasured cook, but gaining a gardener!"

She had winked saucily and closed the kitchen door on a bewildered, befuddled cook who knew that every word of advice offered not only made sense but was what she had been longing for since the day Sergeant Sydney Willis walked straight-backed into her life.

But a little shove? She doubted it. It took more than that, for hadn't Mary Strong shoved and pushed and manoeuvred for nigh on twenty years before she'd finally got Will Stubbs to the door of All Souls? And to the best of Tilda's knowledge, he had never asked those important words. More like it was Mary who suggested it with a firm "*Or else!*"

But wouldn't it be grand if Sydney popped open a velvet-lined box and popped the question at the same time? Tilda yearned.

Once she had longed for a young man — a dalliance, even, but now she was fonder of Sydney than she was prepared to admit, because Sydney was flesh and blood and not a lover who fleeted through the pages of a romantic book and walked into a perpetual sunset with a wide-eyed virgin on his arm.

The knocker on the outside kitchen door came down firmly, once, twice. Tilda patted her hair into place and put another log on the fire before opening the door.

"Sydney dear, come you in out of the cold!" Smiling, she offered her cheek for his kiss, knowing he had no little velvet box in his pocket; wondering what was in the attaché case and large cardboard box he carried.

Sighing, she kissed him back.

"I suppose you'll be wondering where I was, yesterday afternoon?" Sergeant Willis asked, puffing on the pipe Tilda had given him permission to light.

"Of course I didn't! There's a war on. Regular Wednesdays can't be taken for granted!"

Of course she had wondered! For some time now, her friend had spent every one of his afternoons off with her. But yesterday had come a phone call telling her how sorry he was not to be able to keep their date, and would it be possible for him to call in later — probably tomorrow evening?

So here Sydney was, sitting contented beside the hearth, and about to tell her what had happened to break their weekly routine.

"For granted? Oh, I had my half-day same as always, but I went to Leeds. It was business, see, that came up urgent. You'll remember my mother's house came to me when she passed away?"

"Aye." And that it had stood locked and untouched since he returned from the compassionate leave he was given for the funeral. Tilda knew all that; had warned him the Government might take it for bombed-outs, and had he thought that any ne'er-do-well could break in and help himself to anything that took his fancy.

"Well, after what you said, my dear, I offered it for letting — to someone with references, of course."

"And you've found someone?"

"I have. A very respectable lady who teaches at the local infants' school and her not long married to a soldier. Things being what they are, and not so much as a pan nor a tea towel in the shops, she was very pleased to take it on furnished, and at a pound a week!"

"Then it must be a great relief to you, Sydney." A relief too that he hadn't spent the afternoon with some other woman!

"It was. I spent yesterday afternoon with the young lady, and liked her. She paid me a month's rent in advance, an' all!"

"And she's taken everything over; sheets, towels and the like? Did you count everything, Sydney?"

"Not I! For one thing, there wouldn't have been time and for another, she has an honest face. I've an instinct, Tilda, for honest faces. Anyroad, we shook hands on it and she promised to take good care of the house, though she insisted that all things personal, or anything of sentimental value, I should take with me. Only right, she said."

"So that's what's in yon cardboard box then, and the attaché case," Tilda smiled. "I've got to admit I was a bit curious — specially when you didn't tell me right away."

"In the box are photographs, Mother's Bible and a few china ornaments. The attaché case — well, it was always where mother kept her important papers, tucked under the bed so she could lay her hands on it quick if the siren went. And there's her wedding ring and engagement ring and her wristwatch and pearl beads. Not what you'd call the crown jewels, but they were hers, Tilda, and precious."

"Then you must take good care of them, Sydney. Such things money can't buy." Tilda was smugly pleased now that Sydney had explained away yesterday afternoon and taken her into his confidence as well. "A cup of tea, perhaps?"

"A cup will do very nicely," he smiled, knocking out his pipe in the hearth, leaning back to rock to and fro in his chair, contentment on his face. "Can I ask a favour of you — *two* favours?"

"Of course," Tilda smiled.

"Then can I leave the box and case with you for safety? There's precious little privacy in the sergeants' mess and nowhere to lock anything away. Would it be a bother, Tilda?"

"Of course not!" She flushed with pleasure. "I'll put them in the bottom of my wardrobe. They'll be safe there."

"Then secondly . . ." He reached for the little attaché case, placing it on the tabletop, snapping it open. "Will you accept this as a token of our friendship?" He popped open a small box to show a shining garnet ring, nestled into a bed of faded velvet. "It was Mother's . . ."

"But are you sure?" She could scarcely speak. "Something so precious, I mean!"

"I'm sure, Tilda. Mother was always going on at me to find a nice young lady, but I never got around to meeting the right one. She would have approved of you, I know."

Shyly he lifted her right hand. Clumsily he pushed the ring on her third finger.

"I would like to hope that one day you'll do me the honour of wearing it on your left hand . . ."

"Oh — *Sydney*!"

Tilda's eyelashes fluttered, the floor swayed beneath her, and she was obliged to cling to the back of the chair to prevent herself falling in a faint at his feet.

He drew her into his arms, holding her tightly, and she sniffed loudly because her eyes were all at once filled with lovely little tears.

Smiling he pushed her to arms' length and gently dabbed her cheeks with his handkerchief. Then he kissed her hard and long, leaving her breathless.

"You've made me very proud and happy, Tilda."

She smiled tremulously and gazed straight into his eyes.

"Does this mean we're engaged, almost?"

"Do you know, lass," he laughed, "I think it almost does!"

Tilda Tewk's cup of happiness was full to overflowing and as she smiled a silent goodbye to loneliness and longing, shining droplets of pure joy splashed from it, all over her kitchen.

"I think, dear, we'd better have that cup of tea before it's stewed black!" she whispered.

CHAPTER
SEVENTEEN

It was amazing, Keth thought, that after so long away he should be given the same room on his return to Bletchley Park; a room with both beds made up with cotton sheets and grey blankets; a room with a shining, untrodden floor and a small table on which a gramophone once stood.

Footsteps clumped down the same passage and stopped outside.

"I've come to unpack you," said the soldier who stood there.

"It's all right — I'll do it myself, thanks."

He knew it was the duty of the batman to see to his cases and place shirts in drawers and uniforms on hangers, but he wanted to do it himself. Slowly and methodically, to buy time to sort out the muddle in his head.

"Dinner still at seven-thirty?" he asked amiably.

"It is, Captain."

"And can you tell me where Flying Officer Robertson is? He and I once shared this room." Shared it in another life, that was; before Castle McLeish and the stone house and Clissy. Before Natasha, who was dead.

"Posted overseas, sir, about six weeks ago."

"And taken his gramophone and Glenn Miller records with him!"

"Well, where he's gorn he'll be able to buy all the records he wants." He lowered his voice. "The US of A, rumour has it. Washington."

"The lucky dog!" Keth bit on a smile.

"Yes, sir. Well, if you're sure I can't —"

"Quite sure. I take it we are still allowed to use the phone without filling in a chit in triplicate?"

"Oh, yes. But getting through is another matter."

Getting through. To Daisy. Now, he only had to open the door, walk no more than ten paces along the passage to where the phone hung — with Daisy at the other end of it.

Why then had he delayed picking up that phone, in the certain knowledge that, as soon as the GPO allowed, he could be telling her he was back, and that he loved her.

Was it really because he was spinning out the minutes, telling himself that as soon as he had unpacked and settled in he would allow himself that call, like leaving the cherry on the iced bun for the last bite?

Or could it be that deep inside he knew he was free to speak to Daisy only because Natasha had died. Was he denying himself that phone call as a punishment? Yet if he made a bargain with God never to speak to Daisy again, it wouldn't bring Natasha back, nor Hirondelle.

He dug a hand into his trouser pocket, taking out shillings and sixpenny pieces. He would call Daisy *now*! He had waited months, would have given anything to be able to speak to her, so why was he acting like this? Daisy was real and warm and alive! What happened six nights ago at Clissy-sur-Mer belonged to the past and nothing he could do or say would change it! He wrenched open the door and walked, heels slamming, to the phone.

"Can you get me Liverpool, Lark Lane 1322?"

"Your name, please?"

"Captain Purvis."

"I don't have a line to Trunks, sir. There'll be a delay. Can I call you back?"

A delay. He might have known it. All right — so he would hang around. He didn't want to eat, anyway. A drink, maybe, just to take the edge off the pain that nagged inside him and wouldn't go away. Pain, was it, or apprehension? Foreboding?

Natasha! I'm sorry!

Like a petulant child he slammed the door. Weren't we at war, for Pete's sake, and didn't people get killed all the time? The Lancasters that flew from Holdenby Moor killed civilians; the skipper of the submarine *Selene* gave orders to fire torpedoes to sink ships — and sailors died.

But those aircrews and submariners rarely saw the results of their actions as he had seen Natasha gunned down with bullets meant for himself. She should not have been there but she insisted. In her

302

seventeenth year, she argued, she was no longer a child.

Yet the most sick-making thing was returning to the stone house to be told They now had a second naval-type Enigma, and quite by chance! If you could describe a calculated act of heroism as chance!

He stowed his cases one inside the other, then heaved them on top of the wardrobe. The bare room looked more welcoming with his toilet things above the wash basin and his dressing gown hanging behind the door.

He placed two photographs on the table where once a gramophone stood; one of his mother, the other of the Clan the last Christmas they were together. Kids, all of them. Then he took the silver-framed photograph of Daisy in uniform, looking at it with disbelief.

She was only a telephone call away, yet in the tangle of thoughts that filled his mind she was as far from him as if the Atlantic still lay between them.

"We're very busy tonight, sir," he was mildly reproved when enquiring about his trunk call, so he apologized and said he understood, propping open the door of his room, determined not to lay on his bed for fear of falling asleep.

He changed into his slippers. Slippers were a luxury in England. They bit into the meagre allowance of clothing coupons and, like dressing gowns, could be done without, Keth supposed.

His own he had bought in a Washington department store, crammed with all the luxuries people in Britain only thought about occasionally, and with a sigh. Washington. Safely distant from the war, where almost anything was still obtainable.

The ringing of the telephone made him start, then hurry to pick it up.

"Purvis."

"I have your Liverpool number on the line, sir. Will you place one-and-six in the box, please?"

Fumbling in his haste, Keth did as she asked.

"Press button A, caller . . ." The coins fell with a clatter; the disembodied voice told him to go ahead.

More shakily than he would ever have thought, he said, "Hullo? Can I speak to Wren Dwerryhouse, please?"

"Daisy — Cabin 4A, is it?"

"That's right."

"Hm. Sorry, but her disc says she's not in quarters. Lyn's out too. Can I take a message?"

"Please. Will you tell her Keth rang, and that I'll try to ring back later. She *is* on earlies?"

"If she's on D-watch then she is. She isn't in the late-pass book so she'll be in by ten-thirty — okay?"

Keth thanked her and replaced the receiver. And it *wasn't* okay! For months he had thought of little else but speaking to her, only to be told she was out! Of all the damn-awful luck! His stomach contracted. He ought to have had something to eat, but it was too late now. Moodily, he began to undress. He

304

would take a shower, get into his pyjamas, then rebook the call.

What a letdown! What a flaming awful war this was! How long was it going to last? Would they ever be married? The summer of 'forty-one they planned it should be. Saturday, 21 June, the day after Daisy's coming-of-age.

He snatched up soapbag and towel, making for the showers, hoping there would be hot water, knowing he wouldn't care if it ran icy cold. Wasn't there a war on, and who was Keth Purvis to expect hot showers?

All at once he wanted nothing less than to get his hands around Hitler's throat and throttle the life out of him. He wanted to do it for Natasha; for husbands and wives parted; for Tatty, for war widows. But if he were truthful, he wanted to do it because anger blazed white-hot inside him.

And because Daisy had been out when he phoned.

"So, Aleksandrina Anastasia Petrovska, what does it feel like to be one of the masses?"

"To be working class, you mean?"

"What else would you call it when you go out to work — *for money*!" the Countess snorted.

"To tell the truth, Mama, it wasn't at all bad! There's a lot to learn, but learn it I will! And I *am* helping the war effort."

"War effort! It's another name for daughters doing what they want to do instead of doing their duty!"

"My duty to you, Mama — isn't that what you mean?"

"I have been alone all day. No one called, no one telephoned!"

"But I can't telephone you! The phone must only be used for the surgery. Think what would happen if there was an emergency and you and I were chatting on Ewart's phone!"

"Ha! So it's Ewart now, is it?"

"It has always been Ewart, and you know it!" Anna tried hard to keep the irritation she felt from showing. "He's a family friend, as well as being our doctor."

"Yes, but now he is your employer, don't forget! The position has changed!"

"I work for Dr Pryce because the Ministry of Labour said I must find a job and because there was need for a clerk at the surgery. That I know Ewart is very convenient. It means I am not afraid to ask questions."

"Working amongst the sick is not the place for a countess born. You will catch colds and pick up nits!"

"Both are easily dealt with, Mama! Now — how soon will dinner be ready? I'm hungry!"

She was *very* hungry; had barely found time to eat the sandwiches she took with her.

"How do I know? Your cooking lady could not come in. She telephoned to say her husband is home on leave!"

"But there is leftover meat and gravy from yesterday; surely you could have peeled a few

306

potatoes and cleaned some sprouts. There are plenty in the garden."

"I don't cook! I am the Countess Petrovska!"

"Then after tonight, Mama, you are going to have to sing for your supper, because if the vegetables *at least* are not prepared, you will go hungry! All the young ones are in the armed forces or doing war work; men of my age are being called up to fight now. Would it hurt your dignity to peel a few potatoes?

"The world you knew has gone, Mama; your Czar is gone! England is our country now, and we must all do what we can to help. Igor is doing war work and you must not be so selfish!"

"Selfish! I never thought to see the day when my own flesh and blood would speak to me as if I were an imbecile!" The Countess rose to her feet. Shuddering with hurt dignity she left the room.

"Then don't act like one!" Anna called to the retreating ramrod-straight back.

Sighing, she opened the kitchen door, annoyed to see the blackout curtains had not yet been drawn, feeling not one jot of remorse for her behaviour. She had enjoyed her day, even though there was much to be learned.

"Dinner will be ready in half an hour," she called to no one in particular, determined not to go upstairs to apologize. Her mother would come down when hunger forced her to!

It was too dark to pick sprouts so reluctantly she reached for a precious tin of peas, breathing deeply, determined not to let her mother spoil her day in which so many people she knew were pleasant to her and genuinely pleased to see her.

When surgery was over and Ewart out on home calls, she had opened cupboards and drawers, trying to familiarize herself with what went on. It had been a shock to find each patient's details in a bottle-green filing cabinet and warily she picked out her own, wondering how much of her medical history and the unpleasant details that went with it had been left behind by Dr James. But there was nothing there that anyone in Holdenby couldn't read or did not know already; details of her weight, age, the number of her pregnancies and miscarriages and of her stillborn son. Nothing more, and for that she was grateful. It wouldn't do for Ewart Pryce — for *anyone* — to know the dreadful details of her marriage.

But Elliot had been dead these fifteen years and on the day of his funeral she had silently vowed never to let a man hurt her again. Nor would one. Anna Sutton was her own mistress now, and but for the war and the constant complaining of her mother, she was content with her widowhood. That she was young enough not only to marry again but to have children, as her mother constantly reminded her, made her all the more determined to remain in charge of her own destiny.

She cut the potatoes into small pieces to enable them to cook more quickly and save fuel for the war effort — a hint gleaned from a Ministry of Food leaflet. And when she had set them to boil and laid the kitchen table, she would kick off her shoes and light a cigarette.

She deserved one!

At 23.00 hours and with uncanny timing, Keth's Liverpool call came through. Hardly had the coins been pushed into the box than a voice said, "Dwerryhouse speaking . . ."

She had received his message and was waiting beside the phone. Her voice sounded impatient and breathless.

"Hullo? Is it you, Keth?"

"Sweetheart!" He was in control of his feelings now, though his heart thudded loudly. "I'm back . . ."

He had been going to say so many things, had rehearsed them time and time again, yet nothing would come.

"It's really you?"

"It's me. Bad penny, turning up again!"

"Darling! You're doing it again — ringing me up out of nowhere and saying you're back!" She was weeping. "Are you going to stay long enough this time to marry me?"

"Fingers crossed — yes."

"You sound distant, sort of."

"I am. Two hundred miles away!"

"*Peculiar* distant, I mean. Are you back at the same place?"

"Yes. Arrived five hours ago. Been trying to ring you."

"Yes, I know. There was a message. Sorry, Keth, but I'm crying . . ."

"I can hear you. Sniffily, like always and, darling —"

"Your three minutes are up." The impersonal voice of the operator cut in.

"Oh, *no*!" Daisy gasped.

"Do you wish to remain connected?"

"Yes, please!" Keth scooped up the three sixpences he had placed in line on the top of the coin box.

"Place one shilling and sixpence in the slot, caller." A voice so ordinary, so casual, giving them three more minutes together.

"Hullo?" Daisy called.

"I'm still here, darling. Now listen! We've just wasted three minutes dickering about and I love you, *love you*, do you hear me?"

"I love you too! Keth, can't I try to ring you back?"

"Can't give you my number — you know I can't. But I'll ring you tomorrow night — will six be all right?"

"Any time after one o'clock. I'm on earlies!"

"I'd worked it out. I love you, by the way!"

"I love you too! When will they give you leave?"

"Don't know. You know what they're like here . . ."

"Couldn't you manage a seventy-two-hour pass?"

"I'll try. Might even get seven days when I've got myself settled in."

"Darling, I want you so much. Write me a letter before you go to bed?"

310

"I will. And you write to me too. Same address as before. Remember it?"

"Mm. I'll write every day! Oh, *hell*!"

A long string of pips. Their time was up.

"Keth, I love you!" Daisy had time to call above the noise before the line went dead.

"Love you, love you, love you," she whispered to the receiver in her hand.

Then she slammed it down and took the stairs two at a time calling, "It's really him, Lyn! He's back!" She closed the door of cabin 4A behind her, leaning on it, eyes closed, cheeks flushed. "Did you hear me, Carmichael! *Keth is home!*"

"So that piece of paper the duty Wren shoved under the door wasn't someone playing nasty little tricks?" Lyn laughed. "That bloke of yours has crossed the Atlantic more times than I've had hot dinners! Did he say where he's been?"

"He can't do that; not over the phone. But I know it was Washington and he's back at the same billet again."

"At Bletchley Park, you mean — that signal school near London? Any chance of leave?"

"He didn't know. But don't you realize, Lyn, that this morning I thought he was in Washington — and he isn't! I can't take that in yet, never mind leave! And I'm starting to cry again. Why do people cry when they're happy?"

"I don't know, but stop it or you'll make a mess of your face!" Lyn commanded. "Blow your nose, then we'll go down and and see if there's any standeasy left."

"Standeasy? I couldn't eat a thing! And I've promised to write to him tonight."

"Okay. Stay here if you like, but *I* need a cup of tea! And Dwerryhouse," she said softly, hand on the doorknob, "I'm glad for you, I really am."

"Thanks, Lyn," Daisy sniffed as the tears came afresh. "He's home," she whispered, wonderingly. "Keth's back. He just phoned. He *did*!"

"It's only me!" Julia tapped on the door of Agnes Clitherow's little sitting room.

"Why, Miss Julia — come in, do. I was just going to build up the fire."

"I'll do it! And such news! I just had to tell you! I'm on my way to Keeper's Cottage. Alice has been on the phone. Keth is back, would you believe?"

"In England? Oh, my! Did he ring Keeper's?"

"No. He rang the bothy just after breakfast and Polly rang Alice and Alice rang me!" Julia rose to her feet, placing the fireguard in position again.

"Well, they say good news always comes in threes, don't they? First the bells ringing for El Alamein, then Polly's boy home. What do you suppose we'll get next?"

"With luck, a wedding at All Souls," Julia laughed. "Daisy's or Drew's, I don't mind which! Now you're all right, Miss Clitherow? Anything I can do for you before I go?"

"Bless you no, Miss Julia — but thanks for calling in."

"Then I'll fly! If there's any more news from Alice I'll let you have it when I get back. Tell Tilda, won't you, when she brings up your tea?"

The door closed with a bang and Agnes Clitherow smiled. Rush, rush, rush! Miss Julia would never change! She hadn't even stayed long enough for what could be the third piece of good news! Cook, wearing that nice Sergeant Willis's ring, though not *quite* engaged, she'd insisted, pink-cheeked with happiness. Tilda with a gentleman friend of her own at last!

There were days, she thought, pulling her shawl close, stretching her slippers to the fire, when everything was so splendidly right with the world — war, or no war. Just imagine *three* weddings at All Souls. Daisy's, Sir Andrew's and Tilda's!

She smiled to see Julia striding across the lawn towards the stile at the edge of the wild garden, then closed her eyes to daydream about wedding hats. And spring weddings . . .

Kitty spread her fingers fan-like, wiggling them, blowing on them.

"Help yourself, Tatty." She nodded in the direction of the bright red nail varnish.

"Could I?"

"You know you can. Feel free. Anything you want."

Kitty Sutton shared her make-up with her cousin. There was so little of it to be had here, and she was so happy, so in love with Drew, that it was only right and proper, she reasoned. If red nails and a dab of perfume made Tatty just a little bit happier and eased her own conscience at the same time, then swell!

"You're going out with Bill tonight, aren't you?"

"Mm. Can I have some perfume, too? Bill can't see my nails, but he'll like the scent."

"You're fond of that air-gunner, aren't you, honey?"

"Very fond. Or I'm fond of the way it is for me when we're together." With Kitty, she didn't have to pretend.

"But you're not going to fall in love with him just because he reminds you of Tim?"

"No — though what I'll do when he leaves, I don't know."

Bill would go, nothing was more certain. His time spent convalescing on the outskirts of London could end tomorrow. He was beginning to accept his blindness, his face. Soon he would be sent to the surgeon who was doing so much to help men like him; already Sam was there, having a new nose built. He had written, full of hope, joking about being one of McIndoe's guinea pigs: "I suppose I'll just have to get on with life again."

"Y'know I'm real proud of you, Tatty." Kitty bit on her words. She had nearly said that she didn't know what she would do if anything happened to Drew. "I'm glad you and me are here with Sparrow." She stopped again, for fear she said that living in the little white mews house made her separation from Drew bearable. "And I'm real proud of your Bill too. Remember when that could have happened to Bas — the fire at Pendenys, I mean. Mom says she doesn't think of Bas's hands as scarred. Whenever she looks at them even now, she says, she offers up a thank you because it could have been so much worse. Bas could've been badly burned, like your airmen, or even killed. And Keth, too, helping get him out . . ."

"You got a letter from Bas this morning, didn't you?" Tatty surveyed her left hand and the bright red nail varnish. "How is he?"

"He hopes to get furlough for a week, he says. He'll dump his kit at Rowangarth, say hi to Aunt Julia then he'll be off to the kitchen garden like there was no tomorrow. Gracie sure is giving him the runaround!"

"She'll say yes, though," Tatty smiled. "You like her, don't you?"

"Like her a lot. She'll fit in just fine back home. Mom's ever so pleased that Bas has gotten around to some serious flirtin' though he couldn't marry Gracie without his Commanding Officer's permission, even though he's turned twenty-one and in his right mind."

"That's stupid," Tatty murmured, breathing on her nails.

"No. Not really. Reckon the US Army considers itself to be *in loco parentis*, sort of, and makes it kind of difficult for GIs to get married. After all, some of the girls here are real taken up with our soldiers and their smart uniforms — apart from all the money they've got to throw around!"

"Well, there's no risk of Gracie acting the gold-digger," Tatty defended, "but if she did marry Bas, I hope they'd have the wedding at All Souls and not in Gracie's parish. Wouldn't a Rowangarth wedding be lovely, and Uncle Nathan marrying them?"

"Yes, and you and me could be bridesmaids. Your mom gave Mrs Dwerryhouse two ball gowns, remember, so Daisy could have bridesmaids without spending clothing coupons. We could use them again for me and Drew, and Gracie and Bas and — oh, gee, Tatty! I'm sorry. Me and my big mouth! Why don't you belt me one when I talk so tactless?"

"Because the world didn't stop spinning the night Tim was killed; because there are thousands and thousands of women like me who've got to get on with living, and a lot with children to bring up alone, on a pension. Our war widows don't get as much money as they do in America, Kitty. And like I said, Bill being around helps me a little to accept the way things are."

"Yes, and you'll have to face it again when Bill goes and your daydreaming has to stop."

"So I'll get hurt again? So what? I've only myself to blame for the predicament I'm in. But oh, Kitty, it's so easy to pretend and I'm not hurting anyone — only myself."

"Okay — so I'll be there, if it happens, with a shoulder to cry on — y'know that, don't you, honey?"

"I know it and I'm lucky really. Even though I'm an only child, I've got the Clan, haven't I?"

"You have. All the way!"

She turned to see Sparrow standing there. Sparrow never stood on ceremony when entering a bedroom.

"Two things," she said, her face serious. "One — your supper is ready and you'd better get it quick, since Tatty's orf out, doing her Florence Nightingale bit. And two, Keth's home!" Her face broke into the widest of smiles.

"*Keth!*" Kitty shrieked. "Who said so?"

"Your Aunt Julia, just now, on the phone."

"Did she have any news of Drew? Why didn't you call me?"

"Because she only had three minutes and I wasn't wasting half of it getting you downstairs! And she'd have told me if there'd been anything."

"Keth home again?" Tatty said so softly that it made Kitty reach for her hand and squeeze it tightly.

"Home! *Again*. Now are you going to get your suppers, or aren't you? And I'll give you the Rowangarth news whilst we eat!" And, seeing the sudden sadness in Tatiana's eyes, Sparrow didn't talk about Daisy and Keth getting down the aisle at last, because even though it was the first thing that sprung to her mind the second she put the phone down, there were things you just couldn't say. Not

317

when Tatty would give almost anything just to see Tim again. "Off you both go."

She switched off the bedroom light, because it was one of her unwritten laws that a minute of wasted electricity was a minute on the duration of hostilities. And in one minute, the life of someone like Tim Thomson could be saved.

"One of these days," she said so softly that no one heard her, "that man Hitler's wickedness is going to catch up with him."

And when it did she hoped with all her heart that Emily Sparrow Smith was there to see it. And to cheer!

"Well, that's got young Bas's bed made up," Mary Stubbs smiled, taking a box of chocolates from behind her back with a flourish. "And look what he brought, for you and me to share! He's a lovely lad! Bet he's in the garden now, giving a tin of tobacco to Jack Catchpole. Seems they can get almost anything in their canteen at Burtonwood."

"Maybe that's why Gracie's leading him such a dance," Tilda laughed. "Happen Jack's glad for it to be that way, the amount of tobacco he gets. She'll say yes, though." Tilda, with a man of her own, and a ring to prove it, was in love with life and especially with young lovers. "Mark my words, once Daisy and Keth get wed, there'll be Drew and Kitty and Bas and Gracie following on behind."

"Have you given any thought to your own nuptials, Tilda?"

"Not a lot. There's no hurry."

And Tilda Tewk told lies too, because since she became almost engaged to Sydney she had thought of little else!

"But you'll have plans in mind?" Mary wanted the chance to wear her own wedding finery again. "And one thing you ought to do, Tilda, is to buy your hat now; before *They* put hats on the ration! One morning, the Government's going to wake up and realize that hats still don't need clothing coupons and the very next Sunday it'll be in the papers, sneakily, on the day shops are shut, so no one can rush out and buy one!"

"So what do you think I should buy — if I was of a mind to, I mean?"

"A straw, that's what! You can't beat a good straw hat, boater shape. Then you can trim it to match whatever colour your wedding dress is."

"But where can you get silk flowers these days?"

"Same place as I got mine! And if they're sold out, I could always lend you the blue ones from my own hat — and I know for a fact that Alice still has the pink roses she wore when her and Tom got wed. But take my advice, Tilda. Be prepared!"

"Hm. We'll see . . ." Since she and Will Stubbs got wed, Tilda frowned, Mary had become just such another know-all as her man! Not that for once she wasn't right. It mightn't be a bad idea to get a hat whilst there were still hats in the shops.

And say not one word to a soul about it, of course. Not even to Mary!

CHAPTER
EIGHTEEN

Keth was coming home on the fourth. Just for seventy-two hours, from Friday till Monday, but Polly and Alice were in a tizzy; Alice especially, because she wasn't at all sure the Wrens would give Daisy leave.

"Surely they can't refuse her!" She addressed her remark to Tom, behind the evening paper.

"They can, love, but I doubt it."

"They'll have to get the banns seen to this time around or they're never going to get down the aisle!"

"They will," Tom soothed, folding the paper, because when Alice had a bee in her bonnet reading was impossible. "So stop your worrying. You don't want a winter wedding, now do you? At Rowangarth, you've always said it would be. Beautiful, you said, with a marquee on the lawn and the trees green and all the flowers out."

"I'd settle for a winter wedding and the reception in the conservatory!" Alice snorted. "Though tonight I'd be content with the banns being read, and knowing Keth was stopping in England long enough this time for them to be married decent! And did I say *reception*?"

No bride had a reception now. Not even a wedding cake, rationing being what it was. A plain sponge cake, if they were lucky, with a cardboard cake on top of it, decorated to look like the real thing. You could hire them from Creesby bakery. All wrong!

"Bonny lass, receptions don't matter. Our Daisy'll be married in white — you've seen to that — and she's got a going-away costume, an' all."

"Mm . . ." True, few brides wore white in wartime, unless they could borrow, and few had a going-away outfit either.

"And you won't feel like a mother hen that's lost its only chick the day I give her to Keth?"

"Once, Tom, I might have, but all I want now is for Daisy to be happy. She and Keth are right for each other. I knew it the minute that little lad walked into our kitchen all those years ago. They've grown up together. I know Keth like I'd know my own son — if I had one."

"You do have one, Alice."

"Drew, yes." She smiled and her eyes softened. "But what I meant was *our* son — yours and mine, Tom. Would you have liked a lad of your own?"

"Of course. What man wouldn't? But we had Daisy, and a share in Drew's growing up. I'm not complaining."

"I'll grant you that, but I'll feel a lot happier when I know our Daisy has got some leave. You *do* think she will, Tom?"

"Oh, Alice Dwerryhouse — come here!" He pulled her onto his knee. "And give us a kiss while you're about it."

"And you, Tom Dwerryhouse, ought to act your age, canoodling before the six o'clock news!"

She kissed him, nevertheless, and smiled into his eyes, touching his face with her fingertips as she always did when she was extra fond of him.

Then she jumped to her feet, ordering him into the back kitchen to wash his hands and to get from under her feet so she could get supper on the table! As if she hadn't enough on her mind, what with Daisy's leave and the banns to be worried about!

"And with Keth and Polly here to Sunday dinner, you'd better get me a brace of young pheasants if you chance across them!"

"A couple of birds it is!" Tom called back, smiling because Alice was happy.

Alice always was when she had something like a wedding to worry about!

Daisy tapped on the blue door with "Knock and Enter" painted on it, poking her head round it, saying "Hi!" to the Wren who sat behind the desk. "Ma'am wants to see me . . ."

"Sit down. There's someone with her at the moment. Shouldn't be long."

"About my leave — you haven't seen any chits flying about, have you?"

"Not with your name on them, Dwerryhouse."

"But I haven't seen Keth for ages!" Daisy whispered hoarsely.

"There's a lot of applications for Compassionate in at the moment. The soldiers are getting leave from North Africa, now, don't forget. There are some who haven't seen their bloke for *years*!"

"Keth's only got a weekend! Surely Ma'am'll let me have a seventy-two!"

"Don't know. Like I said —"

The door of the inner office opened and an officer left. Daisy and the Wren behind the desk rose automatically to their feet.

"Is that Dwerryhouse? Come in, please," called Daisy's Divisional Officer.

"Ma'am?" Daisy whispered.

"Sit down, won't you?"

Sit down? They always told you to sit down when there was bad news! Daisy balanced on the edge of the wooden chair.

"Application for Compassionate?" The Third Officer was holding Daisy's request form. "Oh dear. A seventy-two-hour pass?"

"Please, Ma'am. I haven't seen my fiancé for ages. He's just back from America and —"

"Sorry, Dwerryhouse — no can do!"

Daisy sucked in her breath and blinked her eyes rapidly.

"A seventy-two is out of the question. You'll have to make do with a forty-eight, and that's against my better judgement. The C-in-C's going to blow his top if ever he gets to know how much Compassionate I've been dishing out lately!"

But the Commander-in-Chief never would, Daisy thought, smiling broadly. The Admiral had better things to do with his time than bother about forty-eight-hour passes!

"Thank you, Ma'am!"

"Pick up your leave pass from the Regulating Office. No travel warrant — sorry. You'll have to pay your own fare!"

"That's all right, Ma'am!" Daisy wished she could stop grinning. Twelve and six for a Forces' return to York wasn't going to break the bank — not her bank, anyway!

"Getting married?" The officer was looking at the sapphire cluster on Daisy's left hand.

"No, Ma'am — but we're going to see about getting the banns read."

"Have a good weekend, then."

Daisy said thanks again and that she would, then closed the door behind her.

"You knew, didn't you?" Daisy grinned.

The Wren behind the desk was smiling too. "Have a good time," she said, winking.

"You bet! 'Bye . . ."

Daisy's mind raced ahead to Saturday, when she went on leave, and to the day following, when she *should* return to Wrens' Quarters. But Monday started a week of night watches, didn't it, and herself not on duty till midnight? So if Lyn were to manipulate her discs on the board beside the phone to show she was anywhere but snatching another day's leave, she could match her leave period with Keth's. It was all a case of the popular eleventh commandment. *Thou shalt not get caught!*

She hugged her delight to her. Home, to Keeper's, and Keth meeting the twelve-thirty train at Holdenby Halt. She did a little skip, then turned to smile brilliantly at her Petty Officer.

"Forty-eight hours, Marjie — plus Monday up until midnight! *Oooooh!*"

And Marjie smiled her lovely smile and said she was very glad, which was decent of her, considering she hadn't seen her own fiancé for almost two years.

Daisy sat down at her teleprinter, taking in deep breaths; letting them go in little puffs of delight, watching with affection, almost, as a coded signal clicked onto her machine. Then she closed her eyes.

Please, Lord, don't let anything awful happen between now and Saturday, like Keth being sent back to Washington before I've seen him and touched him and kissed him. Please . . . ?

Keth handed his warrant to the ticket collector, who didn't recognize him, then looked around him in disbelief because he was back, conditions fulfilled, in Holdenby. And alive! The road outside the station should have looped round a corner to give him a glimpse of his home, but today was grey and cheerless, with mist hanging low over Rowangarth trees and only one more hour of December daylight left.

Tomorrow, Daisy would be home. She would catch the first train out of Liverpool and be here a little after midday, which gave him time, he supposed, to sort out his thoughts and his alibi. From America to Southampton by flying boat of Coastal Command and from there to the signal school in Buckinghamshire.

France had never happened. He knew of no one called Gaston Martin nor of a small village called Clissy-sur-Mer, and must do his utmost to forget a dark-eyed, dark-haired child code-named Natasha, and the Englishman, Hirondelle. Had he died under torture or did he swallow his D-pill? It would be an act of bravery, knowingly to take it, for who but a brave man could decide the exact moment of his death?

Natasha, in her seventeenth year. Daisy had been seventeen when first they knew they were in love. Daisy at seventeen, secure in the love of her parents; Natasha alone but for Madame, her parents at best in a concentration camp. And this late afternoon in early December, Keth Purvis was free to walk home because a girl had died. A girl's life for his and an Enigma machine.

"Keth!" A small car pulled up beside him; Julia Sutton's shabby Baby Austin, the Reverend at the wheel. "Good to have you back! Hop in!"

"I'm expected then?" Keth forced a smile.

"Goodness, yes! The Rowangarth women are clucking like broody hens! How are you — and more to the point, how long are you staying in England this time?"

"Long enough. I want to see you, Reverend." All at once it was the only answer. "Can you fit me in?"

"Of course! Alice is determined to have the banns called."

"No. Daisy and I will see you together about that. You see, I've got to tell someone — get it off my chest — straighten things out. Only I signed the Official Secrets Act and if I tell you, it's treason; could cost me my life . . ."

Nathan Sutton stared into the gloom ahead and then, without shifting his eyes he said softly, "And would you trust me with your life, Keth?"

"Yes, sir, I would."

"Then I'm free for an hour from ten o'clock tomorrow."

"And Daisy should be on the twelve-thirty train, so that will fit in nicely. Good of you, sir."

"No problem. I try to give myself an hour Saturday mornings, if the weather is fine; like to walk up the Pike, take a look down at Pendenys, though heaven knows why! Care to walk with me? I'm usually at the crossroads at ten."

"Then thanks. Between you and me, sort of?"

"The confessional, if you'd like it that way."

"I would. Crazy, isn't it? Soon I'll see Mum; tomorrow I shall meet Daisy and we'll start planning our wedding. Everything should seem set fair, only it isn't."

"Priests are good listeners," Nathan said as he stopped at the top of the lane that led to the bothy.

"See you tomorrow, Keth — and it's good to have you back!"

He drove away, wondering what it was all about. Certainly nothing seemed wrong between Keth and Daisy. They were planning a wedding, weren't they? No. It had to be something far more serious than that because Keth Purvis was a troubled young man; so troubled, in fact, that he was prepared to commit treason to ease his conscience. Something to do with the war, most likely; Keth's war. Something he shouldn't talk about, yet could not live with, and so serious it could only be told to a priest. But that was what wars did to young men — and to women too, he thought as he drove beneath the stableyard arch to garage the car.

He shivered. There was a touch of frost in the air. Tonight, the sky would be cloudless and clear; tomorrow morning would be fine and cold, with nothing to prevent him taking his walk up the pike. With Keth.

"Say all that again," Lyn Carmichael demanded, "without gabbling! And for Pete's sake, stand still!"

"Sorry! I'm still in a tizzy; still can't believe it. Keth's always turning up, out of the blue. It's getting to be a habit!"

"And one of which you approve! But tell me again about your leave so I can fix it for you in quarters."

"I'm due back Sunday night, but I won't be back till Monday. Just put my "In Quarters" disc up, will you, and tell duty-Wren I'm in the lavvy, or something, when she does rounds?"

"So you'll make York for ten-thirty? Will Keth be there to meet you?"

"No. He'll be sleeping at Keeper's but having meals at the bothy with Polly. It's only fair. She's his mother, after all. Hope I'm not too late getting into York. Want to get the noon train to Holdenby."

"With Keth waiting there for you. I can just see that little station."

"Of course — you've been to Keeper's Cottage, haven't you? And you'll be there again, provided my foot-loose fiancé stays in England long enough for us to get married. You'll have to hold on to some of your leave for the wedding, Lyn."

"No, Daisy." Lyn turned her back to look out of the window.

"What do you mean — *no*? You and Tatty are my bridesmaids. Mam's done your dresses! Lyn, you promised!"

"Sorry, old love. At the time there was nothing I wanted more, but you're going to have to find someone else to wear that dress. Kitty, perhaps . . ."

"So that's it! You won't face seeing Drew and Kitty together!"

"I *can't* face it! I've never made any secret of it — I'm still keen on Drew. Look, Dwerryhouse, it was bad enough when I ran into him at the Pierhead. What it would be like seeing him and Kitty together is something I won't even think about!

"And another thing, your precious Clan will be there, hadn't you thought, because they're all in England now, and they'll all make it to Rowangarth for your wedding — even if they go AWOL to do it!"

"Lyn — okay. Be jealous of Kitty, I can understand that, but don't be jealous of the Clan. The Clan isn't just six people grown up from childhood together. It's something far more precious; something I can't explain. Even Aunt Julia couldn't explain it. It's Us, sort of, against the world."

"I'm not knocking the Clan, Daisy. If anyone's at fault, it's me. I can't forget Drew; I don't want to. And what's more, if Kitty ever sent him a Dear John letter, guess who'd be there to help him pick up the pieces?"

"I'm sorry, I truly am. I feel just the same way about Keth, so who am I to tell you to forget Drew? I shall miss you, though. It won't be the same if you're not there, Lyn."

"No, but at least we've got the matter of your bridesmaid in ice blue out of the way, and the drill for over the weekend. And there'll be no trouble as long as you're waiting outside Epsom House for the night watch getting off the transport on Monday. What will you and Keth really be doing, Daisy? Will you both leave Holdenby on Sunday and spend Sunday night in Liverpool?"

"D'you know, I hadn't thought about it! It's certain we'll have to behave, since Keth is sleeping at Keeper's, but I hadn't given *that* much thought!"

"You're slipping! I think about little else — Drew and me, I mean, in Auntie Blod's spare bedroom, sinning on that fat, feather mattress!"

"And then Kitty walks in and catches you!"

"No. Funnily enough, Kitty isn't there; either real or imagined. When I'm sleeping with Drew, she just doesn't exist. It's as if she never had. That's the way it gets you when you're mad about a guy you can't have," she whispered.

"I'm sorry, Lyn. Times like this I feel that Keth and me have no right to be so lucky. I'm sorry I ever introduced you to Drew."

"Don't be. I wouldn't have missed Drew for anything. Things were going fine — then Kitty happened. He's spoiled me, you see, for anyone else. Can you understand that?"

"Yes. It was the same for Aunt Julia. Mam was getting to think she'd never marry again. She was a long, long time getting over Andrew MacMalcolm. Nathan Sutton waited eighteen years for her."

"Wish we weren't on lates! We could have gone into Liverpool and done a pub crawl — got as tight as two ticks!"

"Hey! I don't want to get right, Carmichael! I want to stay cold sober and eke out every second till I see Keth again."

"Okay. You do your thing, ducky, and I'll do mine!"

Mad, fighting drunk. It was the way she wanted to be every time she thought about Drew and Kitty in bed together. And Lyn Carmichael had no one to blame for it but herself!

Hands in pockets, shoulders hunched against the cold, Keth waited at the crossroads. He had slept only fitfully and had no appetite for the fried egg and bread his mother prepared for his breakfast. She had remarked on it.

"Reckon a walk up the pike with the Reverend will do you good, son — give you a bit of an appetite. You'll be talking about the wedding?"

"Not really. That'll keep for when Daisy gets here. He mentioned he was taking a walk this morning, so I asked if I could go along. It's a long time since I've been to the tops."

"It'll be cold and windy up there!"

"Like you said — blow the cobwebs away. You don't mind my going out, Mum?"

"Course I don't. And bring Daisy over, won't you, as soon as you can decently manage it?"

Polly wanted to talk about the wedding, needed to know a time and date and to plan well ahead so she could ask the warden for time off. But Keth had been no help at all.

"For goodness' sake, lad!" she had eventually exploded. "What's the matter with you? You want to marry Daisy, don't you?"

"You know I do, Mum. Only the time is up to Daisy, and when she can get time off, though I'm sure they'll give her marriage leave. Don't worry. It'll be all right this time."

He crossed his fingers and laughed, and his mother had told him to get himself off and out of her way; that some folk had work to do and to give her kindest regards to the Reverend and not to forget he was meeting Daisy at the station at half-past twelve!

Good old Mum! Keth lifted his head, then smiled as Nathan Sutton approached, waving, from the direction of Denniston House.

"Am I late, Keth?"

"No, sir. I was a bit early. Mum chased me out of her kitchen. I'm eating at the bothy and sleeping at Keeper's, you see. Good of you to invite me along."

"You want to talk?" Nathan dug his hands deep in his overcoat pockets, taking the wind head on.

"Yes. It's about where I've been and what happened there. Daisy — everyone — thinks I flew over from Washington, but that isn't strictly true. I flew here, of course, but by way of France."

"Ah . . ."

"When they sent me back to Washington, I was really cheesed off — applied at once to be posted back home. They agreed eventually because they wanted something doing; something I knew more about than most. I didn't know what They'd got in mind for me. They just said my application to return to the UK had been granted — with conditions attached — and that I'd been promoted to captain."

"Conditions pertaining to an undercover job, if I'm not wrong?" Nathan said softly, staring ahead.

"Yes. The back-room job I do now required me to sign the Secrets Act; I had to sign it a second time and was verbally warned not to talk before I went to France."

"You parachuted in?"

"No, submarine. They flew me out by Lysander afterwards."

"You're sure you want to tell me, Keth?"

"I'm sure. I've got to talk to someone. There'll be no luck for me till I do!"

"That bad, is it?"

"Afraid so. Someone was killed, you see, and I can't help thinking it was my fault."

"How come?" Nathan Sutton sensed the tenseness in Keth's voice; his need to talk.

"Because I wanted to get back to Daisy — leastways, that's how I look at it. If I hadn't been in France then my contact wouldn't have been there, waiting for the Lysander with me, the night I left. Going to pick up the — the *package* was part of the deal and I accepted it because I knew it was the only way to get home. So here I am, safe and sound. Soon I shall see Daisy and in a couple of months we hope to be married. Everything set fair, you might say, except for one thing. My contact is dead and I'm sure the bullet that killed her was meant for me. Poor little Natasha . . ."

"She was called Natasha?" Nathan drew in his breath.

"No. That was her codename. She had false papers. Her real name was Hannah Kominski. Her

334

parents were Jewish, but she wasn't. Mind, she was dark — dark as me," Keth shrugged, "but she said her nose saved her. It was tiny and tip-tilted. She was adopted, you see. Her Jewish parents wanted a dark-haired child; when there was a risk of them being deported from Paris, they got false papers for their daughter, then sent her to a life-long friend."

"And what happened?" Nathan asked warily.

"No one knows. Natasha hadn't heard from Paris for more than a year. But let me tell it right from the start, if that's all right with you, sir?"

"The beginning is usually the best place to begin, Keth. But before you do, can I ask something? How old was your contact?"

"Only a kid. Sixteen — going on seventeen. She shouldn't have been mixed up in that sort of thing. It's one of the reasons I feel so bad about it."

"And who gave her her codename?"

"No one. She chose it, she told me. It was all she knew about her real mother — the one who gave her up for adoption. The Kominskis told her only that; that her birth-mother's name was Natasha."

"I see. Go on, Keth — right from the beginning . . ."

Nathan Sutton felt apprehension. From the beginning, he had asked, but did he want the entire story? Come to think of it, did he want to hear any of it?

Yet Keth needed to unburden, and who could he trust but a priest? But why, Nathan thought, as they reached the plateau and paused for breath, did it have to be here, at the spot from which they could look down on Pendenys Place — his brother Elliot's inheritance, had he lived!

Damn Elliot! he thought, as Keth's voice pulled him back from his brooding. And no man — especially a man of the cloth — should damn the dead, even though Elliot had been damned from the moment he was born!

"Sorry, Keth," he heard himself saying. "Let's start down, shall we — get out of the wind?"

And Keth said it was a good idea; that he'd forgotten how cold it could be on top of the Pike.

Then he said softly, "I suppose it all started at a place in Scotland called Castle McLeish. Not unlike Pendenys, really. Heavily guarded, and very secret. Once I got to McLeish, there was no going back, so I suppose that's where I should start. I'll try to be brief, but there are things you've got to know. And when I've told you I want you to give me your opinion — no, dammit — I want more than that! I want you to tell me that not all of it was my fault; that Daisy and I will be getting married only because someone died helping me to get home!"

"You want absolution? So tell me — *all* of it! And, Keth — thank you for trusting me . . ."

The Holdenby train gave its customary three toots as it rounded the curve. Just one minute, one beautiful, breath-holding minute, and it would clank and judder and shudder to a stop and Keth would be there! Keth was home, and soon they would be touching and kissing and loving.

But nothing was so urgent now, because Daisy knew, deep inside her, that this time Keth would stay in England long enough for them to be married. At All Souls. In the spring.

They were slowing, passing the crossing gates. Five more seconds! Keth Purvis, I love you!

She jammed on her cap, reached for her respirator and took a long, shuddering breath. He was there, waiting at the ticket barrier, hands jammed in the pockets of his civilian trousers. She hadn't dreamed it. He *was* home! They were together again!

"Hi, there!" Bas called, and Gracie spun round, startled, which was stupid, because she had been expecting him ever since she knew Keth was back in England and coming home on a seventy-two-hour leave pass.

"Hullo yourself!" Carefully, to give her silly heart time to stop thumping so hard, she picked up her hat in which lay four brown eggs. "Look," she offered. "They're laying well now they're out of the moult."

Hens! A guy really needed to talk about hens when he hadn't seen the girl he was crazy about for more'n three weeks!

"Good to see you, Bas." She was in control again. "My, isn't it cold?" She offered her cheek.

"Sure is." It wasn't her cheek he wanted to kiss!

"Have you seen Daisy and Keth? They're home."

"Yup. Just now left Keeper's."

Great! he thought. Talk about hens and eggs and Keth and Daisy! Don't say you've missed me! Don't kiss me, Gracie, else I might get around to thinking you're as nuts about me as I am about you!

Unspeaking, he followed her up the path, then opened the gate for her.

They were half-way up the lane when he said, "Gracie! You and me have got to talk!" Taking the hat, he laid it carefully on the ground then, hands on her shoulders, he turned her to face him, making her meet his eyes. "Okay — so we've had the hens and eggs bit and the 'Good to see you, Bas' and the 'Isn't it cold?' bit. So tell me, what's with the courting? You wouldn't say you love me — said you wanted to be courted and I'm trying my best! But I can't take frosty cheeks and I can't take seeing Keth and Daisy so happy and Drew and Kitty. What's so wrong with you an' me being happy too?"

"We don't know each other, Bas! Keth and Daisy, and Drew and Kitty have known each other all their lives! What if we made a terrible mistake — had you thought of that?"

"Not for a minute! I've loved you since I first saw you. That's where it started for me, and that's all that matters. Reckon we've got all our lives to get to know each other!"

"But that's just it, Bas! *Have* we got all our lives? You and me both, I mean. Did you know that a girl in the WAAF younger than I am was killed the night of the hit-and-run raid? Less than two miles from the bothy, that girl died. It could have been me! It could have been the bothy that bomber crashed on and not the Parish Hall!"

"Oh, I see." He stood back from her as if all at once he didn't want to touch her, she thought wildly. "So you could've been killed that night. So right now, you could be sitting on your cloud, looking down and wishing like mad that once — *just once* — you'd said, 'I love you, Bas Sutton.' And you could be wishing like mad that maybe it might've been good to be married, even for so short a time!"

"All right! So it wasn't me!" All at once her Lancashire common sense wasn't making any sense at all. "But have you ever stopped to think, *just once*, that you couldn't marry me anyway? You know you'd have the devil's own job convincing your Commanding Officer that I was a fit person to marry you. You *know* you'd have to ask his permission!"

Even as she delivered her last trump card, she knew she was lost, that she *wanted* to be in love.

"So who does the marrying around here, then? And is he goin' to snitch on us to my CO? And who's my CO to tell me whether or not I shall marry when I'm half English and have two passports to prove it?"

"I was only trying to point out, Bas, that it —"

"That it would be no trouble at all, once your folks were happy about me and once I've written to Mom and Pa telling them about it."

"So you haven't told them about me yet!"

"Of course I have. I've told them about Rowangarth's land girl that I take out a lot, and I sent snaps of you. Only thing they don't know is that I'm so gone on you it makes my head buzz! And there was no need to tell them, anyway, because Kitty already did it for me, would you believe?"

"I'd believe anything Kitty said or did!" The smallest smile lifted her lips. "But had you thought that a girl gets married in her own parish? It wouldn't be your Uncle Nathan who married us — even though I like him a lot."

"Okay — so we get hitched in Rochdale! We'll go to Gretna Green, if that's what it takes!"

He reached for her again, because he couldn't bear not to be touching her and because she couldn't flounce off and leave him whilst she was safe in his arms.

"Bas!" She moved her head sharply because she knew he was going to kiss her and if he kissed her the way he always did, anything could happen! "We aren't even engaged yet!"

"So? But if I asked you to marry me and you said you would — even in the dim and distant future —" he hastened, "then that *would* make us engaged and I could take this signet ring off my little finger and put it on yours for everyone to see!"

"I don't want your signet ring, Bas!"

"Okay! So I'll borrow one off Aunt Julia till I can get Mom to send a ring over — will that do?"

"No! What I mean is that I'm a gardener and I

know your parents gave you that ring when you graduated, and it wouldn't be fair if it slipped off my finger and got lost — that's what I meant!" Goodness, he mustn't think she was angling for an expensive ring! "And d'you know something, Bas? Daisy and Kitty will both be married at All Souls and have their receptions at Rowangarth and I'm sure Mum and Dad wouldn't mind it being here — our wedding, I mean. If I said I'd marry you, that is . . ."

"All right. So tonight, when you an' me go out and I ask you to marry me, what will you say?"

"I — I'd say," she dropped her head and he placed a forefinger under her chin, tilting it so she had to look at him. "I'd say first that I think I love you . . ."

"Only *think*?" he whispered gently, indulgently.

"No!" She took a deep breath. "I *know* I love you, Bas Sutton. I've tried hard not to, but it isn't any use! So I'd say yes, if you asked me to marry you! But not all in a hurry," she rushed on. "You'd have to ask my dad — it would only be polite, after all — and as for your folks in Kentucky —"

"My folks will be real pleased. They'll like you a lot. I know Kitty does."

"Bas — I'm late for work!" She would regret this moment of weakness when she came to her senses!

"Okay. Take the eggs in to Tilda, then I'll walk back with you. I've got some tobacco for Jack, anyway. I'll give it to him, then ask him if he'd mind you showing me the garden."

"But you've seen the garden! Heaps of times!"

"So I have. But I've suddenly decided not to wait till tonight. I met you in the kitchen garden and I guess it's there I should ask you to marry me!"

"You're an idiot, Bas Sutton." She bent to pick up her hat. "You say the nicest things. I suppose it's why I love you."

"Hallelujah! I wait for months, then be blowed if you don't say it twice in the space of a minute! Now hurry up and get rid of those eggs, then we can get down to the business of deciding where and when we'll be married."

"Do you remember when we met, Bas?" It was all she could think of to say.

"You bet! It was a Saturday and Jack had gone to a wedding. It was warm and sunny and you had no shoes on. And your shirt — and I remember it well — was *very* unbuttoned. You smelled of roses and newly cut hay and —"

"Bas! I smelled of manure. I did! I remember wondering what you'd think of me — smelling so awful, I mean."

"So you cared what I thought even then?" he smiled, helping her over the stile.

"It seems," she said softly, "that I must have. I guess I loved you too — but my Lancashire common sense kept telling me I didn't — *couldn't*."

"Then from now on, Gracie Fielding, common sense of any sort is taboo! Let's make up for lost time and be crazily in love? And, darling — do you know that on a miserable winter afternoon with your nose all red from the cold and soil beneath your fingernails, you are the most beautiful woman in the world?"

"Right now, Bas, with my red sniffy nose and dirty hands, I *feel* the most beautiful woman in the world. And d'you know what? I think I'm going to cry. I really do . . ."

Nathan Sutton placed logs on the fire, then closed his eyes as if to shut out what Keth had told him, glad of the time alone to sort out the jumble in his mind. It wasn't, he acknowledged, what Keth had actually said, though that in itself had been hard enough to take in. Nor was it that Keth had committed treason, almost, by telling him things which should have remained unsaid.

What had really thrown him was that Keth had unknowingly chanced on something he would rather forget; that all at once a being who had been more shadow than substance was unbelievably real. She was Tatiana's half-sister; Drew's, too. What was so awful was that she had been found too late. The baby who became Hannah Kominski was almost certainly the child of Natasha Yurovska and his own brother Elliot, Nathan brooded. The servant in black, Elliot had called her, and he had made her pregnant.

So quietly, with only Anna, himself and the Countess knowing, Natasha had been taken back to London and from there into obscurity; hidden away until her sin had been born and adopted into respectability. Because the sixteen-year-old girl with hair like Keth's — Mary Anne Pendennis hair — had almost certainly been fathered by his brother, Nathan acknowledged. Only a chance in a million had found her, and now she was dead.

Thank God Keth did not know; that to him the young girl with the codename Natasha had been an unwanted baby, born to an unmarried Russian mother and adopted by Russian refugees to be reared in the Jewish faith. He had pushed the shock of realization into the deeps of his consciousness and tried to concentrate on Keth's tormented words, comforting him, telling him not to shoulder the blame for her death.

"If it hadn't been you that night in Clissy, Keth, it would have been someone else. You did what had to be done. It happens, in wartime."

Yet Keth had told him nothing about why he was sent to France, nor about what he brought back with him except to say that it would help save many lives.

So in the cold light of day, Nathan urged, couldn't it perhaps have been in the order of things that the life of one young girl, no matter how precious, should be balanced against the lives of many? Was it God's doing or Keth Purvis's fault or merely the whim of uncaring Fate?

"I think, Keth," he had said gravely, "that some things we must accept as God's doing and try not to question our faith. And don't think that because I am a priest," he urged, "that God's will is Holy Writ and that I have never questioned it. I questioned it many times during my war. Before our soldiers were sent into battle, many of them came to me to receive the Sacrament because they needed to believe in God and that He would take care of them. To some it was a desperate plea: 'God, I don't want to die!' To others it gave peace of mind, but to me, who gave them bread and wine, it was the certain knowledge that many of them were going to their deaths.

"Having faith isn't just believing; it's believing in God, as I had to, even when I didn't agree with that war nor that God had allowed it. Natasha's death, and that of Hirondelle, were for a purpose and honest doubters like you and me must try to accept it.

"And in all your self-condemnation, have you never once thought that it was in the order of things that you should live that night? Perhaps Himself knew better than you or I how important that package was."

"Mr Sutton, that thing I went to collect *is* important, yet all I can still think about is that I'm alive and able to marry Daisy, only because a toss of the coin — Fate — decided Natasha should die, and not me."

"Fate, Karma, God — does it matter, Keth? Faith is accepting what Life throws at you, as that young girl did the night in Clissy — and hoping there's a heaven, a hereafter, at the end of it. You can't change anything, you know, by being miserable, and something unspeakable isn't going to happen to Daisy because you are alive and Natasha is dead. That's what really bothers you, isn't it?"

"Yes, it is. Daisy could get blitzed again; anything could happen to her."

"Certainly it could. And to you and Drew or Bas, or Tatty down in London. It happened to my father and to Reuben and Jin and Mrs Shaw. If anyone has got to shoulder the blame for that girl's death it isn't you, nor the man who sent you to France. It was, *is*, the fault of the madman who started this war."

"Hitler," Keth said flatly.

"Yes. So hadn't we better leave Hitler to God, because when all's said and done, God is where the buck stops . . ."

And Nathan knew with absolute certainty, as the voice of his wife called him back from the past, that almost seventeen years ago a child was conceived in lust; a child who would grow into bravery and be at a place called Clissy-sur-Mer at a time when Fate decreed she should be. Only he couldn't have told Keth that; couldn't even confide in Julia, who was now invading his thoughts, cupping his face in cold hands, saying, "My, but it's a raw one out there. I do so hate grizzly winter! But I've done my duty and called on the Countess at Anna's behest and sat with the lady — just as Mother would have done."

"Then tonight, darling, you'll have your just reward because Keth and Daisy are coming to talk about having the banns called and weddings and all things nice! How does that suit you?"

And Julia said it would suit her very nicely, then sat on the floor at his feet, her fingers spread to the warmth of the fire.

"And do you know, darling," she said softly, "that I am so very lucky? Keth and Daisy married in the spring and Drew and Kitty soon after, I shouldn't wonder. So why, in all the awfulness of this war, have I the right to be so contented? I wish you'd tell me, Nathan."

"I wish I could, but I can't. I only know that we must accept the happiness — and the sadness — that chance our way, and live them or bear them the best way we can. Does that sound smug, Julia?"

"Smug? You'll never be that, Nathan." She reached up for his hand, placing a kiss in its palm. "And I must go and see to the supper, because Mary has taken the afternoon off to go to the dentist and Tilda is out with her Sydney. But I think I'll have a cigarette first."

She took a packet of Lucky Strike from her pocket, revelling in breaking the seal to sniff their slightly toasted flavour. Twenty cigarettes all at once was heady stuff, and may heaven bless a GI called Bas, and the canteen at Burtonwood.

"Bas brought a tin of Spam with him. I'll make fritters of it, I think. And he brought a tin of peaches, so we'll be absolute pigs and scoff the lot. Supper is at six, by the way. Bas is taking Gracie to the Creesby dance."

"Bas sees a lot of our land girl when he's here," Nathan murmured, all at once happier for Julia's presence.

"Bas and Gracie are as right for each other as Drew and Kitty, and Keth and Daisy." Julia seemed to have her heart set on three Rowangarth weddings.

"I think that since Bas has brought me tobacco, I just might have a fill. Anything you want me to do, Julia?"

"No thanks. Enjoy your pipe; I'll go and see to the blackouts — shut out this awful gloom. Supper won't be long," she smiled, thinking of tinned peaches in thick syrup; realizing it was an age since the Creesby shops had any for sale. Dear Bas. She did so want him to fall in love and be happy.

CHAPTER
NINETEEN

The bell sounded urgently for the second time; distantly the orchestra began to tune up. Hurriedly, drinks were finished, then the theatre bar was empty save for Tatiana and Bill Benson.

"Are you ready?" She reached for his stick, placing it in his hand.

"No. Wait. Look — do we want to see the rest of it? Can't we just stay here and talk?"

"I suppose they'll let us. Shall I get you another beer before they close the bar?"

"No, thanks. I want us to talk because I'm leaving."

"*Leaving?* A bit sudden, isn't it?" He couldn't leave, not when life was becoming almost bearable again.

"It's my eyes, Tatiana. I've been seeing things, lately."

"But you didn't tell me!"

"No. It comes and goes. And only light and shade, most times, though once or twice I've made out shapes — I think."

"Then that's marvellous!" She really meant it, even though she didn't want him to go. "And you're going to hospital to get it seen to?"

"Not exactly. I'll be having tests to see if there's any hope. If there is, I'll go to this place out in the country — some old house that's been made into an eye hospital. Sister said they've had a lot of experience with injuries like mine, so I'm in with a chance — well, with one eye."

"Then I'm glad for you."

"Want a cigarette? I got a packet today."

"Please — if you can spare one. Shall I light one for you, Bill?"

"Think you'd better. I still burn my nose sometimes. And that's daft, when you come to think of it — my nose being already burned, if you see what I mean."

"Don't!" She flicked her lighter, then touched his hand, giving him the cigarette. "I'm going to miss you. Is that selfish of me?"

"No. And it'll be nice being missed. I'll ring you, if that's all right?"

"Of course it is. And I'll write to you. You could get someone to read it to you — till you can see, that is!"

"Till pigs start flying!" He drew hard on his cigarette. "Anyway, do I really want to see again? Maybe it'd be better if I never saw the mess I am now."

"What do you mean — mess?" Suddenly she was angry. "Stop being a whinge, Bill. At least you're alive!"

"Hell, Tatiana — you call this living? Burned *and* blind!"

"You can touch and hear, can't you? You can walk and talk?" she said harshly. "Tim would be glad to be burned and blind, and the way he looked wouldn't worry me at all!"

"Tim?" His head shot up. "Who's he then?"

"Look — I'm sorry. Truly I am. I didn't want for you ever to know."

"Tim? Someone who's dead?"

"Someone I loved, who was killed." She reached for his hand, but he snatched it away.

"I see. So you do your caring act because of him?"

"I do it — started to do it, I mean — because I thought it would help *me*!"

"Tell me about him." He felt along the table top for the ashtray and crushed out his cigarette. "If you can bear to, that is!"

"All right! I'll tell you! I *want* to talk about him and that's good, because once I couldn't have!" She took a slow, shuddering breath. "His name was Tim Thomson . . ." All at once her voice was gentle, her anger gone. "He was from Greenock and a sergeant air-gunner, like you are. And like you, he had fair hair and was just about your age. You want me to go on?"

"Aye . . ."

"I'm half-Russian, but you know that. What you don't know is that my mother and grandmother fussed over me and made my life a misery. They wouldn't let me be ordinary like other girls, so when I met Tim it was — was just wonderful. I'd sneak out to meet him. Daisy and Gracie used to alibi me and it wasn't a schoolgirl crush. We were lovers and I'm not ashamed of it. I'm glad, in fact! At least I have something to hang on to."

"I'm sorry, and it's fine by me if taking me around helped you. You should've told me, though."

"I didn't want to because — don't you understand? — you became Tim! I'd touch your hand, and it was his hand I was touching. I'd take your arm to guide you, and it was Tim's arm. He and I used to walk close — thighs touching, always holding hands. I wanted to walk close to you, Bill, only I didn't dare. Do you think I'm mad?"

"No, lassie. Anyway, it helps to be mad in this world."

"I'm sorry if I've hurt you, Bill. I do like you, I really do, and being with you has been great."

"Like being with *him*, you mean? Aye, it's easy to pretend, isn't it, when the one thing that matters — his face — isn't there!"

"Oh God! I *have* hurt you." She took his hand and held it tightly so he couldn't pull it away. "I'm truly sorry. Please try to forgive me."

"Oh, I can forgive you. Easily. Y'know, we're a peculiar pair, you an' me. There was someone in my life too. Can I touch your face, Tatiana?"

"Y-yes . . ."

He reached out with his hand, and she took it and laid it to her cheek. "Friends again, Bill?"

"Friends." He traced the outline of her nose with a forefinger, then ran his fingers through her hair.

"The nose is right. Hers was like yours — short, and tippy-tilted. But your hair is too long. She wore hers rolled up — because of the uniform, you see. Regulations."

"She was in the Forces?"

"Aye. A WAAF corporal."

"And you loved her a lot? So why isn't she here now?"

"She's not here because she's married. I think her man is in the Navy, but I don't know. I don't even know her name. Like I said, it was a peculiar kind of loving."

"Do you want to tell me?"

"She was a parachute packer. We'd draw our parachutes the last thing we did before we went on ops — but you'd know that. There's this stupid joke, you see."

"Yes, I know! What if this chute doesn't open? Answer: bring it back. We'll gladly change it!" Tatiana supplied.

"Well, I always went to her — the corporal — for my chute. It was a part of the ritual. You'll know about the ritual too."

"Before aircrews take off, you mean? Things they always did or said for luck? Tim's crew used to pee on the tail wheel. Another crew used to count the engines on their plane — to make sure some thieving sod hadn't nicked one of them, they always said."

"Aye — well I always went through the what-if-it-doesn't-open routine with the WAAF corporal and our navigator always took his teddy along. We called him a great Jessie, but we wouldn't have taken off without that bear!"

"And your corporal?" Tatiana prompted gently.

"*My* corporal! That's a joke. She didn't know I existed really; was just being nice to a crew that mightn't make it back to base. And she wouldn't have considered me — even if she hadn't been married. She was classy. Everything about her was top drawer. The minute I heard your voice, Tatiana, you were her, and because I couldn't see you I could go on with my daft crush. You sounded so like her that I almost came out with the what-if-this-chute-doesn't-open joke. I suppose I was glad I couldn't see you — in case you didn't look like her. What colour is your hair, by the way?"

"Dark brown and my eyes are brown. Are you going to be disappointed when you can see again?"

"So you'll want to keep on being friends?"

"I said so, didn't I, Bill? Said I'd ring and write? If the hospital isn't too far away I can come and visit at weekends. We'll keep in touch — word of a Sutton."

"So we can both go on with our daft pretendings?"

"Why not?"

He was trying to smile, but his lips were still cracked and scabbed. She laid a finger across his mouth.

"Does it hurt still?"

"Only when I laugh! And, Tatiana, I wouldn't let things get out of hand, only I'd like fine to have a friend — have *someone*. I've been a loner all my life. Was sent to a children's home because my mother wasn't married. You don't belong, in an orphanage. They gave me a bed and clothes, and I never went hungry like a lot of normal kids did. I'm not complaining. I managed just fine — only I didn't have anyone of my own. It's why I'd like us still to be friends."

"I'd like it too. And I promise never to call you Tim and you must never come out with the parachute joke — okay?"

"Granted, soon as asked." He held out a hand and she took it, and held it.

"And, Bill, don't worry too much about not having folks of your own. Families can be a bind. Mother's all right, but my grandmother is awful and I know my father didn't like me very much. I wasn't a boy, you see. I'm much happier being with Sparrow and Kitty.

"And I think they want us to go — they're putting the chairs up. Shall we sit in the foyer till the show's over? I'll write my phone number down so you can let me have your new address. And I'll give you my Holdenby address and phone number so someone can always get hold of me for you."

She gave him his stick, picking up the cap he had left on the table, offering her arm. Then she smiled at the elderly lady who was emptying ashtrays, because all at once the anger that had been inside her since the morning on Holdenby Pike when she found *K-King* was gone.

She wasn't happy, but all at once she felt a glow of peace. It was almost as if, she thought, she had fought her feelings far too long and was glad to give up the struggle. She would never know complete happiness again, but the relief she felt now was a beginning.

One day, she would tell him all about Tim; how wonderful it had been and how grateful she was for having had such a love. One day. When she was brave enough.

She wondered if Bill would tell her about his corporal too, or if he would confess she had been an invention of the moment so that she, Tatiana, should not feel too bad about using a blind air-gunner as a crutch. She hoped he would believe, when chips were down, that she needed him just as much as he needed her. A peculiar pair, he had called them. They were that, all right!

"Glass door ahead," she said, taking his arm, holding it tightly. "Then two steps down . . ."

"I'd forgotten how it blows here in winter! Straight from Siberia!" Daisy, her arm through Keth's, took the wind head on.

"Let's go to the stableyard. It'll be sheltered there, and we're early anyway. I want to talk to you."

"Mm. Me, too. There isn't a lot of privacy at Keeper's. Really, we should be up the Pike now, but it'd blow us inside out if we were! And it's only just December. Imagine three more months of this!"

"Three months, then we'll be married. Careful." He gave her his hand as she climbed the stile, then hand in hand they ran across Rowangarth's lawn, stumbling in the blackness, making for the darker mass they knew to be the stable block. And the blackout, though awful and sometimes frightening, did have its compensations, like now. It helped you to cross, unseen, someone else's lawn and take cover in the shelter of someone else's stable block, with never a soul seeing you.

"Ssssh," she whispered. "Mary and Will might hear us."

"Not them." Keth unbuttoned his overcoat, pulling her close to wrap her inside it. "Now — before we see the Reverend, are you sure you want us to be married on my next leave?"

"Idiot! I'd marry you tomorrow if I could. Are you trying to wriggle out of it?" she teased. "Are you going to disappear to Washington again? Or will it be Timbuktu next time?"

"I'm staying." Mentally, he crossed his fingers. "I'll be waiting at the church some time in April — you do want it then, darling?"

"I do. Summer would have been a better time, but I can't wait till then. Let's have a spring wedding, when everything's fresh and green. We can't have much of a reception but if it's cold, Aunt Julia says, the conservatory will be just fine. I think she wants to take a snap of the Clan in there. She always said she would; always believed you'd be home to make up the six." She reached to kiss his chin. "I still can't believe you're back, and you're still a bit quiet. Darling — did something awful happen on the way over? Did you make the crossing by sea? Was the convoy attacked? I know how awful it is in the Atlantic. The Government keeps a lot back from the press, you know."

"Sweetheart, nothing happened on the way home!" Silently he begged Natasha's forgiveness. "I had a good voyage over." That at least was true. "And I'm not quiet, exactly. It's just that I can't take it in. I never thought they'd send me back."

But you are back, and nothing, absolutely nothing, happened between Washington and Holdenby! Clissy never was! No one can turn back the clock!

"Hell, but I love you!" He kissed her fiercely. "Do you know how much?"

"Mm." Eyes closed, she snuggled closer. "Shall we hear the banns? Will it be the first reading tomorrow?"

"I should think so. But they'll be read out at Eucharist and that doesn't finish till twelve. We have to get the York train and there's only one on Sundays. We've got to have one night together . . ."

"I felt awful, telling Mam and Dada we both have to leave tomorrow, but I can't wait for you till April."

"Nor me. It's murder, sleeping on the other side of the wall from you."

"So we'll creep out of church once we've heard the first calling. We'll sit at the back so's not to

358

cause an upset, and had you thought — it'll be read from the pulpit immediately before the sermon, so we'll miss that?"

"Devious woman!" He kissed her again. "And you're right, darling. We've been apart too long!"

"But we're on our way now. Just think. I publish the banns of marriage between Keth Purvis and Daisy Julia Dwerryhouse of this parish. If any of you know cause, or just impediment, why these two persons should not be joined together in Holy Matrimony, ye are to declare it. This is the first time of asking!"

"You know it off by heart!"

"And so I should. I've said it over and over in my mind when you were on the other side of the Atlantic and I wanted you so much. What else do you think kept me going? I've imagined it so often: All Souls, you and me, and Tatty and Kitty in their bridesmaid dresses."

"Kitty? I thought you'd asked Lyn?"

"I did, only now she doesn't want to be bridesmaid. You can't blame her, I suppose."

"Drew, you mean?"

"Drew! But Kitty's an absolute darling and so open and honest that you can't help loving her. And she's so right for Drew."

"So it'll be their banns next?"

"I suppose so, though Aunt Julia would have a double wedding in April if she could. They seem to be hanging back, though. I think Kitty is waiting to see if the wedding dress her mother bought will make it across the Atlantic safely, and anyway, it isn't as if they're desperate. They're lovers, you know. They were in bed when he asked her; Drew told me so."

"No kidding? Doesn't sound like Drew's style. He was such a serious little boy."

"Yes, but Kitty's changed him a lot; that, and over two years in the Navy! And why shouldn't they? That holier-than-thou lot have forgotten what it's like to be young in wartime. But kiss me, please, then we'll have to go. Eight o'clock Aunt Julia said, so best not be late. And, Keth — I do so love you."

Lyn Carmichael plucked an envelope from the letter rack. From Auntie Blod, of course. Automatically she searched for any bearing Daisy's name, but there was none; only a folded piece of paper pushed behind the criss-crossed tape. She knew what was written on it, even before she unashamedly read it. *Dwerryhouse. Call from Drew Sutton.*

Once, such a message would have sent her shooting to the stars, but now all she could think was that Drew's ship was in dock, probably for thirty-six hours, that Daisy was on leave and that Kitty was in London. All very nice, except Drew was in love with Kitty and even if he phoned again, she could not trust herself even to answer it, ask him how he was. Even to hear his voice would hurt, and could she trust herself not to ask, "Why did you do it, Drew? Knowing how much I loved you, why

360

did you fall in love with Kitty?" Yes, and sleep with Kitty and ask her to marry him!

She slammed the cabin door, sent her cap spinning across the room, then climbed onto her bunk to read her letter.

Dearest Lyndis,

I suppose it would have been better if I'd phoned you, but things like your mam and dad getting married are best written down, to my way of thinking.

Jack has asked me in a letter to marry him. As soon as the war is over and he can get me a passage, he wants me to go to Kenya to him. I've written back and told him that yes I would, and gladly, and wouldn't it be good if you could sail with me so we could be a real family for the first time . . .

Lyn laid down the letter, then closed her eyes tightly. Everyone was falling in love and getting married! Everyone but Lyn Carmichael, that was!

"Oh damn, damn, *damn*!" she hissed, then buried her face in her pillow and wept.

"I swear, Bertie, this is the best New Year present I could have gotten."

Amelia Sutton put on her reading glasses, opened the letter, then sighed with pure pleasure.

"And that, to my certain knowledge, is the tenth time you've read it!"

"Yes, but it isn't every day our son gets engaged, now is it? Think, Bertie — we mightn't have had him. He could have died in that fire with your mother and —"

"But he *didn't*! He got out of it with only burns to his hands. Forget Pendenys, darling; it's in the past. The Army has got the place now, and I hope they keep it! And are you sure you're completely happy about Bas? It came as a bit of a shock, you can't deny it."

"Not really. Kitty said time and time again in her letters that Bas was smitten. She really likes Grace. *Why* must there be this awful war? *Why* can't a mother be there when her son and daughter get engaged? We could've had engagement showers for them and there'd have been all the fun of planning weddings and —"

"Because our kids have chosen English partners and haven't you said all along that Drew and Kitty were made for each other, even though they are cousins?"

"*Second* cousins, Bertie, which reminds me that they both share a great-grandmother."

"And what has Grandmother Whitecliffe to do with it?"

"Her *jewellery*! You know they have to go on a waiting list in England for engagement rings, and wedding rings, when you can get them, are only nine-carat gold? So isn't it a relief that Julia was left the family jewels? Kitty's wearing one of the old rings, and now so is Grace. It's lovely, them both having old Sutton rings."

"But Grace didn't want a ring. Seems she still wears hers on a chain round her neck most of the time."

"And she chose a very simple one. Bas was most disappointed that she picked out a dress ring of garnets. Garnets are only semiprecious, Bertie."

"So it seems Sebastian has chosen wisely; a pretty girl who likes simple things — and who was shovelling manure when they met! She should fit in well here at the stud!"

"I think we should drink a New Year toast to them all right now. You can't know what a relief it is to a mother when her children make happy matches!"

"But you've never met Grace! We know nothing about her except that according to your besotted son she's a mixture of Lana Turner and Betty Grable!"

"She's lovely and they'll both be on the wedding snaps when Daisy and Keth get married. I mustn't forget to send those reels of colour film in the next food parcel! Why are there such awful shortages in Britain — even wedding dresses!"

"Because they're a small island at war, and most things have to be brought in by sea. We are more self-sufficient, here."

"But films for cameras . . . ?"

"That's because every bomber has a camera in it to film the raid, so civilians must do without. And should we drink a toast yet? There's still a few hours of 1942 to go."

"Not in England! It's New Year already there. Remember that last New Year I was unhappy and afraid because our children would be going to war? Yet they've ended up in England and are both safe and sound and happy, with Julia and Nathan *in loco parentis*. Anyway, the champagne has been cooling for ages and I really do want to wish them both a happy marriage and send my dearest love to them all over there."

And Albert Sutton smiled and surrendered, because when women got the wedding bug, there was nothing a man could do about it. It came as something of a comfort that his brother Nathan was a fellow-sufferer, because Julia would have the bug as well, over Drew and Kitty.

Darling, mischievous Kitty. How quiet the place was without her. Albert wondered where she was, and what she was doing and if she knew how much he missed her.

"Take care, kitten," he whispered.

Kitty sighed, stuck down the envelope, then planted a lipsticky kiss on the back of it.

"Writing to Bill, are you?" She smiled at Tatiana, sitting cross-legged on the bed opposite.

She tried never to mention Tim Thomson or even Drew, and it had been real hard not to tell her that a large parcel had arrived from Kentucky. And that Aunt Julia had opened it and hung a wedding dress in white slipper satin in the Rowangarth sewing room, next to Daisy's.

"Mm. They haven't decided yet if there's any hope for his eyes. I've got a feeling, though, that this year is going to be a better one all round. Last night, when I went to Cheyne Walk to wish Uncle Igor a happy New Year, he thought so too. You'll have to come with me to meet him. He isn't so crusty these days."

"Sure. I'd like that." She wouldn't really, Kitty thought; not if he was as peculiar as the old Countess. But she could be liberal with her promises because she was going on tour soon for three weeks.

She liked touring, taking shows to servicemen and women in out-of-the-way places, yet now there was Drew and it wasn't a lot of laughs when his minesweeper docked and she was miles away with ENSA and very often nowhere near a telephone.

She thought yearningly about the wedding dress at Rowangarth and wanted, suddenly, to wear it; to be married at All Souls. With luck she might get pregnant quickly, then she could give up her war work and put show business on the back burner. She wanted lots of children.

"I heard from the courier from the Russian Embassy that things are really desperate in Leningrad." Tatiana said. "He says whole families are dying of cold and starvation. There is no electricity and sewers don't function. They've been holding out against the Germans for so long that to eat a rat is a luxury now."

"Tatty — *don't*! Rats? Surely not?"

"Seems there's nothing else. He said all the cats and dogs were eaten ages ago."

"Then why won't they give in?" Kitty thought of a child, desperately hungry, having to eat vermin! "Wouldn't it be better if they did?"

"It would, but they won't; not if they're like Grandmother Petrovska. Once, she couldn't even bring herself to think of the peasants — her word, not mine — who had killed the Czar and taken her houses to live in; even yet she refuses to call Leningrad by its proper name. But now she prays for them every night on her knees. She says she is proud of them and that the Czar would have been proud too. D'you know, Kitty, in Russia there is a bomber squadron crewed entirely by *women*? They are based at Stalingrad. Imagine women being aircrew! How lucky can you get?"

"Crew a bomber? Think I'll stick to tinsel and grease-paint, if you don't mind!" Right now, Kitty thought, she missed Drew so much that even the thrill of the footlights was beginning to wear thin. "Wonder what Drew is doing now?" She couldn't keep his name from her lips.

"Keeping safe, I hope." Tatty stuck a stamp on the envelope addressed to Bill Benson. "And let's go downstairs and share Sparrow's fire. It's freezing up here."

"Let's!" Kitty Sutton could not get used to the English cold and houses were not centrally heated as they were in America. Then she thought of the tour ahead, and of draughty, makeshift dressing rooms, and performing in aeroplane hangars or barns, even, with the wind whistling through every crack and under every door. "Perhaps Sparrow will have enough milk for cocoa. I must be getting old, Tatty. I never used to feel the cold when we came over every year at Christmas."

"We weren't fighting a war then, and coal was cheap and easy to get. And there were servants at Pendenys who did nothing else but keep fires going all over the house — even in the bedrooms!" Now domestic servants were all on war work and coal was rationed to one bag a month to every household. "But don't worry, Kitty. We're past New Year now; winter is half over — and that's the phone! Hurry, it might be Drew!"

It wouldn't, of course, Tatiana thought as Kitty hurried downstairs. It would be Aunt Julia, making sure everything was all right at Montpelier. Dear Aunt Julia . . .

"So that's it!" Julia put the piece of paper bearing the wedding date into her pocket. "Saturday, the seventeenth of April at two. I'll tell Nathan to write it in his diary. In ink!"

"Surely it'll be a case of third time lucky," Alice sighed. "It's a pity we can't have a slap-up do, but we mustn't grumble. April is a lovely month for a wedding."

"Yes, and surely Drew and Kitty will be next? It gives me such a wonderful feeling seeing *two* wedding dresses hanging in the sewing room."

"In that case I don't suppose you could make room for two more — the bridesmaid's dresses, I mean? They take up so much space in the little spare bedroom."

"Sure. Next time I'm out in the car I'll call for them. It's a pity that Daisy's friend can't be bridesmaid."

"Can't be? I think Lyndis was looking forward to it — until Kitty happened, I mean. But that's war for you. Feelings running high. Lyn falling for Drew and Drew falling for Kitty. But then who wouldn't fall for Kitty? She's so beautiful and funny and happy. Makes me feel old, Julia. I'll swear it isn't five minutes since the entire Clan used to sit round this very table eating new-baked bread with honey. Like a swarm of locusts, they were! And little Tatty always tagging on behind and begging to be allowed to play with the others without her nanny being there all the time."

"And now she's confounded us all by going off to London and sticking it out in spite of the bombing. I wish she could find another boyfriend, though I think she really loved that young airman.

"But we were talking bridesmaids. I believe Kitty will be standing in for Lyn. They're about the same size and height. It seems a pity not to have two when we have two lovely dresses going begging. I think we should offer them around in the village afterwards. If anyone knows of anyone getting married it would save their clothing coupons."

"A good idea, though why Daisy wants to wear flowers in her hair, I don't know! Her confirmation veil is there, good as new, yet she insists she won't wear it," Alice frowned.

"I think it's a lovely idea," Julia defended. "Flowers, worn ballerina-style, and white ribbons flowing at the back. Have you got any white ribbons, Julia?"

"Now where am I going to get *any* ribbons with none in the shops? Mind, I've an idea I have some somewhere from when Daisy was an angel in the nativity play, if I remember rightly. I'll have a good root through the· sewing drawer. Washed and pressed, they should come up good as new. But a circlet of *which* flowers, Julia?"

Alice set the kettle to boil, because talking ways and means and weddings was thirsty work.

"There should be white narcissi still out in April. Those in the wild garden are always late. They would do nicely for the bridesmaids. But as for the bride — I think Catchpole will come up trumps!"

"Not orchids!" Alice stopped, teapot poised.

"No. But the cymbidiums will be flowering then, and I'll defy anyone but an expert to tell cymbidiums from orchids! He told me he has half a dozen pots putting out buds. Said if he had a date to work to he could keep them back or force them forward, as the case may be."

"But that would be marvellous! Does Daisy know?"

"Not yet, but I'm sure she'll like the idea. A little later in the year Mother's white orchids should be flowering. I shall tell Drew to get his skates on, so

Kitty can carry a bouquet of them." Julia smiled fondly. "Mother would have liked that, don't you think — Drew's bride carrying the white orchids."

"Not would have — *will* like it, Julia, because she'll be there in spirit, believe me."

"Of course she will! Oh, I do wish Drew and Kitty would set a date, or at least have the banns read. Don't they know there's a war on? Anything could happen!"

"Well, it *won't* happen! And seeing Keth and Daisy married will make them wonder what's been keeping them, just see if it doesn't. And wait until Kitty sees that beautiful dress her mother has sent over! She'll get the message!"

"If Kitty can stay in one place long enough to get around to it. She's on tour again, would you believe? Doing twenty performances in two weeks! Pity she had to be based in London. When she was in Liverpool she and Drew saw quite a bit of each other. Now they are like Box and Cox! When Drew's ship is in, Kitty is on tour!"

"Well, let's see Daisy safely down the aisle, then we'll think about getting Drew married!" Alice smiled wickedly. "What that young man seems to forget is that he's got *two* mothers, and both of them want to see him wed! Now let's have this tea, before it gets stewed!"

"I suppose it would be nice if Drew were to get married in his uniform," Julia smiled dreamily. "After all, he's the first Sutton since Cromwell's time not to join the Army. And who will give Kitty away? Her father will be stuck in Kentucky, not able to get over, and Nathan will be marrying them!"

"Then who but her brother?"

"Bas! But of course! And, Alice, had you thought? We haven't given any attention, yet, to Bas and Gracie, and them engaged!"

"I hadn't forgotten them. Daisy seems to think that when they do get married, it will be at All Souls too. I think Gracie is very fond of Rowangarth and she'd like her wedding here, if her family agrees."

"Oh my goodness! Three weddings in the family. Now won't that be just something?"

It was at that moment that Tom, on his way to Rowangarth with a brace of cock pheasants for Tilda, paused to look in at the kitchen window. He had thought to call in for a sup of tea, this being the time Alice always put the kettle on. Yet when he saw them, all dreamy-eyed, he knew it could only mean they were talking about one thing. When women had *that* look in their eyes, it was best not to disturb them! After all, Tilda would have the kettle on too.

And then he smiled, realizing that Tilda often had *that* look in her eyes these days and her with a ring to justify it — even though it was, as yet, on the wrong hand.

He shook his head. Women and weddings. They went together like moonlight and music — or beer and baccy, come to think of it! Either way, there was no separating them, so best not try!

CHAPTER
TWENTY

1943

It had been, up until now, the worst February anyone could remember, yet today was mild, with a pale sun promising that spring was not far away.

"Look, Mama!" Anna pointed to a clump of crocus buds in a sheltered corner. "Doesn't it make you feel good to see them?"

Today was Sunday, Anna's day off from the surgery, a day she devoted entirely to her mother's whims and fancies. It helped ease her conscience for leaving her alone every day whilst thoroughly enjoying working at the surgery. That she had at last brought order to the business side of the practice and sent January's accounts out on time amazed her, for who would have thought Anna Sutton had the intelligence to hold down a job? It delighted her that Ewart Pryce seemed grateful for her help, and didn't hesitate to tell her so. Never before had anyone praised her. Elliot found fault with everything she did; the fact that she had not given him a living son made him threaten to divorce her; her brother made it plain she had made a mess of her life, marrying money instead of one of her own kind. But best not dwell on that today, because today snowdrops lay in drifts in Denniston House woods and the glossy leaves of wild arum were opening. And hadn't she seen hazel catkins and, high on Holdenby Pike, a blaze of yellow to tell her that, even in February, gorse flowered?

"You are quiet," she said, pulling her mother's arm through her own. "Shall we go back?"

"No, I thank you." The Countess pulled the collar of her sable coat higher. "I am quiet because I am thinking."

"But you're not worrying about Tatiana and Igor? The bombing in London is easing off now." Some nights even passed without a siren being heard.

"Why should you think I am worrying? Can't an old woman be quiet with her thoughts?"

"Just as long as they are happy thoughts — and they should be, Mama, with the news from Russia so good. Were you thinking about Leningrad?"

"I was thinking about *St Petersburg*, if you must know, and that perhaps I judged the peasants a little harshly in the past."

"The Communists, Mama? But you said you would never forgive them!"

"Nor will I, for taking my homes as though they had a God-given right to them!"

She still winced to think of peasant boots clumping across her carpets; peasant women rifling her wardrobes whilst their men sawed up her beautiful furniture to burn in *her* firegrates.

"To the victor the spoils, Mama," Anna reproved gently.

"Yes. It was always so. Yet now that man Stalin has stopped the Nazis, is even beginning to fight back, I fear I shall never see my Russia again."

"Beginning to fight back! But what they have done is nothing short of miraculous! Your St Petersburg belongs to the Russians again, and Stalingrad too."

"You are right, Anna. I used, sometimes, to think that if Hitler defeated the Bolsheviks, then one day I would be allowed back to St Petersburg. But if that happened, this country too would be occupied, and the British treated no better than the people of other defeated countries.

"And why you think me quiet is because I must admit, I suppose, that those Bolsheviks deserve Russia now. God Himself knows they have fought for it and starved near to death for it. They have proved themselves. It is their turn now."

"Don't upset yourself, Mama." Anna patted the hand that lay on her arm. "We have a good life here. People are kind to us and treat us as if we belong. And we are going to win the war. I'm sure of it!"

Olga Petrovska lapsed into silence again, because she wanted to think, now that St Petersburg was free from the threat of Nazi jackboots, that soon the rest of Russia would be liberated and there would be food again for the children, the sick nursed and the dead decently buried. No matter how much she despised the upstart revolutionaries who presumed to rule Mother Russia, she had to admit that those same men and women had fought like devils for every street, every house, every heap of rubble, even, to take back what Hitler laid waste to.

Soon spring would come, and in St Petersburg they would hear the cracking of the ice on the River Neva and the snow would melt and the sun shine again; and maybe then the Germans would counterattack to try to retrieve their losses. Yet the people of Moscow and Stalingrad and St Petersburg had known victory and it would take more than a bewildered, battered Wehrmacht to snatch it from them.

"I wonder," she said, because suddenly the silence had become too long, "if Tatiana will visit Igor today?"

"There was a fair few at church this morning. Must be the sun that brought them out," Tom remarked as Alice took off her Sunday hat and gloves and laid them on the table at the foot of the stairs.

"Aye." People, Alice thought, who had once been a bit haphazard about Sunday church now attended regularly. It was the war, she supposed, because when push came to shove it was God who held the scales that balanced life against death.

Mind, she had to admit that of late, Himself had been listening to prayers said in English; things were going better for the Allies: North Africa completely under the control of British and American troops; the Russians starting to fight back and civilian deaths from air raids down to their lowest for many months. "Do you know, Tom, I think things are starting to look up for us. Are we winning, do you think?"

"I wouldn't say winning exactly; there's a fair way to go yet, lass. But at least we're starting to win a few battles. Think I might walk down to the pub for a quick pint. What time will dinner be ready?"

"Same time," Alice said absently. "Don't be late."

Daft of him to ask, Tom thought as he headed for Holdenby. Sunday dinner was at one o'clock sharp. Always had been; always would be.

He wondered what Daisy was doing, because it was better than thinking that in eight weeks she would belong to Keth; wondered too why women took such delight in weddings. Alice was skipping around like a two-year-old these days, with hardly a care in the world. The wedding dresses were made, the banns read and a date set. Everything was under control as far as she was concerned. The only thing to bother her was the wedding cake, or the fact that there wouldn't be one. It was, she said, a crying shame that a bride couldn't have a decent cake to cut on her wedding day and Hitler had a lot to answer for!

But then she wouldn't be his Alice, Tom thought as he climbed the gate of Home Farm cow pasture and made for the narrow, rutted lane that led to the village, if she didn't have something or someone to worry about.

Dear, precious Alice . . .

376

★ ★ ★

"Well, what do you know!" Lyn looked over the top of the newspaper. "Somebody tried to kill Hitler!"

"*Tried?*" Daisy was all at once interested. "So what went wrong?"

"Dunno. Seems he's got his own private plane and somebody sneaked a bomb on board in a case of wine. It didn't go off, though. Still, better luck next time!"

"Which goes to show that he isn't as popular as he thought. He's been clobbered in North Africa and in Russia. Bet he wonders what's hit him. It really couldn't have happened to a more deserving person. But do put that paper down, Carmichael! It's sunny outside. Let's go for a walk in the park — after all, it might be snowing tomorrow."

"All for it." Lyn reached for her coat and gloves, hoping that Daisy wouldn't go on too much about the wedding. She had so wanted to be bridesmaid and now it would be Kitty who would wear the ice-blue dress and flowers in her hair, and walk up the aisle behind Keth and Daisy, her hand in Drew's.

There were times, she brooded as they made for the park, when she wished she had never met Drew Sutton. But they were fleeting, futile wishes, because she would never stop loving him, not even when he was married to Kitty.

"I wonder what Drew is doing," she said against her better judgement.

"He's due in any time now. And he always asks about you when he rings. I'm sure he'd be pleased if you'd come along like you used to, Lyn. It doesn't seem the same without you when I meet him at the Pierhead."

"Better I didn't. Then the pair of you can talk about Rowangarth and weddings without worrying about me being there."

"Lyn — you aren't still upset about Drew? I thought you were getting over him. And I do want you to be my bridesmaid. I haven't asked Kitty yet, you know."

"Then you better had, because I've definitely made up my mind. I won't be there. And not because of Drew," she hastened. "I *am* getting over him. I just think it would be better all round if you had Kitty, that's all."

And I tell lies too, Daisy Dwerryhouse . . .

"Now then, lass." Jack Catchpole glanced up with something akin to a smile as Gracie carefully closed the door of the orchid house behind her. "Just having a look at these buds. They'm doing nicely."

"Aren't you worried, Mr Catchpole — about them not flowering in time for the wedding? Or even flowering too soon?"

"Nay. Reckon we've got it just about right. They'll be at their best on the day, if I'm any judge."

"It's exciting, isn't it? And I suppose it won't matter if they flower a little early, because orchid flowers last for a month, don't they?"

"A month at least. But these here aren't exactly orchids. They'm cymbidiums, the poor relation."

378

"Wonder which colour Daisy will have."

"Well, with luck there'll be three to choose from. Pink, tawny and greeny-white. It's up to her. The bridesmaids'll have to make do with what's left over."

"Aren't you looking forward to it, Mr Catchpole?" Gracie's eyes shone, because she too was in love.

"Weddings, lass, I can take or leave, though I'm pleased about the flowers. Shall look forward to doing them, and buttonholes for the guests. Mind, young Drew and Keth won't wear buttonholes, them being in uniform.

"But what about you, Gracie Fielding? You'll not be interrupting your apprenticeship, will you, by getting wed? Be a crying shame if you didn't leave here a time-served gardener at the end of the war. Had you ever thought of going into gardening? Better'n working in an office, any day of the week!"

"Tell you the truth, Mr Catchpole, I haven't let myself think that far ahead. Can't believe, sometimes, that Bas and I are engaged. I had a lovely letter from his mother, and I've written back, but really — and I know this sounds awful of me — I'd like us to wait till the end of the war when Bas's folks can get a passage over, and be married here at Rowangarth. And I know I should get married in Rochdale, in my own parish," she rushed on, "but everything good that's happened in my life — except Mum and Dad and Grandad — is here at Rowangarth. I'm going to hate leaving it."

"But you won't be leaving it, lass! The Kentucky Suttons came over here every summer and Christmas when Bas and Kitty were bairns. You'll be a part of what Bas's dad calls the twice-yearly migration. And had you thought how grand it'll be, living on a stud farm in Kentucky? A well-heeled family you'll be marrying into. You'll want for nothing, and that's a fact."

"Don't think I hadn't thought about it, Mr Catchpole. I wouldn't want the money to come between us. I've never had any, you see, and I might not be good enough for them. I suppose it's why I want to wait — just to be sure."

"Sure! But you'm sure of your feelings for young Bas, aren't you? Goodness knows you ought to be, the time you kept the lad dangling!"

"Yes. I'm sure about Bas."

"Then what are you bothering about? You've got the makings of a good gardener, you'm pleasant and eager to please, and you'm polite, as well as being a right bonny lass! And Mrs Amelia isn't a snob. They don't go in for things like that in Kentucky; Bas told me so."

"Maybe so, but Bas has always had money . . ."

"Aye, and it hasn't spoiled him, now has it? Bas grew up with brass; you'll just have to learn to get used to it."

He took out his tobacco pouch, inspected the contents, then pushed it back in his pocket.

"By the way, Gracie, it's been a while since Bas was here. He doesn't come as often as he once did.

Has he got himself caught, then, leaving the camp without a pass?"

Jack Catchpole had become used to the regular tins of tobacco Bas brought. He was missing them now.

"Nothing like that. When he first got here, you see, the airfield wasn't operational. Bas was with the advance party, and things were quite relaxed. But now the bombers are there and they're flying ops — *missions* — all the time. They do their bombing in the daylight. It's been on the news."

"Ar. Hitler'll be wondering what's hitting him these days. The Americans bombing him by day and our lads bombing him at night. Getting a bit of his own back now, but serves him right for starting it in the first place!"

"We-e-ll, talking about Bas — I wonder if I could put in a bit of extra time next week? I'd come in earlier, if you like, and see to the boiler and light the potting shed fire. Or I could stay half an hour late each night, if that's all right with you? Bas has a pass for next weekend — legitimate — and I'd be really grateful if I could have Saturday afternoon off."

"Coming next weekend, is he?" Catchpole's face broke into a wrinkled smile. "Well, he's alus welcome in my garden, tell him. And as for working extra — there isn't a lot we can do this time of the year, the ground being cold and wet. You'm welcome to Saturday off, the whole day, if that's what you'd like."

"Like it! Oh, *thanks*, Mr Catchpole." Pink-cheeked with delight she wrapped her arms around his neck, kissing him soundly. "You're an old darling, you really are! Tea in ten minutes!"

And with that she was off, happy as a skylark, he thought, touching his cheek in amazement. Bless my soul, what next, he chuckled, thinking she smelled like a peach that grew against the walls, all warm and soft from the sun — even though it was February.

"Eeeeh," he sighed, heading for the potting shed, thinking with pleasure that when young Bas came next week, his tobacco pouch would be full again! War or no war, life had its compensations.

Daisy and Drew sat in the foyer at the Adelphi Hotel, glad to be out of the wind that whipped the Mersey into white horses.

"Glad I'm not at sea," Drew grinned.

"Mm. Times like this I'm glad it's fuggy in the teleprinter room. The cabins at Hellas House are freezing. Roll on spring!"

"Can't come too soon, eh? How many weeks to go?"

"Eight — and twenty hours! As soon as it's April, I'm going to start crossing the days off like I used to before Christmas, when I was little."

"Do you realize Mother was right? She always said that Keth would be home; that she would take another photograph of the Clan together again.

Some photograph! Everybody in their wedding finery and the sun shining!"

"Mm. I go all goose pimply just thinking about it. Did you know the Ministry of Food allows extra rations for weddings? Not a lot, mind, but Mam said that at least there'll be sandwiches to hand round, even if there can't be a cake. Mam said Tilda was ever so piqued that there'll be a wedding at Rowangarth, and no real 'do' to follow it.

"But if there hadn't been food rationing and all the shortages, we could have had the best reception ever. Gallons of champagne and be blowed to the expense. All that money I've got, I mean. I could have paid for the reception and Mam and Dada needn't have worried about it."

"I keep forgetting your money, Daiz. You never mention it these days."

"What's the use? I have no clothing coupons, and food is rationed and wine and spirits hardly exist — nor jewellery. And no pots and pans nor curtains nor carpets. Nothing in the shops. I remember Dada telling me not to write too many cheques when I got my cheque book, the day I was twenty-one. He'd be glad to know how well I'm doing. Now not a word to Mam and Polly, but on my next crafty weekend we're all going to Morris and Page."

"That snooty shop you used to work in?"

"The same! And I shall take that cheque book and buy them both a really nice wedding hat. Mind, I'll have to be careful when I write the cheque. Polly still doesn't know about the money, though I'm determined to spend some of it. But can we order? I'm ravenous. I suppose it's thinking about the wedding that makes me so hungry."

"Ravenous? You sounded like Lyn then. She was always starving. How is she, by the way?"

"She's fine," said Daisy hastily. "And I've just remembered!" *Change the subject!* "Auntie Blod is going out to Kenya just as soon as she can get a passage. Lyn's father has asked her to marry him. She said yes, of course! Isn't it lovely and isn't it rather sad too, Auntie Blod waiting all those years for him, I mean?"

"Like Uncle Nathan, waiting for Mother? That was sad."

"Mm. By the way, Drew." Deliberately she concentrated on the menu. "You know Lyn can't be bridesmaid after all, so I've written to ask Kitty if she'll step in. She's the same size and height as Lyn and it's a pity to waste a dress after Mam went to the bother of altering it. Trouble is, Kitty hasn't written back yet."

"She won't have. She's touring for two weeks. I miss not ringing her when we're alongside, Daiz. I wish she were still based in Liverpool. And why can't Lyn be bridesmaid? I thought she was looking forward to it."

"Y-yes, we-e-ll — it isn't so easy now, getting time off. If she were just a telephonist there'd be more chance of swopping her leave around, but the other leading Wrens don't seem keen to change with her.

And I think I'll have American fritters, please, though I suppose it'll really be fried Spam. What are you having — fish?"

"Suppose so. Where are you having your honeymoon, or shouldn't I ask?"

"D'you know, Drew, we haven't got around to talking about it, for some reason or other. There aren't a lot of places we can go. The seaside is out — all that barbed wire on the beaches, and even minefields in some places. I suppose we could go to Winchester. We stayed at a super hotel when I went there to see the solicitors about getting my money."

She lapsed into dreaming then about seeing Beck Lane just once more, and the little red-brick house she was born in, and Willow End where Keth had lived; Morgan and Beth's grave, too.

"The bluebells should be flowering in Beck Lane in April."

"Bluebells?" He wondered what bluebells had to do with honeymoons.

"Bluebells," she smiled, cheeks pinking. "Sort of special for Keth and me."

And though Drew still did not understand, not another word of explanation would she offer about the place where bluebells chimed.

Lovely, long-ago Beck Lane, where she and Keth grew up, she thought yearningly; the place lovers returned to.

Winchester! Why hadn't she thought of it before?

CHAPTER
TWENTY-ONE

Kitty sat barefoot at Sparrow's kitchen table, her pretty pink toes wriggling with delight as she sorted letters into piles. From Drew — by far the largest pile — from her parents in Kentucky, from her brother at Burtonwood Airfield and from Daisy in Liverpool. Just one from Daisy, and written in a haze of happiness, she shouldn't wonder.

"Just look at all those letters, Sparrow! Gee, but it's great to be home! The more I'm on the road, the more I love coming back to Montpelier! And could I have a bath, please?" A real bath, she meant; not one taken standing in ankle-deep water behind a flimsy curtain. "And I've just *got* to get my hair trimmed and washed and my nails need doing and isn't that Tatty? Hi, Tatty! I'm home!" she called as the door banged.

Home! Sparrow grumbled silently. The house was like a bear garden already, the well-ordered peace shattered. Kitty came into the place like a wind blowing off the river and her smile was like the sun coming out from behind clouds. Small wonder Drew was besotted by her. "Do you want your supper now, or a bath?" she sniffed.

386

"Supper, please." Kitty jumped to her feet as Tatiana came in, holding wide her arms, hugging her.

"So what's news, Kitty?" Tatiana was always glad when her cousin was back. "I've missed you, by the way."

"Not half as much as I've missed you and Sparrow and my nice soft bed! And guess what? Bas and Gracie are engaged, though Gracie still won't name the day."

"I know. Aunt Julia told us last night. And Gracie has got one of Great-Grandmother's rings; a garnet one — so it's official. Aunt Julia is really pleased about it. She likes Gracie a lot."

"We all do. And okay, I'll shift this lot out of your way," Kitty smiled, as Sparrow hovered with tablecloth and cutlery. "In fact I'll read Drew's letters later when I'm in bed, I think. Right now, I'm starving. What's for supper?"

"Woolton pie and stewed plums." Sparrow opened one of her precious bottles of Victoria plums only on special occasions and the return of Kitty Sutton to the little mews house was special. "And there's custard, an' all. I managed to sweetheart a drop extra from the milkman."

"How was your day, Sparrow?" Tatiana asked when they had said grace and unfolded their serviettes. "Found any exciting queues?"

Queuing was becoming an occupation. On a good day, a dedicated hunter could return with a piece of fish, two tomatoes, and an orange; the orange, if she had a child's ration book that was. Oranges, when there were any to sell, were saved for children.

On a very good day, of course, there might even be five cigarettes at the end of a long wait, or a small amount of pipe tobacco. Sparrow did not smoke, but she always took the cigarettes, sharing them between the milkman and the nice barrow boy who let her have apples, when he had them, and cabbages, fresh from Covent Garden.

"Nah. Never went out this morning. My own fault, mind. I got listening to a talk on the wireless. Ever so interesting."

"So tell us," Kitty demanded.

"Well — it seems that this time we're really going to have a country fit to live in when this war's over. Homes for heroes, and all that stuff. Mind, that's what Lloyd George promised last time, but they threw them heroes on the scrap heap after the Armistice — no jobs, no nothink!"

"But mightn't it be different this time?" Tatiana offered.

"Seems it's going to be. We're going to be what they'll call a social state when it's over and done with. A bloke called Beveridge is working on it. Men coming back from the Forces will go to the top of the queue for a house, and there's going to be a free medical service. No more doctors' bills. Poor people will be able to be ill and it won't cost them a penny; not even if they has to go into hospital, it seems. And free false teeth and spectacles! You wouldn't believe it! I got so tied up listening to it that I clean forgot to go out queuing! Mind, it's nice of somebody to think of it, but it would never work."

"It might," Tatiana frowned. "It would be wonderful if they at least gave it a try." Tim would have been pleased about free doctors. Hadn't he once said his granny died because she couldn't afford to pay the doctor to call?

"Wonderful. I'll grant you that," Sparrow sighed. "And I'm sure that poor people and old people would be glad of it. But will someone tell me," she demanded mournfully, "which poor bleeders are going to pay for it all, because there's nothing for nothing in this world. Never was. Never will be. So who's for plums and custard? Victorias come all the way here from Rowangarth — what more could you want?"

Free spectacles and false teeth that fitted, supplied a small voice inside her. Ever so nice, that would be. Yet more to the point, she supposed, was the fact that people using too much gas and electricity were to be prosecuted according to the newspapers, and that cuts in the clothing coupon allowance had been announced.

"Who wants to scrape out the custard jug?" she beamed, tired of dismal thoughts. "And then help me wash and dry the dishes!"

"Well! Now there's a turn up for the book! Guess what?" Kitty glanced up from one of her letters. "Daisy says that her friend Lyndis can't be bridesmaid after all and would I mind standing in for her? She says she and I are the same height and shape, roughly, so how about it?"

"I think it's a great idea." Tatiana knew the reason for Lyn's refusal. "Hope you'll be able to get time off."

"Hope so too because I'd just love to be there. Daisy says there's a dress, so that's no problem."

"There are two. Daisy's mother made them from ball gowns Mother didn't want. Well, no one gets dressed up for dances these days and it seemed a shame, all those yards and yards hanging there doing nothing. They look lovely. Mrs Dwerryhouse has made a really good job of them. I'm wearing the rose-coloured one and the other is pale blue. Do say yes, Kitty."

"You bet I will! Daisy says Drew is going to be Keth's best man. A dummy run, she says, for our own wedding, and when are we going to get on with it?"

"And when are you?" Tatiana plumped up her pillows, then lay back, hands behind head. "If I were in your position, Tim and I would have been married long ago. D'you know, when I knew that two of our bombers from Holdenby Moor had been shot down that night, I was frantic. The telephone lines were down and I couldn't get through to the aerodrome. So I made a vow — a bargain with God, really — that if Tim was all right, then I'd run away to Scotland and marry him there. You can get married in Scotland, you know, before you are twenty-one, without your father's permission."

"But it wasn't to be. Poor old love," Kitty said softly. "I feel awful, y'know, being this happy when you are so sad and alone. I try real hard not to come out with things that would upset you. I wouldn't hurt you for anything, Tatty."

"I know. And things are getting better now. Mind, I could be like Aunt Julia and wait years and years but I think I won't ever get married. Bill has helped a lot. At least I don't go hysterical now when I see an RAF uniform or hear a bomber fly over."

"But mightn't you and Bill get serious one day?" Kitty was happy and wanted Tatty to be happy too.

"No. But we are friends — special friends — and I like him a lot. He's in hospital now. There's a chance he might be able to get his sight back but it seems there's quite a bit of healing still to do before they can operate. He's near Cambridge, and not too far away. I plan to visit him next weekend."

"Well, I think you're an absolute brick. I'm glad you've grown up. You were real spoiled as a kid. The Clan had to plead with your Mom to let you come to play without your nanny. Always hovering, that nanny!"

"Well, I've severed the umbilical cord. I suppose you know Denniston House is mine, but I won't ever live there unless Grandmother Petrovska goes back to Cheyne Walk when the war's over. I'll bet Mother is glad, really, that she's got to do war work. At least it gets her out of the house. She likes having money she's earned herself. Grandmother thinks it's all wrong that Mother and Dr Pryce should work so closely together. She thinks they should have a chaperon, I'm sure of it!"

"*Wha-a-t?*" Kitty yelled. "Doesn't she know that chaperons went out with the dodo?"

"Not the Petrovska, though she isn't as bitter about those Bolsheviks who kicked her lot out of Russia. Think she's quite proud of the way they stood up to Hitler, even if there are ten families of them living in her precious house now."

"Mm. Guess I'd hate it if someone took the stud off us. I sometimes have to think real hard to realize I'm never going back there — well, only to visit. Rowangarth will be my home when we're married."

"But you'll like that, won't you? And Kentucky isn't all that far away — well not when the liners and flying boats get going again. And had you thought? Gracie will be going to Kentucky to live."

"Yup. It'll be a bit of a wrench for her. But Mom will be real pleased to have her and she'll be able to fuss over her and not miss me so much. And we can always have Clan reunions like before. We'll soon sort something out, Tatty. All I want is to marry Drew and have this war over and done with."

"Then why don't you have the banns called? Wouldn't it be lovely if Uncle Nathan did the first calling the day after the wedding, on the eighteenth?"

"Then I'll tell you something, Tatty — if you promise not to get upset. We *will* be married quite soon. Mom sent me a wedding dress from back home, only she didn't tell me she'd posted it just in case it got sunk on the way over."

"And it's arrived?"

"It's at Rowangarth, hanging in the sewing room with Daisy's. Aunt Julia won't tell me what it's like, except that it's lovely."

"Then Gracie and I will be your bridesmaids, Kitty. We'll wear the rose and blue dresses again," Tatty said matter-of-factly. "You couldn't make it June, could you? Everything is so lovely at Rowangarth then. Heaps of roses, and very light nights."

"Oh dear. I think I'm going to cry — you being so lovely about everything, I mean." She reached for Tatty's hands and held them tightly. "Tell you what — let's always stay together — the Clan, I mean. When we've forgotten all about this war, let's still meet, even when we're old. The Suttons are such special people. I'm glad I'm one and I'm glad I'll still be a Sutton when Drew and me are married.

"And don't feel too hurt at Keth and Daisy's wedding, will you, Tatty? Because if you feel like running away from all the happiness, come and tell me and I'll understand, honest I will."

And Tatty said, "Thanks. If it gets too much, I will. And d'you know what? I'm glad I'm a Sutton too."

Down below, from where she sat in the kitchen rocker, Sparrow heard their chattering and smiled into the fireglow, as if the answer to the question she wanted to ask would be written there, clear and bold.

But it wasn't, because she wanted to know when the war would end, and how many of the precious Clan would come safely home. And more than precious they were to her, for she had known them all from childhood and loved them like her own.

And they *would* be all right! Nothing could, *dare*, happen to any one of them because Rowangarth had paid in full last time. That last hideous war took both Rowangarth's sons and the lovely doctor, too. God couldn't let anything so awful happen again — could he?

She threw a log into the kitchen grate, dulling the glow, sending sparks snapping up the chimney. Pictures in the fire indeed! Angry for even allowing such thoughts, she opened wide the staircase door and called, "The water's good and hot now for baths! And only six inches, mind! There's a war on, don't forget!" She clumped back to her chair and started it rocking furiously.

As if anyone in her right mind could forget there was a war on!

Keth lay on his bed, hands behind head, wishing he had a wireless to help relieve the silence. The small bare room seemed even smaller with no one to share it.

Immediately dinner was over he had booked a call to Liverpool, then blocked open the door with his slippers so he should hear the ringing of the phone at the end of the corridor outside.

Today, he brooded, they were told of enormous shipping losses in the Atlantic which could not be allowed to continue. Recently, a slow-moving convoy had been mauled almost to pieces. Twenty-one ships sunk in the space of twelve hours was not acceptable. Mr Churchill made his feelings about it very plain, because Intelligence had disclosed that Hitler was known to have told a contingent of wounded soldiers from the Russian Front to take heart. Soon, he promised them, the Fatherland's top-secret weapon would be in action; a weapon so deadly that the outcome of the war in Germany's favour could never be doubted.

It was most urgent, the Bletchley boffins were told, as if hitherto unaware of the importance of their work, that signals passing in code between German submarines in the Atlantic should be broken. The winning of the war depended on it.

They must concentrate too on signals gathered in from the airwaves around Peenemünde. Such a name, Keth recalled thinking, had its advantages. It held a surfeit of the vowel "e", and "e" was the most common letter in use. It could be picked out from a pointless jumble because of it. That vowel was the point at which code-breakers began. Peenemünde, on the shores of the Baltic: what was happening there of such importance?

He reached for the envelope on the locker beside him. Better by far to read Daisy's letter again and again than dwell too much on the frustrations of each unbroken code. Soon, he hoped, the machine so many had died for would be copied and reproduced; only then would U-boat signals be read as easily as those of the Luftwaffe and the Wehrmacht.

My darling Keth,

Today has been clear and bright — the brighter for knowing that 17 April is one day nearer. I love you.

Had you thought about Winchester for our honeymoon? The bluebells should be flowering in Beck Lane in April. I love you, love you.

Saw Drew last night. He's fine and sends best wishes. He's missing Kitty a lot. I think they will be next down the aisle. I love you and want you so much.

The telephone began to ring. Keth ran down the passage to snatch it from the wall.

"Your call to Liverpool, Captain Purvis." Such mundane, magic words.

"Lark Lane 1322. Dwerryhouse." As if she had been sitting on the bottom stair, waiting, Daisy was at the other end of the line.

"Darling! It's me and I love you!"

"Love you too, Keth."

"Winchester sounds marvellous. I'm nearer there than you are. Why don't I book it from the eighteenth?"

"What about the seventeenth?"

"York suit you — the Station Hotel? Shall we have the bridal suite for one night — live dangerously and passionately?"

"Fine by me! By the way, I love you. I keep on saying it, don't I?"

"Don't ever dare stop! What are you wearing now?"

"Pyjamas and dressing gown and I've just washed my hair. It's still wet."

"I adore you with wet hair. And don't even *think* of bringing pyjamas on our honeymoon!"

"I won't. By the way, I love you."

"What was that? Speak up, that Wren!"

"I said I love you," she yelled, not caring that the entire hostel could hear her. She wanted them to know; wanted the whole world to know.

"And I love you. Take care of yourself."

The pips were interrupting. Three minutes gone and tonight the operator wasn't going to offer them three minutes more.

The line went dead and Keth gazed smiling at the receiver for several seconds before replacing it, because for so short a time that black, impersonal thing had held Daisy's voice.

Me take care, he thought. So what could happen in the back-room quiet of rows and rows of ordinary huts?

"Nothing!" he said out loud to the photograph at his bedside. "And by the way, Wren Dwerryhouse, I love you — just in case you didn't know!"

All at once the drab, empty room was a good place to be. In just a few weeks, he and Daisy would be married. What else mattered?

"It isn't right!" Alice jabbed a finger at the offending column in the newspaper. "Taxing folks' simple pleasures, just to pay for this war! Take a look at that!"

Tom picked up the paper as commanded, because when Alice jabbed a finger, you took notice!

The Chancellor of the Exchequer needed a hundred million pounds, it would seem, without having to increase income tax. Alice was right. What better, then, than to tax things people wanted least to do without?

The price of beer increased to an astronomical fifteen pence a pint; cigarettes to cost two shillings and fourpence for twenty; three pence on cinema seats and a shilling on theatre seats. And whisky was to go up to one pound, five shillings and sixpence! Now *that* was a laugh, because he would gladly pay that much for a few bottles for Daisy's wedding. Trouble was, there was little whisky to be had anywhere!

"He's laying it on a bit thick." Tom couldn't deny it. "This war has got to be paid for, though."

"Then let them pay that started it!" Alice was peevishly glad she neither smoked nor drank whisky and rarely went to the theatre. "As if I haven't enough on my mind without having to bother about what the Government is up to!"

398

"Then if I were you, bonny lass, I'd leave the worrying to the Government, and concentrate on things nearer home."

Tom knew Alice in all her moods and how best to sidetrack her. Wedding talk, up until the seventeenth of next month, at least, could be guaranteed to drive even what the newspapers printed out of her mind!

"Y-yes, I suppose so, though how I'm to provide enough sandwiches, much less the sit-down I'd always planned Daisy should have, is beyond me." A niggardly amount of margarine, butter, sugar and tea — that was all they were to be allowed towards a wedding reception. You'd think the people at the Ministry of Food had been asked to donate the extra from their own personal rations! Only three weeks to go, and so much still to do.

Thank heaven she had Daisy's wedding dress and the bridesmaids' dresses back at Keeper's Cottage once more. Now, when she lost patience with the war, all she had to do was climb the stairs and see them and touch them to make her feel better, even though in September the war would enter its fifth year. And how many years more it was going to take after that be blowed if Alice Dwerryhouse knew!

It wasn't just Hitler to be sorted, she reasoned. When he was finished with there would still be the Japanese to settle, and they occupying most of the Far East. And what was so awful was the way they had laughed, and called Japanese soldiers funny, short-sighted little fellows, though now everyone knew differently.

Japanese soldiers fought like madmen and preferred death to surrender. The war, Alice was forced to admit, could go on for ten years, with Daisy nigh on thirty before the Wrens finished with her! Unless, of course, she and Keth decided to start a family right away. The Wrens would soon send her home then!

How lovely, in all the turmoil of this war, to have a grandchild, Alice yearned. Mind, baby clothes were hard to come by. Clothing coupons must be surrendered even for essentials such as nappies. And as for prams — well, a mother-to-be had to get her name down pretty sharpish for one of those and a right rickety thing it would be when eventually she got it. Not a bit like the perambulator she had bought for Daisy. A pram of that magnificence, Alice reasoned, could not be bought now for love nor money, and it as good as new in an attic at Rowangarth!

Good as new! So what was to prevent Daisy using it for her own children? A little old-fashioned it may be, but sound and solid and craftsman-made, and with a shine on the bodywork to proclaim its pedigree, even twenty-three years on.

Alice's broodings became reality, almost, and she was pushing that pram again along the lane to West Welby village to phone Julia. And Daisy inside it as bonny a bairn as ever you did see!

"And what, all of a sudden, have you found to smile about?" Tom's words crashed into her daydreaming.

"Oh — nothing. Just women's thoughts . . ."

"Wedding thoughts?"

"Happen, though I was thinking, if you must know, that it's a crying shame that prams and cots and even babies' potties are hard to come by now."

Grandchildren! So that was what Alice was thinking about! A natural enough progression, he supposed, from weddings, according to a woman's way of thinking! Not content with seeing Daisy wed at last, now Alice wanted grandchildren about the place!

"I think, bonny lass," he said softly, because it was difficult to keep the smile from his face, "that things like prams and potties — *and grandchildren* — are best left to Daisy and Keth, don't you?"

"Well, of course they are," she said indignantly. "As if I'd ever dream of interfering! But when they do get around to it, Tom, there's a grand pram at Rowangarth that no amount of money could buy today, had you thought?"

And Tom was obliged to say that he hadn't, and reached for her and held her close because it was an amazing thing that he loved his Alice every bit as much as on the day they were wed, all those years ago.

"Had *you* thought," he smiled, "that you and me are going to have to be thinking about our silver wedding before so very much longer?"

"It is amazing how cheering a little good news is," Olga Petrovska said as she sat with her daughter in the conservatory at Denniston House, gazing into the twilight.

"Good news?" Anna was always grateful for even the smallest uplifting of her mother's spirits.

"The paper said that Stalin is claiming over a million dead Germans since Hitler invaded Russia."

"He's probably exaggerating. It's probably only half that number, though half a million is a lot of young men!"

Anna was grateful that this far, Tatiana had escaped injury, or worse, in the London bombing. She could not share her mother's delight because to her way of thinking, it didn't do to tempt Fate.

"Yes. It is sad that Stalin's son has died in a prisoner-of-war camp. Do you suppose he died of natural causes?"

"Most likely. Stalin's son would be worth more alive than dead to the Nazis. But I'm surprised you show sympathy. I thought you disliked Stalin."

"I dislike all Bolsheviks, but I am a mother and I too know what it is like to lose a son — yes, and a husband. Poor Peter; poor Basil. I wonder if those godless Bolsheviks gave them a decent burial. I doubt it . . ."

"Please, Mama — let's not talk about such things? We lit candles for their souls — we still do. We can do no more. And isn't it splendid news that Tatiana will be home for three days for the wedding?"

"Splendid indeed. Your daughter, Anna Petrovska, can find time enough for her friend's wedding, but rarely visits otherwise. But that is the young for you!"

"Tatiana is on war work, Mama. I'm proud of her. She has stood up to the bombing very well. She gets very little time off and what time she does get she is entitled to spend as she wishes." Anna's words were softly spoken, but their impact was not lost on the Countess.

"I suppose," she shrugged, "it will be pleasant for once, seeing her dressed as befits her station in life. She is the granddaughter of a count. If we were still in St Petersburg she would go to balls and have made her curtsey to the Czarina and be married and have children in the nursery."

"If we were still in Petersburg, Tatiana would not have been born. Now, what will you wear to the wedding?" Anna changed the subject with a firmness her mother had come, recently, to recognize. "Promise you won't wear black?"

"I am still in mourning for —"

"No! It is twenty-five years since the Czar died! Even the Romanovs who survived have long been out of mourning! Why not wear your grey silk? You could lighten it with lavender or mauve — they are both secondary mourning colours," she hastened. "And I'm sure Julia will be able to loan you a pretty hat; Lady Helen had a great many, and they are all there still."

"Olga Petrovska does not wear borrowed hats! I have hats of my own!"

"Yes! *Black* hats!" Anna was losing patience. "And you will *not* go to Daisy's wedding in a black hat! I mean it, Mama!"

"You have become very bossy, Anna Petrovska, since you joined the working classes!"

"You think so?" The thought pleased her.

"I do indeed! You have far too many opinions! Women should not have opinions!"

"But this is 1943! We are at war. Daisy is in the armed forces, Tatiana and Kitty are on war work, and Gracie too! Women are liberated now!" And not before time, she thought, though she had the good sense not to say it.

"Yes! Liberated to march and salute like men! They'll be wearing trousers next!"

"Women wear trousers all the time! What is so wrong in that?"

"Trousers are for men! Women should act prettily and wear ball gowns and —"

"And women — girls — would look completely ridiculous on a gun site or being a conductress on a bus or helping to make planes in *ball gowns*! Oh, Mama — if only you would try to move with the times and not live so much in the past, you wouldn't be so unhappy. Couldn't you find something to do to help? Your own daughter is very happy working in a surgery. I see people less fortunate than myself there every day of the week. And Ewart is a considerate man to work for. He is glad of my help and is kind enough to tell me so! It is nice to be appreciated. Elliot never gave me one word of praise!"

She stopped, horrified, because not since the day the earth covered his coffin had she allowed herself to speak his name.

404

"So you still think of that monster," Olga Petrovska hissed.

"Very rarely!" Anna took a deep breath, fighting for control. "I don't know what made me speak of him!"

Yet she did know. She compared him often to Ewart Pryce, who was charming and kind. She had shut men out of her life the morning the body of her husband was covered with a blanket and taken away. Never again, she vowed, would a man be allowed to humiliate her. Never would she allow herself to love. Not that what she had felt for Pendenys's heir was love. She knew now that it was the need to be taken; be rid of her virginity.

Yet Elliot had not taken her in love. She knew on her wedding night she was to be the provider of a son and she had failed Pendenys. Even while she carried Nicholas, Elliot was unable to keep away from women. Natasha Yurovska was seduced by him; sent away in disgrace to have his child — his *illegitimate* child — and Natasha was probably only one of many. How many by-blows had Elliot Sutton fathered?

"Nor I. But you were eager for him," said the Countess, tight-lipped. "There was nothing Igor nor I could do about it."

"There was, Mama. Igor did not like him, but you wanted me to make a suitable match and Clementina Sutton needed a title in the family! But it's over and done with! I'm older and much, much wiser." And attractive though she found Ewart

Pryce, she would never again let her heart rule her head! "And it's getting dark. I'll see to the blackouts, then make a pot of tea. I think the rations will run to it."

"I would like that." Olga Petrovska's good humour returned, for there was still the picture of Adolf Hitler and his lick-spittle Mussolini in the morning paper to gloat over, the German leader's face showing signs of strain because of defeats in Russia. She was pleased about that.

She shifted her gaze to the window to look towards Holdenby Pike and the setting sun. It made her think of sunsets in St Petersburg; of trees silhouetted against a flame-coloured sky and the River Neva afire with scarlet. And she knew she would give much to stand at the window of her first-floor salon and see it just once more.

"*Tcha!*" She shook her head free of such thoughts, because she knew she could never go back there. Those who had found favour with the Czar, God-rest-him, were no longer welcome in Mother Russia. And anyway, her beautiful house on the banks of the Neva was probably a heap of rubble now!

Julia wriggled herself comfortable on the hearthrug at her husband's feet, knowing she should draw the blackout curtains, reluctant to do so because a perfect April day had given way to a beautiful sunset and she wanted not to have to shut it out.

"Isn't it splendid," she smiled, "that Drew is getting leave for the wedding? And Kitty has just come back from a long tour so surely she'll be in London for a while."

"Knowing Kitty, she'll get here somehow," Nathan smiled comfortably. "She's going to be bridesmaid, don't forget. Pity Daisy's friend couldn't make it. I thought she was a nice girl, what little I saw of her."

"She won't be coming because it's my opinion she was very fond of Drew and I don't suppose she'll want to meet Kitty."

"*That* fond? Are you sure?"

"Daisy is. She told Alice that Lyndis was very cut up when Drew and Kitty got engaged. It was a shock all round, come to think of it."

"But you're glad about them?" Nathan probed.

"You know I am! Kitty's a delight. She and Drew will be perfect together. They'll have beautiful children."

"I think you should let them get down the aisle first. They aren't in any hurry, it would seem."

"Maybe not. But wait until Kitty sees that gorgeous wedding dress! I'd lay odds they'll be married before the summer is out. Imagine," Julia sighed, "a June wedding . . ."

"What is it that gets into a woman the minute she scents a wedding? You and Alice have been full of it ever since Keth got back home! And it won't end there, will it?"

"I'm sure I don't know what you mean," Julia said huffily.

"Yes you do. First Daisy, then Drew. And after that there'll be no peace for anyone till Bas and Gracie are married as well!"

"And Tilda!"

"Tilda! How could I have forgotten her? I take it her sergeant is still keen?"

"Oh my word, yes. But that ring is still on the wrong hand! I've often thought how good it would be if Tilda stayed on as our cook when she's married and Sydney worked with Catchpole when the war is over. He gets on very well with Jack."

"Julia! One wedding at a time! And I'm surprised you haven't mentioned it before now — had you realized that the Clan will be together again on the seventeenth?"

"Sssssh! I haven't said it out loud because I didn't want to tempt Fate. Don't think I haven't thought about it, because I have — and I cross my fingers every time I do!

"But if you hear in the village of anyone willing to give a few hours' help in the house, let me know, Nathan?" She reached for a cigarette, mentally blessing Sebastian, inhaling deeply. "There'll be Kitty and Bas staying, and Drew, and I'm trying to persuade Sparrow to travel up with Tatty. She's practically one of the family, yet she's never seen Rowangarth. And Keth will have to sleep here the night before the wedding, because he can't stay at the bothy and he can't have Alice's spare room because Daisy will be home, and they can't meet on the day of the wedding."

She drew deeply on her cigarette, blowing out smoke in little puffs, all the while making mental calculations.

"It's going to mean extra work for Tilda and Mary, and they'll want time to themselves for the wedding."

"Then ask Ellen, why don't you? She always helps out and she knows the ropes here. Don't forget she was Rowangarth's parlourmaid before Mary's time. She might be hurt if you didn't ask her."

"You're right, darling!" Ellen, who was now mistress of Home Farm kitchen with grandchildren of her own. So long ago, it seemed, Ellen trained up Mary before she left to get married. "That's one problem solved, anyway. I do hope it doesn't rain on the day!"

"Why should it? And might I say, Mrs Sutton, that it's Daisy's wedding we are talking about. You aren't interfering too much, are you — offending Alice, I mean?"

"Of course I'm not! Alice and I have always shared things, good and bad. I've had a share in Daisy just as Alice has shared Drew with me. Alice is the sister I never had and there were times when I don't know what I'd have done without her."

"And times, sweetheart, when she needed you just as much," Nathan said softly.

"Celverte, you mean?"

"Celverte. I married Giles and Alice, don't forget, in the convent chapel. Did you ever think, on that day, that you and I would be married or that Tom would come back from the dead?"

"Never. Yet here we are, all of us happy." She reached up to clasp his hand. "Sometimes I think that I'm too happy and that something awful will happen, because of it."

"But why should it, you foolish woman? Goodness — if everyone thought like that, life would be pretty miserable, wouldn't it? Life is full of ups and downs; it's the way things are! Now for goodness' sake, give Ellen a ring! They're well over lambing now at Home Farm and she'll be pleased to be asked."

"I'll do that, then I think we'll have a drop of the Bourbon Bas brought us. It's amazing, isn't it, that Bourbon actually originated in Bourbon County, in Kentucky?"

"What amazes *me*," Nathan laughed, "is the amount of things he's able to get. You don't think the young devil is in the black market, do you?"

"Of course not! It's just that Uncle Sam sees to it that American troops overseas don't go short. Bas has grown up into such a fine young man. Wouldn't it have been terrible if Keth hadn't been there that afternoon to get him out of that fire at Pendenys?"

"But Keth *was* there. He was probably meant to be, so stop your worrying! Ring Home Farm, whilst I pour."

410

"You're right. You usually are! And did I ever tell you, vicar, what a very comforting person you are to have around?" In the doorway she turned, smiling, loving him. "And since it's courtesy of Uncle Sam, make mine a big one, will you?"

CHAPTER
TWENTY-TWO

"So that's it!" Daisy closed her suitcase. "All packed and ready. Let's hope there are no hiccups this time."

"Hiccups! Listen, that Wren! You are going home to be married tomorrow. Your bloke will be waiting at York, but if he isn't, you'll get the train to Holdenby Halt, where he *will* be there to meet you!"

"Don't say things like that, Lyn. What if they cancel his leave? What if he's halfway across the Atlantic at this very moment? I won't believe any of it till I've got that ring on my finger!"

"Check! You've got the ring, haven't you?"

"I've got it." Daisy unfastened the top two buttons of her shirt, pulling out the chain on which hung the wedding ring Keth had brought back from Washington. The *first* time!

"Right! Now listen!" Lyn placed her hands on Daisy's shoulders. "And look at me when I'm talking to you! Keth *will* be at the church! Tomorrow, you'll be at Keeper's Cottage and the next day, Kitty and Bas and Tatty will arrive, and Mrs Sparrow!"

"No. Just Sparrow — Mrs Emily Smith, really," Daisy said, her voice wobbly.

"Well, anyway, the Clan will be together again after God knows how long, and Gracie and Catchpole will be busy with flowers and your mother running around in a tizzy. It'll be wonderful, Daisy, and I wish with all my heart I was getting that train with you!"

"I know you do, and I'm sorry. It's my fault that you met Drew. I wish you hadn't, truly I do."

"I wouldn't have missed one minute of it! We almost made it, Drew and me. It was just one of those things, old love. Now what say we go downstairs, get some grub, then go for a walk in the park. It's a lovely evening!"

"Or we could walk down to the pub in Lark Lane," Daisy brightened. "They might find us a drop of under-the-counter gin if we tell them we're having a hen party!"

"Some hopes! Some hen party!" Lyn laughed, all at once in control of her emotions. "But I'll tell you what, let's be devils. Let's skip supper and go into town and see what they've got to offer at the Adelphi. Live dangerously!"

"And risk running into Drew? The *Maggie* might be alongside. She's due in. Drew's coming to the wedding, so she's got to be."

"Not due till late tonight. Had it from my friend the despatch rider. She still tells me Drew's movements. I haven't the heart to tell her it's all off. Life's a bitch, isn't it?"

"Not today it isn't! Tell you what, Lyn — you remember I came into some money when I was twenty-one?"

"I remember, you lucky so-and-so! A thousand pounds, wasn't it?"

"Y-yes . . . Well, when I was last home I bought Mam and Polly their wedding hats, and money no object! It was almost the first time I'd been able to spend any of it, things being what they are. So why don't we have a slap-up meal on me, and be blowed to the expense? I bet you anything that Drew and Bas and Keth'll be having a stag night on Friday, so why shouldn't you and me have a hen party?"

"Why not — if you're sure you can afford it, Daisy."

"Of course I can! And we'll tell that nice waiter I'm getting married on Saturday and I'm sure he'll find some wine under the counter for us. So is it on then — a skylark ashore?"

"It's on! We'll paint Liverpool red — well, pink round the edges," Lyn laughed. And if Drew Sutton's ship docked earlier than they'd thought, if he just happened to decide to spend the night at the Adelphi Hotel as he very often did and if they just weren't able to avoid him — then what the heck?

She wanted — *needed* — to see him. It would hurt like hell and pretending she didn't give a damn would make it a whole lot worse. And just to rub salt in, she would ask about Kitty and demand to know when they were getting married. She wanted to see him so desperately that it would be worth all

414

the pain. She would put on an Oscar-winning performance, and smile as she did it!

"It'll be funny, you being Purvis when you come back," she said, her voice surprisingly nonchalant.

"It'll be wonderful, Lyn. Just imagine — no one saying, 'Er — Dwerry-*what*? Could you spell it, please?' When I was little it was such a long name when I was learning to spell it and print it out that I longed to be called Smith! Purvis will suit me very nicely! So let's get weaving. We can catch the five o'clock tram to Lime Street if we shift ourselves!"

"But what if Keth rings? You were worried, remember?"

"Well, I'm not worried any more! Like you said, he'll be home! And, Lyn, I do so wish . . ." Wish you were coming to Holdenby with me tomorrow, she had been going to say. "Wish I could tell you how glad I am that Ailsa Seaton put me in Cabin 4A."

And oh, Drew Sutton, much as I love you there are times when I could hit you!

Trouble was, she loved Kitty too . . .

Luck had been with her all the way, Daisy thought, but wasn't this the most important journey of her life; more important even, than the day she travelled to Winchester on her twenty-first birthday to meet Keth in Beck Lane?

She was going home to be married. Keth would be there to meet her, though whether at York or Holdenby Halt she had yet, in her imaginings, to decide. York would be lovely, but on the other hand, she thought as the train left Leeds station almost on time, to have Keth waiting at Holdenby, where once Mam had kissed Dada goodbye and which hadn't changed one bit since, was her most favoured choice.

Keth would not be wearing his uniform, of course. He had bought civilian clothes in America and looked absolutely gorgeous in them. He looked gorgeous in his uniform too. In fact, whichever way she looked at him made her stomach contract. She hoped it always would; hoped they would be like Mam and Dada, who still exchanged calf-eyed looks and kissed sneakily when they thought she wasn't looking.

She placed an elbow on the window-ledge, resting her chin on it. Lambs in the fields; the hawthorn hedges along the track coming into leaf. York in twenty more minutes — provided they didn't have to stop to let another train carrying things more important than passengers thunder past.

Tomorrow, Kitty and Tatty and Sparrow would arrive. Aunt Julia had been saving her petrol coupons so she could meet them at Holdenby, Mam said, though heaven only knew how she was going to fit them into her Baby Austin and all their cases too.

She wondered when Drew would appear. Would he meet up with Bas in Liverpool tomorrow and the two of them travel together, or would Bas hitch a lift all the way? Bas was good at hitching lifts. He did it a lot.

She let go a sigh. Keth *would* be there. She had worried about it until Lyn told her she knew it would all work out just fine. Third time lucky, she insisted.

"Now off you go and have a wonderful time, Dwerryhouse," Lyn smiled as they parted. "I'll think about you both on Saturday and send you my love. The gorgeous Keth will be waiting for you at York, I promise he will!"

But Keth wasn't here, Daisy frowned as she crossed the bridge at York station and made for the side platform at which the Holdenby train always stood, puffing steam. Lyn hadn't got it right. Maybe she'd got it all *wrong* and Keth was on his way to Washington or Sydney or Timbuktu! A wedding arranged, and no bridegroom. Daisy Dwerryhouse, left waiting at the church!

Oh, *please* let him be there at Holdenby Halt.

People all around her were hurrying. Hobnailed army boots clattered over the footbridge; beside the barrier, which she could see now, people waited. Keth wasn't amongst them. Ahead to her left the Holdenby train waited. She turned where the bridge divided, heard a voice calling her name. She stopped, heart thudding.

"Darling!" He was there! He *was*! They hadn't sent him away again!

Then she was in his arms, and people bumping into them and not caring because to see lovers meeting was a happy thing and nobody minded their cases being in the way.

"I thought you'd be at Holdenby." What a stupid thing to say when she really wanted to shout, "I love you, Keth Purvis!" Shout it high into the roof so it echoed all around the station and all of York heard it.

"Just got here, fifteen minutes ago. Been checking up on your train. Should have been home last night, but —"

"But you were busy fighting your way off the Washington plane!" It didn't matter what she said now because he really had come!

"No. We'd best get out of the way," he laughed. "We're causing an upset here."

He picked up the cases and Daisy took their respirators, following him to the Holdenby platform, demanding to know what had delayed him.

"Had to stop overnight in London — see a man."

"What about?" She stopped, taking his arm so he had to stop too and face her. "You're not being drafted again?"

"No, nothing like that. I had to deliver something."

"You're sure?" The tingling was there, at the back of her nose. "What did you deliver?" She didn't trust that lot Keth worked for.

"Papers. Mind-your-own-business papers. Honestly!"

"We-e-ll . . ." she said grudgingly as he picked up the cases again, striding the length of the little train, grunting with satisfaction as he found an empty compartment at the very end of it.

"Now tell me you love me."

418

He heaved the cases on the rack, slammed the door, then opened wide his arms.

"I only love you if you're not going overseas again," she sighed, closing her eyes, parting her lips.

"To the very best of my knowledge, my doubting Daisy, I'm stuck as a boffin Somewhere in England for the duration. Hand on my heart I am!"

"As long as you're staying long enough to marry me, then I'll take your word for it."

"Why shouldn't I be at the church?"

They laughed as the train started with a lurch, flinging them off balance to sprawl on the seat.

"I don't know why exactly," she shrugged, when they had smiled at the Minster as they clanked past it. "It's just, I suppose, that since you got back you've sometimes sounded a little preoccupied. And I know I asked you if anything had happened on the way across and you said it hadn't, but I still get the feeling you aren't telling me everything."

"Idiot!" He kissed the tip of her nose. "I promise you I haven't a care in the world — except that I'll fluff my lines on Saturday."

And I can't ever tell you, my darling, that between leaving Washington and arriving back at the stone house, Clissy happened, and Natasha. I won't ever forget Clissy, because I almost didn't make it home. But maybe one day I'll tell you — when They say I can . . .

"I don't care what you do, as long as you put my ring on the correct finger. It's been hanging round my neck far too long."

"I suppose they've all got wedding fever at Rowangarth."

"Mm, and loving every minute of it. You'll have to sleep at Aunt Julia's, because the dresses are in the spare room at Keeper's. But Bas and Drew will be there too. Lyn said she supposed the three of you will have a bachelors' night out."

"We probably will if we can find any beer." He laid his arm round her shoulders and she snuggled close. "How is Lyn, by the way?"

"Is she getting over Drew, you mean? She says she is, but she'll be a long time forgetting him."

"It'll be good to see Kitty, for all that. Last time I saw her was in Kentucky. She'd just left dance school and so thrilled about landing her first part in a musical. In the chorus line, of course! Her father didn't approve of a Sutton going on the stage, but she could twist him round her little finger."

"Just like she twisted Drew. I wonder when they'll be getting married?"

"There you are! Almost there! Nothing changes," Keth smiled as the engine driver sounded the customary three hoots. "Brattocks Wood any second now. Remember you stood there and waved to me as the train passed? Seems a long time ago."

"It *was* a long time ago; six years! Another life! But you're home now, and we'll be married on Saturday."

"And nothing will stop us this time."

420

He crossed his fingers as he said it for all that, because when there was a war on you lived each day as it came and took nothing for granted.

That much at least he had learned!

CHAPTER
TWENTY-THREE

"Well, that's Kitty and Tatiana and Sparrow arrived," Mary announced. "Didn't realize Sparrow was so little and old. She really is like a chirpy London sparrow."

"She must be nigh on eighty," Tilda considered, "though Miss Julia said no one rightly knows. So what is she doing now?"

"Kitty is showing her the house, then they're going to take a turn in the garden after tea. Those cherry scones smell good, Tilda. Just like old times again."

"Only because Mrs Amelia sent some glacé cherries in one of her food parcels. But today and tomorrow are cherry-scone days. They'll be cool soon, then you can take the trays up. They'll all be ready for a cup of tea."

"Wish her ladyship were here. She always enjoyed afternoon tea in the conservatory. She'd have loved having the family home for the wedding."

"She'll be with us in spirit, Mary. She's never far away. There isn't a day goes by that I don't think of her. Maybe, if Drew and Kitty set their minds to it we could have another wedding come summer."

"When is Drew arriving? And still no word of young Bas, either, though he's expected. I've seen to both their rooms, and Keth's. Miss Julia said she was sorry about all the extra work, but it's no bother at all with Ellen coming to give a hand. It'll be just like the old days, when there used to be *real* dinner parties." Mary was in a remembering mood.

"In the old days, food wasn't rationed!" Tilda grunted. "It's a sin and a shame that neither Daisy nor Drew will be able to have a proper do. There's only four bottles of champagne left in the cellar, three of them for Drew's wedding and one for when peace comes, though it'll be past its best if this dratted war isn't over soon. Nearly four years it's been going on. Last time, it was over in four years. But we must look on the bright side. At least Rowangarth hasn't had any telegrams like last time."

"Yes, and you'd never have met Sydney, if you think about it, if there hadn't been a war. Be back for the teapot and scones!" She whisked out and up the kitchen stairs before Tilda had time to reply.

Yet Tilda *had* thought about it. Often, she admitted as she sliced the scones and spread them thinly with a mixing of butter and margarine. And right thankful she was that Sydney had been in the kitchen garden that day, and her in search of apples for a pie. Fate. She glanced at the ring on her right hand and wondered if the time hadn't come to transfer it to a more suitable finger.

Dear Sydney. He was well worth the long, anxious wait!

"Couldn't have timed it better, Gracie." Jack Catchpole removed his empty pipe and stuck it in his jacket pocket.

The cymbidiums had flowered on time, as if they had known there was to be a wedding, and the sky was clear and blue and another good day tomorrow, an' all, if he was any judge of the weather.

"When will you make a start on the flowers?"

"Early in t'morning, lass; soon as it's light. Orchids don't wilt. Got the base ready made for Daisy's little headpiece, and Tatiana and Kitty'll be no bother, having flowers wired on to Alice bands." And thank heaven for florist's wire, of which he happened to have a closely guarded stock, still.

"Daisy wants the pink flowers, doesn't she?" Almost automatically Gracie reached for the spray, pumping the handle, knowing after three years of Mr Catchpole's stern tuition that plants of the orchid family liked humid conditions.

"Ar. T'other two'll have to make do with the tawnies and speckleds, and I've got clippings of the dress material Alice and Polly will be wearing. I'll match their flowers as best I can."

"It's going to be a lot of work for you, Mr Catchpole."

"Wedding flowers is alus a last-minute job. I'll manage."

424

"Then couldn't I come in early too — give you a hand?" Gracie was eager to see the making of the bouquets and headdresses.

"But I gave you the day off, lass."

"Yes, but I'd rather be here. I wouldn't get in the way."

"We-e-ll, if you'm sure." Not that she knew much about such things, Catchpole considered, but she could fetch and carry and keep him supplied with tea. And she was pleasant to have around. "And if you won't want to be with your intended. When's he arriving, by the way? Young Drew's here already."

"Yes. I've seen him." Heading hand-in-hand with Kitty in the direction of the Pike. "Bas should be here any time now."

"Ar." And the sooner the better, the elderly gardener thought with relief, him being down to his last fill of tobacco. "Them white orchids of her ladyship's should flower in June — wonder if Drew and Kitty'll decide to set the day for then. Lady Helen would have wanted Drew's bride to carry them to her wedding. And then it'll be your turn, Gracie Fielding!"

"Mr Catchpole! I haven't had time to get used to being engaged yet. And talking of angels, look who's here!"

She was blushing bright pink and a GI was carefully closing the high iron gate.

"Well, off you go and meet him then! And close that dratted door behind you," he called to no avail, because Gracie was already running down the path.

He shook his head in mock concern, deciding he might as well set the kettle to boil since there'd be little sense out of his assistant for the remainder of the afternoon. He clamped his empty pipe between his teeth in anticipation of the gift to come, then chuckled with pleasure. Having a land girl foisted on him for the duration hadn't been such a bad idea after all!

"Now then, young Bas," he called. "You've comed, then, and just in time for tea!"

A long, pleasant pipe of tobacco, taken with a mug of tea in congenial company and with his beloved garden coming awake after winter, was Jack Catchpole's idea of heaven on earth.

War or no war, life still had its moments!

"There, now." Alice gave a final rub to the white shoes. "Nobody would know them from new! Lucky you were able to borrow them, Daisy."

"I'm the fourth size-five bride to wear them, Mam. Maisie in Cabin 4 bought them for her own wedding — shoes weren't rationed then — and after that her cousin wore them, then a girl in Cabin 6! They've walked up and down a few aisles!"

"Never thought I'd see you wearing borrowed shoes to your wedding, our Daisy — but that's what war does to folk!"

"At least they'll take care of the something borrowed."

"So they will! Something old, something new, something borrowed and something blue!"

426

"Well, Maisie's shoes are borrowed and my dress is new and if I wear Aunt Julia's christening brooch, that'll take care of the something blue."

"Hm, but something old?" She would have to set her mind to that, Alice frowned. "And there's something I want to give you, love. Reuben wanted you to have it in his Will. To Daisy Julia Dwerryhouse, the granddaughter I never had, twenty pounds to be paid to her out of my bankbook on her wedding day, if I'm not here to see it. That's what he wanted," Alice said softly, her voice all at once wobbly.

"Dear Reuben. I loved him so," Daisy whispered. "I wish he could be there tomorrow, and Lady Helen too. I'll put the money in the bank, Mam, and when things are back in the shops again, Keth and I will choose something special with it. Twenty pounds must have been an awful lot to Reuben."

"It was. Nearly a quarter's pay when he was a keeper. He was a grand gentleman. He loved you a lot."

"I'm very lucky, aren't I, Mam, being brought up with so much love, I mean, and you not knowing any affection at all?"

"I'll grant you that, but you and your dada and Reuben made up for it. It was a lucky day for me, Reuben speaking to Miss Clitherow on my behalf when her ladyship wanted a housemaid. He knew I was miserable with Aunt Bella, and such happiness I've had since!" She sniffed, then blew her nose loudly. "Ah, well, there's nothing like a wedding for making you count your blessings! Is Keth still at the bothy?"

"Yes, though he'll be leaving soon. Polly will have to get on with the girls' suppers. She looks lovely in her frock and hat, don't you think? Mr Catchpole is making her a spray to wear and you'll never guess what he's decided to use."

"Don't suppose I will. He won't have a lot of choice of flowers, though, this time of the year."

"Maybe not, but he's got loads of polyanthus — every colour under the sun — and he thought them appropriate. Polyanthus, you see, for *Polly* Purvis! He's really enjoying doing the flowers, Gracie said. Suppose he's getting his hand in for Drew and Kitty's wedding."

"Kitty," Alice frowned, "hasn't tried on the blue dress yet. There'll be no time to shorten it now, if it's too long!"

"It won't be, Mam. She and Lyn are the same height."

"Then what is she doing about shoes?"

"She takes the same size as Aunt Julia. She's wearing a pair of hers — silver evening shoes, I think. And Tatty is wearing her gold dancing pumps, so what else is there for you to worry about?"

"The reception, since you ask!" Alice was astride her high horse. "Sandwiches and a cup of tea isn't what me and your dada would have chosen for our daughter's wedding breakfast! And imagine not having a wedding cake!"

"Mam, there's a war on! No one has wedding receptions because no one has any food. And does it honestly matter? I'm one of the lucky ones who'll wear a white dress, and all my friends will be there and where is lovelier than All Souls and Rowangarth?

"If there hadn't been a war on, I could have paid for the reception myself. We could have had anything we wanted and bottles and bottles of champagne. If we wait till the war is over we could still have it, but Keth and I don't want to wait, Mam. We want a wartime wedding! I'm happy about tomorrow. Truly I am."

"We-e-ll, I suppose we'll have to make the best of things."

"We will. It'll be the best wedding ever and my dress is so beautiful. Thanks, Mam, for all the work you put into it."

"Oh, away with your bother, though I'm not entirely happy with the way it's going to look."

"Mam! It's perfect!"

"Nothing wrong with the dress, but it should have a petticoat! I won't have you walking down the aisle with your legs showing through your dress. Imagine what folks would think!"

"But I haven't got a long white petticoat and you haven't got one! A long petticoat would take too many clothing coupons, anyway. I can manage without one."

"No! The more I think about it," Alice frowned, "the more sure I am it needs a petticoat. Now watch those potatoes. Tell your dada when he comes in that I've gone to Rowangarth and I won't be a minute!" With a banging of doors she was gone.

Daisy lifted the lid of the potato pan, then prodded the bubbling cabbage with a fork. Nowhere near cooked, which gave her time to climb the stairs to the small spare bedroom and look at the dresses hanging there. She had done it so many times since she got home yesterday, just to reassure herself that it was real and she *was* getting married at last.

On the windowsill lay two buttons and a reel of white thread. Only in the morning would the buttons be sewn on. Mam didn't believe in completing a wedding dress till the day of the wedding. Dear, lovely Mam. Tomorrow, Dada would give her to Keth, but a part of her would always belong to Mam. Nothing could ever break the bond. Dear sweet heaven, she was so happy!

Tom and Keth walked into the kitchen just as Daisy put the vegetables in the slow oven to keep warm.

"Where's Mam?" It was the first thing Tom asked if Alice was not there.

"Gone to Rowangarth to see if she can lay hands on a petticoat." Daisy offered her mouth for Keth's kiss. "She's determined I must wear one. She's rushing herself half off her feet, Dada. You'll have to tell her to slow down or she'll be exhausted tomorrow."

"*Tell* her, lass? But Mam's having the time of her life, worrying and fussing over your wedding — her and Julia both! And when they've seen you safely down the aisle they'll have the time of their lives again, fussing and worrying over Drew and Kitty! Take note, Keth," he grinned. "Women are queer cattle!"

"I'll risk it for all that," Keth said, just as Alice arrived, breathless and triumphant.

"There now! I knew there'd be something, somewhere! Julia knew exactly where to find it. The Suttons never throw anything away!" She held it up with a flourish, an Edwardian waist-petticoat in finest cotton, frilled with deep bands of broderie anglaise. "I wonder how many balls her ladyship wore it to — and her laced into her tight corsets, an' all! What do you think? And before you say anything, Daisy, it doesn't smell fusty. It's been put away with lavender bags — only needs a bit of pressing."

"It's beautiful, Mam. Are you sure Aunt Julia doesn't mind?"

"Course not. There were ever so many. I picked the one I thought was the right length and it takes care of the something old bit. Now lay it on the bed, love, then we'll get on with the supper. Sit you down, Keth. I suppose you and Drew and Bas'll be out for a few bachelor drinks tonight?"

"If Daisy doesn't mind . . ."

"Of course she doesn't mind," Alice answered for her daughter. "Now let's get this food eaten. Polly will be down as soon as she's seen to supper at the bothy. The warden and the land girls are doing the

431

cooking tomorrow so she can have the day off. And we must be specially kind to her," she rushed on, handing out plates. "She'll be thinking about Dickon tomorrow, don't forget!"

"We'll all be thinking about Dickon," Tom said softly. "And, lass — slow down! You'll be meeting yourself coming back from the church if you're not careful!"

"Slow down? Not likely! I've been looking forward to this wedding for years and I'm going to enjoy it! And how about you, Tom? You'll be out tonight, it being Friday?"

"We-e-ll, I had thought to go to the pub — buy the platoon a pint to drink the bride and groom's health."

"Good!" There was no room at Keeper's for men underfoot tonight! "Just as long as none of you arrive back the worse for ale!"

"Chance would be a fine thing," Tom said gloomily. "The beer allocation doesn't go far nowadays with those soldiers from Pendenys supping it as though there's no tomorrow. Y'know, Keth, no one has ever found out what goes on there. Is it something secret, same as you're doing?"

"Haven't a clue. Probably it's some government department that's been bombed out of London."

"Oh, I doubt that. They're too heavily guarded for an ordinary government department. I heard that even the troops who guard Pendenys can't get inside the house. It wouldn't surprise me if they'd got Rudolf Hess locked up there!"

432

"Dada! Even Rudolf Hess doesn't deserve to be locked up in Pendenys! And it really doesn't matter what goes on there. There are offices where I work so secret they have armed sentries outside the doors, but no one bothers," Daisy shrugged.

Keth said nothing, though he was almost sure Pendenys Place was exactly like Castle McLeish and the stone house in Argyll, and that no outsider would ever know what went on there.

It made him think of Clissy again, and of a child who called herself Natasha . . .

"Keth!" Daisy was passing a hand in front of his eyes. "You were miles away! What were you thinking about?"

"I — oh, nothing important. Just wondering what really goes on at Pendenys."

"And . . .?"

"And I'm still none the wiser," he smiled, the turmoil inside him in check again. "Probably a load of boffins, trying to invent something to counteract the secret weapon Hitler is always threatening us with!"

"And wasting the taxpayers' money into the bargain." Tom was willing to let the matter drop. Tonight he had better things to do and tomorrow was Daisy's wedding. And anyroad, Pendenys Place had always been a mite peculiar! Even before the Army took it!

Tatiana awoke to the drone of aircraft engines, remembering she was at Denniston. Nothing changed. The sound of returning bombers was still like an alarm clock.

She swung her feet out of bed, then pulled aside the blackout curtains, gazing into the sky, opening the windows wider, her keen ear picking out the different tone of the engines. In the early morning they made a different sound, because the bombers were lighter, with bomb loads dropped and fuel used; a lower, almost tired sound, as if they were relieved to be back.

Last night's raid had been a long one, the squadron taking off earlier than usual, though she had refused to let herself count them out. Now, at five in the morning, they came back in ones and twos, circling the aerodrome, waiting permission to touch down.

One flew past, dangerously low, and she flinched to see its black underbelly so clearly. The old Whitley bombers were gone now, replaced by the newer Halifaxes. Halifax bombers were better protected, with an extra gunner. She knew all about them, though she had yet to catch sight of the even more deadly Lancasters that Mr Churchill said would carry the war to the very heart of Germany.

She pulled on trousers and a thick jumper, then walked, shoes in hand, down the stairs. This morning, whilst the bombers were landing, she would go to the top of Holdenby Pike; see again where she and Tim had been lovers and where his bomber had crashed. Then she would send her love to him, tell him she missed him still, and wanted him. And if she were lucky, he would let her know he was there, and that he loved her too.

The morning was sharp as an April morning should be. She breathed in its scents, glad she could think about Tim now without a choke of tears hurting her throat. Her tearing grief and anger had gone; only the loneliness remained.

Bill Benson had helped. She sometimes wondered if there really was an order of things; that though Tim was gone, someone had been sent to comfort her. Not that she loved Bill nor wanted his arms around her, nor his mouth on hers. What she first felt for the wounded air-gunner was compassion and by just being there Bill had forced her to face things from which she had tried to hide. It was because of Bill that she could take part in Daisy's wedding today with a heart free from envy. She would listen to the words of the service and in her mind she would hear, *I Timothy take thee Tatiana*, and Nathan would pronounce them man and wife. It would be like a blessing on their brief loving, and she would be content.

She reached the sheltered side of the pike as a bomber flew over. It was a straggler, its wheels already down for landing. A dicey touchdown it would be, because one of its four engines was not working, its propeller feathered. And waiting beside the runway would be ambulances and fire tenders and those who watched dry-mouthed with apprehension.

One of them is in trouble, Tim. A Halifax, with an engine shot up . . .

She held her breath as the stricken bomber disappeared from view, all the time listening, waiting, willing it to make a safe touch down.

He's just fine, Tatiana. He'll make it . . .

Tim's voice inside her head, telling her not to worry.

"I love you, Tim Thomson," she said, smiling softly.

From the east came a pale yellow glow as the sun began to rise, tipping the morning clouds pink. Above her a curlew called; a warm, burbling summer-call to its mate below. Then it descended as she watched it and she knew that Tim knew she was there.

"Daisy and Keth are being married this afternoon, Tim. You never met Keth, did you? I'm wearing a rose-pink dress, and flowers in my hair and the gold dancing pumps I was wearing the night we met.

"I have to go now, but I'll come again tomorrow — say so long before I go back to London." She turned to walk past the bushes that in another life sheltered their loving, hesitating at the spot where the rear turret of Tim's aircraft once lay, severed in the crash from the fuselage of *K-King*. "See you, Tim. The wedding is at two . . ."

Keth blinked open his eyes, stretching, wondering at the unaccustomed softness of the bed, realizing he had slept the night at Rowangarth. He wanted to pull back the blackout curtains, let in the day, but he was reluctant to leave the bed; wanted to think about today, at two, and Daisy.

Daisy Julia Dwerryhouse. He called back their first meeting; actually remembered it, though he had only been four and a bit. You remembered certain days because they were very bad or unbelievably good, and the day he first saw Daisy, sitting in the biggest, shiniest pram he had ever seen, was a good day for remembering. She had reached for his jumper with a baby hand and pulled it, laughing into his face. Even then she was beautiful; even then he loved her as the sister he never had.

That special day he and Mum piled their belongings on the back of a green-painted lorry and were driven from Cornwall to Willow End Cottage. Dad had got a job. After tramping the roads for almost a year and only writing letters to them when he had three-ha'pence for a stamp, Dickon Purvis had landed a job in Hampshire; one that came with a house, free firewood and fifteen shillings a week.

That job gave back their respectability, though they were hard put to it, sometimes, to make ends meet. When the Great War ended, a man with a job considered himself lucky to be free from parish relief and the stigma of the means test.

Then Dad and Mr Hillier died. One of the very bad days, that, and Mum sitting stricken, not believing it, and Daisy's Mam always there with drippinged toast and sympathy for a small boy.

Mum worrying about losing Willow End; worrying about keeping out of the workhouse. Julia MacMalcolm telling them there were jobs for them all at Rowangarth; a *position* for Mum at the bothy, and free food and a wage, too, looking after Rowangarth's garden apprentices. Respectability again.

And now he held the King's commission and Daisy was very rich, but he wouldn't think about Daisy's money; today especially he would not think about it.

Are you awake yet, darling? Perhaps she was still asleep, pink-cheeked, her long, fair lashes circles on her cheeks. She was beautiful to wake up to. He had done it often, gazing down, chin on hand, at her warm, sleepy loveliness, and after today at two they would be together every night the war allowed. Daisy, to have and to hold till death did them part. His, for all time and if time stretched beyond the grave, his into eternity.

Today he must not think of Natasha.

I'm sorry, Natasha. I'll never forget that today at two wouldn't be happening if it wasn't for you . . .

He threw off the bedclothes, then drew back the curtains to look down the length of the linden walk and across the lawn to the wild garden and the trees that blocked Keeper's Cottage from his sight. Above the pike the sun was rising. April 17. An unbelievably good day, and easy to remember.

★ ★ ★

Brattocks Wood was green-cool and smelled of things growing. An early sun, still low in the sky, threw long shadows through the trees and below them, in the unbelievably green April grass, primroses grew, and drifts of windflowers, bending in a gentle breeze.

Ahead, at the end of the wood, Daisy could hear the rooks circling and calling; coaxing young fledgelings from the nests. It was the rooks she had come to see; tell them about this afternoon at two, and how crazily happy she was.

A young pheasant, its tail still not grown, ran across her path, and above her, through a gap in the trees, swallows circled high. A good sign, that. The higher they flew, the better the day.

She closed her eyes to make her wish. She always did it on first seeing the little birds, returned to England's greenness from the Mediterranean sun. First-swallow wishes never failed her. She crossed her fingers and closed her eyes.

Please let Keth come home safely at the end of the war, little swallows.

It was all that mattered. She and Keth together for always like Mam and Dada; on this beautiful April morning it was the most important thing in the world.

She opened her eyes, uncrossed her fingers, let go her indrawn breath — why did she always hold her breath, when she made a wish? — then ran the length of the woodland path to where the elms stood. Squinting upwards she whispered, "Good morning, rooks," then, because the grass was wet with dew, she leaned her back against the trunk, holding her arms behind, palms inward so she was connected to the tree, and upwards to the very top, where the rooks nested.

Rooks, it's Daisy Dwerryhouse and I'm home on leave and this afternoon, at two, Keth and I are going to be married. At last.

Mam has made my dress and it's so beautiful and soft. And swishy and rustly too. Tatty and Kitty are bridesmaids and Drew is to be best man and Bas a groomsman.

They're all wearing their uniforms. It's only right, really, when there's a war on. You won't know about the war, rooks, but it's because of the war and food being rationed that I can't have a proper reception. But I don't mind. Just as long as the people I love are there it'll be a lovely wedding.

Fly over All Souls at two, will you, and wish us luck? I'll come again, soon; let you know how things went.

She turned to smile upwards, and her happiness reached right to the topmost branches and scattered up and on and out to dance along the pale beams of sunlight. The years of separation and loneliness were gone as if they had never happened. She gave a small skip of joy then hurried home. Mam would know where she was, because Mam told things to the rooks too. Secrets, sorrows and joys; told them all.

She looked down to see the drift of windflowers again. White, fairy things that opened when the

440

swallows came. Wild anemones, really, carpeting Brattocks Wood with a dance of wedding day happiness.

She dropped to her knees, picking a bunch to take back for Mam so that tonight, when she and Keth had left for York, the flowers would remind her of a windflower wedding and of how much her daughter loved her.

"Where on earth have you been?"

Mam was pressing Dada's uniform to wear this afternoon because Dada said that since uniforms were to be the order of dress, then be blowed if he wasn't wearing his, an' all!

Mam said it was only to show off his three stripes but really it was because Dada didn't own a sober grey suit; had never had one. A head gamekeeper wore his best tweed keeping suit on important occasions and his boots and leather leggings. Mam would have preferred the keeping suit, but Dada was adamant.

"Been, Mam? You should know without asking."

"Ah. Had a word with the rooks, then?"

"A word or two. And did you know the swallows are back?"

"I did. They're early this year. Saw my first on Thursday afternoon, just before you got here. Did you make a wish?"

"Of course!" She handed Alice the flowers. "For you, Mam."

"Oh, bonny lass!" Alice upended the iron, tears pricking her eyes.

"Mam! Don't dare cry on my wedding day!" Gently, Daisy dabbed her eyes. "No tears today?"

"No tears," Alice sniffed. "And anyway, they were happy ones." She smiled at the windflowers. "You used always to bring me little posies when you were a bairn, and I'd put them in the kitchen window — dandelions, daisies, buttercups . . ."

"I remember. You put them in a china mug; one with the handle broken off."

"And I've still got it," Alice said softly. "Wouldn't have thrown it away for anything!" She pulled out a chair, standing on it, reaching to the back of a high cupboard. "There! Didn't I tell you!" She brought it out with a flourish, filling it at the tap, arranging the flowers, placing them on the windowsill.

"They'll remind you tonight that I'm very happy and that I love you very much," Daisy whispered.

"They will. And they'll remind me what a pleasure you've been to Dada and me and how lucky we are you're marrying such a grand young man."

"Where's Dada?"

"Out. Took the dogs and said he'd walk the game covers before breakfast, but he's mooching, really. You know how he mooches when there's something he can't cope with. Put the kettle on, there's a good girl. I'm almost finished now."

"Can't cope with?" Daisy was all at once apprehensive. "Is he nervous about the wedding — making his speech?"

"No. Truth known he can't cope with losing you — because that's what he thinks, I'm sure of it. He hasn't said anything, mind, but I know my Tom and I'm sure he's thinking that he's giving you to Keth this afternoon — sort of final."

"The old softie! Tell you what, Mam — when you and Polly have gone to the church, we'll have a little chat, him and me."

"What about? You'll not tell him what I said!"

"Of course I won't. But those few minutes together will be a good time for me to tell him — and thank him."

"Of course it will, and I'm glad you've thought on to remember how much he's always cared for you, Daisy."

"How could I not remember? Now let me get on with the breakfast or I'll be all sniffy! And talking about putting the kettle on — that's Dada outside. I've never known anyone like him! He can home in on a boiling kettle as if he's got radar! Toast and marmalade, is it to be?"

"Aye! Toast and marmalade, when it should be ham and eggs, drat the war!"

"Mam?" Daisy coaxed. "You won't go all weepy this afternoon? Promise? Just be happy for Keth and me?"

"Of course I'll have a little weep, but no more'n most women at any wedding! The bride's mother is allowed a few tears! Ready for something to eat, love?" Alice turned to smile at Tom, who looked uneasy and out of place. "We'll have plenty of toast for packing, just in case we don't have time for a bite before we leave for the church," Alice said comfortably. "Don't want any stomachs rumbling in the middle of the solemn bits. And what are you thinking about, Tom Dwerryhouse, that's making you so vinegar-faced? Not going to rain, is it?"

"No. We're in for a fine day. But if you must know, I was thinking that it seems like only last week our Daisy was a baby in her pram at Windrush. Can anyone tell me," he demanded, forcing a smile, "just where did all the years go?"

CHAPTER
TWENTY-FOUR

"What do you think? Will it do?" Gracie asked anxiously. "I've never decorated a church before."

"It'll do just fine. It looks great, darling." All Souls' font was filled with cherry blossom; on the altar stood shining copper vases of white narcissi, their scent heady. "Daisy'll be real pleased. But when will it be our turn, Gracie? Wouldn't a summer wedding be wonderful? *This* summer, I mean."

"Hey! There's Drew and Kitty first!" Gracie pulled shut the heavy oak door, blinking in the bright sunshine.

"We don't have to wait for them. We could have a quiet affair, if that's what you wanted."

"Then what about your parents? They'll be missing Kitty's wedding. Is it right they should miss yours too?"

"We could have our wedding over again, in Kentucky — you could have all the trimmings; a white dress, the lot. Mom would like that!"

They had come to the place where the bomber crashed, grown over with grass and wild flowers now; a green space where once the village hall stood.

Gracie looked away, because this morning it made her think of her vow never to marry in wartime yet here she was with Bas's ring on her finger and him trying to persuade her down the aisle!

"Yes — we-e-ll. We haven't talked over much about things yet. You know what I mean — *that* side of things."

She looked at her shoes as they walked, because she knew her cheeks were blazing and because thoughts of sharing a bed with Bas had taken up far too much of her time lately.

"Then hadn't we better? Right here and now?" They had turned off the village street and were walking along the lane that led to Rowangarth stableyard and the bothy and Keeper's Cottage. "Couldn't agree more; *that* side of things has got to be talked about. I want kids, and I hope you want them too."

"I want *your* children, Bas, but I think I'd rather wait till the war is over."

"Good! That's one thing settled! And would it be so terrible for us to get married fairly soon? Keth and Daisy are doing it, and Kitty's wedding dress has arrived. By the way, how much of a family would you like?"

They were leaning elbows on the gate, now, gazing across Home Farm cow pasture.

"At least two, Bas, if we can afford them."

"We can. The money side of it won't be a problem."

"And you won't ever think I'm marrying you for your money, because I'm not. Will I tell you something?"

She moved closer so their shoulders and thighs touched and the lovely, familiar wanting feeling started on the tip of her tongue, then shivered right through her.

"The day Lady Helen died, she'd been telling me about the night she met Sir John. They must have been so in love, and I remember hoping that one day I would fall in love with someone like him; tall and fair with grey eyes. Yet here you are, Bas Sutton, not a bit like him and I love you very much."

"Even my hands, Gracie?"

"Especially your hands." She held one to her cheek. "They remind me, you see, that we might never have met. Now will you kiss me, please, and point me in the direction of the bothy? I've got less than an hour to get myself ready!"

"Okay. Guess I'd better be getting back to the church, anyway. And darling," he whispered huskily, lips on hers, "you *will* think about what I said?"

"There are times, Bas, when I can think of little else!"

She pushed him away from her, then ran down the lane and through the bothy gates without even turning to wave, because Sebastian Sutton was dangerous to be near when the mood was on him. And if ever the mood was on them both, and at the same time too, then heaven only knew what might happen! Maybe a quiet summer wedding mightn't be such a bad thing after all!

Oh, my goodness, she thought, taking the stairs two at a time, flopping weak-kneed on her bed.

She was shaking all over! She always was when Bas was around. Never get married in wartime, indeed! She must be out of her tiny mind!

"Right! See you in church!" Alice put down the phone. "That was your Aunt Julia. She's on her way now. The wedding car has just left with Tilda and Mary and Miss Clitherow. It should be here in about ten minutes for me and Polly."

"Good old Julia," Tom smiled. "She's enjoying this wedding."

"And so she should," Alice sniffed. "We've waited a long time for today! Now, let's have a look at you." She picked an imaginary speck from Daisy's gown then bent to adjust the hem, giving it a gentle tug from behind. "Those flowers look lovely on you. Glad you decided not to wear a veil."

"I always said I wouldn't; never wanted to walk down the aisle all shrouded. I want to look at Keth, not hide my face under a veil!"

"Then mind you walk with your head up and your back straight!"

"I'll be very dignified, I promise, though I'll feel like hitching my skirt up and running like mad to Keth's side. You're sure he's at the church?"

"He's there, and Drew with him and Bas getting folk into their pews." She gave a tweak to the daisy brooch with sapphire petals. "Something blue. I wonder, when Julia gave you that at your christening, if she ever thought you'd wear it to your wedding."

"That was a long time ago, Mam!"

"Aye, and I'll soon have a daughter-in-law," Polly smiled, touching Daisy's cheek. "And I'll tell you now, love, if I'd hand-picked you myself, I couldn't have chosen better. I'm glad about you and Keth — and grateful for the posh hat. Folk won't know me when I walk into the church!"

"You look a treat," Tom said softly. "You pay for dressing, Polly Purvis."

"Thanks," Polly smiled gratefully, knowing that Tom realized how she was missing Dickon; how much she would have liked him to see how well his son had done. "I wish that car would come. I'm restless as a kitten!"

"Won't be long." Alice knew exactly how she felt. "You'll remember to lock the front door when you leave, Tom; slip the key in your pocket and not under the stone, and —"

"Mam! I'm leaving by the back door. We never use the front!" Daisy protested.

"Then today we will. No bride leaves this house by the back door! And I'm sure there was something else . . ."

"There is. You haven't asked yet if Drew has the ring safe in his pocket!"

"He has, Tom. Julia checked! Now the car will be here soon, then it'll go to Rowangarth for Tatty and Kitty, then come back for you two. Such a carry-on! Why they could only let us have one car I don't know!"

"Because they've only been allowed petrol for one car." Tom put his hands on Alice's shoulders, turning her to meet his eyes. "And it's there, outside, so be off the pair of you!"

He kissed her cheek, taking care not to disarrange her hat, then kissed Polly, too.

"Well — best be going." Alice's cheeks were bright pink. "Now let's have a last look at you, Daisy Dwerryhouse. Turn round slowly . . ."

"Mam! I look beautiful! I feel beautiful! Now will you and Polly get into that car?"

"Yes. But oh, Tom — how did you and me manage to get such a beautiful daughter?" All at once, Alice was close to tears.

"With no trouble at all, lass, as I remember it," Tom grinned. "Now will you go? You'll throw everything out of kilter if you don't and the bride will be late! See you at the church," he called, watching through the front-room window as the car reversed into the bothy lane, then made off majestically in the direction of the village.

"Ah, well. Ten more minutes and then it'll be our turn. Why don't you take the weight off your feet? Mam said you weren't to sit down and get creases, but if I fetch the high stool from the kitchen you can drape your skirts over it, sort of."

"I could do with a sit-down, Dada. I seem to have been on the go since the crack of dawn. I can't believe it, now it's almost time. But I'm glad of these few minutes on our own. I want us to have a talk." Carefully she sat down, arranging her skirts around her. "I want to tell you you were right, all those years ago."

"Right, love?" Tom lowered himself onto the sofa, feeling out of place in the parlour, wondering why they weren't spending these last few minutes in the cosiness of the kitchen.

"Mm. It was when I was little — when Aunt Julia and Drew were staying with us in Hampshire."

"Oh, aye . . .?"

"It was when they told us Drew and I were brother and sister."

"I remember. The womenfolk thought it was time Drew knew that Mam was his real mother — his birth-mother."

"That's it. I remember having a fit of temper, and running out."

"But you were only a bairn. You'd not long started school."

"I was six, almost. Anyway, I couldn't grasp the fact that there had been someone else in Mam's life before you! I understand now, because Mam thought you had been killed, but at the time I hated her!

"You told me it was possible to love twice, but differently — just as it happened to Aunt Julia. You were in the far woods, in the keeper's hut with the little iron wheels on it, and you sat me on your knee and talked to me."

"Well, I'm blowed. You *do* remember!"

"Not all of what was said that night, but I remember you telling me that I was only a little girl, but one day I'd know what love was like — between a man and a woman, that is. You said one day I'd find the man I wanted to marry and you hoped I'd love him as much as you loved Mam, and she loved you."

"And you'd already found him, did we but know it!"

"I had. You said I was to remember that night, and what you'd said. And you *were* right. You're a lovely, lovely man, and oh!"

She jumped to her feet, sending the stool skittering across the room, sitting beside him in a swish of skirts.

"Hey up, lass! Be careful of that frock!"

"Oh, never mind! Let's have a snuggle like we used to! I'll tell Mam I got the creases in the car!" She slid her arm through his, laying a cheek on his shoulder. "And thank you for being such a wonderful father. I know you think you'll lose me, but you won't, I promise. You'll always be my lovely Dada. I'll love you every bit as much as I love Keth, only differently! Thank you for always being there. I hope you haven't had too many regrets over the years."

"No regrets, lass — well, happen just one, this afternoon."

"Tell me?"

"That your mam and me weren't blessed with another half-dozen, every bit as good as you, our Daisy."

"Did you want a big family?"

"We were so happy being together after all that had happened, we decided we'd accept what the good Lord chose to send us, be it one or many. And what He lacked in quantity, He certainly made up for in quality!" Reluctantly, he got to his feet, holding out his hands, kissing her gently. "Now let's have a look at you."

He straightened the circlet of flowers she had knocked askew, smiling because now he knew she would always be his lass; that neither marriage nor all the money that had fallen into her lap would change her. They stood there, not speaking, until the banging of a car door outside interrupted their precious, private thoughts.

"It's here!" Tom handed her the bouquet of pink orchids, smiling gently. "Out you go. I'll check the back door, then I'll be with you. Careful how you walk down the path!"

The back seat of the car was covered with a white sheet. The driver smoothed it, then handed her into the roomy depths. Tom locked the front door, slipped the key into the pocket of his battledress top, then got in beside her.

The time had come. He was giving his daughter in marriage but he wasn't losing her; only sharing her with Keth, who loved her as much as he did.

"It's a grand day for it," said the driver, as they drove slowly up the lane.

"Aye," Tom smiled. "It's a grand day all round!"

The bridesmaids waited at the churchyard gates; Tatty looking exquisite in dull rose satin; Kitty head-turning beautiful in pale blue. Gracie arrived, pink-cheeked from running, gasping, "Thank goodness she isn't here, yet!" telling them they looked absolutely marvellous before hurrying inside.

"There you are!" Bas whispered. "I thought you weren't coming. You're to sit with Polly at the front."

"Couldn't I sit with the other land girls?" Gracie did not want to be thought pushy.

"No! Aunt Julia says you're family now, and you're to sit with family. I'll join you later, when I've got everybody settled. By the way, darling," he leaned closer, "lots of people have said how beautifully you've decorated the church. Thought you'd like to know."

"Polly! You look lovely!" Gracie whispered, slipping into the pew. "Your hat really suits you!"

"Daisy chose it — paid for it too," Polly whispered, pinking with pleasure. "There's a lot here . . ."

"The whole village, I reckon, and most of the bothy. There's nothing like a wedding for filling a church!" Gracie looked down at her watch. "It's almost time. Ooh, Polly, isn't this lovely?"

454

"It is. Just look at our Keth." She nodded in the direction of her son who sat, ramrod straight with Drew beside him, in the front pew. "His ears have gone red," she whispered. "Always have done, ever since he was a little lad, when he's bothered. He'll be all right once Daisy gets here."

"What time is it?" Keth whispered, dry-mouthed.

"One minute to go," Drew whispered back, his throat suddenly hoarse because he was thinking of Kitty and how they must get their own wedding arranged. He'd waited long enough!

Nathan, on his way down the aisle, nodded in passing. Behind sat Alice and Julia. Keth turned to smile at them and they smiled back rather smugly, as if getting married happened every day of your life.

"You okay, Keth?" Julia asked.

"I'm fine, but Daisy's late . . ."

"She isn't! It's only just two."

Keth checked his watch again, then there was a movement from the back of the church, and a murmuring.

Nathan took his place to the right of the lectern, then made a little movement with his hand. Keth and Drew sprang to their feet as if they were on parade.

Someone hurried down the side aisle, to whisper to the organist, who was Winnie Hallam's cousin. She straightened her back, smiled blissfully, then began to play.

The bride had arrived. Heads turned. Daisy stood at the top of the aisle, her arm in Tom's.

There was a sigh, another murmur. Keth turned, just to make sure she had come. Then he pulled in his breath at the loveliness of her, the way she held her head, the skirt that swished around her as she walked. Daisy, his love. It was happening, at last.

The bride paused to smile at her mother and Julia, then turned to smile at Polly. She was exquisite, Keth thought; no longer Daisy who would flounce off in a huff at the least provocation. She had grown into the most beautiful woman in the world, and she was his.

Their eyes met and she smiled gently, her cheeks pinking. She turned to hand her flowers to Kitty, then took a step nearer to Keth, moving a straying lock of hair.

He noticed that the sapphire engagement ring was on her right hand, saw too that she pulled her tongue round her lips as if she were nervous.

All at once, things he hadn't been able to focus upon became clear. The white blurs on the altar were narcissi; the dance of colour on the chancel steps came from the sun, shining through the south window.

The thudding inside his chest became less noisy; only he could hear it now. Kitty winked at him; Drew gave him the slightest nudge of support.

"Dearly beloved," Nathan opened his prayer book, "we are gathered together here in the sight of God . . ."

456

Polly looked at Gracie, then touched her ear with a fingertip.

"He's all right now," she smiled.

Keth, Gracie thought, was looking at Daisy as if no one else were there, and all at once she knew that if the Reverend asked if anyone else would like to be married whilst he was about it she would cry "Yes, please! *Me!*"

She felt a hand reaching for hers. Bas had joined them. She twined her little finger around his, smiling tremulously.

". . . and in the face of this congregation, to join together this Man and this Woman . . ."

Kitty noticed that the flowers she held in each hand were shaking. She wasn't nervous or anything — maybe a bit envious that it wasn't she and Drew standing there, being married. She had thought, when their loving first began, that it was thrilling and very modern to sleep with Drew without being married. It had been their secret, yet now she wanted to stand in the face of a congregation and be married to Drew. It would be sad that Mom and Pop couldn't get over for the wedding, but nothing was normal these days, and it would be just breathtaking to be married from Rowangarth and have Uncle Nathan pronounce them Man and Wife.

She stared at the back of Drew's neck. She would stare until he turned round so she could form her lips into, "I love you." And she did love him;

desperately and without reason, and hoped that when they were married they would be very careless and start a baby right away, because carrying Drew's child was the most precious thing she could think of.

But this was Daisy's day, and Keth's, and Nathan was asking Keth if he would have this Woman to be his wedded Wife. And would he love her, comfort her, honour, and keep her in sickness and in health, and Keth saying loudly and firmly that he would.

"Daisy Julia, wilt thou have this Man . . ."

They would speak to Uncle Nathan, Kitty thought fiercely, would ask him to start the calling of the banns tomorrow! Besides, she had a beautiful wedding dress hanging in the sewing room at Rowangarth and it sure was stupid not to want to wear it!

She smiled gently to hear Daisy's soft, clear, "I will."

"Sorry I'm late." Ewart Pryce joined Anna who sat alone at the back of the church, her mother's very sudden headache forcing her to go to her bed and miss the ceremony. "Sick visit."

Anna smiled, tilting her head the better to see the bride and groom.

"Tatiana looks very beautiful," he whispered.

"She does."

Her daughter's eyes were gentle, her lips tilted in a small smile. Perhaps, Anna thought, she was coming to terms with the loss of her airman. Maybe

458

now she was getting over the pain. Anna understood about the pain — not of loss, but of betrayal.

Tatiana fixed her eyes on Nathan Sutton's face. Such a dear man. Why couldn't her father have been like him?

Daisy was repeating her wedding vow. It was the part Tatiana had waited for; her promise to Tim.

I Tatiana take thee Timothy . . .

She held her breath and shut out the words, "so long as ye both shall live", because she knew now that even death could not keep Tim from her heart. Their love had been fierce and brief, but it made no difference. That love would outlast the years; would stay golden until she was too old to remember or to dream.

She wondered if Daisy felt as happy as she did.

Keth fumbled a little when he put the ring on Daisy's finger and she smiled into his eyes to let him know it was all right, then manoeuvred her thumb behind it to push it the rest of the way. Darling Keth. Now they were married and the congregation singing "Love Divine, All Loves Excelling".

A kind of triumph beat inside her head. She loved him so much. She was so lucky. Her cheeks were burning, but she didn't care. She slipped her hand into his to follow Nathan into the vestry, and Mam and Dada and Polly and Aunt Julia, and all those she loved best followed behind. She wanted them, all the lovely people in her life, to witness the signing of the register.

They pushed into the little room and Nathan smiled and said, "I think, Captain, that Mrs Purvis would like to be kissed!"

Daisy closed her eyes. It was a wonderful kiss; gentle and a little disbelieving and without passion. She would remember the relief of it always.

"Mam, Dada!" She held out her arms to her parents. "Are we married? Did it really happen?"

"It happened, our lass," Tom said. "Mam and me heard every word of it!" He had thought to feel great sadness at Daisy's wedding, but he had not. "You're wed, all right!"

Alice smiled across the vestry table at Julia, a smug we-made-it smile. She had not let fall the obligatory tears and as Daisy and Keth made their promises had known only happiness for her daughter.

"She's yours now." Tom shook Keth's hand. "Look after her."

"I will, sir." Then he folded Polly in his arms, smiling gently. "Thanks, Mum. For everything."

The singing stopped. The congregation waited. The organist waited. The iron sneck on the vestry door clicked and lifted.

Winnie Hallam's cousin began the Wedding March with great gusto. It was the favourite of all her organ pieces and she played it with a triumph that filled the little church and went crashing upwards to the roof arches.

"Here we go, darling!" Daisy smiled brilliantly into Keth's eyes, then they walked slowly up the aisle, smiling to left and right because everyone in that dear, familiar church was a friend. Behind them walked Drew and Kitty, hands clasped, then Bas and Tatiana, and she so beautiful, so serene.

Polly, her arm in Tom's, walked proudly in her splendid, expensive hat and Alice took the arm Nathan offered and smiled, eyebrows raised at Gracie as they passed; a your-turn-soon smile that made Rowangarth's land girl blush hotly.

Of Julia there was no sign. She had hurried up the side aisle and was positioned, camera at the ready, at the door.

"Can we have a lovely smile from the bride and groom, please?"

Julia had a precious roll of film in her camera, courtesy of the PX canteen at Burtonwood Airfield, which would not only take twenty-four wedding photographs, but take them *in colour*. And today, Julia exulted, as Daisy and Keth stepped aside to let the congregation leave the church, she had her Clan together at last! All six of them to stand laughing into the camera as they had done in a long-ago Christmas. Teenagers, then, dancing to the gramophone and Kitty teaching them the tango, which was all the rage.

Now they had gone to war, and doubly precious because of it, and what better a time, she thought as she arranged bridesmaids and parents into a group, than today? Because Daisy's wedding was one she would remember with joy, and it made her wish all the more for Drew's.

Then she gave the camera to Will Stubbs, who knew everything there was to be known about taking photographs in colour, and went to stand at Nathan's side, to be snapped with Daisy and Keth and Polly and Alice and Tom on the church steps.

She reached for her husband's hand, smiling into his eyes, whispering, "Isn't this a wonderful day, Nathan? We must do it all again soon!"

Daisy ached with happiness. Swallows darted in an April sky; from the direction of Brattocks Wood, a cuckoo called. Her world was so beautiful that it seemed wrong a bomber should fly over low, to remind them that days like this were rare and soon they must all go back to war. She turned to smile at Tatty, who was watching it out of sight, and Tatty smiled back as if she could read her thoughts.

"'Bye." Tilda kissed Daisy. "Got to go. See you soon. And Daisy, love, you look absolutely beautiful."

Warm, romantic tears misted Tilda's eyes and if it hadn't been for Sydney, who was coming to Rowangarth later, she would have felt very envious.

"Me and Tilda are going back to get the kettles on and the sandwiches set out," Mary added. "And you look a dream in that dress!"

Everyone was enjoying the wedding. Daisy gave her father a slow, conspiratorial wink. There could

462

be no wedding bells, very little food to offer and clothing so severely rationed that a bride in white was a rarity these days. Yet today was the most wonderful of her life. She and Keth married at last and the entire village there to wish them well; to enjoy a day of make-believe, almost, in all the awfulness of war.

"Keth," she said, so softly that he had to bend close to hear what she said, "I love you very much." She didn't care who was watching, reading the words on her lips and nor did Keth.

"I love you too, Daisy Purvis. You look very beautiful."

"Smile, please," someone called, as those lucky enough to have films in their cameras gathered to snap them.

"That's the car arriving." Keth nodded in the direction of the gates. "Think we'd better go."

He offered his arm and they walked slowly down the church path, pausing at Reuben's grave.

"Hullo," Daisy whispered. "Thank you for the wedding present. I'll come and see you before we leave . . ."

The driver of the wedding car said he was sorry; that he had only enough petrol in the tank for one journey, and would it be in order if the bridesmaids got in too?

So they pushed giggling into the back, their skirts getting in the way and none of them caring.

People who had confetti threw the last of it; everyone smiled and waved, then took the short cut through the churchyard and past Home Farm to Rowangarth stableyard where it was only a skip and a jump to the front door.

"Isn't this all just wonderful?" Kitty beamed. "Don't you just love an English wedding on a beautiful English afternoon in April?"

"I'm all for it," Keth laughed, "and I'd like to do it all over again — when you and Drew get married. When is it to be, Kitty?"

"Well, you'll not tell Drew one word of this." Kitty beckoned them close, speaking in a stage whisper as only she knew how. "We haven't *exactly* discussed it — well, not at length — but between you guys and me, I'm going to suggest we have a talk with Uncle Nathan; ask him to get things moving."

"And about time too!" Daisy glanced at her watch. "I've been married for twenty-eight minutes and I can highly recommend it! But you've got the man, your wedding dress made it safely across the Atlantic, so what's keeping you? And there are two bridesmaid's dresses available, free of clothing coupons for anyone who wants them — and the white orchids flower in June."

"Sounds good. I'd like the folks to be there, though, but they couldn't get across. Guess you can't have it all ways — not when there's a war on — and I sure do want Drew and me to be married," she sighed as they turned into Rowangarth drive.

Daisy gazed serenely at her new ring. Two more months, then another Rowangarth wedding! Even

464

with a war on, things seemed to be taking a turn for the better.

"Isn't this the most *beautiful* day?" she sighed.

Rowangarth had stood witness to many weddings. Many brides had come here as lady of the big house, to run it in the grand style and provide it with an heir and, almost always, to learn to love it as if they had been born a Sutton.

Kitty loved it already, Julia thought. The Suttons had almost, one late December night, broken their link with Rowangarth, but just in time Drew was born to carry on the line. The war would be kind to Drew; she knew it inside her. He and Daisy both would come home safely. Soon, she was sure of it, Kitty and Drew would marry and have children. Rowangarth was perfect for families.

She rose from the stone seat in the linden walk. The lindens were budding yellow-green. The sycamores and willows had already leafed and daffodils grew in great gold drifts beneath the trees of the wild garden. Cherries frothed pink and white and the grass, cut yesterday in the late afternoon before the dew fell, smelled headily of summer to come.

Rowangarth had risen to the occasion; put on a show for Daisy's wedding so the war should seem a long way away. Julia hoped the bombers would stay grounded this afternoon, then for just a little while, those who wanted to could pretend the war had never happened.

It *had* happened, though. There was Drew in sailor's rig, Bas a smartly dressed GI, Keth in Army uniform. Even the father of the bride wore Home Guard khaki. The war, she sighed, could never be all that far away. Tomorrow most of her Clan would have gone back to it.

"There you are!" Alice, hat slightly askew, hurrying towards her. "Isn't this a grand day? All the sandwiches gone but plenty of tea left!"

"I had a word with Nathan earlier on. He's going to tell everyone that if they'd like to come back tonight, we'll get the gramophone out and have a bit of a dance in the hall. I don't want things to go flat, and it might when Daisy and Keth have left."

"That's a lovely idea. Sure you can put up with them all?"

"Of course I can! I wonder where Nathan is? Haven't seen him in ages."

"No. You won't have. He's in the study, Mary said, with Drew and Kitty!" Mary missed nothing.

"Alice! You don't suppose they're talking weddings!"

"I'd like to think so. Why else would they be in that musty old room when they could be out here in this lovely sunshine?"

"Alice — excuse me! I'll just go —"

"No you won't, Julia Sutton!" Alice was very firm. "If it's banns then it's parish business! Never you mind about Drew and Kitty. Seems they're getting it sorted at last. What about over there, then?" She nodded in the direction of the sundial

466

where Ewart Pryce and Anna talked and laughed. "They've been together most of the afternoon. He sat with her in church — I saw them as we came out — and she had a lift here in his car, an' all! Those two'll be getting themselves talked about!"

"Then I hope they do!" Julia wondered why on earth she hadn't thought of it before. "Anna deserves a break after *him*!"

"*That* man's name is not to be mentioned on my daughter's wedding day! But what if something did happen between them! The Countess wouldn't be best pleased. The Petrovskys have never had anything so middle class as a doctor in the family!"

"No, just a lying, cheating, womanizing pig who shall be nameless as requested. Well, good luck to them, say I! Ewart is a very nice man — though I don't suppose there's anything in it . . .?"

"There might be. They work together, don't forget! And just look at our Daisy! Sitting on those steps, all in a dream. She'll get that dress messed up!"

"It doesn't matter! She won't be wearing it again," Julia laughed. "She looked so beautiful, walking down the aisle. Weren't you proud of her? I could have burst into tears, thinking about her christening. Wasn't it lovely that she wore the daisy brooch?"

"I could've burst into tears an' all, but I managed not to. And I really don't want her getting grass stains on that frock, Julia. I'd thought to ask Gracie if she'd like to wear it — when they name the day, that is — to her wedding. It took a lot of making. I'd like to get my value out of it!"

"Goodness! Drew and Kitty, Bas and Gracie — maybe even Anna, too! Is there something in the Holdenby air, all of a sudden?"

Alice said she didn't know, but wasn't it lovely to think that in spite of the war and all the heartache it brought with it, nothing could stop people falling in love and getting married and — oh, touch wood! — having babies, too?

Daisy sat on the stone steps that lifted one level of lawn to another and tried to sort out the lovely muddle in her head. This feeling inside her — how could she describe it? Was it rainbows or an apricot sunset or birdsong at dawn? Or was it snow on Christmas morning, or the blackbird that always piped Sunset at the top of the old oak in Brattocks Wood, or the first snowdrop or the smell of baking bread?

This feeling was a mixing, she supposed, of all the things that squeezed her heart with tenderness, and the singing happiness inside her; the giddy realization that she and Keth were married at last.

Keth crossed the grass towards her, stopping to store the picture of her in his mind. Her skirts billowed around her like the petals of a blowsy white rose, her bouquet of pink orchids lay at her side. She was quite alone in her world of dreaming, a small smile on her face, her eyes tenderly blue.

"You were miles away, sweetheart!"

"Up on a pretty pink cloud," she smiled. "Don't topple me off it just yet, Keth?"

"No fear! Sounds good. Move over, and I'll join you," he laughed. "But should you be sitting there? Your mother says you'll get a cold in your bottom." He held out his hands but she did not take them.

"Shall I tell why I'm really sitting here, darling — apart from having a lovely, quiet think, I mean." She pushed a silk-stockinged foot from beneath the froth of white. "My feet hurt, if you must know, so I thought I'd slip my shoes off. I've been wiggling my toes in the grass — it's lovely and cool. They fitted when I put them on, but they're starting to pinch now. Suppose that's what happens when you wear borrowed shoes!"

"Daisy darling!" He laughed out loud. "You're the richest woman for miles around yet you walk down the aisle in borrowed shoes! There's a lot of your mother's common sense in you, I'm glad to see."

"Keth! Not today! No money talk on my wedding day! And common sense has nothing to do with it. The fact of the matter is that shoes cost five coupons a pair, and Wrens aren't given clothing coupons! And I suppose I'd better put them on again." She searched beneath the folds of silk and the embroidered frills of her something-old petticoat to pull them out in triumph.

"Here — let me?" He bent to put the satin shoes on her feet, smiling into her face. "Everybody's congregating in the conservatory. Your father is going to make his speech, and then I'll have to toast the bridesmaids — in tea!" He picked up her flowers, then took her hand in his.

"D'you know, Keth, I was sitting there, trying to think about this afternoon at the church, but I can't remember a lot about it! I suppose when I've got to go back, I shall lie on my bunk wanting you like mad and then I'll be able to remember how it was today. But right now it's just one lovely bright blur of happiness."

"Then let's keep it that way? No money talk, no thinking of going back, till we've got to. And by the way, I love you very much."

What a snap, Julia smiled, pushing her camera back into its case. Daisy sitting on the steps, a long slim ankle extended; Keth smiling into her eyes, putting on her white wedding shoe. So romantic, and they'd been so taken up with each other they hadn't even known it was being taken. She waved as Kitty and Drew came towards her, demanding to know where they had been hiding themselves.

"Tell you later, Mother!" Drew grinned. "We're going to do the speeches. I've got to reply on behalf of the bridesmaids."

Frustrated, Julia raised an enquiring eyebrow in the direction of the bridesmaid in palest blue, but she laughed teasingly, her violet eyes full of Kitty-mischief. And it wasn't until Tom had wished the bride and groom health and happiness, and thanked the bridesmaids for being so beautiful, and Drew had made his carefully prepared reply that he said, "And now, everyone, if Keth and Daisy will forgive me for stealing just a bit of their thunder, Kitty and I would like you all to know that tomorrow, if you're at church, you'll hear the first calling of our banns.

"We hope to get married in June — if the Navy and ENSA permit it — so don't any of you put your wedding finery back in mothballs just yet, because I hope we're going to do all this again in the very near future! Now, Mother, does that please you?"

And Julia hugged him fiercely and said it did, and what had been keeping them? Then she folded Kitty in her arms.

"Darling! I'm so glad! When exactly is it to be? You can't know how happy I am!"

"Probably June the nineteenth — or thereabouts. And Aunt Julia, you just can't be as happy as me!"

Everyone was smiling and laughing and shaking hands because young Sir Andrew was getting wed at last to a tomboy of a girl the people of Holdenby had seen grow into a beautiful woman. She would never hold a candle to Lady Helen, mind, but she was a right grand lass and young Drew was smitten with her and that was all that mattered!

"Now whilst I've got you all here!" Julia called above the tumult, "I want to take a snap of the Sutton lot! I took them as teenagers, here in the conservatory, and I want a snap of them all today.

"Tilda and Mary are bringing up fresh pots of tea and before I forget, those of you who would like to are welcome to come tonight — about eight — and we'll wind up the gramophone and have a few dances. I hope you'll be here, because this is such a wonderful day that I'd like to keep it going a little while longer!"

"Just look at her," Alice smiled to Nathan as Julia arranged the bride and groom, the bridesmaids, the best man and the groomsman into a group. "She's waited a long, long time to take that photograph. Her Clan, and may heaven help anyone who harms one of them!"

And Nathan, who always carried a clean, carefully folded handkerchief in his pocket for emergencies, took it out and dabbed away the single tear she was unable to prevent.

"She's very happy today. And you, dear, dear Alice — no tears on Daisy's wedding day!"

"It wasn't a tear, Nathan; just a lovely little squeeze of happiness that got away! And if you'll excuse me, I'll go and give Drew and Kitty my very best wishes. Poor Kitty! She's just gone and landed herself with two mothers-in-law!"

Nathan watched her go, trying not to think too much about 19 June, because he had just realized that both he and Tom would have to endure two more months of wedding-talk.

He must find Tom, commiserate with him, and ask him if he could explain what got into the heads of two normally sane and sensible women when the words "wedding in the family" were mentioned!

Then he laughed out loud, because whatever it was, it made them both very, very happy!

472

CHAPTER
TWENTY-FIVE

"Have you enjoyed today, Anna?" Ewart Pryce stopped his car at the gates of Denniston House, not because the crunch of gravel might awaken the Countess or Karl, but because he wanted to kiss her. Dancing with her tonight made him finally admit that she was much more than a clerk who was pleasant to work with and good to look at. They had spent most of the afternoon in each other's company and danced almost every dance together. The village would have noticed and remarked upon it with an indignant, "Well, did you see the pair of them?" or maybe, "And about time, too; her a widow these fifteen years and him well into his forties and still unwed!" He hoped it was the latter.

"Every bit of it! I don't think I've danced so much since Petersburg — and that's more years ago than I care to admit. Elliot didn't like to dance."

"Your husband?" He said it warily because it was the first time she had mentioned him.

"You sound surprised, Ewart." She wished she could see his face, but even though her eyes had adjusted to the complete darkness, there was only the blur where his profile should have been. "But then, my marriage wasn't a good one. It's the best-known secret in Holdenby, and before your time. I married a man — I was too young, I'll admit it now — who couldn't keep out of other women's beds. It's why I never remarried. Afraid, I suppose."

"So why are you telling me now?" He asked it gently.

"Because today, I suddenly felt free. It happened in the churchyard — when Daisy and the bridesmaids took their flowers there, after the reception."

Anna had thought it a lovely gesture. Daisy laid her flowers on Reuben's grave, Kitty had given hers to Helen, whispering without the least embarrassment, "Just thought you'd like these, Aunt Helen — and to tell you that Drew and me are getting married in June."

"But it was Tatiana who made it all happen. You weren't there, Ewart, but it was when Tatiana gave her flowers to Father-in-law. She put them on her grandfather's grave when I'd expected she'd have put them on Elliot's, yet I knew she wasn't being unkind nor disrespectful. She'd got her priorities right, you see — did something we didn't expect of her. All at once it made me realize what a fool I'd been all those years."

"I don't understand, Anna. Tell me."

"I'm trying to say, Ewart, that I've been the so-called grieving widow for far too long. I wouldn't let myself think about Elliot; wouldn't have said his name, even, if I could have helped it. I felt safe that way, you see. No man could get through what he thought was my unhappiness. I sheltered behind it — not grief, but bitterness — because I was too afraid to defy Mama."

"The Countess thought you should stay in purdah for ever?" he said, surprised.

"No. She often reminded me that I was still young enough to marry again and have children, but she didn't really want me to. Not after Elliot. So I told myself that I didn't want another husband. The least line of resistance, I suppose, because I might have burned my fingers a second time."

"And the churchyard, Anna . . .?"

"Tatiana left home. It took a lot of doing. Today she turned her back on her father and laid her flowers on her grandfather's grave. That took courage too, and it made me realize what a spineless creature I'd become and that Elliot could never hurt me again unless I let him. It took a gesture from my daughter to make me come to my senses — so thank you for helping in my rehabilitation tonight."

"Me? How come?"

"By taking me home, for one thing."

"No problem. Common courtesy," he said uneasily.

"But there *is* a problem — for me, that is. I hoped, you see, that you would kiss me goodnight."

"Ah," he murmured gravely, not a little surprised by the new, forthright Anna. "And what is so wrong in a goodnight kiss?"

"Nothing. But I asked myself whether I wanted you to drive me home because suddenly I didn't care what Holdenby thought seeing us leaving together, or whether it was because I wanted you to kiss me."

"And which was it?" He pulled in his breath, not knowing what to say.

"What do *you* think, Ewart?" She said it softly, anxiously. "Do you think I've gone quite mad?"

"Yes, I do," he laughed, pulling her into his arms, "and it suits you!"

His mouth found hers. It was a brief, gentle kiss. Then he wandered his lips to her closed eyelids, to the hollow beneath her cheekbone and the tip of her nose, hearing the intake of her breath, knowing she was as nervous as he was.

"Now kiss me again, please?" She cupped his face in her hands exactly as the front door opened and a voice called in Russian, "Is that you, child?"

"No, Karl. Tatiana is staying the night at Rowangarth — you know she is," Anna called back in English so Ewart should know what was being said.

"Then are you all right, little Countess?"

"I'm fine, Karl. Dr Pryce has brought me home and I'm saying goodnight to him." Her cheeks blazed. She felt like a little girl, caught doing something very wrong. "Oh dear," she whispered forlornly. "I'm so sorry, Ewart. Perhaps I shouldn't have said what I did. Whatever must you think of me?"

"Since you ask," he said softly, touching her cheek, "I think you are a lovely lady whose company I have enjoyed for the best part of the day and just wished a very pleasant good night."

"Yes, but —"

"No *buts*! See you on Monday. Goodnight, Karl!" he called as the footsteps of the old Cossack crunched towards them. Then he turned the car and drove whistling home.

"I've got the kettle on," Tom said as Alice came downstairs in dressing gown and knitted slippers. "My, but it's been a grand day! All Souls will never see a bonnier bride!"

"It seems no time at all since I was pushing her in her pram to Welby post office to ring Julia up. Yet here we are — come full circle, you might say."

"She looked real smart in that going-away outfit you made for her. Things sometimes fall a bit flat when the couple leave. It was a good idea to clear the hall for a bit of dancing." He reached for his jacket. "Think I'll take a look at the dogs and make sure Gracie has locked the hens up. Might just have a fill of tobacco . . ."

Yes, and brood about Daisy who is Keth's now, Alice thought as the door closed behind him. And wish, as I'm wishing, to turn the clock back to the day we carried her to church to her christening, with Julia standing godmother; wish her back to us, Tom, that little lass who was all ours. Bring back a time before she was left all that money and before war came again. We hadn't a lot to live on, but we were luckier than most. Luckier than Julia, who still cried inside her for Andrew; luckier than the men who tramped the roads as Dickon once did, looking — *begging* — for work. We've all come a long way, since then . . .

She lifted her eyes to the mantelpiece and Daisy, in uniform, smiled down at her. Beside the clock stood the handleless mug of flowers. Was it really only this morning her daughter had picked them?

Alice reached for a flower, dabbing the stalk dry with her handkerchief. Pretty little windflower, to remind her of Daisy's wedding.

She took down the big, heavy Bible in which once she pressed Tom's buttercups; now there would be another memory there. Carefully she laid the wild anemone between pieces of tissue paper, then closing the pages over it she smiled, turning to the damp-spotted flyleaf on which everything important in her life had been recorded.

Daisy Julia Dwerryhouse, she had written. *Born 20 June 1920 at Keeper's Cottage, Beck Lane, West Welby, Hampshire.*

Smiling, she took the inkpot from the dresser, dipping in her pen to record the windflower wedding.

Married 17 April 1943 to Keth Purvis at All Souls, Holdenby, Yorkshire, she wrote painstakingly.

Then she smiled again and wondered what her daughter would say when she opened her overnight case and found the nightdress. The very special nightdress.

"We wowed them all, didn't we?" Kitty laughed. "You and me, I mean, announcing our wedding date!"

"Don't think so, really. People have been half expecting it for ages."

They were sitting in the intimate darkness of the conservatory. Drew had specially chosen it, because there were no bulbs in the lights in case anyone should unthinkingly press the switch and illuminate the entire place. Conservatories were like churches, he supposed; windows too big and too high to be blacked out.

"It'll be lovely in church tomorrow, hearing Uncle Nathan call our banns — real romantic." She sighed ecstatically. "Good old Mom, sending my dress. I've tried it on, y'know, and it looks lovely. Aunt Julia said did I want to borrow Aunt Helen's veil. We're going to have a look at it before I go back; see if it's okay after all those years."

"I'm surprised Mother didn't wear it. Her first wedding was in wartime, like ours'll be."

"She told me about it. She wore white orchids in her hair and a blue dress that wasn't even new. I've often wondered how she felt — thinking her war was over, I mean; celebrating the Armistice, then that telegram coming, saying Andrew was dead. She must've hated the whole world."

"I think she did. She just walked out of the ward without even asking permission and went to the hospital he'd worked in. She wouldn't believe he could be dead, but they gave her his kit and his instruments. It was all very cruel."

"Darling," Kitty snuggled closer, "you'll always be careful, won't you? I couldn't take it if anything happened to you."

"Well, I'm not going to say nothing will happen to me — that would be tempting Fate," Drew said softly, kissing her. "But I've got a better chance than a lot of making it to my demob."

"People like Tim Thomson, you mean?"

"Like Tim. Aircrews and fighter pilots take a terrible mauling — and our merchant seamen, in convoys. Besides, everybody on board reckons a boat as small as the *Maggie* isn't worth a torpedo and a darn sight harder to hit than a carrier or one of the battle wagons."

"You're only saying that so I won't worry, but I will. I shall worry more than ever now that we've set a date. You *will* take care, darling?"

"I will. It's going to be all right! Just eight weeks to go. There'll be no end of leg-pulling when I get back on board."

"So don't tell them!"

"It isn't as simple as that on a boat as small as the *Maggie*. They'll find out when I put in for marriage leave. It's so small you can't change your mind without someone knowing!"

"But you like it — you said you did."

"I do, sweetheart. I wouldn't mind seeing the war out, minesweeping. If only you could be based in Liverpool again, life would be a piece of cake."

"I'll fix it. Once we're married I'll stand a good chance of getting near you on compassionate grounds. And do you know where my brother is? He and Gracie were last seen heading in the direction of the wild garden. What do you reckon they're up to?"

"Not a lot! They were probably taking a short cut to the bothy. Gracie has to be in by eleven and it's quarter-past already."

"Gee! It's all happening! Daisy and Keth, then you and me, Drew, and Bas and Gracie dithering on the edge. Y'know, I was worried about Tatty and her with no one to love today. But she was just fine, as if she's coming to terms with things. Wish something good could happen for her, too."

"Tatty's okay — in her own way. She's half-Russian, don't forget. When she was little and unhappy, she'd say it was her Russian soul needing to suffer."

"Tatty's as English as you an' me." Kitty dismissed her American half. "She has a friend now. Not serious, but there are people in London who take out badly wounded men — mostly aircrew. Some of them have dreadful injuries, and it helps rehabilitate them, sort of. That's how Tatty met him."

"There you are, Kitty. Her Russian soul, doing penance!"

"No! There's more to it than that, I'm sure of it. He has no folks of his own, I believe, so Tatty seems to have taken him over. He's called Bill, and he was blinded."

"Hell! That's bad. How come you know so much about him?"

"Because Tatty and I room together at Montpelier, don't forget. Tatty's changed from that spoiled brat the Clan had to drag around. They were lovely days, though."

"Hope Mother's photographs come out all right. She's never had a colour film before. It'll be good to have another picture of us all, six years on. Hope Bas can come by another reel for our wedding."

"He will. And Mom will slip a couple in the next food parcel she sends. Poor love. Wonder how she feels, not being at her daughter's wedding? Are we being selfish, Drew? Ought we to wait?"

"Yes, we *are* being selfish and yes, we ought to wait." He held her more closely, laying his cheek on her head. "But there's a war on, my darling, and love won't wait for wars."

"Guess it won't, at that." She sighed blissfully, wondering how any two people could be so happy, and that happiness go unnoticed by the jealous gods. "The next eight weeks are going to be the longest and loneliest of my life."

"We really ought to go." Daisy leaned her elbows on the table. "We're the only ones left — we shouldn't take advantage."

They had arrived late, the Holdenby train being held up a mile outside York station to give way to a train carrying tanks, shrouded by camouflage netting.

They were too late, said the clerk at Reception, to order dinner. Chef had served all the meals his food rations allowed for that night. She was sorry, but . . .

Then her eyes lit on the coronet of pink orchids Daisy carried and she asked them, in a whisper, if they were just-marrieds, ringing the dining room from which Maitre d' arrived to escort them to a corner table, apologizing that Chef had very little to offer so late in the evening and they would appreciate that the Station Hotel was as much plagued with food rationing as the next establishment.

For all that, though, the table cloth was starched, the cutlery gleaming and the serviettes folded into rosettes. Scrambled egg, Daisy thought, would have tasted like food of the gods tonight, though it was Spam salad in the end!

"I thought you'd never get round to it." Keth rose to pull back her chair, picking up the handbag she had left on the floor, whispering, "There's confetti all over the place!"

"Kitty, up to her tricks, I shouldn't wonder!" Daisy didn't care who knew they were just married. "It's been such a wonderful day. Do you suppose we could book a call to Keeper's — let them know we've arrived?"

"No!" Keth took her arm and guided her to the door. "We'll ring tomorrow, when we get to Winchester. No intrusions. Tonight, it's just you and me. And you don't want carrying over the threshold, do you?"

Daisy said she did not, since he would probably drop her, and they had just switched on the satin-shaded bedroom lights when a glance behind them revealed a smiling wine waiter, carrying a bucket and two glasses.

"Compliments of the management, Captain."

"Goodness! Champagne!" Daisy gasped.

"Afraid not, madam. We've had none of the good stuff since Dunkirk. But it's fizzy and comes with best wishes."

He popped the cork with a flourish, then retrieved it from a corner of the room, asking Daisy if she would like to have it as a souvenir.

But not even after three glasses of the wine was Daisy prepared to cope with the nightdress that lay in tissue paper at the top of the overnight bag. She held it up, smelling its lavender scent. It was of silk, with lace-trimmed shoulder straps and baby-blue ribbons threaded through the bodice and hem.

"Wouldn't you just know . . ." She sniffed loudly and blinked away a tear. "Mam put it there; she must have. Aunt Julia wore it then gave it to Mam when she and Dada were married. How lovely that they wanted me to have it."

Hand-stitched, Daisy knew, for a young nurse marrying her doctor, on leave from the Army. Mam had made it in secret in the sewing room at Rowangarth, long before she and Aunt Julia decided to be nurses and go to the Front. It was soft and sensuous and weighed nothing at all. Carefully she draped it on the bed.

"I don't think I should wear it, for all that. It must be nearly thirty years old, and so precious. Silk is very tender stuff. I'd hate to rip it or anything."

"Put it on, darling — please? For me? And throw me my pyjama bottoms, there's a good girl." He undressed quickly then watched as she draped her pale-blue dress and jacket over a chair.

"We've waited a long time for tonight."

"Mm." Daisy unfastened her suspenders, rolling down her precious silk stockings with studied care. Keth unhooked her brassiere, dropping it to the floor, kissing her shoulder.

"There now. Put it on . . ."

The nightdress slipped and slithered over her breasts, her hips. It fell almost with a sigh to her feet. Keth stepped back, his eyes sweeping her from head to toes.

Daisy Dwerryhouse in Wren-issue black stockings and knee-length knickers was nothing but a delight. Daisy Purvis, wide-eyed in diaphanous silk was beautiful beyond believing, and she was his.

"Now take it off," he whispered. "You're right. We wouldn't want to damage it."

She shrugged it over her shoulders and it fell in a drift of white to her feet. Without speaking, he lifted her in his arms and carried her to the bed.

Tatiana, Sparrow and Julia and the cases, crammed into the little car to drive to Holdenby Halt. Kitty and Drew, Julia supposed, were halfway there already, having elected to walk to the station across the fields. Julia prayed silently that if the Baby Austin reached there, it would have sufficient petrol in the tank to get back to Rowangarth. She had hardly driven her car during the past month, to save precious petrol for the wedding and to drive people like Sparrow who was not able to walk far.

Now all April's petrol ration was gone, she didn't have enough to get to York, but must park the car at Holdenby station and take the train there to make sure that Sparrow, at least, had a seat on the London train.

"I'm glad Aunt Julia's car is so tiny," Kitty beamed, her arm through Drew's, "and that we had to walk."

"What do you mean — had to? We both wanted to. Mother wasn't fooled."

"It's been the most wonderful weekend." She held up her lips to be kissed. Every sentence Kitty spoke was punctuated with kisses. "If our wedding is half as lovely as Daisy's, I won't complain."

"It will be. I guarantee it. It'll be warm, and the garden full of flowers. And there'll be a June moon, and nightingales singing and —"

"I've never heard a nightingale. What do they sound like?"

"Pure magic. If we're lucky there'll be one for our wedding. Now stand still and let me kiss you. Then we'll have to run like mad or you'll miss that train."

"Nothing I'd like more! I felt just awful leaving Rowangarth. I think we should start a baby as soon as we can, then I'll be able to give up my war work with a clear conscience, and live at Rowangarth all the time."

"Scheming hussy." He loved her so much, could think of nothing he wanted more than to have children with her. She was so beautiful, such fun to be with, so very easy to love. "It seems so long to our wedding."

"Sixty-two days, darling. They'll just fly past. I hope I'll get a couple of tours. They'll help the time go more quickly. Sparrow has a calendar in the kitchen at Montpelier. I shall cross off every day. It'll be like waiting for Christmas, only better."

"Do you mean it — about having a baby? Don't you think we should wait?" They were hurrying now towards the fence that separated Brattocks Wood from the railway line. The waving place, they called it. From there it would be only minutes to the station. Trespassing on railway property, really, but everyone did it and no one, as yet, had been caught.

"Wait? This war's going to go on for ages. If we wait, we'll be past it. And I don't want a nanny, Drew. I want to bring up our kids myself. To my way of thinking, there's no point in all that morning sickness and looking like a beached whale if you're going to hand them over to someone else the minute you've pushed and shoved them into the world!"

"You've got it all planned, Kitty Sutton. And do you realize that you'll still be Kitty Sutton after we're married?" He stopped just before the sweep in the track around which the station could be seen, and took her in his arms. "Shall you mind?" he said when they had kissed, then kissed again.

"Not a bit," she said sunnily, "as long as you and Rowangarth are part of the deal. Now let's run!"

Julia and Sparrow and Tatiana were standing amid a litter of cases and carrier bags when Drew and Kitty arrived on the station platform, just as the signal fell with a loud thunk.

"There you are," Julia scolded. "One day, someone is going to get caught on that line. There's a notice saying trespassers will be prosecuted." She smiled when she said it for all that, because it was hard to scold Kitty, even when she deserved it.

The train let out three hoots then appeared round the curve of the line. The stationmaster, who was now the porter too, because so many of the London and North Eastern Railway's staff were away at the war, called to everyone to stand away from the edge of the platform, if they pleased! Then the train screeched and shuddered and clanked to a halt and Drew picked up two cases and walked the length of the train to find a compartment in which they all could sit together for the last few miles.

He found one at the end of the train, settling Sparrow in a corner seat from where she might see Brattocks Wood as they passed. She leaned back with contentment, thinking of the weekend she had lived with *real* gentry; having her meals cooked and served to her and being deferred to by that nice Mary and Tilda — Ellen too — as if she were not a Cockney sparrow who had never in her life before gone further afield than the hop fields of Kent.

She had taken tea in Miss Clitherow's own little sitting room and drank from her rosebud cups and talked of times past when the Prince of Wales had been a right lad and his mother so taken up mourning her Albert that she never noticed what he'd been up to!

"You'll be coming again for Sir Andrew's wedding?" Miss Clitherow had asked. "I shall really look forward to another chat, my dear."

And Sparrow said too right she'd be here and nothing was going to keep her away, her having known the young gent from being a little lad of two, and entitled!

"Sparrow. Wake up," Tatiana was whispering in her ear, and Emily Smith forced open her eyes and sat up with a little snort and said she hadn't been asleep at all, and were they in York already?

The station was a bustle of servicemen and women, and kitbags and cases, and lovers parting, standing hands clasped tightly, grateful that the train was late arriving.

Kitty reached for Drew's hand, whispering to him not to be sad, that next time they met it would be June.

June. A magic word that rhymed with moon and can't-come-too-soon; a word that hinted of honeysuckle and roses and newly cut grass and a nightingale singing, perhaps. June, when Helen Sutton's white orchids would flower and she would carry them to the church where Uncle Nathan would marry them.

"I think," Drew frowned, "that we should position ourselves strategically, sort of, so we've got three chances of getting at least one seat when the train comes in. Can you stay here, Mother, with Sparrow? Tatty — how about going to the end of the platform? Kitty and I will wait somewhere around the middle. First one to get a seat grabs it and sticks to it like glue — okay?"

"But how will Sparrow know where Kitty and Tatty are?" Julia demanded. "It won't work."

"I agree with Drew," Tatty said at once. "Now if you get a seat, Sparrow, sit tight and one of us will come along the train to find you. I suppose we'll have to be content just getting on it. Let's spread out, shall we?" She held out her arms to Julia. "Hasn't it been wonderful?" she smiled. "And we're going to do it all again soon!" Then she turned to Drew, kissing him. "So long, sailor. Stay lucky!" Then she picked up her case and walked, straight-backed, to the end of the long platform

490

from where she hoped to find at least one seat. For Sparrow.

"That Tatiana," Sparrow said softly, "is a little queen. I thought she'd be real miserable seeing Daisy so happy, but not a bit of it! She's got Sutton spunk all the way down her backbone! Now give us a hug and a kiss, young Drew, and watch what you're doing when you're after those mines. They make a nasty old bang, you know!"

"I'll take care, Sparrow. When we're sweeping, the hatches are battened down and Knocker and I are safe below decks. You take care. I'll be seeing you in June, don't forget."

They kissed affectionately; an old, wise woman who had watched Drew grow up, and a sailor who was soon to be married.

"I don't want to leave you," Kitty whispered, when they had taken up their position, and Julia and Sparrow and Tatiana were lost to them on the crowded platform. "All these people *can't* be getting on the train!"

"Don't think so." Drew threaded his fingers through hers. "Some will be here with platform tickets, meeting the train, and quite a few will get off at York. Hope so. Don't want Sparrow to have to stand all the way to London."

"She won't. Someone will give her a seat. I'm going to miss you, though. Thank goodness we'll be busy. It'll help pass the time. I know we've got a three-week tour planned, though I don't know where we'll be going. Wouldn't it be just wonderful if we took in Liverpool?"

"It would be nothing short of a miracle if the *Maggie* was alongside at exactly the same time! We'll survive. It isn't all that long to June. I'll be going back first train out of Holdenby in the morning. Should be leaning on the rail waving ta-ra to the Liver Birds this time tomorrow."

"Daisy'll be back there from her leave by the time you dock again. Shall you call her?"

"I always do. I'll take her to a flick or a meal. She'll be in need of cheering up, I shouldn't wonder."

"And Lyndis . . . ?" Kitty whispered.

"Just Daisy. Lyndis doesn't come along any more. She's been promoted — works at Flag Officer's place now."

"You were fond of her, though."

"Very fond, Kitty, but it's you I *love*, you I'm going to marry!" He bent to kiss the tip of her nose. "You looked absolutely beautiful. I've never seen you really dressed up before. I wanted to shout, 'I'm going to marry the bridesmaid in blue! Isn't she just something?'"

"Wait till you see me in my wedding dress. I tried it on. Lady wanted to see if it needed any alterations, but it was just fine. And I'm wearing Aunt Helen's veil. I don't suppose it's bad luck to tell you that. We were amazed. It hasn't yellowed one bit!" Kitty was happy again. Indeed, she was forced to admit, there were times when she was real sorry for Daisy's friend Lyn!

Movements on the platform told them the train was coming. Soldiers and airmen and sailors shouldered kitbags; ATS girls, WAAFs and Wrens picked up their cases. Lovers kissed fiercely, desperately.

"It's coming," Kitty whispered. "Tell me you love me."

"I love you, love you. I always will!"

The train stopped. Windows went down with a clatter, hands reached out for door handles. The waiting crowd surged forward as doors banged open. From one, four nuns stepped sedately down. Drew pressed forward to see four empty seats.

"Here!" he hissed, trying to fill the entire doorway with his body, then pushing in to sprawl on one seat and cover another with Kitty's case. "Quick, darling!" Securing a seat on a wartime train was a mixing of brute force and good luck and, ungentlemanly or not, Drew Sutton was learning.

Kitty did not follow him. Instead she jumped on a trolley intended for mailbags and sticking her first and second fingers into her mouth, let out an ear-splitting whistle in Sparrow's direction. Then she turned and sent out another for Tatty's benefit, waving frantically.

"Will you *get on*!" Drew yelled.

Kitty jumped down and with a series of sweet smiles, "Thank you — most kind," and one or two well-aimed elbow jabs, reached Drew's side. Taking off her coat, she laid it with her gas mask on the remaining seat. Then she stood glowering in the doorway, determined to keep all three seats empty until such times as Sparrow and Tatty arrived to claim them.

Sparrow, amazingly, arrived first with Julia struggling behind with her case.

"Well done, you two!" Sparrow beamed. "Strewth! I haven't been in a scrum like that since the General Strike!" She flopped into a seat as Tatiana, red-faced, joined them.

"Stick tight to my seat, Tatty. Just got to say so long to a sailor."

Drew held out his arms. Kitty went into them, winding her arms around his neck. "I love you, darling. I don't want to leave you," she whispered huskily.

"It'll be all right, sweetheart. Don't forget that next time we meet it'll be for the wedding. Just take care of yourself." His lips lingered on hers.

"I love you. I always will."

"See you in June," he whispered throatily.

Doors were being banged. The train was late and there was no time to stand idling. Kitty stepped into the compartment, leaning out of the window for one more kiss.

"Don't wait to wave me off. Go now, Drew."

"Okay. Love you." Like Kitty, Drew disliked final, faraway goodbyes. He turned and walked away, followed by Julia.

"Don't look back, Mother," he said as they reached the barrier, handing in platform tickets. "It's bad luck."

"Yes." It had been the same in her war. "They all got seats and together too. It's going to be very quiet when you've gone back, Drew. Wasn't it an unbelievable weekend? Your turn next!"

But for all that, she felt an awful flatness; as if she had run miles and couldn't go another step. Drained. A sudden, inexplicable low, was it, that must surely follow so magic a high?

When Drew had gone back to his ship, she would talk to Alice about it. Alice would be sad too now that Daisy was Keth's.

"Don't look so unhappy, Mother. Everything's going fine. We're winning the war, and you and Lady have another wedding to arrange. And look — there's our train!"

The little Holdenby Flyer stood at its usual side platform, free of shoving crowds. It always left on time and was rarely late. Not for the Flyer the glamour of hurtling from London to Edinburgh or Perth. No one ever pushed and struggled to claim one of its hard, turn-of-the-century seats. It made the journey from York to Holdenby Halt and back five times a day, except Sunday, with an extra late run on Saturday nights in the summer. The Holdenby train was as reliable and enduring as Rowangarth, Julia thought fondly. Come hell or high water or war, even, it was still there.

"When do you suppose they'll arrive?" she asked when they were settled in window seats.

"About eleven, allowing for delays. They'll be fine. The Tube will have closed for the night, but I gave Kitty money — told her to get a taxi at King's Cross."

"Mm. Gracie gave Tilda two eggs, so she did chopped egg and chive sandwiches for the journey. And Catchpole provided apples from the loft. Jack enjoyed the wedding, I think. He was very proud of his florals. He'll already be planning yours and Kitty's."

"Will Gran's white orchids be in time for June?"

"They will! If they get too far forward, Jack will hold them back and he'll give them a push if he thinks they won't flower in time. Old-fashioned gardeners like Catchpole have a trick or two up their sleeves. Kitty will have white orchids, I promise."

All at once, her vague sadness had gone. Indeed, she wondered what she'd had to be sad about. But just briefly, it had seemed as if something had slithered over her grave.

Now, just to talk of those very special orchids dispelled all gloom, because they had been her mother's flowers, left behind to remind them that Rowangarth endured. And Drew would marry Kitty and have children; Sutton sons and daughters. And the sons would be dark like their mother, and the daughters fair and grey-eyed like their father.

The Flyer gave a warning hoot that it was about to depart. Soon, they would be in Holdenby and they would drive back to Rowangarth on the teaspoonful of petrol she was sure could be all that was left in the tank. She wondered if she should ask the garage to take one of next month's coupons, just this once, then decided against it. There was a war on and even to run a private car, no matter how small and shabby, was a luxury, and until the end of the month she would walk. Or cycle!

"They'll be on their way now," she said, as they left the station, and Drew smiled at the Minster as they passed it, then thought of Kitty and how much he missed her already, sending his love to her in great warm waves, hoping there wouldn't be a raid on London tonight, and that the train wouldn't be stopped at a station miles outside, because trains, if at all possible, were prevented from entering any station being bombed.

He sent his thoughts high and wide. *Take care my darling. See you in June.*

"Goodness, weren't we lucky?" Tatiana asked as she offered packets of carefully wrapped sandwiches. "Getting seats, I mean. And wherever did you learn to whistle like that, Kitty? I always meant to ask you to show me how. You were the best whistler in the Clan. Who taught you?"

"One of the stable lads back home. I'll show you how if you'll tell me some more Russian swear

497

words. He taught me how to spit too. I could spit further than —"

"That will be all!" Sparrow fixed them with a gimlet eye. "There'll be no whistling in Montpelier — t'aint seemly for young ladies to whistle. Besides, it's unlucky and we want no bad luck between now and the wedding! And we want no spitting, either, and no swearin' in Russian!"

"No, Sparrow," they both said.

"And if you don't mind, I'll save my sandwiches for later. Think I could do with forty winks." She took off her hat, folded her arms and closed her eyes. "Give me a nudge, Tatty girl, if I start snoring."

Kitty gazed out of the window. Soon, they would have passed Doncaster. The engine driver, frustrated at the lateness of his departure from York, seemed determined to make up the time lost. Every click and clack of the wheels was taking her further from Drew and tomorrow at this time, HMS *Penrose* — Drew's beloved little *Maggie* — would put out to sea and danger. It wasn't fair! Wars were awful! Look what the war had done to Tatty and Tim!

She closed her eyes so tears that were pricking should not come, and pretended to sleep so she could think of a wedding gown in white satin and of two dresses in pink and blue, that Tatty and Gracie would wear on 19 June.

Then she thought about the calendar hanging behind the kitchen door at Montpelier Mews. She would ring round 19 June in red crayon; would

498

cross off every day between now and then and whilst she was away on tour — which she surely would be — Tatty would make the crosses for her.

She was so happy — almost all of the time, that was. Sometimes her American half reached out to the white, sprawling house in which she was born, and the white-railed paddocks and the horses. And Mom and Pa, of course.

One day, Bas would go back there and take Gracie with him, but Kitty Sutton would exchange Kentucky for Rowangarth, and Drew. And Drew was worth the home-sickness. He was her life now, and anyway, Kentucky would be just a hop and spit away once the liners had finished being troopships and planes could fly the Atlantic without the risk of being shot down.

In eight weeks she would marry Drew, and the bombed houses and streets and churches wouldn't matter quite so much, nor the shortages, either. One day the war would end and the killing and maiming stop, and until it did there was Rowangarth, safe and unchanging to come home to. And always there would be Drew. Kitty and Drew, for ever.

"You wouldn't believe the quiet," said Tilda. "You can almost hear it!"

"Yes, but it's been almost like old times," Mary smiled. "There's nowhere in this Riding to better All Souls and Rowangarth when it comes to a wedding. And I see," she glanced sideways at Tilda's left hand, "that you'll be walking up the aisle before long. When did it happen, then?"

"We were sitting in the conservatory — taking a bit of a breather from the dancing, you'll understand — and Sydney happened to remark that it might be nice if one day him and me could do the same as Daisy and Keth. Mind, I said not till the war was over, but I wouldn't mind being properly engaged, for the time being.

"So he took my ring off my right hand and put it on my left one and said now I must call him my fiancé, since it's official. He said he's going to ask Mr Catchpole if he can work at Rowangarth when the war is over. Mind, it don't do to make too many plans when there's a war on."

"Be nice if you and Sydney could get one of the gate lodges," Mary considered. "Miss Julia would find a house for you both. Estate houses come vacant all the time. Miss Clitherow could have one of the empty almshouses any time she wanted. Mind, if ever Leeds got blitzed, *They* would take the almshouses for bombed-outs without so much as a by-your-leave, and Miss Julia not able to do a thing about it!

"But never mind about the old war! It didn't spoil the wedding, did it? And we'll be busy again in a couple of months. Sparrow says she's coming to Drew's wedding; nothing's going to keep her away. Do you know, Tilda, she told me she hasn't eaten so well since war started and that up here, in the wild north, folks don't know how lucky they are. I told

500

her that Mrs Amelia's food parcels helped a lot, but she said that in London they could go to draw their rations only to find the shop had been bombed!

"We're very lucky," Mary admitted, not at all like her usual critical self. "Will's too old to be called into the Army and since I'm married the Labour Exchange said I'd better keep on with my job at Rowangarth — just as long as I don't change it without asking their permission. As if I would!"

Mary was unusually mellow, Tilda thought, but maybe it was because of the wedding. Weddings always made women weepy and soft inside — herself not the least of them. Yet what Tilda could not know, and Mary had chosen not to tell her, was that Will had leaned close in the church and whispered that she looked like a bride all over again in her wedding frock and hat. And he had taken her hand and squeezed it and smiled at her with calf eyes, which was very unusual for Will Stubbs, who wasn't one for fancy words and gestures.

She smiled to remember how Will had asked her to wear her wedding nightie when they were undressing for bed after the dance, though she felt sad, next morning, that he had changed back to the Will of old and turned grumpily on his side and said it was his morning for a lie-in, when she whispered there was nothing she would like better than a tray of tea in bed, it being Sunday.

Ah, well. There was always Drew's wedding to look forward to, Mary sighed.

When Kitty and Tatiana had been to say goodbye and to tell her to look after the rose-pink and blue dresses as they would be needed again very soon, Alice climbed the stairs to the spare bedroom where she had hung Daisy's frock. She wanted, she told herself, to inspect it for stains — especially round the hemline. A sponge and a press, and it would be like new, especially since she had got it into her head that Gracie might like to wear it. Daisy wouldn't mind a bit and it would be lovely to see it used again — and again, if needs be! A girl deserved a white wedding, even if there was a war on!

It was then she saw the envelope, one corner tucked beneath the daisy brooch which had not yet been put back into safe-keeping. It was addressed to Mr and Mrs T. Dwerryhouse, in Daisy's small, neat writing, and the flap was not stuck down.

Cheeks suddenly pinking, breath indrawn, Alice took out the single sheet of paper.

Dearest Mam and Dada,

This is to say thank you for everything; for my lovely day and for having me and putting up with me for twenty-three years and being such wonderful parents.

I love you both very, very much and I always will. Bless you both, and take care.

Love always and always,

(Mrs) Daisy (PURVIS!!)

"There you are!" Tom was standing in the bedroom doorway. "Happy, now?"

"Who put the letter there?"

"I did. Daisy gave it to me, just before they went off. Said I was to give it to you if you got a bit weepy. That's why I left it with the dress."

"Have you read it, Tom?"

"I have. Short, but very sweet. She's a good girl. She'll always be our lass. We haven't lost her."

"And we never shall," Alice said softly. And if, in the next few days, she got just a little bit weepy, then she only had to look at Daisy's picture on the mantelpiece and the windflowers beside it. "I wonder, Tom, if they'll wait to have a family or if they've decided to start one right away."

"Now then! That's private between the two of them!"

Yet, Tom cogitated as he went downstairs in search of a fill of tobacco, there weren't many things could please him more than having a little lad in the family.

West Welby village, when Keth and Daisy reached it, seemed to have hidden itself from the war in the deeps of the New Forest. On the surface, nothing had changed except cottage windows, criss-crossed with brown paper. Unchanged too stood the church where, just after the Great War, Alice and Tom were married and where, a year later, Daisy had been christened.

At the far end of the village green was the little general store and next to it, the post office from which Alice once made her phone calls to Julia.

Hand in hand they walked past the yellow stone school where Daisy had laboriously learned to print her name, feeling badly done to because it was so long, wishing it could have been short, like Keth's.

And now she was Daisy Purvis, who had laid the coronet of wedding flowers on Dickon's grave and stood solemnly by as Keth took a snap of it so Polly should know it was being cared for still.

Mum's all right, Dad. One day I'll bring her to see you when the war's over. Daisy is with me. We were married on Saturday . . .

Then he turned, holding out his hand to her, smiling, saying they should go and look at Beck Lane and see if Morgan and Beth were all right too.

At the churchyard gates he stopped, checking that the precious film in his American-bought camera was properly wound on. Then, lifting it to his eye, he took another picture of the church and the gravestones around it, a final goodbye to the father who drowned, trying to rescue a Labrador bitch from a flooded river.

They linked hands, each saying a silent goodbye, then walked back across the green to the little lane that wound a mile through hedgerows to the top of Beck Lane.

"If I had a pound note for every time you and I have walked up and down this lane, I'd be a rich man," Keth laughed, glad he had been to the churchyard.

"If you're going to talk about money, then don't dare!" Daisy warned. "Not on our honeymoon, not

504

till the war is over. I've only bought two wedding hats, you know, and taken Lyn out for a meal once or twice, but when cars are on the market again I shall buy you one, Keth, and nothing you can say will stop me! Now, no more money talk!"

"Okay. Promise! Tell me you're happy, darling."

"You know I am." She went into his arms, holding him close. "It's all so wonderful. I don't want to go back to Hellas House."

"Ssssh! No war talk, either! Tell me you love me?"

"I adore you. You know I do. Let's go and tell Morgan and Beth we're married?"

They walked slowly, hands still clasped, the afternoon sun warm on their faces and Daisy recalled how, almost two years ago, she had waited for Keth at the place where bluebells chime; where once they laid Morgan the spaniel. And Dada, lovely Dada, held a little funeral for him and they said the Lord's Prayer and sang "All Things Bright and Beautiful". Morgan would get into heaven without any bother at all, Dada comforted, because heaven wouldn't be heaven, he had reasoned, without dogs in it.

They found the little grave marker at the side of Beck Lane. On it was chiselled B & M, and the date, 1926, because Beth had been laid there too, not long before they left Beck Lane to live in Yorkshire.

"Dada had that little stone put there for Beth and Morgan. I couldn't have just left them there, all alone, when we went to Rowangarth. He always made things come right. You'll be like him, won't you, Keth, when we have children? And are we going to have children, or are we going to wait? I don't mind one bit, though I think I'd like to see the war out in the Wrens. Mind, Aunt Julia and Andrew didn't have a child, and she was left with nothing . . ."

"No, but she got Drew, and everything turned out fine for her in the end. And Daisy, sweetheart, I want us to wait to have a family. It wouldn't be pushing our luck if we waited. It's likely I'll spend my war code-breaking in some unsung back room."

"And they won't be sending you to Washington — *again*?"

"I'm almost certain they won't. I'm on a new project now."

"Like what?"

"Like a new project," he teased, tweaking her nose, wishing he could tell her.

He closed down his thoughts, shaking his head clear of Clissy-sur-Mer and Tante Clara and Natasha. Remember them with gratitude always, but not on these few precious days that were his and Daisy's alone.

"Ha!" She wrinkled her nose at him, because she knew that not for anything would Keth tell her what went on in the so-called back room he shared with other boffins.

"Look! They're flowering! They must have known we were coming!" Keth pointed to a swathe of blue beneath the trees.

"And Beth and Morgan can hear them chiming, too," Daisy smiled fondly. "Aren't they beautiful? The bluebells at Rowangarth were still in bud when we left."

"So they were, but it's much warmer down here; no bitter east winds like at home."

Home was Rowangarth now, and not the cottages that stood empty at either end of Beck Lane: Keeper's Cottage, in which Daisy had been born on a June afternoon, and Willow End, where once Keth lived with Polly and Dickon.

"Are you going to take a snap of the lane, darling, for Mam and Polly to see?"

"If you think they won't be shocked by the state of it — the houses, I mean . . ."

The paint on Keeper's front door was peeling; its path was weed-choked, the doorstep unscrubbed. In the two years since they were there the front gate had fallen from its hinges and lay unmoved, which only went to show, Daisy reasoned, that absolutely no one came here now.

"I can't believe there wasn't so much as a weed there once." Daisy nodded to the tangle of brambles and nettles that had taken over Dada's vegetable garden. "Maybe you shouldn't take a snap, Keth. Maybe we should leave Mam and Polly with their memories."

They walked slowly towards Willow End, older than Keeper's Cottage, and thatched like so many homes in the New Forest.

"Look at that rose! I remember Mam planting it!"

By way of a celebration, Polly Purvis said, on account of Dickon finding a job and them all being together again. Half a crown she paid for that rose, a vigorous climber, its label promised.

Now it had grown to cover the window of the room in which Keth once slept, then rambled up and on, to tangle with the decaying thatch of the roof.

Daisy turned to gaze the length of Beck Lane, grown over with grass because neither feet nor wheels passed up and down it any longer.

"Definitely no snaps. We can tell Polly her rose is doing well and we needn't mention Dada's vegetable garden. Let's tell them everything is fine — and Beth and Morgan, too."

"We'll do that." Keth pushed open the sagging gate. "Shall we stay a while? The stone bench is still there."

Daisy recalled the rough stone seat where Polly and Mam sat on summer evenings, knitting or talking or maybe just sitting, eyes closed, faces to the sun.

There had been no talk of war then. Their children would grow up without the fear of killing and maiming. Their generation — Tom and Dickon's — had paid the final instalment. No more trenches, not partings, nor widows bringing up children alone. That's what they once thought on those summer evenings.

Daisy and Keth sat close, lifting their faces to the sun as Alice and Polly had done.

"I'm glad you booked the same room in the same hotel." Daisy broke the silence.

"I told them we'd had our wedding night in that room and we particularly wanted it again."

"Keth! How could you? It wasn't our wedding night. We weren't married!"

"All right — so we jumped the gun two years ago."

"Well, all I can say is that I hope there's no confetti about or they'll wonder what we're up to!"

"Why should they? We know we're married, so what the heck?"

"Yes, but what about the other time?"

"What about it?" Keth teased. "That was all of two years ago!"

"I wish you weren't so good to look at, Keth Purvis. When you smile like that, I go peculiar inside!"

"Want me to make love to you?"

"Yes, but not in Beck Lane. It wouldn't be right, would it?" It wouldn't. Not when the wraiths of two children might witness that loving.

"Why not?" He kissed her softly, then smiled again, so she could hardly bear the need inside her.

"Because — well, we were kids here . . ."

"So when we're apart and it's winter and I'm in my back room and you're in your hot teleprinter place, you wouldn't want to think back to this afternoon in Beck Lane? Y'know something? I've never made love to a Wren in a bluebell wood." He got to his feet, holding out his hands to her. "You know you want to. You've got that look in your eyes."

So she closed her tell-tale eyes and lifted her mouth to be kissed. Hands clasped, they walked up the lane, past the little marker with B & M 1926 on it, and into the deeps of the beechwood, where bluebells grew thickly.

"I love you, Daisy Purvis," he said huskily.

She didn't speak because she was fixing the time and the place and the earthy woodland scents in her heart so that when they were apart and her need of him was almost too much to bear, she could call back these moments and live them again, and again, and again . . .

CHAPTER
TWENTY-SIX

"Well, what d'you know!" Daisy shook the newspaper indignantly. "If that isn't just our luck!"

"So tell me? Keth stood in the bathroom doorway, shaving brush poised, taking in the rounds of her shoulders and the high, firm breasts, not quite covered by the sheet.

"It's Mr Churchill! Hasn't he just told Parliament that from Easter Sunday, church bells can ring again! Says it's in the light of changing circumstances."

"Circumstances like what?"

"The invasion, I suppose. You were in America, Keth, when we were waiting for that lot to invade us. We were expecting it any day. It wasn't funny. People talked about the invasion as if it were fact, and only the date was uncertain.

"Anyway, bells hadn't to be rung, except if it started so the changed circumstances, I imagine, means we won't be invaded now."

"Then why, Mrs Purvis, are you looking so put out?"

She smiled briefly, sunnily, because she still felt a shiver of delight whenever he reminded her she really *was* his wife. Then she resumed her glaring at the newspaper.

"Because if they'd shifted themselves, we could have had wedding bells. I always wanted wedding bells!"

"Then would a nice, soapy kiss make up for it?"

"Don't you dare!" Giggling, she pulled the sheet over her head — as if all this would last for ever he thought, briefly sad, because on Saturday, in three days, they would leave for London. And at Euston he would find her a seat on the Liverpool train, then go back to Bletchley Park and the black-painted iron bed with its grey blankets.

It didn't bear thinking about. To awaken in that spartan room after the delight of finding Daisy beside him was going to take a bit of stomaching.

"Shall you be able to wangle a couple of days for Drew's wedding?" he called from the bathroom.

"You bet! As it happens, I'll have just done a week of nights, so I'll be able to use my two rest days. No bother at all. It'll be rotten, though, for Lyndis when that happens." She was leaning against the bathroom door, now, her dressing gown tied tightly at her waist.

"Did Drew play fast and loose with Lyn?" Keth splashed his face with water. "He was such a sobersides when we were kids."

"Not a sobersides, exactly," Daisy defended. "He was brought up in a household of women. It was why Aunt Julia sent him mornings to Nathan, at the vicarage. A bit of masculine influence, I suppose.

512

Drew was more what you'd call serious, really. The Navy has brought him out a lot."

"And Kitty!"

"Kitty was the best thing that could have happened to him, but before that, he was quite gone on Lyn and she was mad about him. If Kitty ever dumped Drew, Lyn would be there with a shoulder to cry on. I wish something good could happen for her."

"She's a real good-looker." Keth frowned. "She could have any man she set her cap at. So why doesn't she?"

"Because she's Lyn and because she still loves Drew. I think she always will. As they say, life can be a bitch!"

"And life, as I see it from where I'm standing, can be one big, beautiful bowl of cherries! So hurry up, get your bath, make yourself prettier, then it'll be time for breakfast. You've got fifteen minutes!"

"Bossy boots," she pouted, opening the white leather makeup case which had been Keth's coming-of-age present, thrilling still to see so many pots of cream, and lipsticks and mascaras and face powder. There was even a bottle of perfume in it, and no one, but *no one*, could buy perfume in the shops. "What have you planned for today?"

"Salisbury," he said without any hesitation.

"Is it far? Can we hitch there?"

"Not in civvies. Drivers only stop for uniforms. We can get a train."

"Why Salisbury?" she called above the noise of running bath taps.

"Because I haven't seen the cathedral, except on a painting; because I've always wanted to see it, and because I want to look at something — well — *enduring*, sort of." When he was back amongst codes and ciphers and clicking *bombes*; when he was alone again and wanting Daisy, it would be good to think of such a place. "They do say that Salisbury Cathedral has one of the three original copies of Magna Carta. It's what this war is all about, really; the right of ordinary blokes to live their lives the way they want to."

"Well, aren't you just the poetic one, Captain Purvis, and here's me, thinking you were a cold, calculating mathematician! And I hope we *don't* see Magna Carta! I hope they've got something as precious as that hidden away till the war's over! Wouldn't Hitler just love to get his grubby little hands on it! There now, will I do?"

She wore a blue skirt and flower-patterned blouse. Her legs were stockingless, her feet in flat sandals. She looked, he thought, too young to leave home, let alone be a married woman with more than two years' service in the armed forces.

"You'll do very nicely," he smiled, locking the door behind him. She was much, much too beautiful and he didn't want to leave her. "I suppose," he said, shifting his eyes from the tantalizing glimpse of her breasts, "it'll be

514

scrambled dried eggs again for breakfast. And fasten your top button, please!"

He gazed at the greeny-brown mark in the hollow of her throat. All women in uniform had them, visible only when they exchanged collars and ties for civilian clothes. The mark was caused by the rubbing and staining of the front collar stud. The verdigris in the copper did it. He had a similiar stain, yet he resented Daisy's neck being marked in so masculine a way.

"And it might be bacon and eggs and sausages and tomatoes and lots of fried bread!" Daisy teased, buttoning her blouse obediently. "Won't it be lovely when we can buy all the bacon and eggs and marmalade we want, and have butter on our toast again? How long is this war going to last?"

"We said no money-talk or war-talk," he said softly, stopping on the half-landing to kiss her nose. He loved her nose too. It was ever so slightly tip-tilted and quite perfect. She was beautiful all over. She would have beautiful children for him. One day . . .

Drew rested his arms on the top rail, eyes narrowed against the shine of setting sun on water, feeling the smack of the bows against the turbulence of river meeting sea.

The outline of Liverpool's docks began to grey and fade, even though at half-past nine it was still light. In June, when he and Kitty were married, the day would only give way to twilight at eleven at night.

So long a day was strange still, yet even the sceptics who said that to push the clocks *two* hours forward should never be allowed, were coming round now to the realization that double-summertime not only saved electricity for the war effort, but was a boon to drivers, who were allowed only dangerously small lights.

June 19. His wedding day, and Kitty's. Seeing Daisy so happy made him long for it all the more. Sad that Uncle Albert would not be able to give his daughter away and that Aunt Amelia couldn't be there, but it was as Kitty said: what was to stop them getting married all over again in Kentucky? By the time the war was over they would deserve a second honeymoon, anyway, though she hadn't said how another white wedding would look if they'd had a baby meantime.

Lovely, mischievous Kitty. Lady Kathryn Sutton. She would love Rowangarth as much as he did and of course they would have children. A lot, he hoped.

"Attention on the upper deck!" The bosun's pipe keened. "All hands to darken ship! Darken ship!"

Drew straightened his shoulders and made for the cubby-hole that served as a wireless office. To darken ship was really to black out the ship, exactly as civilians had to, except there were no curtains to pull; just hinged metal porthole covers to be swung into place and made secure with large butterfly screws. And no lights — not even the glow of a cigarette end — permitted on the upper deck.

Small, circular portholes led his mind to Rowangarth, and the tall window on the half-landing and the big, bow windows on the ground floor. At Rowangarth now the sinking sun would be touching those leaded, diamond-paned windows and his mother would probably be sitting in the conservatory, wondering about all the lovely fuss and counting the days to the next upset; to his and Kitty's wedding.

He thought of Daisy. In two more days she would be back in Liverpool, in quarters at Hellas House, and missing Keth. He would phone her when next they came alongside; suggest they meet so she could talk about Keth and he could talk about Kitty and each comfort the other, though Daisy would have Lyn were she in need of a shoulder to cry on.

Dear Lyn. He still felt bad about her, though he had never said he loved her. They had been friends; good friends, though if Kitty hadn't happened, he might have asked Lyn to marry him.

For him, Lyn had been an experience along the way to loving. She it was who made him aware of his manhood, want to do away with his virginity. Lyn had attracted him, bewildered him, left him wondering why he hadn't slept with her. Then Kitty came back into his life, and took it over.

I love you, Kitty Sutton! He sent his thoughts high and wide to a little white house near Hyde Park. I want you; need you near me all the time. I want this war over and you and I real people again, doing what *we* want to do!

The bosun's pipe wailed again. A disembodied voice ordered the stand-down watch to the galley. Drew's soaring thoughts hit the deck at his feet with a hard slap.

There was food to be eaten, a watch soon to be kept, a war to be endured. Only when the war was over could he and Kitty be real people; only then would their lives be their own to live as they wanted.

Till then, 19 June were words to be whispered like a prayer, worn like a talisman. 19 June was fifty-nine long, lonely days away, and he wondered how he would live through them.

An elderly porter walked the length of the platform calling, "Liverpool Exchange! Exchange station!" Though depleted by war, station staff took it upon themselves to call out names of stations because all had been removed when invasion seemed imminent and Authority had not yet said when they might be put back.

Daisy stepped off the train. It was almost midnight and the train late arriving by two hours. Buses and trams would have stopped now; a taxi would be hard to find, its petrol allocation for the day used up long ago.

She lifted her case, shouldered her respirator, then walked quickly to the barrier. With luck, she might be in time to cadge a lift on the transport which should, almost any minute now, be emptying off A-watch and filling up with D-watch, their stint over.

She ran from the station and across the road, her case a dead weight; then down the street to turn left at the first corner. There was no transport outside Epsom House.

"Have the watches changed yet?" she gasped to the Marine sentries at the sandbagged entrance.

"Not yet, Jenny." One of them noticed her case. "Been on leave, then?"

"I've been on my honeymoon," she whispered disconsolately, unable to stop the outpouring.

"Oh, dearie me. Well never mind, girl. You'll soon be back in the convent with your nice Mother Superior!"

The two men chuckled, even though the joke about Wrens living an enclosed life with mothers superior to guard their virginities was as old as the hills and as boring as cold toast without butter.

"Soon be back," Daisy echoed, lowering her case to the ground, clenching and unclenching her left hand, which was numb with the weight.

The transport rounded the corner and stopped outside. The door banged open and A-watch got out to disappear one by one through the very small doorway.

Daisy heaved her case on the step of the camouflaged bus with the blacked-out windows and said, "Hi, Tommy. Got room for one more?"

"Who is it, then?" The driver knew every Wren on every watch, but it was dark inside the bus.

"It's Daisy Dwerryhouse — I mean Purvis!" she smiled wanly.

"Ar yes, queen. You've been on a week's Compassionate!" Tommy nodded. "Shove your case out of the way behind the door. No need to heave it onto the rack. Had a good time then — er — what did you say it was now?"

"Purvis. And yes, I had a lovely time. We've been staying in Winchester." Best tell him. Tommy liked to know what his girls had been up to.

"Why Winchester?"

"Because Paris gets a bit crowded at this time of the year!" She tried to laugh, but the ache she had felt the moment the train pulled out of Euston station was still there, like a tight ball of tears waiting to burst. "As a matter of fact we decided on Winchester because I was born near there and because it's near to a lot of nice places."

"Oh, ar," Tommy said, then got out to stretch his legs and have a chat with the sentries.

Daisy chose the front seat, the better to see Lyn when she got on at the Pierhead at the end of her watch. She breathed deeply and heavily, eyes closed against tears that threatened.

She wanted Keth. Why had he stood there white-faced as her train pulled out? Why hadn't he said, "Don't go!" Why hadn't she said, "To hell with the lot of them!" and refused to leave him?

Because, urged the small voice of reason inside her head, they were no longer Keth and Daisy

520

Purvis. They were names and numbers again. You belong to *Them*, the faceless ones. You do as you are told because to disobey an order is mutiny. You belong for the duration of hostilities!

D-watch, freed from the deeps, began to climb on the transport. One or two recognized her in the darkness, and asked if she had had a good leave. No one chortled, "You've had it, chum, you've had it, never mind!" After marriage leave, it simply wasn't done.

"Everybody on, then?" Tommy banged shut the door and started up the bus, pointing it in the direction of the Pierhead to pick up D-watch from Flag Officer's.

Lyn was almost last on. Daisy called "Hi!" and Lyn said, "Hi!" as if she had never been away, sitting down beside her, saying, "Tell me about it when we get back, uh?"

Daisy was grateful for her understanding and for the hand that found hers and held it tightly.

It wasn't until they had closed the door of Cabin 4A behind them that Daisy gasped, "Damn, damn, *damn*! I don't want to open that case, Lyn! It's got all my honeymoon things in it!"

"Keth, sort of . . .?"

"Yes, and coming back here it's as if none of it happened." She began to pace the floor, hugging herself tightly. "It was absolute heaven — and now this." She looked around her, shrugging helplessly, shaking her head. "I miss him already. I hate this bloody war!"

521

"Come downstairs for standeasy?" To the large, cream-enamel pot of ready-milked tea, and slices of bread and jam always there for late watchkeepers.

"It would choke me!"

"It won't. Bet you haven't had any food inside you since this morning and if you want to lie awake all night listening to your empty stomach making noises, then I don't! I'm the one with rank up in this cabin and I'm *telling* you to! And if you do, I just might give you a letter — *two* letters!" Lyn opened her locker, handing Daisy an envelope with a Holdenby postmark.

"From Mam!" Daisy tore it open, at once feeling better because there *was* another world away from all this; there was Keeper's Cottage and Rowangarth and Brattocks Wood, where the rooks nested and windflowers still grew. One day, she would leave uniforms and watches and partings behind her. One day, the war *would* be over.

Dearest Daisy,

Dada and I were real pleased to read the letter you left behind and we want you to know we were so proud of our girl on her wedding day. I think it is we who should thank you for twenty-three lovely years. We wouldn't have missed one day of them.

Be happy with Keth. God bless you both.

With our dearest love,

Mam and Dada

522

"From Keeper's," Daisy smiled. "They're such old loves. I shouldn't act up, should I?" She took the back of her hand across her eyes. "Keth and I are lucky, really. There might even be a call from him tomorrow night. He isn't all that far away now."

"He isn't. And if you're going to go all sniffy on me, then you can't have this!" Lyn produced a second letter with a flourish. It was addressed in Keth's writing to 44455 Wren D. J. Purvis. "At least he got it right. Didn't you notice? Your mother is still calling you Dwerryhouse!"

"Keth!" Daisy read the postmark: Salisbury. 5.30p.m. 21.4.43. "Oh, Lyn! We spent a day in Salisbury. He must have posted it then so I'd have something to come back to!"

"So read what he's got to say, then we'll nip downstairs smartish before the gannets get the lot!"

"No." Daisy pushed the envelope in her pocket. "I'll read it when I've opened my case and got undressed." She wouldn't mind so much, now, seeing clothes she had worn when she and Keth were together. He loved her, it was all that mattered, and besides, she would see him soon at Drew and Kitty's wedding. "Come to think of it, I could do with a slice of bread and jam, and, Lyn — thanks a lot!"

"What for?"

"Oh — for being you, and for being here. I won't whinge any more! Promise!"

They clattered down the stairs, the letter almost burning a hole in the pocket of her jacket; a letter from Keth — from her husband!

"What-ho! Here comes Dwerryhouse, all pink-cheeked and starry-eyed!" The good-natured teasing had begun. D-watch was demanding its pound of flesh. "No need to ask if you've had a good time! Tell us about it!"

"We-e-ll," Daisy laughed, "if I ever find out who sent those awful telegrams, there'll be trouble! They'd have made a sailor blush! And secondly, from this night on, the name is Purvis! P U R V I S!" She spelled it out slowly, happy again. "Just one thing I *will* tell you! I can thoroughly recommend marriage! You should try it!"

Almost as soon as the words slipped so carelessly out, she was sorry because her eyes met Lyn's and she knew she had hurt the one person who couldn't try it. Because Lyn was in love with a sailor who was going to marry someone else! And she would have to tell her, before so very much longer, about Drew's wedding. On 19 June. All cut and dried!

Oh, Flaming Norah!

When she had opened her case and taken out her spongebag and dressing gown and slippers, Daisy closed the lid on the clothes she had worn on her honeymoon, first showing Lyn the hand-sewn, blue beribboned nightdress.

"Mam made it for Aunt Julia when she married Doctor Andrew in the last war," Daisy smiled. "Then Mam wore it when she married Dada."

"And you kept up the tradition?" Lyn held it up. "It's absolutely beautiful!"

"Tradition? Me wear it? Not likely," Daisy giggled, blushing red. "I was too afraid it might get torn. Well, it *is* silk and it *is* rather old! Afraid I just left it on the bed, and every night the chambermaid draped it out so beautifully, when she turned down the bedclothes. I felt such a fraud, and her thinking I was wearing it!"

"She thought *what*?" Lyn hooted. "When there isn't so much as a crease in it! Chambermaids aren't stupid, you know!"

They began to laugh, and it was like old times again; well, almost . . .

She was so lucky, Daisy thought as she listened to Lyn's even breathing in the bunk above. She was married to the man she loved and who had a better chance than a lot of coming safely through the war. So she would count her blessings, try very hard not to let herself admit how much she needed Keth's arms, his mouth on hers, his body close. Instead, she would pull the blankets over her head, switch on her torch, and read his letter again.

Wife, darling,
This is to remind you that I love you; to tell you that I always did and always shall and hope

525

you are missing me as much as I know I shall miss you when our leave is over. I will try to ring you either before you go on watch or after you come back to Hellas House. Somehow, I will get in touch because I shall need to tell you I want you and to hear you say you want me too.

Remember our lovely day in Salisbury when you read this. Remember always you are mine.

I love you.

Keth

One more reading, and she would know it by heart. Her first letter from the husband she wanted so desperately that her whole body ached from it.

"I love you too," she whispered. "For ever and ever and ever . . ."

She closed her eyes, and lifted her lips for his kiss.

CHAPTER
TWENTY-SEVEN

"Get yourselves downstairs sharpish. Supper's ready!" Sparrow called. "Or else I'll . . ."

"You'll what?" Kitty called mischievously.

"I'll not show you what I've got in my pocket. Something from Rowangarth. Something," she added slyly, "you've been wanting to see ever since the wedding."

"The snaps have come!" Tatiana was first down. "Do let's see them. Haven't they been quick coming?"

"You can see them when you've washed your hands and got yourselves to the table!" Sparrow said, her voice sounding sterner than she meant it to. "And I want no salady fingermarks on them. They're to go back to Rowangarth. We'll have to stand in the queue for a set, your Aunt Julia says, things being what they are."

Films for cameras were in short supply as were materials for developing and printing them. As with most things — prams, cots, vacuum flasks, engagement rings, tomatoes, oranges, lipsticks and cigarettes — they had either to be queued for or obtained only after a long wait on a list — months, sometimes.

"Have you seen them, Sparrow?" Kitty was still not used to the privations of wartime Britain. "Have they come out all right?"

"Better than all right." They were the first colour films Sparrow had seen and nothing short of miraculous to her way of thinking, and wouldn't you know you could only get them in America, where, she sighed, you could get most things else. "Your Aunt Julia says she has another reel put away for your wedding, Kitty."

"And Mom's sure to slip another couple into the next food parcel," Kitty smiled. "For my wedding! Forty-nine days to go. I shall die!" She stopped suddenly at Sparrow's warning glance. "Gee, I'm sorry, Tatty! Here's me going on about getting married and there's you, all alone!"

"Don't worry. I'm fine." Tatiana smiled, just to let them know she *was* all right about Daisy getting married, and Kitty too, because when Uncle Nathan said the lovely words he had made it come right for her. "I felt very close to Tim all day and I'm sure it was the same for Tim."

"Your Tim is —" Sparrow bit on the words that slipped out before she could think to stop them.

"Dead? Oh, no. He's as near to me as I want him to be and he was very, very near the day Daisy and Keth were married. So let's see the snaps," she said very firmly so the two of them would know the

528

matter was closed and she wasn't going to burst into hysterics and weep all over the precious photographs.

"Watch your fingers." Sparrow passed a photo of the bride standing at the porch of All Souls with her father. She was smiling at him and he at her; a secret smile that said she was very happy. And Tom looking at his girl with such undisguised love and pride on his face that Tatty whispered, "Isn't that a beautiful picture? D'you know what — my father never looked at me like that."

"Now then! Don't be coming it!" Sparrow pursed her mouth into a *moue*. "You didn't ever know your father, miss, so don't say things like that!"

"I know I didn't know him a lot, Sparrow," she said softly, "but what I can remember of him, I know he wouldn't have looked at me like Mr Dwerryhouse is looking at Daisy. I know things about my father —"

She stopped, hurriedly passing the photograph to Kitty, remembering Uncle Igor said she must never tell a soul what they talked about in the kitchen at Cheyne Walk.

"Sure, honey. And I know things about him too," Kitty said absently, almost all her interest focused on Daisy and Tom. "He was spoiled rotten by Grandmother Clementina, and if he'd had his backside walloped when he was a boy, Pa said, he'd have been a whole lot better for it! But forget Uncle Elliot. He's history!"

"Let's," said Tatiana gratefully, "and just look at this one!"

So they smiled and sighed and made little ooh-ing noises over the photographs and quite forgot their supper which was as well, Sparrow said much later, since it was salad and not anything she had queued for and spent hours over a hot stove cooking.

"Are you going out tonight, Tatty?" Kitty asked when they were washing up after supper. "Have you got another wounded airman to look after yet?"

"Not since Bill went into hospital, but I think Joannie will soon find me someone. Are you going anywhere?"

"No. I shall stay in and hope Drew's ship is alongside and that maybe he'll get to phone me. It's awkward, booking your number then having to hang around outside the phone box, waiting for the operator to ring back. Drew says there can be quite a crowd of sailors, waiting for calls. I suppose if there's no glass in the phone box, they can hear everything that's being said."

"Drew won't care about that."

"No. But tell me about Bill. Last time he wrote, he was still having medication and tests."

"Last time *the nurse* wrote, he said he'd soon know if anything could be done for him. I hope so. I think he'd be grateful to have just a little sight back, though it'll be awful for him in a way — seeing his face, I mean."

"But you don't mind the way he looks, Tatty?"

"No. But then, it isn't my face, is it? Anyway, I might drop him a line tonight. I've told him about

530

the wedding and all the family getting together. He hasn't any family of his own, so he likes to hear about mine."

"And shall you keep in touch with him, even though he might always be — well — blind?"

"Oh, yes. I'm his family now." Tatiana's voice was very firm, very sure. "In a roundabout way I need Bill as much as he needs me, but don't ask me to explain it, because I can't."

"But you aren't — well —"

"I'm not in love with him? No, nor he with me. Maybe one day I'll tell you why we seem to get on so well together — when I know for sure myself, that is. Right now, though, all I'm sure about is that I'm glad I met him."

And more than that she wouldn't say, so Kitty settled herself in the kitchen rocker opposite Sparrow, closing her eyes and wishing that not only had HMS *Penrose* docked today, but that Drew would be able to phone her. Just for three minutes. Three minutes would be enough to say, "I love you. Take care. I miss you, I want you, I need you . . ."

She closed her eyes and set the chair rocking, daydreaming about a satin wedding dress and Drew, and Aunt Helen's white orchids and Drew, and Uncle Nathan saying "Do you Kathryn Norma Clementina take this man Andrew Robert Giles . . ." Such a mouthful. And the church would be cool and smell of musty old prayer books and dusty hassocks, and Gracie would decorate it as she had done for Daisy.

531

Kitty smiled just to think of warm June days and Rowangarth garden filled with flowers and summer scents. Such a pity Mom and Pa couldn't be there, but they understood, they had stressed over and over again in their letters. They were so good about it that sometimes she felt guilty not waiting until they could cross the Atlantic. Trouble was, she couldn't wait. Oh, they had been lovers, but she wanted to be married to Drew so that people would know they were lovers. That was the awful thing about doing it before you were married; having to be sneaky and not telling anyone — or hardly anyone. Once they were married, though, people would not only know it, but expect it. It was the reason she wanted to be properly married to Drew; that, and to be with him all her life and have his children — not only the three they planned, but probably one or two more they hadn't planned!

"Do you want to hear the news or are you asleep?"

"I'm not asleep, Sparrow."

"I thought you wasn't! You had a very saucy smile on your face, Kitty Sutton!"

"Mm. I was thinking about me and Drew and us having children. As a matter of fact, we were just —"

"Spare me the details! Things like them are between husband and wife!"

"I know. But we will have children. Drew will want a boy for Rowangarth, anyway, so we've no excuse. I think, though, we'll have quite a large

532

family. Rowangarth's big enough, heaven only knows, for ten kids! I wonder where Drew is right now." She closed her eyes. The chair ceased to rock.

"I think she's asleep," Tatiana mouthed.

"I'm not surprised. She was dead beat when she came in," Sparrow whispered. "It's this tour. She wants to go, real bad. They've been getting the dancers and chorus line into shape — rehearsing all day. She reckons she has a good chance of being picked. Middle East, so rumour has it." Sparrow tapped her nose with a forefinger. "But they'll not be told where they're off to till they're well on their way. Security, see . . ."

"She won't be in any danger, though?"

"No more'n our own troops out there. And the fighting's over, near as makes no matter, in Egypt. Those Desert Rats deserve a bit of attention now they've kicked Rommel out.

"All them prisoners we've taken. Thousands of 'em," Sparrow sighed. "How are we to feed them, I'd like to know, when we haven't enough food for ourselves?"

"I think a lot of them have been sent to Canada, Sparrow. The food situation isn't so bad there. But how will Kitty get to wherever she's going? And when?"

"She'll fly, she seems to think. If there's a plane with room on it they'll go that way — and all their gear and props. It'll be the same coming back. They'll have to take pot luck, she said, but that's what she joined ENSA for. It isn't all glamour, it seems. Singin' to our lads, bless 'em, from the back of a lorry, sometimes, and the sun melting their greasepaint!"

"She wants desperately to go, though. Said it would help pass the time to the wedding. I'm to cross off the days on the calendar for her, whilst she's away. I do hope she'll be all right — Drew, too. Nothing can happen to either of them, can it, between now and the wedding?"

"Now why on earth should it? It'll be safe enough in North Africa, if that's where Kitty's going, and why should anything happen to Drew? He knows what he's about! That little minesweeper is a lucky ship, he said. But it's your Russian soul again, being awkward!"

"Maybe it is. I sometimes think I'm a bit like Jinny Dobb."

"Then think on this, my girl! That Jinny used to read teacups and tell fortunes, according to what your Aunt Julia told me. Her didn't have second sight, to the best of my knowledge! 'T ain't Christian, believing things like that! You arsks the good Lord to see as how's everybody's present and correct at that wedding when you say your prayers tonight. Say 'em in English, an' all, and tell that Russian soul of yours to bugger orf!"

"I will," Tatiana laughed, wishing all at once that Sparrow had been her grandmother, and not the Petrovska. "It's just that I worry because I love them both so much; want so desperately for them to be happy."

534

"And they *will* be." The old woman cupped the young face in her hands, gazing into her eyes. "And so will you, one day. Sparrow knows it."

"Bless you." She gathered Sparrow to her, kissing her fondly. "And you're right. We're going to have another lovely wedding. I shall wear the ice-blue dress next time, and Gracie will wear the rose one. Aren't we lucky, having them? Mrs Dwerryhouse said we should let it be known around Holdenby that any bride who wants to borrow them for her attendants can have the use of them if they fit. Clothing coupons are a menace!"

"There'll be a lot of things passed on before this old war is over, Tatty girl. Daisy walked down the aisle in borrowed shoes, and she was one of the lucky ones! I wonder," she sighed, "what she is doing now? Missing her Keth something cruel, I shouldn't wonder. Them old Blimps who started this war can't know how miserable it's making the young ones!"

"It wasn't they who started the war, Sparrow. They just let it happen! Hitler's to blame for it and I hope they hang him when it's all over!"

"You and me and a million others!" Sparrow chuckled. "Or maybe they should lock Hitler in a room with half a dozen women from the East End what have had their homes bombed. Now that *would* be justice!"

The creaking of bed springs above her told Daisy that Lyn was awake. "Want a mug of tea?" she offered. "I'll nip down and grab some breakfast if you like."

Breakfast in bed was against Ma'am's rules, but everyone working late watch did it, and no one asked questions on seeing a Wren in curlers and dressing gown creeping upstairs with tea and toast.

"Would you, *cariad*? There's lovely . . ." Lyn closed her eyes.

"Now don't nod off again. I've something to tell you when I get back!"

"If you're pregnant, I don't want to know!" Lyn pulled the blanket over her head.

"Idiot!" Daisy grinned, closing the door behind her, wondering, for all that, just how she was to tell Lyn. Casually offhand, or straight and to the point?

She was still wondering when she returned with two mugs and two plates.

"Here you are. I managed to get some jam!"

"Aaagh!" Reluctantly, Lyn sat up in bed, arranging her pillows at her head, reaching for the large, fat mug. "So what's news?"

"There was a note on my hook last night when we got in. Drew phoned. He's ringing again this morning. I'll maybe go out with him if they aren't sailing on the early tide . . ."

"Okay. So Drew's alongside. That's news?"

"No, but what I have to tell you *is*, so watch your tea!" Straight and to the point it would have to be. "He's getting married."

There was the smallest silence.

"Well, of course he is. He's been engaged for ages. Weddings usually follow engagements." She blew on her tea, sipping it carefully.

"It's on the nineteenth of June. At All Souls. Kitty and Gracie are being bridesmaids. I'll be there on an AWOL weekend. Don't know if Keth can manage it yet." Daisy picked up her toast, but did not bite into it.

"I suppose Kitty'll be borrowing your dress?"

"No. She's got one of her own. Her mother sent it from Kentucky."

"I see. Well, that would appear to be that then! Uncle Nathan trying the knot, is he, and jollifications at Rowangarth afterwards?"

"Yes."

"And Kitty will have a bouquet of Rowangarth orchids, the white ones?"

"They usually flower in June."

"Well — good luck to them. I envy Kitty, and not only for getting Drew. I envy her that lovely little church and Rowangarth and the garden. I wish you'd never taken me to Keeper's; wish I'd never seen any of it.

"When they first got engaged I was hurt a lot. Then I got to hoping, then wishing, that something would happen to break them up. Not Drew getting killed, nor Kitty. I wouldn't wish that. But I didn't want them to marry. I used to lie in bed, working out ways and means. Bloody silly of me, wasn't it?"

"No. Perfectly natural. I'd have felt really vindictive if Keth had found someone else in Washington. I used to dread it, in fact."

"Well, he didn't. He came back and married you and I'm sorry I ever wanted Drew and Kitty to split up. I still love the bones of him and I want him to be happy."

"I know you do, Lyn. I know I couldn't have loved anyone but Keth, so I won't say that I hope one day you'll find someone else. I want you to be happy, though."

"Thanks, Purvis old love. Reckon I'll muddle through." Lyn raised her mug. "Cheers, Drew and Kitty! All the best!"

"If I see Drew this afternoon, I'll tell him you wished him all the best."

"Tell him I wished them *both* all the best. And now I've got news for you! I'm going to Kenya!"

"Carmichael! You're not going foreign!"

"Of course not. I'm going with Auntie Blod when the war's over. Might as well. She wants me to and I didn't get on too badly with my father. It'll be as good as anywhere, though I'd have liked Auntie Blod's cottage. She said I could have all her furniture when she left, but her landlord wants to sell it when she hands in her rent book. He thinks there'll be a lot of English from Lancashire and Liverpool who have made money in the war and have it hidden under the bed and don't know what to do with it. It wouldn't surprise him, he said, if

538

some of them didn't want to buy a Welsh cottage fairly near at hand for a weekend home."

"But if you're looking for somewhere to live, the Army will be handing Pendenys back to Nathan when the war is over and there'll be ever so many cottages empty there. If you don't really want to go to Kenya, why don't you think about asking him? I'd love to have you near Keth and me."

"Mm. I remember we passed a gatehouse at the top of Pendenys drive. That was a cute little place. Might suit a spinster just fine!"

"Lyn! You wouldn't want *that* gatehouse! Elliot Sutton crashed his car just by there! When Jinny Dobb had had a couple of sherries, she used to swear blind his mother's ghost haunted the spot! *Not* the gatehouse!"

"Not anywhere around Holdenby, Daisy. Too near Drew and Kitty, don't forget. I'm not that much of a fool!"

"Sorry! Just didn't think. I'm selfish, I suppose, not wanting you and me to split up when the war's over."

"Never mind. And that's the phone. Bet it's Drew, for you!"

It was, because the duty-Wren called up the stairs, "Purvis or Dwerryhouse! Whichever you're answering to! It's for you!"

And when Daisy returned to the cabin, having arranged to meet her half-brother at the Overhead Railway, Pierhead stop, Lyn was up, in slippers and dressing gown and brushing her long chestnut hair. And she was smiling.

"So how is the war at sea, Drew?"

"I think we're winning. Rumour has it that Dönitz lost five of his U-boats recently. Seems the Admiralty is getting its act together in the Atlantic at last. But where are we going, Daiz? Fancy a coffee?"

"I'd love one, if we can find one. Tea would do. I'd just like to sit and gossip about my wedding and talk about Keth, if you don't mind."

"Don't mind a bit, if I can get the odd word in about Kitty, and *my* wedding!"

The waitress, when they had found a café, said she was very sorry, but coffee was off. Used up their month's ration a week ago, but she could manage a pot of tea for two and, she looked around furtively then lowered her voice, "I could do you a scone."

She liked to do a scone for the armed forces, since her granddaughter was a WAAF corporal and her two grandsons both in the Middle East, which gave her a fondness for young men and women in uniform.

"That would be lovely," Daisy smiled, taking off her cap, hanging it on her chair. "Remember cherry-scone days at Rowangarth, Drew, and Mrs Shaw?"

"Mm. I often think, on watch. When I'm listening out, I mean, and there's no one about. Remember Windrush?"

"Yes. And Beck Lane and Keeper's and Willow End. Keth and I went there to have a look at the old place. It was so sad, but the dogs' grave was still there. And the bluebells were out . . ."

She lapsed into remembering. She would never have thought to have done such a thing — not in a bluebell wood. Things like *that*, Mam had said, in one of her confidential chats, were very nice indeed, but not to be talked about because bedroom secrets were special between man and wife.

And what about bluebell wood secrets, Mam? I wish I could tell you how very nice indeed that was . . .

Daisy smiled her thanks to the waitress, grateful to her for interrupting such lovely, cheek-pinking rememberings, then stirred the tea leaves in the pot.

"How's Kitty?" She sliced the scones, then jammed them. "Getting excited, I suppose?"

"She is, but about going overseas. She wants desperately to be picked for the chorus line. She won't feel she's done her bit for the war, she says, if she doesn't do at least one overseas tour.

"I told her she was already overseas — her coming from Kentucky, I mean — but that doesn't count, apparently. She's half-English anyway, she says, and come the nineteenth of June, she'll be a hundred per cent English! So that brings us to the wedding," Drew grinned.

"Yes! First mine and Keth's, then yours and Kitty's to look forward to. It's so wonderful, forgetting the war for just a little while. Where shall you go for your honeymoon, Drew?"

"Haven't decided. Maybe Scotland. Kitty says it doesn't matter one bit since we had our honeymoon at Ma's, in Roscoe Street. I'm afraid the future Lady Sutton is going to raise a few North Riding eyebrows with her forthrightness, Daiz."

"And shall you mind?"

"Of course not! I wouldn't change one bit of her! Come to think of it, the entire Clan has done very well, except for Tatty. Poor love. I wish she could find another Tim."

"I think she maybe has, only in a roundabout sort of way. Don't mention it unless she tells you, but one of the wounded airmen she takes out is very like Tim."

"She told me. Bill."

"That's him. He's even an air-gunner. They seem to hit it off. She won't marry him, of course. Not because he's so badly burned — Tatty isn't like that. But he isn't Tim, you see, and Tim was her first love. You never forget your first love. I've been lucky. I married mine."

"Which brings us to Lyn, I suppose . . ."

"She was your first love, Drew?"

"Not exactly, but I do remember when you and she came running like mad to the Overhead stop that first time I met her, thinking even then what lovely legs she had. It wasn't long after that I wondered what it would be like to sleep with her. It might have been Lyn, if Kitty hadn't crashed into my life, but from then on, there was no one else for me. She's completely honest and so very uncomplicated. And very, very beautiful. But how *is* Lyn, by the way?"

"Planning to go to Kenya with Auntie Blod — with her *mother* — when she and her father get married," Daisy laughed. "Well, you know what I mean!"

"When?"

"When the war is over and they can get sailing tickets. I suppose she might get to like it, though she wasn't very happy there as a child. I shall miss her. Kenya seems so far away."

"But you'll be able to fly there, to visit. You can afford it, don't forget. You're very offhand about your money, Daiz."

"I suppose I am, but it isn't real yet. Just figures. How can it be real when there's nothing to spend it on? Maybe I'll think differently about it when the war is over." She plopped a sugar lump into his cup, then passed it to him, not wanting to talk about the money. "I've seen Kitty's wedding dress. It's beautiful."

"I spoke to her last night — had six minutes. She's excited about the tour. Says she'll die if they don't take her. I think I'm landing myself with a stage-struck wife."

"No you aren't! Kitty was always an actress, even when we were kids. She loved to be centre stage. By the way, Aunt Julia's had our wedding photos developed, Mam said, and there are two really good ones of the Clan. I'll see them soon. I've got a crafty weekend coming up. It'll be strange, seeing us all grown up. Last time we were together we were teenagers. Even then I knew Keth and I would marry one day."

"Well, I hadn't an inkling then that Kitty and I would get together. She was just a kid with long curls who could run faster than any of us and make us all laugh a lot. And I seem to remember that Tatty was teaching her to swear in Russian. She was just my cousin from Kentucky — then six years later she's there in a dockside warehouse — and *phew*!"

"Lovely, isn't it?" Daisy sighed, holding up her left hand, all at once serious. "If only the war could end soon — but it won't, will it?"

"I don't think so, Daiz. We've got to see Hitler off first — get back into France. And then there'll be the Japs to reckon with. There's a war on in the Pacific too."

"Lordy, we'll be old by the time we're demobbed! That's one thing I can't forgive this war for. It'll have taken all our young years. And that was a selfish thing to say, wasn't it, when there are thousands of men like Tim who've got no chance at all of seeing the end of it?"

"And thousands of women like Tatty."

"We're lucky, aren't we, Drew?"

"All things being equal, I reckon we've both had our fair share of it. And did you know that when it's over, we're all to be released by numbers? They're going to take into account when you joined up, so it'll be first in, first out. We're all to be given a demobilization number, and it isn't a buzz. It's gen. The skipper told us!"

"My, but that'll be the day! Let's drink to them, Drew." Daisy held up her teacup. "To our demob numbers!"

"Will you put those snaps away!" Nathan looked at Julia over the top of his reading glasses. "If you've looked at them once today, you've looked at them twenty times!"

"I know, but they are so lovely! And that's two sets I've got now. I left the negatives with the chemist in Creesby. He's going to do more, but it'll take a month. But do look at my Clan! All of them at war!" She reached for the black-and-white photograph of almost seven years ago, comparing it with the one taken in colour at Daisy's wedding; Tatiana in pink, Kitty in blue, Drew, Keth and Bas, handsome in uniform. And as for the bride, that little baby who cried angrily at her christening only yesterday, it seemed; so very beautiful. So happy, the six of them, laughing into the camera as if there wasn't a war on.

"And will you look at this one? I just snapped them. They didn't know. See, darling. Keth is putting on her shoe."

Obediently Nathan looked. He had admired it at least six times and had to admit it was very good. Daisy, flopped on the stone steps, her gown and train billowing around her; beside her a bouquet of orchids and her foot extended; Keth holding a white wedding shoe.

"To go from the sublime to the ridiculous, Julia, not five minutes before you took that, Daisy told me her feet were killing her, and what could you expect in borrowed shoes? Does Kitty have any white shoes?"

"I don't think so and she hasn't been issued with clothing coupons. But don't worry. We have the wedding dress and the veil, so we won't let a pair of white shoes bother us."

"You're enjoying these weddings, aren't you?"

"Oh, *yes*! And there's Bas and Gracie, too, don't forget. There'll be two bridal gowns Gracie can choose from, and we can trot the bridesmaids' dresses out again. Y'know, darling, if you don't let this war intrude too much, life can be very pleasant at times!

"Now will you be all right if I pop over to Keeper's? I've decided to blow the coupons on a new dress for Drew's wedding and I'm going to have a look through Daisy's paper patterns. I can buy the material for seven coupons, which is what I'd have to give for a shop dress, but Alice will make one so much better! Won't be long, darling. Just a few minutes!"

She was gone with a banging of doors and he looked through the long, low window to see her crossing the lawn with the agility of a woman half her age. A few minutes? At least an hour, when they had sighed and exclaimed over the wedding photographs again, and put Drew's wedding to rights, never mind going through paper patterns and discussing in great detail what the mother of the groom would wear!

Dear Alice. Dear Julia. Was it really more than twenty-five years since he married Alice and Giles in a chapel in Celverte in another war? Alice pregnant with her rape child; Giles marrying her to claim that child for Rowangarth. And in the background, the sound of German field guns.

He closed his eyes, calling back Giles, the cousin he had grown up with — more like a brother, really. And Giles dead less than an hour after Alice's boy was born; a son for Rowangarth. Drew, whom he would marry to Kitty in little more than a month.

He reached for his tobacco and pipe. Julia was right. If, sometimes, you could shut out the war, life could indeed be pleasant.

Through the open window came the scent of the first lilacs and the sound of birdsong. He struck a match and held it to his pipe, sending contented puffs of smoke to the low, cracked ceiling.

Then he thought of Julia, and how very much he loved her and the war, all at once, was a long way away.

CHAPTER
TWENTY-EIGHT

Kitty burst into the kitchen, struck a dramatic pose, and said, "Guess what, you guys! Just *guess what*!"

"You're half an hour late for supper!" Sparrow scolded.

"I made it! I'm going; actually going on active service, but don't ask me where!" She collapsed into the rocker, fanning her face. "I'm in the chorus line *and* I'm to pack a long frock 'cause they've given me a couple of solos too, would you believe it?"

"I'd believe anything of you, Kitty Sutton, once you've set your mind on a thing! When are you orf, then?"

"Don't know. But I've got to be packed ready for Tuesday, and talk has it we'll be pushing off around the seventh."

"Well, if it's Egypt you're goin' to, you'd better watch out for sand flies and mosquitoes and scorpions — apart from blokes as haven't set eyes on a woman in years!"

"Oh, Sparrow!" Tatiana laughed. "Of course our troops have seen women! What about nurses? They've got army nurses and —"

"Nurses is ladies; chorus girls is fair game. But if your mind is set on it, Kitty Sutton, then good luck to you, 'cause there'll be no living with you till you've got some service in. Maybe when you get back you'll settle down and put your mind to your wedding! When will you be back?"

"Well, given we go on the seventh for three weeks, that'll be the end of May, give or take a day or two for delays. So then I'll only have two and a bit weeks to wait. Guess I'll just about last out!"

"Then you'd better get yourself to the sink and wash your hands, 'cause me and Tatty's sick of waiting. Supper'll be ruined!"

"How will you be getting there?" Tatiana asked, when plates had been taken from the oven and order restored in Sparrow's kitchen.

"I'm almost sure we'll be flying. That's why I don't quite know when we'll be leaving. A group of travelling players isn't all that important, so we'll be given cargo space nobody else wants, I guess. But we'll get there, somehow!"

"Won't flying be just a little bit dangerous?" Tatty frowned.

"No more than living in London, getting bombed. Once we're across the Bay of Biscay we'll be flying over safe territory. Spain and Portugal are neutral, don't forget."

"Ar, but General Franco has leanings towards them Nazis. They were on his side, don't forget, when there was civil war in Spain!" Sparrow felt duty-bound to point out the dangers.

"Ye-e-s, but Portugal likes us and we'll maybe go into the Mediterranean over the Straits of Gibraltar — we'd be in friendly airspace then. Don't forget that all the north of Africa has been cleared. It's safe, Sparrow. They wouldn't send us otherwise. What is there to worry about?"

"Gerry fighter pilots over France, for one thing, and Italy an' all. Them Wops!" Sparrow was becoming vaguely worried.

"The Italians won't be all that much of a nuisance. Their navy doesn't like leaving port, everybody knows that. And I guess their air force won't be worried about one cargo plane with Red Cross markings on it."

"Ah, well . . ." Sparrow gave in, defeated. Happen the girl was right about the Italians. Hadn't wanted to fight us, anyway; only declared war because Mussolini wanted to get on the right side of Hitler! "I hope you knows what you're doing, girl."

"I do, Sparrow, and I'm sure the pilot will know too. I want to go and the sooner I get there, the sooner I'll be back and can really start looking forward to the wedding."

"Ar . . ." Sparrow's eyes took on a yearning look because she had enjoyed Daisy's wedding no end; enjoyed being given one of the best bedrooms at Rowangarth, even if the place was so big she'd got lost a couple of times. "Such a lovely wedding that was, and yours to look forward to in seven weeks, Kitty."

"Seven weeks and a day, Sparrow. How will I survive till then?"

"You'll survive 'cause you're a Sutton! And you'll still be a Sutton when you marry Drew, had you thought, though I suppose you'll be a milady."

"Just as long as Drew marries me, they can call me what they like. And are you ready for my next bit of news?"

"There's more!" Tatiana gasped in mock consternation.

"There's a show opening at the Haymarket, tomorrow. Noel Coward. *This Happy Breed*."

"Noel Coward," Sparrow sighed. "Now I like 'im. 'E's that witty and smooth with it. Hey, Kitty girl, you 'aven't landed a part in it?"

"No, worse luck, but I've landed three tickets for Monday night. A friend got them for me and I thought it would be a little celebration — me going on active service, I mean. Is it on, then?"

"I'll say!" Tatiana laughed. "Thanks a lot!"

"They're not orchestra stalls or anything posh — but we'll be able to hear all right."

"Who wants orchestra stalls, then? I ain't got no mink and me tiara's at the cleaners!" Sparrow grinned. "Of course it's on, girl, and thanks ever so!"

"That's settled, then. Let's hope there won't be a raid to spoil it. So shall we get on with the washing-up, then I can go up to the attic and start sorting my clothes out. And if Drew rings, yell upstairs, won't you?"

"Do you think he will?"

"Oh, I always *think* he will, but I guess he'll be back at sea by now. I wonder if he's put in a request to see his skipper to ask for marriage leave?"

"He'll have it all seen to," Sparrow soothed, pouring a kettle of water into the washing-up bowl. "Don't you worry none. Lately, y'know, I've had the feeling that we're winning at last. Rommel kicked out of North Africa, the Russians fighting back like mad things and our bombers orf in their thousands to drop 'em on Germany. I'll bet Hitler's sorry he started the war!"

"Hitler," Tatty said softly, "will be safe enough from our bombs in his Eagle's Nest. And last time we sent a thousand bombers out, twenty-five of them didn't come back. That's nearly two hundred men lost, Sparrow. I wish we had pilotless planes."

"Would that be possible?" Kitty demanded. "Because if it is, they want to get on with it, and get a few into the air!"

"I don't think it is," Tatiana sighed, "but just think of it — being able to bomb a target and not need aircrew to do it! Now wouldn't that be something?"

Keth booked a call to Daisy, then lay on his bed to clear his head of codes and dead ends and frustrations.

Today had been a bad one, because there had been a panic, again, about the Peenemünde place,

552

with all signals gathered in from the area of the Kiel Canal to be given rush-immediate priority.

Something was going on there. The pilot of a photo-reconnaissance plane had returned with strange pictures that made Whitehall jumpy — or so the buzz had it. But the trouble with this place was that you were only ever told half a story — left hands and right hands, sort of. It made Keth wonder if the spy-masters in Whitehall would become so perturbed about Peenemünde they would order raids by Bomber Command. Or would Castle McLeish take a sly hand in things?

He emptied such thoughts from his mind. He had done all *They* asked of him, had returned from Clissy with an Enigma machine, and now he broke enemy codes; did it all day, every day, until his mind became a muddle and sometimes nothing made sense. All he could be certain of was that *They* would never send him to France again! They could call him coward, write *Lacking Moral Fibre* across his army records in red ink if that was what pleased Them. Because Keth Purvis was not cut out for derring-do! All he wanted was for the war to be over and to live with Daisy in a world where tomorrow was not a dirty word.

The phone rang and he hurried, shoeless, to answer it.

"Lark Lane 1322. Duty-Wren speaking. Daisy who? Oh, you mean Dwerryhouse! Daisy's on watch till midnight. Can I leave her a message?"

"Sorry. I should have remembered," Keth smiled, all anger gone. "Can you tell her that Keth Purvis phoned, and that he — he —"

"Loves her?" she giggled. "Will do! Byeeee . . ."

She replaced the receiver and reached for the message pad.

Purvis. Cabin 4A. Keth loves Daisy. Message timed at 21.20-B/30/4/43.

Then she stuck it, still smiling wickedly, on the hook below Daisy's name.

"So, Gracie lass, you've comed!" Jack Catchpole chuckled. "And here's me thinking you'd gone to be Queen of the May!"

"Oh, my goodness — it's May Day, isn't it? Is there anything I'm supposed to do — like washing my face in the morning dew?"

"That's midsummer morning, for daft spinsters who think it'll make the young man they're after notice them! Don't apply, in your case! But you'd better go round all the greenhouses and see to the ventilation; open the windows and let some air in. Don't do to let 'em get steamy — 'cept the orchid house, that is!"

"How are the orchids coming along?" Gracie asked when she had opened windows and doors and sniffed the heady scent of green things growing.

"They'm doing nicely."

"They'll be flowering for the wedding?"

"There, or thereabouts, lass. If they look like getting too forward, us'll put the pots somewhere

554

cooler, and if they're backward, us'll give 'em a bit of coaxing. Kitty'll have her bouquet."

"Wouldn't Lady Helen have loved seeing Drew's bride carrying them to her wedding?" Gracie sighed.

"She'll know all about it, mark my words!" Someone like her ladyship didn't just die, snuff out like a candle flame and be gone for ever. Oh my word, no! Lady Helen was here watching. And smiling, like as not. There'd be some part of her in the white orchids Kitty carried on her wedding day!

"You think so, Mr Catchpole?"

"I know so, Gracie Fielding, so away and get that fire lit, and the kettle on to boil. I feel like a sup of tea!"

And Gracie, who was the soul of tact, did not remind him on that first morning in May that tea, in the kitchen garden, was never taken before ten-fifteen, because if she did and he got huffy about being corrected by a subordinate, he would likely find it difficult to turn a blind eye when she slipped back to the bothy to collect Bas's letter.

"Tea coming up!" she smiled.

"Well, wasn't that just something?" Kitty gasped. "Did you both enjoy it?"

"Too true!" Sparrow set the kettle to boil and Tatiana took three china mugs from the white-painted dresser and the cocoa tin and saccharin tablets from the cupboard. "I'd never have thought that someone as la-di-da as Noel Coward could do a working-class accent. Cor! All the troubles his family had! The General Strike and him bein' out of work and then the King upping and orfing with his American piece! And then *another* war coming! I could sit through it again! Makes you proud to be a Londoner!"

"I loved it too," Tatiana smiled. "Thanks for taking us, Kitty."

"Well, it's a goodbye present, sort of. I didn't tell you, but I'm leaving tomorrow — sooner than I thought. Seems there's transport for us all. I believe it's a hospital plane, going out empty, returning with troops they can't operate on over there. Not a word to anyone, mind!"

"As if we would!" Sparrow clucked. "No need to tell me that careless talk costs lives! So when are you leaving?"

"There'll be a van collecting me and my trunk around ten in the morning. Don't know where we're leaving from, but it's my guess we'll not hang around, it being a hospital plane."

"I shall miss you, Kitty." Tatiana liked having her cousin around. "But three weeks will soon pass, and I'll cross off the days on the calendar."

"Thanks. And will you post some letters for me, at intervals? I wrote them to Drew because I don't know how it'll be when we get out there — letter-wise, I mean. I've given him the hint I'm on my way — between the lines, sort of — and I've asked him to keep writing to me so I'll have a big pile of letters to come home to."

"I'll miss you too, girl. It'll be like heaven without all the noise you make!" Sparrow scolded, her voice all at once wobbly. "If Drew rings when you're gone, what am I to say?"

"Just tell him I'm on my way. You'll not be able to tell him where, because I don't know myself. He'll understand. And give him my love and tell him to take care, won't you? Oh dear, now I know I'm really going I feel a bit peculiar."

"You'll be right as ninepence, girl! You'll have such tales to tell when you get back. And watch out for them camels! I did hear they can give you a nasty nip if they don't take to you!"

"I'll be careful, Sparrow. Truth known, now the time has come I'm not at all sure I want to go! I'll be miles and miles away from Drew, and had you thought, it might not be the Middle East? What if it's Australia?"

"It won't be, 'cause we haven't got any troops there and if we had, the Australians would entertain 'em for us! Now drink that cocoa down and get yourself orf to bed! You're tired out — all that worrying and rehearsing! A good night's sleep is what you need, my girl!"

And Kitty was bound to admit that probably it was.

"I shall think of you and Tatty and this little white house when I'm away," she murmured. "When the sand flies are biting and the camels are nipping, I shall think of Montpelier and Rowangarth. And the wedding . . ."

557

"You do that, girl. And me and Tatty'll think of you all the time."

"And cross off the days on the calendar and look forward like anything to the nineteenth," Tatiana smiled.

"And my opinion, for what it's worth, is that you and Drew should get down to the business of a family right away! When you and he get wed you'll be her ladyship," Sparrow pronounced, "and it don't do for a titled lady to be kicking her legs in the air and singing saucy songs! Rowangarth needs kids in it, and Gawd knows, there's room enough there for a football team!"

"Drew would be a lovely father; just like Uncle Nathan if he and Aunt Julia had had children. But it's up to you and Drew, isn't it?"

"Guess it is, Tatty. But since we're on the subject, I'd like to start a family, war or no war. I'm not cut out for being an actress. Oh, I'm a show-off, but there's no star quality in me. Pa said I should stick to horses, but Mom stuck up for me when I wanted to give the stage a try. Guess she knew I'd have to get it out of my system sooner or later!"

"That's settled, then!" Sparrow said matter-of-factly. "Now away off to bed, and straight to sleep! Tomorrow's another day, don't forget!"

"I'll set the table for breakfast, if you'd like," Tatiana said when Kitty had climbed the stairs. "And I'd like to write a letter to Bill before I go to bed. Is that all right, Sparrow?"

"Course it is. It's just that that young madam has been burning the candle at both ends lately, and she's tired out. The sooner she falls for a baby when they're married, the better. She can leave all that stage nonsense behind her, then, and go to your Aunt Julia and have her little one at Rowangarth. Now wouldn't that be lovely?"

And Tatiana said it would; that it would be quite the nicest thing that could happen. And she smiled as she said it, even though her heart cried out for Tim's child.

Telegraphist Drew Sutton did not know that when HMS *Penrose* docked on Tuesday, 18 May, that the day would make so great an impact on his life.

It started ordinarily enough. He had closed down the receiver, taken off his headset and collected his mail, amongst which was a postcard of palm trees and a pyramid, silhouetted against a garish setting sun.

Guess where I am! Take care of yourself, my darling. I love you. K.

After which, his opposite number had borrowed a morning paper from a dockyard worker to read of the shattering of the Mohne and Eder dams in Germany's industrial Ruhr by a squadron of Lancaster bombers.

"S'trewth, Andy! I'd rather blow up mines any day of the week! Bouncing bombs? What next!"

And Drew, busy brushing his best uniform and pressing his collar, agreed with him. Flying a huge bomber at a height of sixty feet at over two hundred miles an hour wasn't for him! Yet no matter how he admired the crazy bravery of those crews nor how sick the loss of fifty-six airmen made him feel he had little time, this morning, to think too long on anything but Captain's Requestmen at which he was due at 09.00 hours.

He had never before attended a requestmen's parade, but he had never before needed to ask for marriage leave. On a large ship — one of battle-wagon proportions — "Requestmens" was a big affair, with the Captain's secretary in attendance and a Writer, and the Master-at-Arms in charge of the comings and goings.

On a small ship like the *Maggie*, where everyone knew everyone else and how often he changed his socks, it was much less formal and Drew's skipper acknowledged his salute with a nod, said, "Off caps, Sutton. At ease," and that was really all there had been to it.

The skipper knew his telegraphist well; had heard rumours of his coming wedding and wasn't in the least surprised when he asked for seven days' Compassionate. He had said, "Granted!" rather formally, then smiled and held out his hand and wished Drew well.

At that moment, when Drew returned his cap to his head, saluted, said, "Thank you, sir," and done a smart about-turn, he was just about the most contented rating in the entire Home Fleet. His leave was approved, Kitty would be home by the end of the month and Daisy was on "earlies"; would doubtless meet him at the Pierhead this evening. A very satisfactory state of affairs he was bound to admit — until he met the first lieutenant.

The first lieutenant, the second-in-command — the Jimmy as he was known on the little minesweeper — smiled cheerfully, said, "Congratulations, Sutton!" The very young officer who had done the morning watch and supervised the docking of the ship with much efficiency was in need of tea, a shower and a change of clothing in that order. "I've only just heard!"

"Thought the whole ship's company knew, sir," Drew grinned. "They've been pulling my leg about it for weeks!"

"They have?" The first officer looked mystified. "Funny, but I only knew myself an hour ago. Came in the mailbag from Flag Officer's. Your draft chit, I'm talking about."

"Draft chit?" Something vicious slammed into Drew's stomach. "*Me*, sir?"

"Sure. See for yourself." He dipped into his pocket and brought out a memo. "There you are. D/WRX 805 Telegraphist Sutton A. R. G. You're made up to leading-telegraphist."

"But I haven't even sat my leading-tel's exam yet. Is there some mistake, sir?" There *was* a mistake! There had to be!

"We-e-ll, acting leading-telegraphist, actually. But you'll get your hook up and the pay, of course.

Barracks are crying out for leading sparkers, it seems."

"I'm to go to barracks?"

"That's it. Pack your kit, then pick up your leave pass and rail voucher. You're on seven days' embarkation!"

"But sir, I've just seen the skipper. He's given me seven days' Compassionate! I'm getting married next month!"

"Then I think you'll have to bring the wedding forward. Anyway, good luck, Sutton, and all that!"

He was gone, then, in the direction of the galley and Drew stood quite still, watching him. The first officer was younger than himself. A decent chap, but still wet behind the ears, and too bloody cheerful by half!

Drew shook himself mentally, collecting his shattered thoughts, trying to make sense of it all. He'd been on the *Maggie* three years, had thought to see out the war on minesweepers in home waters. Well, that was what *thought* did for you! Seven days' embarkation, then down to barracks and overseas! Flaming rotten Norah! *Now*, of all times!

"Knocker!" he hissed, all at once mobile. "What do you think? They've only stuck a hook on me and given me seven days' Embarkation!"

"Nah, Andy mate. They can't do it! You're getting hitched!"

"They can, you know! I'm to go to Flag Officer's — pick up the necessary. Then it's barracks, and another ship, and you're missing the point! You

562

aren't given leave joining another ship; you get it when you're going foreign! Jimmy said I'd have to bring the wedding forward, but I can't!"

"Bloody 'ell. Your girl's gone off to Egypt, hasn't she? When's she going to be back, then?"

"Too late! She'll be on her way home and I'll be on my way out! Ships that pass . . ."

"You're sure about all this, Andy?"

"Too right! I saw the memo from Drafting Office."

"But it doesn't have to be a foreign draft. You won't know for sure till you get to barracks."

"It mightn't, but I'm not taking bets on it."

Drew's mouth had gone dry and his tongue made little papery sounds when he spoke. He wasn't afraid. Like his Chiefie said when he joined up — no use worrying. When your number was up, that was it, so enjoy yourself meantime. And it seemed his number still wasn't up. Nothing had changed, except that there wasn't going to be a wedding next month. No wedding. It took a bit of getting used to.

He'd had a good run, for all that. Three years in home waters and regular leaves. And no long spells at sea, either. He'd expected, all things being equal, to have to go foreign — but not yet! Not till Kitty came back! If she only got home for one last night together, he could live with it.

The turmoil inside him became worse, as if all the dismay and anger he felt had torn through his body and ended up in his stomach.

"Want a hand with your kit?" Knocker brought him back to reality. "I'll lash up your hammock, if you like."

"Thanks. Reckon I'll nip over to Flag Officer's while I've got my number-ones on." Find out if it was true; if the seven days' embarkation leave meant what he thought it did. "Won't be long, Knocker . . ."

He paused to look at the old-fashioned sepia photograph hanging outside the wardroom door. It was of Margaret Penrose, mother of the trawler owner from whom the Admiralty had commandeered this boat. In war, Authority took what it wanted without shame or apology, though they had, in the case of the fishing smack, dubbed it HMS *Penrose* by way of mitigation. The *Maggie* she had affectionately become, and every crew member smiled at the photograph, or winked in passing, because Margaret Penrose had watched over the fishermen before them and would continue to keep an eye on the navy lads who now sailed in her namesake.

"I'm in a right mess, Mrs P," Drew whispered. "And there's nothing you can do about this one!"

Then he hurried down the gangway, through the dockyard in the direction of the Liver Birds and the large building on top of which they perched.

He was going to miss those funny, fat birds; miss Liverpool and his runs ashore with Daisy. And more than that; much, much more than that, he was going to miss Kitty.

564

As if to rub salt in the wound of his bewilderment, he found he was passing the dockside warehouse in which they had tumultuously met. Lovely, mischievous Kitty. Beautiful and adorable and heaven to love.

A great lump rose chokingly in his throat. He felt sorry, not for himself but for her, and how great her disappointment when she learned there would be no wedding. Not yet, anyway.

He left the docks behind him, turning right, crossing the road, not knowing why he was hurrying so when if he had one iota of sense in his head he'd be putting off the moment that would take him away from the *Maggie*, from the Liverpool dock at which they almost always tied up; away from Daisy and all the runs ashore they'd had together.

He ran up the entrance steps towards the row of lifts on his left. A light was flashing above one of them and he went to stand by it, following its progress down, floor by floor.

It came to a stop. The doors banged open and a Wren stepped out. She was tall and slim. She had freckles across the bridge of her nose and on her high cheekbones. Her hair was the colour of a ripe conker.

"Lyn!" he said softly.

He saw her pull in her breath and then she smiled and said, "Well, hullo, Drew! Good to see you. Going up the dock road," she said by way of explanation. "Dental parade!"

"And I'm going on leave. Got my hook up — looks as if I'm going foreign."

He shouldn't have told her; should have said he was going to Slops, or to the Paymaster's Office. Anything but that.

"I'm sorry," she said. "Will it — I mean —"

"It's put paid to the wedding, if that's what you mean. Kitty's gone overseas on a three-week tour. I'll be long gone by the time she gets back." He shrugged, trying to smile, but it was a poor effort.

"Look, Drew — it maybe won't be as bad as you think. You mightn't be going overseas — just another ship. You always get a draft somewhere different when you get rank up. And Daisy and Keth had to wait, remember, but it came out all right for them in the end."

She could feel her cheeks burning. He was still every bit as good to look at; she still wanted him. More than ever now, because he belonged to Kitty.

"Yes — well — I'll know more about what's going to happen when I get to barracks." She was the last person he needed to see. When his heart and his mind were full of Kitty, Lyn had got out of a lift he'd been going to get into and it shocked him to think he might have liked to take her for a drink to talk about times past. Or was it really to straighten his conscience? "Daisy said you're going to Kenya with Auntie Blod."

"Yes. As soon as it's all over and we can get a passage." She held out her hand, in control of her emotions once more. "I don't suppose we'll meet again, Drew, so all the very best to you and Kitty. Take care, sailor — wherever it is you're going."

"Thanks, Lyn. And you too." He wanted to tell her he was sorry about Kitty, except that he couldn't be sorry about loving her. It was impossible *not* to love Kitty. Yet he wanted to thank Lyn for the fun they'd had; tell her he hoped that one day she would find someone she wanted to spend the rest of her life with. "All the very best, Lyn," he said. He took the hand she offered, and held it briefly. Then she was gone without another word and he stood to watch her go.

"I mean it, Lyn. Take care. Always," he whispered, but already she was nowhere to be seen.

When the transport, which had already taken on D-Watch at Epsom House, stopped outside the Liver Building to pick up the outgoing watch, Lyn sat down heavily without a word.

"You all right, Lyn? No fillings?" Daisy asked.

"No. I saw Drew, though. He was coming in as I was going out. Couldn't avoid him."

"The *Maggie*'s in, then? Suppose he'll be ringing."

"Then if he does," Lyn cleared her throat noisily, "be prepared for a shock, because he told me he's got his hook up, and you know what that means?"

"Y-yes. Promotion means a draft. I shall miss him! I'm glad about him being a leading-hand, though."

"There's more to it, I think. He said he was going on seven days' leave and he might be going foreign at the end of it."

"He might. But then he might be going to pick up another ship in the Home Fleet."

"They don't give you seven days just for changing ships."

For a moment, Daisy said nothing, then she gasped, "Lyn! What about the wedding?"

"That's what I was trying to say. He said he'd probably be on his way overseas by the time Kitty got back."

"Oh, dammit! Why did she have to go on an overseas tour? They could have got married if she'd been around!"

"Well, if you put it that way — why don't you blame the Admiralty for sending Drew abroad? Kitty wasn't to know, now was she?"

"You're sticking up for her!"

"No I'm not, Purvis! I'm sorry for them both, as a matter of fact. Surely you remember how awful you felt when Keth was sent back to Washington without so much as a by-your-leave?"

"If they'd given him seven days' embarkation, at least I'd have been around for us to be married! But you're right. I should be sorry for them both, and I am. I think Drew will ring me before he goes on leave. Maybe he'll know more about what's going on by then."

"He's sure to. And I'm sorry to be the one to have told you this . . ."

"I know you are, Lyn. It isn't your fault. It isn't Drew's fault, nor Kitty's either. It's the war that's to blame — and that bloody Hitler!"

For the rest of the way back to quarters neither spoke, but hardly had they sat down to eat their kept-warm lunch than Daisy was called to the phone.

"Daiz? It's Drew."

"Lyn's told me. Where are you now?"

"In the phone box at the dockside. I'm getting the four-fifteen from Exchange station to York."

"I'll be there as soon as I can!"

"You're sure?"

"Of course I'm sure! See you at the station. We'll talk then, Drew; have a good old whinge — okay?"

"Fine, Daiz. See you . . ."

"I'm going to see Drew off," Daisy told Lyn. "He's getting the afternoon train. You can come if you'd like to — for old times' sake, I mean . . ."

"No. Thanks all the same. Drew and I have said our goodbyes." She couldn't take another. "Off you go! See you later!"

Stupid of her, really, Daisy thought as she sat on the tram that swayed towards Liverpool, to have asked Lyn to go with her. This morning's chance meeting must have knocked her sideways; to have wished him goodbye must have taken a lot of doing.

It was half-past three when she bought a platform ticket, then ran the length of the Edinburgh train in search of him. She saw him, then calling his name, ran into his arms.

"Drew!" It was all she could say because the sight of him hurt too much and it was he who broke the trembling silence.

"I've got a seat and dumped my kit. Glad you could come, Daiz."

"I don't believe it!" she said, when they had settled themselves on a seat on the platform opposite the open door of the compartment. "I mean — banns read, everything organized then wham! You've got your hook up and on your way to barracks."

"And on embarkation leave, I'm almost sure of it. They don't throw seven days at you if it's a simple drafting job from one ship to another."

"So what will you do?"

"There's nothing I can do except hope like mad it won't be too far away. What if I'm going to be based at Trincomalee? Ceylon is half a world away! I expected to go foreign sooner or later, mind. A couple of months later, and it wouldn't have been so bad, Daiz. We could have had the wedding and a few days together, at least. I'm almost sure Kitty is in Egypt. I had a card this morning with palm trees and pyramids on it."

"It's going to be awful for her when she gets back and finds what's happened. Is there any way you can get in touch?"

"Don't think so. I can write to her care of ENSA, but we agreed that letters would only follow her

570

around from one place to another. I said I'd write as usual to Montpelier. She said she wanted a pile of letters to come home to! Crazy, isn't it?"

"I must say you're taking it very well. I was devastated when I realized Keth had been sent back to Washington. You couldn't apply for a commission, could you, when you get there? There might be a chance, that way, of getting back home."

"Afraid not, Daiz. Reckon half the Fleet would be at it if that kind of fiddle worked! No — it's the way the cookie crumbles, I suppose. The *Maggie* was a great little boat to be on; quite a cushy number, really. There are blokes who've been overseas since the war started. I've been one of the lucky ones. It's just that I'd have liked us to be married before I go."

"Drew — you're such an old love. You never get steamed up about anything. Now me — I explode at the drop of a hat, yet you're so reasonable about everything. And here am I so happy with Keth only a phone call away and poor you who can't even say a decent goodbye to Kitty!"

"Can't be helped — but guess what? I went to Slops with my chitty and they gave me hooks to sew on everything — even my working overalls!"

"Then you'll have to take them to Mam. She'll do it for you. Do they know yet at Rowangarth? Have you been able to ring them?"

"No. I'll just turn up like a bad penny. Mother's going to be pretty cut up — especially about the wedding. She's been wanting me hitched for ages. Anyway — how's married life, Wren Purvis?"

It was obvious now that until Drew's train left, they would talk about anything but a wedding that wasn't going to be.

"Well — though I know I shouldn't say it, I might rather get to like it. Trouble is, they're noted for being skinny with leave at Keth's place. I felt badly done to when he had to go back; I even mentioned trying for a draft to Bletchley Park, but they won't let husband and wife be on the same base, for some stupid reason. Keth wants me to stay where I am, and after what's happened to you and Kitty I'm going to count my blessings and be content with phone calls and be grateful for any leave we can scrounge together."

"Yes — and when I'm feeling sorry for myself, I shall think of Tatty and Tim, and tell myself that at least Kitty and I will be married one day."

"Well, knowing your fiancée as I do, Drew, it wouldn't surprise me one bit if she didn't chuck ENSA, join the Wrens, then volunteer for an overseas draft to wherever you are!"

"Then you'd have to stop her doing anything so harebrained! There's one thing that never happens, and that's an overseas draft to where you want to be. Even Kitty couldn't work it!"

"Want to bet?"

They laughed for the first time, and some of the tension left them.

572

"Have you got anything to eat on the train, Drew?"

"No, but it doesn't matter. I'm miserable enough leaving the *Maggie* and Liverpool. Might as well be hungry too."

"Then shall I try to get through to Rowangarth, or Mam; tell them you're on your way?"

"Best not. That would really put the cat amongst the pigeons! Can't you imagine the mothers, and the consternation. Think it'll be best if I just walk in on then, then do the explaining afterwards. Poor Mother — and Lady too. The last I heard from home was that they were planning a new dress for Mother for the wedding. Everyone was really looking forward to it. I feel so awful, spoiling everything for them."

"Now listen! It's none of your fault — nor Kitty's. Like you said, it's the way the cookie crumbles. Keth and I planned to be married in the summer of 'forty-one, and we were almost two years adrift. Can you wait for two years, Drew?"

"I'd wait for ever for Kitty — but the war won't be over in two years, Daiz, and we both know it. There'll have to be a second front, and then the Japs to see off . . ."

"See what you mean, old love. It's a swine, isn't it? The last war lasted four years, and this one's gone almost that long already."

"Well, unless somebody shoots Hitler, it's going to drag on a whole lot longer. Sorry to be such a whinge, but I'm not the best company in the world at the moment."

"I know how it feels." Daisy reached for his hand, squeezing it tightly. "And all that matters, really, is that you take good care, wherever it is that you're going. Tatty and I will keep an eye on Kitty for you, and try to cheer her up."

They sat unspeaking, hands clasped, because there didn't seem to be any more to say. Daisy was content enough just to be close, because only heaven knew when they would meet again. She thought of Kitty, and how awful it would be for her when finally she knew that Drew had gone. Oh, damn the war! Damn it, damn it, *damn* it!

Tears, angry and bewildered, threatened and she sniffed loudly. Drew fished for his handkerchief and ordered her to blow and to smile, please, just for him?

"Suppose I'd better be getting on the train." He got to his feet. "It's filling up and I don't want someone to pinch my seat."

"Suppose you better had." Daisy stood on tiptoe, clasping her arms around his neck, hugging him tightly. "Take care, bruv. Tatty and I will see that Kitty isn't too unhappy whilst you're away. And you *mightn't* be going foreign."

"No. I mightn't. Look after yourself." He laid his cheek on hers, thinking, all in the space of a few seconds, of the way it had been once upon a time when they were young. "Love you, Daiz. Go now. Don't wait. You know I don't like being waved off."

She stood there whilst he climbed on the train, banging the door shut, letting down the window. Then he smiled and blew a kiss and she smiled back, and pretended to catch it.

She turned and walked, aching all over with despair, to the barrier, handing in her ticket, wanting to turn for one last wave. She didn't, though, because you mustn't look back. Not ever. Looking back was trouble.

God, please, *please*, look after him? She closed her eyes tightly, then covered her face with her hands, shaking with silent sobs. She didn't care who saw her. People always cried at railway stations now. It was the war to blame. People understood.

CHAPTER
TWENTY-NINE

The pilot who had guided the troopship to the river mouth climbed down the rope ladder to the small, swift launch that would take him back to shore. Drew, who was familiar with the comings and goings of Mersey river-pilots, watched dispassionately.

The pilot-boat turned, bouncing on its own backwash, and Drew pulled his eyes away. It was leaving, his last link with Liverpool; best not watch it out of sight, because Liverpool was where he had met Kitty, outrageous in a skimpy costume, and he didn't want to see the docks and warehouses fade and merge into the skyline and oblivion.

He had not been able to believe it at first. Even though there were no station names, he knew his train was approaching Liverpool. He was one of a large naval party which filled the entire troop train and it was ironic that out of all the ports of embarkation, Liverpool had to be the one.

Rumours circulated. Such a concentration of naval personnel, it was suggested, could crew an entire battlewaggon. North Africa was their destination, the buzz had it, to take over a captured enemy battle cruiser and sail it back to England. Or Scotland. Either would do.

"Nah!" came the considered opinion of one already dubbed a lower-deck lawyer. "We're all goin' to set up a shore base — well, we've got Suez back, haven't we?" Stood to reason, he said, that once the Suez Canal was free of Jerry mines, they'd need the Royal Navy either end to keep order.

Ceylon, too, was mentioned and Capetown and Hong Kong, but Drew had offered no opinion. Wherever they were heading, he was sailing further and further away from all he loved. Already, once-familiar landmarks had vanished.

The troopship gathered speed. They were approaching the meeting of sea and river. Soon they would be alone, sailing independently of any convoy, keeping a zig-zag course to outwit enemy submarines. Once the ship was at full steam ahead, they could outsail any U-boat that had yet been launched.

"Found out what she is, then?" The question from a sailor who came to join him.

"No. Probably one of the Empress boats." Once, the troopship had been a liner; now its paintwork was in the colours of camouflage and nothing that might identify it was left. Cabins and sleeping quarters had been stripped of all luxury. Eight men would sleep in a cabin intended for two. "Any idea where we're heading?"

Liverpool — England — had gone now. Soon they would be in seas so vast that direction could only be guessed at by the sun by day and the stars by night. Only the troopship's crew would know; those they carried would be told their destination only when it was considered safe for them to know.

Drew placed his bet on the least likely of the speculations; that they were to sail home a captured enemy battleship. The least likely, of course, because it would be a small miracle if it were so, and that kind of miracle didn't happen, especially when there was a war on.

He turned to find he was alone again; alone until 18.00 hours, when Division C-Charlie — his party — were to muster in the mess hall. What were once-elegant dining rooms had been converted to less glamorous messes, though fat cherubs, their gilt fading, still decorated them to remind how it had been.

The Kentucky Suttons crossed the Atlantic twice a year, Drew thought achingly, in such a liner as this. Summer and Christmas; so regular that Uncle Albert called it the twice-yearly migration. Twice a year the Clan came together, safe in their closeness, picking up where they left off as if they had never been apart.

They were apart now. On this last Sunday in May, Kitty would have counted off twenty days in her mind; Tatiana crossed them off the calendar that hung in the kitchen at Montpelier Mews. Maybe now, though, Tatty would have stopped crossing off the days, because she knew there would be no wedding. Everyone knew, except Kitty . . .

Where are you now, sweetheart? Are you on your way home, and who will tell you, when you get to Montpelier? Will it be Tatty or Sparrow? Will they tell you I have gone before you open my letter, and read it for yourself?

The upper decks were almost deserted, partly, he supposed, because smoking was not allowed there. Not in daylight hours because trodden-in cigarette ends made a mess of the immaculate decks and never in the darkness, because the glow from a cigarette could be seen for miles at sea. Most of Naval Contingent 490, Drew supposed, would be below decks, familiarizing themselves with the layout of the ship, claiming their bedspace on the black-painted iron bunks. And, if they had any sense at all, learning by heart the quickest way to boat stations, should the ship be hit; memorizing it so they could do it half asleep and in complete darkness.

They had always said, in reply to Lord Haw-Haw's nasal taunting about Allied shipping losses, that we had never yet lost a troopship at sea, nor were likely ever to do so. Some troopers could steam at twenty-five knots. Drew hoped that this game old lady could do the same, if need be.

How long before they knew where they were going, and what of Kitty's destination? Was her tour over; was she even now packing her trunk? Would they pass, unknowing, she on her way home, he to a place unknown and for God only knew how long?

His body began to pulsate with the misery of wanting her and the need to touch her, kiss her, love her. Kitty of the violet eyes that could tease and beckon and promise. He had lost her, and all for the small red killick anchor that Lady had sewn on the left sleeves of his tunics and greatcoat; the badge of his new rank.

He looked at his watch. Time to go to the converted mess to hear the orders of the day — even though it was early evening and they were steaming into twilight.

Soon, the ship must be darkened. The leading-hand in each crowded cabin — himself included — would be responsible for the covering of the porthole. They would sleep with the door open, he supposed. Luxury liners were air-conditioned; troop carriers were not. Eight grunting, snoring, sweating bodies in that small space, hammocks opened and laid flat on the criss-crossed bunk-springs to ease the discomfort.

He turned from a sea that was changing from green to black, trying to remember the way to where Naval Party C was to muster, remembering instead Kitty's laugh, the softness of her mouth.

How he wanted her beside him!

"I don't think there'll be a phone call now, Julia."

Nathan did not have to say from whom; the only call Julia was interested in receiving was from Drew. It was five days since his leave ended and there had been only one call. From barracks, he said, and he would try to ring again.

Four days later she was still waiting and she knew instinctively that soon there would be a letter. One sheet, hurriedly written, bearing the red stamp and scribbled initial of a censor clerk. Perhaps tomorrow that letter would arrive, or the next day, and it would begin,

Dearest Mother,
By the time you get this I shall be at sea, destination unknown . . .

He had arrived unexpectedly, carrying all his kit and she had been a sailor's mother for long enough to know that full kit — hammock, kitbag, case, respirator and steel helmet — meant only one thing.

"How long?" she asked when they had kissed and hugged.

"Seven days — embarkation . . ."

"Another ship, Drew?"

"Haven't been told yet. Won't know till I'm back in barracks."

His face had told her the rest, though it wasn't until he changed into civilian clothes and they had eaten supper that he explained, finally, that the wedding would have to wait.

The telephone rang and she hurried to pick it up. It was Alice.

"Won't keep you. Any news?"

"Not a word. Look — I'm coming over, all right?"

"I'll put the kettle on . . ."

"I'm just popping over to Keeper's," she called as she shrugged into her coat. "Don't mind, do you darling?"

"Off you go," Nathan smiled indulgently. She had been restless since she saw Drew off at Holdenby; Alice was the best company for her. "Just tell Winnie before you go that if a call comes from Drew she's to put it through to Keeper's."

She almost ran in her haste to get to Keeper's Cottage, yet Alice had the kettle on the stove and a tray set with cups and saucers when she arrived. She hung up her coat, then sat in Tom's chair, holding her hands to the fire that had not long been lit.

"Tom's home-guarding?"

"Isn't he always, these days? I wouldn't care, but the worst of the danger is past now."

"Never say that, Alice. Hitler's a devious swine. You never know what he'll get up to next!"

"His secret weapon, you mean? I very much doubt it exists, or why didn't he use it in North Africa and why are the Russians giving him such a trouncing? And the losses at sea are the lowest since the war started. It said so on the wireless . . ."

Julia relaxed. Nathan was the dearest, loveliest man, who understood and accepted her in all her moods, yet it was here, in Alice's kitchen, she felt safest from her troubles; here, where Daisy and Drew smiled down from the mantelpiece. Because

Alice always understood and could weigh up any situation calmly; could dismiss Hitler's so-called deadly secret weapon in two sentences.

"I wonder when Kitty will be back. If she flies, she should be home any day now." Frowning, Alice filled the brown teapot. "I'm bothered about the lass. I know the way it hit Daisy when Keth just upped and went."

"Upped and was *sent*, don't you mean? But I think Tatty will tell her gently, and there'll be Sparrow for backup."

"And we don't know for certain that Drew is going overseas, do we? Wouldn't we look a pair of softies after all our worrying, if he ends up on Orkney or Shetland?"

"Oh, if only . . ." Julia stirred her tea, her face a blank. "I'm remembering, you see, how war does things to you. War and Fate are stable mates, you know. Drew and Kitty are so in love it sometimes makes me afraid."

"And what does Nathan say to your broodings?" Alice demanded, her mouth pursed into a disapproving round.

"Nothing, because I haven't told him! I haven't got his faith. When my brother and Andrew were killed and Giles died of his wounds, I hated God with all my strength. A parson's wife, admitting such a thing! I wanted to lash out, hurt the whole world. I couldn't accept, as Mother did. Just a little faith, she said, and a little waiting, then she and Pa and Robert and Giles would be together again."

"But you accept, Julia, that there's *somewhere* for us when we die?"

"I try to, but only because of Nathan. I still doubt. That's why I'm so afraid. Sometimes — like now — I think I'm going to be punished, paid back, for all the hatred that was in me. It was years and years, remember, before I could bring myself to go to France, bear to look at Andrew's grave."

"And you came back accepting that it was a young nurse who'd been left a childless widow, and a young doctor who lay beneath that stone. You came home a middle-aged woman, Julia, because in that cemetery you finally found the courage to say goodbye to Andrew — after more than fifteen years! And God doesn't punish people, Julia, so there's no debt for you to pay."

"He punished Elliot, didn't He, for what he did to you and for the life he'd led? Elliot died horribly!"

"Idiot!" Alice flung. "That wasn't God's doing! That was the devil, claiming his own! And Elliot Sutton died never knowing he'd fathered the boy he wanted so much for Pendenys. We've got that son, Julia; you and me and Rowangarth! Drew was sent as a blessing and he's going to be all right! You've got to tell yourself that every time such daft thoughts get into your head. Drew is my son too, and I *know* he's going to come home to us! And so is Daisy!"

"Yes. They'll both be fine." Tears filled Julia's eyes and she held out her arms.

"There now. Let it all come," Alice whispered, gathering her close. "You've been fighting it ever since Drew went back off leave, and don't say you haven't. I wept buckets the day Daisy joined the Wrens!"

She dipped into the pocket of her pinafore and offered a handkerchief and when Julia had dried her eyes and blown her nose very loudly she said,

"That's better, now isn't it? Now will you drink up that tea, Julia Sutton? It's getting cold!"

An excited, sun-browned Kitty burst into the kitchen at Montpelier Mews, dragging her trunk behind her.

"I'm back, folks, and have I got news for you!" Her eyes were bright with happiness. "Oh, my goodness, you'll never guess the half of it. I'm dying for a cup of tea, Sparrow, and I'm starving! Where are Drew's letters? It's so *good* to be back! You'll never believe the greenness of everything here, after all that sand and palm trees! And was it *hot*!"

"For goodness' sake, girl!" Sparrow wailed. "Tatty! Give her a hand upstairs with that trunk!" She turned away, busying herself with the setting of a tea tray.

"Well — don't I get a hug and a kiss?" Kitty gathered the older woman into her arms, holding her tightly. "My, but I've missed you both! It seemed ages, getting back. We did our tour, then went to an airfield where there was supposed to be a plane. But it was two days late arriving and there we were, living out of suitcases, cadging rations off the RAF boys, and giving impromptu shows! What a way to run a war! Where are my letters, Sparrow?"

"On the dresser, and Kitty, there's — we-e-ll —"

"There's something you've got to know," Tatiana finished.

"Like . . .?" Kitty's head jerked up and her eyes took on a guarded look as she paused to draw breath and for the first time, look into two unsmiling faces. "Oh, don't tell me Drew's lot won't give him marriage leave! I can't believe it!"

"Worse than that." Tatty's face was paper white, her eyes round with concern. "He's gone abroad, we think . . ."

"Abroad! What d'you mean — *abroad*? He *can't* go abroad!"

"We-e-ll — maybe he hasn't. We only know he's been promoted to leading-telegraphist, so that means a change of ship. And they gave him seven days' leave — embarkation leave, he said."

"So where is he now?" Kitty whispered.

"We don't know. Aunt Julia phoned last night. She had a phone call from him from Plymouth barracks to say he'd got back all right off leave, then no news for four days. She said that when you get back, will you give her a ring if you can manage to get through?"

"Ring! I'll do more than that! I'm going up there! *Now!*"

"Kitty girl, you *can't*! Not tonight!" Sparrow was clearly upset.

586

"I can! I'll get down to King's Cross somehow, and take the overnight sleeper! With luck, I can be in York in time for the early train to Holdenby!"

"But Kitty! You've just had a long journey and you're tired out!" Tatiana soothed. "Why don't you get something to eat, then I'll help you unpack? Don't you think it'd be better if you rang Rowangarth, first — see what Aunt Julia has to say?"

"Well — I suppose I need a bath . . ."

"That's right! Try to take things gently. Sparrow'll pull the dampers out — get the water good and hot. And things won't seem quite so bad when you've had a decent night's sleep."

"Okay." All at once, Kitty surrendered, her bottom lip trembling. "You *did* mean it? He really *has* gone?"

"We know he had leave and he wasn't best pleased about it," Sparrow sighed. "It's just the sort of thing them high-ups like to do. They did it to Keth, don't forget, but Daisy and him's married now. For all we know Drew might only be gone a few months. Might have been sent to Gibraltar. There's a lot of Navy there, and that's not so far away, now is it?"

"I think I'll read my letters first — upstairs, if you don't mind." She picked them up, scanning the postmarks, arranging them into date order.

"You do that, and I'll book a call to Rowangarth. Then I'll bring you up some scrambled eggs on toast and a cup of tea."

"No thanks, Sparrow. I'm not as hungry as I thought." Her eyes filled with tears. "Just a cup of tea — if you're making one. Tea would be lovely."

"She was trying hard not to cry," Tatiana whispered when she heard the bedroom door close. "It isn't fair! She was so happy and then this has got to happen. Do you think I should go up to her, Sparrow?"

"No. Leave her be for a while. I'll put that call in, then you can take her a mug of tea up later. Give her time. What she needs is a good weep. Leave her be to sort herself out, eh? Happen there'll be news from Drew in her letters — written between the lines, sort of, so the Censor's lot won't cut 'em out. If I know Kitty, she won't be down for long! Mark my words, she won't!"

"No. Maybe not. And let's not forget Drew. Heaven only knows where he is and how he's feeling. Wars are awful, Sparrow. They just take over your life and there's nothing you can do about it!"

"I knows that, girl. I had a war to contend with too." She laid an arm around Tatiana's shoulders, pulling her close. "And we do it in the name of King and Country and being patriotic. I remember that poster we used to have in the Great War. It was everywhere — you couldn't get away from it. Kitchener, with his black moustache and his finger jabbing! *Your country needs you!* I wanted to spit at that face. I was glad when he was drowned. I remembered thinking that that would put paid to his inveigling lads into the trenches to be killed, like my son was!"

"I felt like that too — when Tim was killed. I used to hate the fighter pilot who did it. I think I still do."

"Ah, well. Ain't nothing we can do but keep our chins up and see that Kitty don't get too upset. And maybe we're looking on the gloomy side. Maybe, even if Drew is going abroad, he might get back home sooner than we think. Keth managed it."

"Drew won't, though." They turned to see Kitty standing there. "I've got an address to write to: Division C. Naval Contingent 490. c/o GPO London. Seems to me like there's a whole lot of sailors being sent somewhere, not just Drew. What do you think is happening?"

"I don't know, and that's a fact." Words were cheap, to Sparrow's way of thinking; platitudes a whole lot cheaper. "You've just got to hope and pray and never stop thinking about him and wishing him home. You ain't the only one. There's women with children as have never set eyes on their father — or can't remember what he looks like. You're a Sutton, don't forget, and Suttons keeps their chins up and get on with it!"

"Yup! I guess so! And when I do find where he's gone, I'll just have to put my mind to getting out to him. That guy promised to marry me, and I'm holding him to it!"

Then all at once, the brief, brave show of defiance was gone. Her face crumpled and the violet eyes filled with tears.

"Tea's ready, if you want a cup," Sparrow said matter-of-factly. "And just this once, Kitty girl, you can have sugar in it instead of saccharin."

Sugar for shock, that's what was needed, because Kitty Sutton had had the shock of her young life and was still reeling from it, to Sparrow's way of thinking.

"Thanks a lot. You're both being very kind," Kitty whispered sniffily. "It's just that I can't think straight. All I can do is wonder why it has happened to Drew and me! What did we do to deserve it that was so wicked? But I *will* try, I really will, and if you'll put up with my whingeing until I get my act together, I'd be very grateful."

"Take all the time you want," Tatiana said softly, because she had trodden the same despairing path. Only for her, that path had no end to it.

"So that's it, Mr Catchpole!" Gracie gave a final push to the tubular brass spray that pumped droplets of moisture into the air. "Fat lot of good those orchids are going to be now! Poor Kitty and Drew."

"Ar." Rowangarth's gardener felt very badly done to. The garden was coming up to its best; rosebuds were bursting open, lupins, poppies, honeysuckle and more besides would have been there for the picking on the nineteenth; Jack Catchpole could have put on floral displays to equal the old days, when entertaining was lavish and no expense spared.

590

The Master of Rowangarth's wedding should have been a triumph of flowers and potted shrubs and plants, with even the laburnums behaving themselves and bursting into great golden tassels, right on time. Mind, the last few days before would have been frantic, with lawns to be cut, flowers picked in the evening and placed up to their heads in buckets of water, and himself and Gracie up at cockcrow on the morning of the big day to see to the bridal bouquets and buttonholes.

Now, it was all off. Some fool at the Admiralty had messed up all Jack Catchpole's triumphant plans, not to mention there being no wedding on account of the groom being miles away!

"Ar," he said again, pipe clamped between his teeth, jaw rigid with upset. Young Bas would have been there. He'd have come to the kitchen garden bearing gifts, but no wedding, no tobacco! Catchpole was becoming increasingly agitated because not only had all his scheming and planning come to nothing, but Miss Julia wasn't at her sunniest either! Nor Alice Dwerryhouse, nor Tilda in the kitchen, who had really been looking forward to it since her Sydney had received an official invitation.

He sucked squeakily on his empty pipe and Gracie, aware always of any change of mood in him, said, "I had a letter from Bas this morning. Said he hopes to be over this weekend. Probably Saturday."

"And I suppose you'll be wanting the afternoon off?" The black mood began to lift.

"I wasn't going to ask, Mr Catchpole, really I wasn't."

"No. And blessed is them that expects nothing, 'cause then they'm not disappointed. In your case, though, you can have Saturday afternoon in exchange for Sunday morning, and that'll mean opening up the glasshouses, seeing to the liquid manoor, and hoeing the onion bed."

"Oh *thanks*, Mr Catchpole. No trouble at all!" Even the stirring of the tub of liquid hen manure twice daily no longer caused her to flinch. With three years of Rowangarth tuition behind her she was the equal of any man, Mr Catchpole said, 'cept in the wielding of a spade, and you couldn't expect a woman to dig as deep and for as long as a man! "And the kettle should be coming up to the boil. I'll go and mash the tea."

She had even learned to mash tea, he chuckled, as opposed to wetting, making or brewing it! Gracie had always been a quick learner. He would miss her when she wed young Bas and took herself off to Kentucky. Of course, there'd be Tilda's Sydney looking for a position when finally the Green Howards had no use for him, and very satisfactory he would be, but for one thing. Sydney Willis did not have a lovely little bottom that wiggled when he walked, nor long, golden hair, nor Gracie's sudden, sunny smile either.

On the other hand, Sydney would be better with a spade than Gracie, he thought as he settled himself on his upturned apple box by the potting shed door to await tea and survey his amazingly immaculate garden as he did so.

"If I tell you something, Mr Catchpole, will you promise on God's honour not to tell a soul?" Gracie placed the mug containing the strongest, milkiest tea on the floor at his side.

"Not a soul, lass. Not even Lily." Definitely not Lily, who rarely visited the village but when she did, liked a good old gossip.

"We-e-ll, when I was in York the other night —"

"At the dance, at the Assembly Rooms?" She had asked off early, he remembered, because it was a special one.

"That's it. And who do you think I saw?" She blew on her tea, taking a tentative sip. He felt irritated because he didn't like guessing games.

"Big fat Hermann Goering, pretending he was a barrage balloon!"

"No, softie," she giggled, then seriously, "but I did see Dr Pryce!"

"Oh, ar." So Doctor Pryce going to York was news?

"And guess who was with him? Mrs Anna, that's who!"

"Tatiana's Mam?"

"The same. And she was smiling and he was smiling and he had hold of her elbow, so they must've been enjoying themselves. Then Mrs Sutton smiled at him real lovely. 'I've been really looking forward to seeing the play, Ewart,' she said. She called him Ewart!"

"She would. It's his name."

"Yes, but she works for him, so I think she should have called him Doctor."

"Why should she? Dr Pryce visits Rowangarth as a friend, and happen visits Denniston House, an' all. Think you're reading over much into it, Gracie lass." Catchpole was mildly disappointed. "On the other hand, it would make for fireworks over at Denniston, if they was going out regular."

"Tatty wouldn't mind."

"Happen not. But what about that countess woman? Her wouldn't like it one bit. You know what an old curmudgeon she can be!"

Gracie knew. She had helped Tatty outwit her grandmother many times so she could get out to meet Tim. There would have been ructions if ever the old lady had discovered the part Rowangarth's land girl played in the deception!

"Nothing would please the Countess, Tatty once told me, except a Romanov getting the Russian throne back!"

She lapsed into thinking. Socializing friends maybe, but the way Mrs Anna had smiled and the look in her eyes when she gazed at the doctor was altogether something different. But best let the matter drop.

"I suppose," she sighed, "they were only going to the theatre."

"Happen. And a theatre's a public place, isn't it? Not like Lover's Lane in the blackout. Couldn't get up to any hanky-panky at the theatre, Gracie."

594

"No, Mr Catchpole."

But they could hold hands when the lights went down, she thought, and what was more she hoped they had! Mrs Anna, by all accounts, hadn't had much of a marriage. Maybe she deserved a bit of fun with Dr Pryce, even if there wasn't anything in it!

She drank her tea reflectively and a little sadly, and Catchpole drank his. Reflectively, too, but with thoughts of Bas arriving on Saturday and the heady scent that would waft up when he ripped the seal of the tobacco packet.

A decent lad, young Bas was . . .

When Naval Contingent 490 had been at sea for ten days, everyone knew that neither North Africa nor Alexandria, where it had been supposed they might crew a captured enemy ship and sail it back to home waters, could be their destination. And when, two days later, it was announced that letters could be posted, those bookmakers who had done well on North Africa and Alexandria began to offer odds on destination Panama Canal. And since it was now fairly obvious that the troopship was sailing in that direction, punters were few and far between.

Their letters, they were warned, would be censored before leaving the ship and must not contain information beneficial to the enemy, such as their port of embarkation, how long they had been at sea and where they thought they were heading. Any such letter would be destroyed!

"If we can post letters," said lower-deck lawyer, "it means there'll be mailbags going ashore. We'll be coming alongside, I shouldn't wonder."

"And do you reckon They'll let us ashore for a skylark?" one hopeful demanded.

"Nah! There'll be armed sentries on all the gangways to make sure we don't! We'll be victualling ship, maybe, and taking on fresh water; maybe mail, if our luck runs good." But mark his words, he stressed, a run ashore would be out!

Drew found a corner on the upper deck which was sheltered from a sun that was becoming increasingly hot; so much so that Authority had ordered the wearing of tropical kit: the drill shorts and tops they were given in barracks. The issuing of "whites" had given the game away, though one telegraphist was heard to say that it meant nothing at all; that last time his ship went foreign they had been given tropical kit and ended up, would you believe, in Norway, in January, evacuating British and French soldiers!

Drew was frustrated and restless, and would be glad when 19 June came and was gone, though one day was much the same as another, on board a troopship.

There had been boat drills and physical training to break the monotony; at night there were games of tombola, with the Master-at-Arms turning a blind eye to the penny stakes, which constituted gambling and were forbidden.

There had been little else to do but pass the days as best he could and try not to think that Kitty would be back at Montpelier now, and would know.

Darling Kitty. He had written to her each day, and since letters could soon be posted, he would add yet another to the handful already written and addressed.

My darling love,

One more letter to tell you I am missing you still, and loving you and wanting you till it hurts. No one knows yet where we are heading. The days are long and boring, which gives me all the time in the world to think about you and wonder how you are.

I am trying not to count the days. To do that would be near unbearable. All I am sure about is that I love you more than ever, if that is possible, and when I think of how far apart we are, I try to think of Daisy and Keth and how it all came right for them in the end.

He shifted his position. The sun shone on the sea, throwing up great glares of light, and he mopped his face and neck, rubbing the palms of his hands down his shorts.

Nearby, four sailors were playing cards. They were very young, probably newly joined, getting in their first sea time. They laughed a lot because this voyage was an adventure. None of them cared where they were going. All they knew was that it was to some country that once was only a shape on the page of a school atlas.

Though we still haven't been officially told where we are going, I have my own ideas. I can't tell you, of course; all I can say is that I want you and though I refuse to be sorry for myself, it feels as if a part of me has been wrenched away, and there is nothing I can do about it.

Why, in God's Name, do I love you so much?

Tatty walked quietly to the bench on which Bill Benson sat, taking his hand in hers. He turned, then traced her face with gentle fingertips.

"Tatiana! Good of you to come! Why didn't you say?"

"Wanted to surprise you. Sorry I haven't got any grapes or magazines or anything."

"Magazines aren't a lot of use to a blind man," he finished for her, matter-of-factly.

"I've at least brought you a bar of chocolate." She took it from her handbag, slipping it into his pocket.

"No! You mustn't give away your rations."

"Please have it, Bill. I just had to bring something."

"You brought yourself. That's more than enough. I had a feeling you might come." He was dressed in hospital blues; bright blue suit, white shirt and red tie. "I can make it on my own to this seat now. I sit out here a lot, listening — and smelling," he smiled.

"Bill, your mouth is healing! That was a lovely smile! Any news about an op?" She took off her coat, draping it over the back of the seat.

"No. You know what they're like in these places. Coming on nicely, is all I'm told, and to be patient."

"And can you still see shapes and shadows?"

"Sometimes. If it's sunny outside I have to wear my dark glasses. Mind if I smoke? Day-sister's a dragon — won't allow it on the ward — but night-sister isn't so bad. At least she only turns a disapproving eye.

"What is that smell?" He lifted his head, sniffing. "So many scents out here, and I don't know what they are."

"It's orange blossom." She reached up and picked a spray and he held it to his nose, then touched it with curious fingertips.

"Contrary to what you might think, the flowers are white, Bill. And there are wallflowers beside the seat. They have a lovely scent too. Country people call them gillyflowers."

"And what else can't I see?"

"We-e-ll, there's a huge sweep of lawn and lots of flower beds, and further over, there are trees; oak, ash, beech. You'll see them after your op."

"There weren't any flowers or trees about when I was a bairn. Saw them in the parks, sometimes, but our place just had a big back yard."

"Was the orphanage so very bad?"

"No. Not once I'd left school. I got a job and they let me go on living there. I had a room of my own, then, and better food. The devil you know, Tatiana, is better than the devil you don't know. I worked for the Corporation, street sweeping, but you know all that."

"Yes. And then you joined the Air Force as soon as you were old enough."

"Aye. For once in my life I was someone, but better than that, I was free. Free from charity, that was. It was good being a sergeant, drinking my first pint, learning to dance. And having more money in my pocket than I knew what to do with!" He reached in his pocket for cigarettes and matches and a small, round box. "Just watch this. I can light a ciggie now without burning myself." He struck a match, lit the cigarette, then inhaled deeply. "And this wee box is for matches and cigarette ends — so I won't set the place on fire either!"

"You're getting very cheeky!" She moved nearer and their shoulders touched companionably. "Whose news first?"

"Yours," he said promptly. "It's the wedding soon. Next week, isn't it?"

"That's just it. Since I last saw you, Drew has been sent abroad. Lord knows where he's heading, but there have been no letters for ages. They gave him embarkation leave, but Kitty was in Egypt with her ENSA lot. It was just rotten luck."

"So Kitty's back now? How did she take it?"

600

"Not good. At first she couldn't believe it. Then, when it finally sunk in, she went upstairs and cried and cried. She's trying to make the best of it, though it's hit her hard."

"So Drew will be on another ship now?" Bill knew all about Tatiana's family; looked upon them, almost, as his own.

"Yes. Sailing further and further away and counting off the days, as we were, to a wedding that isn't going to happen — well, not yet, anyway. This war's a swine!"

"I'll no' argue with you on that point, but I'll settle for a look at the world again. If I could just see, I'd be able to get a better job when they chuck me out of the RAF. I don't fancy learning to make baskets!"

"You'll be fine, Bill. I know it!"

"Maybe so. I'd like to know what you're really like, Tatiana. I've got ideas in my mind and I know your hair is long and that the top of your head is level with my shoulder. You're no' very tall, are you?"

"I'm five feet four!" And Bill, though he had never told her, was six feet exactly. She knew it without asking, because he was just the same height as Tim. "Your mouth has healed far better than I thought. And the skin around it looks much healthier. Did they tell you?"

"They don't need to. I can feel the roughness has gone. From my nose down didn't get so badly burned — I had my intercom mask on. Sister says in time it should be okay. A bit pinkish, but not so bad at all. My eyebrows are growing, too. I'm not going to be the monster I thought I'd be; just part of my face scarred. And blind, of course."

He said it matter-of-factly, Tatiana thought sadly, but he'd had time to accept the way he was and maybe come to terms with it; just as she had come to terms with never seeing Tim again.

"Bill — do you ever hear from any of your RAF friends?" All at once, it was important to have something to say.

"No. I was the only survivor in our crew. I bailed out, then the plane blew up just after. One day a crew is there, and the next day it's gone. You don't have time for making lasting friendships in an aircrew mess. And don't think I'm binding; I'm not. At least I'm alive and sitting beside a popsie, sniffing orange blossom!

"Just something I'd like to ask you, Tatiana. When this war is over and we've gone our separate ways, you and me, can we keep in touch, even if it's only Christmas and birthdays?"

"Well, mine's the first of March, and I've not long had my twenty-first."

"And mine's Christmas Day, would you believe? Not what you'd call a happy Christmas present to some wee girl who didn't want me. Seems my grandmother took me to the Home. Said my mother was too young to keep me. She didn't offer a name. All she said was that I'd been born on Christmas Day. There were a lot of kids like me,

602

Tatiana. I didn't feel particularly sorry for myself. It wasn't until the war came and I joined up that I realized what I'd been missing. When I was nineteen all the crew went out on a binge. First party I ever had.

"Just two weeks after, we got hit over the target. Skip made it back home. We saw the white cliffs and thought we were in with a chance, even though it was a wing and a prayer job." He was staring ahead, his eyes fixed in the direction of the scent of orange blossom. "Skip told us all to jump. Think he was trying to keep the plane in the air long enough to give us a chance to bail out, then ditch it in the Channel. But it didn't work — we were on fire, anyway. I'll never be as lucky again, Tatiana."

"Yes," she said softly. "And if you can make it, you'll spend your next birthday with me in Yorkshire, and you can have another party."

"But won't your parents mind — having me wished on them, I mean? I'm not exactly the ideal house guest, now am I?"

"My father is dead — I told you — and my mother wouldn't mind." How could she, Tatiana thought, when since her last birthday Denniston House and everything in it belonged to her!

"Then I'll hold you to that. What like is your house? You've never told me."

"Well, it was supposed to be haunted. An old eccentric lived there alone. When she died it stood empty for years, then the Army took it in the last war, for a hospital. Aunt Julia started her nursing training there, and Daisy's mother too."

"So it's a big place?"

"No. Roomy, but small enough to be homely. It's got a nice garden and a conservatory. You'll like it when you see it."

"*See* it?"

"Why not? Why shouldn't your operation be a success? Why shouldn't you get your sight back in *both* eyes? Don't you think life owes you that much, at least? You haven't had a lot of luck, have you? And there's a nurse on the front steps, waving. What does she want?"

"To tell us it's teatime, I shouldn't wonder. Nothing posh. Just sandwiches and tea and rock buns on Sundays. Guests are welcome. Will you stay, Tatiana?"

"I'd love to. Now off you go! See how well you can make it back. I'll walk behind you."

And Bill, white stick moving from side to side, made it with hardly a stumble.

It was an hour later when Tatiana was leaving, that Sister, who had obviously been waiting, said, "Ah! Sergeant Benson's friend! Can you spare me a few minutes?"

"My train doesn't leave for an hour. Is something wrong, Sister?"

"Not wrong, exactly. It's all a question of next of kin, you see. We like to have a name when someone

604

is having surgery — and in Sergeant Benson's case it's going to be quite a delicate operation."

"I don't think I can help you, Sister. All I know is that he has no parents. I presumed, always, they weren't alive." Not for anything would she tell anyone Bill had been dumped! Unwanted! "What does it say in his paybook? Next of kin is usually written there, surely?"

"Usually it is, Miss — er —"

"Sutton. Tatiana Sutton."

"Well, Miss Sutton, I've seen his paybook and there is no next of kin. Something was once written there, but it has been inked out — very thoroughly! I asked him about it — casually, you'll understand — but he told me just what you've said, that his parents are dead. Has he ever mentioned relatives to you — an aunt or an uncle, maybe?"

"He hasn't — just that his parents were killed."

"Then I'm going to have to ask him. I must have a next of kin before the operation. The surgeon will insist on it. He isn't of age yet, you see."

"No! Don't say anything to him, please. If he'd been all that fond of his next of kin, surely his or her name would have been in his paybook? But I'm almost sure he has no one. It's very sad, isn't it?"

"It most certainly is. I can't believe there isn't a soul in the world he can call his own!" Her eyes showed concern, and disbelief.

"But he isn't alone! He's got me. I care about him. Why don't you ask him if he'd like me to be his next of kin?"

She didn't stop to think, but even had she done so, it would have made no difference, because no matter what the outcome of the operation, she could not let him go on being so alone in so big and sometimes uncaring a world.

"Are you sure, Miss Sutton?"

"Of course. It will be entirely up to him. I live near York — that's my permanent address — but I work in London. I'll write them both down for you, if you'll give me a piece of paper — and both phone numbers. And, Sister — when is the operation to be? Bill said he didn't know."

"We haven't told him yet, but it will be on Thursday. In the morning. If everything goes to plan, that is."

"Thank you for telling me." She handed back the sheet of paper. "There are all the details you need to know, including my date of birth. I *am* of age, Sister — just — so I qualify, don't I?"

And the Sister said she did — *just* — and thanked her and asked her not to ring until the evening on Thursday, if she didn't mind, then rose to her feet, the interview over.

Ward Sister was a busy woman and had no time to spare for anything but essentials — and the twelve young men in her charge in the ward outside.

It wasn't until Tatiana was sitting on the train that she realized the seriousness of what she had done. Provided Bill agreed — and she was almost certain he would — she had become his next of kin;

responsible for him until he came of age at Christmas. And even after then, could she leave him to his own devices, especially when the operation might not be a success?

Bill would be given a pension, of course, and the Royal Air Force would see that he got some kind of training to fit him for the world outside. But would it be enough? Did anything at all compensate for being so absolutely alone in the world?

"No!" whispered a voice uncommonly like that of Tim Thomson. "It most certainly does not!"

Good! she thought, mind made up. Tonight she would remember Bill especially when she said her prayers. And just to make sure that everything went well on Thursday, she would say them before the icon above her bed, too.

Just to make doubly sure!

CHAPTER
THIRTY

"It's an absolutely beautiful morning up there," said Daisy's relief as A-watch took over. "It's a crying shame to have to work in this hole!" She took off her jacket, draped it over the back of the chair then added, "Anyway, have a good weekend, Purvis!"

This was the end of a week of nights for D-watch. Lyn would take the ferry across the river, then hitch a lift to Auntie Blod's; Daisy would tear up the road to Exchange station, trying to look as if she had an official leave pass in her pocket and hoping a passing naval patrol would not see her buying a ticket to York.

Today she should be sleeping after night watch, though it was more usefully spent travelling home — provided a Wren didn't live too far away, that was. It was the nicest thing about being stationed in Liverpool, Daisy had long ago decided: the AWOL weekends after night watches and seeing Drew when his minesweeper docked. Only now, she thought sadly, when HMS *Penrose* docked Drew would not be on board.

Friday, 18 June. Today, the Clan should have been gathering for the wedding, but there would only be herself. Even Keth, last time she spoke to him, wasn't at all sure he could get the seventy-two-hour pass he had hoped for. And it would be useless, they decided, for her to travel to London. For one thing, Keth reminded her, she would spend two of her days travelling there and back — and without an official leave pass, too. For another, which was far worse, she could arrive in London only to find he couldn't get time off to meet her.

It wasn't Keth's fault. The war was to blame for all the unhappiness in the world, and for Kitty and Drew's especially.

Peering into each compartment she hurried the length of the train and found a window seat in the very last carriage. It meant she could prop her elbow on the sill and stare, chin on hand, at the beautiful June day she was travelling through.

She put her luggage on the rack, folded her jacket and pushed it, together with her cap, to join it. Then she began the automatic rolling-up of her sleeves to elbow length.

She sat down thankfully, wishing she could take off her woollen stockings and heavy black shoes. What she could see of the sky was high and blue, and promised another good day. Soon she would be home at Keeper's; home to cotton frocks and bare legs and scuffed sandals. And Mam would be happy with her only chick to cluck over, completely forgetting that her daughter was twenty-three, and a married woman.

A married woman! She was still a name and number and marriage only came into it when the war allowed! Keth wouldn't be home this weekend, she knew it! But Mam would be there, and Dada, and Brattocks Wood all green-cool, and the rooks in the elms at the end of it.

She rested her chin on her hand. The train had started on time; with luck she might get the noon train from York to Holdenby. The door slid open and two soldiers with kitbags pushed into the compartment, each finding six inches of seat, then wriggling from side to side until they had established sitting space. There was no room for their kitbags on the luggage rack so they leaned them against the door. At least, Daisy thought gratefully, no one else would try to squeeze in. Ten bodies, plus luggage, was more than enough for a compartment intended for eight.

"Anyone mind if I open the window?" she asked and when no one objected, she tugged on the leather strap and pulled hard on the "Down" handle. The window did not move. She didn't know why she had expected it to.

She turned to sit down again. Her share of the seat had shrunk. She took possession of what was left of it, then wriggled her bottom until her rightful space was once again established. The compartment would be very hot and almost certainly smoke-filled by the time she left it at York. She thought longingly of Brattocks, and of the top of the pike where even in summer a breeze blew.

She closed her eyes just for a moment then awoke, gazing around her stupidly, raising an eyebrow at the ATS corporal opposite.

"We've just left Manchester. Hope it wasn't your stop."

"No — York." Daisy's mouth tasted awful, as if it was stuffed with cotton wool. It made her think of the pump in the back yard at Keeper's and water so cold you had to drink it slowly.

"Been on nights?" the corporal asked.

"Yes. Look — if I drop off again, give me a shake at York, will you?"

The corporal said she would; that she was going all the way to Edinburgh. She said it with a smile and all the time fingering the diamond ring on her left hand. Going to Edinburgh to be with her fiancé? Or was she going home to be married?

It made Daisy think of Kitty and Drew, so she shut down all thoughts of tomorrow and closed her eyes and thought instead of Mam's kitchen. Mam's kitchen was the safest, sanest place in the world and soon she would be there. She closed her eyes, but sleep did not come again.

"So what are you two going to be doing tomorrow, then?" Sparrow asked as she spread toast with a mixing of butter and margarine. She wanted to know especially what Kitty would be up to; she was worried about her, truth known. Kitty was taking things far too calmly.

Apart from an outburst of weeping the night she got home from Egypt, it was as if she had shut the war out of her life; shut Montpelier out, too, and herself and Tatty. Stiff upper lips were all right as far as they went, but a bout of door-slamming and the occasional burst of tears would have been more in order to Sparrow's way of thinking.

"I shall be going to see Bill at Cambridge," Tatty supplied.

"You went last week, didn't you?"

"Yes. But he was still bandaged up and under sedation after the op. He should be back in his usual ward tomorrow, and maybe with good news. Would you like to come with me, Kitty? Bill has no one of his own. He'd like to have two popsies visit him." Even though he couldn't see them! she almost said, recalling last Saturday when she had tiptoed down the surgical ward, glancing at names above beds, stopping beside that of Sgt W. Benson to see Bill's face half-covered in bandages. He'd been lying without a pillow and she thought at first he was asleep. Gently she had taken his hand and he said, "Hi! Who's that?"

"Tatty. Does it hurt terribly?"

"No. I'm high on pain-killers, actually. Feel a bit doped up and I've got to try not to move my head. No jitterbugging, or anything like that."

"I can see you're over the worst! Have they told you anything yet?"

612

"Do they ever? I won't know till the bandages come off — what's it like out there, by the way? It's as black as pitch under here."

"It's a lovely day, and if you can't move or sit up, how do they manage to feed you?"

"Drinking cups. I feel like a big baby. And by the way, thanks for being my next of kin. Sister told me about it. They've written your address in my paybook, so it's all official. Do you realize what you've done, Tatiana Sutton?"

"No. Tell me."

"You have just assumed responsibility for me until I'm twenty-one. You've saddled yourself with a millstone!"

"I wouldn't call you that, exactly." She pulled her chair nearer because there were so many bandages she wasn't at all sure he could hear very well.

"All right, then — a poor, stray puppy dog, and blind, at that!"

"Then behave yourself and stop whining or I'll have you sent to a dogs' home!"

"Don't make me laugh," he whispered, lips twitching. "I've got to go real careful for the first five days. After that —" He made a small shrugging movement with his shoulders.

"After that you'll be able to see," she said firmly. "You know you will."

"I don't know anything of the sort," he said softly. "All I know is that my condition is satisfactory and that next week, if you come, the bandages should be off. They won't tell me any more. It makes me think —"

"It makes *me* think that *you* seem determined to think the worst and next week, when I come, I hope you'll be back to your usual obnoxious self again!"

"I'll be that, right enough, and let's face it, if it hasn't been a success I'm blind, aren't I? Just as blind as I was when I took a tumble out of that plane!"

"We'll talk about that next week. How long will they let me stay?"

"Not long. I keep dropping off. It's the dope, I suppose. It was a long way to come just for half an hour . . ."

His voice had become thick and slow and she guessed he had been given something not long before she arrived. She bent close and said, "I'll stay a little longer. Have a sleep, if you feel like it. And I'll come next week . . ."

She took his hand and held it tightly and his mouth moved in the smallest of smiles.

She had looked at the wall clock and saw it was half-past two. If things had gone right, this time next week she and Gracie would have been waiting at the church porch for the bride to arrive . . .

And now it was almost next week, and Sparrow demanding what they intended to do, because she wanted Kitty not to be alone tomorrow.

"Sick visit? No thanks, Tat old dear. Wouldn't make a very good visitor — especially if they give

614

him the thumbs down when his bandages come off. I'll find something to do."

"I'll phone the hospital and ask them to tell Bill I can't come," Tatiana offered.

"You'll do no such thing! You said you'd go, and go you will!" Sparrow insisted firmly. "What concerns me most is you, Kitty Sutton! I'll not have you moping tomorrow!"

"Then what do you expect me to do? Dance a can-can, will I, all around the mews? I should be getting married tomorrow, Sparrow, and I'm not. Okay — so I accept there's a war on and there are people worse off than I am — but please let me be just a little bit miserable? When half-past two tomorrow comes, don't expect me to be the life and soul of the party? Actually, I did think of going to Rowangarth. There's still time to pack and get to King's Cross and be in time for the overnight train."

"Oh, but I wouldn't recommend that! Being at Rowangarth and no wedding would make things a whole lot worse," Sparrow cautioned.

"Maybe I shall want to feel worse! Maybe I shall want to cry my eyes out! What's so wrong with being fed up because They've sent your man overseas?"

"Because if everybody who's badly done to in this war went around crying and making a fuss, this country would be floating on a sea of tears! Why don't you think of Drew instead, and how awful he's feeling, and miles and miles from home, an' all!"

"Guess you're right, Sparrow! But I bet I'm the first Sutton to be jilted at the altar!"

"Drew hasn't jilted you, so don't be such a drama-drawers! Drew can't be there because the Navy has sent him somewhere else and there's nothing he can do about it!"

"Sorry, Sparrow. Sorry, Tatty. I'm acting like a spoiled brat, aren't I? At least Drew is alive. I'll have to tell myself that when things get a bit much. I'll get over it. Daisy had to."

"Yes, and now they're married," Tatiana soothed. "And so will you and Drew be — and maybe a whole lot sooner than you ever hoped. Don't be sad, Kitty. Please don't be sad."

And Kitty said she'd try not to be, and she would be just fine, honest she would, once tomorrow had been and gone — and she'd had a letter from Drew, telling her he had got to wherever it was, safe and sound. And had given her a hint as to where it was so she could start making plans to get to him — by whatever means it took!

There was a loud knocking on the door outside. Knocks on the door came twice a day, when the postman called. Any other knock meant a caller, of which there were few, or a telegram. Sparrow's aversion to the small yellow envelopes in which telegrams came was a throwback to the last war.

"I'll go," she said.

Tatiana looked at Kitty, and raised an eyebrow. Kitty shrugged. "Probably Joannie," she said. It wouldn't be Drew. How could it be Drew?

616

"Well I never! And me thinking you were a telegram. Come on in, soldier!"

"Bas!" Kitty ran to him, arms wide. "Bas! Oh, bless you for coming!"

"I had a seventy-two-hour leave pass — *official* — so where else would I be?" he grinned.

"With Gracie, for one thing. Does she know you're here?"

"Sure does. I saw her last weekend — just a flying visit — and she agreed I should come. She sent you her love — her *very best* love."

"Everyone is so good." Kitty's eyes brimmed with tears and she sniffed them impatiently away. "Making sure I'm not too miserable tomorrow, I mean. I wonder how Drew is taking it," she said softly. "Poor darling. There are no shoulders for him to cry on; just a load of beefy matelots. Drew's got no one, has he?"

"He's got our thoughts. He'll know all the Clan is with him," Tatty said firmly. "If his ship has called anywhere, he might even have had letters, had you thought?"

"Mom and Pa will know by now that the wedding's off," Kitty sighed. "Why was I such a fool, Bas? Why did I do that tour? We could've been married, but I wasn't around. I do so make a mess of things, don't I? Guess it's time I grew up some."

"You went to Egypt because it was a part of your contract with ENSA — you know it was."

"But I wanted to go and it was good, really; all heady stuff. But nothing at all is going to make up for not being there when Drew was on embarkation leave. Think I'm not cut out for the stage."

"Well, you've signed up with ENSA for the duration," Sparrow intervened, "so you'll go on doing your bit to help win the war the best way you can. And like the rest of us, you'll grin and bear it, girl!

"So where you going to sleep, young Bas? Can you make do with the sofa in the parlour? The arms drop down — you shouldn't be too bad." Her eyes ranged all six feet two inches of him.

"I'll be just fine. I've slept in far worse places." He fished in his tunic pocket, bringing out a card. "This is for a week's rations, Sparrow — I fiddled it. And I got a few things from the canteen." He opened his overnight bag, bringing out a tin of ham, peaches in syrup and a packet of coffee. Then solemnly he presented Sparrow with the biggest box of chocolates she had seen since war was declared. "I know you like candies. Hide them away from my little sister, or she'll guzzle the lot."

"Oh, my Lor'!" Her eyes shone with pleasure. "Thank you kindly, darlin'. Goodness! What wouldn't I give for ten minutes in that canteen of yours!"

They all laughed, because Bas's coming had relieved the tension, lifted the gloom a little. Tomorrow, 19 June, would have to be faced and lived through, Tatiana thought, and when it had come and gone, things could only get better. Once

618

Kitty had had a letter from Drew she would begin to accept what wasn't in her power to change.

Tatiana knew. She had lived through something far, far worse.

Daisy awoke with a start, blinked her eyes open, then thought, Oh, my goodness! This is the day! 19 June, at two-thirty at All Souls, by the Reverend Nathan Sutton. Kitty to Drew.

She stretched, then sat up. Last night she had gone to bed early at her mother's insistence, and slept heavily; now, it wasn't quite six, yet she felt impatient to be up.

Quickly she pulled on trousers and a thick jumper, for June mornings could be cold. Then she picked up her sandals and walked carefully downstairs, opening the back door, whispering to the dogs so they would know who it was and not bark.

The sun was not yet out. A mist covered Brattocks Wood and in the distance, Rowangarth's trees rose from a grey velvet haze. Today would be fine. What a city-dweller would call a foggy morning really foretold heat to come.

The birds had finished their early morning singing; now only the rooks cawed loudly, busy, she shouldn't wonder, with their second brood of young.

She walked to the stile that separated Brattocks Wood from Rowangarth's wild garden. The lawn shone with heavy dew and, across it, blackbirds ran back and forth, stopping, listening. Reuben said birds could hear worms in the earth beneath them.

Two wagtails pinked fussily across the grass, tails bobbing. Wagtails always made her smile. She sighed, turning to lean on the wooden fence.

The broom was flowering in the wild garden and the rowan trees and foxgloves, and the first of the buttercups. Such a precious place, the wild garden; so full of memories and all of them happy.

The Clan gathering to lie, hands behind heads, in the grass, squinting up through the trees, talking, teasing. Teasing Tatty most often because she was the youngest, and babied by her mother and nanny and never allowed to get her dress dirty. Tatty was grown up now, and firmly in charge of her life.

Keth joining them, when he had done his paper round; Keth telling them he hadn't got the scholarship to Leeds University that he'd so hoped for. Kitty, doing her imitations. Naughty Kitty, who listened to grown-ups talking then gave a dramatic account of it to her captive audience. So very special, the wild garden . . .

She shifted her thoughts and her gaze to Rowangarth, still sleeping, and from there to the linden walk. Soon, the lindens would blossom and fling their scent to the sky. Beside the lindens, laburnums hung in yellow tassels, tangling with old-fashioned roses and in the herbacious border were peonies and delphiniums and bright brash clumps of poppies. Rowangarth was putting on a show for a bride and groom, and there wasn't going to be a wedding.

She ran across the lawn in the direction of the stable block and, behind it, the kitchen garden, pausing to see that the tall iron gate was unlocked. From the largest of the potting sheds, small puffs of smoke lazed from the chimney. Gracie was already there. Perhaps she too was restless and disappointed. Gracie should have been a bridesmaid; worn the pale blue dress. Daisy called "Coo-ee" and the potting shed door opened wider.

"Hi, Daisy! Come and cheer me up!"

Daisy waved a greeting. Everyone was gloomy. That was what war did to people; let them fall in love and plan weddings, then mess everything up.

"Hi, yourself," she said. "Couldn't you sleep either?"

"No. The birds woke me at five; such a din. So I got up and came here. I'll go back to the bothy at breakfast time — see if there's a letter from Bas. Just come and look at everything." She threw more wood into the little fire grate, then motioned for Daisy to follow her.

"We didn't pick the flowers last night as we intended. No point, was there? But we planned at least four bucketsful for the church. I was looking forward to doing the decorations again.

"And take a look at those." She pointed in mild disgust to ten terracotta pots, filled with lily of the valley, in full, fragrant bloom.

Daisy inhaled their scent, eyes closed. "Gracie, they're beautiful!"

"Oh, sure! We planned to stand them either side of the chancel steps; kept them back, away from the sun — got it just right. And the white orchids too. Mr Catchpole said they would flower at the right time and they have. He's so disappointed. He was looking forward to making Kitty's bouquet. We bridesmaids were having roses; there's so much in the garden now." Her eyes filled with tears. "I'm so miserable for Drew and Kitty."

"I've ceased to be miserable, Gracie. I'm plain angry! I'm real chocker with this war!"

"Me, too, though I'd have missed so much, if there hadn't been one. And that's an awful thing to say," she whispered, "but I met Bas and I came here to Rowangarth and learned so much about being a gardener. I wouldn't have missed that, Daisy, for anything. It's just sad, when you think about it, that it took a war to give me the most lovely memories I'll ever have. No matter what happens, I shall never forget all this."

"I know what you mean. I hated the thought of leaving home. I only volunteered because I got into a foul temper one day and went to the Labour Exchange and filled in the forms. Then I realized I wasn't twenty-one and needed Dada's permission, and I was so blazing mad still that I forged his name. There was hell to pay at home when it all came out, yet I wouldn't have missed it now. I feel rather proud of being in the Forces, I suppose, and when it's all over and I'm old, I shall forget the awful bits, like being bombed and taking orders and night watches. And being away from home." Being away from home was the worst, and being apart from Keth, of course. "But one day I'll tell our children what their Mam did in the war, and Mam will tell them what their Gran did in her war. It's the way things are, I suppose.

"And it's my birthday on Sunday; Mam's too. Hope Keth remembers to send a card."

"Why don't you ask him?" Gracie was smiling, and nodding in the direction of the high, iron gate, and Daisy spun round, her heart all at once bumping.

"*Keth!*" She ran to him, her feet slipping and sliding on the gravel path. "Darling! You made it!"

"But of course!" He scooped her into his arms, swinging her off her feet, laughing.

"But you said you didn't think . . ."

"Well, for once I was lucky! So what have you to say to me?"

"I love you!" She closed her eyes and offered her lips for his kiss. "I've missed you! Do you know, it's two months since I've seen you! And how did you know where I was?"

They turned to wave to Gracie then, hands clasped, made for Keeper's Cottage.

"Mum told me. I knew she'd be up, so I went straight to the bothy. I got the overnight train, by the way, then got a lift from Holdenby on the milk lorry. When do you have to be back, darling?"

"Sunday. I'll have to get the four o'clock from York. I'm on earlies on Monday."

"Then we'll leave together. I'm due back at midnight, Sunday. And I haven't forgotten it's your birthday tomorrow."

She gave a laugh of pure pleasure and then, all at once serious, she said, "Have we the right to be this happy when Drew and Kitty must be utterly devastated?"

"No, but I reckon when there's a war on you take your happiness when it happens along. And it *is* awful for them — I know how I felt when they sent me back to Washington. But things'll work out just fine in the end, like they did for us. Has anyone heard from Drew yet?"

"Not as far as I know. Seems that wherever it is he's going, is a long way away. But we'll think of them both especially this afternoon, won't we?"

"We will."

"And Gracie said that Bas is going to London, so he'll cheer Kitty up. And there'll be Tatty, and Sparrow. I'll be glad when today is over, for all that. But give me another kiss, will you — then we'll go in and surprise Mam. And Keth, I do love you. Take care, won't you? Always take care?"

And he said he would and kissed her again. Then hand in hand they crossed the wild garden and made for Keeper's Cottage.

Tatiana walked apprehensively up the steps of the big old house that was now a military hospital,

624

wondering what Bill would tell her when they met. Last week, when she called, he had been in the surgical ward, but today, with luck, he would be back in his usual bed — with a smile on his face, she hoped fervently.

She tapped on the door of Ward Sister's office, to be told that Sergeant Benson had indeed returned to the ward and yes, it was all right for her to see him and stay for a cup of tea, if she would like.

"Can I go in then? Same bed?"

"No. He's outside. He has a liking for the seat near the orange blossom bush and the wallflowers. He likes the scent, he says."

"So can you tell me —" Tatiana left her question unasked.

"I think it's best he tells you," Sister, grave-faced said, "Why don't you go and find him?"

Tatiana retraced her steps, walking slowly, wondering what to say to a man who has been through an operation and who still might not be able to see. Then she saw him sitting there, his white stick beside him. She cleared her throat, took a deep breath, and walked towards him.

He heard her steps and his head jerked up, then turned in her direction. He was still wearing dark glasses and unease tingled through her.

"Bill! Hi!" she called. "It's Tatiana!"

"Hi!" He patted the seat beside him. "Take a pew. How've you been?"

"Fine." She looked at him sideways. Covering one eye, beneath the heavy dark glasses, was a pad of gauze. She dare not ask about the other eye. She didn't want to talk, really, because her mouth had gone dry and her words betrayed her fear. "What have you been up to, Bill?"

"We-e-ll, Sister on surgical ward couldn't get rid of me quick enough. She said I was a nuisance, but she needed my bed, really. Anyway, they shunted me back to Sister-no-smoking, and on Thursday they took off the bandages. That's all, really, 'cept that I've been sitting here in the sun all morning, sniffing wallflowers."

"But, Bill, isn't there —"

"I know it's the wallflowers I can smell because the orange blossom has fallen now."

"Yes. It doesn't last long."

"You're right. There are petals all over the path."

For a moment that seemed for ever, she tried not to ask. Then she forced herself to whisper, "Can you see?"

"I thought you'd never ask!"

"I was afraid to. *Can* you see?" she gasped.

"With one eye, they can't say yet. Maybe just a bit." He pointed to the gauze pad. "With the other — well, it isn't perfect, but I can see white petals against a dark path with it. They say it'll take about three months, then it should be as good as new."

"But that's wonderful!" Her heart began to thump joyfully and she took his face in her hands, kissing his cheek. "Bill, I'm so glad! What was it like? Tell me about it? Right from the beginning, when they took the bandages off!"

"Well, Sister-surgical-ward was there, and the surgeon. They'd pushed my bed into a room — Sister said there were heavy curtains at the window so the room would be dark.

"Anyway — she took off the bandages and — nothing. 'What can you see?' the surgeon asked and I told him nothing. I felt sick, then bloody angry. 'Nothing at all?' he asked and I told him there was only a white blur to my right.

" 'Good,' he said. 'That's sister's apron.' And then he said, 'Focus your eyes over here. I'm doing something. What am I doing?' I realized I could see a dark shape, then he lifted his arm. 'You've moved your arm,' I said, 'and now you're moving it up and down.'

" 'Splendid,' he said. That was all. It was supposed to be good that I could see his outline, but I'd sometimes seen outlines before the op. I was browned off, I can tell you."

"Poor Bill. Then how," Tatiana frowned, "can you see orange blossom petals?"

"I'm coming to that bit! Next day they took the bandages off again and pulled the curtain aside and I could see a great blaze of light. Leastways, it seemed like that.

"I gave a great shout and before they covered the window again I got a look at the surgeon and I could make out that he was wearing spectacles.

627

When I told him he said, 'Good. Very good, Sergeant.' *Very* good, he said.

"My left eye is still covered, and he said I was to wear dark glasses again and not do anything stupid — like looking up into the sky; things like that. Sister says my sight will improve gradually and could be as good as ever in a couple of months. The left eye they aren't sure about yet, but Nelson did all right on one eye, didn't he?"

His voice was breathless with excitement, his smile was wide.

"Bill, I'm so glad. I truly am! You've just made this awful day a whole lot better. How does it feel — *really* feel?"

"Which? Right now, or long term?"

"Whichever . . ."

"At the moment, just not to have to tap around with my stick is great. And I keep seeing something new. Last night, Sister took me out for the first time since the operation. The light was gentler, she said, and all at once I knew that the ward door was half glass. I didn't know that before.

"I wanted to sit on that seat all night, but she said we had to go in — that she had better things to do than waste her time sitting there with me when there were men who couldn't see in need of her attention. I'm not blind now, Tatiana! I'm going to see properly soon!"

"And you *deserve* to see after what you've been through."

628

"Yes, but the rest of my crew went for a burton. I'd told myself that if the op. came to nothing, then at least I was alive. But I can make plans now, I suppose. You're free of your blind puppy dog, Miss Sutton!"

"Not till you're twenty-one, I'm not! Are you coming up to Denniston for Christmas? The offer still holds if you can get leave."

"What — and frighten your folks? I can't see properly yet, but this morning I'd only to look into the mirror to realize I'm not a pretty sight. I'm disgusting, in fact."

"Well, you really do take the plate of biscuits, Bill Benson! One minute you're glad to be alive and the next you're moaning because you don't look like Clark Gable! I asked you if you wanted to come to Yorkshire for your birthday! Do you, or don't you?"

"I do. Very much. Thanks for asking me. I'll get used to my face, I suppose. It's other people I'm worried about."

"It's nothing to do with other people! And you aren't half as bad as some of the airmen I've taken out, so stop binding!"

"I like you when you get mad, Miss! And I can see enough to realize you are very lovely, Tatiana. Beauty and the beast! That's us!"

"Bill — I'm warning you!" she said severely, looking at her watch. "It's ten past two. Can I tell you about what's bothering me? Can I have a moan, please? It's Kitty, you see. I'm so sad for her."

"The one you should have been bridesmaid for today?"

"Yes. She insisted I come to see you. I'd offered to be around, but her brother arrived on a seventy-two-hour pass, so I said I'd think about her when it came to the time, and send her my love — and to Drew too. I wonder what they're both doing now."

"Wasn't it lucky, Bas — Aunt Julia getting through on the phone, I mean — and just when I was thinking about Rowangarth real hard? She said it was to let me know she and Nathan were thinking about Drew and me, and sending love.

"I asked her what it was like up there, and that did it! She said everything was so perfect that if Hitler walked past the window she'd put a couple in the shot gun and let him have both barrels for spoiling it all! And she said if she wasn't married to a vicar, she'd tell me just where!

"At least she made me laugh. And then she said, 'Chin up. Don't forget you're a Sutton!' And I said I never would. She said, 'Drew's going to be all right. He'll come back safe and sound, I know it. It's just that you'll have to wait a little bit longer, both of you.' I'm glad she's going to be my mother-in-law, Bas."

"Mm. When I phoned Gracie she was spitting mad too. She said the weather was beautiful and the orchids and lilies had come good, right on time. She told me to tell you she'll be thinking of you both. She sounded very wobbly, when she said it."

"She's a love. I'm glad you're going to marry her, Bas."

"Wish you'd tell me when," he said morosely. "But at least I've got a ring on her finger, no small achievement when you reckon that when we met she went to great pains to tell me she had no intention of getting attached to anyone whilst there was a war on." He glanced down at his watch.

"It's a quarter after two," Kitty whispered. "I've just checked. Let's sit down."

They were walking in Hyde Park, she with her arm through his, their steps slow. Walking aimlessly, really. Walking and talking and trying not to think about how it might have been.

"It was lovely getting a letter from Drew at last," Kitty said when they had found a bench. "First Aunt Julia, then not long afterwards the midday post, as if Drew knew I needed to hear from him. It was deliberately vague, as if the ship had docked somewhere, and they'd put mail ashore. If I knew exactly when he had sailed, then figured how many knots they were sailing at, I could estimate how far away he was when he wrote that letter. But it wasn't dated. Maybe it wasn't allowed and anyway, it's a whole big world. He could be anywhere. I wish I knew where . . ."

"You will soon. And it'll probably be nearer than you ever hoped. What say he's heading for the

631

Mediterranean? Or even Gibraltar? Does your lot give shows at Gib?"

"I see what you mean! Maybe there really will be a way to get to him. Oh, Bas, if only . . ."

"Well, if there is, you'll find it, Sis."

"I wish I were pregnant."

"Could you be?"

"I could, but I'm not. Life's a bitch, isn't it?"

"Oh, I wouldn't say that. Maybe it'll be a lot less complicated if Rowangarth's heir is born in wedlock, so to speak."

"I hadn't thought of that. Guess you're right." She looked at her watch again. "Tatty and Gracie would've been arriving at the church about now. I guess they'd have been carrying roses and the church would've been looking lovely — full of flowers. Gracie would have done it for us . . ."

Sighing, she lapsed into silence and Bas did not try to invade that small privacy.

Drew's letter, Kitty thought, had arrived exactly when she needed to hear from him. She had opened it eagerly, thankfully, reading it quickly and then again, more slowly.

My darling love,
    One more letter to tell you I am missing you still, and loving you and wanting you. No one yet knows where we are heading . . .

The letter was with her now. She had only to slide her fingers into her pocket to feel it. She knew it by

632

heart already; a guarded letter, untouched by the Censor because Drew had put nothing in it save that he loved her and missed her and wanted her: *Why, in God's Name, do I love you so much?*

And why did she love him so much in return, and why had they been parted? Which of the cruel fates had seen their happiness and was jealous?

"Bas?" She looked down at her watch again. "We'd have been walking down the aisle now, wouldn't we — you giving me away, I mean? And Drew would have been waiting, and Keth with my wedding ring in his pocket. And Nathan there. I'd have felt very married with Nathan pronouncing us man and wife, you know."

"Sure. I guess Uncle Nathan'd have tied a good strong knot."

"I'm going to weep, Bas. W-would you mind, very much, if I cried all over you?"

"No. Not at all." He reached out for her, his arm cradling her shoulders, pulling her close.

"I shouldn't cry, Bas. Not in public." She reached for her handkerchief. "There are people walking past all the time. But I miss Drew so much, and I don't even know where he is."

"Aw, what the heck? If you can't have a good old weep on your wedding day, when can you?" He laid his cheek on her head. "Let it all come, Sis . . ."

So Kitty wept, because her heart was near to breaking.

Drew had never seen anything quite like it. A sinking sun throwing dances of red on the waters through which they slowly sailed; the great circular sweep of the bay purpling into night, for twilights here were brief. Seagulls, white and well-fed, screeching in their wake; the bridge.

That bridge was really something. They were proud of it, here. "Have y'seen our bridge?" they would ask.

It was winter in this new country, yet the seas had been deep blue, the clouds small and white and high. A beautiful climate, bountiful and benign they had learned yesterday at the lecture.

The currency, they were told, was just like at home. Pounds, shillings and pence and the people drove on the civilized side of the road. None of your continental, wrong-side nonsense here.

He should, he supposed, as he leaned on the ship's rail, be glad the voyage was over. Twenty-four days they had been at sea. It should be good to feel firm earth beneath his feet again but he would be reluctant, when the time came, to step ashore, because the troopship that brought him here was a part of home, and when he left it he would be leaving home; walking down the gangway into a new world and a new life and only God knew for how long.

And tonight, if he allowed for the difference in time; that here it was night when it was morning in England — half a day ahead, almost — then he would be disembarking at just about the time he should have been waiting in All Souls for Kitty. Kitty, carrying white orchids.

He closed his ears and his mind to the babble of excitement all around him, refused to marvel at the twinkle of lights that swept the bay and the strangeness of a country that had no blackout. All he knew was that today should have been their wedding day, Kitty's and his, and that she would be hurting inside every bit as much as he was.

There were sighs, exclamations, ripples of laughter all around him. Heads craned to see that wonder of the new world. When the troopship left the Mersey about a month ago, not one man on that deck had expected to see such a sight, yet now they were sailing slowly beneath the harbour bridge at Sydney. Australia — a million miles away from Kitty.

Drew wished that men could weep.

CHAPTER
THIRTY-ONE

Even the most dedicated pessimist had to admit it: the Allies were winning the war. It had started in the summer of 'forty-three, with the replacing of signposts in rural areas and the removal of anti-tank trenches and barbed-wire entanglements from beaches. Because there wasn't going to be an invasion. Had it been passed by Act of Parliament and recorded in the statute book it could not have been more official. Even a simpleton could work out that Hitler was having such a bad time in Russia that the invasion of the United Kingdom was the furthest thing from his mind.

Then, to add to the air of optimism, the Ministry of Information let it be known that shipping losses in the Atlantic were the lowest for two years. U-boats were being sunk in amazing numbers now. It was like the Battle of Britain all over again, said the man in the street, with the hunting destroyers and planes of Coastal Command seeming to know just where to find the U-boat packs.

It was said that the consumption of large quantities of carrots had enabled our fighter pilots to see in the dark and that, since no one had come up with a better explanation, was accepted as the reason for the heavy Luftwaffe losses. Now people began to wonder what was being slipped into the daily rum ration of our sailors to account for the sudden increase in U-boat losses in the Atlantic.

Nice to think that Hitler was learning what it was like to be on the receiving end. People began to talk about a second front and the end of the war, when not so very long ago it seemed that all was cloud, with never a silver lining to be seen.

Then, all at once, the dim light at the end of the tunnel became a bright reality. Now, the Ministry of Information had something more worth the telling! The Allies had invaded Sicily without casualties. The garrison of three thousand Italian soldiers, tired of a war they had never wanted to be a part of, surrendered without a fight, leaving the Allies wondering what on earth to do with them!

The problem had been solved by setting them to work unloading Allied landing craft full of ammunition and supplies, which they did with amazing cheerfulness.

"Would you believe it?" Julia exulted from the depths of the morning paper. "We've landed on Sicily — that bit at the bottom of Italy, isn't it? Does that mean the second front has started, Nathan?"

"I don't know. It could, though I had always thought it would be either in France or the Low Countries. Does it say anything about casualties?" Nathan remembered his war and the wasting of so many lives.

"None, it says here. Seems the Italian garrison welcomed our lot with open arms! Well, that's a turn up for the book, if you like!"

Julia had accepted now that Drew was a long way away; that probably she would not see him until the end of the war in the Pacific. How many years that might be she would not even think about. This far he was safe and well, his letters cheerful and his new address HMS *Newton*, c/o GPO London.

"Care of GPO London," she had said. "Just like it was when he was based in Liverpool, only he's thousands of miles away, isn't he?"

"I think he might be, Julia, but he'll find a way of letting us know where he is before so very much longer. They always find a way past the Censor, in the end. Kitty seemed more cheerful when she rang, didn't you think?"

"She's getting over the disappointment now. Going on tour to Scotland, she said, with Anne Shelton, no less! She's got no idea where Drew is. All she knew was that airmail letters are taking a week or more to get here. I told her that if she can get time off, she's to come here for Christmas."

"Christmas? But it's only July! They've only just started haymaking at Home Farm!"

"I like to plan ahead." Julia retreated behind the paper again. Looking ahead made things bearable. Tilda had already started her Christmas squirrelling-away; a few spoonsful of sugar each week; prunes, glacé cherries; a packet of raisins from one of Amelia's food parcels. Tilda was sure that very soon someone would kill Hitler and the German population, tired of all the bombing and things going all at once wrong for them, would ask for an armistice. "And do you realize, Nathan, that if this war goes on as long as our war did, it should be over by Christmas?"

"It won't be, Julia love," he said gently. "It can't be."

"So how long do you think?" The end of the war mattered more than ever now.

"I honestly don't know, but *at least* two years, in my opinion. Maybe three. We have to take on Hitler yet in Europe, and then there's Japan. Try not to set your hopes too high."

"That's where Drew is, I know it — well, in Japanese waters. Those Japs fight like fiends; they never surrender."

The door opened and Mary came into the room, carrying letters on a small silver tray. She was smiling the special smile that meant a letter from Drew.

"Letters from our sailor, Miss Julia, and from Liverpool and London . . ."

Julia's doubts vanished at once. Here was news of her Clan and no matter where Drew had been sent, he would come safely home! In her heart she was sure of it.

Three more years, indeed! Julia would rather accept Tilda's version of things. Someone *would* kill Hitler and Drew would be home far sooner than any of them thought.

"Thank you, Mary."

She smiled sunnily. They'd tried before to kill Hitler, hadn't they? Next time, they'd get it right!

"What is this new medical miracle?" Olga Petrovska asked her daughter as they sat over supper. "I read about it in the paper, this morning. Will it do all they say?" Anna should know, the Countess considered. After all, she worked in a surgery, didn't she?

"Ewart and I were talking about it this morning. We invented it a while ago, then the Americans developed it. I suppose you'd call it the best thing since aspirin. Ewart said that one of its properties is to combat blood poisoning from infected wounds. It will save a lot of lives — they've called it penicillin."

"Then that is good, yes?"

"It's very good, though civilians will be at the end of the queue when it comes to giving it out. The armed forces will be given priority. Ewart is —"

"Ewart! Ewart! You talk too much about that doctor you work for!"

"I'm sorry, Mama!" Anna's cheeks coloured. "But you did ask me about penicillin and we just *did* happen to be talking about it this morning!"

"Then you must remember, Anna Petrovska, that you and he are alone together in that surgery. You must be circumspect at all times. The village would gossip if —"

"Mama! We are rarely alone! Patients come and go all the time and Ewart is out a lot on visits. And

640

the village would *not* gossip. Ewart is liked and respected, and I am a Sutton! Besides, he is not a womanizer like Elliot was."

She stopped, laying down her knife and fork with a clatter, horrified that she had spoken her husband's name in the same breath as that of Ewart Pryce.

"So! You are still remembering him, that upstart you married!"

"No. Most times I am able to forget he ever existed!"

"Then take care. All men are the same. It is their nature. Remember you are still young enough to conceive, at forty."

"I was forty-two last month, and well aware of my bodily functions! Penicillin is an amazing new drug, so can we forget it, please, *and* the surgery!"

She was shaking inside. She felt guilty now about herself and Ewart, because her mother had turned it into something distasteful. But then things between a man and a woman had always been so. *Things* was a cross a woman had to accept and bear in exchange for marriage and social acceptance, Mama always insisted! Mama could reduce even a good-night kiss to gutter level. It made Anna wonder how on earth the Countess Petrovska had conceived two sons and a daughter.

"I'll clear away and wash up. Off you go and listen to the wireless, Mama."

Anna was not being generous. She wanted time alone to think very seriously about her position as clerk to Dr Ewart Pryce. Her mother had hinted heavily that her employer was a very attractive man, and the trouble was, Anna sighed, that once directed into war work she would have to ask permission at the Labour Exchange to leave it. Having no children under the age of fourteen, she was considered a single woman and bound by law to work.

What would she then say? "Sorry, but the man I am working for is far too attractive for my peace of mind. I would like to work somewhere else . . ."

To say that would not be fair to Ewart, because it was almost certain he did not think of her as bedworthy. He was a charming, courteous man, who had taken her out a few times and once kissed her good night. Yet the simple truth was that despite her mother's innuendos, Anna did not wish to leave her job at the surgery because she liked doing it; liked the freedom it gave her. And she liked the man she worked for — perhaps just a little too much!

Alice and Tom listened to the nine o'clock news in a state of near disbelief. Indeed, Alice wondered how the newsreader could keep his voice so impersonal and calm.

Not until he had finished speaking was she able to say, "Well, Tom Dwerryhouse, you can say what you like, but Hitler's in trouble now! Imagine! The Italian people telling Mussolini they want a democracy again, and that Victor Emmanuel, suddenly realizing he's King, and telling Mussolini to sling his hook!"

It hadn't been quite like that, of course. Backed by many prominent Italians, the puppet king had ordered Mussolini to go, placed him under armed guard, then had him carted off in the back of an ambulance! Where he had been taken, it seemed that no one knew — or if they did they weren't saying. All that Alice cared about was that a dictator had bitten the dust! It was almost as marvellous as an ounce on the butter ration!

"Now don't get too excited about it, bonny lass. Mussolini never was very bright." Just a stupid, strutting fellow if ever there was one! "I don't reckon he'll be any great loss to Hitler."

"But don't you see, Tom, it isn't just that? Even the Italian people are on the march for peace. You heard the announcer yourself! Demonstrators all over Italy are wanting an end to the war!"

"We all want an end to the war, Alice." Tom reached for his tobacco jar and pipe. "The Italians want it too, but just because our lot have occupied Sicily doesn't mean that Italy will soon be out of it."

"And why not, if that's what they want?" To Alice, it was as plain as the nose on your face. Mussolini was in disgrace, the Italians wanted an armistice, so what was her husband on about? Trouble was, now that the risk of invasion was over, Tom missed the once-frequent Home Guard parades; was not used to having time on his hands. "Go on, then! Tell me! Why can't we have peace in Italy?"

"Because the Germans are there still! Do you think for a minute that they're going to up sticks and away, just because they suddenly aren't welcome? Since when did Hitler ever respect the rights of any country? It wouldn't surprise me if he isn't sending reinforcements there as quick as he can, and be blowed to what the Italian people want!"

Mind, it mightn't be a bad thing at that, he thought comfortably, holding a match to his pipe. Hitler was hard-pressed in Russia, was forced to keep far too many troops in France and the Low Countries because now *he* feared invasion, and didn't know from which direction it would come! He could ill afford to send divisions to hold Italy against the Italians! For once, That Man didn't know which way to turn, and serve him right, an' all! Happen now he was wishing he hadn't started it!

"Oh! There's no pleasing you, Tom Dwerryhouse! All right, so there's still a long way to go, but we're better off than we were three years ago!"

"I'll grant you that, Alice. We seem to have so many troops that we're sending servicemen down the mines now! We're up to full strength, fighting-wise, but we still haven't enough coal for all the factories. I don't think I'd like to have to work down the pit. My dad did, and he vowed I wouldn't follow him!"

"And you didn't, Tom. You went into keeping and I'm right glad you did! But don't spoil it for me, love." For once the news the Ministry of Information chose to release had been worth listening to. Tomorrow the papers would be full of it. One dictator down, two to go — if you could call the Emperor of Japan a dictator! "And talking of Japan —"

"Were we, or are we going to?" Tom smiled.

"Yes. Because that's where Drew is, I'm sure of it. For all we know, HMS *Newton* might be another minesweeper and he's hunting Japanese mines, now that we're getting the better of the German Navy."

"And what makes you think that's where he is?"

"Because he's my son, Tom. I just know he's with the Pacific Fleet. He'll find a way past the Censor, be sure of it! And if you're set on having a forty winks, then I think I'll pop over to Julia's — see if she's got any news."

"She didn't have just before supper!" Tom said, but Alice was already out and away, restless as ever and worrying about Daisy and Drew and Keth; worrying about making the rations spin out and how much longer the war was going to last.

Maybe he'd been a bit too cautious, telling her not to hope for too much too soon. Perhaps he should have been a little more enthusiastic. Wars were hard on women. They carried bairns, saw them into the world and spent years and years watching them grow into young men and women. Having their sons and daughters go to war must be doubly hard for women.

His eyes ranged the mantelpiece from which Daisy looked down, and Drew, and to which had been added another photograph: Daisy and Keth on their wedding day. Happier than a posed photograph, it was Alice's favourite. Daisy sitting on Rowangarth steps; Keth with her shoe in his hand, smiling into her eyes. That match would be a good one. Happen, he thought, as good as his and Alice's.

He closed his eyes and set the chair rocking, indulging in his favourite pipe dream. Alice, pink-cheeked and breathless, running through Brattocks Wood, telling him it had just been on the wireless that it was all over!

What would he do when that day came? Would he join in the celebrations; make for the pub and sink as much ale as he was capable of taking? Or would he walk the rounds of his beat, telling himself it was true, that Julia's precious Clan were all safe, and coming home as soon as maybe? Would he want to weep with relief or would he take an unspoken vow that it would never ever happen again if it was in his power to prevent it?

He didn't know. All he knew was that soon this war would be four years old and maybe only half over. It was a terrible thought and he pushed it out of his mind, thinking instead of the letter that came this morning from Daisy.

. . . I had thought to be on leave at the end of July, but Keth has had ten days approved for mid-August, so I can automatically have mine at the same time as his now we are married.

It is so hot at work, deep in the bowels, which reminds me that an Admiralty Fleet Order was issued that off-duty Wrens can now wear civilian clothes in quarters when not on duty, and for sports. Since walking in Sefton Park must surely be "sport" and I can think of nothing nicer than walking there in a cotton dress, bare-legged, will you be a love and post my flowered cotton skirt and two blouses to me, and my flat brown leather sandals? As soon as possible if it won't be a trouble, because to get out of collars and tie and thick stockings in this hot weather would be sheer heaven . . .

The parcel, Tom smiled, was already on its way, the old brown sandals having first been polished to a high shine. And apart from fretting about the end of the war, Alice had accepted now that Daisy was in the armed forces for the duration of hostilities and looked forward instead to her quarterly leaves — and, of course, to the unofficial crafty weekends the lass seemed still to be getting away with!

Tom blew smoke to the ceiling, watching it drift upward, circling, thinning. It was all wrong that Daisy's generation should be spending the best years of their young lives fighting a war. Had things been normal Daisy would be in her own home, now, with a perambulator to push! Tom closed his eyes, shutting out the war, and considered the delights of

Daisy with a couple of youngsters; two little lads — or lasses — for him and Alice to fuss over and spoil. But war put paid to things like that, and as long as Rowangarth's young ones came back home safe and sound, he'd be thankful for the rest of his days.

He laid his pipe on the hearthstone, folded his arms across his stomach and closed his eyes to think of grandchildren; the lads fair like their mother, the little lasses Pendennis-dark, like Keth. And Alice like a mother hen, clucking with delight, though when that would be only God knew. And He had a very irritating habit of not letting on!

It was the first thing Kitty saw when she got back to Montpelier Mews at the end of her Scottish tour. It sat on the kitchen mantelpiece and even from so far away she could see it was no ordinary letter. With a cry of delight she reached for it, opening it carefully.

"That one has a stamp on it," Sparrow said. "They don't, usually . . ."

"It's from Australia," Kitty breathed, "and it hasn't got a censor's mark on it either."

"He's posted it crafty, if you want my opinion. Let's hope he wasn't caught!"

"I don't suppose he was, otherwise it wouldn't be here. And by the way, hi, Sparrow! Good to be back. Where's Tatty?"

"She's working overtime tonight. It's all on account, I suppose, of the war being so busy in Russia. Fighting back like mad things, them Ruskies is. Will I make you a cup of tea, then?"

"No thanks, Sparrow. A glass of water would be fine! Then I'll go upstairs, get out of this uniform and wallow in my letters. I knew Drew was a long way away. Australia! He couldn't be further away than that!"

"N-no." Sparrow could not dispute it.

"I was secretly hoping it would be Gibraltar, or Malta or somewhere in the Mediterranean. I'd have had half a chance of getting sent on a tour to any of those places. But Australia is out!"

"Yes — well, at least you'll know where he is now. I told you he'd find a way of letting you know, didn't I?" Sparrow splashed cold water into a glass. "And the way things are going, this old war's going to be over before we know it! It won't be long before we start a second front." That much, she considered, wasn't stretching the truth. An Allied landing in Europe was certain. All Mr Churchill and Mr Roosevelt had to make up their minds about was *where*!

"You're right, of course!" Kitty smiled, even though she had her doubts. Tatty's Uncle Igor had gloomily predicted that the war had only run half its course still. Tatty said if he was going to be *that* awful she would find better things to do with her time than visit, only to be made miserable. But maybe, Kitty thought, three more years would see it all ended. Three slow-moving years away from Drew! It didn't bear thinking about! "If you don't mind, I'll pop upstairs, Sparrow . . ."

And read, she thought, all the things Drew had not been able to write in a letter posted on board ship. Now at least she knew where he was. Without even reading his letter, the stamp told her.

She drained the glass in heavy gulps. The train had been hot and crowded and slow. The journey from Edinburgh to London had taken the best part of a day. Porters at railway stations seemed non-existent now, and the manhandling of her trunk at King's Cross had drained the last of her flagging energy.

London, when she reached it, shimmered in a haze of heat, and though there had been a lull in the bombing, the stink of air raids past was still there. The heat of the sun brought out the stench of water-drenched, charred timbers and even the slightest breeze filled the air with the dust of bomb rubble. It made her think of Rowangarth's tree-shaded greenness and a great lump of longing rose to fill her throat with tears.

She took off her uniform, lips set tight against self-pity, then lay on her bed to read Drew's letter.

Darling girl,

First and most important, I love you and miss you and wake in the night needing you close to me. At times like that you are very near and I hear your voice, hear you laugh and forget, for a second, we are so far apart.

How far away was Australia, Kitty frowned. Measured in miles it was half a world away; in longing and needing it was immeasurable.

She had ceased to ask of herself why she had been away overseas when Drew was given his sudden drafting orders. Now she accepted that Kathryn Norma Clementina Sutton could not always take life and shake it and make it notice her. Now she knew she must accept that her wedding and Drew's must wait. She wasn't the only woman in love in the whole of the war; half the women she passed every day in the street were alone and longing, just as she was, for a word from, a glimpse of their man; would give much of what they owned to be able to pick up a phone and say: Darling, I love you, love you, love you.

"And I do love you, Drew," she whispered to the empty room, "and if love can keep you from harm, then you *will* come safely home."

It was later, when they were eating a late supper, that Sparrow ventured, "Well, now — so how is that young man of yours, Kitty?"

"He's just fine, and missing me."

"And he *is* based in Australia?" Tatiana prompted.

"There's no doubt he is, though he didn't mention it, nor his ship's name, nor anything the Censor could object to if it had been picked out for scrutiny."

"But can they do that to civilian mail?"

"They do it at random, I think, just as a precaution. All Drew's letters from his ship are

651

automatically censored, but the one he posted ashore got through all right.

"He had four days off. *Off*, he said, not leave, and spent a long weekend in the Blue Mountains. I've looked it up in the atlas. The Blue Mountains are in Australia, all right. He said it is very beautiful there. Miles and miles of trees and most of them eucalyptus. That's where they got their name from. The new, young leaves have a blue tint to them and to look into the distance it seems like a blue haze over everything — well, that's what Drew said . . .'" She jumped to her feet, pain glazing her eyes over, deliberately pushing him from her mind because just to talk about him hurt. "I'm going to try to get through to Aunt Julia. Perhaps she's had a letter too."

"Be careful what you say on the phone, girl!"

"Of course I will, Sparrow. And at least I know the worst now. Things can only get better from here on, and every day is one day nearer the end of the war."

Then she wondered how many calendars she would tick off, day by day and month by month until that day came.

Take care, my love, she whispered with her heart. Only come safely home and I'll never ask for anything again. Not ever . . .

On 3 September, when the war was exactly four years old, Italy surrendered officially and unconditionally to the Allies; *officially*, that was, since an armistice had been agreed in Portugal weeks ago and signed secretly in Sicily to remain unannounced until the time was right. And the right time to release such stupendous news was on the very day Allied forces crossed the Straits of Messina to land on the toe of Italy, at Calabria. There had been no German military in the area and British and Canadian soldiers landed without opposition. It was as if, Alice said, God was all at once listening to prayers said in English because now things were going our way.

Then more landings took place at Taranto and Salerno. The Allies were in Europe again. The long haul back from the beaches of Dunkirk had begun!

On German radio, the voice of Goebbels was heard hysterically promising revenge, and those who tuned in to Radio Hamburg heard the nasal tones of Lord Haw-Haw warning the British not to be complacent; that Hitler would yet strike the final blow!

The British laughed. Even Haw-Haw couldn't wriggle his way out of this one! Before long, our troops would be the masters of Europe!

Revenge? From which direction was it to come then? Would Hitler produce that much-vaunted secret weapon at last, and scare the daylights out of the arrogant British who had dared defy him? Who did he think he was kidding?

Yet those who worked in secrecy, who broke codes that helped seek out U-boat packs in the Atlantic and kept track of enemy troop movements in occupied Europe, knew that the recent air raid on Peenemünde had not been for nothing; that Bomber Command did not throw six hundred planes into the attack at a whim. What went on at that strange-sounding place code-breakers did not know, but the urgency with which any reference to it was jumped upon by high-ups at Bletchley Park made Keth wonder if perhaps the threatened secret weapon had its base there. Was there at Peenemünde some plane that could cheat our radar? A more deadly bomb, perhaps? Was poison gas, even more horrible and sophisticated than that used in his father's war, about to be used?

Yet it was not his lot to reason why, he insisted. Keth Purvis's job was to break codes, pick out even one word that would point the way to another. To offer a seemingly useless piece of a far larger jigsaw was all it was in his power to do. It was up to the high-ups to place that one word in its order of priority, and not his to worry about.

Yet he did worry. Not for himself, but for Daisy. He often wished her away from a strategically important port that could be blitzed by the Luftwaffe again. When the second front happened — the *real* second front — ports like Liverpool would once more be singled out for attention. Unimportant though he was, Keth knew enough about the war to know it was by no means over.

Take care, sweetheart. He sent his thoughts high and wide, then lay back on his bed, hands behind head, to think of the leave they had just spent together and how wonderful it had been.

He ought, he knew, to be writing letters — but not tonight. Tonight he would think about Daisy and wait for the ringing of the wall telephone at the end of the passage and his call to Liverpool.

His mess bill, he thought, would be astronomical but what the heck? Wouldn't Drew give a great deal just to be able to lift a phone and have Kitty at the end of it? He was wondering just where Drew was when the phone began its ringing.

CHAPTER
THIRTY-TWO

"Who was that on the phone?" demanded Countess Petrovska, nose twitching, because lately there were too many unexplained phone calls.

"Tatiana." Anna pulled the curtain over the sitting-room door against the draughts that blew beneath it. "She's coming home for Christmas."

"Ah." Thwarted, the Countess hugged her wrap closer. She disliked English winters and the English blackout. It had been colder in St Petersburg, of course, but there had been no shortage of wood and coal with which to fuel the many stoves that burned day and night, and no shortage of servants to keep them alight. The days were short now, with the blackout in force at five-thirty, and lasting until breakfast time next morning. "Have we no more coal for the fire?"

"No, Mama. If you would sit in the kitchen, it would be much warmer. We can't spare fuel, really, for two rooms."

"There is coal in the outhouse, and logs too. Why do you keep them locked away?"

"Because I am saving them for Christmas."

"So! Your mother must shiver with cold so your daughter may have blazing fires, when she comes home!"

656

"No, dear — so we shall *all* be warm at Christmas. Tatiana is bringing a friend with her."

"Then I hope her friend does not expect to eat our food, and brings her own rations!"

"Her friend is a man and I am sure he will have a ration card. He's one of her wounded airmen who has nowhere to go."

"Not one of the burned ones?"

"I would imagine so. She did tell me he was blinded but is now seeing very well, so he won't be any trouble. In Russia, remember, no one in need who came to our door was turned away at Christmas. We can't refuse a young man who was wounded fighting the Germans."

"I suppose not. But I shall not like it if his face is disfigured."

"Mama — please look at me?" Anna asked with a softness so steely that the Countess jerked her head up at once. "At Christmas, we shall all eat in the kitchen. I know you think it beneath your dignity, but the dining room will not be used until the warm weather comes again. It is ridiculous to heat a room we shall only sit in for a few hours. I had hoped it would be a happy time, with Tatiana home and Karl joining us at table on Christmas Day and Boxing Day."

"I do not object to Karl. He was a Cossack, and loyal to the Czar-God-rest-him. But I shall not take kindly to sharing my table with a stranger who may not be pleasant to look at!"

"Then will you please consider that it will not be *your* table you are sharing, nor even mine. You will be sitting at Tatiana's table, in Tatiana's house — in which we both live by her favour. If she wishes to bring a friend home at Christmas, then I suggest you are polite to him — or take your meals in your bedroom."

"But my bedroom is like an ice house!"

"Exactly! And there is something else I would like you to know." Anna's gaze did not waver.

"I see! We are to entertain your doctor friend too!"

"No. He can't leave the practice over Christmas, so his sister and her children are coming from Wales to stay with him. What I want to tell you does concern Ewart, though. He has asked me to a dance in Leeds at the New Year — something to do with the hospital there — and I have accepted. I thought you ought to know."

"I see. I suppose it's all right, as long as no one from around Holdenby sees you."

"Mama! I am not asking your permission! I think that at my age I might be allowed to go where I please and with whom! I am merely telling you that on New Year's Eve I shall be out."

"And I shall be alone!"

"No. Karl will be in the house — or you could spend New Year with Igor. If it wasn't for Tatiana's visits, he would be well justified in thinking his family had forgotten him."

"I notice you did not ask him here!"

"Oh, but I did. Two weeks ago, on the phone. He sounded quite touched, but said he had volunteered to be on duty over Christmas so that the married wardens could have time with their families. Now do please try to make the best of things, won't you? This war is awful for us, I know, but we do better here at Denniston than a lot of people. Do try to count your blessings, Mama?"

And because she was at a loss to deal with a daughter who had started to question what her own mother said; who gave orders in a very firm voice and accepted invitations out from her employer, Olga Petrovska held her peace.

But going out to work was the cause of it! That in itself was enough to turn the head of any properly brought up Russian aristocrat! The war was to blame, really. It gave freedoms to women they would never once have dreamed of, and what would happen when their men came back from the war and expected them in their rightful places in the home, heaven only knew!

"I think," she said, "that I will fill a hot-water bottle and go to bed. Bed seems to be the only place I can warm my old bones!"

"A good idea, Mama! And if you put on your woolly bedsocks and pull the blankets over your ears, you should be quite snug!"

Anna rose to her feet, kissing her mother's cheek, wishing her good night, to which the Countess replied with a huffy shrug of her wrap, because this new creature Anna had become must be treated, if not with respect, then with extreme caution.

But she would go to her freezing bedroom and say her prayers and beg the Virgin's understanding of an ungrateful child! And maybe, whilst she was about it, pray most earnestly for an increase in the coal ration!

Sunday morning did not seem a proper time on which to sell saving stamps, Tom considered, but now that most people were on war work, Sunday mornings were the only times Alice could be sure the lady of the house was at home.

Selling National Savings Stamps to stick on a card which, when full, purchased one National Savings Certificate, was Alice's unpaid contribution to the war effort. Her war-work occupation, doing alterations for Morris and Page, had released a seamstress for work in a parachute factory.

Tom didn't much care for the clutter of sewing about the house, but he accepted that it kept Alice busy three afternoons a week and stopped her fretting too much over Daisy, and lately over Drew.

Drew. On the cruiser HMS *Newton*, in the Pacific. The *Newton*, launched at the end of the last war and built solid to last. It had been easy for Julia to look up the details of a pre-war battleship at the library in Creesby. Tom supposed Drew would find a cruiser very big and impersonal after the little minesweeper he'd seemed so attached to. But that was war for you. One thing you were never given was a choice in your own destiny!

"There now! That didn't take too long, did it!" Alice burst into the kitchen on a blast of freezing air, making for the fire. It pleased her to think so much money was being laid aside to help the war effort though she knew it was not only patriotism that prompted the sale of so many stamps at a time when, for once, there was no unemployment.

The truth was that surplus money in the purses and pockets of the working classes was there simply because there was nothing to spend it on. Not even necessities!

"Did you hear any news on your rounds?"

"Aye. Ellen's sister's boy is a prisoner of war, thanks be. They heard officially yesterday." Mind, being a prisoner was not to be commended, but it was far better than missing, believed killed in action. "And Amy Clark as was is expecting. An embarkation leave baby, I shouldn't wonder!"

It irked Alice that Mrs Clark would be a grandmother long before she was. For Daisy to announce that she was pregnant and leaving the Wrens was the only thing of more importance than the winning of the war.

She lifted the lid of the pan in which rabbit stew bubbled slowly. Rabbit again! On a Sunday! She had said more than once that when the war was over, she would never again cook another dratted rabbit. And to which Tom usually replied that if she ever did, he would refuse to eat it!

"I wish," she sighed, "that Daisy could be home for Christmas."

"But she's never been home for Christmas!"

"I know. Every year I keep hoping she'll make it, but she's holding over her long leave till Keth knows when he'll be getting his. Even her crafty weekend will be the week before. And I know I'm not the only mother with a son or daughter called up! All I know is that I miss Daisy something cruel and I want her home! For good!"

"But lass, this won't be her home! When it's over she'll live where Keth lives and works! Hadn't you thought about that?"

"Of course I have!" More than she cared to admit. And she had come to the same conclusion every time; that positions for young mathematicians around Holdenby were few and far between.

"Then why not take this old war one day at a time, bonny lass? Daisy'll be home on one of her crafty visits next weekend, and then there'll be Christmas to look forward to. We won't go short, you know. There'll be few folk who can take a stroll through the woods and come home with the Christmas dinner, don't forget!"

"I'm sorry, Tom. Don't think I don't know that we eat better than most. It's just that this war is four years old and never a sign of when we'll see an end to it. I get so tired, sometimes, of rationing and the blackout and queues."

"I'll grant you that, love, but this war will be over sooner than later. We've turned the corner now. And before long it'll be New Year and 1944. Do you remember when Mr Churchill told us after the battle of El Alamein not to expect too much; that kicking Rommel's lot out of North Africa was only the end of the beginning? Well, come next year, I'm as sure as I can be that we're going to see the beginning of the end, so cheer up! You're really in the doldrums today!"

He pulled her into his arms, holding her close, kissing her, and she wrapped her arms around him and laid her cheek on the comforting roughness of his jacket.

"I know, Tom. I suppose it's with going from door to door with the stamps. People want a chat and mostly they ask after Daisy and Drew. They're good, that way. But it hurts still that Drew is so far away. I worry about him, you know. He's going to be all right, isn't he?"

"The lad will be fine! He's got a young lady at home waiting to marry him! Drew will take care, be sure of it."

"Yes. Of course he will. I don't know what's getting into me these days."

"Don't be worrying, love. This war is harder on the womenfolk. But when things get real bad, why don't you think of *our* war? When our generation had been fighting four years, folks at home were half starved. There was no rationing till it was almost over, and the poor went hungry. This time, at least, we've had fair shares right from the start."

"I'm sorry. I truly am. And on top of everything else, I suppose it's what you'd call my time of life. I'll try to take it one day at a time — and count my blessings, an' all."

"That's more like my girl!" Tom kissed the tip of her nose.

"Yes, and from now on, when things get bad, I'll think of an end to the blackout, and lights blazing from every window in Keeper's Cottage! My, but there'll be many a shilling's worth of electricity wasted the night the lights go on again!"

She smiled, then busied herself setting a tray with cups and saucers, wondering why it was that not so long ago she'd had the most terrible, inexplicable feeling of doom. Time of life be blowed! She was like everyone else; just plain sick and tired of the dratted war!

"Tom," she whispered, her eyes pricking with sudden tears. "Don't ever stop loving me."

Drew lay on the baking sand. On Christmas Day his ship would be back at sea, but for two days, HMS *Newton* was tied up alongside, taking on supplies and fresh water, and the crew, having completed their stint of what was known as "cleaning ship", were given shore leave to discover Sydney.

Drew quickly found Bondi Beach. It was a place he had heard of but never thought to see. Now he could enjoy the luxury of doing nothing; soaking up sun, listening to the cries of surfers and the crash of breakers.

All around him were people who belonged; lovers holding hands, kissing sometimes. Their bodies were young and lithe and sun-browned, but in this strange country December was a part of summer and Christmas dinner could be eaten, picnic-style, on the beach.

He was glad of the strangeness; that there were no frosts nor snow. If he had to be away from England, then this was the place to be.

The sky was an unnatural blue, the sun a blaze of heat. He lay with a newspaper over his face, and it helped shut out the sound of people, allowing him to think about Kitty.

Her letters were arriving regularly now, and she was getting his. She had written — between the lines of course — that she knew where he was. She intended to be as busy as possible over Christmas, and had volunteered to be with a concert party taking a show to an out-of-the-way fighter station somewhere in England.

She had been invited to Rowangarth, but preferred not to be there, she wrote. *Not without you, my darling.* Tatty was going home to Denniston and Sparrow would be spending Christmas alone at Montpelier Mews and glad, she said, of a bit of peace and quiet.

Daisy and Keth would spend Christmas on duty; Bas would try to get to Rowangarth, Kitty had written, and knowing his luck, he'd surely manage it!

Drew spread out an arm and the heat of the sand on its underside made him wince, brought him sharply to earth because he wanted Kitty so desperately he could almost imagine her beside him, her body brown from the sun, her hair curling damply round her face. Sometimes, just to think of her hurt so much that it was like a punishment for wanting her so much. There were even times when he wished they had never been lovers, so desperate was his need of her.

Why had he been sent overseas? Why had Kitty not been there to marry him? Why did the fates play such bloody awful tricks?

He no longer measured the distance between them in miles, but in time. They were a month apart. If she needed him it would take four weeks to get to her — even supposing They would let him go.

He thought about his own war. Being a part of the Pacific Fleet entailed long periods at sea, docking briefly if they were lucky. Most times, they made a rendezvous with a supply ship to take on stores. That in itself could be the highlight of the week; leaning on the ship's rail, watching slings of food and ammunition passing from ship to ship. Then finally the cheer that accompanied the familiar mailbags, their link with home. Letters made his life bearable. He was grateful for the sun, for lights that shone brightly at night, for the genuine kindness Australia offered to visiting poms. But on this December day, he wanted England and the drear of winter; noses red from frost, Kitty in the firelight, Kitty in his arms. He wanted Rowangarth, the crackle of log fires and Tom bringing pheasants for Christmas dinner. He wanted to walk through Brattocks Wood with Kitty; be with her just long enough to kiss her, tell her he loved her.

He sat up, brushing the sand from his hands. Then he took his pen and the postcard he had bought and stamped. It was of Bondi beach and if he were careful, no one need know he had posted it ashore to escape the censor. Not allowed, of course. If he were seen posting it, and recognized, he would be in big trouble.

Carefully he addressed it, seeing in his mind's eye the little white-painted house in Montpelier Mews and Sparrow picking it off the doormat, leaving it on the kitchen mantel for Kitty to find. Then he wrote: *Happy Christmas, darling. Take care of yourself. All my love.*

He signed his name, looking down at the card for a long time as if to impregnate it with his longing. Then he rose and gathered together his things.

He had had enough of sun and the happy din of people being together. He would go to the Fleet Club, get something to eat, then find a quiet corner and drink as much beer as he could decently hold so he might forget his aloneness and incompleteness. Because without Kitty, that was what he was; one sad half of the whole that was Kitty and Drew.

He reached the road, put on his shoes, then went in search of a posting box. Tomorrow, they would sail again, perhaps meet up with the American Fleet or join units of the Australian Navy sailing north on patrol. And when they were at sea, when Australia disappeared below the horizon and the sun bounced blindingly off the sapphire water, it would be Christmas in England.

On Christmas Day on HMS *Newton*, there would be Divisions on the quarterdeck; they would stand capless under a blazing sun, reciting Christmas prayers and singing Christmas hymns. And all the while, he would be longing for Rowangarth, and Kitty.

Listen, God. I don't often ask anything of you, but let there be an end to this war before so very much longer. And more important than that, even. Take care of Kitty?

There was no moon or stars; not the slightest glimmer of light to guide Anna and Tatiana to church. They walked, arms linked tightly, which was the safest way to stay upright in the blackout.

"Do you think Bill will be all right? Grandmother is being too polite. I don't trust her when she's like that," Tatiana murmured as a black shape, more dense than before, told them they were passing the first house in the village.

"Your grandmother understands that Bill is our guest. Russian hospitality demands he is treated with kindness!"

"*Kindness*, Mother! Bill put his foot in it right at the off! Her eyebrows nearly hit the ceiling when he called her Mrs Sutton. My fault, I suppose, for not introducing you both more correctly, but Grandmother didn't have to go to such lengths to explain how wrong he was and that he might call her Countess! I hadn't told Bill about her title."

"Never mind. We got it sorted in the end, and Mama will be nice to your Bill, I promise."

"Why? Did you warn her to watch it, or something? And he isn't *my* Bill. He's a dear friend who deserves to have somewhere nice to go at Christmas because he's had such a rotten time lately."

"Very well. And be careful. It's slippy underfoot."

Tatiana pushed open the churchyard gates, hearing their familiar squeak. She enjoyed Christmas Communion. It was held in the tiny Lady Chapel that was the original All Souls, built hundreds of years ago. Now, it was the only part of the church that could be blacked out, because its windows were small, and set low. Tatiana loved it, felt a closeness to Suttons past in this plain little chapel with whitewashed walls and worm-infested pews.

Only candles burned on the altar and in the sconces on the columns that supported the low beamed roof. The brass jugs had been given their special Christmas polish, then filled with holly. It was so simple; pure, almost, and it made Tatiana think of the yeomen who had been her Sutton ancestors.

Once, everyone believed in God. To them, heaven was real, and life eternal just one step away — the step that separated life from death. She wished her own faith was as strong; wished she might believe that one day, Tim would be waiting for her. Somewhere.

The tiny chapel was almost full when they arrived, and Tatiana sank to her knees. She wasn't very good at praying; not the way it was properly done. On a bad day, she was mutinously silent, blaming God for the war and Tim's death; in one of her better moods, she chatted in her mind to God, eyes closed, as if she were talking to Grandfather Sutton. When she was little and believed in God because grown-ups insisted He existed, she always thought He must be like Grandfather; very old and kind and understanding, with a miracle in every pocket of his Sunday suit. Now she tried to concentrate her thoughts because she had prayers for the asking and it wouldn't do to beg favours if there was no one there to grant them.

Please, God, let this war end soon so there is no more killing and blinding and wounding . . .

Her thoughts wandered to Bill and how he was getting on with her grandmother. He had declined to go to Midnight Communion with them, he being Church of Scotland if he was anything, he said. And Grandmother declined, too, because she wasn't an Anglican and could manage very well with her own prayer book and icon, she'd said primly. Which was all very well, except that she and Bill would be alone for the best part of an hour, which didn't bode well for a happy Christmas.

She peeped through her fingers at the guttering candle flames.

670

And please take care of all servicemen and women and everyone fighting on our side. Look after Drew especially, and Daisy and Keth. And please care for all those who are flying tonight, if anyone is flying, that is . . .

No one should be bombing anybody tonight, she thought bitterly, but she wouldn't mind betting that there would be squadrons in the air. Those who set the targets and ordered raids didn't care at all that it was Christmas Eve.

Her thoughts turned to Tim, who was dead, and she screwed up her eyes tightly against tears and thought of Bill instead, because Bill was a part of Tim, sort of.

She wondered, yet again, who was getting the worst of it at home.

"Countess Petrovska — will you look at me, please?"

The drawing room at Denniston House was warm with logs saved especially for Christmas, the chairs were soft and comfortable and the heavy brocade curtains that covered the glass doors leading into the conservatory glowed richly in the lamplight.

"Look at you, young man!" The Countess jumped visibly, then recovered her composure, straightening her shoulders, tilting her chin. "And why should I do that? Is it a game you play?"

"No. But I would like to talk to you and I'd rather people looked me in the eyes when I'm having a conversation with them."

His voice was soft — respectful, even — so she could not take offence. She had steeled herself to look at his injuries and found them not half so bad as she imagined; nevertheless, she felt ill at ease with him because he was so completely at ease with her. Even when he learned she was a countess, he had quickly regained his composure, smiling, but not apologizing.

"What do you want to talk to me about? Is it Tatiana?"

"Not especially. Only if she comes into the conversation. What I had in mind was yourself. This is the first time I've spent Christmas in a real home, you see. First it was the orphanage and then it was the Air Force. It made me curious to know how real people lived.

"Now I find that someone I thought to be an ordinary person has an aristocratic background, and people like you interest people like me."

"And . . .?" His candour completely disarmed her.

"I'd like to know what it was like, in Leningrad, all those years ago; what it was made people mutiny and kill the Czar. What kind of a place was it? What like was it to live there?"

"In St Petersburg, you mean?" She would never call it Leningrad, proud of its citizens though she had become.

"Aye. Tell me how it was for you. Was the Czar as arrogant as they say and was the Czarina really besotted with that monk?"

"Rasputin?" Mention of that name jolted her into action. "The Czarina was *not* besotted! She was a very religious woman who had a sickly son. That monk deceived her! Peter Petrovsky, my late husband-God-rest-him, always knew he was evil!"

Against her will, she was talking, defending her old way of life, her Czar. Or was it that maybe she wanted to talk to someone about the way it had been — just this once?

"But the Czar-God-rest-him was a good man. Good, but misguided. And he had a terrible cross to bear. His son was sick, might never have grown into manhood — we shall never know now — and his daughters were unmarriageable. The illness that is passed on, you see. Mothers pass it to their sons and daughters carry it, then give it in turn to their sons. Haemophilia. The Czarina brought it with her . . ."

"That's sad," Bill agreed. "And no' so good either for the wee lassies."

"They were Grand Duchesses," the Countess corrected mildly.

"Aye. Whatever. But hasn't it grieved you, seeing those Nazis laying waste to your country? I'd no' like it if they'd done that to Scotland!"

"Grieved me? There were times when I felt almost unbearable anger." She was warming to the young man, in spite of her resolution not to.

"Then tell me — what like was your house? Did you have carriages and servants? I often wonder where I came from but I don't suppose my kin were all that grand or they'd have kept me — or at least had me decently adopted." He said it without bitterness. "You'll mind I was abandoned?"

"No. Tatiana said nothing." Tatiana wouldn't. Tatiana had become so independent lately that she made her own rules.

"I'm no' bitter. It's just that real people — especially people like yourself — fascinate me. They'll be throwing me out of the Air Force soon. I'll have a pension — enough to live on — if I can find a place to rent cheaply. But tell me about St Petersburg — if you'd no' mind, that is?"

"We-e-ll, Sergeant . . ." She relaxed in her chair, head back, eyes half-closed. "To understand our ways you have to understand my people and only a fellow Russian can do that. At times such as this, though, I look back to when we were a family and Tatiana's mother a young girl still in the schoolroom. It seemed, then, that nothing would change, *could* change.

"We had such fine times at Christmas. Church first, and then parties and dancing right through into the New Year. It was very cold. The river froze solid and we would drive miles up and down it on horse-drawn sleighs, snuggled in furs.

"Even though we were at war — the Great War, it was — we never thought things could go so wrong at the Eastern Front that it could be used against our Czar. But he was blamed for it and was forced to abdicate and the Bolsheviks and the Mensheviks fought for power. Like jackals snarling over the

674

carcass of Mother Russia. Not long after, the Czar was murdered, may God rest him."

She shuddered, then crossed herself devoutly, breathing deeply to compose herself.

"If you find it upsets you . . .?" Bill offered, all at once concerned that so formidable a figure could feel so keenly.

"No! I want to talk about it. My daughter says we must make the best of things and my granddaughter is so English that she doesn't care about the way it was! There is only Igor and myself to remember."

"I know about Uncle Igor! Tatiana visits him in Chelsea."

"Yes. He lives there alone and is an air-raid warden. When we had to leave Russia we had only enough money to buy a small house in London. We had feared trouble in Russia since the turn of the century and my husband had gold and uncut diamonds hidden against just such an emergency. Banks did not figure in his plans. What was to be our lifeline if the unthinkable happened was hidden away, and only my husband and our eldest son, Basil, knew where."

"Could you no' have brought it out with you?" Bill was genuinely shocked at such waste.

"No. At the time we had gone to Peterhof, our summer estate, for safety, you see. We just took with us what we could carry, and left — ending up, eventually, in London. Basil and Igor went back to Petersburg. They knew the risks, but still they went. Only Igor returned. They had not been able to get

675

what they went for; just title deeds and my own personal jewellery, hidden in the stables behind the house in Petersburg. The majority of our fortune is still where he hid it, for all I know. They couldn't get back into the house, you see, because the Bolsheviks had taken it over!"

"So if the Communists didn't find it, Countess, maybe it just could be there still!"

"I doubt it. Probably buried under rubble, now. And it was such a lovely house beside the river. We always knew when spring was on the way; the ice would crack with such a noise and we knew winter was almost over."

"And your husband and son — what happened to them?"

"I like to think, Sergeant, that they died defending what was theirs against the rabble, but they were caught by a marauding patrol and shot as looters. *Looters!* They were only looking for what was theirs! Igor escaped, though he had to buy his way out of Russia. I thank God he was the one carrying my jewels or heaven only knows what would have happened to us! We would have been reduced to begging!"

"You all look comfortable enough to me," Bill grinned.

"Then you are wrong! All you see belongs to Tatiana. It comes from the Sutton side of the family and not from the Petrovskys. Did you not realize my granddaughter is rich?" she demanded, on seeing the shock he could not disguise.

"I did *not*! I knew she was no' working class exactly, but I never thought she was well heeled! She never spoke about it, like she doesn't talk about what goes on where she works. I'm beginning to think I'll never get to know her!"

"Do you want to know her, Sergeant — better, that is?"

"If you mean am I in love with her, then no, I'm not! I've got more sense than to think a beautiful lassie like her could ever want anyone like me. Would you, Countess, if you were her? Would you look twice — except in pity — at someone as disfigured as I am?"

He said it not in anger, but with a sad acceptance of what he believed to be true.

"I think you over-estimate your injuries, young man!"

"I know what I look like, though I'll admit there are a lot worse than myself!" He dug his hand into his pocket, and offered a photograph of a handsome, smiling young man. "I've never shown it to Tatiana. There's only you has seen it."

"Then I thank you for your confidence." Against her will, Olga Petrovska was moved. "Are you bitter about it?"

"Not any longer. I was blind, you see, and the day I saw the petals on the path was when I realized how lucky I was. I vowed I'd never complain again. There were flowers growing beside the bench I was sitting on. I'd smelled them, before my operation, but that was all. Then I saw them. Tatiana said they were wallflowers and I thought they were the most amazing things I'd ever seen!"

"I admire your courage, Sergeant! You make me feel very selfish," she choked, her stiff-necked pride all at once deserting her.

"Courage? I'm no' brave. But I was so taken with that wee flower that I drew it afterwards in pencil, and Ward Sister said it would be good for me to try to paint. My hands weren't burned. I can hold a brush as good as the next one. One day I shall earn a living doing watercolours of flowers, just see if I don't!"

"Now there I might be able to help you! In Russia, you see, young girls like me were taught little; only things a lady should be skilled at — flower-arranging, embroidery, piano playing and painting!

"I painted quite well. I liked to do landscapes and some of them hung in our house in Petersburg though I doubt the rabble would appreciate them!"

"Why do you call them rabble?" he demanded bluntly.

"Because I hated them once, for what they had done to our Czar and to my husband and son. But now," she said softly, "I think those people have a right to Mother Russia because they are fighting and dying for her. I would," she sighed, "like to see my dear St Petersburg just once before I die, though it will never be possible.

"But let us talk about your painting. Oh, when I think of all the things we had to leave behind; my easel and paints and brushes amongst them! Sable brushes they were . . ."

"Sssh!" Anna laid a finger to her lips, closing the front door carefully and quietly. "I think Mama and your sergeant have made friends. I'm sure they were laughing!"

"Then they must be tipsy — or Bill's Scottish forthrightness has overwhelmed her!"

"Stranger things have happened." Anna switched on the kitchen light. "And I think we should celebrate, since it's well into Christmas Day now!

"I've got a packet of biscuits — *chocolate* biscuits. Julia gave them to me from one of Amelia's food parcels. I've been saving them for something special, so let's open them now and make a big pot of tea!"

"Let's!" Tatiana laughed. "And let's try to forget the war, just for a few days? And, Mother — I'm so glad you are happy, because you *are* happy. It shows."

"What on earth do you mean?" A tell-tale stain flushed her cheeks.

"I mean I'm glad you are going to the dance with Dr Pryce. You like him, don't you?"

"Yes, I do." Her brown eyes were all at once troubled. "I tried not to. I thought that after your father —"

"That after my father there'd never be anyone else? Not because you cared for him so much, but because you hated him!"

"*Tatiana!* What a terrible thing to say!"

"Why, when it's true? And if you didn't hate him, Mother, then you should have! I know, you see. Uncle Igor told me ages ago how it was between you." Best not mention Natasha Yurovska's child! "He hated my father too — just as Aunt Julia does! Why does she hate him?"

"I don't know." Anna's voice was little more than a whisper. "She has never said as much, but perhaps it's what she *doesn't* say that makes me think you are right."

"I know I am! Have you ever seen the way she looks if ever he's mentioned? I once met her in the churchyard. She turned her head away as she walked past his grave. I wish I knew what caused it!"

"No you don't! Leave well alone, Tatiana, and try not to speak ill of the dead — especially at Christmas."

"Sorry. You're right. It's Christmas! Shall I set the tray with the best china — especially since we're having real biscuits!"

"Do that!" Anna threw back her head and laughed. Then she gathered Tatiana to her, kissing her, whispering, "Happy Christmas, darling, and I'm glad you're glad — about the dance, I mean . . ."

"I said I was. And if he asks you to marry him you should say, "Yes! *When?*" Or maybe *you* should ask *him*. It's going to be 1944 soon. Leap Year, don't forget!"

"We'll see. And, Tatiana, I don't know what Igor told you and I won't ask — but let's not talk about it again? Ever? Now, how about that cup of tea and those gorgeous biscuits!"

"Mm. Good old Aunt Amelia!" Tatiana smiled, realizing she had never before seen her mother so happy — nor loved her so much. "And we'll drink a Christmas toast, shall we, to all our absent ones? To Drew and Kitty and Uncle Igor and Daisy and Keth?"

And silently, and with love, to Tim.

Kitty shivered, pulling the grey blankets over her ears. Here, on this isolated aerodrome, their entire company was billeted in two houses that once housed peacetime airmen and their families. Now families had been moved out because of the danger, and their homes used as living quarters for RAF personnel — and for strolling players passing through, she thought, hugging herself against the cold.

Their one-night show had been a success. They had taken encore after encore; been cheered and wolf-whistled. Tomorrow they would move on in their camouflaged trucks and give a show in a church hall to soldiers billeted in a village nearby.

Tonight she should be basking in a glow of appreciation and applause. Once she had delighted to the thrill of giving her all to an audience, acting out her routine as if there was a star on the door of her dressing room. Show business was all she ever wanted — until Drew, that was.

Drew, angered by the sauciness of her act that night in the dockside warehouse. She realizing she loved him, must always have loved him. Then kissing and making up, and kissing again in rubble-strewn streets. She and Drew together that same night at Ma's lodgings in Roscoe Street. It had been the first time for Drew.

She smiled wryly. "Mom," their daughter would ask one day, "how was it for you and Pa — falling in love, I mean? Was it romantic when he asked you to marry him? Did young men really go down on bended knees in your day?"

Would she say, "No, daughter darling, your pa didn't go down on his knees. We were in bed together when he asked me to marry him, in a shabby room with blackout curtains at the window. There was a war on. There was no time for bended knees."

Yes! She probably would say that unless, of course, motherhood fined her down, over the years, and being Lady Sutton made her watch her p's and q's. But it would be unbelievably marvellous having children with Drew, and Nathan christening them at All Souls' font.

She could have been well pregnant now with their first child, she fretted, laying her hands on a stomach that was miserably flat. Only there hadn't been a wedding, and now she must accept that this would be her life for the duration of hostilities; on

682

tour to out-of-the-way places most of the time, entertaining troops, living out of a trunk. Then back, between times to Montpelier Mews, and Tatty and Sparrow and letters from Drew and Kentucky on the kitchen mantel, waiting for her.

The duration. How long did a duration last? When would Drew be back and where was he now? In port, perhaps, for a few days then back to sea to help fight the war in the Pacific whilst Keth and Daisy and Tatty and Gracie took care of the European end of things.

Those Japs fought real sneaky, didn't they? Look what they did at Pearl Harbor! She'd rather Drew fought the Nazis! She'd rather he wasn't fighting at all and the war over and he on his way home!

His demobilization number was twenty-five. First in, first out! Drew could be on his way home almost as soon as the war in the Far East ended. *When* it ended!

She wriggled a hollow in the sagging mattress, wondering when the rest of the girls would be in. They were drinking in the officers' mess, because it was Christmas Eve. They would come back giggling and switch on the light and wake her up. If she were asleep, that was.

But how did you sleep in a strange bed in a strange house on a strange, blacked-out aerodrome? How did you, when your arms and your body ached for someone you couldn't have? How did you exist until it was all over?

How did a million other women exist? You could understand them going off the rails, she supposed. Men, too. Women alone, cut off from love; men torn from their families, needing the familiar softness of a woman's closeness.

Yet even in wartime, smug society frowned on need and on human frailties, which wasn't fair because she wanted Drew so much; wanted him all the time; needed him so much that sometimes she had to force him out of her thoughts. Why had they been lovers? Why had she known the crazy joy of giving and belonging only to have it snatched away so spitefully?

Faintly, through the stillness, she heard muffled laughter. The bar was closed. The girls who shared this room were being escorted back. They would stand, sheltered by the darkness, kissing, saying a long good night. Then tomorrow they would be away, the brief interlude forgotten, strangers once more.

She turned over, sighing, pulling the blankets higher. She would pretend sleep. She didn't want to talk tonight and anyway, they wouldn't be in just yet. Perhaps a couple of them wouldn't be in at all . . .

Good night, Drew my love. Wherever you are, take care. Remember you belong to me; know that I love you beyond reason and once you are home again, I'll never let you out of my sight, my arms. I love you, want you, *need* you . . .

Julia pulled off her gloves and unwound her muffler, laying logs on the dying fire, smiling up at her husband.

"That was a good turnout for midnight service, wasn't it? Quite a few soldiers from Pendenys, I noticed."

"And some girls from the bothy, though Gracie wasn't with them."

"She's gone home to Rochdale," Julia smiled. "Catchpole gave her Christmas Day and Boxing Day off. She went last night. Bas is on duty over Christmas, she told me, but I gathered we can expect another visit from him around New Year."

"When are those two getting married?" Nathan frowned. "They'll dilly and dally and before you know it, Bas could be moved on."

"So could Gracie. She can be sent anywhere — within the UK, that is. I'd miss her dreadfully, if that happened."

"*You'd* miss her! What about Catchpole? There'd be no living with him if they took his lady assistant from him. I think she's become the daughter he and Lily never had."

"Then let's not talk about such things tonight. I was thinking in church about when the Clan was all together, not so very long ago. Wasn't Daisy's wedding wonderful, Nathan? And oh, *why* did they have to give Drew a foreign draft? I wonder where he is now."

"Wherever it is, he'll be thinking about home, and Kitty."

"Mm. Y'know, darling, for a parson's wife I'm not a very good Christian. I doubt, sometimes. But tonight I felt good when you asked prayers for all our men and women away from home. Drew *is* going to be all right. I got a lovely feeling, in that little chapel. I'm not tempting Fate by saying it, because I just *know*. A mother's instinct."

"Then he'll be fine, with two mothers worrying over him. And since it's Christmas, I think we should have a little snifter, as Aunt Sutton used to say. I've got a bottle locked up in my drawer."

"A bottle of what, and where did you get it? Not the black market? And why is it locked up?"

"It's a bottle of Scotch. The padre at Pendenys gave it to me. I don't know how he came by it, but he doesn't drink whisky, so I fell lucky. Damn nice of him. And it's been locked up for a fortnight so we wouldn't be tempted to open it before Christmas! I'll go and bring it."

Julia had placed two glasses at the ready, kicked off her shoes and was sitting in her favourite place on the hearth rug by the fire when Nathan returned.

"This is lovely, isn't it?" she murmured. "Just you and me together at Christmas."

"I'll be out most of tomorrow at the other parishes." He handed her a glass. "And I want to make as many calls as I can on the housebound. But I should be home well before dark."

"It's all right. I know Christmas is one of your overtime days. We'll combine lunch and dinner and eat at about six. I've arranged it with Tilda. Get a good breakfast inside you and you should last out the day."

"I'll be fine. Amazing the number of mince pies I'll be offered. People must save bits out of their rations all year round just to put on a show at Christmas. I don't know how they manage it. I shall feel awful if I accept, and awful if I refuse."

"Then you'll not refuse! You know it's good luck to eat a mince pie in another's house at Christmas, and good luck to the offerer, so you needn't have a conscience about it." She wriggled herself comfortable, leaning against the arm of his chair, holding up her glass. "Happy Christmas, Nathan."

"And a happy Christmas to you, wife darling." He leaned back in contentment. "So what will you do with yourself tomorrow whilst I'm around the parishes?"

"I shall visit Denniston. Tatty's home, don't forget, and her wounded airman. I haven't met him yet. Then I shall call in on Alice and Tom, probably have a cup of tea there. Daisy and Keth will be home for New Year, so Alice will be having a quiet time — saving her goodies for later. Then I shall listen to the King on the wireless and have a lazy time till you get home. All nice and cosy and middle-aged. I'm glad I'm not young, Nathan. Growing old has its compensations, you know."

"Growing old with you suits me very nicely." He bent down to lay his cheek against her hair.

"Mm," Julia sighed softly because she was, she knew, a very lucky woman. And because of it, she closed her eyes and said a silent, grateful thank you to that God whose wisdom she sometimes doubted. "I love you, Nathan — you *do* know it?"

"I know it," he said.

"Are you sure," Alice said, "that you don't want me to put a match to the parlour fire? It's laid ready."

"No thanks. I like your kitchen, love."

"We'd be more comfy in the parlour, "Alice frowned. "After all, it *is* Christmas, Julia. I'd intended lighting it later, anyway."

"Then leave it for later." Fires in parlours were a luxury, now. "I'd rather sit here and sniff your dinner cooking. Pheasant, is it?"

"Partridge. Tom's got a brace of pheasants hanging in the outhouse for when Daisy and Keth are home. We'll have our real Christmas dinner then." She sighed, settling herself opposite at the table. "Do you remember how it used to be at Christmas, the food, I mean? A pint of cream and a whole cheese from the dairy and the puddings and mincemeat and cake made at the end of summer and stored in the pantry. And all the fruit and chocolates and sherry and port we could afford, just for the asking, in the shops."

"Mm. And the Christmas tree we used to have in the hall. Remember it?"

"That I do! Ten feet high, at least. Quite a to-do there was, getting the tree in. And her ladyship wouldn't have holly brought into the house until the morning of Christmas Eve! She never said why, though."

"I think it was a whim of Grandmother Stormont's; mother to daughter, you know. And talking about Mother's side of the family — how old is Miss Clitherow, Alice?"

"Now what on earth has Agnes Clitherow to do with it? She's all right, isn't she?"

"Perfectly. She isn't as straight as she used to be and she's much slower, lately. But when Mother came to Rowangarth as a bride she brought Miss Clitherow with her, as housekeeper."

"Yes. Of course. I remember it was she interviewed me when I came to Rowangarth to work. It was a good thing she took to me, wasn't it? But what started you wondering about her age?"

"We-e-ll — I suppose I shouldn't say this, but I'm going to for all that! About a month ago she asked Nathan if he would see to things, as she put it, when she was gone. He was quite concerned; said if she wasn't feeling very well hadn't Ewart better have a look at her? But she said she was fine — for her age — just wanted things set to rights — *in case* . . ."

"She's older than her ladyship, that's for sure. I reckon she'd be about three and twenty when she came here. She was a bit young for a housekeeper, I always thought, but she scraped her hair back into a bun, and was always a bit tight-lipped."

"Perhaps she wanted to appear older. Anyway, she gave Nathan an envelope to keep for her with it all set down, she said. Gifts to her friends and her bankbook with enough in it to give her a decent funeral. She asked him if he would take the service, if he possibly could, and would she be presuming too much if she asked to be buried as near to her ladyship as possible, please?"

"Bless the old lass! Wonder why she did it?"

"I don't know. Nathan was quite touched. Said he would do exactly as she wished, then put her Will — I suppose that's what it was, really — in the church safe in our cellar. We had the safe moved out of the church, remember, after the bomber crashed."

"I remember, all right. Reuben was killed that night. But should we be talking like this — after all, it is Christmas."

"Christmas is for remembering. Anyway, Mother was born in 1860, so that makes Miss Clitherow nearer ninety, than eighty. And she looked just fine when I saw her. She's having Christmas dinner with Tilda. Sergeant Willis is invited too. Tilda's quite chuffed about him, you know, though no mention yet of a wedding."

"And Mary?"

"Mary is having the day off to cook Will's dinner. D'you know, Alice, I never thought we'd see the day that Mary got Will down the aisle, and Tilda with a steady man. I think Tilda has plans for Sergeant Willis when the war is over. Undergardener at Rowangarth, no less!"

"It's all very cosy, isn't it — the way Rowangarth lays claim to people? It pulled Tom and me back, didn't it? And gave shelter to Polly and Keth when they had nowhere to go when Dickon died. And when we get Drew back safe and sound, it'll be a lovely new beginning, won't it, with Kitty her ladyship. I think she'll make a good job of it. She loves the old house, you know."

"More to the point, she loves Drew. I wish I knew where exactly she was so I could ring her. She must be feeling very low; her parents and Drew both so far away from her. Maybe we'll see a bit more of her next year, when she's got over Drew not being around."

"Happen we will. Happen next year we'll get that second front over with, and Hitler's hash settled once and for all! There'll only be those Japs then to see to. My, but there'll be such a celebration when that happens! I've often wondered how it will be when Drew marries. Will things here carry on the same, do you think?"

"Almost certainly. Nathan and I were talking not so long ago about leaving Rowangarth, when Drew is finally demobbed."

"*Leaving Rowangarth?* Julia! Wherever would you go? Oh, surely not to Pendenys Place!"

"Most definitely *not* there and anyway, we don't know how long *They'll* be there, once the war is over. As far as I'm concerned, the Army can keep it for ever! But what would you say if I told you Nathan and I had considered having the bothy done up, once the Land Army leaves it?"

"The *bothy*, Julia! Oh, it'd be nice having you just at the end of the lane, but it isn't exactly a gentleman's house, now is it?"

691

"Alice, you snob! But take a deep breath, then think about it. There are more than enough bedrooms for a retired parson with no children; there's a good cellar, attics and all the living space we could want. Decorated and furnished, it would make a comfortable home. And Rowangarth belongs to Drew. He and Kitty must live in it. Besides, the bothy is just about as far away from my grandchildren as I'd care to be!"

"So there's method in your madness! And come to think of it, it could be made quite nice. Needs a new bathroom, of course,and the kitchen modernized. But will Nathan give up the Church, when the war's over?"

"I think so. He'll be fifty-six next birthday. Giles's age . . ."

"My, but we are remembering, aren't we?" Alice smiled softly. "Dear, good Giles who married me to give Drew a name. My husband in name only, though her ladyship never knew it."

"No. I vowed she never would. We were lucky, really. Had you thought that Drew and Tatty could have fallen in love?"

"Often. But it's all right now, isn't it? Kitty's the only one for Drew. And talking about Tatty, have you seen her yet?"

"I called before I came here. She's got her wounded airman there. Such a nice young man. Tatty might bring him to see you. Smile into his eyes when she introduces him, Alice."

"Is he badly burned, then?"

"Amazingly, no. But I reckon he was once quite a handsome young lad, though. He's got plenty of spunk. Now he can see again, he wants to be an artist. Nothing grand, he says. Mainly flowers. He's got a thing about flowers. He's going to the hospital at East Grinstead to get patched up, he says. There's a surgeon there called McIndoe, who's been working miracles, it seems, putting faces back together again; skin grafting and suchlike. Then the Air Force will discharge Bill, because one of his eyes won't ever be right. It's his twenty-first birthday today. That's why Tatty insisted he spent it at Denniston. He hasn't any folks of his own, you see."

"And how is the Countess taking it?"

"Amazingly well, I believe. She and Bill are getting on fine. I think that young man must be quite special if he can charm the Countess out of her uppity tree."

"And has he charmed Tatty, do you think?"

"No. She just likes him because he's Scottish and an air-gunner like her young man was. She's a changed girl, Alice. I hope she'll find someone one day. But where has Tom got to? Surely not doing the rounds today?"

"No. Church parade with the Creesby home guard. Putting on a bit of a show, I suppose, now that they're no longer needed. And Nathan? Doing the parishes, is he?"

"The parishes. And visiting the housebound. And taking Communion round too. Y'know, sometimes I think that man is too saintly for his own good. He takes some living up to, at times!"

"He's a lovely gentleman, Julia. He was a good friend to me when I needed one. We both got lucky in the end, didn't we?"

"We did. Let's hope the young ones will end up as happy."

The young ones, Alice thought as she stood at the front gate, waving Julia up the lane. Daisy and Keth, Drew and Kitty, Bas and Gracie. And maybe, some time in the not too distant future, someone nice for Tatty, an' all. And please God the war would be over soon, and they could all start living their lives again. Already the war had taken far too many of their green years.

Daisy and Keth. Alice closed the door, then held her hands to the fire, looking up at the mantelpiece, smiling, wondering if this time when Daisy came on leave she'd have news for the telling.

"I'm going to have a baby, Mam." It was all Alice wanted to hear. Just imagine! What a way to start the New Year!

She put her hands to her flushed cheeks. Thinking about Daisy and Keth having babies always made her go peculiar. And the times she had sneaked up to the attic at Rowangarth where the big, bouncy pram was still stored under a dust sheet, were almost uncountable.

She was hoping for too much, of course. Common sense told her that. But wouldn't it be lovely? Her first grandchild!

The feeling that sometimes all was not well with her world or maybe, perhaps, that things were all at once going *too* well, left her. Wasn't it Christmas Day and on Wednesday, wouldn't Daisy and Keth be home on leave?

She felt a rare contentment. No more vipers of doubt. The Clan would come home safe and well. No more snakes slithering across her feet. It was her time of life, that was all. It came to all women and you took the good days with the bad and carried on as best you could.

She sat in the fireside rocker, taking deep breaths, letting them out slowly, planning the delayed Christmas dinner they would eat on Thursday with Daisy and Keth.

"Y'know, love," she said to Tom later that night, "I was thinking today about Daisy and Keth."

"Is there a time when you aren't? And lass, no hints and digs about babies when they're home, don't forget! Happen they want a peacetime baby. You can plan when you have them these days, it would seem."

"I wasn't going to talk about babies." Her cheeks reddened because given half a chance she would have. "I was thinking that nowadays it's never Daisy; always Daisy and Keth."

"You think you've lost her, don't you?"

"You gave her in marriage, Tom. If she was taken ill now, it would be Keth they sent for!"

"Oh, Alice Hawthorn — you'll never change!" Tom called her that, when sometimes she looked or acted like the girl he'd courted — and lost, then found again. "Daisy and Keth. Keth and Daisy. When was there ever a time when it wasn't that way? Right from the day Polly and Dickon came to Willow End, they've been a pair.

"Who was it called every morning to take her to school and walked the mile back with her from West Welby every afternoon? Who waited yonder at the lane end with her for the school bus to Creesby, and who did his paper round with him whenever she could? He was the brother she never had!"

"Well, they're husband and wife now." Alice wriggled in her chair, plumping up her cushion, settling her head on it. "I don't know when it was that things changed between them, but they were — well, I don't suppose I should tell you, but —"

"But they were lovers long before they were wed. Is that what you're trying to say?" Tom puffed gently on his pipe, eyes on the fire.

"I am, and you come out with it as calm as you like!" Alice gasped. "Your own daughter and you knew it all along, and said nothing!"

"Why should I? It was their business, when all's said and done."

"And there was me, trying to keep it from you!" Alice began to laugh. "You're a sly devil, Tom Dwerryhouse!"

"I thought you didn't suspect, so I let well alone. And happen I envied them a bit. There were times I wanted you before we were wed."

"And you got me!"

"Aye. Just the once. I was scared half to death afterwards."

"I wish I'd got pregnant, then you'd have had to marry me. There'd have been no nursing, no France for me."

"And no Drew," he said softly. "And I know that what happened was terrible for you at the time but when you look back, that lad of yours — and Julia's — was worth it, especially as it all came right, in the end."

"Yes. It came very right, Tom. Drew looked like his grandfather Sutton, thank God. There was no Mary Anne Pendennis in him. He was born Sutton fair. And then you came back from the dead . . ."

"We're getting serious all at once." He rose to knock out his pipe and lay logs on the fire. "No more looking back, Alice love."

"No more. We've got to think now about the end of the war. It's been going on more'n four years; how much longer, Tom?"

"Give or take a month or two, I reckon we're past the halfway mark!"

"Only halfway!"

"Well, you don't know what might happen. Never mind Hitler's secret weapon — we might have one of our own."

"Then we should use it. *Now!*" Her cheeks flushed with indignation.

She was going to get herself upset again, Tom thought, exactly as the phone began to ring. And nearer fifty than forty or not, she could get to it like a two-year-old, still!

"Tom! Hurry up! It's Daisy! Come and say Happy Christmas!"

He rose, smiling, to his feet. There would be no more war talk now! The lass was on the other end of the phone and on Wednesday she would be home!

He went to stand beside Alice, his arm round her waist, and if he lived to be a hundred and one, he knew that this was one small moment in all his years that he would keep for ever and take out of his memory every so often and say to himself that on Christmas Day 1943, at eight o'clock at night, he knew complete contentment.

Even though there was a war on!

CHAPTER
THIRTY-THREE

1944

"I think I shall return to Cheyne Walk," Olga Petrovska announced on a cold January morning. "Igor has been alone too long," she offered by way of reluctant explanation, "and besides, it is safe there now."

The sky over London had been free of the Luftwaffe for many months, Hitler being far too busy running away from the Russians, the Countess reasoned, to bother about London.

"Are you sure, Mama? Look — I'm late for work. Can we talk about it tonight?"

"As if you care," the elder woman grumbled as the front door banged. "You can't wait to get out of the house, leave your aged mother!"

Anna's hurrying feet crunched the gravel of the drive, sending pebbles skittering. The darkness was complete and would be for another hour, but she was familiar with her surroundings, knew how many steps to take before she need hold out a hand to touch the gates. Then right turn and thirty strides to the surgery outside the village on the Creesby road.

She dipped into her pocket. She had her own key now — useful, since two babies were expected any day, and Ewart could well be out.

The surgery smell met her in a comforting mix of disinfectant and log smoke from the slow-burning stove. This was where she was happiest and if her mother decided to return to her London home there would be little she could do, or would want to do, to dissuade her.

Anna Sutton had begun to know happiness once more; was ready, after so many bitter years, to love again. Once, even to think of the act of coupling would have caused her to close her eyes against the memory of it and shudder. Elliot had seen to that. The husband she thought she loved had married her only to please his mother, and once the baby so necessary to Clementina Sutton's plans was born — a boy, of course — then Elliot would feel free to go his own lusting way again.

Sons, it had seemed, were easily conceived. Elliot's mother produced three in three years, then slammed her bedroom door in her husband's face. She, Aleksandrina Anastasia Petrovska Sutton had had a daughter, two miscarried babies and a stillborn son. And not one of them made in love!

She knew that with Ewart it would be different. Their loving, when it happened, would be a mixing of tenderness and passion. And it would happen. They would know when the time was right and until then a breathless anticipation made her eyes shine and her cheeks to pink too often. The phone on her desk rang, and she reached for it.

"Good morning. Dr Pryce's surgery."

"Anna! Did you find my note?"

"I've only just got in, Ewart!"

"I'm at Banks Farm. We've not long had a fine little boy! I'll be with you in ten minutes. Many waiting?"

"Not a soul — yet."

"Okay. See you!"

That was all; see you. In a few minutes he would be back, tired and in need of tea.

She filled the kettle, then picked up the letters from the doormat. The bell in the waiting room rang. She pulled back the partition and smiled at the first patient of the day.

"Doctor's out on a call, but he won't be long."

Soon he would poke his head round the door and say, "Morning, Mrs Sutton," very correctly, and she would reply, with equal decorum, "Good morning, Doctor."

She laid the letters on his desk, inspected pencil tips and checked the inkwell, all the time wondering why, at an age when she should know better, she had fallen in love again, because since the hospital dance at the New Year, there had been no denying it.

There was no reasonable answer, she supposed, and wasn't in the least surprised to realize she didn't care anyway, and smiling picked up the scribbled note he had left. *Anna. 4.30a.m. Gone to Banks Farm. E.*

She read it twice, then slipped it into her pocket. She kept all his notes, now . . .

Olga Petrovska waited impatiently for the nine o'clock news bulletin. She knew what the announcer would say, had heard it an hour previously, yet still her heart would thud with triumph to hear it again.

St Petersburg had been relieved, the siege broken. After eight hundred and seventy days, the city of Leningrad had been liberated.

Leningrad, Petrograd, call it what they wanted; her beloved city could live again. Many of its most beautiful buildings had been shelled or bombed; perhaps her home beside the river would be no more than a pile of rubble, but the most precious city in all the Russias was free. She turned the volume higher as the pips sounded the hour.

"This is the BBC Home Service. Here is the nine o'clock news and this is Stuart Hibberd reading it.

After two and a half years of siege, units of the Red Army under the command of General Govorov are in full command of Leningrad . . ."

She knew how it would be. People would creep, pale and thin and disbelieving, out of

702

cellars to greet their deliverers. They had eaten bread made from sawdust, cats, dogs and rats; they had endured bombing and bombardment rather than surrender. A million citizens had died, mostly of hunger, and a hundred and fifty thousand soldiers.

Now food and medical supplies could be brought in and gradually, when the wonder and relief had turned from disbelief to triumph, they would set about decently burying their dead, clearing streets, making lights work again and trams to run. Soon, the ice on the Neva would melt and flowers would bloom and trees that lined the broad streets would grow green again — if any trees were left, that was.

Her eyes filled with tears of pride though her Russian soul wept tears of despair, for she would never see her city again nor would Igor, her son. Yet tonight in her prayers, she would ask that Tatiana might one day be allowed to visit St Petersburg, because already in that city a miracle had happened. Who, then, was to say that another miracle might not allow one of the despised aristocracy to return to the birthplace of her ancestors? One day, that was . . .

There was to be an invasion of the continent of Europe; a second front. It was the best-known secret of the war. Britain, whipped and booted out of France, her army plucked from the Dunkirk beaches, was preparing to return.

In Italy fighting raged still. Gradually, the Allies were pushing back the occupying German armies, but still another landing was planned, though none but a few knew when and where.

"That," Tatiana announced dramatically as she laid down the phone, "was Grandmother Petrovska! 'Ay em home! Your mama begged and pleaded! Do not leave, she say, now that London ees being bombed again!'" she mimicked. "Would you believe it? Nothing will be allowed to stand in the way of the duty she owes her son! The citizens of St Petersburg endured far worse than a few bombs, she said, and so can she! What an about-face! Karl is to stay at Denniston because it seems that Mother needs a chaperon."

"A *what*?" Kitty demanded incredulously. "Doesn't she know Queen Anne is dead?"

"Now don't you mock, Kitty Sutton," Sparrow defended. "Chaperons weren't a bad thing. I remember 'em, all right, and decent young ladies didn't go anywhere — not even to the shops — without one! And there was far less hanky-panky, in them days!"

"But Sparrow, Aunt Anna is old enough to please herself!"

"Of course she is, but she shouldn't be living on her own in that great house. There are woods all around. Any old Tom, Dick or Harry could creep out of them trees and where would she be then, without a man in the house to defend her?"

"Probably perfectly safe with Dr Pryce!" Tatiana grinned.

"Not the gorgeous doctor with the lovely Welsh lilt?" Kitty was all attention. "I know she goes out with him sometimes, but I thought that Uncle Elliot would have put her off men for life!"

"My father wasn't a man. He was a monster," Tatiana said quietly, "and I hope she does sleep with Ewart!"

"*Sleep* with him, girl! Your mother is a lady. She don't do things like that!"

"Then it's about time she started, and the best of British to her! I often wondered, y'know, why Aunt Julia hated my father, and then Uncle Igor told me all — or most of it — and don't ask, Kitty! I'm sworn to silence and right now, I am commanded to Cheyne Walk to help unpack the Petrovska's trunks!"

"Then you'll not go, girl! There'll be a siren any minute now. I thought the peace and quiet was too good to last. Hitler's annoyed because he's getting his backside kicked in Russia and Italy. Turnin' his spite on us, he is! Now let's get these dishes seen to and the place tidied up! Then we can fill the vacuum flask and get ready for when Wailing Winnie goes."

There was just room for three, carefully arranged, in Sparrow's air-raid shelter that had once been an inspection pit when the little cottage was a garage. The air-raid drill at Montpelier Mews still pertained. Once the siren had stopped its moaning, they would prepare to go into their bolt hole, though not until the anti-aircraft gun nearest to them in Hyde Park began firing, and its adjoining searchlight began to sweep the sky for planes. That was the moment they would get into the pit beneath the kitchen floor and pull the upturned kitchen table over them. Sparrow had it organized; could have got herself from bed and into it in a minute flat. And half asleep, at that!

"Think I'll nip upstairs and get my letters!" Drew's letters were precious and were taken into the pit by Kitty along with Sparrow's small attaché case, containing her important bits and pieces. Kitty was beginning to accept Drew's absence now; had learned to live from letter to letter with sometimes a card, posted in secrecy to escape the Censor's scrutiny; let her know his ship was briefly in dock in Sydney. Her company was working in forces canteens in and around London at the moment, and she was glad to sleep in her own bed each night in such viciously cold weather.

Tatiana worked more hours than ever before, now the Communists in Russia were allies. Her work as a translator was secret and she shut her mind to it the minute she left her office. She was glad, really, that Grandmother Petrovska had left Denniston House and that the renewal of the bombing of London had not made her change her mind. Grandmother hated Hitler now even more than she hated Lenin and Stalin, because the one lay embalmed in a mausoleum and the other was on

706

nodding terms with Churchill and Eisenhower. Lenin, after whom St Petersburg had been renamed, could do no more harm and Joseph Stalin, though still causing a lot of bother demanding a second front in Europe, had redeemed himself somewhat in Olga Petrovska's estimation.

She would not, Tatiana brooded as she dried plates and arranged them on the white-painted dresser, visit Uncle Igor quite so often now. She had had enough of the Petrovska's bossy ways, and though she had become quite fond of her mother's brother, and admired his devotion as an air-raid warden, she felt she could, in all conscience, leave him in his mother's dictatorial care.

She was just about to say as much when Sparrow hissed, "Quiet! It's them again!"

The Luftwaffe was coming; the sirens rose in undulating wails to warn London. Tatiana sucked in her breath and ran her tongue round her lips. This was not her first air raid, nor even her twenty-first, but her mouth still went dry to hear the awful, tormented wailing.

Kitty gasped, "I'll have to go!" and made for the lavatory.

"Whilst you're up there, open the windows a smidgen," Sparrow called. A window, even slightly open, was less likely to shatter in bomb blast than one rigidly shut. Rather an icy draught than glass all over the bedrooms! She filled the kettle and Tatiana took three mugs from the dresser and the tin marked biscuits. Sparrow removed the small attaché case of important things from the sturdy iron gas oven to place it beside the Thermos flask. "Now then — let's be getting organized."

Together she and Tatiana lifted aside the kitchen table and rolled up the rug that covered the pit cover. Kitty returned with her box of letters and handbag.

"Good," Sparrow grunted. "Just the flask to fill, then all's ready." The familiar siren routine helped ease the initial shock of the alert and they listened, calmer now, to the silence that preceded the dropping of the first stick of bombs. The nearer they sounded, the sooner would the ack-ack gun in the park warn them it was time to take cover. The mantel clock ticked too loudly.

To break the silence Tatiana said, "I'm not going to Cheyne Walk tomorrow either. I haven't had an afternoon off for ages and I'm going to East Grinstead to see Bill. He'll be over his op. by now."

"Your grandma'll be all alone, won't she?" Kitty's tongue made little clicking noises as she spoke. "Doesn't your Uncle Igor have to report when the alert sounds?"

"If he isn't already on duty, yes. But Grandmother is tougher than she lets on. They've got a good cellar that's bone dry, and she'll be down there with her jewel case and icon in that order. She survived a revolution; she'll survive this."

Distantly, the first bombs fell. Sparrow placed the guard over the fire. "That sounds like the docks and the East End again, poor bleeders," she muttered, then lapsed into a listening silence.

708

"I wonder what it was like for Tim," Tatiana whispered. "Him flying, I mean. Did the people he was bombing know he was every bit as afraid as they were?"

The gun in the park began to fire. Two pairs of eyes turned to Sparrow, who nodded and said they'd better be shifting themselves.

"I shall tell my grandchildren about this," Kitty whispered into the darkness when they had manoeuvred the upturned table over them to cover the pit.

More bombs fell, nearer now. No one spoke. Sparrow wondered if Joannie was all right; Tatiana thought about Holdenby and waiting for Tim at the crossroads, then closed her mind to the raid and felt his arms around her and his body close to hers. Kitty thought about Drew and the digs in Roscoe Street and that first night together. Then she thought about Japanese Kamikaze pilots who deliberately crashed their planes on our ships.

Where are you, Drew?

If a bomb hit the house, she wanted to be thinking about him when the awful crash came.

Take care, Drew. I love you. Please hurry home.

"You're looking very pleased with yourself, lass!" Catchpole held his hands to the potting shed fire. "Had a letter from your young man, then?"

"Not yet, Mr Catchpole. Post hadn't arrived when I left the bothy, but I *am* feeling pleased. D'you know, as I was walking here, there were lights shining from Rowangarth windows. Do you realize that the blackout ends earlier every morning now. Before we know it, it'll be spring." The lights had cheered her. "And it's the fourteenth of February, don't forget. Valentine's Day."

"So I suppose you'll be wanting to slip back to the bothy to see if there's one of them daft cards for you."

"I very much doubt it. I tried to get one to send to Bas, but they seem to have stopped making them. Shortage of paper, I suppose. I did manage to get him a birthday card, though. He's twenty-six today. Handy, being born on Valentine's Day; no chance of people forgetting your birthday."

"He doesn't manage to get away so often now." Catchpole said it sadly, his empty pipe in mind.

"No. Last time he came, he said they were flying ops — missions Bas calls them — almost every day the weather allowed. You've got to feel sorry for the Germans, sometimes, what with the RAF bombing them at night and the Americans bombing them in the daylight."

"Ar, but it isn't that simple, to my way of thinking. If 'em don't like bein' bombed then 'em shouldn't have started it in the first place! Isn't patriotic to feel sorry for they Germans, Gracie." He remembered the first battle of the Somme in his war and thought about the grievous shortage of pipe tobacco in this one and had no sympathy at all for the goose-stepping lot who were getting a bit of their own back! "And they've started bombing

London again, haven't they? Us'll have to think of Tatty and Kitty, and be sorry for *them*!"

Chastised, Gracie suggested she put the kettle on, it being mid-February and not a lot to do in soil too wet to dig and greenhouses which could not be heated. And Catchpole, mollified, said that happen just this once the rations might run to an extra mashing and whilst the kettle was boiling, hadn't she better slip back to the bothy, to see if the Post Office van had been?

Her sudden, sunny smile made him think it was a May morning and not halfway through February, and he wondered what it would be like when the war was over and Gracie left to live in Kentucky and he'd have to make do with Sydney Willis, decent though the man was.

He looked at his pocket watch, went to glance at the weathercock on top of the stableyard cupola and check the way the clouds were blowing, shaking his head sadly as he thought that before so very much longer it would be raining again and that little work would be done today.

He sighed and longed for spring which, if you thought about it, wasn't so very far away.

"I'm glad Drew didn't join the Air Force." Julia glanced up as yet another bomber flew low over the house. "They're out almost every night. Another raid on Berlin, I suppose it'll be."

A squadron of Lancaster bombers now flew from RAF Holdenby Moor; made such a noise as they

711

struggled, heavy with fuel and bombs, to make height after take-off. Their four engines made an awesome sound, especially if you happened to live around Holdenby village.

"I suppose it's all a part of the build-up to the second front," Nathan offered, glad to lay down the paper he was only half-heartedly reading because he too had been thinking about Drew and about Kitty.

"Second front!" Julia was tired of such talk; sick of hearing about the secret weapon Goebbels still threatened to throw against Britain. Odious little man! Was there really a secret weapon or did the Nazis intend using poison gas if things continued to go badly for them?

She hoped not. She had stood by, helpless, as young men coughed up their lungs in a yellow spew, fighting death to the end. But in the last war, our side had used it too. We hadn't been entirely blameless.

"I think," she said, "that Hitler hasn't got a secret weapon. It's all part of a war of nerves. He'd have used it against the Russians by now if he had. Lord Haw-Haw was going on about it the other night."

"I thought that man was forbidden in this house."

"He is. I heard someone talking in the cigarette queue in Creesby this morning. They only tuned in for a laugh, they said, but he's uncommonly accurate sometimes. I wish we knew who he was!"

"Does it really matter?"

"Yes, it does! If it's an Englishman broadcasting from Hamburg, then he should be hanged when the war is over!"

"I take it the cigarette queue was unproductive?" Julia was always on edge when she had no cigarettes.

"It was! He said, 'Sorry. All gone!' just three before me. And Bas hasn't been in ages!" She would kill for the toasted flavour of just one Lucky Strike! "I'm giving it up after the war!"

"After the war, you'll be able to buy a packet of twenty any time you feel like it, darling."

"I know, but it's when you can't get them you want them all the more! It's human nature, isn't it? And there hasn't been a letter from Drew for more than a week, either!"

"I guarantee there'll be two in the morning," Nathan smiled, "and, darling, if you go and look in the top righthand drawer of my desk, you'll find a cigarette there."

"Nathan! Where did you get it?"

"I found it on the floor, and tucked it away for an emergency."

"Oh, you lovely man!" She was gone in an instant, her feet clattering along the stone passage.

Nathan smiled. Lovely be blowed! He had taken it from a packet Bas gave her last time he visited. In the heady plenty of two packets of Lucky Strike, she had not noticed the removal of one. And he had another hidden away, for just such an emergency. Sneaky, of course, but there *was* a war on!

Julia returned in a haze of cigarette smoke and contentment, and settled herself on the floor at his feet.

"Do you know," she smiled, "that tonight it was still light at a quarter to six? Soon, it'll be the first day of spring. Are we going to produce our own secret weapon and end the war this year, do you think?"

But on that first day of March only a fool would even begin to guess.

Keth checked with his diary that Daisy would not be on watch, then booked a call to Liverpool. He was tired; too tired to eat. His workload had almost doubled lately. Now, signals came in thick and fast, from the French coast especially. The second front, of course. A signal of no seeming importance could make a vital contribution to an entire whole; that guns were being moved to France — or from France — or that a squadron of Luftwaffe fighters had left the Low Countries and were now stationed not twenty kilometres from Brest. To someone really in the know, one word could be of great significance.

That there would be a landing in Europe was now an accepted fact, but where and when? Those who were party to such a secret could be counted on the fingers of one hand, Keth supposed.

It was April. It seemed an age since last he had seen Daisy but tonight, when his call came through, he could at least tell her he had put in a request for leave. Talking to her was small comfort when all he wanted was to hold her and kiss her and love her. And then he thought of Drew and Kitty so far apart and the wedding that hadn't been, and knew that he and Daisy were two of the lucky ones.

Though the war was going in our favour, how much longer it would drag on was anybody's guess. Europe must be liberated and Hitler made to account for his madness. Fighting a war was considered fair; killing millions of Jews and shooting Russian women and children was not. Winston Churchill had insisted on unconditional surrender from Hitler; had thundered that those guilty of war crimes would stand trial. It was pie in the sky this far, but it raised the spirits of a nation weary of war and made them feel that the terms of any peace treaty would be dictated by the Allies and no bargains made. Unconditional surrender!

Keth kicked off his shoes and removed his tie, lying on his bed to wait for the phone at the end of the passage to ring. He must try not to let his thoughts wander. Lately, he had thought a lot about Clissy and Natasha and Tante Clara. He always thought of Natasha when he was tired or had had a particularly bad day. Probably it was his conscience telling him to count his blessings, or because he knew he was alive because Natasha was dead. Remembering her always was a small price to pay for his life.

"I'm sorry, Natasha," he whispered.

★ ★ ★

"I don't know why people say it's unlucky to marry in May; it's such a beautiful month," Lyn said, face lifted to the afternoon sun.

They were walking in the park opposite Hellas House where once more the trees had greened and the grass was thick with buttercups and dandelions, and ornamental cherries frothed pink and white.

"What do you mean — unlucky?"

"Marry in May, rue the day."

"Nonsense, Carmichael!"

"I know! I'm only telling you what Auntie Blod said. You had a lot of letters today, didn't you?"

"Yes. One from Keeper's, one from Gracie, and —"

"And one from Drew," Lyn supplied. "How is he?"

"Fine. I suppose there isn't a lot of news when you're at sea most of the time."

"Why didn't you say you'd heard from him? Are you afraid I'll go all gaga if his name is mentioned, or something?"

"All right! No need to snap my head off."

"Sorry, love. Had a bad watch, that's all. It's this second front lark. Everybody ringing all over the place. Getting a line to the Admiralty these days is murder. I got a rocket yesterday from the Staff Office because someone was kept waiting for a call! Do they think that pushing a plug into a hole is all there is to it? They ought to get off their backsides sometimes and have a spell on the switchboard."

716

"Everybody seems to be on about the second front. Sometimes I wish it would start, and then I know I don't want it to because there'll be terrible casualties."

Daisy picked a dandelion head, white with seeds, and blew them away like little parachutes.

"Little things please little minds!" Lyn said tartly, picking fluffy seeds from her jacket sleeve. "But what I'd like to know is why are we giving it out on the news bulletins that we're sending reconnaissance planes over Brest and St Nazaire, and bombers too? Are they being softened up for a landing, because if that's the case, our lot aren't being very discreet about it."

"Maybe we aren't going to land around Brest. Maybe it's going to be Holland."

"I was talking to Liz in Cabin 6 this morning and she's just come back from leave. She lives on the Isle of Wight and she said you'd never believe the stuff that's there, around Southampton and the south coast. Rows and rows of landing craft, all camouflaged, and lorries and gun carriers and tanks and Lord knows what else. And troops billeted in tents in the fields — ours and the Yanks! How the Luftwaffe has missed it all, she didn't know! She said you wouldn't believe we've got so much stuff! I wonder when it will be? Are we waiting for tides, do you think?"

"Don't know. I remember that once it was us, waiting to be invaded. After Dunkirk, remember?"

"Yes, and stupid Hitler invaded Russia, thank God! Almost three years ago. Makes you think, doesn't it?"

"Well, all I can say, Lyn, is that I'm thankful Keth is code-breaking and Drew is in the Pacific and —" She stopped, suddenly annoyed for mentioning Drew, then annoyed because she felt she shouldn't mention Drew! "Oh, dammit! I'm sorry, Lyn. I wish I could be sure you've got over him."

"As a matter of fact, Purvis, so do I! If you want the God's honest truth, I don't suppose I ever will. They say you never quite forget your first love."

"*First* love? But you had heaps of blokes once. You told me so!"

"Yes. And I also said I played the field, and you told me not to muck around with Drew's feelings 'cause you didn't want him hurt. Well, Drew was the one to muck around with mine, and *I* was hurt, I'll admit it. Drew really was the first — well, the first I ever wanted to go overboard for. I'd have slept with him at the drop of a hat!"

"I'm sorry, Lyn, truly I am. Sometimes I think it was my fault. If you hadn't known me you'd never have met Drew."

"Maybe not, but I'm glad I did. And d'you know what? If he snapped his fingers this very minute I'd go running — if he was still on the *Maggie*, that is."

"If Drew was still minesweeping in the Western Approaches, he'd be married to Kitty now."

"So either way, Lyn Carmichael's a loser! Oh, what the hell! Have you any money, Daisy?"

718

"Depends how much. I'm waiting for pay day."

"*You* waiting for pay day and you came into a thousand pounds on your twenty-first!"

"Y-yes — well — that money is in the bank. It'll buy Keth and me a decent house when the war is over."

"And a car and a phone!" Lyn dug into the pocket of her belt and counted the money there. "Four and six. How much have you got?"

"A ten-bob note and a penny."

"Then between us we can get a meal at the British Restaurant, catch a crafty half, then see a flick. How about it?"

"Fine by me. If we're sharp about it we can be in Liverpool by four. What's on that's worth seeing?"

"*Casablanca*, or *Now Voyager* — or we could go to the dance at the Grafton?"

"We'll decide whilst we're eating." They hurried back to the hostel. Keth had called last night. It was unlikely he would be able to get through again tonight. "Y'know, talking about Keth . . ."

"Were we?"

"We are now! Don't you think it's funny that it's always Keth who rings me? He can't give me his phone number, and all I know is that he's at a place called Bletchley Park, somewhere down south. He says it's a signal school, but Keth doesn't know a dot from a dash, *and* I have to write to him care of the GPO London."

"So what are you getting at?"

"I think," Daisy said, taking a deep breath, "that there's something funny going on there — like at Pendenys Place. The military commandeered Pendenys at the start of the war, yet no one has found out what they do there; not even the soldiers who guard it! I think Keth's got something to do with undercover work!"

"Idiot! You know very well he's code-breaking!"

"That's what he *says*. But I sometimes wonder when the second front starts, if he'll be a part of it."

"We'll all be a part of it. We'll have to work like dogs, once it breaks."

"I mean actually *there*."

"Now listen! The trouble with you and me, Purvis, is that we're both in need of a run ashore!"

"I couldn't agree more! I'm sick to the back teeth of this war! I want to be with Keth!"

"You were with him not three weeks ago!"

"I was, and it was marvellous. It's why I'm missing him so much. Is it so very much to ask — to be with your husband? I want him with me!"

"You, and a million other women! Anyway, the solution's in your own hands. Start a baby, then you'll be out of the Wrens in three months flat! You aren't pregnant, are you?"

"No I'm not, though Mam would like me to be. I think she can't understand why I've been married this long and nothing's happened. But what the heck! Let's go into Liverpool, then take it from there. How about the Adelphi?"

"You're joking! On fourteen and seven! Besides, I don't think they serve unescorted ladies." And whether or not, Lyn did not want to go to the Adelphi Hotel. She and Daisy had been there with Drew many times and even to walk past it, still made her remember things she would rather forget. "I'll tell you something for nothing, though! You aren't the only one who's sick to the back teeth of this bloody war! Now for Pete's sake let's get a move on!"

They had no sooner opened the front door of Hellas House than they were confronted by an angry Maisie from Cabin 4.

"I'm *sick* of this war!" she flung without preamble.

"So join the club," Lyn hissed. "What's the matter?"

"I've only had my request for leave turned down, that's what! It's because of the second front! There's been this Admiralty Fleet Order and what it all boils down to is that there is no leave! For anybody! It's all stopped except under exceptional circumstances. And I was going to be bridesmaid at my brother's wedding!"

"Well, all I can say," Daisy muttered, "is that this second front is a lot nearer than we'd thought!"

"But it isn't fair! They're going to have to find another bridesmaid now."

"Hang on a minute! Isn't your brother in the Army, Maisie?"

"Yes. And his fiancée is in the ATS. Why?"

"Well, hadn't you thought? If it's really true that leave is stopped for everybody, it looks as if there isn't going to be a wedding anyway!" Lyn offered.

"Oh, bloody hell!" Maisie sat down on the bottom stair and burst into tears. "Oooh! If only I could get my hands on Hitler!"

"Join the queue, lovely girl," Lyn said matter-of-factly. "And why don't you stop your blubbering, and come into town with Daisy and me! We're both fed up too."

"I'm flat broke," Maisie wailed, "till pay day."

"Then tough cheese!" Lyn sailed past her and took the stairs two at a time.

Daisy paused to pat Maisie's shaking shoulders and whisper, "Never mind, love. If it really is true, then we'll *all* be in the same boat. I'll not be able to see Keth either!"

She walked slowly up the stairs, thinking how hard Lyn had become since she'd been made a leading-Wren. That hook on her left arm had made her more forthright than ever, if that were possible. And then, because Lyn was such a love and wouldn't let a little thing like a hook make her so very brittle, Daisy knew what it was really about. Lyn was still in love with Drew!

Poor Lyn. Poor Maisie. Poor Daisy. She closed her eyes briefly.

God, please, please watch what You're about when this second front starts. Please take care of everybody.

Everybody? Now that was pushing it a bit, when you came to think of it!

722

CHAPTER
THIRTY-FOUR

After a year of fierce fighting from the toe of Italy northwards, Allied soldiers liberated Rome. They had feared they would have to fight for every house, every street of the city; instead they arrived to a tumultuous welcome with the enemy fled to the hills.

The news was received with delight in Holdenby. Another capital city liberated, Julia exulted. The seige of Malta over, North Africa cleared of Axis troops; Leningrad liberated, and now Italy free! It was as Alice said as they drank tea in Keeper's kitchen that early-June morning, "We're winning this war, Julia. How long before it's over?"

"I truly don't know. I try not to hope for too much, then when something like Rome happens, it's a kind of bonus."

"But there's the second front, don't forget. I want it to happen," Alice said gravely, "and then I think about the Somme. It was going to be easy, they said, only it wasn't. The courtyard at the château at Celverte — remember it? Wounded laid in rows on the cobbles outside, and no one knowing what to do with them. Soldiers screaming for morphine. I don't want it to be like that again."

"Nor me, love." Julia's hand reached out across the table top. "Thank God Drew is in the Pacific and Keth and Bas not in the invasion, as far as we know. Where do you think it'll be?"

"I don't know. Our lot won't do the obvious. Tom says he reckons it'll be where they least expect it, and I hope he's right. Do you think we'll land on the Dutch coast?"

"We might. I only know there must be thousands of women worried sick right now — here, and in America. Amelia and Albert won't know for certain whether Bas will get sent there. There'll be so many young Americans who'll be a part of that landing."

"Yes, and all the troops from the Commonwealth — coming all this way to fight for a country most of them never thought to see; lads from Canada and South Africa and Australia. Would you in all honesty want to fight for a country thousands of miles away, Julia?"

"Drew's in the Pacific, helping Australia . . ."

"Oh, Lor'! Sorry, love." Alice covered her face with her hands. "I didn't think. We started off being glad about Rome, yet at the back of everybody's mind is the second front getting us all on edge."

"It's the waiting. It's bad enough for us at home, but it must be awful for the troops, not knowing when."

"I don't reckon it'll be long. Daisy should have been home next weekend — one of her crafty ones

— but not when all leave is stopped. Anyone in uniform at a railway station will have to have a leave pass signed by the Holy Ghost, she says, because patrols will be on the lookout for uniforms. She wouldn't stand a chance and she said that somehow, with the second front coming, it wouldn't be right to slope off. When the balloon goes up, everybody will have to stand to for extra duties, it seems. Lord only knows when anyone will be given leave again, she said."

"Nathan says the war won't last another three years. Given a real bit of luck, he says it might be over in two. He was right about the invasion, don't forget. He always said the Germans wouldn't come, when everyone else said nothing was more certain."

"Happen he's got a direct line to the Almighty," Alice smiled. "And I think these tea leaves'll take a drop more water. Can you manage another cup?"

Julia said she could, because when all was said and done there was nothing like a cup of tea, no matter how weak, to cheer people up when nerves were twanging.

"One thing is certain." Julia pushed her cup and saucer across the table. "There won't be any second fronts today, nor tomorrow — not with this awful rain and wind. Catchpole calls it peony weather. Mark his words, he says, the first week in June when the peonies are flowering, it rains and blows and the wind snaps their heads off! Every year he vows he'll never grow peonies again."

"It'll be rough at sea, you mean; that nobody's going to put to sea in a storm?"

"Would you? Even the top brass wouldn't be *that* stupid, would they?" Julia plopped a saccharin tablet into her tea and watched as it rose fizzing to the top. "So I suppose we'll have to be like Katie Scarlett O'Hara. We'll worry about it — tomorrow!"

Julia could not have been more wrong. In spite of rain and rough seas and a near-full moon that slipped in and out of clouds, a thousand heavy bombers took off that night to bomb batteries along the coast of Normandy. And then, as the second hands of many synchronized watches jerked into the first minute of 6 June, British paratroopers landed near Caen. Fifteen minutes later, yet more paratroopers landed, and an alert German sentry raised the alarm.

Three hours on, as a bleary dawn showed in the sky to the east, Field Marshal Gerd von Rundstedt, having been told of the suspicious happenings, turned over in his bed, saying it was an Allied ploy to cover the real landing which, when it came, *if* it came, would be at Calais!

Yet because even a Field Marshal must hedge his bets, the news, for what it was worth, was passed to the bunker in Berchtesgaden where Hitler, having taken drugs the night before, was in a heavy sleep. It was decided not to waken him because no one dared!

At half-past five in the morning came a vicious bombardment from every available battleship in the

726

Royal Navy, saturating the beaches of Normandy between St Germain and Cabourg. An hour later, infantrymen of the United States Army, together with British and Commonwealth assault troops, swarmed ashore at beaches code-named Utah, Omaha, Sword, Gold and Juno.

At nine o'clock it was decided the Führer must be told. He was awakened, to scream hysterically that all Allied forces must be annihilated before midnight. His right arm, raised so triumphantly and so often in the Nazi salute began to shake violently, now, and there was nothing for it but to call a conference of all his war leaders.

At exactly nine thirty-three on the morning of 6 June, the programmes on the Home Service and the General Forces Service were interrupted by an announcement from Supreme HQ of the Allied Expeditionary Force and the people of Britain heard, with a mixing of fear and relief, that the Allies had landed on the northern coast of France.

That was all, but it was enough. For some, it was too much to comprehend as the terse message was followed by advice from the announcer that sets should be left switched on for further bulletins.

Alice was placing a bowl of bread dough to rise when Julia burst into the kitchen.

"Why haven't you got your wireless on? Haven't you heard?"

Alice shook her head, though there was no need to ask.

"It's started! We've landed!"

"What did it say?" Alice whispered.

"Only that it's happened and there'll be more news bulletins. In the north of France, it is . . ."

Julia turned on the wireless. Automatically Alice filled the kettle.

"You'll stay for a cup?"

"Best not, thanks all the same. I'll have to be off. Nathan's gone to open up the church. He says there'll be people wanting to go there — perhaps say a prayer, sit quietly . . ."

"Aye." The wireless was playing classical music. Alice switched to the Forces Service, then turned off the gas beneath the kettle. "I'll cover up this dough. It'll be an hour yet, rising. Think I might pop to church myself."

"Right! I'll see you later, love." Julia turned in the doorway, smiling nervously, quickly, then was gone.

Alice took a pad and pencil. She would leave a note for Tom, walking the rounds of the wood, checking his snares. If he was near, he would call in for a sup of tea any time now.

Tom,
   Invasion started. N. France. Gone to church.
Back soon. A.

She placed a carefully levelled spoon of tea in the little brown pot, then took Tom's mug from the dresser, setting it beside it. She did it with precision as once she had laid out instruments when she was a nurse, in another war. Doing things in an orderly manner helped keep her calm then, just as it was calming her now.

She slipped a corner of the note beneath the teapot, laid a towel over the bread dough, then put on her hat and coat, fastening each button slowly. Then she took a deep breath and closed the back door behind her, remembering not to lock it.

She had heard the noise of battle and knew of its aftermath; knew, like then, that many men would be wounded today. And killed. She could no longer do anything about broken, bleeding bodies nor gently close staring dead eyes, but at least she could pray for those men on the beaches in France; pray with all her heart and soul.

As if her own son's life depended on it, she quickened her steps.

Kitty and Tatiana spread the 6.30 City edition of the *Evening Despatch* on the kitchen table, reading the inch-high headlines that said the invasion was going well in Normandy, that tanks were already ashore.

"It says they're slashing inland and everything's going to plan," Tatiana breathed.

"Yes, and did you know that eleven thousand planes and four thousand ships were in it! Didn't realize we had that many between us! Gee, what a sight it must have been! Bet those Nazis wondered what'd hit them," Kitty exulted.

"Look! It says that Berlin has given out a report that Allied troops have landed on Guernsey and Jersey too, so that's them out of Britain. I hope it's true!"

The Channel Islands had long been a thorn in the flesh of mainland Britain. The occupation of what was almost a part of the United Kingdom had been a bitter pill to swallow.

"We went in at low tide to miss mines and underwater traps and things — sent minesweepers in first, it seems. *Seventy*, would you believe? HMS *Penrose* would be there, bet you anything you like." For once, for just a few fleeting seconds, Kitty was glad that Drew was no longer on the *Maggie*.

"Well, second front or no second front," Sparrow snapped, "you can both shift yourselves! I want to lay the table for supper — that's if you can be bothered to eat it after I stood in a queue half an hour for it, an' all!"

Sparrow had not expected to find the piece of fish they were to eat. She had tacked onto the first queue she came upon, not caring what was at the end of it, because she could not bear to be alone in the little white house with no one to talk to about the invasion.

That the queue provided both someone to talk to and a decent piece of cod into the bargain could only bode well for our lads back again in France. A good omen, that's what!

"How do you suppose," Tatiana demanded, "we know what they're saying in Berlin about our

730

landing on the Channel Islands? Do we have spies there, or something, or is it just a lot of German hot air?"

"Our newspapers don't print hot air," Sparrow sniffed, "leastways not about something as serious as the second front."

"Maybe our lot can listen in, sort of."

"Does it matter?" Sparrow was fast losing patience, even though the news was so good it was almost unbelievable. "All I know is that I want a hand getting this meal on the table and then I want washed up and all put away before nine o'clock. The King is going to be on the wireless at nine, so I'll want a bit of hush. And then General de Gaulle is going to say a few words over the BBC to the people in France. You two can listen to him then tell me what he's on about — all right? And don't forget when you go to bed tonight to say one especially for our lads in France."

Sparrow wondered, for all that, how we knew that Berlin knew what we were up to in the Channel Islands, then decided not to worry too much about it since people in the Government were paid a great deal of money to worry about such things!

What she nor any civilian couldn't know was that at an establishment believed by most to be a signal school, coded messages had been plucked from the airwaves thick and fast, and broken down and pieced together bit by bit. What emerged had been not only the news from Berlin transmitters of the Channel Island landings, but also that Hitler still believed the real invasion was still to come, and was frantically diverting tanks and guns and soldiers away from Normandy to the area around Calais.

The news the staff office at Bletchley Park passed on to Whitehall that early evening of 6 June made the War Cabinet very happy indeed. Hitler, thank God, really *had* gone mad!

As if bewildered by recent events, the Luftwaffe stayed away from the skies over London, and Countess Petrovska, convinced that Hermann Goering now had better things for his bombers to do, announced her intention of vacating her basement room in the Cheyne Walk house for one more comfortable on the first floor.

"Then I think, Mama, you had better wait a while," her son said, his face grave.

"Wait, Igor? But I would like to use my old room again. We are safe enough from air raids now."

"But we are *not* safe! I would feel better when I am on duty if you were still to sleep below stairs. I'm not sure yet, but yesterday I heard about the — *things*. Strange things!"

"*How* strange? Tell me!"

"I can't explain it. I'm only an air-raid warden. I'm not told about such matters, but rumour has it —" He stopped, sucking air through his teeth, wishing he had never begun the conversation. "Rumour has it that some *things* came over — ten, I believe — and one of them reached London."

"Flying things? Strange creatures like dragons?" she snapped.

"Flying things, yes. Strange, too. But one *thing* fell at Bethnal Green — or so I heard. We can't be sure, yet. Perhaps They will tell us, perhaps They won't."

"Talk is cheap, Igor. I do not believe it!"

"Not when I tell you six people were killed and a lot more injured? It was a kind of bomb." Best tell her all. There would be no peace until he did. And if it were not true, he shrugged, then so much the better. "It was a pilotless bomb; a rocket."

"Ha! A bomb that flies! What nonsense. You'll be asking me to believe next that it's the famous secret weapon Goebbels has been threatening us with!"

"I think it might well be just that!"

"Then hadn't you better make further enquiries? It is no use bringing half a story!" The Countess did not like being gainsaid. Already she was heartily sick of sleeping in the cramped little basement room once used by a servant. She did not believe what her son said merely because she did not want to believe it, and until she saw or heard one of the *things* for herself, she was determined to sleep in a more comfortable room.

"Mama! All the rooms on the ground and first floors are locked — with the exception of the bathrooms — and I am not inclined to give you a key! For my peace of mind and your safety, wait just a little longer? It may all be rumour."

He said it heartily, coaxingly, even though he had also heard that the *thing*, whilst it had not made the

733

usual deep bomb crater, had flattened everything in the path of its blast for a radius of a quarter of a mile!

"Very well." She yielded to his wishes because she had no desire to so annoy her son that he insisted she return to wildest Yorkshire. It was better here in her own house. Perhaps in London there was a greater risk of being bombed and strange *things* might from time to time drop out of the sky, but at least she could find company other than Karl's during the day; could worship in her own church and not have to watch her daughter make a fool of herself over the man she worked for! And she supposed that if the people of Leningrad could endure pain and hunger so bravely for so long, then surely she could endure sleeping in a servant's bedroom for a little while longer.

"So, the King has been to France!" Daisy said, folding the newspaper. "I wonder which fool let him go! It isn't a week since we landed there. Anything could have happened to him!"

"Well, it didn't. I'll bet the troops were amazed to see him. But more to the point, how about those flying bombs? Seems they're falling thick and fast on London."

"What do you make of them, Lyn?" Daisy had tried not to think about them, because Kitty and Tatty were in London and Keth not so very far away. "Can we stop them coming?"

"I read something about them yesterday. Seems they're like a bomb with little wings on and they're guided here by autopilot, whatever that is. Trouble is that they seem to be coming at all times of the day and night and it isn't always possible to sound an alert."

"Could they reach other parts of the country?"

"If you mean will we get any of them up here, then I don't think so." Lyn knotted her tie, then shrugged into her jacket. "Anyway, you're safe enough where you're going. You won't hear anything down there in the big hole."

"Aren't you afraid, Lyn, six floors up?" All at once Daisy felt guilty that she worked so safely underground.

"I might be, if ever they start sending them over Liverpool, but till it happens I don't think I'll bother too much!"

"Well, I'd be worried. It must be awful to hear them coming. I believe they have an engine that sounds like a two-stroke motorbike. Then all at once it cuts out and you've only got fifteen seconds to find a bolt hole! It isn't funny, Carmichael! At least with bombers we knew when they were coming and had a few minutes' grace!"

"Come on now, *cariad*, stop your worrying. The RAF sorted them out at Peenemünde, didn't they? Sent nearly a thousand bombers and wiped the place out. The RAF lads will winkle them out again, wherever they are."

"That's what I mean! It wasn't until those flying bombs started coming that they ever told us about the Peenemünde place and how they'd bombed it. We're kept in the dark too much."

Daisy plucked petulantly at a speck of white fluff on her jacket sleeve.

"Well, what I always think is what you don't know you can't worry over," Lyn pronounced with irritating cheerfulness.

"They'll be using poison gas next. And the cheek of it! They're calling those flying bombs V-1s. V for Victory weapons!"

"Now listen, Purvis, to your friendly leading-Wren! The Krauts aren't going to waste their secret weapon on us up here! What they've got they'll drop on the invasion ports on the south coast, and on London."

"Yes! On Kitty and Tatty and Sparrow, and people in Southampton and Portsmouth! How can you take it all so calmly, Carmichael?"

"My word, we are on edge this afternoon! Don't tell me things are getting you down when we can see the light at the end of the tunnel at last! What's got into you? You aren't pregnant, are you?"

"You know damn well I'm not!" Daisy slammed the cabin door behind them, then ran downstairs to await the transport which would take them on watch. "Anyway, smarty pants, I'd like to know how anybody could get pregnant with all leave stopped until further notice!"

"Now there," Lyn was all at once serious, "you've got a point! And I'm not being flippant — truly. Just let's get on watch and be thankful we're not with those men in Normandy!"

"I'm sorry, Lyn. I'm acting like a brat, aren't I?"

"Yes, but I'll forgive you! Reckon if I were married, I'd feel chocker, too, if I couldn't be with my bloke. And had you thought, Purvis, that when we come off watch at midnight, it still won't be properly dark?"

"So what's that got to do with me missing Keth?"

"Nothing, come to think of it!"

She lapsed into silence as they joined the knot of Wrens waiting for the transport. She felt sorry for Daisy, because in a roundabout way, she was in the same boat too. Worse, really, because Drew was at the other end of the world and, anyway, he was in love with Kitty!

"Tomorrow should have been our first wedding anniversary," Kitty sighed. "June the nineteenth. I'm glad we're starting another tour. I'll just grin and bear it and try not to think too much of Drew or my greasepaint will be all messed up."

"Where are you off to this time?" Sparrow asked matter-of-factly, because there were times when sympathy was not in order, and this was one of them.

"We leave for Liverpool in the morning. *Liverpool*, would you believe? We do a show there at the Bear's Paw — it's a sailors' club — then we go to the Isle of Man and from there to Northern Ireland. I've volunteered for overseas, by the way."

"You have *what*, young lady? Isn't that a bit of a daft thing to do? *Overseas* covers a lot of territory! What makes you think you'll land up in Sydney?"

"Not Australia, Sparrow. There's no hope of getting sent there. Where I'll be going is to France. They're asking for volunteers."

"But the second front isn't two weeks old yet! It wouldn't be safe!"

"The King has been, and Mr Churchill," Kitty pointed out.

"They're different. They didn't go there to do a song and a tap dance! And I know we're doing well in France, but I still don't think it's safe."

"I don't think ENSA will send anybody until we've taken a few more towns and airstrips," Tatiana said. "At the moment I don't think our soldiers have any time to stop for a concert."

"Hm. Just as long as you don't go volunteering for anything till you're sure you're going to come back all in one piece." Sparrow was yet to be convinced.

"No one's going anywhere till we're sure we won't be in the way," Kitty smiled. "But I want my name on the list for when we do. Meantime, my trunk is packed for an early start tomorrow and I'm going to have a lovely quiet Sunday. Fancy walking in the park, Tatty?"

"Then if you'll make do with sandwiches for your lunch, I can have a quiet Sunday too." Sparrow liked to read the *News of the World* from cover to cover, Sunday afternoons. "As long as you're back

738

here for six for your supper, a walk in the park will do you both good." It wasn't natural, the way both of them worked; as if each were trying to keep herself so busy she hadn't time to think! Young things like them, she brooded, should be having the time of their lives and not fighting a war and getting bombed. *Bombed!* "And you'll have to keep an ear open for them flying bombs, though I don't suppose Hitler's going to be sending any today, it being Sunday."

"Guess he won't," Kitty comforted, "and anyway, we'll be just fine in the park. And our anti-aircraft guns on the south coast are getting the hang of them now. They've shot quite a few down already."

"Did you know that it's the ATS girls who aim the guns? The soldiers fire them, of course," Sparrow supplied, "but I reckon it's better a woman looking through a gun sight. They see better. I mean, when did you ever find a man who could thread a needle?

"Anyway, if you'd like to take a few sandwiches out with you and get some sun on your faces, I'll do them now whilst you get yourselves washed and dressed and your beds made. Off you go, then! You're missing all the lovely sun!"

"It's good of you to come out with me, Tatty," Kitty said as they turned left at the end of the mews and headed for Hyde Park. "You don't have to, you know — be nice to me, I mean, just because of what tomorrow is."

"Of course I want to be with you. I haven't had a day off for ages. And you can talk about Drew all you want. I shan't mind a bit."

"You're a good guy, y'know. I'm glad you're my cousin. You've improved a lot since you were little. You sure were a nuisance!"

"I remember it all. You all seemed ever so old to me. I longed to climb trees with you and be allowed to get dirty. I especially remember the day we were all in the wild garden, under the trees, and you let me join the Clan. I was so proud. I promised to teach you some Russian swear words, didn't I?"

"Which are still very useful when I want to blow my top," Kitty grinned. "What say we walk the length of the park as far as Hyde Park Corner? There's a pillar box there, and I've got a letter to post."

"Suits me. Did you know that Aunt Julia and Daisy's mother got arrested just near Hyde Park Corner? Let's see if we can find the place, shall we? It was where Aunt Julia met Andrew — her first husband, you know. They'd both been staying at Montpelier Mews, when Great Aunt Sutton was alive that was, and were at a suffragette meeting. Very daring!"

"Can't imagine either of them getting into a fight," Kitty giggled. "Funny, but Mom said she once thought Aunt Julia was never going to get over losing Andrew."

"She's very happy now, though . . ."

740

"Mm. I suppose you can fall in love again — but differently, when you're older. Say, Tatty, how is it that everybody we're passing seems to be a couple 'cept you an' me?"

They were walking along the carriage drive, passing servicemen with their girls, laughing as if there wasn't a war on and that tomorrow, when most of them would have parted, was a whole world away.

"I'd noticed," Tatiana said softly. "Tim and I were a couple once. On the Friday night we were together; next night — well, you know what happened."

"I do. How do you live with it? I don't think I'd want to go on living if anything happened to Drew. He's going to be all right, isn't he?" Tears filled Kitty's eyes. "Sorry, Tatty, but you did say I could talk about Drew."

"I did, but you're not to cry! He wouldn't want you to. And look how quickly a year has passed. Before you know it he'll be home!"

"Sure, sure." Kitty dabbed her eyes. "It's just that today and tomorrow are going to be a little bit much. I'll be fine, though, once I'm on tour."

"There's the pillar box, at the top of Wilton Place." Tatiana pointed to the opposite side of the road. "Now put a big lipsticky kiss on your letter and post it to Drew with a big smile — okay? And then we'll go and sit by the Serpentine. And mind the road!" Tatiana called as a Jeep carrying far too many GIs hooted at Kitty as it roared past.

"Hi!" Kitty waved and smiled because after all, one of those soldiers could have been Bas.

She kissed the back of the envelope, leaving the mark of her lips there, then slipped the letter into the bright red box.

"Come home soon, Drew," she whispered. "Come home safely."

It was then that she heard the sound and knew with dreadful certainty what it was: one of those bombs overhead!

She squinted into the sky. It was all right, wasn't it, as long as they passed over? She stood, waiting to cross the road. Tatty was looking up. Tatty had heard it too.

The noise stopped; it really *had* stopped! How long before it hit! Fifteen seconds, that was all!

"Kitty! Get down!" Tatty was shouting. "*Kitty!*" She was screaming now. "Get down — *down*!"

Tatty on the other side of the road under a tree, face down, arms over her head.

How many seconds more? Seven, six, five? God! She couldn't move! Where *was* the thing! With a cry she hit the hard pavement just as the roar, the flash, a vicious blast of air hit her.

"Rowangarth," Nathan said, lifting the telephone.

"That you, Reverend? It's Sparrow . . ."

"Hullo, there! We've got a bad line. You sound faint."

"No! It's me as feels faint! It's Tatty and Kitty!"

"I'll get Mrs Sutton."

742

"No, Reverend. We might get cut off! There was this bomb, see? I heard it coming. I knew they were out in the park. I went looking for them, Hyde Park Corner way. A flying bomb, it was . . ."

"And where are the girls?" His mouth had gone dry.

"Oh, the damage!" she rushed on. "The ARP lot were there, digging! A bomb on a church, it was. The Guards Chapel at the barracks, near the Palace."

"Sparrow! Were the girls in the chapel?"

"No, but nearby, in the park. A warden told me if they were alive they'd have been taken to St Bartholomew's."

"Bartholomew's? But that's a long way away . . ." He was sweating. He didn't believe any of it. They *must* be all right! *Listen, God, they've got to be!*

"They takes 'em where they can find a bed. There were a lot killed. At morning church, see? More than a hundred dead."

"But tell me what happened to Tatty and Kitty?" Please, not the pips? They mustn't be cut off!

"I rang Bartholomew's. They'd been taken to casualty, both of them!"

"And they're all right?" This was a nightmare!

"They're in there and that's all I know. They're alive, or they'd have been taken to a mortuary! I'm sorry, Reverend, but I'm not next of kin. The ward sister wouldn't tell me nothing! Mrs Sutton and Mrs Anna are going to have to come down here!"

"Yes! Of course." They could catch the midnight from York! "I'll see to it, don't worry. What will you do, Sparrow?"

"I'm going down there. Somebody's got to be with them! I'll find out what's going on. I'll say I'm their grandma!"

"Take care, won't you?" She was too old for shocks like this. "And, Sparrow — thank you!"

"Nah! I'm sorry it had to be me as told you. Don't ring. I won't be here. I'll have to be orf now!"

"Then mind how you go. Bless you, Sparrow."

He replaced the receiver. His hands were clammy and he ran the palms down the sides of his jacket.

"Who was that?" Julia, standing behind him. "It was London, wasn't it? What's happened, Nathan?"

"It was Sparrow." There was no way he could spare her. "One of those flying bombs. Tatty and Kitty were hurt. They're in hospital, but they wouldn't tell her any more. She's going there now . . ."

"Where, Nathan?" Her lips were so tight with fear they would hardly move.

"A warden said it was St Bartholomew's."

"We've got to go. Straight away! Can you get us to York — and Anna, too. She'll have to be there. Have you enough petrol?"

"I'll ring her now, darling. I'll take you both."

"Can't you come? Oh hell, no! A funeral tomorrow, haven't you, and a wedding in the afternoon?" A special licence job.

744

Her eyes darted around the hall as if she were a small, cornered animal, he thought, trying to run away from it all.

"Sit down a minute, Julia. Do we have anything — a snifter of brandy, perhaps?"

"No. There's only whisky, and I don't want that. I'll be all right. Give me time . . ."

"I'll ring Denniston."

"No! Ring Keeper's first. Ask Alice to come." She wanted Alice here.

Nathan picked up the phone. The exchange answered at once.

"Hullo, Winnie. Can you get me Keeper's Cottage, please, then immediately afterwards, can I have Denniston?"

"Yes, Vicar. I'm ringing Keeper's now."

Alice answered quickly. Her voice sounded brightly expectant. Nathan supposed she must think it was Daisy ringing from Liverpool.

"Alice, it's Nathan. There's been an accident. Tatty and Kitty. They're in hospital. Julia asked me to tell you."

"I'll come right away."

"Bless you." He replaced the receiver and at once the phone rang again.

"I'm trying Denniston now, Mr Sutton. They aren't answering yet. I'll keep ringing. Is something the matter?"

"I'm afraid so." No point in holding it back. Winnie had already put through the London call. She would suspect. "Tatty and Kitty are in hospital.

There's been an accident. Mrs Sutton is going to London on the overnight train. I've got to tell Mrs Anna."

"There's still no one answering. If she isn't in, that Karl won't pick the phone up. He never does. Why don't you hang up, Reverend, and I'll ring round places she might be? What shall I say?"

"Just that Rowangarth would like her to ring as soon as she can. Do you think she might be at the surgery?"

"Possibly. She might be in the garden, or gone for a walk. Don't worry — someone will have seen her."

"Thanks, Winnie. Try to keep it low-key if you can."

Footsteps hurrying along the kitchen passage. Alice, red-faced from running.

"I let myself in, Nathan. There's no one about, in the kitchen."

"They're both out."

"Where's Julia? What's happened?"

"Upstairs, I think. Sparrow rang. It was a flying bomb. Tatty and Kitty have been taken to hospital is all she could say. They wouldn't tell her anything. She's going there now; says she'll say she's their grandmother — she might learn more then. I'm trying to get hold of Anna."

"What about the Countess? She's in London. Shouldn't she be told?"

"Oh Lord, no!" Julia, coming downstairs, clinging at each step to the banister rail. "Not the Petrovska! She'll go there and start giving orders!"

"She's family. She's got a right to know. And those nurses won't take any nonsense from her," Alice said quietly. "Now come with me to the kitchen. I'm going to put the kettle on and you're going to have a cigarette and a cup of tea before we do anything! Are you catching the overnight?"

"Yes. Nathan can't come . . ."

"He can't very well leave three parishes without a priest, now can he?"

"I'll ring the bishop early tomorrow." Nathan ran his fingers through his hair. "Maybe he'll be able to help."

"Or you could ask the army padre at Pendenys to stand in, in case of emergencies. I'm sure he would and you know him well enough to ask him."

"A good idea, Alice." Nathan was glad of her calm common sense.

"Then you'd better get yourself a sup of tea, too. You look as if you could do with one! Just put a call in to Cheyne Walk, then come and sit you down for a minute or two." Alice was a firm believer in the comfort of the kitchen. "And don't forget to take Montpelier key with you, Julia, in case Sparrow is out."

"I shall go straight to the hospital." Julia sat down in the rocker beside the fire, gripping the wooden arms tightly. There was a shaking inside her that was like a silent sobbing. "I wonder if they're badly hurt."

"You'll soon know," Alice said, tight-lipped, going about the business of setting the tray with a clean cloth and arranging cups and saucers and milk on it. Being busy helped. "Now come and sit down, Nathan, whilst the tea mashes. Did you book the London call?"

"I did. Winnie said to leave it all to her. She's being a brick. No one's answering at Denniston, nor at the surgery. But then, it is Sunday . . ."

"Drink this tea whilst it's hot," Alice ordered. "And there's sugar in it."

"You know I don't take sugar," Julia choked.

"You do, this evening! Now then, tell me?"

"There was a flying bomb. Seems it fell on the Guards Chapel, near Buckingham Palace. They don't make craters, those things. They explode outwards, I think. The blast does the damage. Sparrow said Kitty and Tatty had gone to the park. They'd be nearby when it fell."

"Yes. And they're in hospital now, getting taken care of! Where did you say it was?"

"Bartholomew's."

There was a small silence as Julia's eyes met Alice's. Neither spoke. There was no need to.

"They should be all right, there," Alice said.

"There'll be no one to answer the phone," Julia said dully, "when Nathan takes us to York."

"There'll be Tilda when she gets in. I'll stay here, till she does. Now finish that drink, then I'll come upstairs and pack a case for you."

"You don't have to." Julia's hand was shaking and tea slopped into the saucer.

"No, but I will. It won't be the first time I've done it!

"You'd better travel light," she said when she had settled Julia on the window seat in the bedroom. "Spare underwear, slippers, dressing gown and your brolly. Will you try to get a sleeper?"

"No. It'd be a waste of money."

"There'll be food at Montpelier, so you'll not have to bother about rations and likely you'll only be away a couple of nights."

"I think they should both come home, Alice . . ."

"And they will, just as soon as they're fit to travel. The hospital will be glad of their beds, I shouldn't wonder."

"Yes, and I can look after them. How will we let Amelia and Albert know? What will I say?"

"We'll worry about that, Julia, when we know what there is to tell them."

"And Drew will have to be told."

"Yes. When we know. Will the fawn skirt and brown sandals be all right? And you'd better take a cardi. It can get cold at nights."

The phone rang and Julia jumped to her feet, clattering down the stairs, only to return dejectedly.

"That was Winnie. She managed to get Karl to answer but all she could get out of him was, 'She go Harrogate.' He understands English, all right, but he won't make the effort to speak it!"

"Never mind. Winnie and me between us will make sure Anna is told. I'll make you a sandwich and do you a flask for the train. And I'd better run a bath — help relax you, because goodness knows when you'll get the next one!"

"A bath would be nice." Julia's voice sounded strange, and far away. "I can't think straight, you know."

"Of course you can't. It's human nature to worry and think the worst, now isn't it? Just take it as it comes. You'll find things aren't as bad as you thought when you get there."

"Yes. You're right. And bless you, love, for being here."

"No trouble. All you have to do is get yourself on that train and leave everything else to Nathan and me. We'll get hold of Anna, don't you worry none! Now straighten your shoulders, *norrrse*," she mimicked in Sister Carbrooke's Scottish lilt. "Face up to it, MacMalcolm and Hawthorn!"

"Oh, Alice!" A sob was hurting her throat, but she swallowed hard on it and forced a smile. "Just be here when I get back, that's all."

"You know I will." It wasn't easy being matter-of-fact, Alice thought, when all you wanted to do was shake an angry fist at heaven and demand, *Why*? "Just get yourself into that bath and I'll see to your sandwiches!"

She walked slowly downstairs, then crossed the wide, high hall where Nathan sat on the chair beside the phone, eyes closed. On tiptoe, she continued down the wooden stairs into the kitchen, pulling the blackout curtains, switching on the light. She had spent so much time in this kitchen, and almost every day of it a happy one. She looked at the fireside rocker where Mrs Shaw sat so often. Dear Cook. Gone, now.

Almost without thinking she opened the drawer where the knives were kept, had always been kept, then reached for scrubbed-white breadboard. So safe, so achingly secure, this kitchen. It hadn't changed since she left it. And please God it never would, and that everything would be all right in that London hospital.

Strange it should be St Bartholomew's.

The overnight express made good time and was amazingly only twenty minutes late into King's Cross. That they had not been held up along the track nor shunted into a siding boded well, Julia thought. What was more, she had found a taxi more easily than she had thought to so early in the morning. The nagging fear inside her lessened. She was here now, and soon Nathan would join her. Everything would be all right.

She hurried into the building, trying to tell herself it was just any old hospital, trying to keep her thoughts under control. She took a deep breath, following the arrows that pointed to Casualty.

Her old, soft shoes made no noise on the marble floor. She walked as quickly as she dared. A nurse must never run, except in the direst emergency. The glass doors ahead were propped open and even from so far away the hospital smell met her and

751

reminded her; made her want to run away from the turmoil, go back to Rowangarth's safeness.

She saw Sparrow at once, sitting on a hard chair, and with her the Countess. They both looked old and defeated, though Olga Petrovska's back was ramrod straight.

Sparrow jumped to her feet with a cry of relief. Julia hugged her close, then held out a hand to the Countess, kissing her cheek.

"Is my daughter not with you, Julia? Why is she not here?"

"We couldn't get through to her last night," Julia said patiently. "We rang round, but she wasn't in. Nathan will find her. She's bound to be on the first train out this morning. She'll be here soon. Tell me what happened."

"Me and her ladyship's been here most of the night. They told us nothing!"

"But they're both all right?" Julia sat down beside them.

"I was able to find out that Tatiana was taken to the operating theatre. I shall not leave until I have seen her!"

"What kind of operation?" Julia whispered, knowing how it could be. She had seen shrapnel wounds before.

"I was not told!"

"All I can say for sure," Sparrow said sadly, "is that there was this flying bomb. I heard it go over, then the engine cut out. A terrible explosion! I went out looking for the girls; knew they'd be somewhere

752

near. Such a mess, there was. It hit a church. More'n a hundred killed. People at prayer — it's sinful! I was a long time finding out which hospital they were in. Didn't ring you, till I knew . . ."

"Well, I'm here now, Sparrow. Thanks for everything you've done. Did you manage to find out anything about Kitty, Countess?"

"Only that she was brought here and that she's somewhere else now. You can find nothing out! Who do they think they are, these people?"

Just overworked nurses, Julia thought, trying to do their best; probably longing to take off their shoes for five minutes, or snatch a cup of tea.

"They're very busy." She bit back the words she wanted to say. "I'll go to the desk. Maybe they'll be able to tell me where Kitty has been sent. If we could only be told how serious it is — though at least they're both alive."

"The nurse over there." The Countess nodded in the direction of a young, fair-haired girl. "You might get some sense out of that one!"

Julia cleared her throat loudly. The nurse looked up from the book she was writing in. She was young and there were dark rings beneath her eyes; had probably worked all night and was still on duty, Julia thought.

"My niece was brought here but I believe she's been moved, now. Kitty Sutton . . ."

"You've no idea which ward?"

"Sorry. I've just got here from Yorkshire. It was the bomb that fell on the chapel, I believe . . ."

"We have a Kathryn Sutton listed. The address on her identity card gave Montpelier Mews. Are you her mother?"

"No, but —" Julia took out her own identity card, "I'm her aunt. She's engaged to my son. Her parents are in America and I'm her next of kin whilst she's in England."

"Ah, then you'd better see Sister. It says here she was admitted to Ward C6. If you go through those doors," she pointed, "then turn left and straight ahead, you'll come to it. Sister will be able to tell you more. We're so busy, you see, especially since those flying bombs started."

"Yes, I'm sure you are," Julia smiled, all at once wanting to tell her that she knew exactly how it was. "Thank you for your help, nurse."

"So you've found where she is?" Sparrow said when Julia returned, the relief on her face obvious.

"Yes. Ward C6. I'm to see Sister. And I'll try to find out more about Tatty, Countess. Do you want to go home, Sparrow? You look very tired."

"Not bleedin' likely. Like her ladyship 'ere, I'm stopping till I find something out! They tells you nothing! You'd think you was asking them to give away state secrets!"

"It's the way it's got to be, I'm afraid. And if you're sure you want to stay, Sparrow . . .?"

"I'm stoppin'." Her chin jutted defiantly. "We're *both* stoppin'."

"Right then." Julia swallowed hard. "I'll try not to be too long."

She hurried away, anxious to see Kitty, get news of Tatty. The corridor was long and narrow and little more than a trolley's width, but then Bartholomew's was a very old hospital. The smell of disinfectant was stronger as she looked above each set of portholed double doors for the ward number, then set off, heart thudding, for the end of the passage, relieved she would soon know; glad beyond believing they were both being taken care of.

Blighty wounds, she smiled softly. In her war, a Blighty wound meant a soldier would be sent home to England to be nursed; Kitty and Tatty would be coming home to Rowangarth the minute they were well enough to travel.

She pushed open the doors of Ward C6 and looked about her. The nurses were busy; best she should stand here until one of them noticed her.

Ward C6, St Bartholomew's Hospital. Did Andrew once walk this ward? When he was doing extra duties to save money for the practice he hoped to buy, did he walk through the doors behind her, stop beside each bed? Was something of him still here?

Help me, Andrew. I'm so afraid.

But Andrew lay in a cemetery in France, at Étaples. He had gone. She must not try to call back a ghost.

A passing nurse stopped, asking if she were lost.

"No. I'm trying to get a few words with Sister," she said softly. "Is she too busy to see me, do you think? I'd be grateful for just a couple of minutes."

"What name shall I say?"

"Julia Sutton. I'm here about Kitty Sutton. She was brought here yesterday — the bomb on the Guards Chapel."

"I'll see what Sister says. Won't be a tick."

Julia stood unmoving, willing herself to be calm, remembering how it was, how it would always be. You never forgot being a nurse. She looked to her left and right, noting each bed and the carefully enveloped corners. Hospital corners, they called them. How many beds had she and Alice made — in another war?

"Sister says she'll see you." The nurse, breaking into her thoughts, bringing her back to here and now. "Her office is halfway down on the left." She was gone before Julia could thank her.

She pulled her tongue round her lips, counting each bed, not looking at who lay in them. Then she saw the open door. From behind the desk, a young woman rose to her feet, her face pale; beneath her eyes the tell-tale smudges. There was a thin, faint outline of lipstick around her lips. Julia noticed it as the nurse shaped her mouth into a smile. She looked too young, she thought, for responsibility such as this.

"Mrs Sutton? Please sit down. My relief will be here at eight, so —"

"I'm very grateful, Sister. I won't keep you. If you could just tell me where my niece is." She offered her identity card. "I'm her next of kin — well, in England, that is. How badly was she hurt?"

"She was admitted yesterday afternoon. Look — I'm sorry. There's no other way to say this. She didn't regain consciousness. Kathryn Sutton died this morning, at 5a.m."

Dead? Kitty *dead*? The walls began to tilt, and the floor beneath Julia's feet. There was a rushing in her ears so loud it made her dizzy. She grasped the edge of the desk, holding on to it tightly. The face before her swam and shimmered and became that of Sister Carbrooke.

Take a hold of yourself, norrrse!

She pulled in her breath, holding it, breathing out in harsh gasps. When she opened her eyes, the room had stopped tilting and the Sister was holding a glass of water, guiding her hand to it.

"I'm so very sorry, Mrs Sutton. Just sit quietly for a while."

She placed the glass to Julia's lips. The water was very cold. She gulped at it and some dribbled out of the corner of her mouth and ran along her jawbone and down her neck.

"That's better. Just a little more . . .?"

Julia shook her head, turning it away, pulling the back of her hand across her mouth.

"Thank you, Sister." It surprised her she could still speak.

She laid the palms of her hands on her lap, trying to relax them, gulping air into her lungs, fighting the silent screaming inside her.

"Dead?" she said dully. "But she's so young . . ."

"Yes." Ward Sister knew there was nothing else to say, that platitudes at times like this were obscene. She reached for the shaking hand, holding it tightly.

"Mrs Sutton, when Day Sister comes on duty, I'll go with you — I mean, do you think you could . . ."

"She's in the mortuary, isn't she? You want me to identify her."

"Are you up to it just yet? Could you, do you think?"

"Yes. I was a nurse in the last war — at the Front."

Her words were harsh with pain. Each one hurt just to say it, yet she had to say them to reassure the young Sister that she wouldn't make a fuss. Later, she would. When there were arms to hold her whilst she cried out her anger and disbelief, she would do it. When Nathan came.

"Then I'll give you her things first."

She took a large brown paper bag from the cupboard behind her. It reminded Julia of her war and how they tied cloths over their hair and pulled on protective gloves to remove the stained, lice-infected uniforms from broken bodies. Then they wrote the soldier's name and number on the bag in black crayon . . .

"And there's something else."

Sister unlocked a desk drawer, taking out an envelope, tipping the contents onto the blotting pad on the desktop. Kitty's watch, her gold locket and chain, her English identity card, an opal and pearl ring.

"This was my grandmother's." Julia picked up the ring. "Kitty is engaged to my son."

She returned it to the envelope with the other things. The identity card was stained with blood and she opened the brown paper bag, slipping the envelope inside, trying not to look at the clothes.

"Will you sign for them, please?"

Julia took the offered pen. She was amazed at the firmness of her hand. But it was all right for the woman who had taken over her mind and her body; the woman who knew how to behave in a hospital ward and would stand there as someone pulled back the sheet that covered Kitty's face. That long-ago woman — Julia MacMalcolm, she was called — would do what was required of her with discipline and calm.

Only later could Julia Sutton weep.

Julia held Sparrow's hand tightly all the way back to Montpelier Mews, listening to the quiet sobbing, wishing she could weep too.

They had left the Countess at the hospital, sitting erect and slab-faced on the hard wooden chair. Fear had flashed in her eyes when Julia said, simply, "Kitty's dead. I've just seen her . . ."

Sparrow had jumped to her feet with a harsh cry, but Olga Petrovska closed her eyes, bowed her head then crossed herself whispering, "God have mercy." For a while she said nothing, then lifting her head she whispered, "Go home, Julia. I shall stay — for Tatiana."

"Yes. Wait with Tatty . . ."

"You need something for your nerves," Sparrow said, unlocking the familiar white door. "And there's nothing in the house but tea."

"Tea will be fine." Julia lifted the phone, putting it down again. "Nathan will be out," she said, almost to herself. He had a funeral in one of the parishes at eleven, then a wedding at two. She picked it up again and asked the operator for a trunk call to Holdenby 195.

"It's best I ring Alice," she said tonelessly. "Nathan could be anywhere . . ." There was a better chance that Alice would be in.

"Sit down, girl. Kettle won't be long."

Sparrow put a match to the fire. In June it was only lit in the evening, to heat the water, but Julia was shaking with cold.

"Can you tell me what happened now?" Sparrow asked when they were seated at the kitchen table, hands wrapped round mugs of strong, sweet tea. "Can you bear to?"

"There's nothing much to tell. I should have asked how badly hurt Tatty was, but I couldn't think straight. All I remember is seeing Kitty there, very still. I only saw her face. There was dust in her hair, but someone had washed her face. She looked very beautiful. I wanted to say, 'Kitty, it's Aunt Julia. Wake up,' but instead I just kissed her — for Drew. I'll have to go back to the hospital, see the almoner, get — get —"

"Do what's necessary," Sparrow whispered, her tears all spent. "Make arrangements. You're taking her home to Rowangarth?"

"Yes." Julia pushed Drew from her mind, refused to think of Albert and Amelia. Later, but not just yet. "Today, by the date, should have been their first wedding anniversary."

760

"Yes. She said. That's why her and Tatty went to the park. To keep her spirits up, I suppose."

There was a long, aching silence until the phone rang to shatter it. Sparrow jumped to her feet.

"That'll be your call." She passed the receiver to Julia. "My Gawd, but bad news travels fast."

"Holdenby 195?" Julia whispered. "Alice?"

"It's me. What's news, love?"

"I should have phoned Nathan, but he'll be in and out all day. Thought I'd best ring you."

"Yes. Anna's on her way. She should be almost there by now."

"Good. The Countess was at the hospital when I got there, and Sparrow. Tatty is in the theatre now and oh, Alice — Kitty's dead!"

"No! *No!*" It was a cry of utter pain.

"I'm sorry. I don't know how else to say it. I haven't taken it in yet. I'm just numb. I want to cry and I want to be angry, Alice, but I can't feel anything."

There was a pause then.

"It *is* true, Julia? There couldn't have been a mistake?"

"It's true. My lovely Kitty . . ."

"But what am I to tell people?" Alice was crying softly.

"Don't tell anyone but Tom — not till Nathan knows. He should be back at Rowangarth at about half-twelve. I'm sorry to put the burden of it on you . . ."

"Who else but me? I ought to be with you."

"Dear God, I wish you were. Ask Nathan to ring. There'll be things to be done, but I can't cope with them. I want someone to hold me, Alice."

"I know, love. I'll see that Nathan's told. He'll know what to do."

"They gave me her things. In a brown paper bag."

"Oh, please, *no!*" Alice was remembering too. "Julia — what are we to do?" Her voice was little above a whisper.

"I don't know. And me telling you — that's just the start of it. Where will it all end? So many people — so much grief."

"Is Sparrow with you?"

"Yes. I won't go back to the hospital till Nathan rings. He's got a wedding this afternoon, but if he could try to get through before then . . .?"

"Winnie will help. She'll get a line for him." There didn't seem to be anything else to say except, "I'll be thinking about you. All the time. And, Julia — take care, love . . . ?"

"Is there any more tea?" Julia held her hands to the fire.

"I don't know about tea — when did you last eat?"

"O-oh — on the train, I suppose. I'm fine. Couldn't eat."

"I'll do you some milky cocoa, and a few fingers of toast. What did Alice say? How did she take it?"

"Shocked. I don't think she believed it at first. It'll be sinking in now, though. She'll catch Nathan between the funeral and the wedding. He'll ring as soon as he can."

"And Mrs Anna? What news of her?"

"She's on her way. She'll go straight to the hospital. Y'know, I thought the Countess would make a fuss at the hospital, but it seems she didn't."

"No. Speak as you find — she was all right with me. I suppose it was a case of the Colonel's lady and Judy O'Grady bein' sisters under the skin, sort of. She was as worried as me."

"Sparrow! I want to go to church and beg that none of this has happened. I want it to be yesterday again so I can make a bargain with God — my life for Kitty's."

"Well, He don't hold with bargaining and you can't go out, anyway. The Reverend'll be ringing, don't forget. And will you stop that pacing up and down and have a good cry, girl? Let it come. Sparrow understands . . ."

But Julia could not weep. The pain inside her was too great. Later, perhaps, when Nathan came, but not just yet.

Tomorrow, she would weep.

CHAPTER
THIRTY-FIVE

Alice was sitting at the kitchen table when Tom came home for his dinner. There was no smell of cooking, and breakfast dishes lay unwashed in the sink. She lifted her head and he saw she had been weeping. She rose, arms outstretched, whispering his name and a fist slammed into his belly.

"Bonny lass." He gathered her close, hushing her, praying silently and urgently, though for what, he couldn't be sure.

"Julia phoned, Tom. We're to tell Nathan — she couldn't get hold of him, you see."

"Tell me," he urged. "Tell me, love."

His mouth had gone dry. He didn't know whether the shaking he felt was his own or Alice's.

"Stay with me, Tom? Be here when I tell Nathan?"

"I won't leave you. What is it you have to tell him?" He realized he must coax the words out of her — words he didn't want to hear. "What did Julia say?"

"Kitty," she said dully "She's dead . . ."

A great rage took him. He clenched his teeth, his jaws, because there was an animal cry of pain in his throat, near choking him. Kitty's face flashed into his remembering and at once it was gone and Daisy's face was there.

"No!" he yelled. "Dammit, *no!*" He closed his eyes tightly and when he opened them he was looking at the wall opposite and the faces were no longer there.

"It's true. Julia said so. Tatty's hurt. They're operating on her."

"Sit you down, lass." He guided her to the table. "I'll get you a cup of tea."

Tea! When Kitty was dead! Damn stupid idea! Likely Alice didn't want tea, but he had to do something sane and safe and ordinary, or he would beat the wall with his fists, shout obscenities.

"Please, Tom. And you have one, too. There's some cheese in the meat safe. I'll make you a —"

"No! I'll see to it. I'll have a sandwich if you'll have one."

"Suppose I better had." Even though it would near choke her. "Will you tell Nathan?" The phone might ring at any minute and she wasn't brave enough to say the words again, not even into an impersonal black receiver.

"I'll tell him. Where can I find him?"

"He's busy in the parishes. He'll be home soon, I think. Mary and Tilda don't know yet. Winnie Hallam left a message for him to ring me, or Julia . . ."

"Hush, lass." He covered the teapot with the cosy, then brought cheese and bread from the pantry. "I

765

know you don't want it, but a bite and a drink inside you will help."

"Yes." She watched him cutting the bread in thick slices, then pushed back her chair. "Think I'll ring the exchange — just check . . ."

"You do that, bonny lass."

Tom looked at the piece of cheese, wondering how long it would have to last, not caring, listening as Alice said, "Hullo, Winnie. Can you give me Rowangarth, please? Engaged? Is it the Reverend?"

Tom looked up. Alice was standing in the doorway, her face wooden.

"Nathan's home. Winnie got him through to Montpelier with hardly any bother. You wait hours and hours for a trunk call, but when it's bad news there's always a line!"

"Aye. Happen he'll ring when he's spoken to Julia. Try to eat summat, lass."

"At least neither of us has to tell him." Alice broke off a piece of bread, pushing it into her mouth, wondering why it tasted so awful. "Shall I go over, do you think?"

"No, lass. Give him a bit of breathing space. Drink your tea up, then give your face a bit of a wash, eh?"

The mantel clock had just chimed one when the dogs began to bark.

"It's him!" Alice ran down the path, arms wide. "Oh, Nathan!"

For a moment they held each other close, then Alice whispered, "She's told you, then?"

"She's told me." His voice was soft, but his eyes were bleak with pain. "Sorry I've been so long coming, but there were things to see to."

"I'm sorry, Nathan. There's nowt we can say, 'cept it just doesn't bear thinking about." Tom held out a hand. "How did they take it at Rowangarth?"

"Badly. All three of them have watched Kitty grow up, you know. Miss Clitherow seemed to take charge. She held her head up and it was as if she were trying to do what Mother-in-law would have done. I didn't want to leave them, but —"

"You must go to Julia. How was she, when you rang?"

"In a terrible state. She broke down and Sparrow had to tell me. I'm getting the two o'clock from York. I rang the Army padre at Pendenys. Thank God he was there. He's running me to Holdenby station, then he'll take the wedding, he says. He's a good chap. I think the bride will understand."

"Of course she will! Are you packed yet?" Seeing his distress made Alice forget a little of her own. "Is there anything me or Tom can do?"

"No thanks. Just pop over to Rowangarth later, and see how they're getting on, could you — try to cheer them up a bit?"

"You know I will, Nathan. Are we to tell people?"

"Best that you should. I tried to get the surgery, but Ewart was out. I don't know if Anna has been able to get in touch with him, but Sparrow said

Tatty was out of the theatre and as well as could be expected."

"Then we'll just have to hope and pray she'll pull through. This is a terrible war. I thought Rowangarth had more than paid its dues in the last one, but I was wrong. Are you sure there's nothing I can do? Have you eaten, Nathan?"

"No, but Tilda is making sandwiches for me. I'll eat them on the train. I should be there before dark."

"And you'll be careful? Those bombs — you don't know where they'll fall. They come without any warning."

"I'll take care, Alice. I'm an old soldier, don't forget."

Tom opened the back door, walking down the path with a man who all at once looked every one of his fifty-six years. "Tell Julia we'll be thinking about her all the time — and Mrs Anna, too. Has anybody thought to tell young Bas?"

"All taken care of. Jack Jeffries — the padre from Pendenys — said he'd use the army network to get in touch with the CO at Burtonwood. People have been very kind."

"Then don't forget — any time of the day or night — me and Alice will be here. You've only got to ring."

"Please go home, Mama. I'm here now," Anna whispered, "and you look so tired."

"I'm all right. I shall stay."

"But they've told us all they can. Tatiana is out of the theatre and as well as can be expected. They won't let us see her until she's over the anaesthetic. You've been here for almost twenty-four hours. You must rest."

"I have dozed a little. I will wait." She set her mouth stubbornly, and Anna knew not to argue.

"I wonder how Julia is now. Do you think I should try to find a phone and ring her?"

"I think not. Perhaps she is resting — trying to sleep; she's best left alone. She has Mrs Sparrow."

"Yes — and Nathan will be with her as soon as he can. Poor Julia. I try not to think it could have been both of them."

"Then close your eyes, Aleksandrina Anastasia Petrovska, and give thanks your daughter is still alive. And pray for Kitty's soul too."

"Yes, Mama." She closed her eyes, but she did not pray. Instead, she thought of last evening when everyone was frantically searching for her. Gone to Harrogate, Karl had said. Only he knew where she really was. She should have travelled to London last night with Julia; been here to comfort her. Perhaps, before she could pray for others she should ask forgiveness for herself.

She bowed her head, crossing herself devoutly as once she had always done; once, in another life.

Blessed Virgin, hear my prayer . . .

Nathan called Julia's name as he opened the door of the house in Montpelier Mews and she ran to his arms, holding him tightly.

"Darling! Thank God you've come!"

"Sssssh." He laid his cheek on her head, making little hushing noises. "I'm here now. Just be still and let me hold you." He felt her relax a little against him and whispered, "I'm so sorry, darling; so very, very sorry. I should have been with you. Thank heaven for Sparrow."

"Yes, but will she listen to me?" Sparrow clucked. "Oh, no! She needs her bed, but all she does is walk up and down like a creature possessed! She won't even cry! What's wrong, will you tell me, in having a good weep?"

"I want to, but I can't. I want to scream and slam doors, but it's as if it isn't happening to me," Julia whispered. "It's all bottled up inside me like a great pain. How will I tell them? What do I say to Albert and Amelia? How can I tell Drew? And me! What about me? I loved her. I'd die for her, God knows. She was one of my Clan. I've lost a child, Nathan!"

"Darling, darling girl! You can't carry everyone's grief. The burden, yes, of telling them, but not their pain. Learn to accept your own first, and live with it — then help me through mine? I need you, Julia, every bit as much as you need me."

His voice faded into a whisper of despair and Sparrow tiptoed out of the room, closing the door behind her, leaving them to their shared grief, her body shaking with silent sobs.

Julia gave way to tears, then; sobbed out her misery and outrage and hurt, and Nathan rocked her gently in his arms, holding her tightly until she could weep no more.

Holdenby was shocked and silent. Death had come violently again to the little village at the foot of Holdenby Pike. As Jinny Dobb always said, bad news travels fastest, and soon everyone knew that Kitty Sutton had been killed and her cousin fighting for her life in a London hospital.

Young, she had been, with eyes full of mischief and as bonny a lass as you'd find in a day's march; so full of life it was near impossible to think of her dead.

Sir Andrew's wife, she should have been, and all the village had looked forward to a wedding the war prevented. How would young Drew take it, and her parents in Kentucky?

A Pendenys Sutton Kitty's father had been, and now the ill-luck that tainted that great ugly house had claimed another of them. Pendenys Place had been cursed from the day its first stone was laid.

Now the lass would never be wed at All Souls. Soon they would bring her home to rest with the Rowangarth Suttons, for surely they wouldn't lay her on the other side of the path with Edward and Clementina and Elliot? Surely Rowangarth would claim the lass who would have been Lady Kitty, but for the dratted war? A strange, waiting stillness settled on Holdenby. People spoke of her in whispers, remembering a young woman with Mary

771

Anne Pendennis hair and eyes the colour of wild violets . . .

Tilda remarked on the mischief in those eyes as she sat, eyes closed, in the kitchen, remembering the little baby from faraway Kentucky, who cried angrily and loudly as the Reverend christened her in the church in which, twenty years on, she should have married Drew.

"They'll be bringing her home tomorrow," she whispered to Sydney, who had been a great comfort to her. "Miss Julia has asked there be no flowers — just from family. So long as people come, that's all she wants."

"It's a sad business. A bit of a lass . . ."

"This war's no respecter of women and children, Sydney. Happen those flying bombs will be falling here before so very much longer. And we laughed, didn't we, about Hitler's secret weapon?"

"Don't fret. The landings are going well, Tilda. We'll have the launching sites overrun soon."

"Happen." Too late for Kitty, though. "It's getting late, Sydney. You'd best be getting back to Pendenys."

"Will you be all right on your own?"

"There's Miss Clitherow. I'll manage. But will you do the rounds with me — check the windows and doors?"

Once the nightly round had been no trouble at all; now it was as if the war were very near, just the other side of the bothy. It made Tilda look in corners, beyond the night shadows.

"No trouble. And I'll look in on the old lady, bid her good night."

"She'd like that. You're a good man."

She closed her eyes, sending up thanks she had been in the kitchen garden that day in search of cooking apples. Then she added a small, special prayer for Drew, who would not know yet.

Gracie and Bas sat on the highest point of Holdenby Pike, looking down on the village and Rowangarth and, further away, at dark, secretive Pendenys Place.

"It was good of them to let you come," Gracie whispered.

"Hell! She's my sister! If they'd said no I'd have gone AWOL!"

"Ssssh." She lifted his hand to her lips, kissing its palm. "I meant because of the landings, and no one getting leave. Mr Catchpole was doing the wreaths when I left; just two, for family. I didn't want to stay and watch him."

"Family! I can't get Kentucky out of my mind. Imagine Mom and Pa getting that letter; imagine them not being able to be at their daughter's funeral! I'm still not sure if they'll know yet. No transatlantic calls now, and even though we could've got permission to send a cable, Aunt Julia said no; that it would be too terse and cruel."

"Who wrote to tell them, Bas?"

"Uncle Nathan. He wrote to Drew, too. Aunt Julia was too cut up. I guess parsons have a way of keeping hold of their feelings. He's taking the service tomorrow — insists . . ."

"I'll be there. Everyone from the bothy who can get time off is going."

"You'll be with me, won't you, Gracie? You're family now and besides, I guess I'm not as brave as I thought. When I got here, Kitty — Kitty's — well, she was already there, in the great hall. It threw me."

"Yes. I remember Lady Helen being there too. I went to say goodbye to her, but I'm sorry about not seeing Kitty, Bas. I just couldn't, not with her so still. I want to remember her at Daisy's wedding, in blue, and she and Drew telling everyone there they were going to be married in June." Tears filled her eyes afresh. "Sorry, darling, but I'm weeping again. Can't seem to stop."

"'S okay. Feel like I want to weep too. Guess guys can't let go, though, can they?"

"Yes, they can." She reached out, drawing him close, laying her cheek against his. "For their sister, they can."

She gentled the back of his neck as his sobs came.

"Mother — you look dreadful," Tatty whispered. "When did you last sleep?"

"Don't know." Anna smiled fleetingly. "My goodness, but you gave us all a bad time," she chided fondly, looking at the mound encasing a broken right leg and the arm suspended like a stiff white pot. She tried not to look at the bruised, lacerated face; her daughter's once-beautiful face.

"I'm thirsty. Can I have a drink?"

Anna reached for the spouted feeding cup, tilting it gently.

Tatiana ran her tongue round her lips then said croakily, "I think I shall live into old age, Mother. Today, Sister said I'm off the well-as-can-be-expected list, and I'm comfortable now. She said maybe they'll take the sling off my arm tomorrow. I'll be able to wriggle about in bed a bit then. My face is a mess, isn't it?"

"Darling — *no!*" They said she hadn't seen it yet!

"It is. I've been feeling it. Okay — maybe it'll heal in time and anyway, they can do things now . . ."

"Tatiana, don't get upset. Your face feels bad because it's still swollen and bruised and —"

"And stitched. I know about that too. And, Mother — I don't care, because I'm alive. Kitty wouldn't care, nor Drew, if all that had happened to her was a broken leg and arm and her face a bit of a mess." There was a small silence that seemed forever, as Tatiana's eyes met those of her mother. "I know about Kitty. She's dead, isn't she?"

"No, oh, *no!*" Anna jumped to her feet, white-faced, wide-eyed. "They shouldn't have told you! Not yet!"

"They didn't tell me. I heard it for myself . . ."

"How? You couldn't have!"

"I did. It was when I didn't know where I was. I felt all floaty and dizzy and there were voices, sort of high up above me. I remembered the bomb and wondered if I were dead, or dying, so I tried hard to listen."

"And?" Anna pulled her tongue round her lips. This was the moment she had dreaded, yet her daughter was the calmer of the two.

"And one of the voices said, 'Two Suttons were admitted, weren't they? Which one is this?' And the other voice said, 'This is Tatiana. It was Kathryn Sutton who died yesterday.' So I just laid there, sort of hanging on, wondering about it and if it were really true. I suppose I was coming round after the operation, but I just closed my eyes again and didn't open them for ages."

"I'm so sorry, darling." Anna whispered. "Sister said she would tell you when the time was right, yet you know and you're so calm about it. You're very brave. I'm proud of you and so thankful you're going to get better."

"I'm not calm; not really. I want to scream at the world because of Kitty, but it's as if there's someone inside me not letting me. They keep giving me an injection — for the pain. Perhaps that's what's making me calm, but when I don't feel so floaty I'm going to cry my head off, for Kitty and for Drew. Especially for Drew, because I know how he'll feel when he gets to know."

"Child — what can I say?" Anna's voice trembled on the edge of tears.

"Don't say anything, Mother. What time is it?"

"Half-past eight — at night."

"And Kitty — where is she?"

"At Rowangarth now. Julia and Nathan were here, but they've gone back home. It'll be tomorrow. Your grandmother has gone to Holdenby too; just for the funeral. She wants to represent Denniston, and to pray for Kitty, she said."

"Mm. Mother, will you go back to Montpelier, and get some sleep, and come again tomorrow — at the time it'll be?"

"It's at two o'clock."

"Then be with me at two, will you, and hold my hand, so we can say goodbye to Kitty and send our love to Drew?"

"I'll be here." Anna kissed her daughter's cheek. "We'll help each other through it, and think especially about Drew. I'll go now. Try to get some sleep, Tatiana."

"Well, that's it!" Mouth set traplike, Daisy closed the door of Cabin 4A with an angry shove. "I can't go! My brother's girl, my bridesmaid, and the rotten Navy won't even give me a thirty-six-hour pass! All leave postponed till further notice! As if I didn't know!"

"Did you think they would?" Lyn Carmichael sat crosslegged on her bunk. "Was Ma'am as shirty as that?"

"No. Actually, she was very nice about it, but rules is rules, I suppose. Only compassionate leave now for next of kin. Do you suppose I could go AWOL?"

"You could, just about, if you travelled in civvies and if you were on lates and Marjie let you off half an hour earlier to get the midnight from Lime Street. But —"

"But we're on earlies and there's no way I could do it," Daisy said tonelessly.

"You could say to hell with the lot of them and get caught by the Crushers. You'd be in big trouble, then, especially as you've had a formal request turned down. It's a bitch, I know, but there's not only a war on, but a second front too. They'd throw the book at you!"

"So what? I'd get my pay stopped — I've got money in the bank! And they couldn't stop my leave because nobody's getting it anyway."

"You *could* get your leave stopped. They'd hold it over, till leave starts again — which it *will* — and then where would you be when Keth gets his next seven days?"

"You're right, I suppose. Keth can't get leave either. There'll be none of the Clan there but Bas. His lot at least gave him a three-day pass. I'm pig-sick of this war. I've had it, up to here!" She put her hand beneath her chin in a dramatic gesture.

"So! Daisy Purvis doesn't like the war any more! Well hard bloody luck, chum, because right now there are a lot of men and women who would give a lot to be as chocker as you — Kitty Sutton, for one! Grow up, for God's sake!"

"Sorry, Lyn, but I just don't know how to cope with it." Her cheeks flushed crimson and ever-near tears pricked her eyes again. "I can't take it in! And I don't really want to be there, tomorrow, because if I was I'd have to admit that Kitty really is dead — and nearly Tatty too."

"Tatiana's going to be all right then?"

"As far as Mam has been able to make out — you know what it's like these days on the phone. And if I seem to be acting like a spoiled kid, then I'm sorry. It's just that once there were six of us and all was right with our world, except for the war. Now, Kitty's gone. *Kitty*, of all people! I want to be with Drew when he finds out about it! He'll have no one, had you thought?"

"When will he know, do you think?"

"Letters take about a week both to America and Australia. Nathan wrote, telling them. Aunt Julia couldn't face it. But any day now, three people are going to have their hearts broken and I can't do anything about it! All I can seem to do is weep. I've never cried so much in my life — not even when Uncle Reuben died, and Lady Helen. I'm sorry, Lyn."

"I know, love. And tomorrow, when we come off watch, I think you should go alone to the park and cry your eyes out."

"I wish Tatty had taught me to swear. She taught Kitty. In Russian. I could use a few swear words right now!"

Poor Tatty. Poor Kitty. Poor Drew. She began to weep again, softly, despairingly . . .

Drew Sutton leaned on the ship's rail, watching the supply ship transfer victuals and fuel and mail to

HMS *Newton*. They had reduced speed only a little and it amazed him that so complicated a manoeuvre at sea should appear so simple.

Last to be taken on board were bags of mail and a cheer went up from watchers as the sling was pulled inboard. Letters from home; letters from Kitty. There would be a mail-call some time during the afternoon watch, he calculated, when the ship's postman had sorted letters and parcels into upper decks and lower decks and cabins and messes.

When he came off duty, Drew decided, he would pick up his letters, then find some quiet place to read them, and daydream of Kitty and Rowangarth and the end of the war and Kitty, and getting married at All Souls. To Kitty.

He turned away from the sunlight that came blindingly off the sea, blinking in the sudden gloom as he ran lightly down steel stairways to the wireless office to begin his four-hour watch. He felt good, now there were letters to look forward to.

He heard the faraway keening of a bosun's pipe, felt the rhythmic rise and fall of the deck beneath him. They were at full speed ahead again and another stint of duty was about to begin. Soon, when the day ended, the white ensign would be lowered and the ship's bugler would play "Sunset". Another day over; one day nearer to going home.

His watch kept, Drew had showered and changed. The sun was less hot now, and a cooling breeze blew through the porthole which need not yet be closed and darkened. There had been four letters from Kitty; three of which he had read in date order. Now, like the cherry on the top of an iced bun, he would read the last one. Slowly.

He smiled indulgently to see the marks of her lips on the back of the envelope; a bright red, abandoned kiss; turning the letter over, prolonging the moment of opening, scrutinizing the postmark: London. 18:VI:44. Carefully he slit it open, marvelling that it was something she had touched and kissed.

The pages of thin airmail paper crackled tantalizingly as he opened them.

Montpelier
June 17, 1944

My dearest love,
    Today by the day, on Monday by the date, should have been our first wedding anniversary. This letter is to tell you that I wish with all my heart it had been so; that we had been married as we planned to be and that I had had your child. I wish that on our honeymoon we had conceived it; wish that now I had it in my arms, to remember you by.
    I try, in all the hurt of wanting you, to tell myself that a year of our separation is over, that we are one year nearer the day when we will truly be married and know the absolute joy of wiping out the years of loving we lost.

Now, I find comfort in remembering Roscoe Street and where it all started. I live it often in my heart, remembering every word we spoke, every kiss, every touch. I want to weep with happiness that I was your first love. No matter what happens, I know I shall always be that.

I will write to you tomorrow, before I start our tour. Maybe tomorrow the pain of wanting you so desperately will have lessened, though I hope not.

Close your eyes, and know I am kissing you. Whenever things get bad, call for me with your heart and I shall be only a whisper away.

I want you so much, my darling, need you to hold me and make love to me. Please take good care of yourself. You are so precious to me that without you I would die.

I love you with all my heart and with every breath I take.

Your Kitty

He folded the letter and put it back in the pale blue envelope. Then he closed his eyes and touched the mark of her kiss with his lips.

"I love you, too, my darling girl. *You* take care . . ."

"Dammit, I haven't got a cigarette!" Julia jumped to her feet. "I'm going out!"

"Where?" Nathan's eyes were anxious.

"Just out!" Her voice was sharp.

782

"Then I'll come with you."

He knew where she would go, wanted to be there when finally she gave way to the tears she had not shed at the graveside.

"No! I'll be all right!" She sucked in her breath, holding it, letting it out in little huffs. Then she shook her head and dropped to her knees at his feet, laying her head on his lap. "Sorry, darling. Didn't mean to snap. But I'd rather go on my own, if you don't mind."

"If that's what you really want?" He knew her so well that he did not try to prevent her.

"Yes. I need to see she's all right, say good night to her."

"If you're sure? But I'll be there in half an hour, to walk home with you."

"Yes. Do that, Nathan. And you do understand, don't you?" Wearily she pushed herself upright, shaping her lips into a brief smile. "It's just that tonight, I want to do it for Drew."

"Drew would want you to weep for her too."

"I know. But there aren't any tears there. Just a hard lump inside me. I can't cry, but I'm not going to do anything foolish, I promise you. Just give us a little time together?"

He walked to the front door with her, hand on her shoulder, then kissed her gently, watching her go. There was such rage in her, he thought; such despair. Beside the grave this afternoon she had stood alone and apart, fighting her grief. She insisted that it should be he, Nathan, who took the service. She would be all right, she said, only *he* must do it. One last thing, for Kitty.

Then Alice had crossed over to her side and taken her hand, standing close so their shoulders touched. He had been grateful for that gesture, and that Alice understood.

"Come back to the house, love?" Alice whispered afterwards, but Julia had remained after all but himself had left, watching each spade of earth, wincing as it fell on that sad coffin, taking all the pain of it on herself because neither Amelia nor Albert nor Drew was there. Wars did that to people, he sighed; war had even prevented a last goodbye.

He returned to the small sitting room, glancing at the mantel clock. Half an hour he would give her! That was all!

Julia opened the churchyard gate carefully, remembering the creaking that no amount of oiling had cured. Then she walked on the grass at the side of the gravelled path so her footsteps should not be heard. She didn't know exactly why she must be here tonight, at Kitty's graveside. All she could be sure of was that her mind was in torment and she was unable to gather her thoughts together.

But thoughts did no good, nor thinking. Not thinking of what might have been had Kitty and Tatty left Montpelier Mews just five minutes earlier last Sunday afternoon, or five minutes later. And thinking that if someone in an office at Plymouth Barracks had not written out a drafting order with

Drew's name on it or even if Kitty hadn't been in Egypt with ENSA, today would have been different. It was no use saying that today would never have happened. Today always happened just as tomorrow never came, but if only one of the ifs had not been, then today would have been kinder and more merciful.

She walked towards the grave. If there was any comfort to be gleaned then it was the fact, she sighed, that Kitty lay beside Mother. Helen Mary, wife of John.

Kathryn Norma Clementina Sutton, beloved of Andrew. Kitty and Drew no longer. Did he know yet? Had Nathan's letter arrived? How was it for Amelia and Albert? What could she say, do, promise to God, so they may not suffer so much? She had not for one second taken her eyes from Kitty during the service, willing her thoughts and love to her, wherever it was that her spirit roamed. Nathan was sure she was with God already; she, Julia, wanted it to be so but her faith had no substance now. All she could be sure of was that Kitty was dead and lay, now, with the Rowangarth Suttons. She was Drew's. Pendenys should not have her. And she was one of Rowangarth's Clan; she belonged to Rowangarth, even in death.

Julia slipped to her knees beside the rounded mound of moist earth, touching the wreath of red roses to tell Kitty they were really from Kentucky, from Mom and Pa. Then she looked at the cushion of flowers; each one of them picked with the morning dew still on them.

Jack Catchpole had made those wreaths and Gracie brought them to Rowangarth, giving them to Miss Clitherow, then joining Bas who sat disconsolately on the seat in the linden walk.

Bas was the only one of the Clan at the graveside, standing white-faced, his hand in Gracie's. Her Clan had come together briefly for Daisy's wedding. There was such happiness that day, Julia brooded, that she should have known it could not last.

She glanced upward. The sun was sinking over the stable block, the evening clouds touched with apricot. There was such a silence she could hear her own breathing.

"Do you know I am here, Kitty?"

She waited, eyes closed, but nothing moved and there was no voice that answered, "Yes, and I love you, Aunt Julia." No matter how hard she tried, she was unable to snatch the smallest whisper of comfort to help ease the ache inside her or loose the tears she needed still to weep.

A word, a sign — is that too much to ask, God? She wanted no miracles, no parting of the waters; no blinding road-to-Damascus light. All she needed to know was that Kitty was at peace; that she had forgiven the world for what it had done to her.

There was a sound behind her. Someone was coming. She rose to her feet, then slowly turned.

"Did I startle you, Miss Julia?" Jack Catchpole standing there, half hidden by a yew tree.

"No. I heard you coming, Jack. Just making sure everything is all right. Have you come to spray the flowers?"

"No, miss. And happen you'll have to pardon the liberty, 'cause I got to thinking it wasn't right. I said so to Gracie. 'There should be something for her from Drew. She would have wanted something . . .'"

"Something I forgot?"

"No, Miss Julia. Weren't nothing you forgot; just something Drew would have wanted me to do. I've taken the liberty to bring these — from him to her."

He brought his hand from behind his back, offering the flowers. They were fashioned into a wedding bouquet and even in the half-light Julia knew exactly what they were.

"Mother's orchids!"

"Aye. It's June. They're in flower again. I'd have mentioned it, then thought it best I didn't. Two wreaths, you asked for; one of red roses and one of Rowangarth flowers. So that's what I did for you.

"But the white orchids were there, and nowt would do but that I made the lass her bouquet — the one she never carried last year . . ."

The orchids glowed waxily white in the apricot sunset, beautiful beyond believing and she knew they were the sign she had asked for.

"Mother . . .?" she whispered.

It's all right, Julia. She's with me. The orchids are to let you know . . .

Her mother's voice, inside her heart; dearest Mother, who was happy again, with Pa. Mother would take care of Kitty!

"You give them to her, Jack," she whispered, closing her eyes, biting hard on her bottom lip.

He bent slowly, awkwardly, to lay the bouquet beside the red roses.

"There you are, Kitty lass. You couldn't go without your flowers, now could you?"

Julia covered her face with her hands and the tears came, hot and salty. And the ache eased from her heart and the rage and despair. Her shoulders shook, and Catchpole gathered her to him. Not in an act of familiarity between the mistress of Rowangarth and a servant, but as two people, joined in the love of a young girl with mischief in her eyes; an elderly man and a middle-aged, childless woman, sharing a great sadness.

"There now, Miss Julia — you have a cry then. Catchpole understands."

So Julia gave way to great jerking sobs for Kitty, for Amelia and Albert and for Drew; took their grief on herself and cried it out into the June twilight.

"There, there. Don't take on so?" Hesitantly he patted her back. "If I thought you'd be so upset, I'd never have done it. It seemed right, though, at the time."

"You *were* right, Jack and I'm glad you did it. Mother wanted Kitty to have her flowers, I know that now, and when I write to Drew he'll be glad about it. But I was too blind with self-pity to see it.

I needed to cry, but the tears wouldn't come. Thank you for being here when I needed you."

"Well — if you're sure . . .?"

"I'm sure. One day I'll tell you how much those orchids meant to me. Good night, Jack, and bless you."

She listened as his footfalls faded, heard the squeal of the gate. Then she stood, a small sad smile on her lips, drained of all emotion, yet knowing that now she could begin, from this trembling moment on, to learn to live with her loss and help Drew through it. Drew would need all her love and support one day — when he came home to loneliness.

The gate opened again, and Nathan stood there. Half an hour, he'd said, and now he was here. She held out her hand to him, squaring her shoulders, lifting her chin.

"Are you all right, Julia?"

"Not all right. That's going to take time, but I think the worst is over now. See, darling . . ." She smiled down at the bouquet. "I came here full of rage, wanting to make sense of it. I didn't know where Kitty was; if she was a lost soul or if she was at peace." She linked his arm, then twined her fingers in his. "Do you know that Drew worried about those white orchids. When they planned to be married, it was, and he asked me if his gran's flowers would be ready in time.

"I told him that old-fashioned gardeners like Catchpole know how to bring plants forward, or hold them back, and he would see to it that Kitty carried the orchids at her wedding."

"But sadly . . ." he prompted.

"Sadly," she whispered, "we didn't have our wedding, and I forgot, in my self-pity, that Drew would have wanted her to have them this afternoon — a last goodbye, I suppose."

"Yet Catchpole remembered."

"Him, and Mother."

"You think Catchpole somehow knew he must make Kitty her orchids?"

"Yes. Mother told him. She wanted us to know that Kitty is all right."

She let go a shuddering sigh and they walked in silence through the village and past the almshouses to Home Farm lane.

A first star was shining, alone and bright, directly above Rowangarth, and Julia smiled up at it and whispered, "Goodnight, Kitty darling."

"Do you want to cry some more for her, Julia?"

"Yes, but not just now. Catchpole got the brunt of it, I'm afraid. And there'll be more tears to come. I'll have to help Drew over it, and Amelia and Albert, but right now I feel drained. I've accepted now that Kitty has gone from us, and I feel limp and useless."

"My dearest Julia, you were ever the same. Your joys are so joyful and your sorrows so keen. Don't change. I'll be there to share the good times and help you through the bad ones."

"I know you will. Did you know I have a roll of colour film. Bas got it for me and I was saving it for

Drew's wedding. I shall put it my camera and take a photograph of Kitty's grave and when Drew and Amelia and Albert are able to face it, I'll send it to them. Drew will be glad to know that Kitty had her wedding bouquet at the very end."

They were crossing the lawn towards the open conservatory doors when Nathan said, "Perhaps you won't go along with this, darling, but Kitty was so special, so naughty and happy and loved — why don't we give her the white orchids? Why can't they be her memorial so we can always keep her near us — and remember her especially every June when they flower?"

"What a very lovely idea!" Julia said softly. "Of course they must be hers. Not Mother's orchids, but Kitty's orchids. Dear, lovely Nathan. Only you could think of a thing like that!"

"But I didn't think of it. There was this little voice in my ear, actually, and it sounded very much like your mother's. Now let's get inside. You're cold. I can feel you shivering. Tomorrow I'll come with you to the churchyard and we'll take the photograph together. Would you like me to?"

"Very much," she whispered. "And, Nathan — even if I haven't told you so lately, I love you. You do know it, don't you?"

"I know it," he said softly and thankfully. "And I love you too . . ."

CHAPTER
THIRTY-SIX

December 1945

Liverpool had changed. Bombed buildings still stood defiant like blackened, broken teeth, but there was no bomb rubble in the streets now, and on bomb sites there was evidence that, come summer, they would be covered with grass and wild flowers.

The sailor turned his back on the burned-out shell of a church at the top of Bold Street. Best get back to the hotel; get something to eat, then tomorrow say goodbye to Liverpool.

He had been a fool to come, had expected the vibrations of a lost love to be hanging on the air still, and that he had only to call her name with his heart and she would answer him. But she was not there when he stood outside Ma's lodgings in Roscoe Street, nor had he found her on the dockside. The warehouse in which the ENSA concert was held that night was padlocked and deserted.

He should not have come here; should have taken the train to York and not to Lime Street; made straight for Rowangarth and the dearness of it. Yet it had started in Liverpool, and in this bombed, bawdy city he had thought to say his first goodbye, knowing that when finally he got home there would be another goodbye to say; a grave to visit. He had a photograph of that grave, yet still he must face it before he could finally accept that he would never see her again.

He lingered to marvel at the lighted shop windows and streetlights that burned brightly, even though it was only four in the afternoon. Once, there had been no lights; only a blackout so dense you'd wanted to reach out and push it aside. Once, those shopfronts were mostly boarded up because shattered plate glass had been impossible to replace in wartime.

It wasn't wartime now, though. All at once peace came, and not just the amazing peace that fell over all Europe; victory in Europe and mad, frantic celebrations. Britain gone crazy for a week. He had seen it on newsreels in the ship's recreation space; specially flown out there so those whose war had not yet ended would take heart and know that peace was in sight for the whole world.

Peace came sooner than the world expected. When the sailors of the British Pacific Fleet expected their war would be many more years ending, a bomber of the United States Army Air Force flew high over the city of Hiroshima. On its nose was painted the name of the mother of the pilot who flew it: *Enola Gay*. The day was Monday, the date 6 August 1945, the time 08.15 hours. *Enola*

Gay carried one bomb, and one bomb had been enough to wipe out an entire city, kill half of those who lived in it. Three days later, a second bomb was dropped on Nagasaki with the same terrible aftermath.

Those two bombs were in no way ordinary. Their power was drawn from a chain-reaction in uranium; neutrons hitting atoms the papers said, but few had heard of neutrons or atoms or of chain-reaction. All an astounded world knew was that two vicious explosions caused Japan to offer unconditional surrender, and the war had been over.

A vicious wind that blew straight off the River Mersey took the sailor's cap and carried it rolling over and over to the feet of a Wren. She picked it up, looking around for its owner then stopped stock-still. He heard her gasp, "Drew!" then she was smiling and it was as if only yesterday Daisy had rushed into his arms at the Pierhead stop of the Overhead Railway, knocking off his cap in her joy at seeing him.

He walked towards the Wren, and when he was still a few feet away she sent the cap spinning back to him, saying, "Yours I believe, sailor!" just as she had done it and said it four years ago when first they met. "And what the hell," she demanded, all at once in control of her voice, "are you doing in Liverpool? I thought you were in the Pacific."

"Got demobbed this morning in Plymouth Barracks. Hi, Lyn." She was wearing her greatcoat and a muffler, her face pinched with cold; she was the very last person he had thought to meet in Liverpool. "Long time . . ."

He had not thought his voice could sound so normal nor that she could be so little changed.

"So what are you doing here? Daisy's on leave, but you wouldn't know, of course." She turned her back against the wind, pulling up the collar of her coat, pushing her gloved hands into her pockets. "You'll have been quite a few weeks getting back." She was able to look at him now, after the first shock of their meeting. He was thinner. His face, beneath the cold, was tanned and his hair fairer — the sun out there, no doubt. "Keth's on leave too."

"Yes," he nodded, trying to come to terms with being here and meeting Lyn, and not Kitty. And it wasn't that everything seemed different now; wasn't just the lights blazing all over the place nor the absence of barrage balloons overhead or that there were fewer uniforms about.

This place was different, but so was Drew Sutton, because he was no longer the young sailor who took out his sister whenever his ship was alongside; took out her friend, too; might have fallen in love with her if something inside him hadn't insisted that he should wait.

"I don't suppose it occurred to you to ring Hellas House?" Her voice cut into his thoughts.

"I did, actually. Engaged, as usual."

"So what brings you to Liverpool, or shouldn't I ask?"

"Feel free, Lyn. Don't think it was such a good idea, now you come to mention it. I was trying to sort myself out, I suppose."

"Well, there are no traces to kick over, so you must be looking for memories."

He winced at her directness, at the uncanny way she had known.

"Look — you're cold," he said. "We shouldn't be standing here. What time are you on watch? Lates?"

"Yes. On duty at six. Got fed up in the Wrennery without Daisy, so I decided to do a shop crawl — see if I could find a decent tablet of soap or a lipstick. Didn't get either."

"Then would you like to come back with me? I'm booked in at the Adelphi for the night. I'd appreciate someone to talk to — if you want to listen, that is?"

"Why not?" she shrugged.

They spoke little as they walked to the hotel, except he said, "It's strange, seeing lights here. There were lights in Sydney, of course, but I always connected Liverpool with the blackout somehow."

It wasn't until they were sitting in the foyer and Drew had ordered a tray of tea that Lyn said, "They don't work, Drew — sentimental journeys, I mean."

She laid her greatcoat and cap and scarf over the chair beside her, then leaned back, hands relaxed on her lap.

"I realize that now. I should have gone straight home. So where do we begin, Lyn?"

796

"Here and now, I would say. No time like the present. When did you land?"

"Three days ago, at Rosyth. Left my ship behind in Sydney. My demob number came up, you see — first in, first out. They packed us all onto a trooper; airmen, pongos and navy bods, all grinning like Cheshire cats, Blighty-bound."

"What is your number, Drew?"

"Twenty-five."

"Mine's thirty-two. Reckon I'll get out early March."

"Any plans, Lyn?"

"Yes. All cut and dried. I suppose Daisy would mention that Auntie Blod is going to marry my father. She's going out to Kenya as soon as she can get a passage, or a flight."

"You're not going back home, then?"

Things seemed easier, he thought, now they were talking, though she still had the habit of looking him straight in the eyes when she spoke. Direct as ever.

"No. And Kenya ceased to be home when I was sent to school in England. I've no wish to return and anyway, they'll not want me playing gooseberry.

"But to cut a long story short, Auntie Blod's cottage was to come on the market when she left it, but the owner has agreed to sell it to me for four hundred pounds."

"And you're happy with that?"

"Seems a fair price to me. Auntie Blod is leaving all her furniture — just taking a few small, sentimental things with her, so I'm very lucky really.

There's an awful shortage of furniture and pots and pans, and things. People thought the minute the war was over the shops would be full overnight, but I think things are worse than ever now. I'll be very cosy. It'll just seem strange being there without her, that's all."

A waiter brought a tray, setting it on the table at Lyn's side and she lifted the lid of the pot, stirred the contents, then said, "Milk in first?"

"Whatever."

She concentrated on pouring, remembering that he took one lump of sugar and very little milk. "Wish Daisy were here."

"Me, too. How will you manage, Lyn — financially, I mean? Have you a job lined up?"

"Can't apply for a job till I know when exactly I'll be demobbed, but people will be going on holiday again now the war's over and Llangollen is a popular place. I'm hoping to find a job in one of the hotels — receptionist, or telephonist. I've enough saved to put down a deposit and pay my legal fees and I've figured my demob gratuity will be about eighty pounds, so I won't be destitute. My father agreed to guarantee my mortgage repayments with the bank — the least he could do, I suppose. I'll manage fine. What about you?"

"I'll go back to Rowangarth, get used to being a civvie again, make a fresh start. I'll manage."

"Do you want to talk about it, Drew?" Lyn set down her cup and saucer. "Would talking about her help?"

798

"How can you ask that after what happened between you and me?" Drew whispered.

"But nothing happened! That was the trouble, I suppose. I had a crush on you and you loved Kitty. It happens all the time. I'm over it now. You didn't break my heart, you know — just dented my pride a bit."

Liar, liar, *liar*!

"You're a funny girl." He managed a smile.

"Well, thanks a heap! Thought I was really rather something, actually! But are you coming to terms with things now?"

"I thought I was. It was Nathan who wrote telling me. Then Mother wrote, but still I didn't believe it. I thought that if I convinced myself those letters were a mistake, then there'd be one from Kitty next time we docked. But there wasn't.

"Then Mother sent me a photograph of her grave. There were two wreaths on it and a bouquet of orchids. Catchpole made it. Said it was the bouquet she should have carried on her wedding day."

"That's bad, Drew. How did you cope? Didn't it tear you up, seeing it?"

"No. I got used to the fact, though, that I'd have to go to the churchyard and see it when I got home. Only when I'd actually seen her grave, I told myself, would I start believing it. I was thousands of miles away, you see. Distance seemed to cushion it. Then the trooper docked and there were trains waiting for us. Overnight to barracks in Plymouth, just like it always had been. I think that was when it hit me, when I knew I'd got to get my head out of the sand. It's why I came here, I suppose."

"Does anyone know you're back?"

"No. Mother said it would be marvellous if I got home for Christmas, though. She'll be expecting me any day now."

"Home for Christmas! So will I be, Drew. First Christmas leave since I joined up, would you believe? I'm glad about it, really. Don't suppose there'll be another chance to have Christmas with Auntie Blod."

"You'll miss her."

"She'll only be in Kenya. And before long, we'll be able to phone abroad. We'll ring each other up on special occasions and write all the time. And there's Daisy, don't forget. When she and Keth get settled, I'll be able to visit her. We'll keep in touch. We'll have to. I'm to be godmother to their first baby, she says."

"That'll be the day!" He had wanted children too; Rowangarth wanted them. It hurt just to think about it.

"Oh, I don't think they'll wait once Keth gets a job and they find somewhere to live. Keth wants to go into teaching. What do you think about Bas and Gracie getting married, then?"

"I was glad for them. They planned to do it sneaky, you know, Bas insisting that his English passport entitled him to marry in England without asking his CO's permission. American troops have to get permission — I don't know if it's to protect the soldier or his intended.

"Anyway, Bas decided he'd best go through official channels, and once leave started again they had a very quiet wedding. Nathan married them. Just Gracie's folks there, and Julia and Tatty."

"It would have to be quiet, wouldn't it, Drew? Daisy didn't go, even. She told me they had a week in Edinburgh, though. Gracie had never been to Scotland. Seems she's still at Rowangarth and living in the bothy, though now they aren't flying missions at Burtonwood, Bas gets loads of leave. Gracie gets sleeping-out passes, and most times they stay at Rowangarth. Does it hurt, Drew, us talking about Keth and Daisy and Bas and Gracie?"

"It hurts like hell. Is there any more tea in the pot?"

"Yes, but it's gone cold. Do you think they'll let us have a fresh one?"

"We can try. Pity you can't have dinner with me."

"I'd have liked that. I'm starving, actually."

"Never knew you when you weren't! Lyn?" All at once his face was serious, his eyes troubled. "It's all right — you and me, I mean. We can still be friends? No ill feelings?"

"I've told you, clot, no ill feelings!" She held out her hand. "We'll always be good friends, I hope. We'll have to be. I think Daisy's got you in mind as a godparent too, when it happens. Can't be glowering at each other over Nathan's font, now can we?"

801

"Good old Daiz! You'll write to me, Lyn — let me know how things go for you?"

"Of course I will! Anyway, Daisy'll be writing to you, won't she, so I can slip a PS on the bottom of her letters?"

"A postscript. Of course."

"We-e-ll, I might sent you the odd postcard from Llangollen; y'know, Welsh ladies in tall hats — when the Wrens sling me out, that is. Reckon you'd best not order more tea, Drew. I've got to get going."

She rose to her feet and he helped her into her greatcoat. Slowly she buttoned it, then said, "I was only kidding. Of course I'll write. And surely we'll meet up one day, if only at some dim and distant christening. Wherever she and Keth end up, Daisy is going to want her children christened at All Souls."

"Of course. I'll walk with you to the Pierhead. Still at the Liver Building?"

"Still there. One day I'll be able to tell my grandchildren what a very ordinary war I had!"

A waiter appeared with the bill, which Drew signed with his name and room number, and as they went out into the cold of the late-December afternoon, a flurry of sleet hit them. Heads down, they walked toward the riverfront, shoulders hunched against the wind.

"Ouch!" Lyn gasped. "Welcome home, sailor!" and they both laughed.

There were fifteen minutes to go before the watches changed so they hurried up the steps of the massive square building and into the lobby to stand gasping from the cold.

"It seems a long time since I was at the Pierhead," Drew said, less tense now. "Remember Charlie and his cheese sarnies? Is he still there?"

"Haven't seen him in ages. Reckon he'll have retired a millionaire to the South of France now it's over. He made a crafty cheese wad though, didn't he? But best I get up to the sixth floor, Drew." She held out her hand. "I'm glad you're going home to Rowangarth. Once you're there, things can only get better."

Her voice trailed uneasily away and she turned abruptly and made for the lifts.

"Lyn!"

She spun round as he called her name, then walked back to where he stood.

"You will write — sometimes?"

"I'll write, Drew. That's a promise." She lifted her fingertips to her lips then laid them on his cheek. "Take care. See you . . ."

A lift door slammed open and it was her cue to run towards it, away from him. She hurried inside, pressing the button, her heart was thudding. Oh, but she was a good actress! Real smooth she'd been, when all the time there was such a shaking inside her that surely he must have noticed.

Drew was back. Tomorrow he would likely get the first train out. But she wouldn't look up his train time, and she wouldn't phone him in the morning just to say how nice it had been, meeting after so long. She wouldn't do it because she dared not. She wanted him every bit as much, but it would be useless offering her love to someone who still must stand beside Kitty's grave; finally admit she was gone from his life for all time.

Poor Kitty. She closed her eyes and said a fervent thank you for her own life, complicated though it had become again.

The lift whined to a stop, the doors opened. Time for another six hours at the switchboard, though watches were less frantic now, callers less demanding, less impatient.

She would not try to dismiss Drew from her mind. Instead she would wallow in the misery of seeing him again and of knowing he still loved Kitty. It hadn't been fair, that lousy rotten flying bomb.

"Flaming Norah!" she hissed, then pushed open the doors above which "TELEPHONISTS" was painted. "Roll on my demob!"

"It might have been nice," Daisy said, her hand in Keth's, "if we could have had Christmas leave. Lyn's managed it."

"Never mind. Next Christmas we'll both be civilians and, with a bit of luck, in our own home."

They were walking to Denniston House to call on Tatty, who had phoned half an hour ago that they come at once because she had *news*!

"And will we have a baby by then, or be expecting one?" She wanted a child. Soon, she would be twenty-six, and part of her dreamings had been a family of three before she was thirty. "The war is over. There's no reason why we shouldn't. If I got pregnant, I'd get out of the Wrens a lot sooner."

"We'll start a family," Keth said softly, "when I have a job and can provide for one, and a roof over our heads."

"You can be very bossy, Captain Purvis!" She wanted to say how easily they could afford children; that prams and cots and baby clothes would be no trouble at all. But she did not because she was so happy, so grateful that Keth had survived the war. Drew, too. Very soon now, Drew would be home for good. Aunt Julia had heard from him ages ago, telling her not to write any more letters to HMS *Newton*, which could only mean he was on his way home. Not to Kitty, though . . .

"I wonder what Tatty's news is?" Deliberately Daisy pushed away unhappy thoughts. "She sounded very excited. Do you suppose it's got something to do with Bill Benson?"

"There you go! Matchmaking again!" All at once, Keth realized how lucky he had been. His army days were as good as over and he and Daisy had a future once more. Not like Drew. What would he do? What would Keth Purvis have done if there had been a letter to Washington, telling him that Daisy had been killed in the Liverpool blitz? "You know I love you, darling, and that there was never anyone else but you?" he said softly.

"I know it. Sometimes even now, I can't believe it's all over, that I'll be a civilian in six months. Then something reminds me of Kitty, and I'd give almost anything for it not to have happened. How am I to face Drew? What will I say to him, Keth? What words are there to tell him how I feel?"

"There aren't any, so you don't have to try to say them. Just be there for him. Sometimes a hug says more than all the words in the world."

They had come to the crossroads now, and the signpost that pointed to Creesby and Holdenby, its arms restored.

"This was where we used to wait for the RAF transport to take us to the dance, Keth. That was where Tatty met Tim Thomson, at one of the sergeants' mess hops." Tim was dead too.

She clasped Keth's hand more tightly as they crunched up the gravel of the drive to see Tatiana waiting for them at a window.

"Oh, come in do, out of the cold! We've got the house to ourselves and there's so much to tell you!" She laid logs on the fire, telling them to warm themselves. "And you don't want tea, do you?"

They said they didn't, that they would rather talk.

"Good! Then sit down, both of you." She settled herself on the hearthrug, just like Aunt Julia, Daisy thought. "Now, first things first! I didn't buy you a wedding present because there was nothing in the shops. Come to think of it, there still isn't, but this is the first part of it. Bill painted it especially for you both." She gave the picture to Daisy, smiling proudly. "See, it's got its Latin name — *Bellis perennis* — on it, but it's your flower really."

Against a pale green background was a clump of tiny daisies, painted in pastels and framed in delicate gold.

"Bill signed it as well, just in case he gets famous! Do you like it?"

"It's beautiful, Tatty! I didn't know Bill was an artist."

"He didn't know either. It happened when he got his sight back and the first thing he saw was a wallflower, so he drew it as a sort of memento, I suppose. That was when everyone knew there was an artist in him wanting to get out."

"Where is Bill? I'd like to tell him how good it is."

"He's in the loft, painting. He stays there for hours and only breaks off when he's hungry. He sold a set of four flower drawings last week — his first ever — and that's what gave me the idea for yours. Four would look lovely, hung in a group. Would you like to choose three other flowers — sort of special to you both — and then he can get on with them?"

"Tatty, that's marvellous! I know already what one of them must be! I'd like a wild bluebell and one day I might tell you why," she laughed, blushing prettily. "Keth and I will decide on the other two, and let you know. Now — what's the other news, because I know you're bursting to tell? Is it something about you and Bill?"

"No. Bill is a dear friend and we're very happy muddling along together, him living in the flat above the stables and me here with Karl. Perhaps we'll be lovers one day — I don't know. Right now I'm concentrating on my leg and getting it mobile again. I'm riding my bike when the weather allows, and doing exercises. Ewart keeps an eye on me and it's because of Ewart, really, that I've got piece of news number two to tell you."

"Go on!" Daisy demanded, snuggling closer to Keth, slipping her fingers into his.

"Well, there's an operation I can have for my face, he says." She moved a swing of curls with her hand to show the ugly red scar left by the bomb. "I'm glad, really, because I can't always be hiding it behind my hair. It's the operation they started to do for the airmen who were badly burned, and now it's available for everybody."

"You must be very relieved," Daisy sympathized. "I mean, you being so good-looking, then having that happen. How did you feel about it?"

"When I finally got to see my face, you mean? Amazingly it wasn't the shock they'd thought it would be. I hadn't actually seen myself in a mirror, but I could feel. I knew something was very wrong. But then Sam visited not long after that. He was one of the airmen I used to take out and he'd been one of the McIndoe guinea pigs. What they'd done to his face was almost a miracle.

"Anyway, when they finally gave me a mirror, I just took one look and shuddered, then said out loud, 'Not bad. Not bad at all, considering it might have been me who was killed that Sunday.' Drew

808

wouldn't have cared what Kitty looked like, you know . . ."

"No, he wouldn't. When will your operation be?"

"In early summer, I think. There's a queue, and men and women in the Forces get priority, which is only right. I'm really very lucky. I don't mind waiting."

"You deserve all the luck in the world," Keth smiled, "and I hope you and Bill will get together one day. You're such a nice person, things have got to go right for you. Do you remember what a brat you were?"

"I do! Coddled and spoiled. I bet you all used to hate it when I came to play with you!"

"It wasn't you," Daisy defended. "The Clan didn't like your nanny, though. She restricted us a bit — especially when we'd decided to climb trees, or have a spitting contest."

"I remember. Kitty was the best spitter, wasn't she?" Her eyes filled with tears and she dashed them away. "I do miss her. I'm glad I'm not going back to Montpelier. Poor Drew. I want him back home, but it's going to be awful for him." She blew her nose loudly then smiled. "But there's more news, and it's also to do with Ewart. He and mother are getting married!"

"They are *what*? My, but they kept that quiet, didn't they?"

"Not from me, they didn't. But I'm really glad about it."

"But when is it to be, and can I tell Mam?"

"Of course you can. There'll be an announcement in the *Yorkshire Post* tomorrow. Only a quiet affair. They're getting a special licence instead of having the banns read. Nathan is going to marry them and Mother is asking Uncle Igor to give her away — for a second time. She wasn't happy with my father, but she'll be okay with Ewart. She'll be moving into his house and Karl will stay here, so the village won't be able to gossip about me and Bill."

"Tatty! I've just thought! Does your grandmother know yet?"

"She does! She wants Mother to get married in London from Cheyne Walk like the first time — in the Russian church. She's a crafty one. But Mother said no way would she, so with a bit of luck the Petrovska will have a mood on her and stay away!"

"Well! When you said you had news I didn't think it would be that good," Daisy smiled. "But are you sure you'll be all right on your own in this big house?"

"If I'm not, then Bill can move in with me!" Tatty giggled. "Now wouldn't the village go to town on that? And there is another bit of news — for what it's worth. Did you know that the Army is leaving Pendenys at last? Uncle Nathan is to meet someone from the War Office there in a couple of days. The Army will hand back the keys and Uncle Nathan has got to agree that the seals they put on the tower door haven't been tampered with. Grandfather Sutton had all the furniture stored in the tower, remember?"

"Tatty — do you think I could get to have a look at it? D'you know, I've never been in there." Daisy breathed, then thought how peculiar it was that she had enough money to *buy* it! Now that *would* give the village something to talk about!

"I've been in," Keth grimaced. "Once, and that was enough!"

"When there was the fire, you mean," Tatty frowned. "when Grandmother Clementina died? Doesn't it seem a long time ago?"

"Ten years, almost. When I think of what Keth did to get Bas out," Daisy shuddered, "I still get goose pimples."

"So do I," Keth laughed.

Then all at the same time they were quiet because each was thinking back to the way it had been and could never be again. Golden summers before the war and special, sparkling Christmases. The Clan together for all time, it would seem.

Now Kitty was gone and Gracie a Sutton, though she never could, never would try, even, to take her place. Best they should leave the Clan on an enchanted day when windflowers danced for an April bride. Now the Clan could only be a picture in colour; one special moment of complete happiness, a memory to keep in a silver frame.

"We shouldn't be laughing, should we?" Tatty whispered. "Kitty, I mean . . ."

"But we *should*. Wherever Kitty went there was mischief and fun," Keth said fondly. "She wouldn't want us not to laugh."

"I think she would want us to remember her always, especially when we're together." Daisy gazed into the woodflames as if some part of Kitty were there. "If we do that, we're still the Clan, aren't we?"

It was then that the phone rang and when Tatiana returned from answering it, her face was pale, her eyes anxious.

"That was Aunt Julia," she whispered. "Drew's home . . ."

Julia knew her son was home. Mothers' instinct told her to stand at the window on the half-landing and look down the drive. So she stood, breath indrawn, eyes wide, counting off the seconds until he was standing there, looking at Rowangarth as if deciding whether or not it was a mirage. His cap was jammed forward over his eyebrows, his shoulders hunched against the cold. His kit, she knew, he would have left at the gatelodge.

He stood very still and she willed him to look at the window and see her there, and wave. But he did not. All at once he straightened his shoulders, pulled his hands from his pockets and set off on the last long hundred yards.

Quickly she opened the front door, standing on the top step as she always did, as her mother had always done, waiting, welcoming, savouring each second that brought him closer. Then she lifted her hand and he was near enough for her to see his answering smile. She ran down the steps, arms wide, and he gathered her close.

Neither spoke. There were no words for this moment. He was home after more than six years; home to Rowangarth. And Rowangarth would reach out to him and comfort him so the bitterness she knew was there inside him would fade all the sooner and he could begin to live again; to live without Kitty.

Julia clung tightly, not wanting to break the spell, let the world in on this moment so things would be said that were best not said. Beneath the thickness of his greatcoat she could feel his thinness; sensed the unhappiness that stiffened his body.

She took a step back from him, cupping his face, whispering, "Welcome home, son, and oh, darling, I'm so sorry. So very, very sorry."

Unspeaking, he took her hand and together they walked up the steps.

"I'm not used to it yet. Will you give me time, and will you talk about her, Mother?"

"If you want to. She's next to Mother, Drew. She isn't alone. Come into the winter parlour — it's warm there."

He followed her into the little room, sitting down in front of the fire without taking off his heavy coat, pushing his hands into his pockets again as if hugging himself, holding tightly to his feelings.

"I loved her so much. I still love her — I always will. How am I to live with it? How am I to look at a grave that is all that is left of her? You know how it is, Mother. How do I cope with the loneliness?"

"Drew — there is something that must be said so I will say it now. I know how it is; know the bitterness and anger. I raged against the world because I loved Andrew so much I thought my love would keep him from harm. I wasted eighteen years learning that life goes on. It must. The world couldn't stop turning just to bear witness to my grief.

"For sixteen years I refused to visit Andrew's grave. I thought that once I did I would have to accept that he was gone. Mother begged me to — Nathan, as well. Goodbye. A word I would not say. I robbed Nathan of so much happiness, but he loved me so he waited."

Drew rose to his feet, unbuttoning his coat, shrugging out of it. He did it without speaking, as if he were trying to pick words from the jumble in his mind.

"Mother — it took you a long time; perhaps that's how it will be for me. I so looked forward to this moment of coming home, knowing I'd been lucky and made it through the war. I wanted to stay alive because there was a future for me with Kitty. Now, she's —"

"She's at rest. She's with the Rowangarth Suttons. I am asking — *begging* — you to go to her;

814

to say hullo, then say goodbye. Do it now, Drew, because if you don't you'll only be half alive and when you have done it you'll be able to start living again. Be thankful, as I should have been, for the short time you had together, then let her go."

"I don't want to forget her." He would not shift his gaze from the fireglow.

"And she would want you never to forget. If only you will say goodbye, Drew, then we can all talk about her with happiness and without fear of hurting you. Do you know what Jin Dobb said to me once? She told me I would love again and I was angry. How dare she presume, I thought, even to think there was anyone who could measure up to Andrew?

"But she said there was first love and last love and all kinds of loving in between and that one day, if I would let myself, I would be happy again. I'm not saying you must love again. I just want you to know that I went through it too. What I am saying must seem harsh and cruel, but I have said it for the first and last time."

"But how could I love anyone as I love Kitty?"

"You can't! Kitty was your first love and first loves are precious and never to be forgotten. But there is last love, too. Oh, Drew, it tears my heart out to say this, but I love you so much that it must be said. Don't put off that last goodbye?"

"All right — so I'll go. I'll go now because I want to. But there'll be no comfort for me, doing it."

"There will, Drew. Something will happen — a sign. It happened for me when I went to Andrew's grave. A blackbird started singing in that cemetery at Étaples; just like the one that sings Sunset on the oak in Brattocks. It sang his goodbye to me."

"Blackbirds don't sing in December, Mother."

"There'll be a sign for you; something will happen and you'll recognize it for what it is."

"We'll see . . ." He walked to the door, opening it, then turning to look at her. "I'll go before it starts to get dark."

"Shall I come with you?"

"No. It's between Kitty and me."

He closed the door deliberately, firmly. She listened to his slow footsteps, then ran after him calling, "Drew! Your coat!"

But he did not hear her and she reached for the telephone with a shaking hand. She wanted Nathan, and he wasn't here.

"Can I have 195 please, Winnie?" she asked tonelessly.

"Drew's home," she whispered when Alice answered, "and I think I've just done something awful. I begged him to go now to Kitty's grave. I told him the longer he left it, the harder it would be. Should I have done it, Alice?"

"I think you should." Alice's voice was low and even. "There was no living with you after Andrew died. You and your stubborn refusal to say a decent goodbye."

"Yes, but do you think I went a bit far with Drew?"

"I don't know, Julia. Only you know what passed

between you. And happen it wasn't so much what you said as the way you said it."

"I begged him to go and see Kitty. Maybe it'll be no comfort to him, but at least he'll have been. I feel dreadful for all that. Wouldn't you think that at my age I'd have learned some sense?"

"Is it so wrong to want to protect your son from going through what you did, then? Is he there now?"

"Yes, and I want to go to him, help him."

"No! He's a man! For six years he's fought a war; let him fight this battle like a man! It happened to me too, Julia. Do you think I don't understand what he's going through?"

"But I told him there'd be a sign; something to give him comfort. Twice, Alice, when I was desperate, the people I loved sent comfort to me. At Étaples Andrew sent me birdsong, and when I was in torment over Mother, Gracie brought me a white orchid. Surely there'll be something for Drew?"

"If he's to have it, then it'll be there for him. How did he seem?"

"Lost. He's thinner too, and there was such despair in him. I dreamed of this day; prayed for it. Drew home safely from the war was all I ever wanted, yet now the day has come there seems nothing for me but an incredible sadness — and of my own making, too."

"Julia, *listen*!" Alice sighed. "If it's a sign you want, then here's what your mother once said to me. I was pregnant with Drew and still hurting over

817

Tom being killed. Giles was very ill and did I but know it, there was worse to come.

"But I asked her, that day, how she had always been so brave, been such an example to us all when often her heart must have been near to breaking point. And she said she wasn't brave, just commonsensical. There was an old saying, she told me, that went something like there being nothing we could do to prevent the birds of sadness from flying over our head, but we didn't have to let them build nests in our hair!"

"So what are you trying to say?"

"I'm telling you to buck up; that Drew's need is greater than yours. You've got to be brave — and commonsensical — for him. All right — there's a bird of sadness around, so watch it! Put your chin up! You're a Sutton!"

"You're right, Alice. I can't stop life from hurting Drew, but I can be there when he needs me."

"Yes, and happen when he wants a shoulder to cry on. Men need to weep, an' all, you know."

"Yes. I'll be there. Can you tell Daisy Drew's home?"

"Tell her yourself, she and Keth are with Tatty. Give them a ring, why don't you? Then tell yourself you've got Drew safely home, then take it a step at a time."

"Yes. He went to war a boy and he's come home a man. Bye, Alice. Thanks for listening . . ."

818

Alice smiled at the receiver as she put it down, even though her eyes brimmed with tears.

"A man, Julia," she whispered. "And what's more, I reckon that between us, we've made a right good job of him!"

Drew closed the back door quietly, crossing the stableyard, skirting the kitchen garden, making for Home Farm Lane. He took a roundabout route so no one need see him and stop him and shake his hand. Afterwards, maybe, but not just yet.

He opened the churchyard gate carefully, remembering the noise it made, then walked down the path to the four yew trees, all the while looking up at the church clock.

That church was older than Rowangarth, even. Inside it was the tomb of one who had helped conquer England with William. All the land around had been his reward and he built a stone house and a sturdy, square church. The church remained, but the Suttons, Yorkshire yeomen through and through, replaced that house with Rowangarth, in Elizabeth Tudor's time.

He turned his head abruptly so he was looking at the plot where generations of Suttons lay. On the right of the wide path, the old Suttons; on the left the Suttons of Pendenys Place — Aunt Clemmy, Uncle Edward, and between them, Elliot.

His eyes ranged ancient Sutton gravestones, the names on them near-obliterated by wind and weather. They read like a history book.

There lay Gilbert, and Mary his wife, and John, the grandfather he never knew, and Giles, his father, once married to Lady.

There was Helen, née Stormont, his beloved grandmother, and beside her, a grave unmarked but for a simple wooden cross.

He gazed at it for several seconds before the lettering on it stopped blurring, then he smiled sadly, his heart thudding with pain.

KITTY
1.11.20 – 19.6.44

That was all. Next June, probably, when Uncle Albert and Aunt Amelia came over from Kentucky, there would be a stone to mark where she lay, but the simple cross told those who walked by that here was Kitty of the violet eyes and the Mary Anne Pendennis curls. Kitty from Kentucky, outrageous in a black and crimson costume and fishnet stockings. Kitty sharing her bed with him in Ma's lodging house in Roscoe Street; his first lovely love.

"Hullo, you," he whispered, so only she might hear him. "I'm home."

The churchyard was still and quiet. Already the light was beginning to fade. He straightened his back, looking down, listening with his ears and with his heart, but he did not hear her voice nor her laughter. Kitty was still and silent, but then Kitty was a summer creature; warm and vibrant and soft as a June sunset, sweet as a haymaking day. She wasn't here for him because she was in her winter sleep. Not until the swallows came and honeysuckle flowered and wild, white roses; not until the lindens blossomed scentily would she be there laughing, the sun on her face and teasing in her eyes.

There would be a sign, Mother said; but even in a stillness so complete he could almost reach out and touch it, there was no small sound of comfort; no feeling of warmth or hope was there for him.

"We didn't say goodbye, my darling; just, 'See you. Take care. I love you.' No one ever said that word in wartime, so I'm here to say it now.

"Goodbye, my darling Kitty. We were so special together. D'you know, sweetheart, right up until now I wanted it not to be so. I told myself that all those letters that came, telling me, being sorry for me, were just a bad dream. Even when your own letters stopped coming, I was so sure there was an explanation and that you would be there, waiting, when I came home. And you are, my love, and I'm home and — and . . ."

The tears came then; tears a man shouldn't cry. Hot, bitter tears that ran down his face unchecked because he wanted her to have them. They were all he could give her now; Kitty, who had died on a summer day posting a letter with a lipsticky kiss on it.

He pulled his sleeve over his eyes, touching the name on the cross as if he were touching her cheeks, her closed eyelids, her mouth.

"See you," he said softly. "I'll come again tomorrow. I'm glad you're beside Gran . . ."

Lights were shining from windows in the village now, and as he walked along Home Farm Lane he could see the south side of Rowangarth and lights there too. Little beacons of hope, were they, trying to tell him something, give him the sign he looked for?

He shifted his gaze to the sky. It was streaked with wintry red and bare black trees glistened wet against it. High in that sky, in the distance, was a flock of birds, black birds; rooks coming home to roost after a day foraging fields opened up by the plough; Rowangarth's rooks. Once, they had left. Once, when everything was going wrong, the rooks flew away to nest in some other place. It was bad luck for Rowangarth.

And when they left, at the lowest ebb ever that Grandmother could recall, she feared that with the death of her son Giles and a baby too weak to feed, almost, there would be no more Suttons at Rowangarth.

Yet on the day of Giles's funeral, the rooks returned cawing and quarrelling, to the elm trees they had left a year ago, and the sickly baby — himself — began to feed.

And the rooks had stayed and were circling over his head, calling to tell him they were there still; that they knew Rowangarth's sailor was home.

Should he go to Brattocks, stand beneath the elms? Daisy told things to the rooks; Lady too. He

822

didn't know how they did it, but maybe just to stand there would be enough, and the rooks would understand.

He was climbing the fence into the wood when he heard laughter and put two fingers to his mouth to whistle loudly. Then he began to run towards them, Daisy, Keth and Tatty; those people he cared for most were there for him, just as the rooks were, as Rowangarth was. He waved and called, "Hi!"

"Hi, sailor!" Daisy threw herself into his arms, laying her cheek on his, rubbing the back of his neck with her hand. "What are you doing out here without a coat?"

"Been to see Kitty," he said, holding his arms out for Tatty, seeing the vicious weal on her right cheek.

"Welcome home," she whispered, "and I do understand."

"I know you do. Thanks for writing."

He held out his hand to Keth, who shook it warmly, then laid an arm across his shoulders.

"Your mother told us you were back, Drew. We came looking for you."

"Shall we come to Rowangarth with you?" Tatty asked.

"No. I'm going to see Gracie and Catchpole, first, thank them for Kitty's orchids, and then I'm calling in on Lady. Why don't you all come over after supper, though. We've a lot to catch up on."

"If you're sure?" Tatty hesitated.

"I'm sure. I'll ask Gracie to come and if you want you can bring your airman along, Tatty, if he's still at Denniston."

"He is, and he's not my airman. Bill's my friend. Tim sent him . . ."

"Right! We'll see you later, Drew." Daisy didn't want the conversation to become complicated, even though she knew that tonight, Kitty's name would be spoken a lot and Tim's, too. Tonight they would be glad, just being together and tomorrow would be another day. "We'll set Tatty on her way. I'll tell Mam you'll be calling, Drew?"

"Sure. In about half an hour. I want to catch Jack before he packs up for the night."

He smiled, and all at once it was a real smile that didn't hurt, because he was home and Kitty had been there, fast asleep beside Gran. Today, he had fretted inside himself, yet now he had said a proper goodbye to Kitty and he would go again tomorrow to say hullo.

He turned to wave to Keth and Drew and Tatty, then made for the kitchen garden, to say hi to the newest Sutton.

And then he would go home. To Rowangarth.

CHAPTER
THIRTY-SEVEN

Holdenby, September 1948

"Not going home for your dinner then, Sydney?"

"Not today, Mr Catchpole. Mrs Willis has packed me sandwiches. She's gone to York. Something, she said, about buying a christening present for the baby."

"Ar." Catchpole jammed his straw hat on his head. "Then I'll leave you to it. See you in forty-five minutes."

He walked slowly, inspecting his garden as he went. Sydney Willis, married to Tilda Tewk, was a gardener with great affection for orchids and that being so, Catchpole knew he could, when the time came, hand over the key to the orchid house and know that the collection built up by his father and grandfather before him would be in capable hands.

He had been lucky finding Sydney Willis, he thought, as he closed the ornate iron gate behind him; their shared passion for orchids had led a sergeant in the Green Howards to his garden and a friendship established with Rowangarth's cook.

That was during the war, of course, when Pendenys Place had funny folk in it and was guarded day and night by Sydney's regiment, though not one of those soldiers, Sydney included, ever discovered quite what it was they were guarding. A rum do all round, that. It was a good day when the Army packed up and left and handed the place back to the Reverend, him being the rightful heir.

Catchpole walked slowly and with dignity as befitted a head gardener, thinking about that war and the vegetables he and Gracie had grown for the war effort. Gracie from Rochdale. One of the best apprentices he ever had and by far the bonniest. Now she was Grace Sutton and lived in Kentucky with young Bas, and had a lad of her own. Gone to America with a boat-load of GI brides and her given priority because she was expecting. He'd heard that Gracie and Bas would be sailing over for the christening. He hoped so. He missed the lass, even though Sydney Willis was satisfactory in every way.

But you couldn't have it all ways. Gracie had made his war bearable; she deserved to be happy. Only right and proper, when you came to think about it, that she should meet her husband in this very garden. It gave him a great pleasure to think about it. Indeed, there was times, like now, that he knew near contentment, he thought as he opened Lily's kitchen door and was met with the smell of cooking. Steak and kidney pie. There was no mistaking it.

★ ★ ★

Sydney Willis, too, was a contented man. He unwrapped his immaculately packed sandwiches and thought of Tilda, as near perfect as his mother had been, and all he could ask for in a wife.

Tilda liked being called Mrs Willis. It so pleased her, she had whispered confidingly on their wedding night, that she wouldn't care if he never called her Tilda again!

He had fallen on his feet when the Army dispensed with his services after giving him a gratuity, a grey pin-striped suit, two shirts, a pair of black shoes and a brown trilby hat. And a civilian ration book and clothing coupons, of course, because rationing had not vanished overnight as most folk thought it would. Even now, some foods were still hard to come by.

He opened the top button of his trousers. He was putting on weight. Middle-age spread, Mrs Willis had said sternly, but he replied it was tender loving care and good cooking, and he was all for it!

He unscrewed his bottle of cold tea, tilting it to his lips. The garden looked well. A little sad, now, as summer came to a close, and in need of a good tidy-up and a pruning-back once the last of the apples and pears and the plums were picked. There was something comforting about being a gardener, and being a gardener in Rowangarth's employ was especially so.

He thought about his wife, a good woman and a cook without equal, for whom he cared deeply. He hoped she was having a good day in York.

★ ★ ★

Tilda Willis — née Tewk — pulled off her gloves elegantly and sighed contentment. Here she was, a married lady at last, taking tea and a toasted teacake in Betty's Café. She smiled up at the waitress; these days, she wanted to smile at everyone.

She bit into her teacake, little finger extended, recalling as she often did, the most wonderful day of her life. Just as the war ended she married the man she had been waiting for these thirty years past. Sydney Willis. Better by far than all her romantic fiction heroes. Sydney was flesh and blood and not a figment of her frustrated longings.

Alice made her wedding dress, then together they shopped around for an exactly right hat. Alice would know it, she insisted, the minute Tilda tried it on.

Tilda had asked Tom Dwerryhouse to give her away, but he declined, saying she had met her Sydney in Rowangarth kitchen garden, and that the honour should go to another far more fitting.

So Jack Catchpole walked her down the aisle, wearing his Sunday suit, a rose in his buttonhole, and a very important smile.

Such a lovely day with Sydney in his uniform, his sergeant's stripes blancoed brilliantly white and she carrying a finger-spray of gypsophila and pink carnations, exactly as Mary had done.

A honeymoon in Bridlington, then home to the tiny lodge at the stableyard gates, and since she was still Rowangarth's cook, she reckoned she had the best of both worlds and never forgot to give thanks every time she went to church.

And at such times, she asked the good Lord to sort something out for Sir Andrew, because when the Reverend and Miss Julia moved into the bothy, the poor lad would rattle around that house like a dried pea in a tin can.

She wiped her fingers on her serviette and let go a sigh. She would never forgive Hitler for that flying bomb. Poor Miss Kitty, so young, so still beneath her white marble stone.

Yet something *would* happen for young Drew, because didn't Mary insist he got letters from a young lady and sometimes rang one up — long distance. Tilda fervently hoped it was so. She wanted the Master of Rowangarth to be as happy as she was. She had been there the night of his birth, watched him grow into a fine young man who had gone to fight for his country. Now, she wanted him wed and happy, with bairns of his own and a son or two for Rowangarth.

It was more than four years since Kitty died; two years since the wooden cross was replaced by a gravestone and a memorial service held in All Souls, and every one of the Suttons there, except Gracie and Bas, Gracie being not long on her feet after the birth of her first.

Drew seemed happy enough now; giving his attention to Rowangarth, walking the rounds of the game covers with Tom, getting the estate houses in Holdenby smartened up, now that building materials were allowed for repairs again, and paint once more on sale in the shops.

But happy enough wasn't good enough! She wanted Rowangarth to be as it was when first she went to work there; before the First World War, that was, and a year before Sir John died. Splendid dinner parties there'd been and Mrs Shaw and Ellen and Mary and Bess and Alice, aye, and young Tilda Tewk, rushed off their feet and loving every minute of it.

Yet soon, when the Reverend and Miss Julia moved into the bothy and she and Mary had left for their homes each night, Drew would be alone in that great house, 'cept for Miss Clitherow, poor old lass. Deaf as a post now, and her bed moved into her little sitting room since she could no longer manage the stairs.

But she was game to the end; said that if the good Lord allowed and Sir Andrew, too, she would end her days at Rowangarth, dying, if she could manage it, peaceful in her sleep, then be laid to rest as near to her ladyship as made no matter.

But all things change, Tilda sighed. That young kitchen-maid was nearer fifty now than fifteen. And a married lady, thanks be!

Tatty opened the door of the stableyard flat, then walked quietly to where Bill Benson sat at his easel beneath the skylight.

"Hi, hen." He looked up and smiled.

"Am I disturbing you?"

"No. The light's gone — going to call it a day. Only one more to do now."

"You're going to have to get a move on, aren't you? If those cards are going to be printed and boxed and in the shops by Christmas."

"They're for *next* Christmas and these six designs are going to keep body and soul together for the next six months!"

Bill's first commercial commission. Six designs for cards; holly, Christmas roses, snowdrops, mistletoe and robins, with *From an original by William Benson* printed on the reverse.

Tatiana flopped on the sofa that served as a bed, watching as he cleaned his brushes, returned his pots of colour to their ordered lines on narrow shelves. His orphanage upbringing had planted the seeds of tidiness in him. Everything in its place. She had remarked on it.

"I like order," he'd said, "and think — if I hadn't got my sight back, there'd have had to be a place for everything and nothing moved. Blind men can't see unfamiliar obstacles."

"But you *can* see, Bill, and you're doing well."

"I can't complain; and you had your operation and beautiful as ever again. It was a lucky day for me when a lassie volunteered to take a blind airman to the theatre."

"Reckon we're lucky for each other. I've come to tell you Karl is making tea, so if you want a cup, feel free. Don't hang about, though, because I'm going to see mother, soon. She knows where I can borrow a cot."

"A cot!" He went to sit beside her. "Why on earth do you want a cot?"

"We-e-ll, this morning I phoned Kentucky. You know Bas and Gracie and their little one are coming over for the christening? I asked them to stay here, and they said yes. I thought they could have the guest room and sleep the baby in the dressing room off it. So now I'm after a cot!"

"Thank heaven! I thought you'd gone broody," he grinned, getting to his feet, holding out his hand to her. "And I could do with a cup of tea. Thanks, hen."

"Did I ever tell you," Tatiana said as they crossed the cobbled stableyard, "that when Denniston House was a hospital in the other war, your flat was the nurses' common room — when they had time to sit down, Aunt Julia said. Both she and Daisy's mother were nurses here. And before that, an old maiden lady lived here alone. She was a bit strange, I think. Aunt Julia was scared stiff of the place when she was young; thought she was a witch. I suppose that if I live here alone for long enough, people will think that of me too."

"You, a witch? Away with your bother! You'll not end up a maiden lady! For one thing you're too attractive, and for another, you've got money! What about Drew? He'll marry one day."

"Marry me, you mean?" Tatiana stood stock still, her cheeks flaming. "*Drew . . .?*"

832

"He'll have to marry someone — have bairns to pass that estate to — and his title."

"I see. The Keir Hardie in you is surfacing again! Jealous of him, are you? So what are you doing, then, living here and painting pictures? Why aren't you out campaigning for your shirtless ones, getting yourself into politics?"

"Because I like being here painting pictures and I'll stay until you decide to kick me out!" he grinned. "Besides, you'd miss me if I wasn't here, admit it."

"Yes, I think I would!" *Think?* Of course she would miss him. He was almost Tim. Sometimes he *was* Tim and she wondered how long it would be before they were lovers. "But do hurry, Bill. I've got to call in on Aunt Julia, let her know Gracie and Bas will be staying here. I hope she won't mind."

"Of course she won't! And, Tatiana," he said softly as she reached for the doorknob, "I'd miss you too. I'll not be leaving, if that's all right with you?"

"Fine!" she said over her shoulder, very offhand. "And I don't have designs on Drew, nor him on me. We're fond of each other, but we both know we wouldn't mix. And besides," she added, almost as an afterthought, "I think I've got a penchant for Scottish air-gunners!"

"Where's Drew?" Alice stirred her tea noisily because to her way of thinking the place was altogether too quiet.

"Gone to see the architect. You don't mind us sitting in the kitchen, Alice? Tilda's having the day off and I told Mary to go home. I can manage my own supper."

"I like the kitchen, though it's unnatural quiet. Are the plans for the village hall coming along all right?"

"Seems Creesby Council has no objection to a new building, provided it doesn't take up more square feet than the old one. The parish council has decided it's to be called the Memorial Hall," Julia smiled.

"In memory of Lady Helen, and Kitty?"

"Yes. And of Uncle Edward and Reuben and Jin and Cook. It'll be built in stone again, but the space put to better use. Amelia and Albert have promised to come over for the opening."

"Nathan not back from London yet?"

"He's staying the night. The contract has been signed, now, on Cheyne Walk. I'm glad he decided to sell it. It was always a white elephant. Why Aunt Clemmy ever bought it I'll never know."

"I suppose because it was fashionable then to have a second home in London and Mrs Clementina had money to burn, didn't she? Nathan will have called next door, on the Countess?"

"He has. She and Igor are rubbing along, it seems. The Countess is inclined to have memory lapses, Igor told him, and thinks she is back in St Petersburg again. Igor does nothing to disillusion her; says she's almost happy, when she's back in her house beside the River Neva."

"She was a funny old stick. Will Nathan be staying the night at Montpelier Mews?"

"He will. Said he'd check up that everything's all right, now that no one's living there. He intends calling on Sparrow whilst he's down there. She's happy living with Joannie, and as bright as a button still. It was best, though, after what happened, that she didn't live there alone."

"Shall you keep Montpelier, Julia?"

"Oh, yes! It doesn't cost a lot to run it and it'll always be there, when we want to go to London. Besides, it's got too many memories for me ever to sell it."

"Aunt Sutton would be glad about that. She loved that little house."

"Mm. But she loved France better — and horses and her little snifters of brandy, bless her. Such a lot has happened since you and I first went to stay there. It was 1913, wasn't it — thirty-five years ago and you and me out looking for a Suffragette meeting?"

"And finding one — and trouble."

"Finding Andrew. And so much water under so many bridges since then. We're getting old, Alice."

"So we are — but I'd still not change a thing, except Kitty, perhaps . . ."

"Darling Kitty. Drew's beginning to accept it now, I think."

"He should be married. I wish he'd find himself a nice girl."

"He will, one day."

"He needs a bit of a push, for all that! Four years is long enough!" Bas and Gracie were happy, and Keth and Daisy, Alice reasoned. Tatty had even found a kind of contentment. It wasn't right that Drew should be alone. "And when you and Nathan move into the bothy, he'll feel it — all on his own, here."

"But he won't be alone entirely. There'll be Tilda and Mary."

"So they won't be going with you to the bothy?"

"No. They belong at Rowangarth, which reminds me — do you think Polly would like to work for Nathan and me? I know she's happy in her almshouse, but —"

"Aye. Reuben's old place," Alice smiled fondly. "Are you planning on asking her?"

"If you think she wouldn't mind."

"She'd welcome it. Polly has worked all her life and having nothing to do is wearing a bit thin, I'm sure of it. Said she didn't want to be round at Keth and Daisy's all the time, seeing if they wanted anything doing — offering to baby-sit."

"Then I'll ask her. I wouldn't expect her to live in. A few hours a day would be fine. Nathan will be getting the bothy garden back into shape once he's retired, and I can manage the housework. It's only the cooking that bothers me."

"I reckon Polly'll be glad to oblige. She knows that bothy like the back of her hand. Lord knows she lived there long enough. It'll be like going home for her. When do you expect Nathan back?"

"Tomorrow, on the afternoon train. I'm glad the Cheyne Walk house is sold; maybe now Father-in-law's estate can finally be settled. It had to wait till the Army left Pendenys, though."

"It'll seem funny, Creesby Council having the place. Pity Nathan and Albert couldn't sell it."

"They can't. It's entailed until Bas gets it, though if I know Bas he'll give it away. And Creesby Council isn't having it, exactly. They're paying a peppercorn rent — five guineas a year — in return for keeping it in good repair. They're putting a caretaker in on the top floor, I believe — where the nursery suite used to be."

"And what about the stables and outbuildings?" It fascinated Alice to think that Pendenys Place estate, once Mrs Clementina's pride, should be broken up. But then, who would want to live in such a great, unhappy house?

"Nathan's almost certain that a market gardener is going to lease them — and the gardener's house and kitchen garden."

"And the rest of the estate houses and lodges rented to ex-servicemen with families." Nice of Nathan, that was. Just the kind of thing he would do. "I wonder what really went on there in the war, Julia? Was it being kept in case of emergency, do you think?"

"What! All those soldiers guarding an emergency! No. I think there were goings-on. Spying. But we'll never know. I went round the place with Nathan when he got it back. It was amazing. They hadn't left a thing behind. Not so much as a scrap of paper, or a notice on a wall. There'd been a real professional clearance. You'd never have known they'd been there, except that everything seemed faded and in need of decoration. And Creesby Council won't do that — not when they are only using it for storage."

"Oh dear. The end of an era, you might say. And Pendenys was built with such high hopes; so proud and haughty," Alice sighed.

"A good riddance to it! Don't know what I'd have done if Nathan had wanted to live there. We'll be very snug in the bothy — next-door neighbours, you and me, Alice."

Next-door neighbours, Alice thought fondly as she walked back to Keeper's Cottage, smiling to see the rowan saplings Jack Catchpole and Gracie planted in the war, six feet high now.

Nice that Gracie and Bas were coming over for the baby's christening and that Lyn and Tatty and Drew were to be godparents. Alice thought of the christening gown she had so thankfully made; started it the minute Daisy said she was expecting though she'd been a bit worried, them not starting a family as soon as Keth was demobbed.

But she was a grandmother at last. Such a lovely feeling. All she could ask for now was for Drew to fall in love again and give her the excuse to make another christening gown; threaded with baby-blue ribbon, of course, because Rowangarth needed a son.

She wondered about Lyndis and Drew, then closed down her thoughts. Of course she wanted Drew married, and of course he would marry, one day. And until that happened, she was determined never to interfere or say one word about it in Drew's hearing, even though she had a moral right. But only he would know when the time was right, though she hoped with all her heart it would be soon.

Foxgloves, Daisy thought, was a beautiful house. The name had first attracted her and then she fell completely in love with it. It stood alone in a narrow lane, off the Creesby road, and from upstairs windows she could see Ewart Pryce's house, and sometimes Anna in the garden.

What she liked about it most was the kitchen. It had a tiled floor and a table with a scrubbed-white top with eight wooden chairs round it. Foxgloves also had four bedrooms and a large attic and off the kitchen, a door that opened onto stone steps and a whitewashed cellar.

There was a sitting-room, of course, though scantily furnished, and a dining-room completely empty of furniture. Tables and chairs and sideboards were still in short supply and people with wartime gratuities in their pockets and wartime savings too, were paying far too much for secondhand furniture. Floor covering, rugs and yardage for curtains were still hard to come by. The Board of Trade still insisted on dockets for essentials, such as beds and linoleum for floors, but the meagre allowance had gone nowhere in Daisy and Keth's house.

Nathan had come to the rescue with floor coverings.

"Take what carpets you want from Pendenys," he offered, "if you can find any the moths haven't got at!"

They were lucky. Most of the carpets survived six years of storage. The floors at Foxgloves were luxuriously carpeted, the rooms bare, until Julia offered a kitchen table and chairs and two amazingly soft sofas. Nothing was ever thrown out at Rowangarth and the attics could be relied upon to yield up things long forgotten. They would suffice, Julia said, until better could be bought, because the phrase "For the duration" had been quickly replaced by "When the shops are back to normal."

In one aspect, though, they were very lucky. Daisy had put her name on the list — everything important was on a waiting list now — for an electric cooker. Waiting time, said the man behind the counter, would be about a twelve-month. Then he espied her condition and immediately, because she was an expectant mother, the time was cut to three months and the cooker, mottled grey and white, stood there in splendid newness. It made her very happy, but these days practically everything made her happy.

She walked softly outside to stand beside the pram Alice had triumphantly produced from Rowangarth attic, eliminating at once the perambulator waiting list.

"Always said it would last a lifetime," Alice exulted, loving its old-fashioned solidity, its splendid chromium-plated handles and mudguards and a hood and apron kept from cracking over the years with applications of Mansion polish and a smear of linseed oil from time to time. "Paid a fortune for that pram when you were born, our Daisy. Now at last we'll get a bit more use out of it!"

Daisy looked down at her sleeping child, at its soft, fine hair and eyes already turned from newborn-blue to brown. Keth's hair, Keth's eyes, Keth's long, black eyelashes.

The christening was to be on Sunday with a bit of a do afterwards at Rowangarth. Aunt Julia had insisted, because if the September afternoon turned a little cold, she said, there would be the conservatory to fall back on. Daisy agreed at once, because they had very little crockery — not half enough for guests — and seating only for ten, if you included the sofas.

There would be sandwiches to eat, and Mam had baked a christening cake because people weren't so reluctant now to buy food on the black market, there being no seamen's lives at risk in the Atlantic any longer.

She sighed contentment because on Friday Lyn was coming and it would be like old times again in Cabin 4A, only better. But soon, Keth would be home from Creesby Grammar School where he taught mathematics and physics. He would peep the horn of his second-hand Austin to let her know he'd arrived — just once, and gently, so as not to awaken Bump, who might be sleeping — then they would kiss urgently as if it were Beck Lane all over again, and the floor carpeted with bluebells.

"Idiot," she would chide, reluctantly pulling away.

"I've missed you," he'd say huskily as if he were newly home from Washington, and a war on still.

"The baby," she said when they had kissed, and kissed again, "must be given a name! Do you want the little thing growing up thinking it's called Bump?"

She had not wanted their unborn child referred to as It, or He-or-she. Bump they named her pregnancy and Bump the baby still was.

"It's Mary, surely? We agreed, didn't we?"

"But are *you* sure, Keth?" She placed vegetables to cook. "I was to have first choice of a girl's name — you a boy's. Mary-what, is she to be? Her second name is up to you."

"Then would you mind if I chose — Natasha? Mary Natasha. It goes well, don't you think?"

"Y-yes, it does, but why Natasha? It's Russian, isn't it?"

"It is," he said gravely.

"I see," she said, though she didn't see at all, and moved to stand beside him, taking his hand so he

842

should know she wasn't being awkward about his choice. "Am I to know why?"

"If you'll tell me why you chose Mary."

"Because it's a lovely name," she said softly. "It *goes*, sort of; a name for a servant or a queen. Mary sounds right, somehow."

"Then I would like Natasha because it sounds right with Mary."

"And you're sure that's the only reason?" She was looking down at their clasped hands now.

"Must there be any other reason?"

"For a name like Natasha — yes!"

"Then I can't give you one, darling." He said it firmly, flatly. "I just want it."

There was a pulse of apprehension beating in her throat, so she turned abruptly to lower the heat beneath the bubbling pans.

"Who is — *was* — she, Keth?" Her eyes were on the cooker still, because really she didn't want to know.

He moved to stand behind her, hands on her shoulders, because he couldn't bear not to touch her.

"I can't tell you — not yet." He said it so sadly that she turned to reach for him, laying her cheek on his chest.

"Something happened, didn't it? There's a part of your war you don't talk about."

"But you've always known that." He manoeuvred for safer ground. "I'm still bound by the Official Secrets Act, probably will be for a long time. Things aren't really back to normal, yet. The Communists, I mean, clamming up on the West again."

"So now they're our enemies?"

"You know what I mean, Daisy." He still held her. He didn't want her to flounce out of the kitchen because she still flounced, sometimes.

"I don't care too much about Stalin and the Russians and the bother over Berlin. What I *do* care about is your not telling me — and I don't mean about Bletchley Park. There's something else, isn't there?" Maybe *someone* else. "When you came home from Washington the second time — just before then, wasn't it?"

"Why do you say that?" She had moved away from him, now, with the width of the table between them, her eyes sending out a challenge, her cheeks flushed.

"Because!" Her mouth had gone button round, her chin tilted like Daisy's of old. "There *was* someone, wasn't there?"

"No, darling. *Something*." He walked toward her carefully, because all at once she was a ticking, unexploded bomb, ready to go off. He took her hand again and because she did not snatch it away he said, "Come into the front room?"

"Only if you'll tell me. I won't have secrets between us, Keth."

He guided her to the soft, sagging sofa, carefully placing an arm behind her.

"Some secrets must stay secrets, darling girl."

"Not when they're called Natasha!" Her body had stiffened again and he knew there would be no placating her.

"What do you want to know?" he asked warily.

"About *her*! There was a woman, wasn't there?"

"No." He wasn't lying to her. Natasha had been little more than a child.

"Keth — *please*?" There was a trembling on her voice now. She wasn't going to explode. She was hurt, which was worse. "This is our little girl's name we are talking about."

"No! It's more than that!" All at once he didn't care. Be damned to the lot of them at Castle McLeish and the stone house! He took a shuddering breath. "There *was* someone, and Mary is going to grow up looking very like her — brown eyes, black hair. I can't forget Natasha. I mustn't — ever.

"But Mary is going to grow up, Daisy, and I'll make sure she does! It's because of Natasha I'm here now. Natasha had a Russian mother and she was sixteen when — when she died. And that's all I can tell you!"

"France, wasn't it?" Somehow she knew it had been France.

"Yes." He felt her body go limp against his; knew she was weeping. "Maybe one day They'll let me talk about it; maybe some day I'll go back, find out the whole truth about what happened — but not yet."

"Mary Natasha." Daisy fished for her handkerchief. "Mary Natasha Purvis. It sits nicely, Keth. What are we to tell people, though? They'll ask, you know."

"Then we'll tell them they are names we like, that's all."

"Names we *both* like." She whispered a kiss on his cheek. "Now let's get our supper before she wakes up and wants feeding. And, Keth — I won't ask again, I promise."

Jack Catchpole looked up from his apple box seat beside the potting shed door, then smiled broadly.

"Lass! You've comed, then!" Bas Sutton was walking towards him, a small boy high on his shoulders. Behind them Gracie was carefully closing the high iron gate as she had done so many times before. "Eh, but it's grand to see you!" He completely forgot his head-gardener's dignity and took her in his arms, kissing her cheek warmly. "So this is young Adam, then?"

"Say hullo to Mr Catchpole." Bas deposited his son on the path and the small boy looked up with his mother's blue eyes. His legs were sturdy and he had good hands, Jack thought; hands to hold a spade.

"'Lo, Mr — Mr — 'Lo, man." Gravely he offered a hand.

"Hullo, Adam." Catchpole squatted on his haunches, chuckling. "It's a big word for a little lad."

Gracie laughed, though all the time looking around her. "Where's Mr Willis?"

"Day off." Jack Catchpole hadn't wanted anyone else here today. Not with Gracie expected.

846

"Tell you what, Mr C. Adam's just had his afternoon sleep — can Bas take him round the garden — tire him out a bit?"

"Course he can!" Dogs, unless on the end of a lead and accompanied by a responsible adult, were not allowed in his garden; cats doubly so. But Gracie's lad was welcome to the run of the place.

"He's a fine bairn," he acknowledged, placing his pipe between his teeth. "How old is he?"

"Two and a bit, and a playmate due in December," she smiled.

"Well now." He hadn't been quite sure and hadn't wanted to comment, babies being private things. "Married life suits you, lass. How is Mrs Amelia these days, and Mr Albert? Bad blow for them, Kitty was."

"Yes, and made worse because they couldn't get over to her funeral. But when her stone was put there, it did Mother-in-law good to see it, and the memorial service in All Souls seemed to give her comfort. Adam has helped a lot. He adores his gran-gran. I think they might start visiting regularly again, now they're both accepting it."

"Well, you tell them from me that Kitty'll have her bouquet every June. D'you know, lass, we call them Kitty's orchids, now; not milady's."

"That's nice." Gracie got to her feet, hands in the small of her back. "Can we walk a bit — I'd like to see the orchid house?"

"You'm welcome, but there isn't much of a show now. Want to have a word with her ladyship, do you?"

847

"Not exactly." How well he understood her. "But I'd like her to know I've been."

When they got there, Gracie espied the green-painted folding chair, leaning against the far wall.

"Do you suppose she'd mind if I sat on her chair?"

"Nay, not her. She likes folk to come here. If I've got a bit of a problem I sit on that little chair and nine times out of ten it sorts itself out. But how about you, Gracie — no need to ask if life's being good to you. You'm thriving on it. Stopping here long, are you?"

"A week with Tatty, though I'll be seeing everyone, of course. Then a week at Rochdale. We're sailing back on the *Mauretania*; better for Adam than flying. I want to be back home before I'm seven months, though."

"So Kentucky's home now?" He felt vaguely cheated.

"It is, Mr C, though I'll always be a Lancashire lass from Rochdale and there'll always, *always* be a part of me here in this garden. It's my happy place. I often call it back, and I'm picking strawberries again, or planting cabbages, or barrowing manure," she giggled. "Do you know, the day Bas and I met, I'd been shifting manure and I smelled awful!"

"Ar," said Catchpole, content again.

"And I never thanked you, Mr C, not properly. I left in such a rush when I was offered a passage over, so I want to thank you again. It was wonderful here. It wasn't right I should have been so happy — not with a war on. But I was. I'm a time-served gardener, too; no one can ever take away what you taught me. And it was here Bas and I met. This garden — and you — will always be special."

She reached to kiss his cheek and he turned away to pick off a decaying leaf because all at once he was so full up he didn't know what to say.

"Ar," he said, a bit sniffily. "Think you'll find time to decorate the church up a bit for Sunday? There's plenty of flowers still, and you alus enjoyed doing it. Won't be too busy with the babbie, will you?"

"Not at all. There are plenty of willing helpers. Tatty is real taken with Adam."

"Think she's going to marry that artist fellow as lives in her stableyard, then?"

"I think she well might, now she's getting over Tim."

"Tim? Who was he?"

"He was a secret — had to be. Daisy and Drew and I knew about him, though. He was killed on the pike the night the bomber crashed on the village. I think that was why she went to London. She met Bill there."

"And young Drew — how long's he going to be getting over Kitty? Isn't right he should be single still. What do you make of him, Gracie?"

"He'll be fine. Tatty told me he was very cut-up when he came back from the Pacific, but he's always been friendly with Daisy's friend from the Wrens.

Lyn visits Foxgloves quite often. I think Daisy hopes they'll get together one day."

"That'll be the red-headed lass. She came here with Drew last time she visited Keth and Daisy. He wanted flowers for her to take back to North Wales."

"So fingers crossed, then . . .?"

They sat in contentment, each with their thoughts. He remembering a smiling girl in her new Land Army uniform, eager to please, boiling the little iron kettle on the potting shed fire. Strange, but the enamelled mugs still stood on the top shelf beside the bottle marked Poison. He'd never had the heart to use them, after she left . . .

Gracie smiled at the white orchid plant, though there were no flowers on it now. And she remembered Lady Helen sitting on this very chair, telling her about a seventeen-year-old girl in a blue ball gown who fell instantly in love. Nice, really, that her ladyship had slipped away gentle, with a white orchid in her hand . . . She rose to her feet and Catchpole asked her if she'd got a bit of backache.

"No — but I get the fidgets if I sit too long. I suppose I'd better see what that son of mine is doing. Mustn't have him running all over our seed beds, Mr C."

He smiled, then left her, knowing she wanted a while alone, realizing how much he missed the lass from Rochdale who had taken the place, for a little while, of the child he and Lily never had.

Gracie sat down again, remembering. Polly's cooking at the bothy; driving in the blackout to the

RAF dances at Holdenby Moor; Tatty meeting Tim, Tatty losing Tim. She and Drew going dancing.

Hot summers, bitter winters; her ladyship still and peaceful in the candlelit great hall; meeting Bas with manure on her boots.

And Daisy and Keth's wedding, and Rowangarth kitchen garden. She and Mr Catchpole safe from the war outside behind walls nine feet high. Once upon a time, that was.

She folded the little green chair, lingering her fingers over its roughness. At the door she turned.

"'Bye, Lady Helen," she whispered. "It was nice being here again. I'll come and see you next time we're over — when the baby is born. Just wanted you to know I'm real happy with Bas and to tell you I'll never forget you."

She turned to see her son running down the path towards her and it was 1948 again. She glanced around the warmly moist glasshouse once more, then closed the door firmly behind her.

Wouldn't do to let in cold air. Not into Mr Catchpole's orchid house!

"Let me take a peep at her — please? I won't waken her," Lyn Carmichael pleaded.

"You won't recognize her. It's a month since you were last here; babies grow a lot in four weeks," Daisy said knowledgeably. "Her eyes are really brown now — just like Keth's. Pendennis eyes. But go and see her, then I think we should eat whilst we've got the chance. Keth stays later Fridays —

tries to catch up with himself so he doesn't have to bring marking home.

"It's only salad tonight; something quick so we can natter," Daisy smiled when Lyn returned, misty-eyed. "Pull up a chair and give me the Llangollen news — like any gorgeous hill-farmers in the offing!"

"You can't wait to get me off the shelf, can you? Hasn't it occurred to you that I just might be happy in my job and in my own little house and not having to please anyone but myself?"

"No it hasn't, because it isn't true! You're still hankering after Drew so don't try to deny it. This is Dwerryhouse from the bottom bunk you're talking to now!"

"Okay. So I'm still nuts about him." Lyn helped herself to salad, arranging it carefully on her plate, selecting a small piece of meat with irritating slowness.

"Well — go on then," Daisy clucked. "What are you going to do about it? It's 1948, remember. Leap year. You could propose to him!"

"Could I, now?" Lyn put down her knife and fork, resting her chin on fisted hands. "And be slapped in the teeth again? I once practically offered it to Drew on a plate; told him I loved him. But he didn't take me up on the offer, and he didn't say he loved me, either."

"Drew was always a cautious little boy — serious, too . . ."

"Yes, and caution flew to the four winds, and he seriously went to bed with Kitty the very night they met up again!"

852

"Kitty is dead," Daisy said softly.

"Yes, and I'm sorry; for her and for Drew. Kitty being killed gave me no satisfaction."

"I know. Remember she and I grew up together, Lyn. There was something magic about the Clan, like we'd be together always. Twice every year we met up and it was as if we'd never been apart. Kitty getting killed knocked me sideways, too.

"But Drew doesn't want to be alone. He's accepted things now. I know him so well and it would only take one small step on his part — or a bit of understanding on yours."

"I won't play second fiddle to a memory." Eyes on her plate Lyn began to eat again, indicating the matter was closed.

"But you wouldn't be second fiddle! Nathan and Aunt Julia are happy together. You can love twice, she once told me, but differently. She won't ever forget Andrew. How can she when he was once her reason for living? And Nathan accepts that, because he knows that the second time around can be just as good."

"It took your Aunt Julia eighteen years to make up her mind, though! You said it did! I can't wait that long for Drew. I'd shove off to Kenya first, out of his way. They want me to, you know. Auntie Blod is always going on about it!"

"*Kenya!* You really do take the plate of biscuits!" Daisy's knife and fork clattered to the table top. "I've never heard such nonsense! You and Drew get on fine, don't you, whenever you're here? You go out together, and —"

"We go on walks, that's all. Walks round Rowangarth garden, walks in Brattocks Wood, walks to the top of the pike! I thought Holdenby Pike was a snogging spot, but for us it isn't! And neither of us talk about the old days. It's as if that part of our lives is taboo."

"But you laugh a lot when you're together, don't you, and he's always pleased when you come to stay. Softee, softee, catchee monkey, don't they say?"

"Maybe so, but Drew's no monkey and I'm sick of walking on egg shells!"

"Then *do* something! Go in at the deep end and if it comes to nothing, then at least you tried!"

"Yes, and then I can creep off to Kenya with my tail between my legs and marry the first bloke out there who asks me!"

"There are times," Daisy hissed, narrow-eyed, "when I could thump you, Lyndis Carmichael! For two pins I'd — Listen! That's Keth!" She stopped, sliding her eyes to the window as a car horn sounded.

"You said he'd be late."

"He usually is, Fridays. I suppose it's because you're here, Lyn. And what do you know — he's got Drew with him!"

She said it smugly; like a cat that had just found cream in abundance, Lyn thought as she felt her cheeks flush.

854

"Great!" She found her voice, pushing back her chair as the kitchen door opened, saying, "Hi, Drew."

"Lyn! Good to see you!" He smiled, holding out his hand, kissing her cheek. "Not interrupting your meal am I, Daiz? I was coming out of the surgery when Keth passed; he insisted I come along, say hullo to Lyn. He's putting the car away — said he wouldn't be a minute."

"Now why's he doing that? He knows we're going to Tatty's, tonight!"

"Are we?" Lyn's eyebrows arched.

"Yes. Tatty's a godmother, too. Apart from anything else, you'll have to decide between you which of you carries Mary. And why were you at the surgery, Drew? What's wrong with you?"

"Nothing, touch wood. I went to register — you know, for the National Health Service. Aunt Anna reminded me. It'll be a good thing — free doctors, I mean. And free medicine. Well, that's what Ewart says, though he's going to be a lot busier. But about Denniston — can anyone come along?"

"Feel free. It's open house at Tatty's."

"Then your car or mine, Daiz?"

"We'll walk," Keth said from the doorway. "It isn't all that far to Denniston. Shall we wait for you, Drew, or will you just arrive?"

"Expect me when you see me. And I'll have to be going. Dinner's early tonight. Mother and Nathan want to be at the bothy by half-six. The decorator is calling to have a look at the place. Mother's tickled pink because he's actually got some wallpaper! Things are looking up!"

"Keth, you idiot!" Daisy wailed when Drew had left. "You should have had him pick us up here! Now, he might get interested in what's going at the bothy and not turn up at all. And Lyn's only here till Monday!"

"Sorry," Keth smiled. "Forgot Daisy's usually on the matchmaker tack when you and Drew get within striking distance!" He kissed Lyn warmly, hugging her close. "You'll have to get used to it I'm afraid, because once Daisy Purvis over there gets an idea into her head, there's nothing anyone can do about it! Good to see you, for all that! Had a good journey?"

"Changed at Chester, Manchester and York as usual, but otherwise fine! And worth all the bother just to see Mary."

"Mary Natasha," Daisy said softly.

"Well now, there's posh!" Lyn grinned, the fluttering inside her under control again. "And if you don't mind, I'll nip upstairs and unpack. Same room, is it?"

"Yes, but this time you've got a chest of drawers. Mam lent it to me, till I can come by one. Thank goodness she gave us my bedroom furniture!"

Then she grinned at Lyn because it was almost like old times again and what did furniture — or the lack of it — matter anyway? Far more important than waiting lists for wardrobes and chests of drawers were Lyn and Drew.

Now that really *was* something to worry about!

CHAPTER
THIRTY-EIGHT

Because it was the christening of a baby girl, Gracie had decorated the church in pink and white. White roses, pink roses; large white daisies, pink dahlias and late-flowering honeysuckle. For a little while she had been Rowangarth's land girl again; Grace Fielding who would never fall in love until the war was over.

She smiled up at the husband who stood beside her at All Souls font, their son on his hip; Sebastian Sutton from Kentucky. He had walked through the kitchen garden gate and common sense flew over the wall! Bas smiled back. Adam stuck his thumb in his mouth, then laid his head on his father's shoulder, eyelids drooping.

Beside him stood Tatiana and Bill, little fingers linked, and Polly Purvis who thought of Dickon and wondered what he would have made of his first grandchild, whilst on either side of Tom stood Julia and Alice; Julia thinking what an absolutely beautiful day this was turning out to be and Alice, smugly pleased with the lace and satin christening gown she had sewn by hand.

And then her mouth rounded into a *moue* of concern, as she fervently hoped that Daisy and Keth would get more use out of the christening gown than she and Tom had had out of that expensive pram! She leaned forward to catch Julia's eye and received a wink of approval.

Dear Julia. Alice's mind swooped backward in time and they were young again, and foolhardy, and the whole of London theirs! Going on for forty years ago and two wars to face, did they both but know it.

Julia smiled at her husband, who had finished reminding the godparents of their duty to the baby who lay in Lyn's arms and was asking of her, "Name this child?" Dearest Nathan, who would never have children of his own because he had loved too long and too patiently.

And when Lyn said, "Mary Natasha," Nathan's eyes met Keth's and for the space of a second there must surely have been only the two of them there, so long did that second last, so alive was it with meaning and understanding and approval.

Natasha? Once, Julia frowned, there had been a Natasha at Denniston House who was sent into secrecy to have Elliot Sutton's child. Natasha Yurovska. The servant in black, he'd called her. And go back to your dark little hell, Elliot Sutton! There is no place for you here today! She shook him from her mind, concentrating on the words of the service.

"Mary Natasha, I baptize you in the Name of the Father and of the Son . . ."

Nathan, gentling the baby's head with holy water; Mary Natasha flailing her fists, letting go a cry of outrage as befitted Tom Dwerryhouse's grand-daughter. Daisy smiling at Keth; Keth smiling at his daughter; Nathan giving Mary Natasha back to Lyn; Drew watching every movement.

What was he thinking? Was it, perhaps, of a child that was his and Kitty's? Julia willed him not to raise his head and look to his right through the open church doors to the white marble stone, sending her love across that same font at which Drew had been christened, telling him silently that she understood, begging him not to wait as she had waited.

They were singing a hymn; one Daisy particularly liked. "All Things Bright and Beautiful". It was her very favourite, she had said as a small child when they sang it in Beck Lane for a spaniel called Morgan. So long ago, yet only yesterday.

Then Alice and Tom and Daisy coming home to Rowangarth and Polly, too, and a dark-eyed boy called Keth, and she saying goodbye to Andrew, and Nathan asking her to marry him.

Don't close your heart to a second loving, Drew? Love can happen twice, I promise you. Kitty will always be your first love, but there is last loving, too, and all kinds of loving in between. Jinny Dobb said that and Jin knew what she was about.

The Sunday School children, who always came to christenings, were leaving, blinking in the September sunshine. Lyn walked slowly, carefully, with her goddaughter; Drew placed a hand on her elbow to guide her down the steps.

"My word, but she well and truly cried the devil out of her, eh?" Polly said, and Alice laughed and said you couldn't mistake that yell, now could you? To which Tom agreed wholeheartedly, because only a Dwerryhouse had a flash temper like that, and hadn't the baby's mother had one, an' all?

Daisy, who once rushed out in a fit of rage and volunteered for the Wrens! And if Mary Natasha Purvis ever did a damn-fool thing like that, she'd have her grandad to contend with!

Daisy, so beautiful in motherhood yet still the little lass he had more than once taken on his knee to kiss away her tears. She was Keth's now, and lived in a fine house on the Creesby road. He missed her, yet Alice said you never lost a daughter and told him not to act like a great daft lummox, because she was only a cock-stride away!

Alice smiled into Julia's camera, wanting this lovely day to go on and on. Alice Hawthorn had come a long way since Aunt Bella's, had found complete happiness, because who in her right mind could ask for more?

Silly little tears pricked her eyes and she blinked them sternly away. This was a happy day, a cherry-scone day, for surely Tilda would have baked those special scones for the christening tea, now that glacé cherries were in the shops again.

The baby began to cry. Lyn handed her back to Daisy and Tom said the bairn had had enough of fancy frocks and christening water and folk fussing over her, and wasn't it time to get back to Rowangarth and wet her head in a proper manner?

"Tired, darling?" Bas whispered and Gracie said she was, just a little, but wasn't it worth crossing the Atlantic just to be here? And Bas agreed and said how about doing it again, next year, and having another christening at All Souls whilst they were over?

So they all got into cars and made for Rowangarth, because now that petrol was back in the pumps again, cars dust-sheeted for the duration were back on the roads, though to see a brand new model was still a rarity.

Will Strong, under his wife's close supervision, had set up trestle tables in the conservatory and grouped basket chairs and wooden chairs about the garden. And Tilda and Mary laid the tables as carefully as they had done for one of Rowangarth's long-ago dinner parties, using the best linen and china, because hadn't the war been over these three years, and weren't things going to get better again? Soon? With luck?

Happen by next year, Tilda sighed, food would be completely unrationed and she could send her order to the grocer at Creesby with sugar and butter and tea and lard on it — as much as she wanted! And when that happened, Rowangarth might have grand dinner parties again — if ever Drew got wed, that was.

Nathan Sutton sat a little apart, teacup and plate at his feet, wondering how soon he and Julia would be able to move into the bothy — by Christmas, maybe? — and when, after that, he could write formally to the bishop, confirming his retirement.

It was just as he decided that next year's harvest festival would be his last as parish priest that Tatiana and Bill came to join him.

"Can you talk, Uncle Nathan, or are you having a quiet moment?"

"Yes, I can talk and no, I wasn't in deep contemplation; just thinking about when I shall retire."

"Then I hope it won't be just yet." She settled herself on the grass at his feet. "We're going to be married, you see, and we want you to marry us. And don't say you hope we know what we're doing!"

"No. For a long time, Tatty, you've known *exactly* what you are doing! Might I just say, though, that you've kept it very dark. Why so sudden?"

"We-e-ll, I said to Bill the other day that if this winter is going to be as cold as the last one, he'd be a lot better moving into Denniston, and be blowed to what the village — or the Petrovska — said. I didn't care, Uncle Nathan, that Holdenby would think we were sleeping together, because we probably would be — and it's none of their business, anyway."

"Aaaah," Nathan said to give himself time to recover his composure. "Well, you see —"

"Look, sir, it didn't happen like that — not exactly." Red-faced, Bill interrupted. "I agreed with Tatty that the village would talk, and I said that that being the case, then we might as well be hanged for a sheep, as they say, and share a bed.

"Mind, that being the case, it wouldn't be fair on any bairn that might happen as a result, to be labelled illegitimate. It's no' fair. I never knew my father; was put in a home when I was a week old. A bairn needs to be born in decent wedlock!"

"I agree entirely," Nathan murmured, feeling the need to say something, but not at all sure what.

"So he said, would you believe," Tatty breathed, "that it was a case of no wedding — no *nothing*! And I thought about it and suddenly knew I wanted to be married to Bill and have a baby as sweet as Daisy's. Today, at the christening, I was completely sure we're doing the right thing."

"So I'm going to have a word with Tatiana's mother — it's only polite," Bill smiled.

"Mother will say yes, anyway, and bless you, my children! She's so potty about Ewart she's still high on a pink cloud! We're hoping to have a Christmas wedding, no bridal gown or bridesmaids; just a quiet affair with only people we like there.

"I shall ask Uncle Igor to give me away — I've got quite fond of him — though if he does, then the Petrovska will insist on being there, too!"

"And why shouldn't she be, you awful young miss? She'd be very hurt if she wasn't asked," Nathan admonished mildly.

"Suppose you're right. And she isn't half as bossy these days. But if she makes a fuss about my not wearing white, I shall just ignore her, because I don't qualify for virginal white, you know."

"I know about Tim," Bill said gently.

"Well, never think of yourself as second best," Nathan said very firmly. "Julia had Andrew, but she and I are very happy. I just accept him as a part of her life. If you do that, Bill, things will work out fine, because second time around it can be just as good — but different."

"Bless you, Uncle Nathan. I do so wish you'd been my father. You're such an old love!"

"Well, you can have me *in loco parentis* if you want. And might I offer a fatherly word of advice? Postpone your honeymoon until the wedding — if you haven't already, I mean —"

"No, we haven't, Uncle Nathan, and I suppose we can count up to ten for a few weeks more, and Bill can stay in his garret just a little longer. We thought it would be nice to have the wedding some time the week before Christmas. I don't suppose you could marry us in the Lady Chapel? It's so lovely and old and enduring. All the early Suttons would have been married there, before the church was made bigger, and grander."

"The Lady Chapel it is," Nathan said. "Just right for a cosy Christmas wedding. Anything else you'd like?"

"Can't think of anything, but I'm sure there'll be something," Tatiana smiled sunnily. "And till we've told Mother, could you keep it to yourself, do you think?"

"My lips are sealed. And I'm so glad about you both. It's marvellous news. I know you'll be happy together."

"We will, sir," Bill said very seriously.

"Yes, we *will*. And we'll leave you in peace now, Uncle Nathan. Just wanted to be sure you'd still be available." She kissed his cheek, smiling into his eyes. "Y'know, I wouldn't feel married unless you'd tied the knot. See you!"

Nathan watched them go and for the first time in many months he thought of his brother.

"Y'know, Elliot, it's a pity you'll never know what a lovely young woman your daughter has grown into," he whispered inside him. "You'd have been so proud of her . . ."

When Rowangarth was quiet again and chairs and tables had been cleared away and the sun was slipping redly behind the stableyard roofs, Lyn Carmichael rose to her feet.

"Well — everyone's gone but me. The party's over, as they say. Care to walk me back to Foxgloves, Drew?"

"Be glad to. I seem to remember," he said obliquely, "you asking me that once before."

"Yes, before —"

"Before Kitty," he supplied, gravely.

"Mm. I asked this sailor to see me back to the Wrennery. I'd never dated him before — not him and me alone exactly. Usually his sister was there."

865

"But *that* night . . .?" Drew prompted, very quietly.

"We-e-ll — the night in question, Wren Carmichael made a real fool of herself. She asked this sailor, who'd usually doled out brotherly pecks to the cheek, if he would kiss her good night, as in properly. And when he did, the aforesaid Wren completely lost her head, offered her virginity on a plate and told this sailor she loved him. Best forgotten, wouldn't you say?"

"But I've just remembered it!"

"And now I'm remembering that once you told me about this linden walk and the seat on it and the scent of linden blossom. I said would I ever get to smell your blossom and you said if I was a good little Wren, I might. But good little Wrens didn't have a lot of fun, did they? The one we're talking about was too damn good, wasn't she? Still, I've got to see your linden walk at last, though I can't smell anything."

"No. You're a couple of months too late."

"Ha! The story of my life! Not only do I miss the blossom, but when eventually I get to sit with you beneath the linden trees, all I get for my pains is a frozen behind! That seat is uncomfortable *and* cold!"

"I'm sorry. So which way shall we go? The long way round or the short cut through Brattocks to the crossroads and the Creesby road?"

"Whichever," Lyn shrugged, hugging herself tightly, because not only was she cold but she was shaking inside. And that was because if something didn't happen tonight to clear the air she was packing up and going to Kenya! No messing!

"What is it, Lyn?" He took her arm, guiding her towards the wild garden and the stile at the near end of Brattocks. "I watched you today in the church. You looked so sad. Has something happened? Want to tell me about it . . .?"

She remained silent for all that, because they were passing Keeper's Cottage. There was a light in the front room window and she knew exactly what it would be like inside, because she had stayed there, hadn't she, with Daisy. In another life, that was.

"What is it? Once, we were friends, Lyn, and we agreed, didn't we, to be friends again? You said so yourself, the day we met in the Liver Building. And we've got on fine, you and I, ever since . . ."

"Oh, sure. And every time I come to stay with Daisy and Keth we meet and chat like old friends, and you kiss me good night as friends do — a brotherly peck, like always. It's the same mixture as before. Friends! That's all you and I ever will be!"

She walked ahead, and because the trees threw dark shadows and the moss that grew at the side of the path was damp with dew, she slipped and would have lost her footing had not Drew taken her elbow, and steadied her.

"Careful." He was still holding her. "And I'm sorry the way you feel about us, I mean. Don't you want to tell me?"

"About why you thought I looked sad in church? I hadn't realized it showed! But yes, I *was* sad — or maybe it was self-pity. Mary Natasha is so beautiful that I wanted her, or one like her, of my own! I envied Daisy and Keth; envied them that child and their happiness too! And I wanted to conceive a baby with a man I loved; wanted all the morning sickness and yelling and shoving and pushing that baby into the world! And every time Daisy puts that little one to her breast I go cold, I'm so envious! That's what I've become! An untouched, unloved woman who aches for a child inside her!"

Unspeaking, he let go her arm and there was such a silence between them that she could hear the thudding of her heart and the harshness of her breathing.

Above them, a night cloud shut out the last of the sun and a flock of birds wheeled above them, cawing as they settled down to roost for the night.

"Rooks!" she hissed. "Daisy tells them things, doesn't she, and Daisy's mother, too! Rooks keep secrets, I believe, so how about if I tell them one! Want to hear it, Drew Sutton?"

She walked away from him towards the elm trees, heels slamming in anger, not caring about the slippery path. Then she stood feet apart, hands on hips, looking up into the green darkness.

"Hey, you lot! I believe you listen to things! Then get an earful of this and hear it good, 'cause I'll not be passing this way again! I'm leaving, going to

Kenya to Auntie Blod because I can't take any more!"

She sucked in a deep breath, holding it, letting it go noisily, but it did nothing to ease her torment.

"There's this bloke, you see. I fell for him — a real hook, line and sinker job — first time we met. I thought he just might have had feelings for me too, so what d'you know? I offered it and no strings attached — except that perhaps he might have said he loved me too!

"But he didn't say it because he knew, somehow, that I wasn't his grand passion. He met her not long after, his cousin from Kentucky, and you can't blame him for the way he fell for her. He'd loved her all his life, only he hadn't realized it!"

She stopped, shaking with anger and despair, and her words swirled around her, then spiralled up to where the rooks roosted. And she covered her face with her hands and leaned against the trunk of the tallest tree, because all at once she felt weary and drained.

The tears came then; straight from the deeps of her heart and they caught in her throat and turned into sobs that shook her body from top to toes.

"Lyn? Don't cry? Please don't cry?"

He reached for her and because she did not turn from his touch he stepped nearer and took her into his arms, cupping her head with his hand so her cheek rested on his chest.

"Ssssh. It's all right. Let it come . . ."

"Drew! I'm s-sorry. That was a bloody awful thing to do!"

"It wasn't. But if it was, I deserved it."

"No! No, you didn't and can I borrow your hankie, please?" she sniffed.

"Sure. Be my guest." He pushed her a little way from him, dabbing her eyes, then giving her the handkerchief, telling her to blow her nose.

"Good job it's getting dark," she whispered croakily. "I must look a mess . . ."

"Yes, you must. Your mascara, I shouldn't wonder, is all over your cheeks — and my shirt front too — as well as your lipstick."

"It isn't funny, Drew. I meant it. I did love you. I still do. It's why I'm going away."

"You *can't* go. What about your job, your house? What about Daisy and Mary Natasha?"

"I'd pack my job in, go for a couple of months — see if I liked it. Then if I did, I'd come back and sell up. People are going crazy for holiday cottages in Wales."

"But you didn't like Kenya, you said; never wanted to go back, you once told me." He said it softly, coaxingly, as if reasoning with a child.

"I didn't — don't. I'd stay here if just once you'd say you love me, even though you didn't mean it. And if sometimes you would kiss me properly like that night outside the Wrennery when Daisy wasn't there . . ."

They began to walk, then; past the waving place where the railway line ran alongside Brattocks

Wood; climbed the boundary fence to stand at the crossroads beside the signpost. Away from the trees, it was lighter.

"You look just fine — your mascara, I mean," Drew said.

"That's okay, then. Daisy won't be asking questions, will she, when I get in?"

They walked slowly, reluctantly, as if both knew there were things to say before they got to Foxgloves, though neither knew where those words would lead.

"I'm sorry, Lyn, that you were hurt so much. Listen — those brotherly pecks we've been having lately — I thought it was what you wanted. I didn't realize that — that after Kitty, you'd gone on carrying the torch for me, sort of. And that morning I rang Daiz to tell her I'd got engaged, you spoke to me, too, and sounded glad for me — said you hoped we'd both be happy."

"Yes, and then I sat on the bottom stair and cried my eyes out. The entire Wrennery must've heard me. You thought I was a good-time girl, Drew? It was the impression I liked to give, till you . . ."

"It would still have been Kitty," he said softly. "She knocked me sideways."

"I know. And I wasn't glad about what happened to her. When she died, all I could think was that it could have been me or Daisy, in the Liverpool blitz. It was damn awful luck. I tried not to think about you, and how awful it would be when you got to know.

"But I *was* sad about Kitty. I had to bottle everything up because Daisy was in such a state, kept weeping and wanting Keth, but there was only my shoulder for her to cry on."

"There's a seat a bit further down — I think we've got to talk, Lyn." He took her hand and they walked to the new wooden memorial bench. "When I came back from Australia and got my demob, I didn't go straight back to Rowangarth."

"I know you didn't. We met, in Liverpool. It was blowing, and raining icicles. You seemed lost, like you were looking for something."

"I was. Or maybe I was convincing myself that she really wasn't there and never would be again. So I stayed the night, then caught the first train out next morning.

"But Kitty wasn't at Rowangarth either; not in the conservatory nor the wild garden. All I could find of her was a wooden grave-marker with her name on it. It was like a goodbye."

"It must have torn you apart, Drew. Are you ever going to forget her?"

"No. She happened, and I can't begin to pretend she didn't. But at least I've accepted the way it is. Mother told me she wasted too many years raging against the world after Andrew died. She asked me to try not to do the same.

"When finally she went to France to his grave, she had to accept he was dead, she told me. So I was luckier than she was. At least I was spared the bitterness. All I have to contend with now is the loneliness."

"And I've just made a right mess of it, haven't I?" Lyn sighed. "My performance just now in Brattocks must have shocked you, invaded your privacy. Sorry if I embarrassed you."

"It shocked me, yes, because I'd never really realized how you felt. Even when you started visiting Daisy and Keth and we met up again and —"

"And *walked*, and *talked*!"

"And walked," he laughed, "and talked like old friends."

"All very nice and chummy, wasn't it — till I put the cat amongst the pigeons!"

"Amongst the *rooks*! But are you really thinking of going to Kenya?"

"Thinking, yes, but I won't go. And, Drew — before the soul-searching stops, this is your chance to cut and run; give me a wide berth next time I visit Daisy. Because I won't change."

"You must have loved me a lot," he said softly.

"I did. I do. I always will. And if you can still bear to have me around after tonight — well, you don't have to marry me. If sometimes we could be — well, closer, sort of. It's just that I'm sick to the back teeth of being a virgin still."

"Oh, Lyndis Carmichael!" He laid an arm across her shoulders and pulled her closer. "What on earth am I to do with you?"

"Like I said — you don't have to *marry* me . . ."

"Oh, but I do! You *can* love twice, Mother said, but differently. So shall we give it a try, you and me? Knowing that Kitty will always be there and that sometimes people will talk about her just because she was Kitty, and a part of how it used to be, at Rowangarth?

"Knowing that every time you and I walk through the churchyard or down Holdenby main street, we shall see her there, beside Gran? And can you accept that every June, Catchpole will take white orchids to her grave and that she was my first love? Knowing all that, will you be my last love, Lyn?"

For a moment she said nothing because all at once there were tears again, ready to spill over and she wouldn't weep; she *wouldn't*!

"That really was the most peculiar proposal I've ever had!" She blew her nose noisily. "Come to think of it, it's the *only* proposal I've ever had! It — er — was a proposal?"

"It was, but I think I'd better start again. I want you with me always, Lyn. Will you marry me?"

He still hadn't said he loved her, she thought wonderingly, as a star began to shine, low down and bright in the sky. But he *would* say it. She could wait, because now tomorrows were fashionable again, and people could say the word without crossing their fingers.

"I think if you were to kiss me," she whispered, "like properly, I'd say 'Thanks. I will.'"

Their mouths touched; gently at first and then more urgently, and as she pulled away to catch her breath she looked over his shoulder at the star; first star; a wishing star. So she closed her eyes, searching with her lips for his, wishing with all her heart for a child with clinging fingers that was little and warm and smelled of baby soap. Two children; maybe three.

"I think," she said shakily, "that we'd better tell them at Rowangarth — make it official."

"I think," he said softly and solemnly, "we better had. Then we'll call at Keeper's and tell Lady and Tom, then I'll walk you back to Foxgloves, so we can tell Daiz. Bet it'll be a bit of a shock." He reached for her hand, lacing his fingers in hers.

"Not a shock," Lyn whispered tremulously, "but she *will* be glad for us."

It seemed right, somehow, and very comforting that as they kissed again, a new crescent moon should slip from behind a cloud to hang over Rowangarth's old, enduring roof, as new moons always had; and that from the top of the oldest oak in Brattocks Wood, a blackbird began to sing sunset.

As it always would.

The publishers hope that this large print book has brought you pleasurable reading. Each title is designed to make the text as easy to read as possible.

For further information on backlist or forthcoming titles please write or telephone:

In the British Isles and its territories, customers should contact:

ISIS Publishing Ltd
7 Centremead
Osney Mead
Oxford OX2 0ES
England
Telephone: (01865) 250 333 Fax: (01865) 790 358

In Australia and New Zealand, customers should contact:

Bolinda Publishing Pty Ltd
17 Mohr Street
Tullamarine Victoria 3043
Australia
Telephone: (03) 9338 0666 Fax: (03) 9335 1903
Toll Free Telephone: 1800 335 364
Toll Free Fax: 1800 671 4111

In New Zealand:
Toll Free Telephone: 0800 44 5788
Toll Free Fax: 0800 44 5789